MUTINY'S CURSE

A Novel

Dan L. Thrapp

All scriptures are taken from the *King James Version* of the Bible.

Mutiny's Curse
ISBN 1-58919-949-9

Published by RiverOak Publishing,
a Division of Cook Communications Ministries
P.O. Box 55388
Tulsa, Oklahoma 74155

DEDICATION

For Grace, Margie, Jan, in the order of their appearance.
And, of course, for that other wonderful woman. . . .

ACKNOWLEDGMENTS

Many thanks to Dan Thrapp's friend and colleague, author Dale L. Walker. This novel would not be in print had it not been for the advice, practical help, and encouragement that he so generously gave to the author's daughter.

FOREWORD

Because the plausibility of the basic theme of this work may be questioned, these are the facts:

The possibility of Fletcher Christian's escape from Pitcairn and subsequent return to England is summarized succinctly in the authoritative *Dictionary of National Biography*, the standard British reference work, Vol. 4, P. 278. It is implied or defined in numerous other works.

This is a novel. It is not history. Yet it does *no violence* to the historical record. Everything in it, not historically based, is reasonably possible from the *facts* of the historical record and can be so defended.

Where historical characters are portrayed, they are consistent with the actual personalities, so far as the records reveal these. The Indians and other indigenous people behave consistently with ethnological studies, and their activities are true to history.

All of the geography is portrayed accurately. I have visited most of the sites and studied them firsthand. The delineations are valid for the place and time.

Many of the incidents are based upon history; the facts have not been tampered with, except to the extent a fictional narrative demands.

Mutiny's Curse is a novel—plausible, sound, and reliable within its historical and geographical framework.

Dan L. Thrapp

BOOK I

Then said the LORD, Doest thou well to be angry?

JONAH 4:4

CHAPTER ONE

His name was Christian, though his faith was not. He felt himself complete and apart, believing there was neither Heaven above to reward nor pit below to punish. He was a man: one who could handle his own life, if it could be managed at all; though on this dank morning of April 28, 1789, his confidence was somewhat shaken. He paced the aft deck of His Majesty's armed vessel *Bounty* as she wallowed in the South Pacific swell, her sails slatting and banging against her masts, awaiting the winds of dawn. She made her way slowly now, her bottom rolling with the copper sea, eight leagues southwest by south of the island of Tofua.

A great struggle warred within Fletcher Christian, which belied his calm countenance. Injuries, fancied or otherwise, boiled within. He had suffered significant cruelties inflicted by his captain, progressing through simple indifference to callousness into sheer brutality. He was not alone in his suffering—every man on board had been abused without exception, down to the lowliest seaman.

Below the angry seaman, in a cabin separated from the deck by a scant fourteen inches of beam and plank, lay the harsh taskmaster, William Bligh, lieutenant of the Royal Navy and acting captain of the *Bounty*. Oblivious to the thunderheads of hatred gathering round his ship, he slept peacefully, enjoying dreams of the honors and certain advancement awaiting him in England upon completion of this tedious and exacting mission.

To an empire that had come to understand that strength and power rested not on arms alone, but upon economic muscle, the endeavor was of no little importance. The already enormous profit from the West Indies plantations might be increased further if costs could be shaved. How better than by inducing African slaves to live on breadfruit, a cheap substitute for expensive manioc, wheat, and other foods? Grown upon trees as large as English oak, the fruit came in loaf-sized bundles of butter-gold; generations of Polynesians had come to depend upon it as an Englishman on bread, and hence its name.

manioc-cassava-
plant grown in the tropics for edible root stock.

Since breadfruit was native to islands of the Southern Ocean and would grow only from sprouts and shoots, the *Bounty* expedition was undertaken to transplant them and required a conscientious, able man of ruthless drive. William Bligh fit such requirements.

Escape from Bligh, the sole cause of his agony, obsessed Christian now. This very night he had intended on quitting the *Bounty* aboard a makeshift raft of a spar and a plank or so, ferreted to him by William Purcell, the ship's carpenter. Under cover of darkness he might have embarked on this crazy contraption, had not circumstances conspired against him. The night was quiet and the sea calm—perfect conditions for reaching land safely. Unfortunately, the beauty and stillness of the night brought most of the ship's company on deck to enjoy the fresh air. It soon became obvious that it would be impossible for Christian to slip away. Christian finally cast his plan aside, but the desperation that fathered it, he could not.

"Hound! Dog," he had been called within the hearing of the men, and worse—he whose birth and education were higher than the captain's. To be used like a dog was even more cruel than the insult. Small insults—trivial injustices taken separately but growing in sequence—when heaped together on this endless voyage, had become insurmountable in his mind.

The cruelties and the blindness of the ship's commander against the company had brought the master's mate and acting lieutenant Fletcher Christian now to the edge of an abyss—in defiance of the Royal authority and in violation of his duty.

He glanced upward, beyond the cro'-jack, his eyes sweeping by habit the tracery of standing rigging, running lines, masts, spars, and canvas that moved the ship. A predawn gust filled topsails and topgallants briefly. John Mills laughed raucously as he told a favorite tale, breaking into Christian's black thoughts. The sound grated on his nerves.

cro'jack- the lower cross bar (yardarm) on the third mast, the mizzenmast.

With brassy purity, two bells sounded in the coming bright dawn. Five o'clock by landsman's time.

topsails and topgallants- upper sails, usually second and third counted up from the deck.

Christian moved beyond the sound of the old man's voice. His injuries beat upon his brain insistently—there had to be a way out. He turned to the wheelman, young Matthew Quintal, a London wharf rat who bore no love for Bligh, nor any other.

Christian whispered, "Quintal, how do the others?"

"About what, sir?"

"The treatment, man! The floggings! More abuse with every hour! . . . and the soft, lovely lasses, each left behind on Tahiti."

Quintal licked his lips.

"As you do, sir, I've not a doubt," he replied, cautiously.

Christian thrust his face closer.

"Would they help me seize the *Bounty*, Quintal?"

Quintal appeared stunned and unable to speak. Then a sharp glint of something—vengeance?—came into his eyes. He sighed, "Aye, sir," almost with relief. "Churchill. Mills. Maybe Martin, even. Most of this watch would be with ye, Mr. Christian. They've had enough, as I have. I can still feel that last floggin'. An' the others, sir, they've had their fill of th' cat an' meager rations, I would swear!"

cat- cat-o'-nine-tails-
a whip of nine knotted cords fastened to a handle used for punishment by flogging.

"Be quick, then. Go forward. Send me Churchill. Martin too." Christian peered along the deck. "Ellison! Take the wheel." The youth responded with a cheery, "Aye, aye, sir!" Leaning upon the starboard rail between the guns, Christian impatiently awaited the men. New hope and purpose inflamed his mind, swept aside the webs of indecision.

No taller than a boy, Isaac Martin trotted aft, touching his forelock respectfully.

"We shall seize the ship; are you with us?" The harshly whispered words only hinted at the boiling cauldron within. Martin's small eyes widened in surprise. He steadied himself at the rail. Ship's officers did not discuss mutiny with seamen.

"Ye've been flogged and starved!" Christian pressed. "Ye have no love for the captain. Can ye stand this ship to England, with more of the same? Six months. Perhaps a year? There's no help for us, Martin! We must seize her!"

Thirteen years of Navy discipline enveloped Martin. His sharply-honed instinct for self-preservation made him back away, panicked by the notion, not the immorality of it.

"I ain't the man for it, sir," he protested. "I know ye've suffered, but I do me duty, Mr. Christian. I'll have none o' it. Unless," he shot back over his shoulder, "ye can bring in the others. Ask Matt! Charles!"

Christian watched him go, helpless to avert a possible disaster. It was the Master-at-Arms Charles Churchill treading down the deck like a wolf who reassured him. Churchill swung the eighteen inches of reef point, his trademark. The crack of its tarred strands against his canvassed thigh punctuated his every impulse.

Prodigious muscles bulged beneath his jacket. He nursed a grinding hatred of Bligh, barely kept under control since his flogging for a brief desertion in Tahiti.

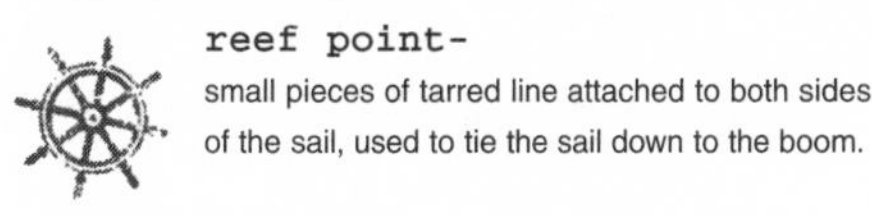

reef point-
small pieces of tarred line attached to both sides of the sail, used to tie the sail down to the boom.

"Quintal told me," he greeted the officer, his tone of near-respect. "I'm with ye. So will be most of the watch, Mr. Christian. But we must be swift. Have ye a plan?"

"No," admitted the officer. "Not yet."

"We must breach the arms chest. Coleman has the key. He'd never join us."

Christian's quickened eye lighted upon a shark's fin, skimming silently along the waves and holding close to the vessel.

"Tell him ye have need of a musket to shoot a shark," urged the officer. "Once the chest is open, arm those we can trust. Four of five are enough. Put a man on guard over the chest, mind you. There'll be an effort to retake the ship. I'll join you below. Hurry, man!" Churchill ran forward, collecting old Thompson, Alexander Smith, Frenchy Williams, Muspratt, and old John Mills. Behind the mizzen, Christian knotted a cord securely about a heavy iron fid, at hand to wedge a topmast, should it require bracing. He slipped the loop around his neck and beneath the shirt, his assurance against the gallows. If the mutiny failed, two would drown that day. Christian meant to take Bligh with him into the sea.

Churchill's party bounded down the companionway to the main deck. The locked arms chest rested atop the hatch near Coleman's cabin. The master-at-arms rapped respectfully; his fellow conspirators lurked beyond view.

"Eh?" growled Coleman testily, opening the door. "What is it ye want, Charles? Out with it!"

mizzen- mizzenmast-
the third mast from the bow in a ship with three masts.

Churchill softly requested the key.

"For God's sake, what for? It's scarce dawn!"

"A shark, Joseph. To shoot a shark. Evil fortune it is, clinging to us all th' night."

"Ye'd wake a man to kill a bloody fish? Have ye no senses?" Coleman turned back toward his bunk.

Churchill glanced at the set faces of the men behind him. He must get to the weapons quickly. "Mr. Christian's orders, Coleman."

The armorer stared blankly at him.

"He couldn't delay it, eh?" he grumbled. "Well," he turned and snatched the brass key from its hook, tossed it to Churchill. "Have your fun. Ye'll have little enough if the captain hears of it. Mind you return the key—but later on."

Silently the men sped to the hatch. Sprawled across the arms chest lay the most worthless of the *Bounty's* five midshipmen, John Hallet, dead asleep at his watch. Christian, having joined the men, rattled the boy's head against the planks. "*Hallet!* What the devil are you about? Your watch is on deck. Get your arse topside before I report you!"

Galvanized, Hallet bounded up the stairs. Churchill fell to his knees, fitted key to lock, and bared the weapons. Christian snatched up a cutlass, the others muskets, bayonets.

Christian addressed surly old Matthew Thompson. "Guard well the arms. Give them only to those we can trust; defy the others. Lads, follow me!" He ran up the fore hatchway to the deck where Hallet and the equally incompetent Thomas Hayward were seized and placed under guard. Christian and his mutineers, now under the shadow of the noose, moved swiftly down the deck. The officer improvised as he ran, though none would have suspected, so swift and certain were his orders.

He directed Quintal and scar-faced John Sumner to capture Fryer, the sailing master, who hated Bligh but whose sense of duty was iron-riveted. He sent Alexander Smith, the genial seaman-philosopher, to guard the aft hatchway. The ship all but secured, there remained only the focal point of the entire plan—the captain himself.

Christian summoned Churchill, Mills, and Tom Burkitt and sped down the main companionway. The starboard cabin's door was slightly ajar and Captain Bligh slept on his back, snoring contentedly. Christian moved in silently. Just as Christian pressed a cutlass to the captain's throat, his brilliant blue eyes popped open and his naturally pallid face drained to chalk. With startled disbelief he stared upward at his chief officer.

"What!" A sudden pulsing corded his thick neck above his flannel nightshirt. "What is this?" Christian's blade pressed him back.

"Not a word, sir," he warned, "or 'tis death! Not a word, mind?"

"Have you lost your wits?" Bligh roared. Despite cutlass, bayonet, and two muskets braced against him, he loosed a bellow that would have seared a deck. Christian jabbed him.

"You'll get no help, sir. We've seized the *Bounty!*"

"Why, that's mutiny—*mutiny!*" gasped the captain.

"Mutiny it is, sir," agreed Christian, " . . . or justice."

Christian felt the iron fid, heavy, reassuring against his chest. Three bells rang distantly, five-and-a-half o'clock; oddly this note of sanity on a mad morning further braced his will. The daylight filled the cabin. Bligh's face flooded with pink, save for the jagged white scar slashed across his cheek.

"Fetch a cord," Christian ordered Churchill. A sounding line from the deck was cast to bind the captain.

"You *cannot* take my ship!" Bligh grated, "Nor escape from me. You are mad, Christian! Let us have no more of this . . . this nightmare!"

"What's done is done," Christian said. "Your vessel is taken, Captain Bligh, by your own fault not ours. Over on your belly, now." He knotted the stout cord tightly about Bligh's wrists. "Up!" he commanded.

The *Bounty* rolled in the slight swell as they gained the deck. Ellison had abandoned the wheel. Bligh, observing this, roared at him from habit, "You worthless soul, get back to the helm or I'll flay you alive!"

Young Tom seized a bayonet, ran to Christian, saluted with a flourish that brought for the first time this morning a smile to the officer's face. "Forget him, Mr. Christian. I'll stand sentinel. Gladly, *gladly*, sir!"

"Right." Christian turned to order the sixteen-foot jolly boat broken out.

jolly boat-
a small boat, used for general purpose work.

Ellison danced a sailor's jig before the bound captain, lunging with bayonet feints.

"You'll make half of us jump overboard before we reach Endeavor Straits, will ye? Now the sharks shall have their reward, Captain Bligh!"

Tom skipped around the officer, stroking the steel blade affectionately, grinning wickedly.

"'Dancing is good for the men,'" he mimicked Bligh. "How would *you* like to dance for your men, then, sir captain?" he demanded. "Remember how you made sick old Brown and John Mills dance or not get their grog? Brown! Mills! Come watch the captain dance for you! Dance he does or no grog he gets!" He lanced the bayonet within a hair's breadth of bare toes. Bligh did not flinch.

"Shut up, Ellison!" ordered Christian, wearily. "Go work out the boat with the others. Mills! Amain!"

"One moment, Mr. Christian," cried Bligh, with his old peremptory note. Involuntarily Christian paused, squared, turned, "sir?"

"How many men do you have?"

"A dozen," he shrugged. "Mayhap more. There is much hatred against you, and who knows what's inside a man's mind? Others will join, with success."

"You would set half of the *Bounty*'s complement adrift? On a scarcely-known sea, amongst unsettled islands and savage cannibals? Does murder mean nothing to you?"

Christian thoughtfully bit his lip.

"Aye," he admitted. "The thought of murder does stir me. But despite all your meanness and cruelties, you are an expert seaman, sir, and I think it's not murder for you—only time, for us. You will find safe haven, I wager."

"Christian, 'tis a rude, brutal death you are consigning us to, or little short of it."

Christian returned his stare. Implacability settled like stone across his dark young face. He waited. Bligh's sea-blue gaze bored into him.

"If you go through with this thing, Christian," said the captain at last, his voice cold and low and penetrating, *"may God damn your soul!"*

"God, Captain Bligh?" the young man laughed harshly. "You have claim to such allegiance? Does God wink at your cruelty and greed? Your God is no friend of mine. Nor do I acknowledge Him or any other of your colleagues on this evil day you yourself have brought upon us."

Yet Bligh's thundered curse had jolted Christian's brain and stabbed his soul. For a fleeting instant, the captain had resumed command, once more domineering the deck, authorized by tradition and law to abuse his officers and men as he saw fit. Christian impatiently thrust aside any notion that this arrow might one day prove fatal, though he was plagued by guilt this fated morning. The violation of his rule of loyalty and honor, and of discipline, the laws by which the truest of men live, generated guilt.

A malediction such as Bligh's may destroy a man, not through its own force but augmented by one's imagined sin, if he be impressionable, uncertain, frightened, weak, or unlucky. This infected Fletcher Christian now, at this pivotal moment in his life, but he did not yet understand it fully. There was no time for self-examination—nor the inclination for it.

Shaken, for all his confidence and calm exterior, Christian turned without another word and stalked forward up the deck. Bligh received no further word, knew not his shaft had lodged.

CHAPTER TWO

"Make haste, Charles," Christian called to Churchill, who was overseeing the removal of stored yams from the jolly boat.

"Very well, sir," the master-at-arms replied. "This was a poor bin for roots, but Bligh didn't want the men to steal 'em." He snapped his rope once or twice. "Ought to leave some yams in here," he grumbled, "See if the captain can live on a quarter pound a day too!"

The smile on Christian's face faded. "I don't think the jolly boat will be large enough, Churchill. At least a dozen men must be put into her, perhaps more. Break out the cutter instead."

cutter-a single masted- fore-and-aft-rigged sailing vessel, also a kind of sloop.

Churchill's eyes clouded. "I wouldn't care if founder she did," he muttered. He called to Alexander Smith to rip the canvas cover from the sloop-rigged larger boat. Morrison and others helped, but William Cole, the boatswain and an old navy man, objected.

"If I do it, I'll have had a hand in this business," he argued. "That I do not wish, for I have me family in England to think on. Ye know what the lot of a mutineer's kin is likely to be!"

"Nevertheless, ye'll help break the boat out, William," Churchill ordered. "You can go in here, if you've a mind, but now we need your hand. 'Tis death if ye resist," he added, absently. Cole shrugged, peered aft toward Captain Bligh, then turned to the work with a will.

As the cutter swung over the side, Cole warned. "'Tis a leaky vessel you're putting us into."

"Speak to Mr. Christian," growled the master-at-arms. "'Twas his decision that ye have the cutter instead of the jolly boat."

Staring moodily over the stagnant ocean, Christian felt the iron fid heavy against his breast. He had half a mind to leap into the sea and be done with the whole business. Death would be mercifully swift, his integrity intact. But what of his companions? No, he had brought with him too many men.

"Beggin' your pardon," blurted Cole. "If you put us into the cutter, 'twill be our deaths outright, sir. She's not large enough. Besides, she's a rotten carcass of a boat, worm-eaten and decayed in the bottom boards and strakes. 'Twould be murder to put us into her, sir."

Bligh also had spoken of "murder."

"He let the boat get in that condition, 'twould serve him right," Christian muttered.

"Sir, it's not Mr. Bligh alone that will be going in her."

Christian reflected thoughtfully.

"I wish you were one of us, Cole," he said. "But you are right. I have no wish to be your executioner." Calling to Churchill, he asked, "How many will go?"

"More than I had thought," the other conceded.

"Better give them the launch, then. She's larger and more seaworthy."

"Right, sir, the launch it is," agreed Churchill. He turned his crew toward swinging the cutter inboard and breaking out the third boat, a twenty-three-foot craft, in the best condition of any. The tarred rope cracked again.

"I wish you'd belay that, Churchill," complained Smith. "It sounds overmuch like a neck being broke by a hangman, a notion I can do without this morning."

"Aye," agreed Churchill. "'Tis similar, right enough." A faint smile flitted across his face. He slapped the reef point against his leg twice. "Aye!"

Restless, Christian paced aft, noting that Martin, still on guard over Bligh, was pressing into the officer's mouth a selection of shaddock, a primitive grapefruit grown abundantly in the South Pacific. "He was parched," the seaman explained. The captain's fury and explosive roars had certainly dried his throat. 'Twas like Martin, though under arms and thus irrevocably a mutineer, to try to appear to his captain as not entirely committed. For Martin the wind remained variable. Christian said nothing.

Sturdy and somewhat under medium height, Bligh might have appeared comical—bare-footed, in his nightshirt, and with his sleeping cap askew—but he did not. Somehow the aura of authority had not deserted him, nor would it so long as he drew breath. Yet on this early morning of decision, Christian in his white shirt and knee britches domineered the situation. He seemed taller than ever, and his favorite silver buckles glowed on his black slippers. His dark brown hair was tied back neatly. There was a power and strength about the man, tempered only by his uncertain will. At Bligh's summons, Christian confronted him once more.

"Do you," demanded Bligh, "pretend that you can perform this criminal act and ever return to England?" His quarterdeck voice grew peremptory, even bellicose, revealing again the old Bligh who had precipitated the revolt by his disdain for others. "When I return, Christian, I shall have you hunted down like the dog I took you for—correctly, sir, it appears." The jibe struck home. Christian flushed, raised his cutlass, but withheld the blow. When he replied, his voice—if strained—was courteous still.

"What I shall do and where I shall go is my affair," he said. "I wish only to be rid of you, Captain Bligh. You shall have the boat and provisions and the people who desire to go with you, or as many as you can transport. The sea is not without haven, as well you know. You may escape; I hope you do. I want no blood of yours on my conscience. But whether you reach home is your concern, not mine. You have brought this circumstance upon yourself."

derrick sheaves-
pulleys on a hoist used to hoist boats and unload cargo.

Derrick sheaves rattled and squealed as the launch was lowered to the water that with luck would be its home for weeks to come. A few mutineers and other seaman gathered to listen.

"Mr. Christian," pleaded Bligh, his back tight against the mizzenmast, his tone now almost pleading, "this is the third voyage you have made under me. You have been in the Royal Navy ten years. You are of good family. Have you no regard for authority, no respect for discipline, no remembrance of duty?"

"Captain Bligh, authority has been abused beyond endurance. You have lost the right to demand duty and discipline from others."

With his wolflike gait, Churchill paced aft.

"I don't mean to interrupt, sir," jerking a thumb at the captain, "but them below wants up on deck. Shall we let them surface?"

"Use your own judgment, Churchill. Permit those we can trust to come up. In any case, we must soon decide who shall remain and who must go." Christian stared over the sea, his earlier black depression edging into awareness once again. The sharks, with broad day, had fallen astern.

Permitted on deck were William Purcell, the carpenter, and John Samuel, Bligh's clerk and steward. Samuel brought the captain's clothes and, securing Christian's permission, helped him dress. Old John Fryer, who followed the ancient and honorable calling once pursued by Captain Cook and by Bligh himself, asked to return to the deck which he had quitted at midnight with his watch.

Slightly stooped, his watery eyes scanning the unfamiliar disarray about, Fryer remarked crustily, "I don't know your purpose, Mr. Christian, but I see you have the ship and Captain too. You know 'tis your death warrant?"

"Hold your tongue, Fryer. I've been in torment these weeks past—"

As Christian turned away, Fryer sidled toward Bligh and whispered, "Can I do anything for ye, Captain?"

Bligh nodded toward Christian. "Knock him down!" he urged, but he said it overloud, as was his custom.

Christian spun around, lunging for Fryer who scuttled forward. "Don't let any of those others approach Bligh," he told Tom Burkitt, who by now had replaced Martin. "We'll have the boat ready shortly and be done with him."

"Aye, aye, sir, an' 'twill be good riddance, but I'm sorry that some of the others must go," replied the other.

"There's no help for it," muttered Christian. "'Tis death for all of us, if we come under His Majesty's guns."

Fryer, who had moved forward, approached the boatswain Morrison, as near a friend as the contentious old man had.

"Have ye a hand in this business, James?" he asked. Morrison shook his head, the lank hair dancing. "Will ye raise a party to retake her?" Cautiously the boatswain's mate nodded.

A seaman, Millward, whispered, "I'm with ye too, James. Can we trust others?"

The *Bounty* might have been retaken indeed, for the sense of duty in these loyal Englishmen ran strong, but the majority were determined neutrals. And this, of course, was no one's doing but the captain's, although never would he accept the responsibility for it. Men who wreak great wrongs by reason of their insensitivity cannot comprehend what they have done, and Bligh was such a one as they. The mutineers were not vile creatures. Most of them under different circumstances might have been judged "good" by their fellows. But they were good men impelled to evil acts by a force outside themselves. That force was Bligh.

Churchill's suspicions grew as Fryer moved from one to another. "Morrison!" he bellowed. The boatswain dropped a line and straightened. "What was between you and the master?"

"Nothing, Churchill," replied James Morrison. "We were wondering how many were going in the launch. That was all."

"'That's a lie," cried Alexander Smith, on the other side of the boat. "I saw him and Millward shake hands. They'll have our necks bound in a rope, is what I'm thinkin'."

"Keep Fryer and Morrison below," Churchill ordered. "Tell Thompson to shoot them down like rats if they approach the arms chest." He snorted impatiently, snapped his rope twice, the tiny explosions like distant pistol shots following one another down the deck. In this turmoil a diminutive figure, Bligh's clerk Samuel, darted toward the launch, his arms heaped with papers, books, and clothes.

"Samuel!" Churchill bellowed. "You little rat, come here! Spread them things out so I can take a look."

The clerk halted and defiantly laid his treasures before the bulky corporal: Bligh's journals, his commission, the captain's uniforms. He also had gathered up the timekeeper and almanac, necessary for accurate navigation, some maps, and drawings including Bligh's original surveys of the American west coast and of the Sandwich and Friendly Islands. Most of his collection was snatched from him, except a few spare clothes, the almanac, and the master's journals.

Watching the provisioning of the launch, Bligh pleaded for weapons, arguing his need for protection since what natives were known along the route were particularly hostile. However, only four cutlasses were cast aboard for him.

In the end, 150 pounds of bread, 16 pieces of pork, each weighing about 2 pounds, 6 quarts of rum, as many bottles of wine, 28 gallons of sweet water, and 4 empty water casks were lowered into the launch. The scant provisions comprised about all the weight the boat could manage with her numerous company. Despite the danger, there was now a rush by those abandoning the *Bounty* to take with them the meager provisions they most prized. Already some had commenced to tumble over the ship's side into the open boat. At the height of the confusion, Bligh for the last time summoned Fletcher Christian to him.

"I'll pawn my honor, I'll give my bond, Mr. Christian," he all but begged, "never to think of this if you'll desist. Think of my dear wife and little girls, longing for their husband and father who may never see them again!"

To Christian, whose only god was honor, Bligh's fervent appeal bordered on the blasphemous.

"No, Captain Bligh," he returned, contempt straining against his self-control, "if you had any honor, this would not have come about. And if you had regard for your wife and family, you should have thought of them before you behaved so villainously."

Once more Bligh attempted to speak. Christian shut him off.

"*Mamu*, sir! You live still by my grace. Not another word—not one!" He had picked up the Tahitian expression, for he had a quick ear and agile tongue for language. Now his attention was drawn as Cole sought to intercede on Bligh's behalf.

"'Tis too late, William," he replied. "I have been in hell for this fortnight past. I am determined to bear it no longer." With no further word, he went forward to decide with Churchill who would remain aboard the *Bounty* and who must go. Only the greatest courage, skill—and luck—could bring those in the launch through. But those who remained on the ship faced great risk themselves in seeking new lives in an unknown world. They would forever live in the shadow of the gallows. The choice seemed one of doom.

No able seaman—not one—elected to go with Bligh, although a few murmured that, but for the overloading of the small craft, they might have done so. Those put aboard included Fryer, his mate, William Elphinston, and two despised midshipman, Hayward and Hallet, the latter so terrified at his prospects that Christian was forced to fling him over the rail into the launch. Purcell, the carpenter, went with them and an assortment of others. Thomas Ledward, the surgeon's mate, possessed skills the mutineers coveted. But he also had a wife, family, and prospects of a worthy career at home, so at Christian's order, he was allowed to leave—without his medicine chest, his books, or his instruments.

Remaining aboard were generally the best of her complement. The pick of the midshipmen elected to stay: Peter Haywood, Steward, and Edward Young; also Morrison, an agreeable fellow, once a midshipman himself, who was ever occupied with his notes on native customs; Churchill, bold, demanding respect and given it, though never friendship; and the able seamen, some worthy, a few grading downward toward the dregs. Retained against their expressed desires were Joseph Coleman, armorer; Charles Norman, carpenter's mate; and Thomas McIntosh, carpenter's crew. Michael Byrne, the blind fiddler, was allowed to remain out of compassion.

"Bring the captain!" Christian called to Burkitt, after the other men climbed into the launch. Bligh was marched to the ship's side and his bonds cut. He chafed his wrists, rubbing the puffiness out of them, and hesitated, as though to speak again.

"Come, Captain Bligh," directed Christian. "Your officers and men are in the boat. You must go." He added, pointlessly, since the time for counter-insurrection was long past, "The least resistance will mean your death!"

Nevertheless the captain faced him squarely.

"You believe this will be the death of me and the others?" Bligh asked, with spirit. "As God is my witness, Christian, remorse shall *never* quit you! And, if we live, sir, we shall meet again. I trust under a Spithead yardarm!"

Christian bowed with a trace of a smile. Or it may have been no more than nervousness, a relic of his anguish, now subsided.

"That may be your pleasure, Captain Bligh," he conceded.

Spithead yardarm-
Spithead is a strait and anchorage off the coast of Portsmouth associated with the navy. A yardarm is a timber perpendicular to the mast and used to hang square sails from. Bligh means that he will meet Christian on a navy ship when he is hung for his crime from the yardarm.

The officer clambered stiffly down into the boat. It rocked heavily as he cast his body into it, its freeboard now only seven inches, a perilously slight distinction between life and death, even when the sea was calm. As Bligh grasped the tiller, he seemed forlorn yet somehow still a commanding figure. He directed the men at the oars to pull away. The launch veered astern, clung for a few moments to a line from the ship, holding as to an umbilical cord. Bligh gave the order to cast off.

At the stern rail, Christian directed a ram of rum be served around, while the crew joked about the over-laden boat and its hapless cargo.

"She seems a bit heavy in the stern, eh?" dryly observed Alexander Smith.

"That she surely does, Alex," Ellison laughed. "Eh, Captain Bligh!" he called across the calm water. "Your fat carcass will prove too much for the boat! I'll wager she sinks before you even reach Tofua! Stern first!"

A gleeful howl arose from the clustered mutineers. But not all of the *Bounty*'s remaining crew were so certain.

"I'll be hanged if I don't think he has a chance," muttered Tom Burkitt at Christian's elbow.

"A brave man always has a chance, Tom," said Christian. "Of any man, Bligh is their best hope to reach safety. If I were less confident, I should have taken some other way. Though I saw none—no other, at all." Across his brain there seemed to float a whisper, sighing in the rigging, leaving strange words behind: "*Laich*," it seemed to say, if Christian heard aright. "*Laich anochi iemach.*" He paused, listening. No doubt it was only the wind. He called Young to him.

"Are you prepared to take over the ship?" he asked. He knew Young would prove trustworthy to the new cause, particularly with Churchill prowling the deck. "The wind is freshening. Set the course west northwest. My head is bursting with a thousand devils . . . all thrusting pitchforks. I must go below."

"West northwest it is, sir!" Young smiled, showing the gaps in his teeth.

Before retiring Christian stared seaward once more. The launch had become a distant speck on the wide waters, its oars striking sparks in the early sunlight. The ship's clock sounded eight bells, eight o'clock on this bright South Pacific morning.

CHAPTER THREE

Christian shouldered his way into the captain's cabin. The distinctive odor of its former occupant still lay in the room—an emanation almost tangible, as though Bligh had left the cabin for a moment only. But Bligh would not return. Christian slammed the door, which had not once been closed during the voyage. The captain desired to be ever available to his deck officer. Now Bligh was adrift on the boundless ocean, pitting his courage, his resourcefulness, his inflexibility, his vile temper against the sea, which was his enemy, his friend, and his opportunity. *Bligh*, the mutineer told himself, *is gone to his fate. I am finally rid of him—forever.*

Christian scanned the room without really seeing the instruments, the shelf of books, the neatly hung clothing, the sword upon the cabin wall, the charts open upon the table, the time glass, the sparse and heavy sea furniture crowding the constricted space. He collapsed across the bunk, pressing his piercing temples with his hands. Christian turned fitfully for a time. Finally, he slept, while the *Bounty* rose and fell with the water slapping louder at her plates, straining to gather way as the wind freshened, her sails filling, the spars and masts and stays whining their song.

plates-
copper plates fastened to the sides and bottom of the ship to keep sea worms out.

An hour later, Christian stepped on deck composed, more his old self than he had been for the past forty-eight hours. Churchill greeted him with a twisted grin, handing over the pistol that once had belonged to the captain. "For any soul as needs it, sir," he said. "'Tis loaded and primed."

Christian thrust it into his waistband, and from that day forward never went without it. The pistol was the badge of authority, though he needed it little; his will, his innate leadership, the seamen's confidence, would serve him better.

"We had best collect the small arms, sir, and store them in the chest, with the key in safe hands. Ten muskets, two pistols, two cutlasses besides those we flung to the captain, and ten bayonets, along with the powder and shot in the magazine for the guns. My bunk is made up atop the chest. No one shall get to it, save by leave. Do you wish the key, or shall I keep it?"

"You had best retain it. A few may try to retake the ship, even now. Always keep Tom Burkitt or Smith close by. If we survive, 'twill be through good fortune and vigilance. Vigilance, Churchill!"

"Aye, sir."

The *Bounty* surged forward with the freshened wind, running free. The deck pitched and developed a slight roll. Christian's hair blew, the breeze was fresh and damp against his face, sweeping away lingering doubts.

"A fine, free wind," Christian said and glanced over in the direction of Young—the ablest midshipman on board. Smith, behind them, spun the wheel, correcting how she drove.

"Yes sir, 'tis free, indeed," Young replied.

"Were it not for what happened this morning, the world would seem good." Christian shook his head. "The crew and vessel are damned alike by our act—my act."

"Mutiny can be a beginning too."

Christian laughed. "I did not suspect ye were a philosopher. I wish I knew what is to come."

"So do we all, sir, and 'tis you who shall determine what 'twill be."

"I intend to sound the men, decide what's to be done," replied Christian. "Nothing was planned—would you believe it?"

"Aye, I would," Young chuckled. "Confusion there was aplenty, but of planning—well, even a cob could see there was none. I'm astonished you brought it off!"

"'Twas a jury-rigged mutiny," agreed Christian, "astounding to all of us." He glanced upward. "Best shorten sail, Young. Take in the t'gallants and the main and mizzen topsails. There's no point in driving when we don't know where we're bound."

t'gallants and the mizzen and main topsails- topmost sets of sails on the first and second masts, the second sail up on the second and third masts.

The crew, lolling about forward, abuzz still with the morning's events, roused to Young's "Up, lads!" Cupping his mouth to drive the words along the deck, he shouted, "Clew an' bunt up t'gallants! Stand by to lay aloft an' furl!"

"Aye, aye, sir!" greeted the order as the men swiftly sprang into action. Under shortened sail, the ship lost way from four knots to less than three, the pitching and rolling lessened, and the wind's sweep was muted in moments.

Christian directed Churchill to muster the complement aft, twenty-five mutineers and others, an odd assortment to be sure.

"Clew an' bunt up t'gallants! Stand by to lay aloft an' furl!"-
"Haul in and gather the top most sails! Get ready to go up and roll the sail up and secure it!"

Under the corporal's watchful eye, the men leaned against a rail or stood, arms folded, legs spread to the heave and fall of the deck, waiting to hear the new master. Christian, reading their faces, saw in some a wary optimism, in others deep and gloomy dread.

The avowed nonmutineers were Coleman, the armorer, whose early morning mistake of giving out the arms chest key made the revolt possible; Charles Norman and Thomas McIntosh, carpenter's mates, held aboard for their necessary and valuable skills; the young midshipmen, Stewart and Young; and the blind fiddler, Michael Byrne.

Among those who had no apparent hand in the mutiny were John Millward, 22, and James Morrison, 28, the boatswain's mates.

Christian scanned these faces and the others before him, observing how they stood. He could be sure of tough and ruthless Churchill, young Tom Ellison and John Mills, Burkitt and Quintal of course, Smith, and several others. There were eight who had turned no hand to mutiny, and another nine who had, and seven of uncertain bent. The mutineers had arms, the others none, and that made the difference. Now Christian faced this mongrel company.

"Men," his deep voice had a new note of confidence, "we have acted as Englishmen will always act when oppression becomes too great. We have also created new problems. Our lives can never be the same. We have seized the *Bounty*. We have set adrift the captain and those who wished to accompany him—"

"Only some of them, Mr. Christian—not all!" cried Coleman.

"Aye, Joseph. I know well that you and some others wished to leave but were not able. Bligh will remember. But we have mutinied; we cannot alter that. For us it is the gallows if we come within the grasp of His Majesty's arms, and they are far-reaching indeed. We have several months of grace, perhaps. It could be a year or two before a search would begin."

"But whatever happens, a ship will hunt for us. We must seek out a haven where we can fashion new lives. To find that place, we must have discipline and authority. We must now bestow our loyalties upon someone among us. I pledge to support with all my strength the man *you* choose."

Startled, the assemblage whirred with chatter like a swarm of insects, opinions flowing back and forth without direction. Then Alexander Smith spoke up. "There can be no doubt of it, sir. There's none among us but would follow you, an' none other we would agree to follow. We want you to be our captain, Mr. Christian. You set our course; we'll crew your craft!"

"Aye, sir, that we will," cried several others.

Although hardly surprised, Christian was moved by the unanimity of the decision, even from those who had clearly opposed the mutiny. With that he was content and more. Though he had not been aware of it clearly, the weight of authority forged by ships' commanders from all of history was somehow bequeathed now to him. He was no stranger to the quarterdeck. The *Bounty* was his fourth ship. Often he had served as deck officer and sometimes alone on a night watch held all semblance of command. But when major decisions were required, there always had been another to make them. Command was an illusion—now it was reality. The ship and her company was his responsibility; he could turn to no other, only to the boundless horizons within.

"Very well, then," he agreed, casting aside any foreboding. "Let us fashion a future as best we can. I know there are some who had no hand in this affair. I have no wish to be harsh or oppressive toward you. But come what may, *I mean to preserve this company*. We have two choices: we can endure as an armed camp, one-half ever on guard against the other, or we can openly work the ship together and make our way. I will let you free when the opportunity affords. To conduct ourselves thus, however, I need your undertaking to make no effort to recapture the *Bounty* nor seek to harm us. May I have it? Stewart? Young? Morrison? . . ." He ran down the roster of those doubtful or opposed to the insurrection and secured from each his pledge.

"I thank you all," said Fletcher Christian. "To man the ship we need to form two watches, although we have had three before. This will no doubt be a shorter voyage, and two must do. Young?"

"Aye, sir," agreed Young.

"I will take the other watch myself," Christian announced.

Christian saw to it that his watchdog Churchill was in Young's division and that the uncommitted seamen were in his own.

He directed Morrison to assume charge of the ship's stores and act as boatswain, a sort of foreman of the deck. Tom McIntosh was named carpenter, John Mills gunner, for a cannoneer he was by trade. By high noon the *Bounty* was once again a working ship. The course remained a question. Where to?

"Tahiti, Mr. Christian!" called several voices when he broached the question. A roar of approval went up.

wear-
to turn a vessel round carrying the ship's backside or stern around by the wind, the opposite of tacking which carries the ship's front or head around by the wind.

Perhaps Christian assented because he had no better immediate alternative. Or perhaps because he, too, had beautiful memories of Tahiti, living memories.

"Tahiti it is, then. But we must not plan to remain there. For us 'twould prove suicide." He turned to Young, who was leaning nonchalantly against a swivel gun. "Before your watch goes below, we'll wear ship to southwest by south. When last I took a sight, we were at 175° east and 20° south. If we drop down to 25 or 30, we should pick up westerlies at this season. Both Cook and Bligh found them there."

brail the driver-
haul up the after sail or spanker (a triangular sail at the back of the ship) by the lower corner.

stretch the main and mizzen tops'ls-
unfurl and spread out the topsail, the second sail up from the deck on the second and third masts.

trimmed-
arranged the yard arms and sails in reference to the wind.

"Aye, sir."

"Then we can make our easting to 150° and raise Tubuai, which I am curious about. It is a possible haven."

"Aye, sir. Southwest by south it is."

Young's clear call galvanized the men of both watches.

"Up, lads! Starboard men—prepare to brail the driver! Larboard hands—stretch the main and mizzen tops'ls!" The maneuver required a nice balance between steering way, a play of canvas fore and aft so she did not become unmanageable, and the use of sea and wind themselves to bring her about. Properly braced, the fore course and three topsails would pull her around. She fell off from the wind, then spun about smartly. The foreyards were hauled around to force her bow onto the new, more southerly tack. A steady wind from the larboard beam blew her forward. The starboard watch trimmed main and mizzen yards. Under main and mizzen topsails, the *Bounty* would all but manage herself.

The ship picked up her fresh bone. The starboard watch lay below. Larboard men completed tidying up, coiling the myriad ropes and hauls, for a well-managed ship shows her pride by the neatness of her deck. Christian summoned Morrison and Brown. They trotted aft, touched foreheads respectfully.

"We have no need for breadfruit seedlings now. Take the men who can be spared from duty and begin to clear the main cabin and amidships."

"Overboard, sir?"

"Overboard!" Christian grinned. "Pots and all. Bligh's burden will follow him into the sea. To Brown, the ship's gardener, he said, "What you've done these many months, you now can undo in half as many days."

Brown's face crinkled with laughter. "I was getting right weary of breadfruit, anyway. Some of us saw Bligh's ugly mug in every plant."

fresh bone-
from the expression "carrying a bone in her teeth," when white foam appears at the bow as the ship moves quickly through the water.

When the ship left Tahiti, she had aboard 1,015 breadfruit plants in 774 pots, 29 tubs and 24 boxes, along with a selection of other plants. Among these were the *aveee*, as the Polynesians termed it, considered by Bligh "one of the finest-flavored fruits of the world;" the only slightly less tasty *ayyah*; and the cluster-growing *rattah*, something like a chestnut, which could be boiled and dressed like Windsor beans, a staple in England. There were also the bananalike *orai-ah*, which Bligh held to be "very superior"; the *peeah*, from which the islanders made a sort of pudding; and the *ettow* and *matte*, both sources of a red dye used for tinting garments. To properly care for all these plants, the cabin floor had been sheathed with lead. Over this a lattice held the pots. Since they must be watered regularly and the supply of fresh water was limited on a long voyage, provision was made to drain off the surplus from the containers. Ventilation for the plants was much superior to the crew's, an added source of friction. If the vessel were forced into high latitudes during the winter season, a stove had been installed. This too was a luxury denied the men, some resenting a treatment more solicitous of plants than people.

Now all this carefully conceived work was to be wrecked upon the shoals of altered purpose. A human chain was quickly formed. The nodding plants, in their pots or boxes, were delivered from hand to hand, from aft cabin up the companionway, out through hatch to the leeward side, where they were dropped unceremoniously into the white-capped sea. They floated, most of them, upright for a time, gradually sinking lower into the ocean, a tossing, struggling procession of monuments to human folly. Each weighed from twenty to forty pounds, so the work, which began with spirit, soon lagged, although it would continue until the ship was emptied of her greenery.

Under press of command, Christian had become as different from the confused, unpredictable individual he had been earlier, as fish from fowl. The turbulent events of dawn had faded, although his belly-knot of hatred for William Bligh remained. However, this obsession no longer drove him. He had become a sea captain in his own right, with a handy ship under him and a willing crew to drive her, a law unto himself. This was even more so as a mutineer. He had shoved his guilt into the background along with the ominous weight of Bligh's malediction. With these, somehow, he would have to live, to endure.

The tropic afternoon waned. The sky filled with high clouds, friendly of form, no anger and little rain in them, and the mood of the day quite matched Christian's own. The clouds forecast a good steady seaman's blow, a pastiche of filmy blue and orange, lavender, and pearly gray. It was a mottled sky that roofed this ocean almost every afternoon with soft pastels in contrast to the primary reds and blues and yellows that gave an opulent sensuality to the flora of the islands of this Polynesian world. Just before twilight, Christian watched the dying sun fire the scattering clouds, kindling them until they flared, a blazing cataclysm that burned out quickly as the sun plunged into the western sea and was extinguished.

CHAPTER FOUR

As the last plant was heaved into the brine, the main cabin was stripped of its fitting for the pots; and the officers moved with relief into roomier, more adequate quarters. Christian retained Bligh's cabin. To keep the crew occupied and to impress the natives they surely would encounter, he ordered a set of worn and softened sails cut up and sewn into uniforms. The jackets and breeches were blue-edged with strips cut from Bligh's uniforms. "Nothing has a more beneficial effect on the mind of the Indians than a uniformity of dress," he explained to Morrison, charged with creating the clothing.

"It also has a healthy effect upon us, sir," added the boatswain, "as it betokens discipline."

By the ninth of May, the *Bounty* had entered a region of violent squalls. One swept in from starboard, pelting her with rain, lightning, and great thunder claps, along with a heavy unstable gale. In the midst of the tempest, a blinding flash and rush of wind heeled her half around, threatening to take the ship aback. Her fore topsail split with a cannon shot explosion. Tattered remnants flagged wildly far above the deck.

Christian cried the other watch up, sending men aloft to cut away its shreds, they being cautious lest the deadly whips of wet canvas knock them into the sea. The strips of sail gone, the foremast firmed under its course and ceased the savage shaking that had threatened the vessel with dismasting. After the squall, the captain had a new foresail broken out, and the ship soon was running free once more.

For nineteen days she made her way east, bowling before a wind steady for the most part and breasting the swells rolling against it.

Christian spent many hours in his cabin, poring over thick volumes of Cook's great voyages with their descriptions of winds, water movements, and sprays of islands, seeking clues to an impregnable haven. He was intrigued by the great navigator's description of Tubuai, where Cook charted what he believed was a single passage through an encircling reef, though he had not landed on the potato-shaped island.

Christian knew that his own navigation was not overly-precise, though this did not greatly concern him. He could always fix his latitude accurately by means of the sextant and the *Nautical Almanac*. Longitude was another matter. The *Bounty*'s chronometer had stopped during the morning of the mutiny and was set again, largely by guess. It might be off enough to provide an error of several miles in an east-west fix. The invention of the chronometer, scarcely twenty-five years old, had already proved itself as the one ready means of determining the number of nautical miles or degrees of longitude a ship might be east or west of Greenwich. If the *Bounty* could reach a known position, the chronometer would be reset.

They drove eastward along 23° 21' south, the approximate latitude of Tubuai, knowing that they must raise the island no matter what inaccuracies might attend their longitude findings. Shortly after sunrise on May 28, John Sumner, foretop lookout, said: "Land ho! One point, starboard!" A wisp of cloud was all that could be seen from deck, but from his vantage point Sumner could make out the tip of Teraetu Peak, at forty-three sea miles or more. The *Bounty* continued slowly until 1:30 the following morning when she hove to off the reef west of Point Tepuu.

hove to-
to heave to is to place the vessel in a position with sails adjusted in order to stay in the same place in the water.

Invisible in the darkness, the land made its presence known by the faint scents that floated seaward from any coast. A seaman can ever feel the land, stirring an awareness of danger by night and anticipation of pleasures to come by day, whether it be the spice-laden airs of the Indies, the dull drab wetness of the rocks of Cornwall, or the stink of Bombay. Here, from the unseen island of Tubuai, came a breath of the tropics, surely, but of mystery too, an aura real and tantalizing to excite the soul. Christian felt it. It brought to his mind a flood tide of recollection of the beautiful girl he loved—Mautea, whose lure grew stronger each hour.

With full morning, under canvas reduced to jib and fore topsail so that the *Bounty* scarcely made way, Christian ordered the cutter broken out. Stewart, with six men at the oars probed along the reef, seeking Cook's passage. The West Indian had a brace of pistols, though cautioned by Christian to use them only for serious trouble. The ship in seven fathoms, or forty feet, of water could keep almost abreast of the cutter, which moved slowly toward the barrier reef.

Fortunately the sea was calm, the wind not yet made up. Eagerly the mutineers on the *Bounty* studied the shore, passing the glass from hand to hand.

"There seems to be abundant level for garden patches," observed Young. Tubuai displayed two knots of mountains with gently sloping plains all around. "There are aplenty of coconut palms. That's favorable."

"Aye," agreed Christian, sweeping the land with the telescope, "its western parts appear rocky and barren. It seems populated. I can make out a canoe with a number of men. Perhaps they will show Stewart the passage. Captain Cook marked the channel with a grapnel, though he didn't go through to the beach. If he found little of interest here, I suppose other ships would also avoid Tubuai."

"Particularly with all the pleasures of Tahiti hard by."

"Exactly."

The cutter had now moved in closer to the reef toward shoal water. Cautiously it continued its parallel course, the bow man throwing the lead line ahead and calling out the sounding. The water was brilliantly transparent. Fish of astounding variety and color were oblivious to the cutter save as its shadow broke over them, when they scurried about in wild flight.

"Sir, the Indians in the canoe appear armed," Young said. Christian focused his glass on the craft gliding toward the reef.

"You are right," he agreed. "They have spears, at any rate." He halloed this information to Stewart who waved acknowledgment, still watching closely to see where the native craft would broach the reef, thus indicating the passage. The cutter's crew pulled steadily. Suddenly the canoe shot through a gap in the reef half a mile beyond the boat, then swung swiftly toward the narrow boat as though it were a thing alive, racing for sheer joy. The canoe darted against the side of the cutter. Fifteen of the islanders leapt aboard like monkeys. They were into everything in an instant, one having snatched up a jacket, bounded back into the canoe, gleeful with the prize. Others tried to strip the craft of everything loose. Overwhelmed by the natives and their incredible agility, uncertain whether it was a friendly or hostile raid, many of the whites were all but helpless. The natives made a few feints or threats with their spears, and there were so many of them that Stewart was indecisive.

Not so his more volatile crew. Quintal, McCoy, and Burkitt, more resolute, snatched the spears from some of the islanders, then broke and cast them into the water. These natives, at least, were now as helpless as the whites. The issue decided, Stewart shipped out his pistols, pointed them at the swarm, pulled the triggers. One misfired. The other thundered a healthy roar, frightening the Polynesians. They dove frantically over the side, sweeping into their canoe without visible effort, paddling hastily back toward the gap in the reef, chattering and peering fearfully at the pursuing cutter but slicing through the passageway far ahead of it.

Stewart found the channel three-fourths of a mile wide with depths of four or five fathoms. To starboard on a sandy headland, he saw a rusted iron grapnel, marking this as the passage Cook had discovered a quarter century before.

By midafternoon the *Bounty* was in the lagoon and safely anchored. The cutter was heaved aboard lest the natives pillage it. Christian ordered a heavy guard, warning that unless the ship were attacked directly, fire must be used to warn off interlopers rather than kill. Several islanders had swum twice around the ship at close range in the dark, inspecting the strange creation, but the guard had not fired on them.

With dawn the cutter was lowered once more. The crew rowed the kedge anchor toward land, dropped it, and the *Bounty* was hauled up to it. This hard labor continued until she had been warped half a mile into the lagoon, where she was moored in three and one-half fathoms, about twenty feet, of water off a glittering white beach. The shore gradually filled with curious, gesticulating natives whose shouts came clearly across the still water. Even before the ship had reached her mooring, ten canoes with two to fifteen paddlers in each were launched. Following the lead of the boldest, they soon ringed the ship. Shy at first, they maintained good distance, occasionally sounding a few conch shell blasts.

kedge anchor-
an anchor carried out by boat, dropped into the water, and then used to kedge or winch the ship to the anchored location by means of a large rope called a hawser.

"Sounds like a flock of bloody trumpeters," grumbled McCoy. "If Mr. Christian would give us leave, I'd shoot one or two an' the rest'd leave us in peace."

"I favor that," agreed Mills. "Why he don't want to kill them is beyond me."

"Because if we are going to live on this island, we can't kill them all, and we must make use of some," put in Morrison, testily. "You can't work with dead men!"

"No," retorted McCoy, "but you can have peace and quiet. "At least 'twould put a stop to their ruddy din."

During the night other islanders arrived from their villages on Tubuai, for both the canoes and the numbers of natives had increased vastly by dawn. Their greater strength lent them courage. Shortly after the morning watch, Morrison's repeated invitations at last were accepted. A grotesquely huge old man, a chief perhaps, was paddled hesitantly to the *Bounty*, being delivered there like 300 pounds of tribute. He sat dourly amidships in the narrow craft, his bulk spilling over the sides, his face unsmiling, his eyes fearful. Invited urgently to come aboard, he at last stirred despite his weight, clambering with surprising agility over the side by the Jacob's ladder lowered for him, even though he probably never had seen one before.

"Ain't 'e fat, though?" marveled Ellison.

"Heavy, not fat," corrected Morrison. "With age they become very heavy, like him. I wager some top twenty-five stone. Yet they never lose their grace nor go to belly-fat like Englishmen. They simply grow heavy in all their parts, retaining something of the beauty of their youth."

"Eh?" replied Ellison, wonderingly. Only Morrison would come up with something like that.

Fletcher Christian smiled, winning a grin in return and a heavy sigh that may have been sheer relief that the visitor was not to be sacrificed to the gods of this huge and mysterious vessel. The chief examined everything about the deck with astonishment, but what caught his eye and held it was the livestock Bligh had taken on at Tahiti for food. Hogs, goats, and a dog seemed equally novel to the royal visitor; obviously his people were without animals of any sort. He was delighted when a goat bleated or a pig grunted, nimbly leaping aside when one turned toward him, to the hilarity of the crew. Christian solemnly presented him with an ax head, some cloth, and a few nails. The chief examined each one of the seamen in turn.

"I believe the blighter is counting us, sir," warned Churchill, snapping his tarred rope with nervousness.

"Aye, he may be," said Christian unconcerned. "If he and his men think they can overrun us, however, a little grape should quickly change their minds."

Once the chief had departed, the captain ordered arms distributed and positions manned at strategic points about the ship. They had little to occupy themselves until noon when a great stir occurred on the beach. Warrior-filled canoes shoved off. Of far greater interest to the company, however, was a large craft paddled by a muscular crew of six, with a cargo of eighteen girls, flowers tucked in their hair, which fell in glossy ringlets to their trim waists. As the boat approached, the girls stood erect, beating time with sticks on the sides of the canoes to the singing of one of them, from her dress and manner and deference paid her, a daughter of a chief.

"Eh! Eh! This is more like it!" breathed Tom Burkitt, as the canoe swept like a driven leaf toward the ship.

"'Tis that, Tom," cried Skinner, in happy anticipation. "What they cannot win with spears, perhaps they can with love, eh?"

Churchill was not so fascinated by the girls swarming over the side of the *Bounty* that he failed to notice the approach from the other side of a cloud of canoes, manned with fifteen or twenty men each, conch horns blaring. "Mr. Christian!" he called. "Best look sharp, sir. The women are a decoy and we may have an assault!"

Mills and half a dozen others were ordered to the starboard rail, muskets at hand. Two of the four-pounders were loaded with grape and their muzzles lowered to wreak havoc among the cockleshells, if necessary. Although the natives were without experience with gunpowder, many of the canoes drew off a bit.

Under surveillance of the midshipmen, the women were treated courteously by the crew, and joyfully. The paddlers, aboard with the girls, dove into everything, pilfering whatever they could. One snatched the card from the compass, breaking the glass, and thus drawing Christian's attention.

The officer grabbed the card, to which the powerful native clung grimly. Christian wrestled him to the deck, ripping the compass card from his hands. Grabbing a tarred rope, the captain flogged the native howling over the side, where he tumbled into a rocking canoe. The other islanders fled, men and women alike. Some leapt into hovering craft, others plunged into the water swimming as swiftly as porpoises for the shore.

"Let them go," Young urged.

But this restraint had little peaceful effect. Once the women were clear, the swarming boatmen brought weapons up from the wells of their craft, brandishing them threateningly. One, finding nothing else to steal, slashed the rope from the kedge anchor and started off with it. Christian, his irritation at last overcoming his reluctance, swept up a musket and fired. "Mills!" he roared. "Touch off the grape!"

The roar and havoc of the four-pounder terrorized the natives. Frantically they paddled for shore. The *Bounty*'s boats were lowered swiftly and rowed in after them, armed men eager to further punish the attackers. Approaching the beach the boats met a hail of flung stones, the islanders not paying attention to the rattle of musketry until they saw some of their number spill bleeding upon the sands. Then they fled into the woods. In a moment all were beyond sight.

"Gather up the canoes, as many as you can," directed Christian. "We'll make them fast to the ship. If they want to recover the craft badly enough, they will come after them. We can make peace, I shouldn't wonder."

In the native boats Burkitt discovered a number of cords of coconut sennit, each about two feet long, for use, as Morrison supposed, in binding members of the ship's company.

"Since these waters have no name, sir," called Stewart from the jolly boat, "why not christen this Bloody Bay? This morning's work would make it the right title." And so it was ever after known.

The following morning, the natives still not reappearing, the ship's boats were manned. They rowed across the sparkling lagoon in the cool of the morning, along the coast of the island, eastward inside the reef but well off from the land. Soundings were taken from time to time, testing whether the *Bounty* could be worked along this way. The depths ranged from one and one-half to four fathoms along a fairly restricted channel to the northeast extremity of the island. Here the land was well screened by a cluster of four keys, or low islands, heavily wooded with the evergreen *toa*, trees used to fashion native war clubs and spears. On the main island here, well concealed, a settlement might avoid discovery from passing ships and be defended. They found an abundance of breadfruit, coconuts, plantains, and on one landing many yams and another root called taro. In the lagoon were plenty of fish and turtles. Christian ordered hatchets and other gifts left for the natives, hoping their goodwill might still be cultivated.

"If we could warp the *Bounty* this far along the lagoon, we might establish ourselves behind the shelter of the reef and those isles," mused Christian.

"As you say, sir," replied Young glumly.

"Your enthusiasm overwhelms me," said Christian good-naturedly.

He turned to Morrison, whose views on the natives were usually trustworthy and sound. "What do you think, James?"

Morrison shook his head. "Sir, if I might speak frankly, I have no favorable impression of these people. Begging pardon, sir, I don't see how anyone could favor them."

"What you say has merit," Christian conceded, "and yet I doubt any island in these seas is completely uninhabited."

"Tubuai is close by Tahiti, Mr. Christian," Young put in. "Don't you fear it would be often visited?" It was only about 300 sea miles south of the larger island

and on the track of the westerlies that ships normally would use from New Holland on their way to Matavai Bay.

"It's nearness is an advantage," the captain argued. "With a large, rich, well-populated island so nearby, I doubt whether any commander after a long passage would waste time on small, rocky Tubuai, particularly since it has no good anchorage."

The next afternoon there was still no sign of the natives. Christian ordered a small goat and two sickly pigs landed on the beach at Bloody Bay. Perhaps they would survive. If not, they might provide a feast for the natives. Mollify them, perhaps.

The ship was kedged to the mouth of the channel where she set her canvas for Tahiti. Christian once more mustered the company. Young and Churchill stood beside him as he faced the men, his demeanor serious. "Lads, we shall reach Tahiti in less than a week. But we cannot remain there, as you know. Tubuai will be our retreat." Silence of approval, resignation, or frustration greeted this expected announcement. "I desire that no man among you reveal or even mention the name of Tubuai to any Tahitian. If anyone does so, I shall be forced to punish him severely. If any man of our company deserts on Tahiti, he will be caught and by my order shot. You have given me the power, and I will use it to hold us together."

"Do you mean to keep us captives for the rest of our lives, sir?" demanded Coleman. Fletcher Christian flushed.

"I do not anticipate the future, Coleman," he replied. "I am concerned about today. You will obey, or you will perish."

"I didn't say I would not obey, sir," said Coleman.

Christian moved on. "We would be headed for disaster if we left some of you on Tahiti until the next visit by a British warship. There is no way I could assure you would not reveal our destination. I am forced to take you beyond His Majesty's reach."

Heywood spoke up. "'Tis forever indeed then, sir, is it not?"

Christian's face darkened again. "Forever is infinity. Let us say it is only for now."

Christian's shortness originated from his own indecision. He had not planned for the future. He was forced to seek immediate answers to immediate problems.

"From this day onward, Churchill and four others will be on guard," Christian said, "to see that my orders are carried out. Today we shall distribute the *Bounty*'s goods for trading with the natives among you all, fairly. Tahiti may be the last opportunity you will ever have to trade with them."

"And the women?" added McCoy. "Surely you don't expect us to shun them on Tahiti, sir?"

"Of course not. One purpose in returning there will be to persuade enough native women to accompany us, so we shall each have one of our choice. Women we shall have and other resources for a new, full life."

He directed Churchill to draw lots on the effects of their former companions. To each man was parceled his share, not to everyone's satisfaction, however.

"It seems the members of your mutineers were better served than others," muttered Tom McIntosh, scratching his red hair. Churchill eyed him coldly.

"Do you wish to make a formal objection?" he demanded.

"Now, Churchill, you know 'twas nothing like that," replied the Scotsman, placatingly. "A wee observation, is all."

"Keep such to yourself hereafter," advised Churchill. His tarred rope punctuated his words.

CHAPTER FIVE

The *Bounty* picked up the trades southeast of Mehetia, a lonely rock of an islet forty sea miles east of Tahiti. The ship coasted its southern reaches, its seething wake white and long. She rose to the blue rollers with purpose and by late afternoon was abreast of Tahiti-iti, or Taiarapu, the smaller part of the turtle-shaped main island. Its head, Taiarapu, faced the southeast, its carapace, Tahiti Nue, was crowned by a mighty trio: Mount Orafwanna, reaching upward 7,560 feet, with two smaller companions, Pito-iti and Aorai. Rising at the precise center of Tahiti Nue, this cluster was robed in green to the very summits, though a dozen leagues at sea they cast a bluish tint caused by reflection of indigo water. With sundown the wind had dropped and the ship stood off the land, rolling lazily, awaiting dawn when the trades would carry her inward toward the anchorage.

In the early evening, Young joined Christian on the aft deck, noting that the cloud cover about the peaks of Eimeo had blown away—good weather would hold tomorrow. Forward, Michael Byrne, his sightless eyes closed, played nostalgic airs of the North England he feared he might never see again while Coleman and others sang softly until McCoy, Quintal, and Ellison, anticipating the joys of the morrow, loudly demanded a jig and the decks erupted with spirited tunes and wildly dancing seamen.

With the dawn the *Bounty* hauled her wind and stood in for Matavai Bay, to leeward of Venus Point, a half-mile promontory jutting northward, its feathering of palms rising above the land. The broad expanse of the bay was alive with canoes as joyful natives gathered to welcome the ship and their old friends, many of whom lined the rail of the *Bounty*, grinning in anticipation. The water mirrored the land to westward of Venus promontory and beyond to the point of Arue where overlooking the ocean rose the great *morai* of Paré, the *morai* of kings, the holiest, most revered site on the island or even in the South Pacific. Its stepped pyramid of stone gleamed yellow in the strengthening sunlight.

morai of Pare–
a burial ground and a place of worship for the Paré tribe in which animal and human sacrifices were made.

From the black sand beaches, the cloud of small craft swarmed toward them, mostly single-hulled canoes with outriggers and three or four paddlers. Among them, like great ships of the line, were three double war canoes, almost 100 feet in length, 4 feet wide and 6 deep, bearing from 60 to 100 paddlers each. These craft were fashioned of teredo-resistant planks split from a breadfruit tree, or uru. Hewn with stone adzes, the boards were shaped and sewn together with stout coconut sennit through burned holes, the cracks caulked with fiber and sealed with black gum from the breadfruit. A heavy sea, however, could force the seams, causing the warriors to bail frantically with gourd scoops. In the center were stages for the fighters, with a forward breastwork to shield spearmen and behind them spaces for slingers and their baskets filled with stones large enough to brain a luckless victim.

teredo-
shipworm, wormlike clams that burrow in submerged wood.

Darting about the war canoes like minnows among great fishes were the lighter craft, sculpted in a month or more from single trees with fire and an adze. Most had a beam of eighteen inches or less and a length occasionally of twenty feet. Usually a canoe-maker fired the trunk to burn out its core, finishing the interior with rough coral or abrasive sand.

"They must be making up for war," observed Morrison at the starboard rail.

"Against us, do you think?" Christian asked.

"Oh, no, sir. But they have broken out those war canoes and to some purpose, I believe. In the foremost one are the Areeuoys, however. They do no fighting. They are a pack of fun-loving rascals."

"How do you recognize them?"

"By the flowers in their hair and their tattoos, sir—see, the black spot on their left breasts, and their legs and arms are stippled black. That and their mindless good spirits mark them, sir."

Now a dozen of the happy blades vaulted over the sides of the *Bounty* and darted about the deck, seizing loose articles that caught their fancy, tossing them to their colleagues in the canoes. Christian, annoyed by their thievery, was stayed by Morrison. "Begging your pardon, sir, but it would be best to leave them alone, honored as they are ashore. They won't steal what is of importance, because 'twould be a hindrance to them."

Christian might still have ordered Churchill to clear the deck had not the royal double-canoe arrived then with Otu—now called Tinah—the king, and his wife, Iddeah, and their considerable retinue. Christian called his company smartly to attention. He gave a hand to the royal pair as they tumbled heavily over the side. Tinah, an immense man, the most massive human being on the island, towered nearly a foot above Christian, himself well above average height. Tinah was framed and muscled to match his height, for the hereditary chieftains invariably were huge. Tinah's hair was touched with gray, his countenance gracious, if somewhat solemn.

Iddeah supplied the animation her stolid spouse lacked. She was tall and handsome, her height emphasized by her royal headdress resembling an Egyptian's, a quilted panel of lush black feathers with a two-inch border of white. Over her shoulders hung a semicircular cape, also feathered in black, and a necklace of triple strings of gleaming white sharks' teeth; all of this finery overlay a white tapa cape and white skirt. Respectfully she followed her husband across the deck and stood slightly behind him.

tapa-
coarse cloth made from the pounded bark of the paper mulberry and decorated with geometric patterns.

Morrison interpreted for the ceremony of welcome, even though Christian and several others were fairly versed in the dialect of the island.

"He says he is surprised, sir, to see us return so quickly and where are Bligh and the others?" reported Morrison. "Gets right to the heart of the matter, he does, sir."

"Yes," replied Christian, thoughtfully. "Tell him . . . tell him we met Captain Cook and he ordered Captain Bligh to found a . . . a colony on New Holland. Tell him we left the breadfruit plants there and returned here for hogs, poultry, and other things for the colony. Tell him something like that, Morrison."

"Yes, sir," replied the boatswain.

"He says he is happy to see you back, sir, whatever the reason, and he wishes Captain Cook had returned with you, though I have explained that was impossible. I do not know how much he believed, sir, but I do not think he cares one way or the other. He says little about the livestock but talks of a war between his people and the Attahuru tribe. He says the chieftain dashed the flag sent to circle the island announcing the confirmation of young Otu, his son, as king."

"*Two* kings, Morrison?"

"The custom, sir. The firstborn son becomes king because, being a meld of the old king and his queen, he is thus an improvement over either; but the old king rules as a sort of regent until the young king can take over.

"I see."

"The flag was dashed down and that is a signal for war. I believe, sir, he is suggesting a trade. If we help him with his battle, he will supply the *Bounty*."

"What sort of assistance, Morrison?"

The boatswain again engaged the mighty Tinah in conversation.

"His majesty says that half a dozen men with loud-firing muskets will decide it. He adds that his warriors would be unable to spare the time to gather the provisions until they finish their campaign, another way of stressing his point, it seems to me, sir."

Christian surveyed the ship's company. "You heard, lads. Do any of you wish to volunteer?"

Churchill snapped his rope loudly. "I'll go, gladly, sir," he offered, adding slyly, "It seems a fair trade. If the king will give us provisions, I'll undertake to fight his war for him, if you'll go too."

"I'd like to venture it as well, sir," added Mills. Martin, Thompson, Skinner, Millward, and John Williams also volunteered.

"Tell Tinah that eight of us will come," Christian directed Morrison. "When do we leave? How long will we be gone?"

Morrison questioned the chief.

"His slingers already have flung their challenge at the district of Attahuru, chanting, 'War is begun!' The men of Attahuru have replied, 'The gods protect you in your war,' which is their way of accepting the challenge. 'Twill be necessary to hold rites at the temple of the Great *Morai* at dawn; but they will be brief because the enemy has stolen the red sash of royalty and the ark and other things from the temple, and without them there can't be too extended a ritual. The true purpose of the war is to get them back, I think. Afterward it will be necessary to take three days to reconsecrate the Great *Morai*."

He asked another question of the king, then continued:

"Tinah says the expedition must be sanctified before Eatua Nue, the awe-full god, and his son, Oromattowtua, who presides over war. I don't get all he says, but the expedition should not take long. Say ten days or a fortnight."

Christian nodded.

"Sir," Morrison asked, "the war and rites at the *Morai* will be quite singular. I don't suppose any white man has ever seen them. Might I go observe if I pledge my word to return promptly when it is over?"

The captain grinned. He well knew the seaman's fascination for the native customs and secretly admired his intelligent pursuit of their culture.

"Of course, Morrison. But keep a sharp eye out. Don't break their taboos or you'll end up a sacrifice yourself! They seem addicted to the use of humans as ritual victims. Nor are they overly particular whom they use."

The morning star burned white in the southern sky as the volunteers led by Christian set out toward the shore, each armed with a musket and a goodly supply of powder and ball. *Bounty* seamen rowed them to the beach below the pyramid of the Great *Morai* for the feast of war and the rites necessary to assure success for the expedition. As day exploded out of the east, they approached the sacred structure, where Polynesian people met their gods.

The Great *Morai,* half the size of a cricket field, was fenced with a stone wall almost the height of a man and was cobbled over its whole expanse. At the farther end rose the truncated pyramid, which Morrison called the *ahu,* rising thirteen tiers to a platform forty feet above the pavement. On this stage were representations of the three gods in whose honor the Great *Morai* was built. About the structure was a thicket of upright poles, or *unu.* The tall ones, Morrison whispered, represented masts of ghostly vessels; the shorter ones, the paddles. The broad altar atop the pyramid was littered with heaps of skulls and jawbones of sacrificial victims. Priests sat cross-legged on the pavement, waiting patiently. Carved planks, smeared red, flamed like banners of chivalry against the sky, each denoting a chief's house or district. Because the seamen were honored guests—and most desirable allies—they had stone seats at the back of the courtyard. They watched as a priest before the pyramid, his back resplendent with a cape of parrot feathers, his brown arms upraised, chanted a litany in a language none of the whites had ever heard before.

"Rather elaborate, this," whispered Christian to Morrison.

"Yes, sir. Their mythology is carefully thought out and the people indoctrinated to understand some and be mystified by what they don't comprehend. Like all humans, they need gods. Otherwise their lives are pointless, and no one can stand that. I think that is the whole reasoning behind these ceremonies, sir."

It was Christian's turn for reflection. Speaking softly he said, "Yet we, with our superior knowledge, can see that their beliefs are pointless. Perhaps our 'higher' notions are equally pointless, eh?"

"We can never know, sir. We cannot detect what lies beyond us. We all stand in need and have to take religion seriously, not only with the mind, for it is more than a mental, more even than an emotional thing. 'Twere humans themselves. Religion has got to come out of them. Without personal experience of it, their lives are going to be pretty empty."

"You sound like a bloody vicar," muttered Christian.

A distant drum began its slow throb, booming deeply from the sharkskin head stretched across its open end. From the beach behind the *morai* rose a shout and the tramp of marching feet. The procession filed through the gateway, across the pavement to the altar, bringing hapless human sacrifices. Each was trussed to a pole whose ends rested upon the shoulders of two men. The victims, Morrison whispered, were thieves or other criminals the natives had decided "well deserved to die."

Tinah was seated as the presiding dignitary as there were fourteen sacrifices, one for each district of the island remaining loyal to Tinah and Otu. Each victim was executed in the hope that the gods would favor the war expedition.

"Seems a bloody way to start such an affair," muttered the captain, observing the executioners slipping on the rounded cobblestones greased with blood and human gore.

"'Twill be even bloodier if they win," replied Morrison.

The feast that followed was magnificent: roast pig for all, with a plentitude of coconuts, yams, poi, and other foods. Swollen by several hundred warriors, the throng stuffed themselves far beyond normal human capacity, while drums throbbed, nasal flutes whined, and banners tossed in the slight breeze. By evening, the signs propitious, the war party formed under Terumana, a bulky, powerful warrior bearing a seven-foot *toa* club of glossy black and murderous weight, carved with emblems of past victories. He shared the leadership with Hitihiti, a good-natured hulk well known to the *Bounty* crew since he had once sailed with Cook and loved all Englishmen. There was also Ahutoru, a silent chieftain of unknown ability. Each in turn was introduced to the whites. Morrison interpreted Christian's brief speech informing them that the ship's party was at their service. He would, however, allow no one but himself to lead and command his own men.

Evening fell with a tropic rush, and the war party filed out along the dark coast, hundreds of fighting men armed with spears, slings, clubs, and protected by charms and shields. Almost silently they padded along the satiny pathways on this expedition devoted to murder and plunder and war.

CHAPTER SIX

Late on the third day the warriors, with no more formation than a pack of wolves, worked across the highlands on trails beaten smooth by generations. Christian's party, muskets slung across shoulders and ball and powder packets heavy at their sides, followed three of the leaders, well ahead of the fighting men.

The horde dropped toward the shore, Terumana abruptly halting before a coconut plantation. Before him was the long-anticipated *Marro Eatus*, the "signal for war." It appeared inoffensive. Ribbons of white tapa zigzagged from tree to tree and crossed the path several times. At each tree it touched was tied a young pig. The tapa was a white threat to those who passed; the pigs a bribe to hungry warriors to feast quickly and go home. Neither emblem served. The horde ripped off the tapa. The instant the first fighter touched the *marro*, a sling stone struck his ribs, breaking bone, but his companions burst forward to skirmish with the enemy ambush. The whites milled uncertainly, "not knowing friend from foe," as Morrison later put it, until the enemy, seeing the musket-bearing *Bounty* men, fled precipitately into the mountains. The casualties on each side had been negligible, but war had begun.

Since it was almost dark, Chief Terumana ordered camp be made among the palms. Holes were dug, piled full of sticks and stones, and fires started in each by twirled sticks.

While the wood burned down to usable coals, Churchill stalked the environs of the camp, his musket across his arm, his brow furrowed, Mills keeping pace. "I don't like this business," the corporal grumbled. "These blighters are through with war for today and think of nothing but feasting. If T'towha and his Attahuruans had their bloody wits about them, they would overrun us now!"

"Aye, Charles, that they could," agreed Mills, peering into the darkness. Neither noticed Morrison, until he spoke.

"But they won't," he assured them. "Tahitians only fight with the sun. At night they fear the spirits who always join their enemies. No one can successfully fight a spirit! Darkness, therefore, is a time for feasting and amusement."

Churchill surveyed Morrison coolly, his pale eyes unblinking.

"That being the case," he said, "now would be the time to strike, eh!"

"That it would," smiled the boatswain, "if we could find the enemy—and if we could persuade them to fight. But we cannot."

Cooks worked steadily at preparing the feast of enemy pigs. The oven-pits were paved with scorching stones and fresh plantain leaves. Once cleaned and dressed, the pigs were laid in with the entrails and such vegetables as breadfruit and plantains, the whole covered with leaves and hot stones and a layer of earth packed atop it all so that only a wisp of steam escaped. The flutes played and the party sang their island songs for an hour, until the banquet was ready. All alike gorged themselves on roasted pork.

"I've never see a more scandalous war," muttered Martin, his mouth full of hot meat and breadfruit. "Cast a few stones and feast! No wonder they grin and sing all the time."

"Guard well your muskets and ammunition tonight," warned Churchill. "They may not be willing to fight at night, but they'll steal anytime." The corporal shook his balding head in disgust and slipped out for another look around. He returned before long.

"Morrison," he growled. "I want to talk to Terumana and them other chiefs. Come interpret for me." The boatswain followed him to the blazing fire where the chiefs were stuffing themselves. The Englishmen were offered food; but although Morrison accepted a token, Churchill rudely declined.

"Inform them they must better manage their men tomorrow, else we cannot tell one from another and are bound to shoot our own party." Morrison stared at him for a long moment, then turned to Terumana and conversed gently. The chief stopped chewing long enough to listen, then spoke to Churchill, his mouth still half full.

"He says his men do not know how to fight any other way, and he has no control over them once the battle begins. I believe that is correct, Churchill. They are not disciplined soldiers, you know."

"Does he want his own warriors cut down?" demanded Churchill, angrily. "I've a good notion to get Mr. Christian to gather our men and go back."

"Mr. Christian would never approve, Churchill," replied Morrison. "He depends upon us to do our duty, so Chief Tinah will provision the *Bounty*."

"Duty!" snorted Churchill. "What sort of duty is it to make war with a gang of filthy savages who fight like a cloud of mosquitoes?"

Morrison stared at the ground between his feet. It was Hitihiti, Tinah's half-brother, who broke the impasse, he alone comprehending English.

"Morrison?" he put in, politely. Hitihiti circled his head with a forefinger. "We wear uniform, eh? Badge, eh?" He grinned broadly.

"How would it be," Morrison took up the suggestion, "if we tore up the *marro eatua,* and had each of our fighters wear a strip? Then we could easily distinguish them."

"Do that, Morrison," said Churchill with relief. "Mr. Christian will approve, of course. Make it a broad band—two inches, at least."

The natives gleefully accepted the badge as a uniform, linking them with their English allies. That it would be a target for their enemies never occurred to them. The novelty was the thing.

In the morning cool, while the wet dew corded the stems of tall grass, the war party straggled out once more, the Englishmen surrounded by a multitude, the best and most honored warriors claiming the right of closest association. Each native wore a broad headband, giving the appearance of discipline.

From the advance party wavered a faint cry signaling contact with the enemy, who had withdrawn into a mountain stronghold at a narrow pass. "We can't plan anything save we force them out of there," grumbled Churchill, though it was midday before the pass could be seen clearly enough to be studied. By then the blazing heat and humidity had exhausted the Englishmen. They might have faltered had not the natives fetched them green coconuts, the milk refreshing them greatly.

Christian, Churchill, and Mills advanced and viewed the defenses.

"With muskets they could hold that pass against a thousand," said Christian, "but with only stones for weapons, I don't think they'll be so fortunate."

"Muskets or bows would do it, sir," agreed Churchill.

"It's an odd thing," Mills added. "These people use bows and arrows to play with but not for war. Rogers and his red Indians could show them how to fight!"

"They play at war like they play at everything else," said Churchill sourly.

"Yet they kill," mused Christian.

A short rest renewed the Englishmen, and the war party moved up to the pass, the Tahitians willing for their new allies to go first to meet the enemy. Above them the cave swiftlets darted in and out of their rock-hole nests, and glossy long-tailed birds, sought for royal tiaras, shared the nesting sites.

Christian gripped his musket with both hands, calling, "Let's take it at a run, lads! Follow me!" He burst across the opening before the startled defenders could react, followed by the other Englishmen. Missiles had commenced to shower down, bouncing about like mighty hailstones. No one was struck except Williams. The blow bruised his leg but broke no bones.

Christian and Churchill led the line moving up the scrubby hillside toward the prominence above, screened by rocks and thick bushes. An enemy warrior, to obtain a better view, raised above the parapet. Churchill fired, catching him full in the chest, bringing him hurtling down the slope, end over end, to lie crushed and quivering almost at their feet. The Tahitians from Matavai howled, pressing forward to the very edge of the opening, though none yet dared dash across.

Clambering up the precipitous slope, the Englishmen held their muskets in one hand, swung their shot pouches around to their backs, and pulled themselves upward from clump to clump of stiff growth. The defenders lined their parapet, flinging stones, with hasty and inaccurate aim. Mills shot a second enemy and Martin a third. Thompson wounded a fourth, the musket ball splintering granite before his face, driving rock splinters into flesh and bone.

"Lads," panted Churchill, his face and chest running with sweat, "if the locals was any good, they would climb that rock from the other side and we could roust them. Tell 'em, Morrison!"

The boatswain shouted to Terumana and Hitihiti and saw them cautiously advance, urging their followers along. A few did so. Seeing this, Christian and his men, their weapons reloaded, swung into action afresh, quickly scaled the remaining 100 feet toward the stronghold. The defenders, observing an advance from both sides, howled and fled down the southerly slope of the mountain, leaping from rock to rock. A few more were struck by bullets or stones, but most escaped, demoralized and whipped.

"Not much of a war," muttered Churchill, grunting as he gained the deserted stronghold. "What do we do now, go back?"

Christian talked briefly with the chieftains, Terumana and Ahutoru. Morrison translated. "They say that Tinah will not be satisfied until the *marro ura* is returned, for without it he will not be king of the entire island. We still have not captured their district. They think it best to keep on, sir."

"In that case we must hurry—press them closely, lest they recover."

With the Englishmen in the lead, the war company spilled down the mountainside, occasionally glimpsing a fleeing Attahuruan, though meeting no resistance until they reached the first coconut plantations and a few reed houses.

"Let's burn them!" urged Churchill.

The flimsy structures billowed flames as the attackers surged toward the principal village of the Attahuru. Shortly before dark they were met by a flag-bearing delegation from T'towha, the aspirant for a throne. He would be pleased to meet the invaders in battle in the morning, on the grassed slopes north of the village, weapons to settle the matter of sovereignty.

"Sounds civilized!" said Christian sarcastically.

"'Tis better than fightin' in the mountains," Churchill agreed.

Shortly after dawn, consequently, hordes collided. The defending warriors of Attahuru were bravely arrayed in caps and cloaks of brilliant feathers, but their attire availed them little. The first volley wreaked havoc among the tightly packed enemy. Many had never heard gunfire before and instantly fled to their mountains, erecting a breastworks in a narrow canyon. The assailants moved up against them with Christian, now accepted as a great war chief. When the enemy saw the force with the thunder-weapons ascending inexorably upon their stronghold, they cried in apprehension and dispatched a white flag.

Under Christian's urging, the emissaries were received. Before sunset the rebel chief T'towha with his wife, attended by a flag-bearing priest, came in for a grand council before a blazing fire. He agreed that the *marro* and even more holy ark would be returned, signifying his submission.

"With that, everyone will be pleased," ventured Morrison.

"Everyone? What's everyone to do with it?" demanded Churchill. "Everyone wasn't even with us. *We* ran this campaign and won its battles. *I* had more to do with its success than anyone. The question is whether *I* am pleased." The arrogance of victory was on him.

Christian's eyes narrowed. "In that case you *are* pleased, are you not, Churchill?

Churchill paused, reddened. "I suppose so."

Christian watched him turn and go, saying nothing further.

On the march back to Matavai Bay with the ark and red sash, the rebel chief, T'towha, his wife, and retinue occupied a place of honor. They were formally presented to the delighted king in a sacred ceremony at the pyramid of the Great *Morai*, when the dead warriors of both sides were given to the gods and buried beneath its cobbles. Tinah and Iddeah presided over a mighty feast, with T'towha in excellent spirits and obviously forgiven for his brief revolt. Christian, Churchill, and Morrison sat as honored guests directly before the royalty. Responsible for slaying most of the victims, the Englishmen were adopted into the families of surviving relatives, in accordance with custom, to be treated evermore as beloved kin who could do no wrong.

"Civilized nations might well adopt some of these customs," grinned Churchill. With the happy conclusion of the war, he had assumed a cheerfulness quite out of keeping with his often surly character.

"Aye," agreed Christian, "but then they would not be civilized."

Churchill laughed aloud, the only occasion in Christian's memory he ever had done so.

CHAPTER SEVEN

Provisioning of the *Bounty* proceeded swiftly for several days, Christian desiring to stow as much as possible. Stewart and Young—and the ever-curious Morrison—spent their time with the natives, fishing in the lagoons and reefs, and harvesting the ocean. Christian encouraged Morrison's studies of the natives, as their talents might prove crucial to survival of the mutineers.

Seines, or nets, of huge size were used by many fishermen. More interesting to the Englishmen, however, were the line anglers who fashioned cords from roeva bark, strengthening the fibers by rolling them on their bare thighs and twisting two or three strands together. The lines could hold even dolphin. The hooks were usually pearl shell, circular in form; and although unbarbed, the points curled back upon themselves so that when taken by a fish, a tug on the line would force the point through the cheek and hold the creature fast. Flying fish, dolphin, albacore, and bonito were commonly caught in this manner.

On this morning several canoes, including two double-hulled craft, left in the gray dawn for the open sea, taking the three English sailors as guests. For dolphin and other large species, they first had to catch flying fish for bait. The night before, lines had been set with a white stick weighted with a stone to bob upright when the coconut-baited hook was taken. The fishermen retrieving the devices found a flying fish at almost every hook.

Hitihiti stood forward as the angler. When he spied a school of fish, he ordered the crew to pull down the poles in the bow until the hooks dangled at the surface, while he splashed water from the leaky hulls into the sea to create a fine spray about the bait. As the lure was seized, the crew hoisted the poles while he grabbed the struggling fish with bare hands, a risky, exacting task.

Two twenty-pound bonito were taken quickly, but before their striped undersides had faded under the burning sun, the fishermen shouted excitedly, "*Ah-i-i! Aahye! Aahye!*" The crew hastily lowered hooks into the waters, pointing the canoe down upon the feeding albacore, many weighing up to seventy pounds.

Two seized lines almost at once, sounding at the pull of the hooks and carrying the bows of the double canoe under. The sea washed the length of the vessels, rolling the crew, Morrison with them, into the cold salt water. Coughing out brine, the Englishman, a clumsy swimmer at best, clung to the swamped boat with desperation, though the native crew greeted the mishap with shouts of glee. One raised both hands from the water, each clutching the previously captured bonitos. Righting the craft, the Polynesians flipped their lithe bodies aboard, bailed out the hulls and continued fishing while Morrison recovered.

"Where are the others?" demanded Christian as Morrison returned that evening, bringing a fat bonito as his share of the day's work.

"I don't know, sir. Aren't they returned yet?"

Concern wrinkled Christian's brow. "No," he replied. "No, not yet." He paced the deck, hands folded behind him, peering at the moving sea. The sky was scarcely clouded, a good sign. He bore his dinner to the rail to eat, scanning the ocean anew, his worry increasing. Fully an hour later, a canoe bearing Stewart swung in to the ship.

"We hooked one but lost him," reported George. "It must have been a large dolphin. He snapped the line like a thread."

"Where's Young?"

"Is he not back yet? His canoe also struck a dolphin. The last I saw, it was cutting northwest at a great rate. I'm sorry, sir—I should have kept better watch."

"'Tis not your fault," sighed Christian. "I'm sure he will be found. I just feel a sense of responsibility for the welfare of my men."

"Begging your pardon, sir," Stewart replied, "but didn't your responsibility end when you sent old Bligh off?"

Christian stared at him, demanding honesty as was ever his way. "Go on, Stewart."

"Well, sir, I would not belabor the point, but there is little difference between being towed out to sea by a fish or lingering on to die of boredom on some ocean rock of another's choice." He added, gently, "Some would choose a hasty death at sea, sir."

Christian's face paled. "You may be right, Stewart. God knows I had no alternative—and have none, now!"

Stewart relented, placing a hand upon the shoulder of the young officer. "None has a choice at such a time, I suppose. And you have ever retained our respect and affection. Bligh lacked both."

The night swept in with a velvet rush, bringing the showering burst of familiar tropic stars: the Cross, then the false cross, the pointers to the true, the hazy Magellanic clouds, and the brilliant beacon Achernar. Christian remained long on

Magellanic clouds-
Either of the two small galaxies that appear as conspicuous patches of light near the south celestial pole.

deck, straining to see beyond the reef. At length he went below and fell across the bunk, hating himself for the certain ruin he had brought upon others. Was this the meaning of Bligh's bitter malediction?

It was some time before he slept, although restlessly, until a welcome hail awoke him at dawn. Christian bounded up to the deck as a canoe swept in, towing a huge creature all of seven feet in length. The man in the bow raised his paddle and shouted again.

"Eh, Young!" returned Christian with relief. "Wherever did that great fish take you?"

"Whoosh, man!" cried the young man, "We put a line on th' bounder after midday, an' he begin to tow us nor'west, furder an' furder. He fought hard turble. Soon we were beyond sight o' th' land; an' we paddled th' night, though towin' him; an' by dawn we were off th' reef; an' here we be! Ain't he th' fair beauty, though?"

"Aye!" grinned Christian in relief.

"'Twill indeed be touch and go," sighed Young as he and Christian lazed upon deck one tropic evening.

"True," conceded Christian. "What I foresee is not a colony of castaways, in dread of hostile natives, but a merged kingdom of light and pleasure—and justice too. An ideal principality."

"With you as prince, eh?" laughed Young, instantly regretting his familiarity with his captain.

"I've no wish to be a tyrant," Christian replied. "I'd abandon this colony before I'd allow it to be controlled by force. We have the means to create something new and good."

"British seamen are poor material for it, Christian. They will toss Heaven itself for some delight of the moment—women, rum, and a winning card. Can you build your utopia of such rough material? Everything will progress smoothly until some Cain covets something of Abel's and slays him. Then where's your paradise? Human nature is a rock that you cannot shape by ordinary appeals to reason or humanity."

"But our opportunity is *not* ordinary!"

"Well," Young said, at length, "we had better take plenty of women, I think."

Christian slowly shook his head. "I'm not so sure," he argued. "If we did that, we would create an isolated colony, a thing apart from the native tribes of Tubuai. That could prove disastrous. We should form ties at the outset through our need for mates—to make their society our own."

"With justice our rule, peace in our hearts, and God over all, we will trade enlightenment for women, knowledge for peace, English industry for Polynesian gaiety, iron goods for breadfruit, eh? I hope your vision is fulfilled, but I doubt 'twill ever be. Yet for its success I will pray to Almighty God and his Son, Jesus Christ."

Christian flushed. "God has nothing to do with it, nor Christ. You know I have little truck with such ideas."

"Ye should have. I doubt it will come about short of a miracle."

Squealing pigs, protesting goats of high odor, and complaining chickens came onto the *Bounty* in great numbers as Chief Tinah's orders were fulfilled. Livestock cluttered every available foot of the top deck. William Muspratt, the appointed clerk, tallied 460 hogs, 50 goats, more poultry than he could or would count, and a few dogs and cats to control the rat population of Tubuai.

On the ship, when she eased past Dolphin Bank on the sixteenth day of June, 1789, were besides the seamen, 28 Islanders, including 9 men and 10 women, 8 boys and a girl. Hitihiti came, and Christian had convinced Mautea to join him—after an abbreviated native marriage ceremony. Alexander Smith's Tihuteatuaonoa, whom he mercifully renamed Jenny, and Thomas McIntosh's Mary also shipped out. The other seamen's women would not accompany them, preferring their families to unknown perils in the cold southern ocean.

In precisely one week, the ship raised the peaks of Tubuai and stood in for Bloody Bay, and with the past reception fresh in memory, the swivels and all four-pounders were loaded and freshly primed. Not until the second day, however, did a few shy natives emerge from the timber, bearing aloft a banner of tossing plumes for peace. The Tahitians questioned these natives, five or six, learning that the island was divided into three districts, at war with each other, the enmities deep and bitter. The chiefs were Tinarou, Tamatoa, and Tahuhuatama.

Hitihiti explained to Christian, "It was Tinarou's people alone, not those of the other two, who fought you. Tinarou and his warriors have retired inland."

"How do you think the others feel toward us?"

"They are friendly, I think. Tamatoa wishes to win your support for battles against the other chiefs." He added, "He would like to become your *tayo*, your brother, to strengthen his alliance with you."

"What if we settle in another district?"

"Perhaps if you could become *tayo* to *all* the chiefs, that might end the wars."

Christian laughed. "If only all wars were ended so easily!"

With Morrison and two or three others, Christian went ashore at dawn for the *tayo* ceremony. After a lengthy harangue, Tamatoa presented him with a plantain seedling, the emblem of friendship, and a root of yava, the source of the drug most islanders prized. The chief saluted him with his own name of Tamatoa as, in a *tayo* arrangement, names were exchanged. A seemingly endless procession deposited gifts before Christian. The next morning the captain returned to lavish favors as best he could. He presented the king with hatchets, Tahitian cloth, matting, and the holy red feathers, to bring Tamatoa the best of good fortune.

"Tamatoa's district is too open to the sea," said Christian. "I don't relish any portion of this landing for our colony."

"Me, neither," interjected Churchill. "Why, a ship's broadsides could rake the whole of this slope to the tops of the mountains."

"Exactly. Let's look again at the northeastern portion."

The party set off single file along the beaten red path between walls of high grass burned by the sun until it smelled to Christian like English hay. Insects darted before them, sometimes with a tiny whir like miniature quail. Disappointed Tamatoa was left behind, he dared not enter the domain of his enemies.

By noon the men helped themselves to a banana tree. It was clear and bright; and Christian for a moment thought how sweet and good life was, forgetting the dismal events which had brought him here. They halted again at the seaward edge of a grove of coconut palms. Christian scanned the keys, or low islands, which lay a mile or more offshore. They were timbered and almost concealed the reef beyond, where the rollers swept up, broke, and foamed, their spume glittering in the bright sunlight. Any cruising ship would stand well clear of that reef, which would also shield the lagoon from curious boatmen. Privacy here would not likely be challenged.

"What do you think, Churchill?"

Churchill, as master-at-arms trained to consider matters of weaponry and defense, seemed for once almost enthusiastic.

"'Twill do," he replied confidently. "If we can warp the *Bounty* around to this coast, that is. No larger ship could ever do it. Guns from off that reef could scarcely reach us here. With our cannon we'd hold off any boats they might send in upon us. I think 'twould do very well, sir."

Morrison interrupted softly. "Mr. Christian, sir," he said. "I believe we have visitors."

Half a score of natives filtered through the trees, their brown bodies melding with the background. They hesitated, one apparently a chief wearing a turban, carrying a black war club; his followers were unarmed. He smiled tentatively.

"Tell him we wish to be friends and have no evil purpose here, Morrison," directed Christian. Mills came up and stood beside them.

"He says he is Taroatohoa, the son of Tahuhuatama, and is chief of this region."

"Is he the true chief, or is his father?"

"As his father's son, he is, sir. The father is regent."

Christian nodded. "Sound out Taroatohoa on a possible settlement."

Following a brief interchange, Morrison grinned.

"He says he is delighted, and I believe him. You may take your choice of land; his people will help. He also says he wishes to be *tayo* to you, sir. I would recommend it. Being *tayo* to both him and Tamatoa might end their strife, making them brothers to each other."

"I doubt it," murmured Christian. "Brotherhood doesn't come that simply." He mulled over the problem. "Nevertheless, tell him I am agreed to be his *tayo*. Tomorrow we shall try to warp the *Bounty* along the lagoon to this point, although I'm still not sure it can be done."

CHAPTER EIGHT

Chief Tomatoa, incensed that the Englishmen would settle in his rival's area, pleaded with the young captain to destroy the new *tayo* agreement with Taroatohoa. He showed Christian his endless coconut groves, the numerous breadfruit trees crowned with deep-green leaves, the fruit growing upright on stalks amid the leaf clusters.

Tomatoa pointed to the great orchards of these rich and treasured trees and offered Christian his choice, and the Englishman said, "No!" not for lack of appreciation, but because the survival of his colony was at stake. He now turned his attention to establish the settlement. The *Bounty* was warped four miles eastward with the greatest difficulty, for there was no true channel, the bottom of the lagoon was obstructed by coral growths, and the ship often grounded. 'Twas sheer drudgery, but somehow on the eighth of July she was moored prow and stem with bower anchors in three fathoms half a cable length offshore off the easternmost tip of Tubuai. The sails were unbent, the topgallant masts and yards struck, lowering her profile, reducing the possibility of discovery.

"I would think we should store the t'gallant masts," muttered Churchill. "'Tis true we have no intent to put to sea again, but emergencies may arise."

"What sort of emergencies?" Christian asked.

Churchill shrugged. "I cannot foretell the future." He added, to temper his crustiness, "If we retain them we might permit ourselves an option, until we get settled."

Christian replied. "Aye, they might indeed prove useful in some way."

The captain, with Hitihiti and a few of the company, met Taroatohoa on the beach, the chieftain happily bringing gifts of yams and breadfruit. Smiling, Christian thanked him.

"Now to create a colony—something utterly new in the world!" he murmured. None of his party replied; Stewart gazed through the coconut grove as though he heard the toll of doom. Christian selected for the settlement a flat meadow, 100 yards inland from the cove where the *Bounty* was moored. A creek meandered through it, a screen of timber protected it from the sea, and plunging shot from the mountains could not reach it.

"What do you think, Mills?" he asked the gunner, whose knowledge of frontier forts and cannon was considerable.

Mills rubbed his grizzled whiskers. "It will do, sir. What sort of works were you thinking of? Palisades would be difficult, I'm thinkin', without no yoke of oxen."

"They would, indeed," agreed Christian. "How about an earthen fort, with perhaps a moat surrounding it?"

"We have many hands, if they will set them to it."

"We'll see to that. You draw the plans. The walls must be thick enough and tall enough to protect us from shot."

"Seems to me like so much wasted effort," grumbled Churchill softly.

"Once we dismantle the *Bounty,* we are immobilized," explained the officer, patiently. "Sooner or later His Majesty's ships will come for us. If they discover a slightest clue, they will investigate. If they land a boat, we shall surely be uncovered. The islanders cannot keep any secret, and Tamatoa now has no love for us anyway. That is why we must have defense works."

Returning to the ship, Christian mustered the company aft to inform them of his plans to build a fort. "We shall directly—Where are Sumner and Quintal?" The men, confused, looked at one another.

"Ashore, sir," Muspratt said. Christian felt hot blood flood his brain at this first direct challenge to his authority.

"Why were they not stopped?"

A thick silence settled over the deck.

Finally Muspratt, again, replied. "We . . . it happened while you were ashore, sir," he said. "We had no authority to stop them. Besides, it might have meant a fight."

"Our very survival depends upon obedience to your elected authority," Christian cried. Realizing that this was the wrong tack, he let the matter drop.

The errant pair, their ardent spirits depleted, swam confidently out to the ship in the morning, clambered dripping over the side. Christian harshly summoned them aft. Surly, they shuffled to him.

"Why did you disobey orders and go ashore without permission?" Christian said coldly.

"The ship is moored," Quintal replied. "We are now our own masters."

Christian whipped the pistol from his belt and clapped it to the startled seaman's head. "I'll show you who is master!" Never, since the morning of the mutiny, had he acted so decisively, and he felt the better for it. "We will have discipline and order, or we are nothing, and by God we shall not be nothing while I am master! Churchill!"

The master-at-arms trotted aft. This affair was more to his liking. "Aye, sir?"

"Take these two scoundrels below. Put them in irons until we decide what to do with them." He returned the pistol to his waistband. "We *will* have discipline," he said to Young.

"Well spoken, Captain Bligh!" replied the grinning midshipman, forcing Christian himself to laugh. "You were right, of course, but I fear this is but the beginning. Mutiny, it seems, breeds mutiny. It might be unwise to impose too heavy a punishment. Their gravest crime was curiosity, and they are scarcely to blame for that."

"I'm not angry at them, but they must remember to submit to authority. I will wait until morning," replied Christian. "A night's reflection will do them no harm."

Young nodded. "That is more than fair, sir. Might everyone be permitted to go ashore one day—Sundays, perhaps?"

"We might," agreed Christian, "and after a swift visit to the keys to look after the animals, the men will have liberty for all that day."

Christian promptly got the work on the fort underway, proceeding by trial and error. The forge was got up on deck, and Joseph Coleman, the armorer, set to work manufacturing spades, hoes, and mattocks, heavy durable tools that would outlive their users.

With Tahitian assistance, the gardener, William Brown, set about clearing a patch of sunny, light soil near the projected fort, planting yams and other food stock. The remainder of the company daily labored on the earthworks, a sentinel always posted for hostile natives.

Christian was greeted July 18 by Chief Taroatohoa and his aged father, Tahuhuatama. They brought symbolic gifts of plantains and yava roots. A piece of turf was ceremoniously turned, the union jack raised, the dimensions of the fort laid out, and an extra allowance of grog issued. It was to be called Fort George, after the monarch whose ship they had stolen, whose captain they had set adrift, from whose guns they were in flight, and to whose control most desired never to return. Such is the power of tradition. Young saw the incongruity of it all. "We might call it Fort Cromwell," he jibed. Christian grinned, recalling the battered old castle above his boyhood village of Cockermouth, which misty legend insisted Cromwell had breached with his siege cannon and afterward ruined.

"Above all, we are Englishmen," he protested. "'Tis in our blood and cannot be gainsayed."

"I thought we had elected to become men apart?"

"Englishmen apart, perhaps, but Englishmen still. We mutinied not against George III, but against abuse of his authority."

"I know, sir. Fort George it is. God and King forever! And all that."

CHAPTER NINE

Shrieks and blasts from great conch shells rent the air one morning as the *Bounty* men labored. Scarcely had they taken defense positions when a strange procession wound among the trees, a horde of men, women, and even children, moaning, sobbing, weaving to and fro, their heads and shoulders gashed and bleeding. Morrison, after conferring with Hitihiti, stood enrapt atop the embankment, observing the weird and horrible parade.

"It's all right, sir," he reassured Christian. "Tahuhuatama has died. This is the beginning of his funeral." Morrison shifted uncomfortably. "Sir, could I—that is, I—"

Despite his revulsion at the spectacle, Christian laughed aloud.

"By all means, Morrison."

The boatswain scooped up his note paper and raced away. Stewart, winning an indulgent, approving nod from the captain, followed.

They reached the shore where several relatives preceded the body in their mourning dress of matting, their faces gashed with shark's tooth flails. Horror overtook Stewart, but Morrison scribbled down each detail.

At the peak of an earthen pyramid and beside it, the body of the late chief was gently laid in a grave. The natives waited patiently for the brewing yava, and when the first pair quaffed two bowls each, they quickly subsided into a stupor, their flaccid limbs under continuous massage by their women. Others began a lavish feast, interrupted at times by dreadful wails and scarifications. During the night, more people arrived for the commemoration of the great chief's passing.

The following dawn the mourners began to cut and mangle themselves afresh, many striking their heads with heavy war clubs until blood poured down their bodies, revealing in scarlet rivers their despair at the loss.

Stewart impulsively rose to intercede when Morrison restrained him. "They would not appreciate interference, sir," he warned.

"How you can write about this loathsome undertaking is beyond me," muttered Stewart.

Morrison looked up in astonishment. "Why, sir, we are the first Europeans to witness this!" he exclaimed. "Don't you think such customs should be made a matter of record?"

"I think they should be consigned to oblivion," replied the midshipman.

"Perhaps our ancestors may have conducted themselves in this way. Would that someone then had recorded their customs for us to study today."

Meanwhile, work continued on the new colony. Christian was no idle spectator. He performed a man's full work day after day, sweating with the others, sharing their blisters. His muscles hardened and he drove himself more vigorously than he drove others.

With the fort well underway, Christian, Stewart, Morrison, and three others left on August 20 in the cutter on a reconnoitering cruise around the island. The gaff-rigged boat sailed beautifully, and Christian determined to renew her bottom boards and put her in first-class condition once more.

The reef happily proved to be continuous except for a narrow passage to the southwest, impracticable for a ship, and with the island demonstrated to be a secure-enough base, Christian faced his major remaining problem—the establishment of peace with Tinarou, most belligerent of the three island kings. He had to be won over either by treaty or through force of arms. Apparently Tinarou desired first to fight. A few weeks later a party of Tahitian men, directed to bring in a supply of coconuts, was assailed by some of Tinarou's warriors, one being severely wounded by a flung stone.

Christian instantly ordered Mills to take an armed party in pursuit and, locating the Tubuaians, they fired into them, killing one and frightening the others. This brought tranquility for a few days, though he had no illusions it would last.

"What do you think, Morrison?" Christian asked.

"Begging pardon, it seems to me, sir, as though this is but the start of it," the boatswain replied.

"My problem," Christian mused aloud, "is to make sufficient impression upon Tinarou without confirming him as an enemy."

"Sir, may I make a suggestion?"

"By all means."

"Let us burn his house, sir. This will assert our authority, yet injure none of his people, thus demonstrating our forbearance. Inside the hut I have observed a pair of carved images we might take with us. They seem to be ritually important. If so, he would have to secure their return. He must negotiate."

Christian smiled with relief. "Splendid idea, Morrison."

The images were eighteen inches tall; carved of black *toa* wood; decorated with pearl shells; human hair, teeth, and fingernails; and round each was a tiny hedge of red feathers from some island bird. Christian shook his head with disbelief.

"The contraptions men fashion and put their faith in!" he marveled. "Man's capacity to delude himself is fathomless."

"Yes, sir," agreed Morrison. "With idols or without."

Behind them a pillar of flame and smoke consumed the matted hut.

CHAPTER TEN

With September came a slowing in construction of the massive fort, Young and others sensing a creeping disillusionment and restlessness among the Englishmen, a situation either not detected or ignored by Christian. His energy, enthusiasm, and good spirits remained high, though he stirred ever less response.

One morning a Tahitian boy rushed to the captain to report that the hostile Tinarou, accompanied by a large band of his followers, was approaching through the timber.

Hitihiti talked with the boy. "Captain," he warned, "Tinarou's men are armed but left their lances in the woods. They can seize them quickly, at a signal. It would be well to be wary!"

Christian scribbled a note to Coleman who was aboard the *Bounty*. "Tell the boy to take this to the ship and give it to the gray-hair who guards the cannon."

He had Mills arm a number of men and quietly conceal them atop the earthen walls. With Hitihiti and Morrison, he prepared to receive the oncoming Tubuaians, peacefully or by war, as they chose.

Chief Tinarou approached with a broad smile, indicating the huge baskets of provisions his people bore, aligning the gifts at the feet of Christian's party. Through Morrison he pleaded, tears glistening in his eyes, that his household gods be restored.

"Certainly we have no intent to keep them captive," Christian assured him. "We took them only for safekeeping when you discourteously refused to meet with us." Before he could reply the officer continued: "But I ask that you treat us with friendship."

Tinarou nodded vigorously. With a show of great good humor, he offered Christian a bowl of yava.

"Take care, Captain," warned Hitihiti. Christian declined the offered food. He signaled for the armed men atop the walls to reveal themselves.

Tinarou was no fool. He recognized that the captain was aware of his treachery, and his grin vanished. A quiver shot through his body, he twirled his war club and screamed, while two or three attendants flogged their heads bloody with sharks' teeth to indicate their hatred. Tinarou stalked off in flaming anger for the shore. Coleman, aboard ship, glimpsing the ragged horde, followed Christian's instructions and loosed a warning shot from a four-pounder. The ball whistled above them, driving them in a tumbling panic back into the timber.

"Coleman ought to have loosed grape among them," growled Churchill.

"That would never do," Christian countered. "We are too few and they too many; our stores are limited, and theirs unbounded. We must live with them and not in opposition to them. Otherwise we face disaster."

"I've faced disaster before, sir, and still I live."

"Did ye enjoy it?"

The corporal shrugged indifferently. "'Tis a part of life," he replied. "Ye accept it because ye must. In this life there are the lions and the antelope, and while I have teeth, I prefer being a lion."

Christian called Morrison over. "Wander down to Taroatohoa's village and sound the sentiment there; discover if Tinarou's hostility has spread among them. Perhaps invite the chief to a heiva aboard the *Bounty*. Hurry back as quickly as ye can."

Morrison returned long after dark, clambering over the ship's side and touching his forelock respectfully. Taroatohoa's loyalty was unshaken.

"He accepts your invitation with pleasure—as does most of his household, I am afraid. I don't rightly know how many, sir."

"No matter," Christian sighed in relief.

Taroatohoa brought two sisters and a large troupe of attendants laden with provisions for the feast when he came aboard next evening for the heiva. Christian greeted him as befitted a trusted ally, handing him and his attendants over the rail. They separated as was the Polynesian custom for the dinner, the women drifting aft, the men forward.

The captain recognized many of the dishes, and Morrison explained those that puzzled him. In addition to several types of fish and shellfish, there was the inevitable breadfruit, sliced into orange blocks of a squashlike substance; fried golden bananas, their taste heightened by a mysterious condiment; slippery globs of sweet poi, swimming in a slurry of nutty-rich coconut milk. There were many types of greens and even a bit of baked pork, for the Tubuaians already were making use of the *Bounty*'s largesse. Polynesian eating was an enthusiastic and noisy affair. Brown fingers dipped into swirling coconut milk, grasping at bits of flotsam; heads bobbed forward, the fingers swiftly raised the prize to the mouth for noisy sucking and inhaling, the louder the sounds the more appreciated the dinner.

Torches of bound coconut fibres dipped in vegetable oil cast an eerie light across the deck as the Tahitian heiva-dance followed the feast. It instantly won the rapt attention of the Tubuaians, many of whom had never seen one before, and also of the Englishmen, who had never become blasé toward this living poetry of music and motion and beauty, so typical of Polynesia. The Magellanic clouds cast a soft overlight upon the dances which, by their gentle suggestiveness, welcomed the viewers into a wonderland of delightful patterns, a new glimpse of allurement.

Mautea, the most beautiful of the Tahitian women, entranced them with the undulating, formalized movements, flowing, rhythmic, and impulsive. An ankle-length, close-fitting sheath of glazed tapa, shimmering white, enhanced the sensuous beauty of her form. The lower edge of the skirt was bordered with red, paralleled by a second red stripe ten inches above, topped by a vest of the softest blue, decorated with two bouquets of black feathers, one at each breast. Streamers of feathers hung from her slim waist, and black or red feathers ringed her long fingers. At her shoulders were wings of tapa cloth, shaped like fans, edged in red. To add to her regal height, a turban of tresses piled atop her glossy hair, inlaid with orchids, glittering bits of coral and ivory shark teeth in a serrated pattern of wild originality.

The torchlight flickered upon the swaying dancers, stirring the senses of the lonely seamen. To the Polynesians it was a traditional dance, deep and ritually fulfilling; to the Englishmen it was a foretaste of an enchanted world, whose invitation the dancers extended so fluently.

Christian watched Mautea, loving her as he had never loved another. It was one of those exquisite intervals that visit the young with beauty, warmth, and exultation.

When the crew the next morning presented themselves before the captain, prior to disembarking for the daily labor at Fort George, Quintal himself led the "revolt" which the heiva had generated.

"What is this, a new mutiny?" demanded Christian, good-naturedly, when the party objected to going ashore. He absently fingered the pistol thrust into his waistband, looked them over, one by one. The men, although respectful, were grimly determined. The weeks of severe labor had corded their muscular arms and chests and bellies and made them seem more resolute than before.

"No, sir, no new mutiny, sir," replied Smith, touching his forelock. "We would just like to profit from the last one."

"What do you mean?"

"We want to be rid of this bloody work, sir. Why can we not join with one of these tribes? Feasts and pleasure—that's the life we want."

Christian scanned the set faces before him. "I do not deny what you say, Smith, but soon we will be ashore for good, and things will improve."

"That's in the future, sir. We want freedom now!" A chorus of agreement followed.

Christian felt a temporary loss of words. "What do you propose?" he asked.

"That we join Taroatohoa's people. Surely he would welcome us."

The captain shook his head.

"That wouldn't do, Smith, an' well ye know it. The hostilities between these tribes are too great, and we have already made enemies of Tinarou and his people. We cannot bring their inevitable wrath down on innocent bystanders. If we do not build our own colony, we cannot stay here."

An impasse. Christian, supported by his officers and certain of the men, held firm. The wilder elements remained adamant.

"If this be not mutiny, what is it?" grumbled Christian to Young.

"Aye, sir, 'tis insistence upon their rights against your authority—in that 'tis mutiny, straight enough. But there's some justice on their side too. They do not have th' dream you have. They see no future aside from the pursuit of enjoyment. What else is left to them?"

"Duty, perhaps?"

"Duty to whom, sir? To King? We're outlaws. To you? Respect, an' even affection, perhaps, but *duty?* To your dreams? Their duty, as they see it, is to preserve themselves, an' find what pleasure they can—today. Tomorrow may never come."

"Duty or no, sir, discipline can be enforced." Churchill broke into the officers' discussion as though he were their equal, as in certain ways he indeed had become.

"Perhaps it could, Churchill," Christian agreed. "But 'twould create the identical situation aboard the *Bounty* we wish to avoid. We cannot live in a camp armed against each other."

The seamen refused to work the following day and the third, as well. Shortly after seven bells of the forenoon watch, Smith, with Quintal and McCoy, once more approached Christian.

"Yes, what is it?" asked the captain noticing they omitted the salute of respect.

"We'd like some grog, sir," declared Smith.

"You get grog. Each day, as you ever have."

"More, sir. A double ration."

"Our supply is not inexhaustible, Smith, as you know."

"Neither is our patience, sir," Quintal put in sharply.

Christian coldly surveyed him. "What does that mean?"

"It means we must have more grog, sir, and if it is not given us, we shall seize it!"

"Get forward, the lot of you!" cried Christian. "*I* am master of this ship, and you will obey orders as long as you are aboard. If you prefer to try your luck ashore, go; but without guns. An' if ye have any sense, you'll halt this insubordination!"

The trio shuffled forward. Young spoke to Christian ominously, "They'll have grog, sir, you'll see."

"Churchill!" bellowed the captain. "Take Mills and two or three of the most resolute, go below and restore order. Post a reliable man on guard to prevent their complete looting of the liquor."

He paced the narrow aft deck thoughtfully. "Double the grog allowance for everyone," he called to Muspratt. "We'll see if *that* is effective."

"If 'tis not overlate," replied Young.

It was. By the next day the insubordination threatened all control. Christian, if a visionary, remained a realist in many ways. At four bells of the evening watch on September 10, he ordered the company mustered aft. They massed, some sullen, a few drunk, others cheerful, buoyed by the conviction they had almost become their own masters. The captain surveyed them, grinning ruefully.

"Lads," he said, "as ye well know, we've come to an impasse. We cannot live ashore until the fort is built. It will not be completed if we refuse to work on it. We cannot endure as a company with many determined to pass the days in idleness and drunkenness. The grog will soon become exhausted. Then you would have nothing save yava, and from what I've seen, no civilized man would touch it. You have chosen me as master, and yet ye refuse to obey. So there you have it. I confess I am at my wits' ends—have you any suggestions?"

"More grog!" called a voice, amid general laughter.

It was Joseph Coleman, the wise and dependable armorer seasoned by his forty years and sound in judgment, who replied:

"Mr. Christian, ye've called for opinions. Mine is that this whole thing is wrong, sir. I do not see how a 'paradise' can be established unless the angels are content. Your paradise has flaws an' will destroy itself if ye persist, and soon. I'll wager at least half of us do not like it here. Ye have a minority, sir, an' the only way a minority can control a situation is by unending force. Beggin' your pardon, but I do not think that is in your nature. This solution of yours, Tubuai, is doomed, sir, an' the colony with it."

"You put a gloomy turn to 't, Joseph," replied Young, leaning against the rail. "Situations men despise at first can be solved in the future . . ."

"The future. Aye, the future," said Christian. "We have destroyed our future—unless we create a new one. Where to do that? Where better than on Tubuai? I ask you, men. What is your alternative?"

"Tahiti, sir!" several voices chorused.

"Aye, aye, Tahiti!" shouted others.

Christian shook his head in disbelief.

"That, lads, is *suicide*, and well ye know it," he protested. "With the exception of a handful, there's not a man among ye but would be dead within a year—would swing from a yardarm. We are outlaws! The very first place to be investigated by His Majesty's vessels will be Tahiti. Ye'd be daft—mad—returning there!"

The men returned Christian's stare, unmoved.

Christian spread his hands resignedly. For months his vision of peace, happiness, and security had flowered while he was blinded to the true nature and limited capacity of the men around him. Even so, Christian might have won over enough spirits to continue his experiment for a little longer, had Churchill not abandoned him openly. The next day's conference was decided by the corporal.

"I'm for Tahiti," Churchill announced to the captain's amazement. "I'm frank to say I've had a gut full of this place." He scratched his matted chest, where the gray had touched the curled brown hairs. "I've lived a long life, an' it matters little if it's soon to end, so 'tis ended in pleasure. I've seen both this isle an' Tahiti. For me, 'tis the other."

"In the face of certain death, Churchill?" asked Christian.

"Certain is as certain does," he replied, without concern. "Before I'm hanged I must be caught. Tahiti is large, with many places of concealment . . . "

"And many natives to point them out for searching marines!"

"Mayhap. Every man must die, an' I do not fear it, nor wish to postpone it unduly, although I do not seek it. The future I do not fear—nor anything else. 'Tis Tahiti." He added, as a clear afterthought, "Sir."

Defeat etched itself into Christian's face. For the first time since the mutiny, his vision had narrowed, darkened, a realization that he was floundering toward a fate he could neither see nor predict. "Is this," he murmured in agony, "the curse that Bligh laid upon me—the destruction of the people I most desire to save. Have I doomed myself to this?" He shuddered. The men silently watched him.

"Thataway floats your stick, sir," Mills said, inspecting the captain closely.

Christian looked full upon him. "I do not understand, Mills."

The gunner shrugged. "'Tis a Yankee woodsman's sayin', sir," he explained. "I s'pose it comes from the Indians, Algonquins, likely. A trapper sets for beaver, an' the tie chain is attached to a float, a stick. When th' trap's sprung, the animal takes off with it an' drowns, the float showin' where it is. The sayin' means that's the way she is, an' no man can evade or alter it. The 'stick' is fate, sir. A man's fate."

"My stick," mused Christian. "So my stick floats—but where? To what purpose?" He raised closed fists to his eyes. "*Laich,*" the word of mystery he had heard before, came faintly to his brain. "*Laich, anochi iemach . . .*" So it seemed to say, words without meaning, syllables of no sense. Then, slowly, he recovered his composure.

"Gentlemen," he began softly as they pressed forward to hear his words. "Gentlemen, I will carry you and land you wherever you please. I have one favor to request: grant me the ship, tie the foresail, and give me a few gallons of water, and let me run before the wind. I shall land upon the first island the ship drives to. I have done such an act that I *cannot* stay at Tahiti. I will never be carried home to be a disgrace to my family."

Young spoke up. "Ye sound, Captain, as though you felt abandoned. 'Tis not so! Where you go, I will go, an' others too. We have cast our lots with you, and I for one intend to follow you until death. We shall never leave you, go where you will."

"Aye, sir. There's others of us feel the same," said Alexander Smith.

Christian's expression lightened at this support. "Let us have a show of hands."

Sixteen opted for Tahiti, and nine for some more remote haven, with Fletcher Christian their leader.

"That does it, says it all." The officer sighed. "Those who go ashore at Tahiti will have their share of arms, ammunition, and all else that they desire, providing the ship is left in proper condition for sea."

Directing Young to take charge of the deck, start to unbend the canvas, fill the casks with fresh water, and trim the vessel for departure, Christian went below.

CHAPTER ELEVEN

Refitting the *Bounty* was a simple matter, not so provisioning her. Christian sent seven men under Burkitt and Skinner to gather in hogs enough for their brief voyage. The party returned within three hours, shattered, bloody, defeated.

"We barely escaped with our skins, sir," Burkitt glumly reported. "One chief told Hitihiti they would do the same to you, should you come."

Christian flushed. "Whose warriors were they—Tinarou's or those of Taroatohoa?"

Churchill shrugged massively. "What difference does it make?" he interjected bluntly. "Kill some and 'twould inspire respect from all, wouldn't it?"

The officer made no effort to hide his disgust. "Ye are daft, Churchill!" he cried. "We cannot kill just to see men die. If we slay 'twill be for punishment."

"The savages ought to be learned a lesson on how to greet Englishmen. Parcel out some muskets, and I'll take a party and blow some respect into them—as I've long wished to do."

Christian glanced at him. Despite his aversion, some amusement crept into his expression at length.

"I suppose it's time you got your wish," he consented, in partial surrender, "but I shall go along."

Churchill distributed arms to twenty sailors. With them and the nine Tahitians and four boys, one carrying the tattered union jack, they swarmed ashore and worked inland.

"Sir," said Mills anxiously, "all due respect, but would it not be better to send a man or two in advance, as scouts? An ambush in the timber and we might be overwhelmed."

"Right you are. Take a Tahitian or two and work ahead, but remain in sight." Mills and the natives, however, quickly disappeared into the brush ahead, and the main force entered the timber cautiously, pausing to listen, then pushing on. They had just entered a defile, when the storm broke.

Screeches and howls and a hail of rocks, a sleet of spears fell upon the seamen from all sides. Now and then they glimpsed the warriors, garbed in scarlet sashes and peaked caps of tough coconut fiber, their faces fiercely daubed. Blasts of musket fire blew them backward with some killed or wounded. Yet they regrouped and came on again, savagely pressing home the attack.

Christian swiftly organized the seamen, urging them to hold their fire. "*Stay together, men, an' shoot when you see the whites of their eyes!*" he thundered. The directive was most effective. Soon, the enemy thrust was shattered. The leaping, sweating warriors fled howling.

"They fight with more fury than wit," commented Morrison, wryly.

"That they do, James," Mills grinned, blowing acrid smoke from his gun muzzle. "'Tis not man to man they are beaten. They're whipped because they lack discipline."

Among the slain was Tinarou's brother, killed by Christian himself.

Christian paused for a moment over the man's lifeless body. "He is the only man I have ever killed," he said aloud to himself. He felt no sense of triumph, no pity for the victim, no emotion except, curiously, a passing freshet of confidence in his own power, strangely warming, this capacity to erase another being with utter finality. It was odd.

A score of pigs were quickly rounded up and driven to the fort, and now with provisions aboard, her water casks filled, the *Bounty*, considerably lightened, slipped easily back through the passage and hove to outside the reef, while salt water was pumped into her bilges to stabilize her for the voyage north to Tahiti. At noon her fore course and tops were loosed. She gained way close hauled under a freshening southeasterly breeze. Tubuai, with its kaleidoscopic, bloody battles and dissensions, was but a memory.

The ship hove to off the rounded islet of Mehetia, half a day's run from Matavai Bay, and Muspratt parceled out the trade goods as Christian had pledged: ammunition, arms, liquor, slops, and other desirables, divided into apportionments, all under the watchful inspection of the ship's company. Once fairly divided, they chose the piles by lot. Then the goods were carefully guarded until the vessel anchored in the roadstead for the third—and final—time.

On September 22 the party electing to remain ashore made preparations to depart. It included midshipmen George Stewart and Peter Heywood; Morrison, who was most anxious to further his studies; and Coleman, Norman, McIntosh, and Byrne, none having lifted arms against Bligh. Also deciding to remain at

Tahiti was Burkitt, despite Christian's warning that, as a prominent rebel, his lot would be certain execution. Lastly, young Tom Ellison and Churchill also decided to remain.

"Churchill," argued Christian, "I truly fear for you if you do this. Every effort will be made to capture you—both of us, that we above all be punished. Won't you reconsider?"

"They must catch me first, sir," Churchill replied, his cold eyes sweeping the skyline of the tumbled mountains. "I will not be taken readily."

Remaining aboard the *Bounty* were Young, Mills, Brown, Martin, McCoy, Quintal, and Alexander Smith—a hard lot, unpredictable. But these were not all. Taroameiva, from Tubuai, and his two friends all warmly attached to Christian. And, of course, Mautea.

"Will nothing make you reconsider?" In the cabin he caressed her face. "We may never return to your people, and I fear our course is sure to be even more difficult than what we have already endured."

"Nothing. Your life is my life. I wish for no other."

Later on deck, Christian turned to Young. "Tell the men if they wish to bring a woman they may do so—one woman for each. We will need them with us when we find a location to settle a new colony. Have the men bring them on board after dusk, and then keep the girls below deck when we put out."

"Aye, sir."

"And mind the men tell none of them, not one, we are readying for sea. When they feel the roll from the outer swells, we will be too far from the reef for them to elude us and swim back. This must all be done secretly, mind you."

"Right, sir."

"I'll go ashore and return when the moon comes up."

Those electing to remain on the island wrestled their hammocks, chests, and belongings to the deck, impatient to hit the beach, but their departure was slow and difficult because of considerable surf. Christian boarded a swift canoe, passing other craft already ferrying the giggling women, their glossy hair bedecked with flowers, bringing a fresh fragrance to the weather-battered ship now beginning to stink from goats, hogs, and rotten bilges.

After the captain had paid his respects to Chief Tinah and his wife, Iddeah, he returned to the black-sand beach to sit moodily, flipping pebbles against the surf's white foam. His temper was at one with the sea, its heavy breakers generated by some distant storm lashing against the coast ceaselessly, futilely. A sodden coconut was lobbed again and again against the powdery sands, only to be swept out by the undercurrent back to the sea again. *We are like that,* Christian thought, *tossed about by life with no true direction, little intelligible guidance, until we are smashed, dissolved in the ocean, our elements formless and forgotten.* Yet within him a voice protested: *We are not truly flotsam, or need not be. We have intelligence; we have will. We do not revert to the particles of nature unless we abrogate these powers. We remain an entity, a force, so long as we can exert our talents and our will.* Christian smiled indulgently at his musings.

Stewart and Heywood, their baggage stacked away from the water's edge, interrupted him. Christian was glad they had come. He wanted to talk with the young midshipmen this last evening.

"Will we ever see you again, sir?" asked Heywood.

"'Tis unlikely," replied Christian, slowly. "Somehow you will return to England within a year or so. I can never go back."

"Are you certain?"

"Who knows? No one can predict his fate. I would return to Moorland Close if . . ." His voice trailed off.

"Everyone on the Isle of Man knows of Moorland Close and your people."

"Aye. We Christians are Manxmen, too, and our lineage is a proud one. Some of us have been executed by the Crown—falsely, I might add, until now. Others of us may be, perhaps with more reason!" His jest brought no smiles.

"Courage can lead to glory or the block," said Stewart, his West India eyes glittering. "Equally as well."

Christian was restless, wanting to say what must be said, suddenly eager to have done with it, return to the *Bounty*.

"Peter, I would ask a favor of you."

"Aye."

"When you return to England, there will be an investigation of the mutiny. You and Stewart should readily be cleared. 'Twas my affair, mine alone, and I accept responsibility."

"You had some little assistance," Stewart pointed out. "Churchill, Smith, Ellison—the others."

The captain watched the beat of the surf. "I had no help, George. The mutiny was mine. I conceived it, urged it, executed it—and perhaps 'twill execute me in the end." He paused. "I felt I had no choice."

Heywood attempted to disagree, but Christian continued. "When you are freed, Peter, I wish you would visit my people at Moorland Close. Explain to them the events as you know them, from the day we left England until now. Omit nothing, gloss over nothing, protect no one, defend no action—tell them the truth. If you can speak well of me, do so, but only honestly."

"Aye," said Heywood. "They know thee for a man o' honor an' principle, an' I can only confirm it."

"Truth, Peter, not kindness."

"Aye, sir. The truth it shall be, an' they'll welcome it, I pledge."

In silence the three watched as the sun plunged into the sea beyond Eimeo. A tower of cloud over that island flamed, then faded, drawing in the dusk. Torches of the natives danced along the beach. Christian stiffly rose. "I must be off, now," he said quietly. He shook hands with his friends. "Good fortune attend you."

"May God take care of you," replied Stewart, with deep feeling.

"Let God take care of Himself!" he retorted. "*I* will take care of Christian."

Ignoring the harshness of his words, they accompanied him to the water's edge, where he hailed a canoe.

"Will we see you in the morning, sir?" asked Peter anxiously.

In the dim light Christian shrugged. "'Tis not likely," he replied. He stepped into the craft and was gone.

CHAPTER TWELVE

Young greeted Christian as he clambered over the side. "The plants and animals are all put aboard. As are the women."

"Susannah?" the captain asked about the midshipman's favorite.

"She was first to arrive, thank God."

The rising moon shed ghostly light as the ship stood out to sea, making quiet way under a light breeze. Not until she was clear of the reef and rising to the roll of the open waters did the Polynesians become aware of her movement. They rushed for the deck. Christian watched the developing bedlam with a touch of compassion.

Mautea had come on deck. "They are alarmed," she whispered softly to Christian. "Let me speak to them."

"Young! Mills!" Christian called. "Herd them aft—but kindly, lads! They are of us, now."

Yet fright was their lot. Mautea addressed them quietly, calmly, so that they pressed forward to hear her words above the pounding of the water. While Christian's knowledge of the tongue was imperfect, he knew she was reminding the islanders that they were among friends, that they, too, were people of the deep, accustomed to long voyages. As she spoke, the tension eased. A smile here and there, once a bit of laughter. When she finished the mercurial natives were in good humor—given the shock of their sudden change of fortune.

The *Bounty* set a northerly course and by noon they coasted the atoll of Tetiaroa, twenty-six miles from Tahiti. By evening the ship had come about and was outside the reef of the indented northern coast of the arrowhead island of Eimeo, or Morea.

Aboard were the nine Britons and their women, most with English names bestowed upon them by their mates, less in honor perhaps, than for convenience. The trio of Tubuaians had no women, of course, but the three Tahitian men had made no such error.

Young told the captain that he was concerned "that the lack of women for the Tubuaians may cause difficulty."

"Possibly," admitted Christian, "unless we settle where others may be obtained. We will hope for the best. Set the course northerly," he directed.

"Aye, sir," replied Young, good-naturedly. "By the way, what are we looking for?"

Christian laughed, his good humor bubbling to the surface for the first time in many a day.

"Well, all the natives can report is that we disappeared on a northerly course. Perhaps toward Atafu, 2,000 miles west northwest of Tahiti. "Foul-weather" Jack Byron discovered it twenty-five years ago. So we cannot go there. That leaves us approximately 100,000 other islands that have not yet been raised by Europeans!"

"Let's hope we don't have to inspect them all before we find one to your liking."

"*Our* liking, Young. Don't forget we are in this together."

Young, by training and habit, scanned the fore and main courses and the tops, all pulling full and well on this tack.

"What are we looking for, sir?" Young repeated.

Christian pondered the question before replying. "We require an uninhabited island, off the main track of discovery and above all with no suitable harbor to lure a chance vessel. It should have a swampy or iron-bound coast all around, yet be fertile enough to sustain a colony and sufficiently mountainous to prove interesting, for our party needs stimulus and excitement."

"Have you found any such in Bligh's books?"

"I am still searching. First we shall take a look at the misty isles of the Spaniards, if we can find them. Then elsewhere, perhaps."

Christian had learned from the literature aboard much of what was known about the opening of the southern ocean. The Spaniards, a clannish lot, commenced its exploration out of Callao as early as 1570, permitting little to be known of their landfalls. Dutchmen made important voyages and significant discoveries. The English followed with Byron, then Wallis, Philip Carteret, and Cook with his three great voyages, on the last of which his sailing master aboard the *Resolution* had been Bligh himself. But still the ocean remained too vast a realm to be deprived of all its secrets—and it would not give them up easily.

Over the following weeks, the *Bounty* cruised the restless deep in a seemingly aimless fashion. But Christian had a plan that brought them once again within sight of land. The wanderers observed the cloud over the stupendous atoll of Rangiroa long before its picket of coconut palms became visible from the deck.

Within hours, the ship penetrated the spectrum-tinted lagoon and explored the coconut-bordered white beaches for many miles but found no fresh water. "It's too level and uninteresting anyway," Christian confided to Young. "Our only relief from monotony would be to fight among ourselves."

He then laid a precise course direct for the equator, which they reached by late October, having sighted no further islands of consequence.

The sea remained steady, with only an occasional squall. They were always brief and soon gave way to clear skies filled with innocent clouds. The nights were silent, with no bird cry, although the seamen on watch were urged to listen for them. Neither were there successive lightning bolts flashing in the predawn from some constant direction, indicating the presence of mountains. Nothing but the ocean sky, unending and monotonous.

"We are not only the sole ship afloat in all this sea, but it appears we have seen our last bit of land and must sail on forever," grumbled Mills one bright morning. His remark appeared to decide Christian.

"I've been troubled with discouragement too. We need water." He brought the ship about onto a fresh course.

The *Bounty* plowed southwesterly for days until she approached an egg-shaped isle about the size of Tubuai, identified by its soaring peaks as the Purutea, though later to be known as Rarotonga, the mutineers becoming its first European discoverers.

"It will not do for us," Christian said, "because of its natural harbor, but I suppose we can take on water and wood here."

A canoe skimmed out toward them laden, besides its crew, with gifts of hogs, coconuts, and plantains. The natives bounded over the sides of the ship, their garlanded heads bringing a pleasing perfume and their patter a fresh life to the decks. One gaily beflowered youth, perfect of body and grinning broadly, greeted the captain with a hand on both shoulders in a swift gesture of welcome, fingering the pearl-shell buttons on his jacket and admiring the blue of its cloth.

"Why don't you present it to him?" suggested Mautea. "You will make a *tayo* of him and he will help you."

The captain stripped off the jacket and draped it over the shoulders of the youth. Shouting with glee, he leaped to the rail, balanced there, calling to his friends in the canoes, pointing to his new prize until a musket ball smashed through his body and blew him end over end, dead into the sea.

Silence fell like an instant, smothering blanket over the ship. The Puruteans, speechless with shock, clapped their hands to their mouths. Screaming, they dove into the water, making it boil with froth and fury as they stroked toward their craft, streaked aboard, and paddled with loud wails of anguish toward the shore.

Quintal, his musket still smoking, leaned against the mainmast, reeling with drunken laughter, "Get along you savages!" he jeered. "Steal our captain's uniform will ye? We'll blast ye to the devil, that we will! We're the mutineers o' th' *Bou-u-u-nty!*"

Christian snatched the pistol from his waistband and ran forward.

"Don't shoot him, sir," pleaded Young. "Don't kill the sorry fool—"

Christian, struggled to be free of Young's encircling arms. "He's earned death, the black-hearted dog! He shall have it."

Young frantically sought to block his advance. "Wait, sir," he pleaded. "Wait . . . If you shoot him 'twill be the beginning of the end. Some of the others will stand by him—We'll have a war aboard, sir. Death for all—for you, for me, for the women . . ."

Young's plea for mercy drained away some of Christian's fury. He swayed, ran a hand across his face. He thrust the pistol back into his sash then, side-stepping Young, Christian stepped up to Quintal, leaning drunkenly against the mast, his eyes glazed and uncomprehending. The captain snatched away the musket, lashed Quintal across the head with the stock of it, the thick mat of hair softening the blow, which staggered but did not fell him.

"You murderous fool!" the officer ground out. "You ought to be flogged to death. If I ever see you again with a firearm without my permission, I will kill you. Do you understand, Quintal?"

The violence was over, but its effects could not be erased. Under guard a landing party went ashore to fill the empty casks from a clear-running stream below the falls.

Watered, the ship once again was alone on an endless sea, the steady trades pushing her for better than a week. Any day the ship would raise the Friendly Islands. Christian remembered the year before in these very waters. Then, the *Bounty* had been a tight ship, expertly handled, homeward bound after nearly a

30,000-mile voyage. Christian sighed. Now she was wandering, her grassy hull wallowing almost aimlessly, saved only by the copper plates from riddling teredos, her canvas worn, her paint blistered and neglected, sailing on and on and on.

"Land ho-o-o!"

Martin's wail, raised from the foretop, halted Christian's restless pacing. "Where away?" he called.

Martin paused in his descent. "Dead ahead, sir!" he replied. "Clouds and a mountain under them. We can raise it by evening."

And so the ship stood off to windward during the night and with the dawn moved in to an anchorage amid a cloud of craft paddled out to greet this great "outriggerless canoe," as natives termed the wind-driven European vessels. Without hesitation they stormed aboard, asking for "Totee! Totee!" Christian, puzzled, turned to Hitihiti.

"It is their name for Captain Cook," he explained.

"Cook was here?" cried the officer. He darted below and returned with an open book.

"This must be the island he called Tongatapu," he reported. "Ask whether he left any horned cattle here." Hitihiti turned to the natives and gestured with his hands to indicate horned animals. Several men nodded vigorously, "Yes, yes, they say the animals were left here, and some live still," he translated.

"Since we are only about 100 sea miles from Tofua, we cannot stay here," sighed the captain. "Though we can provision, I suppose."

The *Bounty* resumed her slow progress westward, but it seemed of no use.

"I confess I am becoming weary of chasing mountains," Christian conceded to Young, at last.

"Well then, sir, what do we do now?"

Christian maintained his silence, searching his mind.

"We must find our island soon or perish upon these seas," Young continued. "Listen to the men below! They are drunk again. One day they will tire of all this. And I'm afraid 'twill be very soon."

"You're right, of course. Let me fetch a book I found that may provide us a clue."

The captain returned shortly with a volume marked with slips of paper at several points. Its title was *Account of the Voyages of Byron, Wallis, Carteret, and Cook* by J. Hawkesworth, Volume One of a set of three. He found the passage he sought. "This is Admiral Carteret's account," he explained.

> We continued our course westward till the evening of Thursday, July 2, when we discovered land to the northward of us. Upon approaching it the next day, it appeared like a great rock rising out of the sea: it was not more than five miles in circumference and seemed to be uninhabited; it was, however, covered with trees, and we saw a small stream of fresh water running down the side of it. I would have landed upon it, but the surf, which at this season broke upon it with great violence, rendered it impossible. I got soundings on the west side of it, at somewhat less than a mile from the shore, in twenty-five fathoms, with a bottom of coral and sand; and it is probable that in fine summer weather, landing here may not only be practicable, but easy. We saw a great number of seabirds hovering about it, at somewhat less than a mile from shore, and the sea here seemed to have fish. It lies in latitude 20°, 2' south, longitude 133°, 21' west. It is so high that we saw it at the distance of more than fifteen leagues, and . . . we called it Pitcairn's Island.

Christian closed the book. The swift tropic dusk was upon them. The *Bounty*, in the stillness of the evening, lay almost without movement, her masts and spars a tracery in the early night sky, the harsh cries of the hunting birds stilled.

"What do you think?"

"It sounds well enough, sir, but can we find it?"

"The latitude and longitude are given. I suspect the latitude is in error, though. There is a penciled note on the chart placing it at 25°, 2' south. There may be some difficulty with his longitude also, if his timekeeper was inaccurate, as it may have been on so long a voyage. If we reach the correct latitude, however, we can run down it until we find the island. What say you?"

"You are the captain, sir. If you say 'Pitcairn,' then I am with you. Of course, 'twill require weeks of beating against the trades to reach it. We may have a mutinous crew by the time we get there . . . if we do."

"Perhaps. We can be assured of the loyalty of the Polynesians. Certainly some may prove troublesome. We should lock up the arms again."

"It might be wise."

CHAPTER THIRTEEN

Christian lowered the sextant. "Carteret was near correct on his chart," he mused. "I make it latitude 25°, 4' south. But he was off on his longitude by about 175 miles."

"He caused us trouble enough in locating it," commented Young. Bulky and lonely, the volcanic rock protruded from the sea.

"Trouble? Aye. And if he made its location a problem for us, 'twill be no less so for others. At least, Carteret reported a waterfall, a good sign."

All seven Britons aligned the rail. Reckless Jack Smith climbed to the foretop where he dangled his feet over the crosstrees, passing down his observations.

"She's ironbound everywhere," he reported. "No place for an anchorage on this coast, Mr. Christian."

"Looks similar to one of the Orkneys, that she does," grumbled McCoy. "Hard-edged, stony, fit only for goats, an' humans living in rock huts like wolves!"

"It may not be quite so bad as that, Will," countered Brown. "I can make out timber on't. We'll see for certain when we close tomorrow."

Christian could not quite sort out his emotions. He stared across the water at this mysterious island they had come so far to find. Was this the end of his ambition? The notion was difficult to accept. He reduced sail so that the ship barely made way during the night, directing a sharp lookout lest some unsuspected current or wind bring them hard against dangerous rocks in the dark.

Young had gone below. Christian stretched on a mat aft the wheel, staring into the overhead velvet, watching the great unfeeling constellations on their nightly pirouette—the Southern Cross with its foot in the Milky Way; Sagittarius, Tucana, Phoenix, Capricornus, Canis Major, Columba, and, in the center of everything, the hazy glow of the Magellanic clouds, named for the voyager who had coursed these seas near three centuries ago. *I wonder,* thought Christian, *if he, too, had felt unsure, lost—cursed?* On his great passage from the Straits to the Marianas without sighting even a coral reef, Magellan must have imagined himself upon an endless treadmill, driven by winds to nowhere, sailing in the midst of nothing. Yet all the time he was surrounded by islands filled with life and activity, love and war and death, all invisible to him yet existing all around him and his ships, could he but see them. *Was everyman's life so separated from reality?*

What would the morrow hold? What future lay before them on this forbidding yet alluring island? And perhaps beyond this island, somewhere else?

The smell of the land came with the soft trade winds, mingled with the stale odors of the weary plants, the cooking fire, the tethered goats, the fowls, the stink of a vessel and its company long at sea, the musty stench of unwashed bodies and sunbaked tar, and an oaken vessel with the juices dried out of her. Now these smells were dissipated by the rock, the fragrance of this unexplored land they might come soon to know as they knew themselves.

With the first light, the sun's rays struck the eastern headland and the island's highest point, somewhat westerly of its center, a ridge which Christian calculated at 1,100 feet. It was not the mountainous interior that gripped the seamen, however, but its plunging coasts, the ivory spray flying everywhere along there, indication enough for a sailor that a landing would be impossible unless there was some hidden beach or cove.

"I don't like it," muttered Mills, sourly. "Far's I can see there ain't a grain of sand; an' if we did find a beach, how would we get the stores ashore without th' *Bounty* bein' broke up on them rocks?"

The island's aloofness, even its hostility invigorated Christian, for his part. His voice assumed a new authority, a fresh confidence. An infectious eagerness shone on his face, highlighted by the early sun.

"Break out the jolly boat," he directed. "We'll pull in for a closer look. There must be a way to get ashore. There must be!"

Young directed the putting of the tight little boat into the water. In an aside to Christian he said, "You'd best carefully choose the men to go with you sir. There is an uneasiness growing."

Startled, Christian glanced about hastily. "Uneasiness?" he repeated.

"Discontent, sir. Again I am hearing rumors of Tahiti as preferable to this barren rock."

"From whom?"

"The troublemakers, of course."

Once afloat and warped around to larboard, the craft raised and fell against the ship's sides. Young grinned and nodded as the captain broke up the Quintal-McCoy duo, taking Quintal with him. He watched as their oars raised and fell in unison, the boat appearing and disappearing among the swells. Christian, from his jolly, carefully examined the coastline with his glass.

"I'm bound if I can make out even a nook," he admitted. The seamen, working strongly at the oars, their backs to the land, watched his face intently for any clue to his findings. The boat neared a pair of offshore rocks, then pulled easterly along the north coast, reaching a cluster of wet and gleaming rocks at its tip. Just under it they discovered a difficult, though possible, cove, if the sea should slacken off. They stepped the mast then. Picking up the wind which rose with the sun, they cruised more easily along the southern coast, finding it completely ironbound too.

At the western extremity, they found a second barely possible landing; but the best opportunity was to be discovered along the northwest coast, though it would prove uninviting enough. The mountain above it rose precipitately. Once landed, it would be very difficult to gain the interior, if possible at all. They furled the sail, got out the oars again, and pulled in toward the shore, having found the island about two miles long and half a mile wide, verdant, though ruggedly mountainous, and heavily timbered in its numerous valleys.

"That is favorable," approved Christian, to no one in particular. "I see no sign of inhabitants."

"No, sir," conceded Martin, soberly. "There sure ain't."

"Maybe it proved overmuch for anyone else who ever sighted it," added Smith. "In case anyone ever did."

Christian seemed oblivious to the jibes.

The jolly boat cautiously drew in for a closer view. Christian examined what there was of the beach carefully with his glass.

"The only possibility I detect is at the base of that inlet," he reported. "Let's pull for it."

The boat slipped in close to the spray-beaten shore and revealed a curving nook with a narrow beach, only a few yards wide, at its head. Here, surprisingly, a landing was effected readily. Christian jumped lightly ashore and stood, his fists to his hips, legs spread, surveying the wooded mountains which served to wall off the body of the island as though ever to thwart intruders.

"If there is not too much sea, we could use this cove for a regular boat landing." Unexpectedly Smith agreed heartily, his spirits apparently raised by the ease of landing.

"Right, sir. 'Twas better than I expected."

"Pull the boat well above the tide level. Let's see if we can climb to the interior," directed Christian. He shouldered a musket and worked his way laboriously upward, the others following as they might. After a climb of twenty feet, they made easier way and at last gained a relatively level plateau. From the rim they could see their boat on the beach and the ship standing off a mile or so, her sticks fairly steady in the calm sea. Young was observing their progress through his glass no doubt.

Having caught his breath, Christian made his way westerly across a timbered flat. Here would be a fine place for a village, hidden from the sea by a fold of rock, invisible to any ship cruising the coast. Near the flat was a fairly substantial trickle of fresh water; sufficient, Christian judged, for a modest settlement, one larger perhaps than the company now aboard the *Bounty*. The seamen dropped to the warm, red-brown earth and refreshed themselves with coconuts lying all about.

"There are also plenty of breadfruit," Christian observed.

"Do ye mean we brought all them plants from Tahiti to the ends of the ocean and back for naught?" demanded Martin, disgustedly.

"We did, I suppose," Christian laughed. "Better that, however, than to find a retreat and have to live without."

By evening they were atop a long, curving upthrust that included the highest point on the island. Facing easterly was a great cave with a triangular entrance, eighty feet tall and half as broad, screened well by timber. Christian, exploring its interior, said, "One man, well armed, could keep a battalion at bay here, so long as his powder and shot held out." He turned to Smith. "Build a fire, Jack," he suggested. "We must spend the night somewhere, and here we have shelter in the event of a squall." The date was January 10, 1790.

Lounging about the fire, its flames casting weird shadows on the rock walls, the bearded figures resembled a gathering of pirates which, in point of fact, Christian mused, was about what they were. Rested, warmed, full of coconut and fruit, they all were in high good humor, instinctively relishing the campout, as primordial as those of ancient times when hunters clustered around a fire struck to keep a hostile world at bay as much as to give human comfort.

"Don't ye find it strange, sir, these islands scattered about the ocean, no man can predict where nor to what purpose?" demanded Smith.

"Aye, they are oddly cast, 'tis true," agreed the young captain. "But I have studied something of rocks, and islands such as this are volcanic in origin, I'm sure."

"Ye mean these mountain-islands are volcanoes, like to blow us all into the sea?"

"I judge they are volcanic, right enough, but their activity must have ceased long ago. This island, Pitcairn, appears to be an ancient volcano. You can make out the rim all around save to the north, and ye can discern some of it even there. The mountain must rise steeply from the ocean bed, because we found no bottom only a short distance offshore."

Scuffing a level place on which to lie, Christian made a discovery proving that the *Bounty* men were not the first human beings to have set foot upon the island. Scarcely covered by dust was a stone adze! It was all of ten inches in length and weighed more than a pound, its edge ground to a respectable sharpness, lacking only the haft and the braided sennit which bound handle and head together. A moment later Martin uncovered a second, slightly shorter, but thicker than Christian's. Both were four-sided in cross section, unlike the triangular adzes in use among the Polynesians, but otherwise identical in size and workmanship. Possibly, Christian thought, these may have been more ancient.

"I noted no other signs that the island is inhabited or was lived upon in the past," he said. "But it might be well to maintain a guard tonight. I shall stand the first watch, until about midnight, then awaken one of you."

He leaned upon a boulder at the right of the cave opening, his back to the blowing embers, the silence of the tropic night all about. Christian thought of the stone adzes they had uncovered. Who were the intrepid navigators who originally discovered this lost island? Where had they gone? Were those stone relics all that remained of them—and would a chance artifact be all that would mark this rock as the final home of the mutineers of the *Bounty?* Was it, in truth, their *final* home, or would there be others? This volcanic protuberance in a limitless sea, was it to be the end of a life, his life, which extended from the old world to the new, from the subarctic to the subantarctic? Christian reviewed the people he had known, his family, friends, the women he had loved.

There was, Christian conceded, no glory in his past and little prospect in his future except a hoped-for survival. Survival for what? He shook his head at the puzzle. Some would say to work out his guilt. Guilt? He felt none—or did he? How could one feel guilt for doing what was right, what one must? Yet guilt he felt, beyond a doubt, and being an honest man, he must concede that rather than being erased with time, his one mutinous action, lying deep, had soured within him, tainting his days. Yet this, too, he would conquer, because he must. He was his own man, responsible to no one but himself, servant to no other, no society, no god. Against the rock he squared his shoulders. This would be his kingdom, his and Mautea's, and they would be beholden to no one.

With the first light the mutineers stirred, awakened, yawned into the morning, rubbed their tousled heads, and smoothed their beards. Gathering their weapons they aligned themselves on the apron of the cavern, seeing the mists rise in the valleys, listening to dawn cries of noddies and the diving terns.

"We'll climb the ridge once more," announced Christian, "and examine the approaches for other possible landing sites."

Once the summit was gained, the men scanned the undulating ridges, wealthy with verdure, rippling downward toward the sea. In the distance they could hear the endless roar of the surf. The officer led them south along the spine, the partial rim of the old crater. The center of the volcano had been filled by erosion, fashioning a flat area of red-brown soil, which would be an ideal site for a settlement. The Englishman could find no obvious signs of recent habitation.

"We shall never find a more secure, a more perfect retreat," cried Christian. There were several hearty "ayes" in return, for his mood was infectious.

Just before noon they sat upon the bluff, eating coconut, happy as youngsters exploring an unknown wood. They were free as any person ever can be. They were enslaved solely by their inborn limitations: their desires, their lusts, their ignorance, their prejudices, their unwillingness, perhaps inability to meld another's passions as their own. They had all their loves, hates, and greeds; they were ordinary men.

Scatteringly they descended to the bar and rowed out to the ship, carefully sounding the inshore bottom. It shelved rapidly, so the *Bounty* could be brought quite close. As Christian swung the ship's rail, he was in as fine a mood as he had enjoyed for months. For the moment, any thoughts of shame, fear, or uncertainty were submerged. Once more he was in full command, not of the ship alone, but of himself.

"How does it look, sir?" asked Young.

"Excellent! It will be hard indeed to get ashore what we need and haul it up to the site for a town, but 'twill be well worth the effort. This island is so perfect that 'tis difficult to believe!" He recounted its features, firing Young with his enthusiasm.

"It is fortunate you returned when you did," Young informed the captain. "You were very nearly stranded."

Christian, startled, was brought back to harsh reality.

"Quintal," explained Young, laconically. "He wished to raise sail, ride the trades back to Tahiti, abandon you and the others."

The captain instantly sobered. "He can be vicious, for all his skills. What shall I do? Punish him for treachery? Or forget it, since his plot did not work? The endless dilemma."

"I already punished him, sir. He's in irons below. He also has a sore head and, I wouldn't doubt, a disposition to match."

"Let him remain there then, for a time."

The seamen set about working the whip toward the coast. She was anchored in seventeen fathoms, fifty yards to sea, where unloading commenced. Tedious work it was, with only two boats, the cutter not being fully serviceable because of her unrepaired strakes. Yet the endeavor prospered, if slowly.

CHAPTER FOURTEEN

The clinker-built jolly was lively and responsive, but small, so that the cutter must be put to the limit of its use to get the *Bounty*'s stores to shore. The livestock had to be landed first, and Christian foresaw many trips to ferry the animals and plants. Scarcely had they begun, however, when an untethered goat bounded into the water and swam easily to the island where it nimbly climbed the face of the mountain, grazing happily. At that the captain ordered the rest of the goats loosed, shoved overboard, and they all swam ashore. Delighted with his success, he intended to do the same with the hogs, but Martin stopped him.

"Sir, we will lose some pigs that way," he warned.

"How so?"

"Pigs don't swim like goats, sir. Some of 'em will cut their throats with their fore-hooves, because they raise them over high when swimming."

clinker-built-
poorly built.

"I never heard of such a thing!" replied Christian.

"Maybe you never swam hogs, then, sir."

"No, I never did. There was no swimming water near Moorland Close. I suppose we shall have to ferry them ashore, along with the fowl and all the other stores."

Young cleared his throat, as he always did when about to interrupt with some thought he considered important. Christian waited.

"Couldn't we rig one of the hatch covers for a raft, run a line from ship to shore and unload in that manner, sir?"

"Good thought, Young. Perhaps we could also mount a breeches buoy atop the cliff, anchoring it to the trees, to save us lugging everything up the face."

breeches buoy-
a canvas seat in the form of breeches hung from a life buoy running on a hawser and used to haul persons from one ship to another or from ship to shore, especially in rescue operations.

The ship was warped even closer to the shore and a block attached to a stout rata tree well up the incline, the lines affixed to the mainmast above the tops. Soon a serviceable ferry was created. Even the anvil and John Williams' heavy toolbox were readily transferred by this means. From the landing, the stores were hoisted by the breeches buoy—boxes, bales, casks, coils of line, sails, ship's stores, and even potted plants—to the plateau, where they were heaped about haphazardly.

rata-
long-lived, crimson flowered tree which grows around the Pacific rim.

Emptying the ship proceeded more swiftly than Christian had hoped, and with less dissension, everyone too busy for mischief. Even the Tahitians worked willingly. The women fashioned rude huts on the flat, scouring the land for foods within their experience and to their taste, creating homes as women will, with no outward despair over having cut permanently, for all they knew, the ties with their own people.

"What have you there?" asked Christian one day as Young strolled past. He bore a bundle under his arm, wrapped closely in his jacket. Young flushed.

"Oh, items I thought we could not well do without." He offered the parcel to the captiain then, who raised a corner of the covering and read: *Holy Bible*. With it was the *Book of Common Prayer* of the Anglican Church, both being from Bligh's collection.

"That's a tie with the past we could spare," Christian said, irritably. "Such superstition only leads to trouble."

"Sir, we may base our careers on volcanic rock, but we must base our lives on something more; and these books will assist us. There is not only guilt here, but forgiveness; and one day we may need to draw upon it."

"As you wish," said Christian after a hard moment, turning away.

Eight days were devoted to unloading from the ship most of what they desired or could have need of. Christian thought they also could use much of her oak timbers and her thick copper sheathing, perhaps some of the iron.

"I think we'd better run her aground, strip her, and then figure out how to dispose of her," he speculated.

Brown, the gardener, had busied himself setting out plants of many kinds, noting happily the wealth of breadfruit already growing about.

"That says something about the size of the colony that once existed here," he remarked to Christian. Breadfruit could not be started from seed, only from shoots, and these must have been carried from island to island, the only agency capable of doing so being human.

"How did it get established in the first place, then?"

Brown sighed and spread his hands.

"Some things are known only to the Almighty," he replied. "Among them how this marvelous plant originated."

Christian, a trace of humor in his voice, retorted, "Whenever a hard question is asked, the unknown answer is laid upon the Almighty. 'God knows' is the reply! You'd think He would have been too occupied to attend to such details, even if He cared about His creation, which has yet to be proven."

Young had joined them. Now he cast aside his deference, as he rarely did, wading boldly into the conversation.

"Often have I heard ye talk thus, sir," he gently chided, "and, if you'll pardon me, it ill becomes you. You are a man of judgment and good sense, and one of high principles, too, I vow; but ye are a man like the rest of us, and you cannot be more complete or whole than the rest of humankind. A person, from time to time, must have something greater to lean on. Englishmen call it God."

"Some Englishmen, Young. Most, perhaps; but not all. I count myself free of that, which is based solely on myth as I believe. No one can peruse history, observe the evil that is rampant, the Blighs who abound, see the wickedness in human hearts everywhere, and still believe in some unearthly being who created them and responds to their needs. 'Tis not logical."

"All truth is not logic."

"Perhaps not. But truth, to be believed, must not defy logic."

A shadow of a smile flicked across Young's face.

"As Churchill would say, 'logic is as logic does,'" he said, and all three laughed. Young, like Christian, was widely read for the day and for his profession, though usually concealing it under brusqueness.

"Ye know, sir," he reminded his captain now, "John Donne said that 'no man is an island,' and it may be that no island, not even this hidden morsel of land on an almost unknown ocean, is complete to itself, either. For one thing we have brought Englishmen here; and they, their memories and traditions. And the Tahitians brought theirs; and so there is a relationship established between Pitcairn on the one hand, and Tahiti and England on the other, a binding that girdles the world. Just as no island can ever be truly isolated, since all are rooted in the common rock, so no one, created by God and dependent upon Him whether he wills it or no, can ever be wholly removed from Him. Perhaps God is the connection between peoples who know of Him and those who seek to reject him. I would not too readily turn from God, Captain, for I am convinced He will never discard thee."

Checking the impulse to retort, Christian strode down the steep path to the landing.

By late January the *Bounty* had been emptied of her stores and everything else deemed useful. Even the ship's bell was swung up to the plateau and mounted in a framework to be used as a signaling device for the villagers, its brassy summons audible if one were sheltered from the racket of the surf from one end of the island to the other. On the twenty-third day of the month Christian, Young, Smith, and the other mutineers boarded the ship for a final inspection. She had become little more than a hull. "Let's run her ashore and break her up," suggested the captain. Most assented, though one or two mumbled an objection.

"'Tis a fool's idea," muttered Quintal, thickly. He had been into the dwindling rum supply again. "Th' hulk would be visible for many a year to come, drawing investigation like a rum smell draws drunks."

"You should know, Quintal," retorted Young.

"With the heavy surf, she would soon break up and be lost to view," said Christian. "If we ran her ashore, we might salvage timbers and other portions, should we have need of them." He left silent the thought of most of them that running the *Bounty* onto the rocks instead of more immediately destroying her would prolong the illusion that they were not yet stranded beyond reprieve. The ship, however battered and broken, would lie there still, a link with England, with home. Yet they were men of courage and decision. Fletcher Christian, knowing this, faced them. "Who's for running her ashore, and who is for burning her?" he demanded.

Three only, Quintal, McCoy, and Martin, opted for the flames, the remainder for beaching and allowing the sea to destroy her. They hoisted the anchor a bit then and set a foresail to drive her ashore. Suddenly, amid this activity, a curl of smoke rose from amidships, soon becoming a cloud pushed upward by slender tongues of orange flame.

"That idiot Quintal set her afire!" shouted Young. "Nothing can save her now. We should let him burn with her!"

Tumbling over the side, into the cutter, they pulled for shore. Quintal staggered drunkenly to the deck through the billowing smoke and fire. He waved a bottle, called hoarsely for the boat to take him off, his voice pleading, clearly audible across the heaving waves.

"Let 'im burn!" growled Mills, straining at his oar.

"I say he can swim ashore, if he ain't too drunk, an' if he be, he won't feel the flames or be much loss," agreed Smith.

"He can't swim," replied Christian. Pushing the tiller over hard, he directed the oarsmen to bring the boat about. They stroked swiftly back to the ship, now hugely ablaze. Quintal, too drunk to more than weakly cheer, leaned over the rail and took another long draught, sweat from the roaring fire glistening on his face. Christian leaped aboard amid smoke and flame, snatched away the bottle and shattered it on Quintal's head, then dumped the half-conscious seaman over the rail into the crowded boat and leaped after him. The rowers pulled swiftly away from the doomed vessel.

"He wasn't worth it, sir," said Young, testily.

"I know," replied Christian, his eyes focused on the inferno of the *Bounty*. "But he's one of us. I could not let the flames have him."

"What's the difference?" muttered Mills. "He'll burn sooner or later anyway."

On the shore the party clambered upward through the pungent gloom of smoke and dust, the bay below them aglow with towering flames. The smoke, black with the tar of ropes and planks, billowed westward like masses of hair streaming from a fiery face. The flames leaped up the masts and shrouds and burned at spars, tops, and crosstrees. It lighted the night and would have been visible 100 miles across the ocean, had there been human eyes to see. There were none save theirs. The ship, which had brought them safely to this secret isle on a desolate sea, now was consumed, her mission done, her life finished. With her died the last best opportunity for the marooned seamen ever to regain their accustomed world.

"She won't burn completely. A hulk will remain." Young pointed out.

"Aye. We can fire the bones once more and weaken the hull, so she will fill and sink, but there is no hurry. Time enough and to spare."

Christian turned away. He strode toward the village. Mautea awaited him, watching this tall, responsive, yet oddly remote man coming up the path toward her. She felt for him, now, as always, a devotion she could never define. Only dimly comprehended to others was the structure of their love, building that perfect trust that makes possible the highest human relationship.

He saw her and instantly dropped away the mood of melancholy the burning of the ship had draped about him, for in her was his new life.

CHAPTER FIFTEEN

A clear peal from the *Bounty* bell shattered the morning stillness and summoned the castaways to an assembly before Christian's hut. There was no hurry. The men strolled in from scattered dwellings, the temporary shelters serving them until erection of more durable cottages.

Christian addressed them easily, with the natural leadership so much a part of his nature.

"I thought it wise if we settled certain matters and established a pattern we can live with," he began. "By your vote you selected me as your captain. Here, however, while emergencies may still depend upon a measure of discipline, the need of such rigid authority as we had at sea no longer holds. We have outgrown it."

"A man needs discipline, sir," argued Young.

"Perhaps. The discipline of the sea is one thing. But I believe that here our small group can do without a formal government. I cannot conceive of any situation we could not solve by free and open consultation among ourselves."

"We Englishmen love organization," Young replied, dubiously. "You cannot have organization without someone at the head of it."

"We are no longer Englishmen."

"What are we then?"

Christian hesitated. "Pitcairners!"

"Well," laughed Young, "you are the head Pitcairner, then; and for most of us, you always will be."

The other shook his head, then cast the matter aside. "I think we should now divide the island among us, so each man will know his land, cultivate it as he wishes for his wife and children . . ."

"Simple enough," put in Smith. "Sketch a chart of the island on the dust there, and split it into equal shares."

"'Tis not quite that simple, I'm afraid. Much of the island is mountainous and rocky. We must share the good land fairly or it will mean hardship for some, and discontent. Brown has compiled a chart, outlining the fertile areas. We must mark it out so that everyone gets an equal share and is satisfied with his lot. We must adjust the boundaries until everyone's objections are overcome. Once one expresses himself as content and all sections are assigned, he must abide by his decision and hold to it."

He glanced across the assembled faces.

"There are fifteen men among us. Fifteen allotments should be made, equal in fertility and potential."

"Fifteen? I count nine," objected McCoy. "Nine Englishmen, and that's all that matters. You said yourself there ain't too much good land."

Christian controlled his voice with an effort. "We are fifteen men, English and Tahitian, but men, now heads of families."

Quintal shook his shaggy head. "That ain't right, Christian," he blurted, omitting the respect he had been forced to exhibit aboard ship. "These savages don't understand our way of doing things, and besides there is more of us than them. I say we split the good land among ourselves."

"That would only create chaos on this island," cried Christian. "I cannot agree."

McCoy jammed his sailor's knife once or twice into the earth between his legs.

"For me, land means I share alike with the rest of you Englishmen. Land an' power I've always dreamed of. Land means I eat. My family eats. So far as that goes, th' natives ain't going to starve, we'll see to that. What's land mean to them? Nothing. What they want is plenty o' food, a garden plot, an' a cottage of their own—not land. We ain't deprivin' them of nothin'. They gets what they wants, we gets what we wants. Everybody's happy."

"That is not true. You are creating a difference between people. You are creating slaves who own nothing but live by our grace. That leads to the worst form of oppression. It can only bring dissatisfaction, resentment, and war amongst us."

Williams spoke up. "Even if you divide the land amongst us an' them alike, Mr. Christian," he pointed out, "the natives wouldn't have their land long, because the seamen would figure out some means of getting it from them. 'Twould be fairer in the long run to divide it just amongst ourselves, for we are wiser in the ways of holdin' our possessions and would retain it for longer."

"We are all in this together, we live or die together," insisted Christian. "We must establish a society that is just."

"I'm an Englishman," said Mills, "an' we wouldn't be all over the world if we wasn't superior people."

Christian gestured his helplessness. A vote showed only he, Young, and Brown voting for a fair division among all, the others excluding the natives.

"That makes nine in favor of giving all a fair share and six opposed," Christian wryly reported.

"How in God's name do you figure that?" demanded Mills.

"Three Englishmen and six Tahitians vote for all to share equally, and only six against it."

"For Christ's sake, they ain't got *no* vote, Christian!" cried Mills, in exasperation. "They got no land an' they got no vote. The vote's amongst us!"

"First you deprive them of land, then of a voice. Next it will be their freedom. Then it will be war," prophesied Christian, gloomily.

"How are you going to explain it to them?" asked Young, later.

"I don't know. Perhaps Mautea . . . 'Tis a thankless task."

That afternoon she approached the native men and spoke softly, earnestly, insistently, with them. They talked for a long time before she returned to her husband.

"They do not like it," she said, tears in her eyes. "It is not just the land, but that they are not accepted equally."

"I understand. It would anger me, as well."

"But they will accept it—for now. I cannot tell about the future."

"Nor can any of us, Mautea."

Thus was the wedge driven. Fletcher Christian sensed the disaster it would wreak.

In the cool of the evening, he shouldered a hoe and climbed to his own allotment west of the village. He turned the soil over, testing its character and fertility. It was a rich red-brown, soft to the touch of the hoe and warm beneath the late sun. While he was thus engaged, Young came upon him from the woods.

"How does the land look, sir?"

"Fine, thus far." He was glad Young had joined him. "Why do you suppose the men are so obtuse? Here we have a plain case of right and wrong. And yet these men freely, of their own choice, selected the course that can lead only to disaster. Why?"

Young sat upon a boulder. "Partly greed. Sheer selfishness, if you will. Or, simply because they are human, with all the blindness and stubbornness and stupidity of their kind."

"Are humans always like this? Will they never improve?"

Young stared at the ground, selected a pebble, tossed it, catching it neatly, turning it over, examining it, as though it were a thing important.

"Yes, sir, there is but one hope," he replied. "There is one Power and one alone who can bring men out of themselves, make saints out of sinners. The means by which it can be reached is faith, religion, if you will. That is what we need to develop on this island."

"Oh, for Christ's sake!"

"Exactly."

Christian laid the foundation for his permanent cottage to face the near-completed home of Williams, but 100 yards from it. Instinctively, most of the others followed the pattern until an English-style commons was outlined. Here the women built their cooking fires and gossiped, while the men lounged at their leisure, out of sight of the sea, but never beyond its sound.

From the plateau the distant surf seemed a steady moan, the beat of succeeding waves blending with neither beginning nor end. Down on the beach the crash, the muted groan of the sea was more rhythmical, like a human heart, a heartbeat of the deep, beginning nowhere, ending nowhere. Christian enjoyed the endless boom of the surf, the changing appearance of the ocean; he was lured by its smell, sound, and freshness.

The foundations of the cottages were fashioned from native rock, the beams of rata laid with a floor of planks and mats. The walls were of boards sawn from native trees, and the roofs of thatch. A few had windows made of glass from the *Bounty*, although sliding shutters were more common. The community lived out of doors much of the time for the temperatures, as revealed by the ship's thermometer, ranged comfortably from about 55 to 85 degrees, even though the humidity usually was high.

The frequent showers were ordinarily brief, the steaming brush drying quickly under the sea breeze and the returning sun. Although wild foods were plentiful, most of the men followed the example of Christian, planting taro and other rootstocks "to give substance to the meals," as Williams put it. Running wild, the hogs quickly recovered from their long passage aboard ship; and the goats and fowl seemed at home from the outset. None found any natural enemies on Pitcairn and since few were slain for food, their increase would be substantial. When a rare animal was butchered, the feast became a celebration.

About a month after the cottage building had begun, Young and Christian, beneath a spreading plantain, were silently enjoying a warm afternoon sun.

Christian asked, "Did ye know that Mautea is with child?"

"Truly!" the other's reaction was instantaneous, his delight manifest. "Congratulations, sir. I am happy for you—and so will my Susannah be, take my word!"

"I'll wager Susannah already knows," replied Christian. "Women have a way of knowing such things."

"When is he due?"

"He? What if it is a daughter? Mautea just told me that she feels certain it is a girl. I suppose 'twill arrive in late September, or October. That will be spring. A good time for a new beginning, eh?"

"I'd say such news is cause for celebration," Young replied.

"A feast does seem appropriate. Very well, we shall go and find an animal."

The goats and pigs were feral enough that it was easier to shoot and carry one home than drive it in for a butcher's knife, but neither Christian nor Young were of a mood for an early kill. Instead they wandered eastward toward the unexplored tip of the island.

Young gazed over the cliff toward the beach. "Let's see if we can make it to the beach!" he urged. Slowly, cautiously, the pair worked down the pitch, their progress stirring up clouds of terns, noddies, and red-tailed tropic birds, rising screaming from their nests, swirling like banners around their heads. "Good place for the girls to come egging!" called Young, as he disappeared around a point, having gained the water's edge. A moment later a shout reached Christian.

"Look what I've found!" Young cried with excitement.

Christian inched his way to him within moments, finding his friend standing before a stone wall, protected by an overhang. On the surface numerous figures had been carve by some forgotten passerby. "What do you make of them?"

"I am not sure, sir. That seems to be a man with his arms upraised—perhaps in prayer. Those resemble dancing birds. That might be a thundercloud and perhaps a star up there. But what about the circles and a cross within?"

"I wish Morrison were here. He would have some theory, no doubt, to explain this gallery."

"Aye. But since he is not, we are free to interpret them as we choose."

"And?"

Young delighted in the opportunity.

"Let's say that this figure represents a man at prayer," he said, his quick eye scanning the carvings. "Obviously he was shipwrecked and took shelter here, perhaps during a gale. It is pictured at the left, but the stars, upper right, soon came out; and the next day dawned clear. He climbed the cliff to reach the rookery, for you can see the startled creatures leaping into the sky. No doubt he raided nests for eggs."

"Your imagination is better than his, I've not a doubt," grinned Christian.

Young leaned on his musket, reflecting.

"Possibly his picture presents a philosophical notion. Why, certainly, 'tis truly simple! He is giving thanks for his safe arrival here, discovery of shelter, the provision of food—all the necessities of life."

"But why the circle?"

"Well, I imagine . . . I suppose that represents his view of life: birth, death, success, failure, the four winds perhaps represented by the cross within. The rim of the horizon, the sea, which to a Polynesian must symbolize existence. All is endless as a circle. The continuity of being. We begin in life, and we end in life. He must have thought something of that. These hieroglyphics are like music, a universal language, really."

Christian gazed across the sparkling, empty sea in the island's lee with little movement. "You really believe all that, don't you, Young?"

"Yes, sir, I do," he replied, simply. "I cannot conceive of a life without something beyond myself. I realize my own limitations. My strengths are simply insufficient for this business of living. I must, therefore, draw on outside help in order to get through this existence bequeathed to me."

Christian crossed his arms upon his knees. "We have been on Pitcairn but a short time, really," he said, "and yet I do not feel the peace that has come to you, I admit, but rather at times a twinge of restlessness, an impulse to be gone. How do I explain it? I have here all that I desire and far better than I deserve—a lovely wife, a baby to come, comfort, and some good companions, a tolerable relationship with others—no reasonable desires unfulfilled. This is what every man seeks, whether at Cockermouth or in the South Seas: every man but Christian!"

"I am positive your restlessness is not abnormal, Captain," reassured the other. "It will pass, in time, I think."

Christian scanned the broken shoreline, swept by the sea again.

"I do not contemplate flight from here—that would prove scarcely feasible. But I do not feel that my life is finished, nor that it can be fulfilled on this island, nor will be."

"You know, sir," Young finally replied, "I cannot believe that ye will ever find happiness, a place on earth so idyllic that all your desires may be satisfied. That, in my view, is not the way of the world—or of society or an individual's life. I think you will find contentment only within you, not in a flight to Tarshish or from reality, but acceptance of it. You must accept the fact that a man is not sufficient unto himself, but only an imperfect reflection of Another, and incomplete without that Other."

flight to Tarshish-
a biblical allusion to the prophet Jonah's flight to the city of Tarshish to catch a ship to get away from God's command that he go to Ninevah with a call to repentance for their sin.

Christian, his old irritation flashing anew, leaped to his feet.

"Ye sound like a preacher I once heard addressing a carnival crowd in a field near Moorland Close," he growled. "John Wesley! He and his hymn-singing brother, Charles. A couple of bloody fools I thought them then and consider them still. Their 'message' was the sheerest idiocy, and it has not improved with time. Your words mirror theirs. Let's return to the village. Perhaps we will get a shot at a goat or pig if we gain topside before dark."

CHAPTER SIXTEEN

The coconut torches one by one were lit before the cottages around the commons and the few dwellings off in the bush. Christian observed this ritual of dusk from beneath a twisted *miro* tree where the smell of woodsmoke from cooking fires lay close to the earth. He remembered this pungent odor from far at sea on the *Bounty* when she approached a landfall. The sea, and the wind that carried the scent this evening, also brought reflection. At this season the winds of Pitcairn blew westward; farther south, his sailor's knowledge suspected, they would blow east, for had east winds not brought the *Bounty* from Van Diemen's Land to Tahiti? Probably they circled the globe in the forties and below. The ship had all but rounded the world, and what had she discovered? Islands of some variety. A few communities of people. Trouble. Crime. *Crime?* No, he would not concede that. But revolt is often the cause of justice against tyranny, an action that civilized societies considered crime because it disturbed public tranquility and endangered its stability.

Christian clung stubbornly to that ancient dispute with Bligh as a struggle between oppression: cruelty on the one hand and justice on the other. Assuredly it had been that. But it was deeper rooted still, and Christian's obsession was in some part an oversimplification. Perhaps he feared to face the deeper issue, or possibly this was not yet clear to him. What was necessary, as in every basic human dilemma, was that the matter, like a great sperm whale, must be allowed to surface, blow out its peripheral concerns like foul steam into the clear sunlight and fresh atmosphere of pure reason, cleansing soul and body in anticipation of the truly major contests in the subconscious deeps where problems have their origin. In his case the eruption into mutiny was not a mere lashing out against oppression but the test between absolute independence and absolute authority. This reflected the most fundamental question known to humanity: whether they are creatures of law (and whose law?), or are they themselves the law, or perhaps something in between.

Christian's thoughts had lately focused increasingly on fantasies, dreams of a future found not on this lonely island. He had said as much to Young one day as they lounged beside his taro patch.

"Where then—and how would you undertake it?"

"I wish I knew," sighed Christian. "'Tis only a dream. I would never leave Mautea, nor would she want to accompany me further, I suspect. Especially with the child due at any moment and then a helpless babe to care for." The familiar, boyish grin spread over his face. "Pitcairn forever, eh?" he cried, Young laughing with him.

One bright spring day in the month of October, Christian dallied over his breakfast of fruit, watching Mautea, heavy now with child, going about her tasks with the solidity that had grown upon her in these last days. She was aware of his attention, realized it was generated by his love for her, and was happy with it; but this morning she appeared even more solemn than before.

"Are you sure you feel quite well?" he asked.

She nodded. "Except that I am not comfortable, nor will I be until afterward. Perhaps a feast for our good friends would take my mind off myself. Why not shoot a pig or a goat for our dinner?"

Happy to fulfill her request, Christian snatched up a musket, some powder and shot, and gently kissed his wife. She stroked his smooth cheek. "On your way, stop at Young's and ask Susannah to come by. She can help prepare the dinner—when do you suppose you will return?"

"Early this afternoon, I imagine. The goats are grazing on the other side of the west rim, so Smith reports. They grow wilder every day."

He shouldered the weapon and the light spyglass and walked across the sunlit commons, speckled with dancing shadows. At Young's he found the midshipman hard at work upon an intricate model of a ship he denied was the *Bounty*, although she seemed to Christian to exhibit her lines. He gave Susannah the message. Beyond the upper end of the village, he climbed the ridge to the great cave where he and the others had spent their first night on Pitcairn. All was bright under the spring sun, new, as his love for his wife each day was freshly renewed. Far below he could observe the thatched roofs of the cottages. When would Mautea's time arrive? He put the concern aside; surely she would let him know.

Christian caught up his musket and set out southerly along the ridge, watching for the flash of a goat on the slopes plunging steeply toward the western coast.

Near the southern extremity of the ridge, he glimpsed a movement and stepped quickly into the shade of a *burau* tree, not wishing to alert the quarry. He focused his glass upon it and brought into view not an animal, but the seated figures of Matt Quintal and Will McCoy, apparently relishing the bright day as much as he. Christian snapped the glass closed, fastening its clasp with a crisp click, and made his way down the incline toward the pair. They greeted him with grunts of welcome. Neither had shaved since their arrival on the island and were shaggy as goats and smelled not dissimilar, but they were Britons and his crew . . . and his comrades in exile.

"Pleasant morning," Christian greeted them.

"Like all of 'em, sir," replied Quintal noncommittally.

Sarah must have fed him well this morning, Christian thought. It was a rare event these days to get from him a respectful "sir."

"Or almost, anyways," agreed McCoy. "Makes a laddie wish for a Glasgow fog at times. Ah, well, I do enjoy the sun though, as a good Scotsman must, he sees it so seldom at home." He tested with his thumbnail a ti root from several heaped before him. "You know, Christian, there is good juice in these tubers. If I had a kettle and a coil, I could make some Scotch-Pitcairn whiskey out of 'em! Rum is fine for women and Jamaica buccaneers; but whiskey, properly distilled, is the drink for us northerners. It helps us forget the cold and the rain, an'—"

"An' your duty, your sins, an' your lives!" guffawed Quintal, winking at Christian.

"Aye," Christian replied, scanning the tumbled slopes before them. "We are an ordered little community now, tolerable to each other. Whiskey would destroy that life, and perhaps all of us, I'm thinkin. 'Tis lucky you don't have the makings of a still."

The Scotsman stubbornly pursed his lips.

"Ye talk as if I intended we become sots, Christian. 'Tis not that. Not at all. Just a nip in th' chill of the mornin' an' a dollop at night before bed. Perhaps a glass at noon to hasten the nap. That's all. A solace is what it is, Christian. A comforter for civilized man."

"I thought ye were talkin' of Scotsmen?" snickered Quintal.

McCoy swung a ti root wildly at the head of his companion.

"I'll teach ye who's civilized, ye Cornish tin tailin'," he growled. "As much whiskey would be drunk in Cornwall as in Scotland, if ye had the wit to make it!"

Christian passed on, around the curve of the ridge, at long last sighting a small herd of goats grazing on the exposed slope. The early afternoon sun highlighted a brown and white billy among them. Christian sat on the soft earth, crossed his legs, braced his elbows against his knees, and sighted carefully. He squeezed the trigger, holding his aim as the flint struck its spark, lighting the train of powder, the explosion speeding the leaden bullet through the cloud of blue-black smoke. The goat leaped high, crashed on its side. The others, startled, wheeled and bounded down the hill toward cover.

Christian bled the animal and roughly dressed it. Tying its feet together, he hoisted it across his back. He gained the ridge where the walking was easier and slipping and scrambling down its slope at last, made his way to the commons. It was midafternoon.

At the edge of the green, he saw a cluster of excited villagers before his cottage. A catastrophe? Mautea? He broke into a labored run, the trophy's weight forgotten, the carcass flopping about on his shoulders. The crowd saw him and shouted. Susannah ran to greet him. "He has arrived! You got a fine boy!"

Young, grinning broadly, ran close behind, stretching out a hand to him. "Christian! You're the first old man of the village! Come and meet your son."

"How is Mautea?"

"Fine, I guess. Come on!"

Christian burst into the cottage, slowly approached the mat where Mautea lay, smiling happily, nestling a bundle in the curve of her arm. She lifted a corner of the wrapping to reveal a tiny, reddish face, eyes tightly closed, a minute fist tight against the mouth, dark hair plastered to the forehead. His son! He took his wife's hand in both of his. "You didn't tell me!" he charged, gently. "You sent me away!"

"It is not a man's business, bearing children," Mautea dreamily defended herself. "It was better you were not here. Now I am glad you have returned. Do you like your son? Do you think he looks like you?"

Christian laughed—completely, fully happy. He kissed her softly on the mouth, the eyes, the curve of her neck, whispering into her ear. "I love the two of you. He looks like you and I am glad."

She wrapped her arm around his head and drew him close. "I love you too. I am glad my son is your son. I would have no other."

Young had entered the room behind Christian, standing uncertainly during the reunion, wondering at the ancient miracle, so commonplace and yet so new. Here was a living sign that the colony might endure. This child, the mingled seed of the men of the north and of the women from the great southern ocean, had arrived here, the first of many others who would create a new community, make of it what was possible by their abilities and integrity.

"God!" breathed Young. "We, too, are instruments of Thy creation!"

If Christian heard he gave no sign. Mautea drifted off into happy sleep and so he left her and led the way outside. He grinned at Susannah, already busily preparing the goat, and walked over to a rough-barked tree, leaning against it, staring unseeing at the clouds and the sky, savoring the knowledge that he indeed had become the first father of this community he had founded.

"What about a name, sir?" Young burst in upon his thoughts. "How about Christian? 'Tis a fine one and ought to be preserved."

"I think not," Christian shook his head. "I shouldn't wish to saddle him with a name that to others means mutiny, crime . . . perhaps failure."

"None of these apply to the name of Christian," argued the other, loyally. "Not even 'mutiny,'" he paused. "If not Christian, what do you prefer?"

"'Tis October," Christian pointed out. "But what day is it?"

"Wednesday, I think. No. Not Wednesday. Thursday it is."

"How about Thursday October Christian, then?"

Young laughed.

"If a name suggests character, he will certainly be an original. But won't Mautea object?"

"I think not. She will no doubt name him herself in her own tongue, but I'm sure she will agree to anything in English I suggest. Thursday October Christian it is! Let's have a tot of rum on that, eh?"

CHAPTER SEVENTEEN

Six months later, on a misty dawn in early March, 1791, Young ran toward Christian's cottage on an urgent summons. Mautea slid open the shutter, her face apprehensive, fearful. "Have you seen the captain?" she cried.

"Christian? No, indeed. What has happened, Mautea?"

"In the middle of the night, he gave a great cry and leaped from bed, running from the house. I have not seen him since! Would you search him out?"

Young hastened to the rim of the cliff and peered down at the beach. He saw the *Bounty*'s two boats, drawn high on the shore and covered carefully with thatch as always when idle. Beyond, the waters rolled over the grave of the ship, the hulk sunken with no visible trace. As the sun slipped from a covering cloud, he discerned a distant figure perched atop the needle peak that had come to be called The Rock, just north of the landing. So still was he, so immobilized he appeared almost part of the formation itself.

Young hurried to its base and laboriously scaled the point, joining Christian on his narrow ledge.

"Captain!" he cried. "Mautea said you blasted out of the cottage as though shot from a cannon! Are ye ill? Tell me, man!"

His words appeared to rouse Christian from his wild searching of the sea.

"It was so real. I *know* it was so! Did you not see it too? It cannot have been but a dream!"

The midshipman chuckled indulgently.

"A nightmare? Why, only children have nightmares. What was it like?"

Christian's face was drained in the chill dawn, his lips pale. A tremor seized his strong hands. "The ship!" he mumbled. "Did no one else observe it?"

"Ship? What ship? The *Bounty?* She is gone. We burned her, and the hulk broke up and sank, don't ye remember?"

"I'm not daft, Young," he replied with scorn. "Not the *Bounty*, the vengeance ship!" He tried to collect himself. "I know I dreamed the most of it, but 'twas so real! A frigate of some twenty-four guns came up out of the southeast as though she had rounded the Horn, her shrouds trailing mist, her sails gleaming. Her crew were all on watch, the marines among them. Each man stared to sea, searching in all directions. Only the captain moved, pacing the quarterdeck ceaselessly, his hands clasped behind his back. Then he looked up and I saw his face! The face of evil, the countenance of the devil himself, relentless, remorseless—the face of a man who lives by hunting his fellow men, who never gives up. No mercy, eyes implacable, frozen. My God, what a face! It jarred me awake, and I rushed through the dark and climbed this rock to await it." Christian covered his eyes with his hands.

"'Twas but a dream," said Young, placing a consoling hand on his shoulder. "Look! The sun's up. Mautea will have breakfast ready. Come, Captain!"

Christian did not move.

"Do ye think me mad?" he whispered.

"Mad? You're the sanest man I know. Look! The sea is empty, as it ever is. Come."

"'Twas more than just a dream," he said slowly. "When I reached this ledge, day had barely broken. I swept the horizon with the glass. To the northwest I caught a touch of sail—royals only. But there was no mistake. In the night a ship passed close, within easy vision of Pitcairn, from the Horn bound for Tahiti as she must have been. We were saved by the night. Darkness alone. But one day there will come another."

It was long before Fletcher Christian shook off the icy memory of the vision (for so he believed it to have been), but in the warmth of life with his family and the physical labor he found in gardening, he gradually recovered his optimism.

Both of the *Bounty*'s boats were maintained in as seaworthy condition as the ship's craftsmen could make them. The damaged strakes of the cutter had been replaced and the craft repainted from stores salvaged from the ship so that the boat was nearly as good as new. The two craft made possible a welcome addition of fish and shellfish to the colonists' tables.

Mautea was once again with child, and though Christian often found himself content, dark thoughts afflicted him at times. On one such occasion, Young approached him. A stubborn rain had fallen for two entire days, most extraordinary on Pitcairn, preventing outdoor work.

"Makes one think of London, don't it, sir?" asked Young, dodging in under the dripping eaves.

"Aye," responded Christian, glumly.

The wetness of Young' s woolen jacket smelled vaguely of the sheep-grazed downs of England. He accepted a cup of fresh coconut milk from Mautea, who donned a glazed tapa cloak and announced she would visit Susannah.

"You men are sad today," she murmured, "and will talk of your cold island. We will speak of Pitcairn—and perhaps Tahiti. It is better!"

"I suppose," said Christian after a long silence, "we could go over to Mills' and sit in on a game with those playing cards he contrived. At least they keep the men occupied."

"True. I suppose they need something now that the liquor's gone." He fell silent for a moment. "Another thing that has gone with the rum is the quarreling, or most of it."

"Suppose a woman dies," said Christian. "The wife of someone. Where would he turn for another? He would seize a mate from one of the natives. This would cause great resentment, perhaps to the point of murder. Once the die is cast, the war begun, it will end only when one man is left, for each abuse would lead to another. It is ever so."

"You are gloomy today, indeed!"

"Aye." Again the silence. "I see no hope of avoiding disaster." Christian shook his head. "Ye know, if it were not for Mautea, I would quit this island. I sense a murky future here and along with it an almost irresistible pull onward, I know not where nor why, nor even how. I do not even know what I seek, except contentment, I suppose—a thing impossible to win."

"There is no land of contentment, of that I'm sure," agreed Young. "If it exists at all, it is only to be discovered within you, in your own mind. You find it there only when you learn your true role and resign yourself to it, part of the great design not of your making. You have a part to play. I believe it can be done on Pitcairn as well as anywhere."

"You're not preaching again, are you, Young?"

"I will not avoid it, sir, since I believe it to be of ultimate importance to you as well as to me. Look at your record. Mutiny, Tubuai, Tahiti, Pitcairn. You assert that all these have been failures on our part, perhaps because of some curse from Captain Bligh."

"My 'stick,' Mills calls it."

"I remember. I do not agree with your obsession, but suppose you are right. If they were failures, 'twas because in each case we tried to be our own little gods and rejected the power of God himself to bind us together."

"And you think acceptance of this God would have made a difference?"

"Yes, by giving us something beyond ourselves, something to take the place of kin and country and duty. The three serve very well for most Englishmen, although if the truth be known, they are only a substitute for God. We need Him here, on this island, sir."

"Do you wish to be the Wesley of Pitcairn?" demanded Christian, angrily. "Have sense, man! We are rude and cynical seamen, not gullible women."

"I am no evangelist, but wives or sailors, we are all human beings. Tell me," he continued, "why are you so opposed to even a single service of worship?"

"I don't rightly know. Perhaps I feel I do not need it. I try to be a good man, do right. What more is expected? Am I not fulfilling myself?"

"I don't think so, not completely. We have the duty to accept authority, to submit to it with all our spirit. That, I believe, is the whole thing. There we will find a rest and peace—and strength too. God knows we need all of those." He thought for a moment. "We've not held a service since before the mutiny. I salvaged the Bible and Prayer Book, however, as you know. Let us call worship for Sunday morn."

Perhaps because of Young's enthusiasm, Christian's resistance wilted.

"As you wish," he sighed. "I doubt I'll come myself, however."

Young was not completely certain what a worship service required, but he received assistance from Brown. Together they arranged a makeshift altar in one corner of the commons and placed the *Bounty* Bible open upon it. They had no candles, but Brown's wife helped them arrange *dudui* nuts, bound together within a framework of slender sticks and one end of the bundle lighted. They served very well. At one point Brown looked in the almanac to determine the proper service for this April 24. By some miracle or other, it was discovered to be Easter Sunday—the most significant day in the Christian calendar—in the year 1791.

"Amazin'!" exclaimed Brown. "Most of us go to church only on Easter anyway, if we go at all. Here we have it presented to us, like!"

"Or us to it," agreed Young.

This was the first public event in the sixteen months they had lived on Pitcairn. Perhaps for that reason, every soul came to the service, even Christian, faint disdain upon his handsome face save when he glanced at Mautea, holding Thursday on her lap, watching the rites with interest, perhaps some comprehension. Was the service, because of its popularity, a success, then? Who could tell?

About one year after the birth of her first son, Mautea was delivered of a second, and this child Christian named Charles for his own father. And, as time elapsed, Christian's mind turned more and more to England, his Cumberland home, his family. Frequently he could be found reflecting in the great cave, gazing out over the empty sea.

He and Young had taken to torch fishing at night among the rocks, and Christian, scanning the star-sprinkled sky, would pick out the brilliant guide-stars over the southern ocean. With beacons like these, where could a seaman not navigate! With such friends, Polynesian ancestors had settled the islands of this greatest of seas. They had fearlessly skimmed across the waters in all directions, completing stupendous voyages of thousands of miles in their primitive canoes, with scant supplies or none at all. If they could navigate this way, what should deter an eighteenth-century sailor, with charts and a stout boat, from cruising where he willed? But Christian realized the notion was a fancy only, since he would never leave Mautea.

Christian pored over Bligh's books, the records of Cook and Carteret and other explorers of the Pacific. He calculated that the coast of Chile lay little over a thousand leagues eastward. With the entire length of America bounding the Pacific, and one landfall as good as another, navigation would be no problem so long as he sailed east. But could he do that against the trades? From Cook's chart and from the records of Drake and other freebooters, he found that a few degrees to the south of the lee of the coast of Chile, a mighty current would carry a craft northward to any bay along the coast.

He felt a gentle hand upon his shoulder. It was Mautea who, knowing nothing of books or maps, yet sensed his mind.

"Do you wish to go?" she asked sadly. "Women are made to manage families, men for the sea. If you must go, we shall not hold you."

Christian seized her roughly, drew her to him and kissed her, as much to erase the restlessness, perhaps, as for love, but the love was there too. "I shall *never* leave you, Mautea!" he cried. "*Never!* You are my life, my love. I will never go."

He slammed shut the books, shook his head, and pushed the volumes away. It was fancy only. He was not a man to shirk responsibility, and his clearly was to remain. Thursday was a toddler, his son and heir. Heir? To what? To shattered dreams, a broken reputation and flight from English justice—from himself? A legacy, indeed!

Bitterly he left the cottage and strode to his taro field where he hoed savagely until called to dinner. By then the restless mood had all but vanished.

Several other children had by now arrived on Pitcairn, and Christian and Mautea were expecting their third. As before, Mautea sent her husband hunting as her time neared, but Christian, now aware of her purpose, kissed her tenderly before departure. She clung to him for a long moment, then looked deeply into his eyes, the cloud of pain gathering slowly in hers. "Keep me in your prayers," she pleaded, though prayers to her native gods and to the English God were alike to her. Christian buried his face in her fragrant hair, touched with his lips her shoulders, her fingers. "You shall ever be first in my heart and mind, Mautea," he pledged. "Is that not enough?"

Christian remained at his cave until late afternoon, lost in dreams of what had been, what was and might be, and wrapped, too, in sleep part of the time, for it was an unusually warm day. He wondered whether the new arrival would be a boy or a girl. Mautea desired a daughter, and he rather wished for one too.

Shortly before dusk Christian picked up his musket and shouldered the goat, for he had shot one as his wife had requested. He slipped down to the plateau, pacing toward the village in long, easy strides. This had been a happy day for him, and soon it would be a joyous one for Mautea and his two sons as well. He reached the edge of the commons before noticing the low chanting of the women, all gathered at his cottage. Instinctively he feared something amiss. He began to run and before he reached the house, Young came out to meet him.

"Mautea?" demanded Christian, harshly.

Young braced his hands against both shoulders of his friend. "She's gone, Captain!" he cried, the compassion deep in his voice. "She perished in childbirth. Your daughter is alive and in Susannah's care—"

Christian broke free and bounded into the cottage. From it, after a harsh moment of complete stillness, there burst the wracking sobs of a man in the throes of grief beyond control. The women clustered at the edge of the meadow chorused their own laments, the mourning cries and shrieks of their tradition. Young stood alone on the step, listening to the lamentation of the Polynesians and the anguish of his fried, unable to assuage the sorrow of either, for he knew that in the beginning grief must be borne alone. This was Pitcairn's first death, though there would be many another, Young realized, and perhaps in the not-so-distant future. Not many of them, however, would touch him with the tragedy, the poignancy of this wrenching separation of his two beloved companions.

Later, much later when the mourners had quieted, the burial accomplished, Christian and Young stood together on the rim above the landing. Below them the two boats, pulled above the tide, rested beneath their thatch. The Englishmen were silent. Young observed the fresh creases on the forehead of his friend, of anguish or of determination he could not tell.

"'Tis over, sir," he said at length.

"Aye. 'Tis over." Christian's voice had a bitter edge as though he blamed a fate he could not combat for his tragedy. "Now I am free, I suppose."

"Indeed?"

"Except for the children. Would . . . could—?"

"Aye. Already Susannah loves them as her own."

Christian held his silence for a moment. Then his expression relented. "With Mautea gone I could not remain on Pitcairn. 'Twould seem a sepulchre, a morgue. I should go mad. I suppose there is no hope that ye should accompany me?"

"Where, sir?"

"Who knows? To the end of the earth and then oblivion. My only goal is 'beyond.'"

Young slowly shook his head. "I could never abandon Susannah. Besides, my aches and midnight fevers are returning. Somehow I feel I have not overlong to live. No, I cannot leave this island, nor do I wish to. This bit of rock is where I end my course and, I must say, at peace with man and God."

"He must be considered, too, eh, Young?"

"He must, for on all occasions he considers us."

Christian held his tongue. When he spoke it was as though he had not heard, his mind taking on a fresh tack.

"I'll use the cutter."

"Of course. As you wish." Young sighed. "I'll get Smith to help us launch her when you are ready. Taroameiva and the Tubuaians will help provision her. Smith and I can step the mast and bend the sail; and should ye leave in the dusk, you'll be out of sight and ken by morning. The others, with their carousing, will not miss you until you're well away."

"What if a ship should come? Not a vengeance ship, for I no longer fear such; it is too late for that, I think. But suppose an exploring vessel or wandering craft should raise this island and find you here? Would you reveal my departure?"

Young grinned, reassuringly.

"For us the day you pass beyond the horizon you vanish from our earth. I am not sure what others would relate, but I shall instruct them well, that you died on Pitcairn, through disease or mishap. No one ever can prove otherwise. The natives shall be so taught and come to believe."

Christian remained dubious.

"Can ye make the story convincing, Young? And simple? Take Smith, for instance. A good man at heart, I think, but so flighty that he cannot remember from one day to the next what he was told before."

"It shall be as simple and straightforward as I can make it, sir, though I fear for our peace on Pitcairn once your hand is taken from us."

"With you still here, it should make no difference."

"I am not the man you are, Captain. You were born to be obeyed . . . and loved. Your control was the restraint and guidance we sorely needed. We shall miss you beyond the telling."

"Do you think I should not go?"

"No. A man cannot control his deeps, save in surface ways. Ye must go, so take our blessings, and Godspeed!"

CHAPTER EIGHTEEN

Christian felt a gate had closed upon a segment of his life. He was impatient to move out, explore another field, seek fresh problems he could not yet imagine. It was time to leave Pitcairn.

On Smith's advice, the cutter had been rigged with lugsail, and because the canvas was without a boom, "splendid for reaching," as Smith believed, and suitable for running too. She had been rigged on the pattern of the sexerns, the handy Shetland fishing boats, which one man alone could manage far beyond the sight of land. A short mizzen was stepped aft to drive her and, in the event of some furious squall, to give her way should the mainsail needs be lowered or was blown away.

"One man can handle her neatly now," approved Young. "'Twill take alertness, though, and all your skill. At this season the wind should hold steady aft or at worst come in abeam. Of head winds I doubt you'll have a touch."

Christian stored the boat with fishing lines and pearl-shell hooks, a flat stone on which to build his fire, and wood for burning, three breeves filled with sweet water, and half a boat of coconuts as well, useful for food and drink alike. Susannah had roasted a pig and baked a goat and brought other foods she thought would keep. With Young for company, Christian had pored for hours over the charts compiled by Cook and assembled by Bligh, the finest then in existence of the Pacific, though in truth little enough was known of this great ocean.

In the dusky twilight when the colonists were at their evening meal, on Friday, September 6, in the year 1793, Christian stepped into the cutter and worked her away from the land. As he did so, Young tossed him a tightly wrapped parcel. "It might prove useful!" he called. Christian laid it aside and when later remembered it, he unwrapped it slowly, finding the worn, shiny Anglican *Book of Common Prayer.* He tossed it under a thwart.

thwart-
a rower's seat extending athwart, across a boat.

In the late evening glow, he raised the lugsail and later his mizzen to a variable northerly. He sailed southeasterly through the night, and by sunup Pitcairn was but a charcoal hulk, low on the horizon. By the second evening he was alone upon the great waters. The wind had freshened and the cutter, which he had named the *Isabella*, heeled a trifle. Although he had no way of measuring it, he sensed a current sidling the boat east. If true, that was all the better.

Christian believed he was approximately 2,500 sea miles from the American coast, but he must make approximately 500 south before he would begin his actual run. With luck, he calculated, he would be no more than 100 days at sea, although it was now late winter and that could mean a stormy passage. Squalls, however, might replenish his fresh water, and with his lines he hoped to catch a fish now and then.

He held the tiller easily, for the cutter required little guidance, laid his head against the cappen, his feet braced to a stretcher, and daydreamed as she drove southeasterly. The *Isabella* rode the sea lightly, smartly, as though eager for the adventures ahead, pleased to be free of the island, spirited as a colt. Christian idly recalled his spotted pony at Moorland Close, wondering if she still lived. Perhaps.

To Christian it seemed as though he sailed over a watery desert, for the birds had clung to Pitcairn and there were none about, nor whales nor even flying fish. Of the life of the deep waters, beneath the thin strakes of his boat for three miles down, he could know nothing. His sea was the cold, brilliant world of the sailor; and for an Englishman the sea was home, bred into his bones and blood by the generations extending back into antiquity. It was no marvel that Englishmen carried their flag and culture through all the seas of the world, for they could not refrain from roving. All the continents, all the seas, all the islands lured them, pulled them onward, and ever would. Christian had run away to Marysport and Whitehaven and then to sea at fifteen rather than settling on the farm beneath Cockermouth Castle as his father wished. An Englishman, of Manx descent, how could he have resisted the lure of the deep waters?

As a youth his mind had been consumed by reading, sharing this taste with his relative and neighbor, William Wordsworth, who at last report was beginning to write poetry, *his* roving taking the form of flights of fancy. But, not being a poet, the cold salt sea called loudly to Christian, and he would not ignore it. He was glad he had visited the far ports where strange tongues were spoken. Were it to be done again, he would alter nothing. Nothing. Save perhaps his one act of rebellion—but likely not even that.

He traced the events that had brought him from second in command of His Majesty's armed transport, *Bounty*, to the cutter, *Isabella*, rocking now with the everlasting swells upon the little-known South Pacific.

So many threads had gone to make up the mutiny! The matter of pride, for example. A man had his pride of ancestry and position, true, but also his pride of work, of competence, in the worth of his profession. He cannot overlook lack of trust in his professional duty. A landsman could leave a cruel employer and seek elsewhere to establish his value. But a seaman, on a global voyage, could only endure oppression, fawning endlessly before a callous superior. Or he could revolt. Being a man of principle, Fletcher Christian had no choice.

Bligh had charged that Christian simply was one who would endure neither the authority of God nor captain, king, nor country. Was this true? He sought to embrace his emotions. Of God he had no thought, since he did not believe in his existence. Of Captain Bligh? For eighteen months Christian had loyally served under his captain as he had served other officers before him. Was his revolt against authority? He rejected that notion. To the admiralty and its servants, a man must operate within a framework of rules, regulations, discipline, and Articles of War; mutiny—any mutiny—must be regarded as an uprising against authority. But to the individuals involved, it was not always that simple. There were many complicated factors involved in his rebellion against Bligh: their professional relationships, their views of a seaman's life and work, their personal lives, even their family backgrounds.

What about the authority of king and country? Fletcher Christian was an Englishman, the royal institution and loyalty to his country were part of his very soul. Even now, as an outlaw he would ever recognize the king and his authority. The mutiny had not been against king nor nation nor navy discipline, but *for* selfhood, for the best of the English in him. Being English, he could do no other.

So wherein lay the stick, the burden of guilt, which Bligh had laid upon him? Christian was not superstitious. He did not believe in "curses," as a whole. Did Bligh believe in imprecations? Christian could still see the captain leveling his malediction. Had all that occurred in the four years since been idle coincidence? Tubuai, which had come to nothing; Tahiti where, against his wish, some of the mutineers had been let go to certain death should they be captured; Pitcairn, the colony founded by him with the seeds of its own destruction; the tragedy of his personal life, shattered by the death of Mautea . . .

Somehow on this cold and lonely sea, he felt very close to her, as though she watched his every movement, understood his mind, his emotions, was sensitive still to his moods. He felt her presence now, in the seaborne cutter, more strongly than he sometimes had on Pitcairn, even when beside her. Although he could not explain it, she would remain an inseparable part of him during all the long and perilous voyage.

Within eight days after leaving Pitcairn, quartering south, the *Isabella* had reached a zone where the west wind blew purposefully, although rarely with gale force. She could run before it, showing a white bone at her prow, eagerly making way. There was little to occupy Christian save his own reflections. His foot striking a bundle in the bottom of the craft, he recognized again the parcel Young had given him and once more held the worn brown prayer book in his hands, idly leafing through it. "Forms of Prayer to be used at Sea," it said, as he scanned a paragraph or two: "O Most powerful and glorious Lord God, at whose command the winds blow, and lift up the waves of the sea, and who stillest the rage thereof; We thy creatures, but miserable sinners, do in this our great distress cry unto thee for help: Save, Lord, or else we perish . . ."

Christian's eyes swept the peaceful sky and sea; he observed the steady wind, with no hint of tempest. *That passage is meant for another day, I suppose*, he judged. He tossed the book back under the seat.

After a month at sea, Christian had fallen into routine. He drowsed, half awake, half asleep, most of the day and night. Occasionally he stood to stretch his muscles. He was down now to the last of his meat, and it was beginning to smell with age and mold. Most of his sustenance came from the coconuts. He cracked the shell upon the stone hearth, picked out the white fibers with his knife, chewing them, sucking the moisture out. He was no longer aware when he slept or when he was awake. The endless hiss and wash of the sea had become so much a part of him he no longer heard it, and the wind itself only seized his attention when it snapped a sail with gusts of fury. He baited his hooks and cast them astern, trolling ceaselessly, rarely catching anything.

On the thirty-fourth day, heavy thunderstorms cannonaded the ocean. Lightning cracked from towering piles of cumulus, lancing the water in a score of directions, the jarring thunderbolts reverberating from wind-whipped waves and howling gusts. But the great storm moved beyond him, and he drowsed again, for the wild tempest had drained him of energy. He did not know how long he slept, but he awakened to an ominous sense of danger.

He raised his eyes just in time to see a mighty waterspout bearing down upon the cutter less than a quarter-mile distant. It was perhaps 400 feet in width. Its weaving tower of wind-lashed spume extended from a cloudbank several thousand feet above the surface to the ocean and swept down upon the *Isabella* more swiftly than a horse could run.

Springing into action Christian loosed the sheets free of the cleats, the lugsail whipping wildly downwind. He swung the tiller hard to bring the *Isabella*'s bow around. But he was not in time. The roaring monster fell upon him, spinning him swiftly in its funnel, catching the craft and whirling it down, down into an immense trough, broadside to a towering sea that rose endlessly above, whipped by brine and wind. Heeled far over, lying completely horizontal along the vertical circular wall, the struggling cutter, its sail fluttering free, rose dizzyingly for long moments toward the black eternity of the sky. Christian braced himself with horror, staring directly down into the seething depths of the ocean, waiting imminent destruction.

For the first time in his twenty-eight years, he was completely at the mercy of the elements, man against nature. Nature so fierce, so implacable, so violent that despite his reserves of courage, Christian was shaken to his depths. The boat teetered on the lip of the huge wave, a hair's breadth from catastrophe. A cry escaped him: "Oh, God!" he groaned. "My God, I am lost!"

At that very moment, the *Isabella* was flung to the crest of the great wave and, caught by the reverse of the maelstrom, was blown upright. She slid down the slope of the upsurge toward freedom. In a moment the spout was gone, cruelly hissing its mindless way across the ocean toward the north beyond his sight. "*Laich*," seemed to come, words he had heard before, "*laich, anochi iemach*," and he knew their meaning no more now than before. Shaken to his soul, Christian collapsed into the boat, his face upward to the streaming rain that trailed the spout. The crisis had lasted but moments, though it seemed almost a dividing point in his existence.

The squall had passed. Christian arose to sag against the mast wearily for a few minutes, then set dully to gathering the lines again about the cleats, bringing the *Isabella* around slowly. As she gathered way, the sun briefly came out, a fiery flash of light among the torn and jagged clouds, driving its hot breath upon the broken sea. The night would be clear and cold, the stars burning with their peculiar intensity like the multiple eyes of an overseeing deity peering down upon the lonely boat and its solitary navigator, bound from the island of no return toward an uncertain landfall of the future.

Before full darkness arrived, Christian chanced to glimpse a corner of the prayer book under the seat where he had flung it. At the summons of an instinct he refused to recognize, he picked it up and in the fading light thumbed its worn pages. "An Hymn of Praise and Thanksgiving after a Dangerous Tempest," he read.

"Must have been written for me, this time," he muttered aloud. Holding the book tight to his chest, he turned the open page so the light would strike it and read in a voice skeptical, scornful, and far from devout, yet with a hint of something deeper still:

> O come, let us give thanks unto the Lord, for he is gracious: and his mercy endureth for ever.
>
> Great is the Lord, and greatly to be praised; let the redeemed of the Lord say so: whom he hath delivered from the merciless rage of the sea.
>
> The Lord is gracious and full of compassion: slow to anger, and of great mercy.
>
> He hath not dealt with us according to our sins: neither rewarded us according to our iniquities.
>
> But as the heaven is high above the earth: so great hath been his mercy towards us.
>
> We found trouble and heaviness: we were even at death's door;
>
> The water of the sea had well-nigh covered us: the proud waters had well-nigh gone over our soul;
>
> The sea roared: the stormy wind lifted up the waves thereof;
>
> We were carried up, as it were to heaven, and then down again into the deep: our soul melted within us because of trouble;
>
> Then cried we unto thee, O Lord: and thou didst deliver us out of our distress.
>
> Blessed be thy Name, who didst not despise the prayer of thy servants, but didst hear our cry, and hast saved us.
>
> Thou didst send forth thy commandment: and the windy storm ceased, and was turned into a calm.
>
> O let us therefore praise the Lord for his goodness.

Christian slowly rewrapped the marbled volume in the cloth and tossed it again to the bottom of the boat. "He must have been here," he mused, for the last time before full darkness obscured the moving sea. Christian himself did not know whether he referred to the author of the prayer or the Author of the storm. He forced himself to forget the book, as he had quickly forgotten the tempest.

The morning dawned still and bright. The boat wallowed in an empty sea, awaiting a breeze from whatever direction. Shortly after sunup, ripples, tiny wavelets, swept across the water, forecasting a morning blow. Fortunately it drove in from the west, merging into a gale, and Christian stood away on his course. All day the wind blew hard, but despite its growing fury he left the lugsail up, running driving with the rain, exhilarated by the boat's progress as he exulted in the storm. At dawn of the following day, when it abruptly ceased and the cutter wallowed again under a light, almost imperceptible breeze, he felt drained, somehow defeated.

He had been at sea by his calculation for forty-one days. The rains had replenished his fresh water; thirst was no problem. But on a hot morning, he split a coconut and found it spoiled, its milk dried up, its meat too rancid to be devoured. He shrugged and tossed it overboard, opening another. It too was rotten. Quickly he opened others, three, four, and found each unfit for use. Salt water had soaked into them and his food supply, deemed sufficient yesterday, was wiped out almost completely today. The truth dawned slowly. He was now little more than halfway from Pitcairn to the continent, supplied with water but with only a week's supply of food, even with stoic rationing. The animal carcasses were long since gone.

He possessed the lines and hooks and some scraps of food, which he carefully collected. He must waste nothing. Early in the voyage he had caught two or three small fish, more for amusement than food, but now he trolled in earnest, baiting the hooks with bits of rotten coconut. "Even if they don't see it, they cannot miss the smell," he grumbled. He had taken to discussing his problems aloud, not realizing before how the sound of a human voice shored up one's sanity.

Either there were few fish in these seas, or they cared not for spoiled coconut, for Christian caught nothing and felt scarce a nibble. Of birds there were virtually none. Once a wandering albatross, white with black touches, glided in from aft, cocking its head and yellow bill to observe the boat and its solitary passenger, its black tipped wings outstretched twelve feet across. It seemed suspended in the air, motionless, beyond reach of his flailing oar, mysterious, aloof, yet curious. Perhaps, he thought, it's looking for galley scraps. "Well, so am I," he told it, glumly. He might have shot the creature, but to no purpose for he would not have been able to recover it. No, they were two forlorn wanderers, and he let the bird come along for the company both seemed to desire. Once or twice he caught a glimpse of a dark brown stinker or the flash of a distant storm petrel, soot black, erratic in flight, dipping between rollers and completely lost to view, then rising again in its endless quest for sustenance.

The first three days of his harshly reduced diet were agonizing. He was plagued with hunger such as he had never known. It contorted his belly, goaded his mind toward a decision to eat the last of his food at once; but then the torture lessened, though his strength ebbed. After ten days he felt so debilitated, he was unable to properly work the boat or move about unless there was an urgent need. The *Isabella* idled along before the lightest of breezes. Christian sensed a current also moving her, but he could not judge its strength, nor even its direction. He slept more often, though for briefer periods. Day and night melded into spans of being half awake, then asleep again. He was tortured by dreams of the most grotesque nature. He wondered, *Was this what death would be like, a merging from this life into black unconsciousness?* 'Twas too deep a problem to concern him now; he could not concentrate on any subject for longer than a brief period.

One cloudless night he dreamed of an elegant repast in London with his brother, Edward, the successful barrister. It was at a fine restaurant in the West End; he could not remember its name. But he vividly sensed the food, the wine, the laden table, endless succulent dishes that beckoned him but dissolved in his dream before reaching his lips.

Amidst this illusive luxury, a fog of warm and stinking spray engulfed him. A sucking, shattering blowout alongside the boat brought him sharply awake. Across the moonlit water, the booming whale spouts sounded all around in the suddenly turbulent water. In the ghostly light, great flukes raised high above the boat, then struck the surface with the explosion of a sixteen-pounder, drenching him with the splash. Huge proportions of dark shapes wallowed across the bow. All about he could hear the noisy exhalations of enormous creatures. One massive head loomed over the boat while Christian cringed. The eye of the sperm whale glittered in the moonlight with a malevolent sheen, appeared to examine the craft's helpless occupant as though speculating whether such puny prey would be worth devouring, then suddenly was gone. With a great thrashing of tail flukes and blowing of air warm enough to generate a misty fog, the whales swam on. Soon they were cavorting across the great swells of the Pacific, lost to sight . . . and then to sound.

Christian, exhausted, fell asleep and awoke at dawn, stiffened, damp and cold. He attempted to rise. Dizziness overwhelmed him. He clutched the mast and clung to it until his brain cleared. Now he knew he was starving, but it brought no alarm to his mind, nothing but acceptance and resignation. If he were to starve, so be it, and quickly. 'Twould not be swift, however—that he knew. Perhaps a stupor would wash over him, detach his mind from its shriveling body until both plunged into nothingness. If hope had gone, why did he not cast himself over the side and have done with it? He was not such a man, and there burned within him that strangest of qualities—hope. Hope for what? He did not know, could not imagine. But hope. Hope shored up by a mystical belief in his power to surmount somehow every peril, every difficulty, every evil. Even this.

No, he would not destroy himself, though not through fear of any later punishment; for he believed in none of that. This life was all he would ever have. When it ended he would be poured into blackness and an emptiness without consciousness. Then why not now? But no. Not now. Later, when he had finally spun his life out. Not yet had he done that. Not quite yet.

One morning, an eighteen-foot blue shark, slender as a ship's gun, swam alongside—its curiosity keeping it abreast of the boat, but Christian was too listless to even attempt to capture it. Perhaps the remora fish attached by suction cups to the shark's throat might fish for him, if he could attach a line to it. To capture one, however, required strength, and that Christian no longer possessed. He was in a bitter spiral of decline; the periods of sleep were becoming longer, those moments of wakefulness more brief. Was this approaching death? How could he know? None had ever returned to tell.

In a moment of lucidity, he calculated the *Isabella* had run two-thirds of the distance to the coast, but he was finished, or almost so. He dreamed again of lavish repasts, of Mautea, seeing anew her lovely face, her dark liquid eyes, hearing her words of reassurance, of—hope! He shook himself, his belly aching with its emptiness. The night was chill, and he laboriously searched his mind for the hundredth time for some solution to his suffering. He came fully awake for an instant, clarity returning to his brain, an understanding of how near to insanity he had come. "Christ!" he moaned. "Oh, good Christ, let me die!" He cried blasphemously, with no petition intended.

Yet a fluttering of stubby winks and wet flops about the boat jarred him fully awake. He saw a flippering of life all about. Dimly he became aware that a school of flying fish, chased perhaps by a dolphin, had sought haven on the *Isabella*.

Greedily Christian seized one and with his knife slit it end to end and thrust it into his mouth, chewing ravenously on its warm, bloody meat, the juices dribbling through his beard. He must have eaten only briefly and slept. He awoke and continued his unfinished meal, slept again, awoke and ate once more. The quick recovery of his senses was miraculous, yet not a miracle, as castaways and frontiersmen had always found that nothing is so effective as raw flesh to revive the starving. By the evening of the following day, he was mentally himself once more, if physically weak as a child. The *Isabella* sailed on with a following breeze, sometimes strong, then light and puffy.

The fish did not last long. Once consumed there were no others. He lapsed more swiftly than before into his comatose state. Dimly he scanned the eastern horizon for some suggestion of land. There was none. The current, undetected now, pulled the *Isabella* north as much as the wind blew her east. The sky remained empty. The clouds that signaled the presence of high islands would never rise over the continental coast where the air was too dry to form them. The agony in his cramped belly became intense, his moments of consciousness rare, and even his resilient hope sagged. He entered a stupor, which deepened as the endless days progressed until he knew not where the boat drove, nor cared. His life slipped toward a dark and shadowy abyss. Awareness ceased.

So it was that the *Isabella,* washed in from the sea like any other flotsam, was heaved up fast upon a sandy beach beneath towering, scorching mountains, her stern awash still as though reluctant to sever her alliance with the deep, the craft with her unconscious passenger, holding against the shore, in the grip of the land, waiting. For what?

A bearded, wizened, ageless figure, with oddly bowed legs and tattered garb, sped down from his cave with the morning. He peered into the boat with burning eyes to see what treasure the sea had fetched him.

He waded through the surf, clutched the gunwales, and leaped aboard. Grasping Christian's beard, he turned the face upward, the pull not cruel, but firm, relentless. The piercing eyes saw some glimmer of life in that sea-worn countenance. He also saw and stuffed into his ragged garments the prayer book. He dragged the body to the gunwales, leaped into the water, and rolled Christian skillfully across his shoulder. He clambered through the surf to the shore, bearing his burden slowly upward to the cave. The *Isabella,* as though realizing her mission had ended, slid back with the surf into the sea to be washed, no man could say where.

BOOK II

Jonah rose up to flee unto Tarshish
from the presence of the LORD.

JONAH 1:3

CHAPTER ONE

Flickering shadows and blocks of light played above him. Christian thought perhaps they were castings from the flames of hell, but of course there was no hell. That he knew. Then he perceived that they were reflections of sunlight on wrinkling waters; and since he was below them, he must have drowned. But he could breathe easily, drawing warm air deep into his lungs, so he was not beneath the waves. Slowly his mind freed itself from the fantasies of half-consciousness, and he saw that the bright patterns on the smoke-darkened rock above him were cast by firelight. Turning his head with effort, he saw the fluttering blaze at the mouth of the cavern. It was night. He closed his eyes again, but he could smell the pungent, salt-savored smoke of the driftwood burning. He opened his eyes once more and stirred his emaciated body, heavy with stiffness, and aching bones. He felt old and exhausted.

A shadow passed over him, then quickly returned. He felt strong fingers grasp his beard, twist his face around to the light, and he stared into glowing eyes, into ageless features, wrinkled and colored like an English walnut, fringed by whiskers with a light frosting of gray. "Eh, eh, eh?" muttered a voice, busily, as though speaking to no one. It was high pitched, but not too high, and had a positive quality that carried reassurance. "Eh, eh, eh?" it repeated, a touch of warmth this time. "Awake, eh, lad? 'Tis time, 'tis time enough, I'll grant ye. Ye've slept long here, an' who can say how long before it in the boat. I'll get some nourishment into you, lad. In a moment, a moment. Have patience, now."

Dreamily Christian watched the figure dart to the fireside, poke up the flames, and draw out orange coals, making a tiny bed of them on which he placed a large copper cup, stirring its contents from time to time with a stick. He brought the steaming mixture to Christian, propping him against a woven blanket laid along the wall. With a crude metal spoon, he began to feed the castaway. Christian was beyond hunger, beyond thirst. The starvation ache in his body had given way to numbness. He showed little interest in the feeding process until he had tasted a spoonful or two of the soup. Then a ravening obsession seized him, and he reached out for the cup.

"Eh, eh, eh!" warned his rescuer. "Not so greedy, lad. There's enough an' time enough, an' I'll be judge of the rate of flow. Do ye lay back now, and let me be about my business. Easy does it, lad. There, now!"

Clucking like a mother hen and talking busily to himself, the stranger efficiently pursued the task, laying not only the broth in Christian's mouth, but pieces of flesh. "Mussels, they are. Mussels. They'll quickly renew your vigor, that they will. Eat hearty, now. When this cup is finished, 'tis sleep you'll want; an' when you awake, there'll be more of this an' mayhap a bit of meat as well. We'll see, lad. We'll see what we shall see!"

Christian ate and slept and awoke to eat and sleep again; and when he finally roused himself it was broad day, and the sunlight gleamed upon the water beyond the cave. From time to time he could observe a lacework of froth as a breaker lashed at the land, driving its spume within his range of vision. Beyond that sea lay . . . but he would think no more of that.

He stretched, surprised to find much of the ache gone, so swiftly had his body recovered with such a modest amount of food. He stood up slowly, felt dizziness, and sat again; and when his faintness passed, he raised himself once more and stepped to the lip of the cave. From it he could see a length of tawny beach in one direction, lost in the haze of sea and distance; in the other, beach sweeping in a great curve beyond which were two or three rocky islands, like crumbs of a broken land.

A rattling of pebbles signaled the approach of the old man, bobbing quickly into view around the edge of the cave, bearing across one shoulder a quarter of meat and suspended from the other a skin of wine.

"Eh, eh, eh!" he greeted Christian. "Up, eh, lad? How does it appear to ye today? Is the hunger gone?" He cackled with good spirits.

"I don't think 'twill be gone again, ever," said Christian with a slight grin. "I could eat all the food in the world at one table and hunger still for more!"

"We shall see, we shall see. Now build up that fire again from the coals, while I cut off some goat for roasting. 'Tis a feast we'll be having, if the *guardia civil* do not come first to arrest us for theft of the animal. But they will never reach us, for I know how to cover my tracks."

The fire was built, the meat well roasted and washed down with draughts of yellow wine, thin and dry as the desert haze and pleasant to the taste.

"What place is this?" asked Christian.

"Place? Place? This is no place at all. 'Tis a refuge from places. Places are where people are or where they frequent for profit to themselves, and no one frequents here but this old man and you. Does that make this a place? Perhaps, since there are now two of us. Perhaps."

"Surely this land must have a name. There can be no land without one."

The other thought the matter over. He bobbed his head in assent.

"Aye, every bit of land must have a name, 'tis true," he agreed. "That island yonder, the long one, see? They call it Choros, an' perhaps 'twas named by some Indian long since done to death by the race that proved more powerful. Eh, in this world power means superiority, and superiority is nothing else than power, power, power."

"It seems thus, often."

"Always, always. Though power is not always power of the sword, even if those so armed can think of nothing else. This land? 'Tis a kingdom, lad. They call it the kingdom of Chile."

"I thought Chile was Spanish-owned."

"It is. 'Tis one of the kingdoms of the Spanish king, the one most remote, least known, most embattled, and (who knows) most worthless, though a Spaniard opinion might differ."

"It seems of little value to the eye."

"Here, aye. But to the south it becomes green and lush and rich and fertile, with rivers flowing from the mountains to the sea. Beyond them are the forests and Indians who wield a power the Spanish cannot crush. They are too wise to submit to Spanish lies and blandishments and so are free and will remain free so long as they are brave and vigilant."

"If that land is so beautiful and rich, why do you stay here?"

"Why, lad? Why to pluck living flotsam from the sea! What else?"

Christian joined him in laughter, then conceded, "At any rate, 'tis well for me that you were at hand."

Chewing on another strip of roasted goat, he finally asked, "Who are you, sir? Ye live within a Spanish kingdom, dwell in a cave like a wild man, and ye talk like an Englishman with a command of words like a scholar. What is your name?"

The other wagged a long forefinger.

"Names. Places. Why must every fragment of land and each bit of humanity float a banner? A badge? Why cannot I be but 'thou' to you? Ah, but I see I cannot. Your mind is too attuned to mankind's silly practices for that. Call me Ishmael. 'Tis as good a name as any other, more meaningful than most. And yours?"

Again Christian laughed.

"And which of us is bound by formula now?" he demanded. He considered the question for a moment. "I will answer to Fletcher."

"A maker of arrows and barbs, of missiles that fly true and straight and know not what they are about! A good enough choice."

"If I could but live up to it."

"Each man answers a goal, a target toward which he strives, even a Fletcher. 'Tis to select a goal, then use it for your aim."

"Where are you from?"

Exasperation touched the face of the old man.

"Names. Places. Origins. Soon you will ask my age, my wife, my children, the whole baggage man drags about and needs so little of. Where do I come from? Why, like any man, from my mother's womb. Where else?"

Christian's strength returned swiftly, for he was blessed with youth. His muscles filled, rippling flesh renewed itself over chest and belly, his back straightened with newfound health. Animation returned to his bearded face and dark eyes. He followed Ishmael as a boy follows his father, learning from him the secret of breaking mussels from submerged rocks, abalone from overhanging ledges, of running down the half-wild goats, and of concealing the fact from any but the sharpest eye. They saw no other human being during the weeks that followed, nor sign of life save the goats. Occasionally the old man disappeared for a day or two, returning with wine, from where he would not reveal. Christian collected the driftwood for their fires and in the evening listened to his talks of the land in which they lived and of survival there.

"Here we are free, free as may be, but in a trap nonetheless," said Ishmael.

"Why is that?"

"Because we dare not be discovered. The Spanish Empire is a vault, locked by suspicion and hatred against all outsiders and walled by cruelty and steel against those who would come in. To be discovered a foreigner within the empire—without the gold to buy release—means death, as like as not."

"Are there no foreigners, then, in Chile?"

"Aye, of course there are. A few hundred in the cities, scattered here and there like flung grain. But without exception they have purchased their immunity either with gold or with loss of freedom."

"Their freedom?"

"Aye, in some cases, perhaps by marriage, quickly arranged. A foreigner who weds a Spanish woman, or even a Creole, is suffered to remain, almost as an equal, though not quite of course, since to a Spaniard no other than a Spaniard ever fully is his equal."

"You do not like them, Ishmael?

"Eh, eh, eh, of course I like them, lad. They are a people, and so of God. But within each Spaniard is a strange mixture of the primitive and cultured, savage and civilized, cruel and kind, degenerate and noble, the like of which the world has seen in no other race. But to love them is one thing, to trust them quite another. I love them despite their faults; I would never trust them, while I wish to survive."

Christian probed his mind with many questions. "How do you know so much about them?"

"How? How, you say? Oh, I pass for one of them when it pleases me. I speak their language fluently, although with an accent of which I can never be rid, for my tongue was trained for different words. When they ask me where I am from, I say Estramadura; and that satisfies them because every Spaniard has heard of Estramadura; but since the Pizarros, no one comes from there. They know, however, that it is a province half-Spanish, half-Portuguese, with an accent strange to a Catalan's ear. Mine passes for Estramaduran."

Christian traced a pointless design with a stick in the sand. "With all their evil qualities, why then do you like them?"

Ishmael ceased his rocking, his eyes glowing with an almost physical force.

"The Lord said we were to love our neighbors; he did not specify some to love an' some to hate. So we must love all of them, without exception. You note, however, that he did not say that we must trust them. Perhaps he knew a Spaniard or had heard of one."

Christian learned that Chile was a country of a single city and a few towns, a novelty in an empire whose people believed that the city was where civilization flourished and the countryside where it languished.

The single great community was Santiago, 500 miles to the south of this secluded cave. It had perhaps 30,000 residents. Valparaíso, a week by horseback removed from Santiago, on the western coast, numbered no more than 5,000, and Concepción, 300 miles southward of Valparaíso, on the Bío-Bío River which defined the Spanish frontier settlements from lands held by the fiercely independent Araucanians, counted fewer than 6,000. La Serena, 80 miles below their retreat, had perhaps 4,000, while Chillán and Talca, southward of Santiago, filled out the roster of Chile's most favored settlements.

So remote were they from any settlement that the two lived in a world alone, the boom of breakers against the land so rhythmical it quickly dulled the senses. Christian dreamed away the weeks, an unreal existence with no punctuation, neither fear nor anticipation, no enemies—and no friends, aside from Ishmael.

The reflective moments grew, however. He had a growing sense of being a man apart, touched by fate. Deep within his subconscious, the pattern set on that April dawn in 1789 led now to a new stirring in him, a growing restlessness. The featureless plateau on which he existed, a plains of sameness which no active man can tolerate for long, strengthened his growing dissatisfaction. The old man, recognizing his irritation, sympathized but could offer little help, for it was an inner problem, of the mind alone.

"Ishmael," blurted Christian one evening as they finished their meal and dusk crept over the land, "are there roads to Santiago?"

The old man did not answer directly, aware his guest sought not information, but acquiescence.

"'Tis daft, man!" he protested. "Ye would not survive in that place a week."

"Where else, then?"

"Why anywhere? Here you have food, shelter, companionship, idleness. What more is there?"

"Aye, idleness. 'Tis the idleness that nearly drives me mad. My body is idle, my mind is not. The time has come when high risk is preferable to no risk at all."

"Ye speak like a guilty man, Fletcher, one fleeing from something, and that may lead you to destruction. Here there is no guilt, save of mankind as a whole, no remorse—an' no peril, either. Or little of it."

Christian lay back against the warm sand, hands clasped behind his head. The two were silent for a time in the warm covering of the evening.

"I would go to Santiago, Ishmael," he said quietly.

"'Twill mean your death, likely!"

"You have been there and survived. Why cannot another?"

Ishmael gestured impatiently.

"I am practiced in the tongue, Fletcher. I can pass for one of them or be ignored, which is as useful. But you! The first time you opened your mouth, you'd be known for a foreigner, hailed before a magistrate, condemned as a spy and shot within the hour."

"In that case I shall not speak," said Christian with a trace of humor. I will be mute. You can say my words."

"I? I? You would lead me to destruction? Hah!"

"Would you abandon me to certain death?"

Ishmael chuckled.

"You seize unfair advantage, Fletcher. You know I cannot allow you to pursue this mad course alone, even though to go with you may be my own destruction. Being alien you already are a man condemned, and those who travel with you would be of equal guilt in judges' eyes."

Christian's deep voice came from the blackness of despair. "I do not fear death, Ishmael, although I should regret to cause your own. But you are indestructible. I am sure you would survive me, or I would slip away and try my luck on my own. I do not fear to die, Ishmael. I am a man accursed and those who bear this evil do not carry their fate in their own hands. They may, 'tis true, bring disaster upon those whom their lives touch, but this is not always so."

"How do you mean, 'accursed'? I doubt there is such a thing."

Slowly Christian reviewed for Ishmael the turbulent events of his recent life, though about the details he was vague enough.

". . . and so I was condemned by a man whom I may have wronged but who surely wronged me. And 'twas no light thing. Since the moment of his curse, I have brought disaster to many lives. 'Tis difficult to explain, Ishmael, but the conviction that I am set apart from other men runs deep, a terrifying belief I would gladly shed, could I do so."

"Eh, eh, eh! I do not believe in curses, except within a mind that feeds on self-pity. Curses speak of witchcraft and evil and the primitive mind. To rational men they cannot exist, and you are intelligent, Fletcher. This curse is only in the black recesses of your mind. Forget it!"

"I do not speak to convince you," replied Christian. "A curse does not come to all men—to very few, I think. It can be defined no more than love or hate, yet that does not argue for its nonexistence. To a man accursed 'tis real enough. He needs no further definition, no other proof. I have felt the weight of it for years—have you? You cannot argue against what you do not know, have not experienced."

"That belief is surrender to the evil one suspects but cannot demonstrate. 'Tis better to affirm faith in the power of love, the glow of light upon one's life. I cannot prove that a curse is an impossibility, but I know that faith exists, that it crowds out the darkness of despair and brings light an' joy to lives that grasp it. With faith there is no room for darkness or evil or curses. 'Tis by faith I prefer to live."

"Faith in what?"

"In God, of course, and in his goodness."

"I do not believe in God, Ishmael."

"Ye must believe in his adversary, in the devil then, since ye say you hold a 'curse.'"

"The curse is not a person; 'tis a power. Your faith I suspect is not a person either, but a power, if it is anything at all."

"No, Fletcher," said Ishmael, leaning forward. "My God is not an indefinable something that faith attaches to, but One who is real. 'Tis because I know this and know him that I have faith."

"Ye sound like a priest, a preacher, Ishmael!"

"Perhaps," he agreed, after a moment's pause. "It may be that they, too, sometimes perceive the vision that has come to me."

"With all of that faith will ye, then, accompany me to Santiago?"

Ishmael sighed. "Ye test it to the uttermost, Fletcher. But I cannot let you go alone, for curse or no curse, 'twould mean your death. If ye must go, I shall accompany you, though no doubt 'twill mean destruction for us both.

CHAPTER TWO

On the fourth day of their southward journey, the trail they followed wound from the coast through a defile threading a range of small barren hills. Bobbing hats of poncho-clad riders rose into their view. They stepped aside to allow a strange procession to pass. Each bony, wall-eyed horse bore upon its back a rider but brought something else too: after it stumbled a tattered human being, whose long black hair was tied to the animal's tail and whose hands were lashed with rawhide thongs behind his back. Some of the animals towed two or even three of these wretches, their bare or sandaled feet competing for space upon the narrow, stony path—stumbling, falling, dragged remorselessly until they struggled to their feet to keep up with the progress of the horse. In all there were twenty-five or thirty of these hapless beings, mostly men, but including a few dirt-encrusted women. The riders, as dark-visaged as their captives, showed not a shred of mercy, appearing unaware even of the existence of their human flotsam.

After the column had passed, Ishmael seated himself upon a rock at the summit of the pass, his wrinkled face solemn, his wise old eyes following the forlorn column as long as it could be seen.

"My God," breathed Christian, still engulfed in horror. "What was that?"

"Eh, eh," returned Ishmael. "Are you asking me or God?"

Christian remained speechless, his brow furrowed.

"That, lad, was an introduction to the Spanish empire, your first glimpse of the *encomienda* system."

They sat there dressed like the farmer or vagabonds who wandered from *estancias* to villages seeking work, begging a few scraps of food. Each wore a poncho, that universal South American garment devised by Indians before the time of Columbus and quickly adopted by Europeans. These blankets of dingy brown wool had a slit in the center for the head and hung to the knees. Some of the better ones were fashioned with colored stripes, but few wanders could afford such luxury of design. Their hats, bell-shaped, were of cheap straw, loosely woven. A flannel shirt, a pair of loose drawers, and for shoes, a slab of raw bull's hide cut to the shape of the sole and lashed on with thin rawhide thongs completed their wardrobe.

Ishmael and Christian circled La Serena, a coastal town; they rested above it while Ishmael pointed out the features within view, including a few broad cultivated fields toward the interior made rich by irrigation.

"A mud town with little to relieve it," grumbled Christian, mopping sweat from his throat.

"Except the churches," Ishmael replied. "There are seven of them, eight counting the chapel, as you can see. The tall steeple across the street from the market place and plaza is the Cathedral of Saint John. The building resembling a crown with its serrated roof line is the palace of *el corregidor*, governor of this district."

"La Serena appears divided into squares as regular as a chessboard."

"Aye. All Spanish cities are so. Some king once got the notion that the proper way to create a city was to start with a rectangular plaza and run streets at right angles from it. Since then every city of Spanish origin has been laid out so.

The town lay about the head of the larger of two inlets forming the Bay of Coquimbo. "Ships," said Ishmael, indicating the brig in the harbor, usually anchored in about seven fathoms off the place called Tortuga, nine miles by road from La Serena.

"The place doesn't look like much," said Christian.

"Others have regarded it more favorably," replied his companion. "The Indians once captured and burned it. Your piratical countryman, Francis Drake, sacked it, as did Bartholomew Sharp a century later. And now the Spanish find it valuable for the storing of wine, which is contraband since the Crown objects to colonials creating what otherwise might be purchased in Spain. La Serena's history seems to be outlawry." His brown face wrinkled. "We may rest at a plantation on the Elqui River beyond the town."

I thought you feared my discovery as a foreigner?"

"I know the *dueño*. If ye speak not, Paulo will not betray us."

"Yet you trust no Spaniard?"

"This man is Portuguese, not Spanish—an exile from Colonia, brought here from Mendoza because he understands the wine-making. He can be trusted."

It was near dusk when they plodded up a tree-lined earthen lane toward a complex of whitewashed buildings. They passed swarms of Indians coming in from the vineyards, tools athwart their emaciated though still muscular shoulders, heads bowed, eyes dull and incurious, a ragged parade of the walking dead. Here and there among them was a mounted man as vigilant as the laborers were somnolent.

"The principal rider—the man dismounting now before the house—with the silver work on the bridle and saddle is the overseer," whispered Ishmael. "Those other horsemen are *jefes*, his assistants. The darker men on mules are the foremen. They all drive the Indians who are slaves in fact, if not in name, with the whip, stocks, and still worse brutality, as ye no doubt will see. Mercy has no place upon a Spanish *encomienda*, for mercy reduces profit."

A cart, its tortured wooden wheels screeching at the total absence of grease, slowly approached from the direction of the hacienda, passed them, the driver, an Indian, staring at nothing. As the vehicle passed by, Christian glimpsed arms and a foot protruding from its bed. "Look, Ishmael!"

Ishmael glanced at the grisly cargo, then hurried on, saying nothing.

"What was that about?" persisted Christian. The other angrily shook him off.

"'Tis but the day's dead," he muttered grimly. "The wastage from the fields, a price of the *encomienda* system, the children of God returned to God."

"But I don't understand. What caused—"

"My friend, why can't you let me be? I do not wish to speak of it further," Ishmael heatedly broke in. "What's done is done!"

The pair circled the extensive cluster of buildings, passed a peach orchard, and Ishmael left Christian behind a clutter of reeking hog pens while he disappeared for a time. It was fully dark when he returned with another man who silently glided before them, leading the way to a wattle-and-daub hut with thatched roof. Ishmael flashed a spark to a candlewick. With the light he motioned their guide inside. He was Indian, Manuel by name, and of the Picunche people, the old man explained. But what struck Christian instantly was that his eyes were lively, his grin merry, his whole demeanor attracting one to an engaging personality. Ishmael gave him a long draught of wine. Manuel wiped his mouth with the back of his brown wrist, shook hands gravely with both, flashed a smile, and was gone.

"He doesn't appear unhappy with his lot," observed Christian.

"As the son of a *cacique*, or chief, he has it slightly better than the *mitayo*, or field laborer, but do not fool thyself that his life is pleasant. He is but a slave like the others."

"Where did Manuel go from here?"

"He is one of the lucky ones, for he has his own *barraca*, a young wife, and a child or two. His woman, he told me, is ill with the ague, which is why he hurried off. Nonetheless, his life is sure to become a tragedy."

Christian shook his head with disbelief.

"Surely you exaggerate, Ishmael?"

"You shall see, lad. You shall see. I have not told the smallest part of it, and I am an honest man."

Christian awoke as the first light of a clear dawn filtered through the crevices over their pallets. Ishmael offered him a handful of roasted maize and a cup of cold water.

"An *encomienda* breakfast, Fletcher," he laughed. "On this the *mitayo* labors all day until dark. Every day. Sometimes a bit of fruit in season, a morsel of fowl or bite of pork, and a swallow of wine if he can steal it."

A commotion in the near distance startled them. Christian made for the rag that hung across the doorway; Ishmael pulled him sharply back.

"Fletcher, remember that our lives and that of Paulo hang in the balance," he warned. "Swear that no matter what we see, you will make no outcry, attempt no intercession, whatever cruelty takes place, you will observe but not cry out. Our lives, Fletcher, our *lives* depend upon it. Swear it, or I will not let you go!"

Christian, little comprehending the urgency, gazed wonderingly at his companion.

"Of course, Ishmael. I pledge it."

"Come, then," said the other softly, shouldering through the entryway.

He led Christian down the pathway between rows of flimsy, tiny huts, each the home of an Indian family, or sometimes two. They halted within view of a cluster of Indians before a shack. A woman lay prostrate upon the ground, her clothing ripped aside. She lay upon her face, a dark foreman lashing her back with his bloodied whip, while a horseman watched impassively and other men stood by. Even as the brutal scene continued, a figure flung himself from the hut and hurled his body over hers so that the lash a time or two hit his own back. It was Manuel of the night before, then so joyous, lively—now frantic with concern.

"His wife is being beaten because she did not go to work today," whispered Ishmael.

"She, she had a fever! She was ill!"

"She did not work. Now she is whipped for it."

Two of the bystanders, at a word from the horseman, grasped Manuel by the arms and flung him backward, while the lash descended implacably upon the reddening form of his stricken wife. Once more Manuel struggled to his feet and cast himself again across his wife, seeking to protect her body with his own.

Once more he was flung back. Still a third time he struggled forward, blindly in protest. The horseman harshly cried out.

"He says the *indio* cares too much for this woman!" whispered Ishmael. "He says he is too *macho,* too male. He says to—cure him. They will do it. We had better return."

Christian, hypnotized, remained rigid, fixedly staring at the bitter scene. Ishmael's steel grip upon his arm ripped him away against his will.

Once they returned to the hut, now deserted, Christian seemed to awaken from his trance. "What will they do to him, Ishmael?"

"It is the way of the *encomienda,* my friend. No amount of rebellion is tolerated. Manuel's devotion to his wife is perceived as weakness, and he will be punished. Undoubtedly, they will castrate him."

"Surely you jest!" Christian exclaimed in utter disbelief. "Such cruelty can not be possible!"

"Not only possible, but unavoidable," sighed Ishmael grievously. "Nonetheless, the ultimate injustice comes after punishment is meted out. No matter the suffering at the hands of their masters, the slaves must respond by saying, 'May God bless you!' It is a symbol of acceptance, utter submission."

"'May God bless you!'" Christian savagely repeated as he now sat upon the mud floor, Ishmael beside him.

"Even the most cruel master can ask for that," said Ishmael softly. "The Spanish believe themselves to be, Fletcher. That is why they require it."

"*Christian!* From my childhood I remember that Christ taught compassion, mercy, love, forgiveness, kindness, justice, goodness. There is none of that in them!"

"Some would assert so," admitted Ishmael. "Still, they delude themselves. They believe Christianity is a formula, not a way of life. Hence they are little more than pagans."

Christian's savage thoughts tumbled about in his brain.

"I do not believe in God or hell," he growled, "but if I did, I would be pleased. For people who allow such things as we have seen would surely rot in eternal fire. If I could create a hell for them, I'd do it, happily."

"'Vengeance is mine,' saith the Lord."

"Really? Where *is* this vengeance, then? Does your God approve of such cruelty, such barbarity as we have seen? What kind of God is that?"

"You ask how the Lord works, as did Job, long ago. The answer he received was that it is not given to man to understand. Only that God does. I can give ye no answer, Fletcher, only understanding of your anger, and compassion for Manuel—and love for him an' his tortured wife."

"The two sat quietly, each with his own thoughts.

"This," said Ishmael finally, "is Chapter One of the book of the Spanish Empire. 'Tis a blight that extends for 7,000 miles north and south, 2,000 east and west, afflicting millions, frequently with tortures and cruelties that surpass even what we can imagine, in diverse ways, to unimaginable degrees. For brutality feeds upon brutality and deepens as men become inured—and as it fails to solve their problems."

"Well, since there is no hope for these poor people from the 'God of mercy' you believe in and no visible compassion, either, is there nothing left?"

Ishmael flushed. "God does not operate the affairs of men by means of puppet strings! Man is free to be cruel and oppressive—to be evil—if he chooses, but by doing so he becomes destructive, to himself not least of all."

"That is of great benefit, of course," Christian said indignantly, "for the poor Indian, who has suffered abominable cruelties for generations! We speak of the Spaniard and what he does to himself by blindness, avarice, vanity, cruelty, but who speaks for the Indian who is subjected to these evils? What does your God do for him? A man born into filth and degradation, a life of bitter slavery and insupportable oppression, a miserable death—what good is God to him?"

"If God controlled the affairs of men, man would be less than man, an amusing toy for God and little more, valueless for himself and for his Creator. But within each man's life and circumstances, God is available and his love and concern are at hand."

"For Manuel and his wife, for example?"

"Yes, even to them, now and forever."

"Manuel must be grateful," jeered Christian. "No longer a man, his family destroyed, but assured of 'love' and 'concern' from One who would not help him to justice when he so desperately needed it."

"Don't say thus, Fletcher. To doubt is human; to condemn, blasphemy. The evil was done by man, not God. He cannot prevent such deeds without compromising his creation." Changing the subject, he added, "Ye asked if there was no other recourse, and that I cannot say, but the present captain general, whom Chileños call the president because he presides over the *audencia,* or administrative council, has attempted to abolish the *encomienda* pattern, being unable to correct its abuses. He is perhaps in a losing struggle, even though sentiment against the system is rising among a few of goodwill."

"If there be any such within this empire of evil."

"There are, ye may be sure."

"Who is this captain general of noble heart?"

"Ye would not believe me if I told you, so I shall not—at least until the bitterness leaves and your mind opens again."

Christian was silent for so long that he knew Ishmael thought the conversation was ended, but it was not. When he spoke it was with iron determination: "I tell ye, Ishmael, I know no better than you what the future holds, but given survival and strength, I pledge my deepest oath I shall not rest until I see this evil overthrown. I shall never, so long as I may live, lose any opportunity to fight this system, to free these people, and to further the destruction of so rotten, cruel, and inhumane an empire and its instruments!"

Deep within he heard again the words, *"Laich . . . Laich anochi iemach."* Only now they sounded so loudly that Christian looked over at Ishmael to see if he also had heard. He had not. Christian shook his head but could not chase away the inward resonation of the words nor the feeling that somehow he had the full attention of the *Being* who spoke them. He immediately rose in his agitation to pace the confines of the hut until Ishmael said, at last, "Eh, eh, well, we may as well go since you are of a mind to march."

CHAPTER THREE

Ishmael and Christian had passed south from the Chacabuco Mountains and from a distance of fifteen miles they could see the lofty spires of the churches of Santiago. The roadway now was more traveled. They came upon a succession of rude huts, many with traces of whitewash adhering to the brown walls. The people appeared to be Indian or *mestizo*, a lowly, miserable lot, though apparently free. Perhaps, thought Christian, they had somehow escaped the covetous eyes of *encomienderos*, but his companion explained that Spanish were ever free, *mestizos* usually so, and Indians might become free if they had served in the army or were married to women of Spanish origin.

Santiago was a corruption of the true name, Santo Jago, meaning Saint James, and originally added "de Nuevo Extremo" or "of the new frontier," since the Spaniards had extended the border of their empire to the nearby Mapocho River at this point in 1541. Approaching the city, Ishmael and Christian were driven to one side of the highway by a cavalcade of a dozen horsemen, in a column of twos, dressed in blue coats and capes, scarlet waistcoats, and blue trousers tucked into black boots to which were strapped spurs with enormous, many-pointed rowels. Each rider had slung over his shoulder a shortened musket, or carbine, and at his right hand a steel-hilted saber. Their horses were small, deep-barreled native animals with tails squared off two feet above the ground, although the sergeant in command rode a larger mount of obvious foreign breeding. Ishmael bowed as the column passed and Christian followed suit.

"The uniforms, the weapons, the formation are Spanish," confided Ishmael. "The spurs are Chilean. Every Chilean wears such spurs if he can afford them. The Spanish concede them that bit of vanity."

"Aren't they all Spaniards?"

"There are no Spanish regiments in Chile," Ishmael laughed. "Here the officers alone are Spanish or hold Spanish commissions; but the *soldados* are recruited locally, many *mestizos* and even some Indians. Soldiering is an honorable way to keep from starving in this rich country. Some enlist, some are caught by press gangs, some enter the army to eat. Others are forced into it as punishment by the courts. If military discipline does not cure them of their proclivity to crime, at least it controls them."

"Are most of the regulars stationed here in Santiago?"

"No, most of the regiments are on the Bío-Bío River, the frontier with the hostile Araucanian Indians. Some along the coast, as well: Valparaíso, Concepción, Valdivia. The Spanish always fear invasion. I think the threat illusory."

"That's the first time you've mentioned Valdivia. What is that?"

"A fortress city far to the south, the uttermost redoubt of the Spanish Empire. When you stand on Nieblas headland, there you are facing the Antarctic wilderness to the south, wild Indian tribes to the east, the unknown ocean to the west. Only to the north and along the coast is there connection with the empire and with Spain."

"You have been there, Ishmael?"

"Lad, I have been everywhere. Yes, I have been there. I would not go again willingly."

Ishmael, standing within the welcome shade of a haya tree, tossed a small leather purse to Christian. Christian hefted it and found it weighty.

"We might become separated somehow," explained his companion. "You'd best have some coins, but remember, speak not! Shake your head or nod. Say nothing, for 'twould be your death warrant!"

"I'll remember."

"Mind you do not overpay," cautioned Ishmael. "Nothing would so quickly betray you as carelessness about money."

"What are these coins worth?"

"The larger ones are *pesos*, the smaller *reales*, eight to a *peso*. Most of what you need will be counted in *reales*—for bread, a bit of meat, and wine."

Among many other travelers, the two walked with heads lowered, in order to attract as little attention as possible, across the long bridge over the Mapocho leading into the city. Now and then a curious glance surveyed them swiftly, more in hope of finding customers than from suspicion.

They leaped aside as a four-wheel curtained coach clattered by, led by an escort of dragoons and followed by an attendant upon a silver draped horse of good breeding and lines. "Eh, eh, the *corregidor,*" said Ishmael, softly. "The bishop."

Across the flag-stoned plaza, the bishop's carriage rumbled to a halt before a massive facade, the footman assisting a portly, blowing figure to step down into the blaze of sun and heat, a cloud of color—birreta, cassock, sash, and the *cappa magna*, his symbol of authority—all purple. He swatted with irritation at the flies buzzing about his face and waddled into the relatively cool interior of the building.

"He lives well," grinned Christian.

"'Tis not his home! It's the cathedral. Soon the people will come for high mass. This must be Sunday."

Across the plaza the great doors of the cathedral, three pairs of them, were swung slowly open and propped ajar by shabbily-dressed Indians.

"They have buried hundreds beneath the floor," Ishmael remarked. "Ever there are requests to bury more. The churning of the earth under the flagstones continually disturbs old graves and old bodies. The result is that the smell of death hangs heavy inside and the cathedral must be aired before each service or its fetid atmosphere would offend delicate nostrils."

"I think the order of decay appropriate for such a monument to superstition and misplaced trust," muttered Christian.

"Come with me after the people have entered, and we'll see whether the mass leaves you so alienated as you imagine yourself to be. Will ye do it? 'Twill take pluck for one so minded as you, but perhaps it will lift your vision. Eh, Fletcher?"

Christian groaned. "If ye will accompany me afterwards to a *pulpería* for a bottle of wine and a bit of food. You never seem to hunger, but I am not so fashioned."

The deep tones of huge bells summoned the *Santigueños* to mass. Slowly they arrived, almost blackening the plaza. Many were ponchoed *mestizos* or Indians, but carriages and saddled horses bearing the wealthy also drew up. Christian and Ishmael slipped through a doorway with the last to arrive.

The cathedral held many altars, ten of them by Christian's count; and crowds of people blanketed the rough stone floor, which lay sixty feet below the dingy ceiling of the enormous building. Socially blessed individuals sat forward on rough wooden benches, their ladies seeking to fan away the reek of death rising all about, remainders with the stylized ritual of the temporal quality of human life amid dreams of eternity. Behind the fortunate ones huddled their slaves mingled with some *mestizos*, a multitude of Indians, and tattered vagabonds. Christian and Ishmael paused within distant view of the principal altar where they could converse softly with no danger of being overheard.

Having mumbled his prayer and left the foot of the altar, the portly bishop, Don Blas Sobrino y Minayo, was now seated upon the golden-armed Episcopal throne, his vesting underway. He rose, acknowledged the sinfulness of all men with the thrice-repeated *mea culpa*, and the mass got underway, while Ishmael explained the celebration to his companion. Despite his skepticism, Christian watched with growing interest. At one point he asked, "What is a mass, anyway?"

"Why, 'tis to preserve the memory of the Last Supper, Fletcher, a stylized reenactment of the meal at which Jesus commanded his followers to eat bread and drink wine in memory of the body and the blood he was to offer for mankind everywhere. That is the purpose of it: to commemorate and to remind."

"If it was less 'stylized,' it would accomplish its ends more effectively," Christian commented.

"Some would think so," Ishmael assented, slowly, "but then it would be less universal."

Despite his scorn Christian was intrigued by the elaborate ceremony and felt somewhat drawn toward it. This inevitably was countered by his reluctance to believe, and a massive restlessness resulted. Overwhelmed by a tide of emotions he could no longer withstand, he turned and rushed blindly into the glittering sunlight and stifling heat of the plaza. Ishmael followed and found him leaning against a pillar, his white face pressed to the coolness of the stone, his eyes half-closed against the turmoil within him.

"What is it, lad?" asked Ishmael anxiously. Christian did not reply for long moments, then recovered his composure.

"Ishmael, I need food and drink—aye, bread and wine, that's it! Not to celebrate some mythical event in legend, but to rebuild my guts and legs here and now! Can't we find a *pulpería* to serve the likes of us?"

Despite the crowd gathered within the cathedral, the plaza still teemed with people and animals. On two sides it was bound by arcaded, towered buildings with tiled roofs, but low shops and houses bordered it elsewhere. Hawkers and seated Indian women attempted to sell their wares: vegetables and farm produce, leather goods, bits and pieces of finery, combs elaborately carved, mantillas and laces, ponchos, straw hats, and sandals. The pair threaded the assemblage to an open wine shop opposite, whose curtain, drawn aside, revealed a doorway. Christian entered first, his broad shoulders all but filling the entrance. His eyes became adjusted to the dimness, and he made out the proprietor, a sallow individual with lank black hair framing his face like the curtains of a funeral carriage. "*Señores?*" he asked, initially polite to strangers who might be worth the effort. Two or three unkempt Spaniards sat around a cask, rattling leathern cards of huge size, the values rudely painted on the upper left corners. They played silently, diligently for the most part, and it was difficult to see for what, since neither money nor chips lay before them. Perhaps for their own amusement.

"*Señores?*" asked the proprietor again, patiently. He still was unsure of their ability to pay. Christian pointed to his mouth, shook his head silently as a mute, and pointed to his companion.

"*Vino, un poco de pan, queso,*" mumbled Ishmael, quickly enough so that his accent might be lost. As the *tendero* hesitated, Ishmael brought up his leather purse, setting it heavily upon the flimsy counter. The heads of the players swiveled speculatively, then returned to their cards with no comment. But they would remember.

When food was brought, Christian impatiently worked free from the wooden plug with its coating of wax, upended the bottle, took a long draught, and set it before him. He tore away a chunk of bread, chewed it, together with a mouthful of pale yellow cheese, and drank deeply again. He still was troubled by the rite in the cathedral.

"I would not drink so, lad," muttered Ishmael, softly. "'Tis long since you ate; wine on an empty belly might bring carelessness to your tongue. It could prove fatal. Shall we find a shady spot along the Mapocho to finish our meal?"

Christian shook his head. The wine was already firing his mind.

"I'm only tired of endless walking," he whispered. "I'll be careful."

But he was not. On the long trail south, they had lived a beggars' existence, and beggars are not often treated to wine; it had been long since he had tasted it. More than a day had passed since they had eaten. Emotion had drained him. Perhaps the confusion of the morning had led him into recklessness, a disregard for his own fate and that of his companion. At any rate when Ishmael chided him once again about over-hasty drinking, Christian flashed angrily: "Leave me be! I am no boy who must be controlled in his tippling!"

He ignored the instant bedlam his outcry provoked. Ishmael disappeared from before him, fleeing through the open doorway just behind one of the startled gamblers. In only a moment, it seemed, two blue-clad militia bustled into the room, stood before the table, questioning him harshly in rapid, staccato Spanish. Christian grinned at them, took a final draught of the wine, cast the emptied bottle aside.

"Not a word of what you're sayin' lads, do I understand. Not a bloody word. Ye wish to take me with you? Aye, had I a pistol, you could not do it. But I have none! Let's go, then—from the gateway to Heaven by way of a pub to perdition in one bloody day! Let's be off." He arose, swayed, and accompanied his grim escort toward he knew not what nor where.

The ancient jail of the city had tumbled down some years earlier, and Christian was prodded through the Sunday throng of curious strollers toward an imposing new building fronted by a line of Tuscan columns and surmounted by a tower that bore Santiago's only great clock. It nightly struck the curfew hour of nine, after which all of suspicious appearance found abroad were to be arrested and brought in. Many were thus sucked into the huge building, but few emerged. It housed not only people guilty of insignificant transgressions, but also those to be destroyed for greater crimes, real or suspected. Even the Chilean version of the Inquisition, a dying reflection of Lima's murderous ecclesiastical court, was held here, still deadly enough to be dreaded on this remote fringe of the mighty Catholic empire.

Christian was brought before the Sunday sergeant, his face stubbly with two days growth of whiskers, his eyes small and suspicious. After attempting without success to extract information from the prisoner, who did not even comprehend his questions, he nodded for a turnkey to take him two floors below, past barred cells caging prisoners of every variety. At last, with his enormous key, the jailer locked him into a crowded cell, flashed a toothless grin in the flickering lamplight, drawing a forefinger sharply across his throat. Roaring delightedly, he stalked away, his laughter receding with him until he ascended the stairs and was lost to sight and sound.

Impatiently shaking off his fellow prisoners with his halting Spanish, "*No hablo castellano*," Christian sought a corner pile of filthy straw upon which to rest. An army of ravenous bedbugs soon drove him to the naked stones where he sat with his back to the bars, his head beginning to throb as the wine leached from his brain. He held no illusions; he knew Ishmael had spoken truly. He hoped the old man had escaped; and no doubt he had, for Ishmael's survival quotient was high. Christian was aware that his own escape from this vermin-infested sink would only be by firing squad or the garrote as Ishmael had explained happened to virtually every foreigner. Even persons of countries allied by treaty with Spain were so disposed of. Ships of friendly nations were captured or sunk when they strayed within the reach of Spanish canon, for the empire considered isolation a matter of survival in its kind of murderous world.

The Englishman reviewed his adventurous life from the day he had signed on the *Bounty*—Tahiti, the mutiny, Tubuai, the death of Mautea, the voyage in the boat, rescue by Ishmael, and the wanderings southward to this city—all brought up short. His abbreviated existence of good and evil, passion and quietude, life and hope and despair cut off by the contents of one single bottle of cheap wine. What irony!

He was not bitter about it. Rather he was caustic, resigned to the futility, nay the folly of such a life and of existence itself. At length Christian slept. He had no idea for how long. There were no windows in this lower prison, and the light from the lamps ever was the same. His dozing must have continued for quite some time; for his headache was vanished when the massive key grated in the iron lock, the door swung open, and he was motioned out. Beyond the jailor were four soldiers, not at all like the ragamuffins who had arrested him. He vaguely recognized them by the smart dragoon uniforms encountered at the entrance to the city.

Christian was herded by this escort up the stone stairs to a second tier of cells and by another flight to the street level. For the first time he realized now that it was night. The soldiers silently passed the desk sergeant, a different one, though equally unkempt and ugly. Where was he bound? To a magistrate? A firing squad? He neither knew, nor did he care overmuch.

Through the gloom they marched, the dragoons' pace timed with the jingling of their spurs, and Christian's own step measured and silent. His sailor's sense told him it was late, just before midnight, to judge from the stars. At length they approached a great black hulk of a building and entered by a side door, guarded by a uniformed dragoon who stepped aside to allow them passage. Once more they mounted stairs, now of gleaming marble. They passed a long corridor and turned in through a heavily carved door and by way of still another door gained an inner room. It was meanly appointed, although perhaps with the best furniture Santiago had to offer. On the other side of a heavy table covered with reddish embroidered silk sat a square-faced man of stern visage. He seemed to Christian the epitome of the Spanish colonial official except for his eyes, oddly of a lively blue. His powdered white wig was combed and parted sternly, framing a large head in the fashion of the grandees who had conquered and now ruled half the world for Mother Spain. A bulldog chin divided by a deep cleft gave him a grave, almost morose, expression; and tight lips, the sternness of a self-disciplined man. Stark eyebrows brought strange vivacity to this commanding face. The officer's throat was bound with a white silk scarf, his uniform dark blue, heavily embroidered and opened to reveal a red vest of silk.

The official surveyed the prisoner, and Christian silently returned his stare with resignation tempered by defiance, for he was not one to leave this life without pride. The officer motioned the dragoons to withdraw. Their spurs ran beyond the other room into silence. Doors were closed, the sound of iron bars being lowered into place, conveying to Christian the realization that he was trapped hopelessly. He was alone with the captain general, for such the official could only have been, although why so august a personage should be curious about a doomed wanderer he could not imagine. The officer gestured with a muscular hand.

"Sit down, me boy," he said, with a brogue that could only have originated in the north of Ireland. Christian collapsed into a waiting chair, his mouth agape with astonishment.

CHAPTER FOUR

Ambrosio O'Higgins, or Higgins as he preferred to be called, was president of Chile and captain general of His Majesty, King Charles IV, and one of the most remarkable men of the Spanish empire in any age. He was now seventy-three years of age, although his face and vigor would not have suggested so many winters; and in truth, his greatest accomplishments lay yet before him. However he had already become a veteran of countless triumphs over adversity and the obstructionism of lesser men by his intelligence, loyalty, and zeal.

Born in County Sligo, Ireland, and a victim of a wave of political persecution in his homeland, Higgins had followed an uncle, a Franciscan friar who was not without influence at the Spanish court, to Cadíz where he entered the employ of an Irish commercial house. He was sent to Peru where he soon came under the cruel eye of the Inquisition, lost what property he had accumulated, and was forced to move to Chile where he performed several engineering tasks to the satisfaction of military authorities. He then returned to Spain with the maps he had drawn of fortifications and coastal works and so impressed the court that he was recommended to high officials in the southernmost colonies.

Higgins was admitted to the army, initially as an engineer, then as officer of the dragoons. His abilities were such that he soon reached the rank of brigadier and rose swiftly in administrative responsibilities. On November 21, 1787, almost the precise day that the *Bounty* under Captain Bligh raised anchor at Spithead bound for Tahiti, Higgins was made administrator for the Chilean district of Concepción, promoted in due course to his present high position.

Christian was not aware of all this, but he saw something of the man's character in his face, and his respect for him was instantaneous. Higgins surveyed the prisoner calculatingly.

"How came ye to Chile?" he asked, his blue eyes fixed intently upon the young man. Christian hesitated.

"From the sea, sir," he replied.

Higgins laughed, giving his face an Irish and youthful cast. "Most of us do, me boy," he agreed, "unless we be Indians. Are ye then an officer?"

"Yes, sir, although never in command . . . by royal commission."

The older man noticed the hesitation but said nothing. Rather, he nodded understandingly.

"And what then is your name?"

"Fletcher, sir," Christian answered.

The loud-ticking upright clock in the corner showed 1:37 A.M., and Higgins' engineering skills were a guarantee of its accuracy. Finally, the captain general turned back to the young man. "Fletcher, me boy, I'm sure ye comprehend what happens to spies in this land? An' to the Spanish mind ev'ry stranger is a spy."

"Yes, sir, so I've been told," murmured Christian with resignation.

"Eh? Been told? By whom? There's not a man in central Chile, outside the army, who can speak your tongue. Who told ye?"

Christian grimly bit his lip. He had been careless. His thoughtlessness might easily destroy Ishmael, as he had destroyed so many because of the "stick" which scarred not only his own life, but also others'. He looked squarely into the blue eyes across the table.

"It was a mere slip of the tongue, Excellency. I meant nothing by it."

"We have ways, sir, of extracting information."

"Aye. I am sure of it. But in this case, Excellency, having no knowledge I deem of value to you, I could not speak further on it."

Higgins glared at Christian, then slowly relaxed. The grin again lightened his rugged features.

"There are worse sins than loyalty, son," he said approvingly. "I cannot believe ye possess knowledge that would place the empire in jeopardy." He leaned back, surveying the ornately gilded ceiling. Only the ticking of the great clock broke the silence. Higgins toyed with a quill pen, glancing up sharply at his prisoner.

"Where were ye educated?" he demanded abruptly.

Astonished, Christian had expected any question but this. "Why, sir, at the Free Grammar School for seven years and before that at Brigham School and at All Saints in—where I was born. After that mainly at sea, in the arts of navigation and deck command."

"Ye've had more schoolin' than most," mused Higgins. "Has it benefited you? Do you believe in it?"

Startled by such questions, Christian hesitated, then answered honestly: "Why, yes, sir, I believe I do. 'Twould be odd, unthinkable to be without it, your Excellency. A rather barren existence, I should imagine."

"Quite," the old man agreed, nodding his head thoughtfully. "Quite so." His fingers again shuffled the desk furnishings. He leaned forward, clasping his hands, searching Christian's face earnestly.

"I have a son," he said gravely. "He is now fifteen an' lives in the care of the Franciscans at Chillán, not far from where his mother, a fine and lovely woman, abides. I could not, for reasons of state, marry her, but she has ever meant a great deal to me; and from a respectable distance, I have endeavored to care for her and our son." He offered the explanation, not as an excuse, for he was not an evasive man, but by way of preliminary. "I have not seen the boy but once years ago, but I have frequent reports of his progress under the friars and . . . and in other ways."

"How is he known?"

"Bernardo. Bernardo Riquelme. His mother, Isabel, is of an old and worthy family, though not in affluent circumstances by any means. I have never denied the parentage, nor would I; but I thought it inappropriate to bestow upon him my own name, although he is welcome, should he choose it."

"I understand, sir, but do not see how I can be of assistance."

Higgins grinned amiably.

"Me boy is half Irish, half Spanish, and wholly *Chileño*, which means he is wild, grown almost beyond control. He may waste a life that might prove of value to himself and to others without proper guidance. It is my wish that he be educated in either Spain or England."

"Aye, sir." Christian remained warily noncommittal.

"However, there are difficulties. Bernardo is a boy of spirit, if I do say so. Being raised a Chilean, he bears a resentment against Spain because of their long tradition of arrogance toward its native people and the many discriminating edicts against them." He sighed. "England he distrusts less, perhaps because he knows little about it; but he believes it to be a land of cold rain, perpetual clouds, a grim an' grimy place, storm-lashed an' sodden, where any learnin' he might secure would be washed away by water. He coughed slyly. "I must say there is some truth in his conception."

Christian smiled slowly. "He appears a perceptive lad."

"Aye, he is that," Higgins chuckled, "he's a live one, a true Higgins, if I do say so. My task for you, Mr. Fletcher, is to visit Chillán, about 400 leagues to the south, and persuade my son that England is not such a devil's den as he imagines, that a proper education is a necessity for a young man if he is not to become a complete barbarian. Win his assent, Fletcher, to undertake the venture and perhaps accompany him to England yourself. Will ye' accept such a mission, sir?"

Christian considered the matter, reluctantly shaking his head, as though to rid it of an evil memory.

"I am not at liberty to return to England, your Excellency."

Higgins' eyes narrowed in speculation.

"Perhaps I understand," he conceded. "Perhaps. An active man does what he must from day to day. The voyage to England may not be required of you. Of more importance is the persuasion. Will you undertake that portion of it?"

How strange it is, thought Christian, *for this man, who holds the most awesome power in the whole kingdom south of Peru, to plead for assistance with such a problem. To ask for help from a doomed vagabond whose life could be snuffed out as one might extinguish a flickering candle.*

"If ye succeed," continued Higgins earnestly, "I can arrange a place for you in the army until ye master the Spanish tongue an' the ways of the people. I do not forget those who have favored me, sir."

"If I fail?"

The other returned his glance boldly, soberly, the blue eyes implacable. He said nothing, nor was there need.

"Bernardo speaks no English?"

"None whatever."

"And I but little Spanish."

"'Twill require a month, or half again as long, for you to reach Chillán. In addition to your escort, I will send a Chilean qualified to instruct you in the tongue. With diligence you will speak a passable Spanish by the time you reach Chillán. For the rest you must use your ingenuity."

"The mission interests me, as does the future of your son, Excellency. I might add," he said with a trace of a smile, "the alternative appalls me. I accept."

Higgins' expression brightened. He held out a cordial hand and rang a small bell beside the quill stand. Almost instantly a dragoon entered, clicked to attention, and waited.

"This is Corporal Quinn, one of several Irish lads I've maneuvered into the forces here, to everyone's benefit. There is no soldier like an Irish soldier. He will see you to the barracks where you will be outfitted as is proper; you will be given written directives and letters of introduction for those you'll meet along the way. I shall not give you precise instructions, however. You must carry out the mission as you can by your own findings and judgment. I believe your quarters here will prove adequate until your departure."

"An improvement at any rate over the *calabozo*, Excellency," cheerfully conceded Christian. "That place is fearsome, make no mistake!"

Higgins laughed heartily. "So I've been told by other survivors. See, already ye're learning Spanish, usable Spanish. Good-bye and good luck, an' God bless you in your undertaking."

CHAPTER FIVE

Somewhere out on the ragged-edged parade ground, a trumpet blared, shrill and stabbing the darkness, awakening Christian. Men stamped into knee-length *botas*, clapped kepis on tousled heads, and tumbled out into the late night to stand the first formation of the new day. Drill sergeants bellowed out the names; the men reported, standing at rigid attention while the Spanish flag was raised, red-and-yellow horizontal stripes with the escutcheon of arms of Castile and Leon, surmounted by the crown of the House of Bourbon. The flag hung limp, awaiting the first rays of a sun scaling the Andean heights with its accompanying breeze.

On the morning following his meeting with Higgins, Christian leaned against the whitewashed adobe wall of the barracks, the silent observer of this scene enacted every dawn under every flag on every part of the globe. He awaited the return of Sergeant Major Dennis O'Leary and Quinn. They were not long. The morning roll call was perfunctory, as always. Little wonder, Christian thought, that soldiers looked forward to the occasional campaign to relieve the monotony.

The men poured back into barracks, Quinn and O'Leary bringing up the rear. "Like some *maté*, sir?" invited the sergeant, grinning. "It cuts th' mornin' skrug."

"To be sure. What is it?"

"Tea, sort of. From Paraguay. With enough sugar it'll be tastin' welcome. I don't know if it's th' tea or th' sugar a man gets to need at break o' day."

A silent Indian shuffled among the men with a blackened kettle of boiling water, filling each soldier's small dark gourd stuffed with chopped leaves and sugar. The liquid was sucked out through a straw and the drained gourd then refilled as desired. This was a period for gossip, companionship.

"Do you ride, sir?" asked O'Leary.

Christian then laughed, the sergeant grinning with him. "As a boy I had a piebald pony, but that was the extent of it. I don't imagine you would say I'm a horseman now or ever was."

"You'll learn, sir, for you've the build for it," replied O'Leary. "Since you'll head south within a few days, you'd best join the *manejo* class this mornin'. An' in the afternoon, too, if th' early session don't leave you stiff as a tree. *Manejo*—that's what this army calls equitation."

"I thought all Chileans were born riders! Who needs equitation, save me?"

"The army thinks 'tis a way of spendin' time without givin' a man leave to work up mischief. Then with th' desertion an' the Indian fightin', th' army's got recruits ever comin' in. Most of them don't know nothin' about a horse. So equitation classes go on an' on an' on." He stumped away, his great spurs ringing on the stony earth.

Corporal Quinn led Christian to the dozen recruits gathered at one edge of the parade ground. Four armed soldiers patrolled nearby, lest someone seek to escape. Before each new dragoon was heaped a small mountain of equipment. Several mounted *huasos*—the superb Chilean civilian cowboys—expertly handled strings of spirited horses, small, short-coupled, but with traces of their Andalusian forebears. They displayed assorted colors, their hoofs trim, naturally polished, indicating youth and health.

The recruits faced the horses, apprehensively eyeing the animals, which returned the stares. Christian's gazed was fixed upon a silken-coated black.

"Your choice, sir?" asked Quinn, chewing on a twig. "That black? You'd better let me choose for you, sir. He'll bust your bottom, that one will. How about th' bay to th' right?"

"I prefer the black, Corporal."

Quinn removed the twig, leaned forward, spat thoughtfully.

"It ain't just your own funeral, you know, sir," he said. "Th' gin'ral told us to watch over you an' not let you git yourself kilt. You'd best take th' bay."

Each man was assigned a horse, Christian took the halter rope of the bay. The black went to a *mestizo* recruit. Quinn showed Christian how to put on the bridle smoothly, forcing the animal's mouth open with his left thumb and slipping in the harsh bit.

"First thing, you ride around bareback," he was informed. "That's so you get used to th' motion of th' horse, get to be part of him, sort of. Here, just put your foot in my hands." Quinn cupped his great palms and all but flung Christian astride the little bay, which sidestepped nervously but was held close by the Irishman's iron grip on the reins.

The succeeding days were a time of concentrated work for Christian. It was physical, learning the skills and trade of a dragoon, and mental, in a furious study of the tongue and Iberian ways. The captain general had provided an amiable young instructor, Ferdinand. The Englishman learned swiftly, aided by a natural talent for languages and a determination to succeed, but after an initial period of swift learning, Christian lost the momentum and despaired that he would ever succeed in mastering the tongue, despite constant reassurance from Ferdinand. Then after many weeks there came a time when the pieces fell into place with a rush and he suddenly found himself beginning to think in the new language.

Meanwhile, under the guidance of expert horsemen, he physically toughened, developing a bond with his horse and a respect for its noble species that was never to leave him. He wore the issued uniform of a dragoon; his hair was barbered and combed, his beard trimmed. With his naturally dark complexion, he might have passed anywhere for a Spaniard, save that his diction stubbornly faltered over the rolling double "r" sound.

"No matter, *señor,*" consoled Ferdinand. "Even in Spain there are districts where that sound does not prevail, yet people are understood."

Before dawn one midsummer morning in late January, a small party rode out of the post toward the distant southerly frontier. In addition to Christian and Ferdinand, who reluctantly came by direct order of Higgins himself, the group consisted of Quinn and four Chilean dragoons, and two *huasos*. With them came pack animals, a brown mule and a flea-bitten gray gelding.

Sometimes well beaten by the heavy travel, the trail rose by contorted twists up a rocky slope to a pass, crossing a spur of the coastal range. To the east towered the Andes, hoary with snow in their stupendous elevations. Beyond the pass the trail dropped into a thicket, crossing occasional rushing streams. Near one they encountered a dozen *huasos* squatting about fires, surrounded by packs of skin *arrobas* of wine and brandy. Their mules, a hundred or more, grazed in a nearby glade.

"From Rancagua," grunted Quinn. "They go to Santiago."

Rivers ran more water the farther south they moved; the countryside was greener, trees increased in variety and number, and the people seemed more self-reliant and independent, remote as they were from the Spanish administration. Below Rancagua, its plaza intersected by cobbled streets in the form of a cross, and Talca, they swam their animals across the Rio Maule which, according to Quinn, formerly marked the frontier between the settlements and wild Araucania, which no Spaniard dared enter unless part of a fighting command or a criminal in flight. "A lot of the Araucanian power, *Chileños* believe, came from Spanish soldiers who deserted to 'em," Quinn observed, thoughtfully. "I think, though, that them Indians always could fight; an' all they got from deserters was more rank-power."

"Rank-power?"

"Just more soldiers is all."

"Where is the frontier now?"

"Generally along the Bío-Bío River, well below Chillán."

Early in March, the harvest time, the tight little contingent reached Chillán, the major post of the frontier defenses in the south. There were immense herds of horses, quarters for a company of infantry, of dragoons, and a battery of artillery. With the captain general's orders, they assumed quarters as commodious as available at so forward a position.

Overlooking the river was the Franciscan monastery with its adjacent school for nineteen boys. Peach orchards flowed up the hillsides from the stream, interspersed with vineyards and fields of grain, yellow and ready for the scythes. While school and lessons took up the morning, the afternoons were free time for pupils; and the friar directed Christian to a lower orchard as the most probable place to find the young man he sought. He rode the bay slowly down the slope toward the swift-flowing water, whose chatter rose as he approached. It was hot and pleasant in the grove, insects sparkled and slanted through the sunlight; and the horse moved easily, lured by the sound of cool water, its hoofs felted with short thick grass. Christian wondered what sort of boy the president's son would prove to be. He was of an age to have reached the threshold of thought, but was he capable of it? How adamant would he prove in his refusal to go abroad? If he rejected the idea, what would that portend for Fletcher Christian? Christian knew the answer; he smiled grimly. Would Bernardo prove sportive or morose? Intelligent or stupid? Friendly or aloof? He would discover the solution, if he could but find the boy.

He dismounted above a low bluff where the trail dipped down to the river. A human squeal rent the still air, startling the bay, which swiveled its ears expectantly. A flash of color and a young girl, pigtails flying, ran past and disappeared into the orchard. Then a curly-headed youth rocketed after her. Christian thrust a strong arm across his waist and halted him. Bernardo backed away, his blue eyes narrowing.

"*Señor?*" Christian questioned. "*Quien es?* Who are you?" His speech was clear now, though hesitant.

The boy replied somewhat haughtily, "I am Bernardo Riquelme. Who are *you?*"

"A friend, son," Christian replied. "I have come far, from Santiago, . . . to meet you, to talk with you."

The boy's dark, curly hair was cut short above strong shoulders and a sturdy build. Remarkable against his dark skin, his blue eyes reflected a lively curiosity which, while adding to their daring, made his appearance altogether engaging. An independence of spirit cast an aura of leadership about him, despite his short years.

"Why, *señor?* Why would you wish to talk with me? Are you a brigand, an outlaw, perhaps? Have you ever killed a man?" Curiosity overflowed his reserve. Christian laughed, his white teeth gleaming in his dark face, any of his worries resolved.

"I am no highwayman, Bernardo! I came from your father, for it is his messenger I am."

"I have no father, *señor*. My mother lives in Chillán, and she is all I have except a sister, who does not count."

"Sisters rarely do, when they are young. When they become older, sisters assume importance. How old are you, Bernardo?"

"Sixteen."

"A man already, eh? Or soon to become one, I vow."

Bernardo Riquelme was pleased; he thought of himself as a man, of course, but so few grownups shared his view.

"What do you wish to see me about, sir?"

"Here, I have a letter from the captain general of the kingdom of Chile, your father. Can you read what he writes?" Bernardo gravely attempted to decipher the handwriting.

"Handwriting is difficult for me to make out," he conceded. "I can read books better."

"Do you wish me to read it to you?"

"No, I can do it."

His independence was reassuring. He labored on and at length folded the paper again and returned it.

"Well?" asked Christian.

"Sir, I have no father. A mother, that is all. I do not know this man, although no doubt he is a good man." His restless eye searched the orchard for the girl who had fled.

"As you say, Bernardo, this is a good man, and he is indeed your father—ask your mother if it is not so. She will tell you. Will you do that?"

Bernardo's blue eyes rested on Christian's face, then again searched the grove. "If he is my father, what do you wish to talk to me about? I will listen, though perhaps I will not believe what you say since I do not know that he is my father, as you believe."

Christian took a deep breath; he faced the test.

"Although you perhaps are not aware of it, he has kept himself informed about you . . . and your progress. As you are his only son, he wants you to assume a station in life befitting his own; and for that he believes a good education is necessary, one that you can acquire abroad only, in Spain perhaps, or in England. You have reached the age of decision; he wishes you to consider his proposal and, if possible, to agree to it."

"But I am being educated here, by the Franciscans in their school, a very good school, as they tell me."

"A good school I have no doubt, but a preliminary school, Bernardo. It is time to think now of one more advanced, which you will find only abroad."

Riquelme squared his shoulders, spoke firmly, "Sir, I thank you for coming to see me. Please also thank the man who says he is my father. But I am *Chileño;* I will live in Chile forever. I do not wish to go to Europe. Being Chilean, I detest Spain. England does not interest me, either. No, *señor,* I will not go."

CHAPTER SIX

Christian found Bernardo Riquelme much to his liking. The boy may have returned the affection, but he showed a stubbornness and inflexibility inherited from his Hibernian ancestors, the Englishman glumly suspected. Neither his favorite tutor, Father Gil Calvo, or even the father superior could budge the young man, although both supported the messenger from the captain general.

"Don Ambrosio is a staunch friend of the Franciscans," asserted the father superior and urged Christian to move his quarters from the post to the monastery where he would be closer to the boy. There he was assigned a monk's cell, furnished with Spartan simplicity but clean. Its small window opened upon a vista of orchards, the river below, and the high peaks in the blue distance. Every day he shared in the school life of Bernardo, seeking to deepen their friendship. Christian had no illusions about his fate should he fail. Still he had a true interest in the young man whose future, he came to believe, might be an important one with proper preparation.

One afternoon a small cloud of brigands swept down upon a herd of cattle and horses that were grazing about a league away in a field belonging to the monastery. In minutes they killed two of the three herders and ran off the animals. The third herder brought the alarm in a mad rush, clattering into the cobbled yard. The father superior ordered him to alert the military post at once. But Christian, whose horse fortunately already was saddled, gathered up a few laborers, and with a sharp-eyed Indian tracker, set off at a high gallop for the scene of the robbery. Only after they had gone a good distance down the trail did Christian notice Bernardo among his band of avengers, mounted upon his light-gray mount. The Englishman ordered him to return, but the boy withdrew only for a short distance, then stubbornly followed along, keeping up with the pursuit, even though unarmed.

At a crossing of the Rio Chillán, the expedition caught up with the bandits endeavoring to swim the cattle across. On the high ground above the crossing, the pursuers opened fire, downing several of the enemy. It was only then that Christian saw a leader of the brigands make for Bernardo who was riding eagerly toward the action. With no time to load his pistol, Christian thundered down upon the outlaw just as the ruffian tried to seize the boy.

Christian's horse struck the brigand's in the forequarters as all *huaso* mounts were trained to do for handling livestock. The enemy was knocked to the ground where the Englishman pounced upon him, beating him into submission with his emptied weapon.

"This one we will take back with us," he said to the boy. "The military will know what to do with him."

Bernardo's eyes danced. His own narrow escape had roused his blood; and he had found in Christian a hero, the first of his young life.

"They will execute him," he replied. "He is a thief."

"Yes, I suppose so," returned Christian thoughtfully. "I would prefer that inquiry be made as to why he stole. Many things can be resolved if the reasons be known."

"He stole," insisted Bernardo. "Therefore he must die." The implacable Spaniard in him spoke now.

Relieved at their safe return, the father superior listened closely while Bernardo excitedly related the outcome, scanning Christian's dark face as the boy rattled on. This God-sent opportunity was not to be wasted.

"Apparently, my son, you owe your life to your friend."

"Yes, that is true," Bernardo bobbed his head. "To you I am indebted beyond words. I am at your service."

While the expression was a mere formality, the Englishman seized upon it.

"Then shall you go to England?" he asked, searchingly, "as your father wishes?"

Bernardo flushed. He had been trapped. But he was forthright, a youth of his word. "Is it—is it demanded in this way, sir?"

So simply was it asked and so profound was the anguish behind the words that Christian all but allowed him to escape, but his instinct and his pledge to the boy's father would not permit it.

"It may or may not be true, Bernardo, that your life was in jeopardy today," he replied gently. "But my own life is at stake. I am a foreigner and under automatic sentence of death if I fail the captain general."

"You did not tell me."

"I did not want to influence you that way. But if you feel you owe your life to me, you can give me life by acceding to the wishes of Don Ambrosio and pledging yourself to pursue your education in England." He peered at the lovely vista of the broad valley. "It is not as though you were sacrificing your life for another," he continued. "'Twill be only for a very few years—an exceedingly brief time and for your own benefit. You will return better fitted to be a leader of your people."

Bernardo agonized in the heavy silence, tormented by doubts and fears. His face showed, however, that he was fascinated somehow by the new horizons spread before him. Wordlessly he assented.

"Will you come with me to tell my mother?" he asked, shyly.

Isabel Riquelme glided into the light to greet her son as the brass-studded door was unlocked by an elderly servant. Christian's breath was quite taken away by her loveliness. Isabel greeted her son affectionately; and turning with grace, she welcomed the boy's friend. In her glance was a subconscious appraisal.

"Welcome to my house," she said in liquid Castilian, offering her hand, cool, yet with cordiality. "I had heard of your arrival."

"I did not know," he replied, "or I should have paid my respects before this. Were you aware, too, of my mission?"

"Yes, I knew of it. I shall do nothing to hinder you. It has been explained to me, and it is for the best, clearly." Yet her lips trembled, if ever so slightly.

"*Señora,* the invitation which Bernardo has accepted is for a short time only, a few years at most."

"To a mother that is forever."

"Perhaps it seems so. Yet your son will return to you better equipped to face great responsibilities . . . to stir your pride. Ultimately I know you will be happy with his decision."

"That may be."

Christian longed to savor for a few minutes more the company of this woman who had so strangely moved him, but Bernardo had to return to the monastery.

"*Señora,* I am always at your service."

"I thank you for your kindness. Take care of Bernardo. And . . . *vaya con Diós!*"

CHAPTER SEVEN

Bernardo Riquelme went north with Corporal Quinn and his small detachment. Higgins had directed Christian to turn himself over to the commandment at Chillán to await further instructions. As a foreigner he found himself avoided by the officers for fear he might be condemned despite the success of his mission, lest they be marked by an unseemly familiarity with him. But through a remark of the post adjutant, he learned that President Higgins was en route to hold a grand *parlamento,* or council, with the Indians, somewhere south of the frontier.

The Englishman also learned that Higgins, because of the stiffness of his aged joints, or more likely because the challenge had stirred the engineer in him, had determined to come south by coach. Remembering his own journey, he marveled that anyone should imagine a wheeled vehicle could possibly negotiate the steep passes and torturous river crossings. But Higgins could assess for himself its practicality. Pioneering and road building were not only avocations, but a passion with him. If Don Ambrosio had to create a road hundreds of miles southward, he would do so and count it a minor triumph of his administration, no matter what incredible difficulties lay before him.

Christian rode his splash-faced bay four leagues northward on the day rumor insisted that the captain general might arrive. He came upon the astounding coach stuck firmly in the muddy waters of the Nuble River. Truly a mighty vehicle, the coach of state was never designed for the rough horse trails. Bold royal colors of red and yellow were now sadly covered with grime, its sides gashed and scarred by narrow passages through rocky defiles. Men strained at the wheels, riders mounted upon the horses shouted and flogged as their animals strained. At the rear of the coach, soldiers pushed and shoved waist deep in the rolling water. Slowly the vehicle began to move, bounding and lurching up the steep bank to stand, dripping and befouled upon the flat. A gray head protruded from the window on Christian's side and turned upward toward Sergeant Dennis O'Leary, seated beside the coachman.

"Let's be on, Sergeant, let's be on," rumbled a deep voice testily. "It can't be a great deal farther. We had best be gettin' in before dark, methinks."

"Yes, sir," replied O'Leary, saluting automatically, although beyond direct view of the captain general.

The head in the window turned toward Christian, whose bay stood beside the trail.

"Oh, it's you, is it?" demanded the voice, harshly. "Well, come in, sir. Ride a league or two with me, if you please."

Christian tied the bay to the rear step and climbed into the commodious conveyance. It must have weighed at least a ton and swung upon leathern throughbraces in the manner of English coaches. These served as springs, but they did not provide any great comfort. Sitting was like riding a whaleboat in a rough sea, save that the bounces and jolts were not decently spaced as upon open water, but came irregularly and most inconveniently. Don Ambrosio's wig was askew. He clutched his hat firmly in his hand, his muscular legs bracing himself solidly against the seats before him. Huddled forlornly in a corner opposite, his wizened secretary, the bearded Don Tadeo Reyes, sat bruised, silent, inwardly cursing the day he had assumed his post.

Higgins, though wearied, appeared determined, something like a conqueror who has just triumphed over a fearsome enemy. "Blast it all, we've almost made it!" he growled. "How far is it? Three or four leagues? This is the first time," he stammered, between jolts, "that a wheeled vehicle has—has—passed over this God-forsaken trail. But a road is needed here and—and now 'twill be beaten out. Where my wheels have passed, others soon will journey in comfort! Development! Progress!"

"Aye, sir, that it is," agreed Christian, clinging desperately to an upright rod bracing the doorpost. "Progress it is, sir!"

The carriage eased along now across a broad and level meadow. They both cautiously relaxed and talked more easily.

"I met Bernardo upon his arrival at Santiago," said the captain general. "He spoke most highly of you and your diligence on my behalf. 'Tis in your debt I am."

"I endeavored to follow your wishes, sir."

"You did well." Higgins gazed through the coach window at the Chilean countryside slowly gliding past. "As I pledged, I will either set you up in a small business of some kind or secure you an army commission, perhaps as a lieutenant—a rank above where I started forty years ago. There is opportunity here for a man with wit, a civil tongue, and diligence. Which shall it be?"

"I have no talent for business, sir. If the choice be mine, I would select the army."

"I thought as much. I share your views, and bitter experience has demonstrated my own lack of talent for it. So be it, and Godspeed, sir! I shall observe your progress with pleasure, so far as the exigencies of the service permit."

Christian's acceptance among the officers of the Chillán garrison was instantaneous now that he was the acknowledged protégé of the captain general. He was outfitted in the blue dress blouse, cape, knee breeches, and waistcoat with the gilded buttons and scarlet trim of the dragoons. He was also issued polished high boots with enormous spurs that marked a Chilean horseman of the king. He drew side arms, a brace of pistols, a knife or dagger, and a saber with plain black hilt. All of these, completed by cockaded hat and buff gauntlets, designated him an officer pledged to uphold the system he had sworn to Ishmael to destroy. The irony left him sardonically amused and uncertain. He had no taste for treason. Though he was prepared now to serve Charles IV as loyally as he earlier had served George III, the great evils of the system festered within him. He knew that some day, somehow, he must work to bring about the downfall of its wicked practices, no matter what the result for the imperial society. The seed planted at La Serena had taken root.

General Higgins moved most of the troops at Chillán along to his headquarters, twenty-five leagues south at the small village of Los Angeles. Here units from other posts had massed: from Concepción, from the coastal fort at Trauco, and from scattered outposts on the fringes of Araucania. They were 1,500 soldiers of army and militia in all, with 66 officers. Most colorful of all were artillerymen from Valdivia, splashed with gold embroidery, but each unit was garishly dressed. It was a gathering of rich hues, the better to impress the Indians.

Already those Araucanians not actively hostile were gathering at Negrete, eighteen leagues to the southwest of Los Angeles. They numbered, according to informants, 161 *caciques*, or chieftains, 16 aged councilors and wise men, 77 minor chiefs or group leaders, and 2,308 warriors, with women, children, and aged besides.

"Good," approved Higgins upon receiving the information. "With the war still on to the south, 'tis better than I'd hoped." He added for the benefit of Christian, attached to his staff for the operation, "The wild ones keep us honest, and we're certainly the better for it."

Christian found his interest strangely stirred by the wild situation beyond the Bío-Bío. He was directed by O'Leary to a soft-spoken adventurer, Bartolome Borja, as a fount of helpful information, but Borja received him coolly. He would say very little, until the Englishman had confirmed his sincerity, intelligence, and above all, his honesty. Then he gradually opened up, an unrivaled source of facts—mingled with myth, to be sure— but most of them precise, penetrating, and judicious.

Of Borja's background Christian learned that he had an Araucanian wife and roamed openly in that frequently hostile country, trading sometimes with Indians as far removed as the higher Andean passes. He feared no man, gave allegiance to none save his friends, and honored nothing save his word. Thus his circle of friends was a narrow one but most unusual. To be accepted by Borja was to be a man of character. Gradually there formed about him an irregular sort of clan, an association of like-minded men of all races and backgrounds who were not to be taken lightly.

Higgins had an unshakeable faith in Borja and used him frequently as scout, messenger, translator, or councilor, adding to his prestige. Borja spoke no English, but Christian's Spanish was now such that they could converse fairly easily.

"The nature of Araucania?" Borja replied to one of the Englishman's attempts to gather information. "It depends upon who describes it. The Indians don't call themselves 'Araucanian,' but Butal Mapu, or Mapuche, which I use, because '*mapu*' means land and '*che*' people, and they are people of the land. So the Pincunche means the 'north people' and the Huilliche the 'south people.' The Pehuenche are of the high Andes, some breaking over into the Pampa now. Then you get other people. Some believe that the southern Butal-Mapu are a different breed, but I hold they are the same."

"Where are they?"

"South of course. From the Tolten River to the Bueno and even beyond. They speak the same language, intermarry, fight the same, and have identical gods, so why wouldn't they be the same people?"

"What's below them?"

"You break out into the islands, and no man knows who lives there or anything about them."

"How many Mapuche are there?"

Borja looked quickly away, then squarely at Christian.

"Enough. Some say 500,000 or even a million. Perhaps once that was the case, but disease and liquor have killed them off. I doubt you could find more than 300,000 today. That still means a lot of fighting men, and they are the best. Better than the Spanish."

"Why?"

Again Borja hesitated, speaking carefully.

"Maybe you'll see for yourself, *señor,*" he replied. "They have as much courage as the Spanish. And they've got brains about how they use it. They fear not death, nor wound, nor maiming, nor mutilation; and it is a rare Spaniard who can oust those shadows from his mind. When they decide on war, they'd rather fight than eat or even breathe; and it is bred into their bones."

Captain general Don Ambrosio Higgins wished to take his state coach across the Bío-Bío to the *parlamento* grounds at Negrete and impress the Indians with its unrivaled magnificence. But even his iron will and artful engineering were not sufficient to ferry the cumbersome vehicle over the swollen stream. Therefore he mounted a rawboned white horse, larger than the normal run of Chilean animals. Clutching the saddletree with a strong right hand, he let the swimming beast tow him across the stream and then rode majestically to the brightly striped awning, erected over the quarter acre where the council was to be held. The Indian encampment appeared to Christian to extend into infinity.

The emerald prairie, level as a beach, was laid like a carpet from the riverbank to the high mountains in the distance. The great plain was almost barren of trees save for the sacred *canelo* before the awning, without which no council could succeed nor would its decisions have been in any way binding. This *canelo* was fifty feet in height, its trunk so riven with fractures that its cinnamon-colored inner bark showed through.

Troops and Indians were everywhere. The endless herds of livestock grazed out across the plains: llamas with flat woolly backs, long necks, and expressionless faces; a few more-skittish brown animals in the distance that Borja called guanacos, half-tamed; horses of every variety; cattle and sheep guarded by youngsters on horseback. Near the awning a dozen beeves, spitted on poles, roasted above open fires.

Araucanian riders cavorted everywhere. Usually they were armed with lances, fourteen to twenty feet in length and bedecked with feathers. But the councilors were gathered at the awning.

Seated upon a carpeted throne on a small dais, the captain general scanned the ranks before him. They were of a mixed lot, slightly smaller in build than the average Chilean soldier. Their elderly councilors had neatly combed gray hair, the scars of many battles upon their faces and bare limbs. The arrogant young chiefs and braves wore silver earrings which flashed in the sunlight, while a few plumes or feathers drooped from their hair.

Borja stood just behind Higgins to interpret. Christian, slightly to his right, was fascinated by one of the Araucanians, arrogant and perfectly proportioned, of about the Englishman's age. He was taller than most of his fellows. He wore the silver headband and earrings of a warrior chief, but the way he carried his head and his burning stare revealed his authority even more clearly. He stalked back and forth, his mace swinging loosely at his side, restless as though ready for battle at any time with anyone. Approaching the awning, he came face to face with Christian, his dark eyes impaling the Englishman who felt as though twin lances pierced him. The Indian passed on, but Christian would never forget that first domineering stare, free and implacable.

"That's Kolapel," said Borja in an undertone. "I'm surprised he's here. He is almost always at war with somebody, the Spanish or some of his own people. He is a *gen-toqui,* or war chief, and that is the top-rank among the Mapuche when they are at war, which is most of the time."

"Where is he from?"

"He is one of the power Huilliche, the south people. They're almost always away fighting somewhere. It's a tribute to Don Ambrosio they came at all. They like him."

"Why?"

"He doesn't lie to them. They value honor."

Some of the Mapuche bore Spanish firearms, others short bows with quivers of puma hide, many carried long two-handled clubs of murderous weight for knocking enemies' horses unconscious. Some had knobbed or spiked clubs; and a few still carried old-fashioned slings, or even an ancient flint ax, kept for ceremonial reasons. Each warrior trained as a specialist in the use of a particular weapon.

Most wore traditional dress: a bright-colored *makun*, or poncho, spurs strapped usually to bare feet, though head men often wore woolen boots or leather sandals as marks of rank.

"They don't have one overall chief," explained Borja, "unless they agree on someone for war. But his authority ends when the fighting does. That's why all these warriors are here, with none predominant, not even Kolapel. This makes it difficult since the Spanish can't talk to one chief but have to persuade the whole crowd."

A few kegs of brandy had been trundled out for distribution when the council might end. The Indians eyed it thirstily. Borja grunted, "Makes for cooperation, setting that liquor in plain sight."

The captain general turned to the interpreter. "Ready!" he said. He raised himself laboriously to his full 6 feet, 2 inches, inhaled deeply, and spoke, his wise old eyes on the faces of the Indians, integrity in his voice and demeanor.

"Chiefs, my ancient and honorable friends!" he began, his words translated phrase by phrase. Borja gestured as he did, relaying an identical emphasis of word and tone.

"Full of joy and satisfaction I now meet upon this happy ground the great chiefs and principal leaders of the Mapuche. I salute you all with joy. I am ordered by the king, my master, to salute you in His Majesty's name—to congratulate you for the inestimable blessings of peace, brought now to this great southern continent. I have listened patiently to the complaints of some, to the excuses of others, the umbrage that a few have taken, and the plans for revenge of those of you with little perspective.

"Today, however, the sun shines bright and I see with heart-felt joy that a kindly disposition appears in all, to terminate the unhappy differences . . ." His deep voice droned on while the dark faces watched and listened.

"Recollect your situation, my friends, when I was first appointed by His Majesty to the military command of this frontier. There are many amongst you who remember the miserable state in which I found the whole country. Destroyed on both sides of the river, desolate and laid waste. All its inhabitants were suffering the calamities of unceasing furious wars, brought on by their own intemperance and unruly passions. Many were obliged to flee with their women and children to the mountains, and were reduced at last to feeding on their faithful dogs that followed them! The great chiefs and Indians of the Mapuche were witnesses of these things. But before I left you, your houses were rebuilt, your fields smiled with a yellow harvest, and your pastures were richly decorated with the herds of your cattle. Your unruly young men obeyed the voice of the elders, cruelties and barbarisms were abandoned, and a better day dawned for all of you.

"You have rigorously observed the promises you made to me at that time. The Spanish settlements have been most scrupulously spared by your warriors, their cattle not disturbed, and in no circumstance have you broken the goodwill you pledged yourself to maintain. For this honorable part of your conduct, I give you all due thanks. I have therefore recommended the Mapuche to the powerful protection of the king.

"I should like now to send among you Spanish officers whom I trust, to teach you the ways of our people, to watch over your well-being, to guide you, and to report to me any difficulties you may encounter, that we may act swiftly to assist you to correct them. What do you say to this? After you have approved it, we shall open the kegs of brandy here and together drink to our new and more lasting friendship."

Higgins relaxed upon his throne, the long legs stretched before him, his hands folded across his belly. He appeared to doze; but Christian could see that the old man's eyes were lively and alert, scanning the faces before him, seeking to read the reception of his speech. The chiefs discussed it animatedly, nodding heads as though agreement might be near.

But at that very moment, the youthful Kolapel halted before Higgins, surveyed him bleakly, then mounted the dais. From this equal prominence he spoke with equal authority, facing his fellows, his voice just short of a roar. Again Borja translated.

"Mapuches!" he began. "*Toquis*, chiefs, leaders, warriors! Brave men of brave women, from the rocks and lakes and mountains of your hereditary lands! You have heard what this man, speaking for the Spaniards, has said. You have considered it. Now hear me! I speak to you not as a chief, but as a warrior who has fought a thousand actions, who has never known defeat, who brings to you the authority of war, of victory, of experience with these Spanish!

"The Spaniards come with a *canelo* branch in their words, but in their brains and hidden from view the red arrow and the bloodied ax. We seize upon the branch, and they surprise us with weapons. How many times must this be before we learn? We are men, not sheep, not fools!

"Our friend speaks of Mapuche cruelty. We were not a barbarous people when the Spanish tried to overrun us and taught us savagery. Four times in three centuries the Spanish have invaded us, tried to enervate us with Spanish things, and so enslave us. Four times we have had to rise up and throw them out! Now we would have this tragedy occur a fifth time!

"What if we should submit, if the Spanish triumphed finally?

"Remember, Mapuche, what happened when once we did so! We were divided among the Spanish like the cards they gamble with. We were assigned to farms to labor like slaves for these foreign dogs, to work their mines, to herd their stock. Our liberties and our manhoods were swiftly stripped from us. Then the Spanish turned upon our families and seized our women and our children too.

"These things—not friendship, not alliance, not peaceful growth—are what they seek. Mapuches, I say no! I say keep your Spanish officers out of our lands. When the puma stalks a band of guanacos, unless he is young and foolish he does not seek to run them down on the open prairie, for that way leads but to an empty belly. He feigns disinterest; he seems to sleep; while his prey grazes, he creeps among them. When they least expect it, he roars to life and slays and devours! So do the Spanish try, by one ruse or some other, to slip amongst us to engulf us when they choose. We can rule ourselves as we have done for centuries. I say, Our customs are not your customs. We do not desire your customs. We will not be slaves. We are Mapuche! Free men! We are warriors! Let us remain so."

Kolapel swung his mace forward and back, the sharp stones protruding from its blackened head gleaming in the fading light beneath the awning. Higgins sat silent, still as death, listening closely to the young leader.

"This old man says he is our friend, and I believe him, for he speaks with an honest tongue." The voice was more quiet now. "He is not of the tribe of the Spaniards, and perhaps that is why he can be believed. He says the Spanish among us would serve our interests, and I believe him—while he lives. But he has many years within his bones. When he dies, what will happen then?

"Mapuches!" the voice rose again. "We have had centuries of bitter, bloody experience to show us what will happen! In the past we have been weaklings, or fools, when we listened to Spanish blandishments; always it has brought us disaster. Now we hear anew the same old cry of peace, benefits. Are we children to believe this once again, to trade our freedom for a barrel of brandy that is drunk within an hour, after which we awaken to find ourselves slaves for life? Are we stupid? I say no! I say we are not fools but warriors! Men! If we are wise and strong and independent, we will take care that we remain so. Let the Spanish carry their brandy back beyond the Bío-Bío!

Kolapel stalked from the tent and into the crowd of tribesmen, his head visible above the others as he passed through them to his waiting horse. He mounted and galloped away, not looking back. Under the awning the gathered chieftains mumbled, forming their decision. But there was no welcome now in their eyes. They had heard what the young man said. They believed he spoke with truth and wisdom.

"And so," muttered Borja wryly to Christian, "another council goes for naught. And this one, Don Ambrosio told me, cost 10,897 *pesos*. That will sting the king of Spain right in the purse!"

CHAPTER EIGHT

Captain general Don Ambrosio Higgins remained at Los Angeles five days, composing his report to the Crown. In the caustic view of Borja, he was "trying to explain where all that money went and how its expenditure benefited the empire. If he is successful, he has truly kissed the blarney stone!"

"Where did you ever hear of the blarney stone?" demanded Christian.

Borja laughed.

"I've been around Don Ambrosio a long time. But I do not imply that he lies. Being an Irishman, he sees brightness even in disasters."

His duty completed, Higgins led his staff westward toward the almost deserted pueblo of Santa Juano, devastated by the frontier conflicts. It was necessary to cross once more the Bío-Bío, where Higgins speculated on the possibility of floating the treasured coach across the swift-moving stream. "We could do it by cutting logs, lashing them to both sides and rafting it over," he mused to Christian. "'Tis feasible—I'd stake my life on't." He shook his head sadly. "Well, another day."

The crossing was made on horseback, and along the southern bank the destruction seemed limitless. At Santa Juana a few fearful survivors emerged from the ruins to greet the entourage with feeble "*Vivas!*" There was little spirit among them, as though the Higgins party was a mirage. Two or three men clutched a harquebus, one a lance, and the few women each with an infant staring with burning eyes at a strange and hostile world. Higgins dismounted in the plaza, surveyed the ruins, and shook his head sadly.

"Ghastly," he muttered. "Frightful." He noted his aide, Christian, stiffly standing by and added, "Let us hope peace will permit life to return to these poor people."

"Yes, sir," replied Christian. "For both Spanish and Indian!"

Higgins peered at him from beneath black brows. "Still unconverted, eh? That is the ideal, sir, but it's a long way off. You will remember what happened at the council."

The party moved out the following day by a sinuous route subject to a thousand ambushes.

"So the Spanish have discovered," grunted Borja in response to Christian's speculation. "Every trail is soaked with Spanish blood and fertilized with their bones. But they are persistent, the Spanish. The proof is they are still here and possess the land, the Indians are gone and won't return."

"You sound as though you are not a Spaniard yourself."

Borja grimaced. "I am Basque."

"I thought Basques were Spaniards?"

"The Spanish think so, but we know we are not. We were overrun, I suppose, like the Indians—except the Mapuche. They at least are still free."

The escort was quartered on the coast at the Bay of Arauco. Higgins and his staff lost no time inspecting the lightly manned defense works that screened the inlet. Christian had seen fortifications in many parts of the world, had some knowledge of the principles involved, and instantly recognized the mastery shown here. Arauco was superbly protected against any assault from the sea, providing she had the manpower to work her guns. That was the key: manpower and incentive.

His inspection completed, Higgins took Christian with him on an official visit to the mission *encomienda* south of the pueblo. They found the fields little tended, the vineyards unpruned, and much of the wheat harvest appeared to have been lost to the grazing flocks of sheep, burros, and rangy wild cattle. With each discouraging discovery, Don Ambrosio became more incensed. He was in poor humor when they reached the stone mission buildings.

"What is the meaning of all this, Father?" he demanded angrily of the hooded Franciscan superior who received them in his office. The priest spread helpless hands.

"We do what we can, your Excellency," he protested. "We have many Indians, but few to direct them and little resources, as you can see."

"Resources! You have lands, as rich and fertile as any in the kingdom! Indians? Why are they not trained to command their fellows? To improve themselves? To farm? To herd? Are they any better off here than in the wilderness?"

"We try everything, but it is diffi—"

"Father, I don't care in the least how difficult it is! The king's treasury has been taxed heavily to support you. You must do well with what you have."

Higgins continued to fume as they rode toward Arauco. "This station is in precisely the same state it was when Bishop Marán visited it five or six years ago. He was incensed about it too, but the king wouldn't listen and ordered more money poured into this place 'to maintain tranquility and to benefit the Indians.'

Benefit! The Indians are benefited more by a wild life under the devil in their mountain lairs than by a slovenly *encomienda* such as this. But I can do nothing. Nothing! And that worthless father superior knows it well. My hands are tied!"

Christian reflected in the shadow of his superior's storm that the fault lay not so much in the management of the station, but in a system which held little incentive to missioner, to Indian, to faith—assuming the missionaries truly possessed faith.

The following day they descended upon San Pedro, a fortress on the Bío-Bío protecting Concepción and garrisoned by a detachment from that port, drawn up in full dress for review. San Pedro, too, was a battered relic of Indian wars from centuries past.

Concepción lay south of the well-protected Talcahuano Bay, the finest natural harbor Christian had observed on the Chilean coast. It was a key location. They crossed by ferry boats, which Higgins had installed while intendant years earlier.

Like all Spanish cities, Concepción was centered on its principal plaza and most of the houses were one story, built of adobe or other native materials and tile-roofed, the windows covered with iron gratings and glass used only by the very rich. Higgins' party reached the great square with the unfinished cathedral and palace of the bishop on one side, the governor's mansion across the way. The captain general pulled up before the government house and dismounted stiffly, handing the reins to Christian who passed the horse to a guardsman. Without looking left or right, Higgins stalked between files of infantry standing rigidly at attention and barely acknowledged the subservient greeting of the bewigged governor, the bishop, all twelve members of the *cabildo*, and a fluttering galaxy of lesser officials. A visit by the all-powerful agent of the king was not to be taken lightly. Higgins endured the ceremonial, then disappeared inside the palace to be seen no more that day.

intendant-
an administrative official, governor, under French, Portuguese, or Spanish monarchies.

Very early next morning, with mists drifting slowly up the river, Christian was summoned to present himself without delay to the captain general.

Higgins casually returned his stiff salute, sipped at a maté gourd, inspecting him wordlessly. To Christian he appeared fully rested, an amazing recuperation for one of his years. The general tossed across the table a packet of papers that thumped to rest before the young officer. They had been sealed with heavy brown wax.

"I want you to deliver these to Valdivia," he said. He passed across a folded letter.

"Here are my orders to the captain of the *San Ildefonso* anchored in the bay, directing him to transport you south to the fortress. You will report to the commandant, Colonel Diego Aliaga de Lurigancho, deliver the papers, and place yourself at his disposal for the approximate future. He has command of all of southern Chile, a wise and good man, so far as I know. You are fortunate to serve under such a one, and I wish you well."

Christian saluted once more.

"May I take this opportunity to thank you, sir, for your kindness and to assure you of my lasting fidelity and respect?" he said.

Grinning, Higgins reached a hand across the table.

"Were we in County Sligo we could drink to that," he chuckled. "But here 'twould not be seemly, though I thank you for the sentiments. Th' best of fortune attend you, an' may God watch over your progress, as I hope to do meself, should I be spared."

Christian pressed his horse toward the port that lay three leagues northwest. A settlement lay at the narrow neck of the Thumbes Peninsula, which protruded like a thumb, protecting the bay from the great Pacific. The officer found two armed vessels at anchor hard by the beach, the smaller being the *San Ildefonso*, her white canvas loose-hung and airing. His seaman's eye was instantly gripped by her rig: a felucca with the squat, triangular sails of a typical Arabian, the first he had ever seen at close range. How she had been brought round the Horn was a nautical puzzle whose solution he could not guess. Higgins had desired that a swift vessel be tested for courier service on his coast, and somehow she had been sailed here. Like most vessels of the Mediterranean style, she was lateen-rigged on all three masts; as a concession to ocean conditions she bore square topsails on fore and main.

Christian turned his bay over to the corporal who had accompanied him to the waterfront, rubbing the horse's muzzle in farewell. He hailed a crew and was rowed out to the ship, clambering lithely aboard via the Jacob's ladder, happy to step on a deck again, to feel the worn planks beneath his feet. He saluted the captain, one Garcia Rodriguez, and handed him the captain general's letter.

"*Muy bien, señor Teniente,*" the officer said, refolding it. "When do you wish to leave?"

Christian expertly assessed the trim of the vessel, the set of its yards, the lounging crew.

"As you please," he replied. "If your ship and crew are in order, when the wind rises and the tide goes out. Otherwise as you direct. How long is the passage?"

"Ninety leagues, *más o menos,*" estimated the captain, fingering his thick graying hair. "Two or three days, if the saints favor us with good northerlies. Would you prefer quarters below or on deck?"

Having observed a crewman and an officer scratching themselves, Christian decided to sleep topside during the run, thus avoiding various forms of carnivorous life that made sleeping below a torture to one not yet infested. It would be for two nights only.

The *San Ildefonso* lifted her hook at dawn and slid with the falling tide out of Talcahuano Bay, picking up a light northerly that pushed her south on the first leg of the run. She raised the long guardian rocks of Santa María and glided onward, the land like a half-submerged log on the eastern horizon, with a narrow cloud bank as flat as the coast lending a ghostly shadow to its color. It almost seemed to Christian that he was putting out once more aboard the *Bounty* or some other British vessel.

At dawn of the second day the felucca had run out of land, driving southward in her element of sea and sky. The captain occasionally glanced at the fill of the sails to judge the wind, though paying no more attention to navigation than that. Christian asked if he knew where the vessel was and received in reply a nod. Curious, he persisted, "Have you no instruments, sir, to ascertain your precise position?"

"Instruments? *Sí.* Below in the cabin," replied Rodriguez with a catlike smile.

"But you do not use them?"

The captain shrugged.

"There is no need, *señor Teniente,*" he replied gently. "The wind is from the north, we run before it, therefore we make south, always at the same velocity. And when the sun is there," raising his arm to the position of ten o'clock, "we shall bear southeast and make the land as we always do. It is not complicated."

"If the wind should change?"

"She will not change, *señor.* She never changes."

"But if she *should* change, what in that event, *señor* Captain?"

"Then we are lost," he shrugged again. Christian laughed.

The wind, as Rodriguez promised, did not change. At approximately ten o'clock, the felucca altered her course for the southeast. By two o'clock the land had reappeared, ranges of low mountains, close together. The ship made for a point precisely between the uplifts. Just at twilight she bore in for a bay, red and gold colors raised to identify her as Spanish for the coastal watchman.

CHAPTER NINE

The *San Ildefonso* slipped between narrowing headlands and dropped anchor in three fathoms under a battery of cannon from a fortress Christian could scarcely make out in the late twilight. The moon had not yet risen.

"Corral," explained the captain, pointing toward the defense works.

"Her guns would prove an obstacle, but not insurmountable to a determined enemy," Christian replied.

"They are not alone, *señor,*" said Rodriguez with quiet pride. "They are but one battery. There are others."

"How many?"

"Sixteen."

"You mean sixteen other cannon?"

"Not sixteen other cannon, *señor Teniente*. Sixteen other fortresses, in addition to Corral. Every point we have passed and others, too, have their own battery, powerful defense works like this one! It would be a very foolish enemy who would attempt to storm Valdivia."

Christian again spent the night on deck, despite misty rain. From time to time the moon shone through and he could make out the massive breastworks of the great fortress with over thirty embrasures, no doubt each with its twenty-four-pounder. He slept at length, but in the gray dawn a movement on deck aroused him.

A shaggy tangle of black hair rose above the bulwark and a bare-footed creature swung over the side from the ladder. All he lacked was a knife between his teeth to be the picture of a buccaneer. Christian yawned, pulled on his boots, watching the tousled stranger sucking maté with Rodriguez. The Englishman accepted a gourd from the captain.

"This is Piculai, our pilot," said Rodriguez. "He is an *indio,* as you can see. He will take us up the river to Valdivia when he finishes his maté and desires to do so." Piculai grinned, proud of his independence. He sucked at his maté. He was in no hurry.

"Is it far to Valdivia?" asked Christian.

Piculai nodded. "Far enough. Four, perhaps five leagues, but the current is against us, and sometimes the wind. It may take until evening if it rains or the wind dies away."

Bearing a point or two north of east, the vessel moved with the sea breeze past Mancera Island, heavily fortified, and south of the power bastion of Niebla, entering the river. Thin and misty rain fell as the heavy timber on either bank dripped. These woods, Rodriguez explained, were the cause of the fortification of Valdivia in the first place. "The guns deprived the area to English and Dutch pirates who refitted their ships here," he explained.

The brownish water on this dark day teemed with river life. A web of islands, generally low and sandy and supporting dense thickets, spread about them. All day the felucca thrust upstream, tying up briefly when strong cross winds swept down tributaries, ruffling the waters and making headway impossible. There were no settlements, but pirogues and an occasional balsa raft passed downstream all day.

Valdivia lay upon the Rio Calle Calle, a branch of the Rio Valdivia. The banks were lined with mooring, a swarm of light craft splashed about her watery skirts. Atop the hill rose the walls of a fort dominating the river, its parapets lost in the low clouds and rain. Christian could vaguely make out the armed Spanish towers of earlier defenses. Although he never had seen their like, he realized each in effect was an artillery turret. They were perhaps forty feet tall, of cemented stone, tapered from earth to waist so that the turret resembled a monstrous mortar, aiming skyward. *If the towers were well supplied, their defenders alert and determined,* Christian mused, *'twould make capture of the city very costly, even if other fortresses were overrun.*

Following Rodriguez's directions, the Englishman made his way up the hill toward the city's center, the plaza and the defense establishment. Unlike other Spanish towns he had visited, Valdivia was built of wood—the constant rains would melt adobe within the month. The people were active and purposeful as befit those who must dwell in a damp, invigorating climate. They were not dour like the Scots, however, he decided, for as he passed doorways, he heard tinkling merriment and caught the pungent smell of brandy.

With his bundle of dispatches, Christian was ushered into the office of the commander, who sat at a blackened desk littered with papers and maps. Diego Aliaga de Lurigancho was a small man, the Peninsula engraved upon his every feature. He was efficient and alert, his eyes darted here and there, never still for more than a moment. His mustache was neatly trimmed, his person plainly dressed for the Spanish army of that day; he seemed as competent as he was impeccable. His eyes examined both the new arrival and the bundle of papers.

"From his Excellency, Don Ambrosio Higgins, president and captain general," Christian explained. Aliaga nodded.

"And you?" His voice was as neat and definitive as his person.

"Sir, I am to report to you for orders."

Again Aliaga nodded. He tossed the packet to the desk, rang a silver bell, and an officer stepped smartly into the office, saluted at rigid attention.

"This is Lieutenant Edward Christian," he said curtly introducing them. "Captain Mariano Gregorio, adjutant. See that he has quarters and what is necessary. He will remain unassigned for the present." The adjutant saluted once more, his face expressionless, and led Christian from the office. Christian did not know why he had selected the first name of Edward, save that it was that of his favorite brother. He would attempt to honor it.

Gregorio had a prominent Spanish nose and was clean-shaven except for brownish sideburns of some length, his dark hair precisely combed. He had a strong chin and bloodless line of a mouth. His caste-awareness was revealed in a hint of disdain, or contempt perhaps, with which he regarded Christian, assuming him to be a provincial. Probably worse.

"Your baggage, *Teniente?* A trunk, perhaps? Your other uniforms?"

"Only one small bundle of a few necessities, *señor* Captain. It is aboard the *San Ildefonso*, the felucca tied up where the street drops to the river."

"I am well aware of where the *San Ildefonso* is moored, *teniente*," reproved Gregorio, his left brow raised faintly upon learning that the lieutenant, as he suspected, was almost wholly without luggage. He rang his own bell, of copper and smaller than the colonel's. A corporal instantly appeared, clicking to attention. "Show *Teniente* Christian to a room in the officers' quarters," he instructed curtly. "Lend him any service he requires." He turned back to the papers upon his desk. Christian was dismissed.

Through the rain the corporal followed the appropriate two paces behind the officer while trying to guide him until Christian insisted that he walk beside him. "In the darkness no one will notice," he assured him. "How are you addressed?"

"Felipe Guido, *señor Teniente*," adding softly, "from Chillán."

"I, too, have been at Chillán," commented Christian. "The place is quite beautiful."

"*Sí*. And the sun shines there, *mi Teniente*," sighed Guido. "I have a family and many friends in Chillán."

"Why did you leave them and join the army?"

"Sir, I served twenty years in Spain. But at Chillán I was impressed, I did not 'join.'"

"Will you be in service for long this time?"

"*Quién sabe, señor Teniente.*" It was too dark to see the shrug.

The two walked in silence for a few paces, the damp mist glistening in tiny beads on their faces.

"What do you think of your Captain Gregorio?" asked Christian. Guido held his silence momentarily.

Christian knew enlisted men were not to evaluate officers, but having opened the subject, he could not let it lie. "Some officers one likes, some one does not," he observed. "An officer is a man like any other. But I think the enlisted see them more clearly. Do you like your Colonel Aliaga?"

"Yes, *señor Teniente*. I do. He is a strict man, but just."

"Gregorio?"

Guido again walked silently. Christian thought he detected a quick shake of the head. "No one does," the corporal said. "But he is ambitious and has powerful relatives. His star will rise."

They turned in through a darkened archway past a guard, and the corporal led him into a Spartanly furnished room, equipped with a rawhide mattress, two blankets, a table, and chair. A lamp sputtered upon the table. The wet wool of their uniforms smelled heavy in the air.

"Tell me, Guido," said Christian, tossing him a coin, "where does one eat—and drink—in Valdivia?"

"Come. I will show you," replied the soldier, flashing a grin for the first time.

Once more they set out through the wet streets, water running darkly in the ruts and forming pools as black as tar. Across the plaza a light shone through a doorway where a hanging drapery kept out some of the rain and much of the chill. Guido pulled it aside, standing by as Christian entered. He made his way to a table and motioned Guido to a chair, but the corporal firmly shook his head.

"No, *mi Teniente*," he refused. "In this garrison it is not done so. Officers eat at one table, enlisted men at another." He paused a moment. "Here the brandy is warming and cheap, and they have food. If the *teniente* is through with me now, I must report back."

As Guido left, Christian surveyed the room, finding it little distinguished from any public house. Tables, rows of bottles behind a counter, a packed-earth floor, and almost no customers at this late hour. A figure suddenly appeared beside his table. Christian looked up—into the face of the loveliest girl he had seen in all of Spanish America.

Perhaps it was because of his long isolation or her bright contrast to the grim rain, even his own weariness and hunger, that she broke through his consciousness as few women had ever done. The girl stood expectantly before his table. Christian for a moment completely forgot his Spanish, where he was, everything.

If she noticed his discomfiture, Roca Montalván gave no indication; perhaps she was accustomed to this reaction to her beauty. Her native courtesy forbade her remarking upon it, so the strange officer would not be further embarrassed. Roca clearly was a *mestizo*, taller than the average Indian or Spanish woman, slender, and not yet twenty years of age, but with an air of maturity beyond her years. Dark and wavy hair fell to her waist. Her dress was simple, a light-colored blouse of cotton and a full skirt, darker in shade, of the same material. Her eyes were wise, friendly, curious, but not forward; and her lips and teeth were good. His life with Mautea seemed as far away in time as it was in space.

She flashed him a smile, "You will have, *señor?*"

Christian stared at Roca mutely, as though he did not hear her speak.

"You will have, *señor?*" she repeated.

"Ah, yes," sighed Christian. "Food and drink. Meat? Cheese? Bread? Brandy? Wine? Brandy first, I think."

She laughed lightly. "As you wish, *señor*. First the brandy."

She returned with a dark bottle and glass, setting them before him, her skirt brushing his sleeve. The brandy was warming though heavily flavored with anise. He drank it freely.

From behind the counter a heavily mustached, dour individual raised himself laboriously, slowly, and shuffled forward. He waited before Christian's table until the officer looked up. The man, who may have been the proprietor, jerked a thumb in Roca's direction, as she stood slicing roasted meat at the counter. "*El cápitan* Gregorio possesses her!" he said bluntly. With no further word he shuffled back behind the counter and settled down like a huge toad, silent and unmoving.

With the bread, meat, and cheese, Roca brought a jug of *chicha*, the Chilean hard cider, and of this the officer heartily approved. He invited the girl to sit across from him, and there being no other customers she did so, sipping the drink slowly.

Unwilling to examine his motives too deeply, Christian quickly finished his meal and invited the beautiful woman to return with him to his quarters. With little hesitation, she complied.

But when they departed before dawn the next day, neither noticed the heavy carved door to Gregorio's room was ajar, nor could they have detected it in the gloom. After escorting Roca home, Christian returned for the morning portion of maté and bread. When Gregorio appeared, the coolness between them seemed little discernible and easily forgotten. Christian reported to headquarters for duty and was handed by Aliaga a folded parchment of orders.

"This is directed to the commandant at each of the seventeen fortresses about the basin," the young officer was told. "They will give you the results of their own inspections and their needs for the coming season. You will take as much time as required; then, return here with the documents they give you. Take two enlisted men; Gregorio will assign a pirogue and crew."

The sun shone brilliant, if briefly, as the boat nosed into the Calle Calle under powerful thrusts of its paddlers and swung downstream. The craft sliced swiftly through the dark water until, shortly before midday, it beached on the sandy right bank at the tiny settlement called Niebla by Guido. Christian sprang ashore and with the corporal and a soldier named Gomez, made their way over the hills to a major fort, the Niebla Castle.

They approached the defenses from the rear, passing through heavy main gates past the patrolling sentry after he had surveyed their documents, and along a road cut through living rock into the heart of the bastion. Its heart was the gun platform, or shelf, carved from the sandstone of the headland, with space for eighteen forbidding twenty-four-pounders, 60 feet above the Pacific breakers and 20 feet below the well-manned crest behind. It was all but impregnable, if held with spirit, its guns splayed out in a quarter-circle of defensive power able to wreak destruction upon anything afloat in the outer harbor. Its fire field was interlocked with that at Corral across the neck.

Yet these mighty forts were but the introduction to an intricate pattern of defenses that protected one of the finest anchorages of the world. Christian had nothing but admiration for the engineers who had conceived and built this massive system, even though their ultimate strength lay not in their engineering, but in the alertness and determination of those who manned the defenses. He could detect few weaknesses. The fort at Corral might be subjected to plunging fire if heavy guns could be moved through the timber to the hills above it. The jugular of every fort is the supply and garrison ports; but so far as he could observe, these were well protected.

He spent the better part of a week gathering reports. During this time he acquired a solid grounding in Spanish fortification construction, as well as of each of the seventeen major installations, filing the knowledge away in his retentive memory. On the way back to the city, the paddlers made almost better time than the felucca had done, hugging the shores, out of the main sweep of current. It was raining heavily again. He delivered his papers to the colonel, little concerned at the coldness with which Gregorio, as adjutant, greeted and ushered him into the office.

In his quarters Christian made himself presentable, then quickly crossed the plaza through the rain and the wind to the *pulpería*. He thrust aside the curtain and entered, shaking the water from his hat, scanning the room for Roca. She was not there. Behind the counter sagged the proprietor, his drooping mustache even more lugubrious than his eyes, bitter with hatred. He answered gruffly Christian's unasked question.

"The girl is not here. She will not come again. Roca is destroyed!"

The flat monotone took the officer aback, like a cannonade catching a ship unaware. He rocked on his feet, demanded unbelievingly: "Why? What do you mean, 'destroyed'? What could have happened in but a few days?" His voice rose with each scorching question. The other lifted his shoulders slightly, his hatred unconcealed.

"I told you she was Gregorio's woman," he muttered tonelessly. "But she went with you. Now Gregorio has destroyed her. No man will have her now."

Christian stared blankly, struck by a tremor of dread. "What do you mean, old man?" He pleaded, hoarsely. "Where is she? Why do you say, 'Now no man will have her'? Where have you taken her?"

"I take her no place. She is in her room. You do not want her now. No man does, save perhaps Gregorio to scorn and possess, for such he is. A man of deep hatred who must possess what he hates. Such he is!"

Blindly Christian snatched up a lamp and brushed past the other. His pool of light flowed down the corridor with him. He thrust into her room, stood with his back to the wall. A form lay face downward upon the bed, tumbled ponchos heaped about. The figure did not move. From somewhere came a voice, piteously insistent, a voice into which death had already entered.

"Go from me!" it cried. "Leave. I am—I am no more yours, nor any man's. I am no more."

Christian moved forward slowly, clutched her shoulder, and gently turned her to face him. What he saw made him stumble and falter, horror-stricken. What had been a face of surpassing beauty now was clotted with blood and scabs. What left him weak with repugnance was the greater cruelty: her lovely features had been mutilated with cuts that would never heal, scars that would forever erase any hope of loveliness.

He shuddered, turned away, fumbled for the doorway, and ran from the room. Struggling to hold down his stomach as he rushed out of the establishment, he heard the old man calling after him. "She is destroyed. You have destroyed her! You and Gregorio! Agh!"

Fury surged through Christian as he stalked against the rain, across the square, feeling nothing but the horror of what he had seen. He brushed past the sentinel, burst into the adjutant's office. Gregorio still was there; but the colonel had gone. Gregorio looked up as Christian bulled into the room, knowing what he had seen. His perverse smile was touched with arrogance, which only served to further infuriate Christian. He drew up, stared, trying to fathom this creature.

"That is what *los indios* do to women who betray them," said Gregorio without emotion. "They ever treat unfaithful women so. She is Indian; she understands. It is but justice, no, *Teniente?*"

Christian leaped at his throat and bore down with iron fingers. He lifted the pampered officer from his chair, crashed a bony fist full into his face, feeling the cartilage crumble. Gregorio crumpled into a corner and lay heaving for a long moment. He rose blindly, searched beneath his cape for his gloves, and slapped Christian across the cheek with them.

"At daylight," he said, with no hint of pain, only hatred in his voice. "By the river. You have no sword of course, for it is the weapon of gentlemen. Therefore it shall be pistols." He added formally, correctly, "You have seconds?"

Then he turned upon his heel and stalked blindly into the brisk air of the winter night.

CHAPTER TEN

A sprinkling of rain diffused the soft light of dawn, distorting reality and bringing cold wetness to the two groups of men, huddled beneath the giant *coihué* trees. Gregorio, in keeping with the occasion, was in his dress uniform, resplendent with gilt and braid, colorful in blue and scarlet, the plume of his headpiece rising bravely against the gloom. By contrast Christian's group was somber, nondescript. He was silent, as were his seconds, Guido and Rodriguez, save when there was something of importance to communicate. Guido had insisted Christian wear the oversized poncho, drooping in immense folds from his wide shoulders, creating a blocky, haystack figure whose true form beneath this outer garb was indistinct.

"I have never fought a duel, *señor Teniente*," Guido had conceded, "but I have observed many. Each opponent seizes any advantage he can." He indicated the poncho.

"When the count is given, pace off the steps exactly, and turn precisely upon the tenth one," he advised. "Your opponent will try for an advantage, turn a whisper before the tenth count in order to get in his shot first. But do not trouble yourself about that. He is a marksman, for that is a soldier's skill, and if he is accurate, you will have no further concern. But it is likely that he will be so eager to fire first that he may not be accurate. As he levels and shoots, you will be just turning at the count of ten, your poncho will flare out with your turn, presenting him a swirling form of great size. It is most unlikely that he will be able, shooting swiftly, to locate the true target amid the bulk. After he fires you can take your time and kill him, if you wish."

Following Guido's instructions to the letter, Christian felt the tug of the ball as it whipped through the poncho and burned his belly. He was unharmed. He leveled his pistol slowly then, aiming it full at the waiting opponent whose face shone white through the merciless rain. If, at the final moment, he subconsciously permitted the barrel to drift aside or if his aim was simply imperfect, no one knew. He fired and Gregorio, wounded only, was wrenched upon his back, writhing in pain before his self-discipline took command. He lay still as Christian stood above him, surveying his victim without visible emotion, his pistol still smoking. If Christian's gaze was unrelenting, Gregorio's was equally hostile.

"I am not killed, *señor Teniente*," he ground out painfully. "I live. Perhaps we shall meet one day again."

Christian spun upon his heel.

"Let us hope so," he muttered.

Colonel Aliaga returned the salute precisely, sternly observing him.

The Spanish officer accepted the inevitability of duels between hot-blooded young officers, although the Crown sought to eliminate the custom as inimical to efficient management of the world's most powerful empire. But officers, especially striplings, held violent passions, or they would be neither suitable military material nor worthy to enforce Spanish interests.

"Having wounded my adjutant, *Teniente*," he said coldly, "you have placed yourself beyond my province."

"I know, Colonel. I regret it deeply."

Colonel Aliaga sighed. "Until you took vengeance to be your mission, you had done well in the brief time you have been here," he admitted. "It is not my intention to waste a good officer, even a hasty and injudicious one, but for the present I cannot retain you at Valdivia. The example would be bad for morale. Therefore you are ordered to report to Captain Don Guillermo de Tomaroa y Cuernavaca, who is to engage in active duty against the rebellious Indians of the south. You will find, I am sure, *Teniente*," he added dryly, "sufficient action to cool your hot blood. You may take along with you a personal aide, an enlisted man, if you choose. The expedition is already organized. Don Guillermo leaves in the morning. He has been informed."

Captain Tomaroa, a lean, sallow-faced individual, tall and with a waxed, upturned mustache that contrasted with his generally mournful mien, returned Christian's salute laconically, then slumped forward to shake his hand. "We need men who can take advantage of opportunities," he said pointedly. "I'm happy that you are such a one." He said no more about the duel, but Christian was grateful for his approval.

He found the expeditionary force of 138 men ready to embark upriver on a keelboat of shallow draft, two square sails on a single mast; forward on the deck lay coils of cordelle line for towing the boat over sandbars and shallows. A litter of Araucanian plank canoes nuzzled her sides, as though seeking nourishment. They would be used by Indian auxiliaries, scouting the advance. Christian, ordered to oversee the loading of her final stores, swiftly established order out of the confusion, earning Tomaroa's approval as well as the friendship of a red-cheeked young priest, newly out of seminary and as chaplain, eager to save men's souls wherever he could.

Ammunition and store sufficient for a month were taken aboard, packed in mule-size loads and stacked under Christian's direction along the centerline of the deck, the men's equipment piled on either side. Canvas awnings were stretched over the cargo to the rail on either side, shelter for the soldiers from the incessant rain. Officers were quartered below. The men filed aboard that evening, firewood was loaded and boxes filled with sand to provide hearths for small cooking fires. At dawn the heavily-laden craft headed up the broad Pichitengelen River toward enemy country to the southeast.

The channel soon narrowed, the banks closed in. Strong-backed Indians and *mestizos* lined either shore with the cordelles, wading to the waist at times, straining, struggling for footing, hauling the craft along and assisted by pole men working silently in rhythm. At the bow they placed their long poles into the water, seeking bottom, and struggled toward the stern, their effort propelling the craft slowly forward. The work was long and cruel. The men labored in shifts, an hour or two on and twice that off, and the craft was slowly edged along, up the oily, smooth-flowing stream.

Shortly after dawn the next morning, the boat was tied up hard by a grassy meadow whose immense expanse was black with herded horses and mules collected under military order. They would provide transportation for the interior, Christian gathered.

About sixty Indian auxiliaries squatted around small fires, a motley crew, and Christian readily identified the *cacique* because he alone carried a sword and wore a hat with feathers. Others wore a scarlet band about the head to contain their wildly growing locks and also to identify them as friendly. Each wore a poncho and remnants of discarded Spanish uniforms. Except for a few armed with mace or bow, each man carried a lance. This iron-pointed weapon, Guido explained, never was thrown but stabbed from horseback or afoot. When a charge was ordered, the shaft was pressed hard between elbow and side, its point directed by the hand. In addition the Indians carried machetes, the tool of all work in these thick forests and a formidable weapon.

Captain Tomaroa sized up the animals critically, while the vessel was being unloaded. "Not enough stock to move our supplies," he grumbled. "That leaves two choices: we can mount and pack all the men for a short campaign or mount some of the men and more supplies for a longer expedition, leaving the rest here, hoping . . ."

"For what, sir?" asked Christian.

"For a miracle," returned the other testily. "For more animals."

He was silent so long that Christian dared a further comment.

"It is not for me to suggest without invitation, sir. But wouldn't it seem preferable to make the longer campaign with fewer men? Would that not be more likely to produce positive results?"

Tomaroa inspected him leisurely, almost humorously.

"*Teniente*, you do not know the Araucanians. Our mission is to find them. If we do, we will need every single man we can muster and then we shall have none too many. When they strike it is like a comet, and to accomplish anything we need all the firepower we can get." He spread his hands, hopelessly. "Nevertheless, we have no choice, I suppose. I think as you do, but it's an invitation to disaster."

About one-third of the baggage was stacked beneath a *canelo* tree—the "tree of peace," as Guido pointed out—and left under guard. Mules and horses were packed swiftly, the combat detachment formed up and assigned mounts. Christian found himself riding a copper-colored horse with a roving eye and a disinclination to walk when it could trot. Since he was still not an accomplished horseman, he found the endless jogging all but intolerable. The command moved away from the river, a sinewy procession of armed and mounted soldiers. Behind them a ragged convoy of pack animals were goaded along by *mestizo* hirelings with no interest in the expedition beyond the one *reale* a day they hopefully would be paid. Christian found himself at midpoint in the column, heading a company of twenty-eight men, with Guido beside him as aide and general informant into the ways of the Spanish army.

The expedition slowly wound up the trail through the wooded hills toward the region of the Dallipulli. The rain gradually ceased, and Christian could reflect upon his new situation. His meeting in the office of Don Ambrosio seemed a lifetime ago. He was an officer in the Spanish army! True, he was as green an officer as any unlearned stripling from Andalusia, but he had the backing of the most powerful official south of Peru, which would assure a successful future in the army, if he pursued it.

Yet Christian secretly felt closer in spirit to wild Araucanians than the Spaniards who perpetuated an unjust, evil, and all but intolerable system. As an army officer he was an agent in the furtherance of wrongs he saw all about him, but what choice had he? A man must live. If he were not here in this saddle, he would have been executed, dead, and buried. Would that be an improvement? More honorable? No man could tell, not even Ishmael. One clutched grimly to life, rather than seeking out the unknown. He had no fear of death, but no inclination to die, either. Christian shrugged. "*Quién sabe?*" he sarcastically concluded his thoughts.

Once atop the forested mesa he caught up with the captain who soon halted, endeavoring to read a sketch map in the shelter under a *coihué* for it had commenced to rain again.

"Perhaps we can make Tegua before dark," he said glumly. "Six or seven leagues, a third of the way to Dallipulli."

"What's at Dallipulli?"

"Nothing. *Indios*. We will camp there, scouting the environs for Araucanians. Who knows what we may find?" He spoke without rancor, even barren of emotion. He was a soldier; this was soldier's work. Tomaroa splashed to his horse and stepped easily into the saddle, gesturing for Christian to ride with him.

"How will you establish contact with the enemy?" wondered Christian aloud. The captain grinned.

"Fortunately the enemy is quite eager to fight us. We use *bichos*—scouts. We have them out now, in advance and on either side to prevent surprise. The Araucanians have their scouts out too. The problem is not in making contact—it is in making war."

Several *tiúque* birds fluttered up with sudden squawks from the forest, their racket magnified in the dripping woods. Several figures appeared on the trail ahead. Christian felt under his poncho for his pistol, but Tomaroa signaled him. "They are *bichos*," he explained, peering through the rain. "They have picked up someone. A woman, I think."

The two spurred forward, pulling up alongside several Indian scouts clustered about a woman who clutched a bundle in her arms. She stared defiantly at her captors; in her gaze there was no gentleness, only hatred and courage. A scout saluted Tomaroa, jerked his thumb toward her. “She’s Araucanian. We found her in the woods. She was trying to reach Qudpal’s camp. She says she does not know where it is. She is lying, of course.”

“Of course,” repeated Tomaroa, wearily. “What’s in her bundle?”

A scout inspected it.

“Her baby,” he said. “Dead.” He conversed briefly with the woman. “She says she strangled it because it was crying. She feared it would betray her presence. We found her anyway.”

“Bring her along,” sighed Tomaroa. He motioned the column to resume its march. It was late. They would be lucky to make Tegua by full dark.

It rained harder still the next morning so that the force did not reach Dallipulli until the following day. The commander sent Christian with an experienced lieutenant and one company to scout the surrounding area with instructions to “burn any habitation you run across, if you can fire them in this infernal wetness, but not until after you search them for food. An army could starve in this country without confiscating provisions from the enemy.” They found no hostiles but torched a dozen Indian huts.

The next day Tomaroa’s command tracked a sizable enemy band southward to the Rio Bueno, in Mapuche called the “river of the frogs.” The hostiles swept ahead of them, across the river on a fleet of canoes, leaving the Spaniards with no means to pursue them. They appeared upon the farther bank safe from attack, taunting the whites—daring the despised enemy to come across and fight them.

“They know bloody well we can’t reach them,” said Christian, his competitive spirit stirring. “They feel safe enough, I guess.”

“That is true,” Tomaroa flashed his grin. “They do feel safe. But do not be deluded, *Teniente*. They would still conduct themselves so if they decided to fight. They jeer because it mirrors their nature. They will bring us battle, when they choose.”

The scout returned to Dallipulli empty-handed and disgruntled. Three local chiefs awaited the captain: Calfunguir, Auchanguir, and Manquepan, each strongly protesting his loyalty to the Spaniards, his eagerness to serve in any way, but the captain was suspicious. The chiefs volunteered to help hunt down the hostiles led by Qudpal, Cayumil, Tangol—and Kolapel. They said, however, they did not know how large the enemy body might be.

"And if they do know, they aren't going to tell us," grumbled Tomaroa, gesturing toward the *caciques*. "You can't trust those *Indios* beyond your sight."

He ordered them bound, uncertain of what to do with them. He sighed again. He didn't believe them and couldn't be bothered with them. He made his decision, as a soldier would, swiftly. "Lance them!" he directed. At least no superior would ever nullify that order. He turned to other matters.

Christian was perturbed, though recognizing his was not the place to protest, that arguments would carry no weight with the commander. He watched the summary execution from a distance, regretting it still, but aloof as Pilate.

Tomaroa summoned Pailapan, *ulmen*, or leader, of his auxiliaries. The Indian trotted up, eager to please the officer.

"How long would it take your men to construct balsa rafts to cross the river?" he demanded, through an interpreter.

"How large balsas? How many?" relayed the interpreter.

"Enough to get a hundred men across the river, under fire perhaps."

A mixed interchange followed.

"Pailapan says if there are *totora*, reeds along the bank, enough of them, the rafts can be built in a day and a half," said the interpreter. "But he said there should be sufficient soldiers to protect the builders so they can work without interruption. The Araucanians will not like it and may attack."

The captain nodded. The river ran through a series of marshes. There would be plenty of reeds. "Let's be about it," he ordered, setting in motion a night operation back toward the stream. By dawn the infantrymen were in positions along high ground overlooking the watercourse where hordes of auxiliaries labored cutting the *totoras* and bundling them.

These grew in dense thickets, each stem 3 or 4 feet long and slender as a finger. Indians harvested them with knives attached to long poles, drawing them in with hooked sticks, fashioning packets 10 or 12 feet in length. The bundles were lashed together to create their curious rafts, pointed at both ends, each capable of ferrying five to eight men. They were unsinkable by gunfire and too green for torches. The danger was that these were made of reeds still fresh and heavy and would not last long in the water.

"No matter," muttered Tomaroa. "They'll get us across to the enemy, and then they can sink for all I care. Cortez burned his ships to show his men they had to fight or perish. If these rafts get water-logged, they will carry the same message!" He laughed shortly. The captain sat upon a folded poncho, his back against the mossy corrugations of a *coihúe* trunk and focused his glass on the opposite bank, particularly studying several low islands. He looked a long time, then snapped the glass closed and murmured as though to himself, "They are fortifying two of the islands and the opposite bank, all right. It will be impossible to take, if we don't get across before they finish." He arose and went for a closer inspection of the raft-building operation.

"How are the rafts coming? How much longer?"

"Very fast, now," Pailapan assured the officer. "Plenty reeds. Plenty workmen. Plenty soldiers. By dawn we have fifteen, twenty craft done. Enough?"

"I guess so. Twenty would be sufficient. You think you can have twenty ready before dawn?"

The Indian shook his head. "I don't think so."

He was correct. By midnight Tomaroa knew the rafts would not be completed until after sunrise. Now he would have to move his force across the river in broad daylight, against a stiff and determined resistance. If he delayed until the following night, the Indians might complete their defenses. That would be even more devastating than crossing the stream under fire.

At three o'clock in the morning, Mass was celebrated, the soldiers exhorted by the young chaplain to do their duty in defense of holy religion, their king, and their country. Christian assumed he meant Chile rather than Spain, although the Araucanians on the opposite side of the Bueno would have a different idea whose country it actually was. Sipping maté by the smoldering fire, Christian remarked as much to Tomaroa. The Spaniard nodded.

"*Sí*," he conceded. "It is the difference that makes wars. The country truly belongs only to the stronger and more civilized which, of course, we are." Christian pressed the matter no further.

A dim grayness sifted in from the east, signaling the approach of day. The soldiers were formed up, protecting their muskets from the wet beneath thick wraps, for upon their proper functioning would rest the success of the operation and their very lives. Across the wide stream and through the rising mist shown the vague glow of enemy fires.

The men sullenly awaited the launching of the balsas. Behind the infantry twenty-two mounted troopers would follow, swimming their horses across, as would all of the officers save Tomaroa. The cavalry mounted and moved west along the bank a couple of hundred yards to where a gravel bar protruded into the stream. There they halted in a column of twos. At the encampment they had left, out of sight in the dense woods, a guard would remain with the pack mules, bringing them across the river should it become safe to do so.

CHAPTER ELEVEN

Christian stroked the neck of his nervous mount to quiet it. The officer checked his side arms once more, a brace of pistols swathed in cloth, carried on his head to keep the powder dry. Tomaroa had provided him with a lance, shorter than the Indian weapon and far more manageable for a novice; it was strapped under his right leg where he could free it quickly. The captain had advised against encumbering himself with either musket or saber.

Inwardly Christian felt as calm as the placid river before him, though with a faint surging of eagerness for the action to begin. Gone was his doubt, his concern over right and wrong, over life and death, peace and bloodshed. Those things had been tucked away in the dim recesses of his mind. All he felt at the moment was a flooding consuming urge to win—at all costs. It was this mystic, primordial compulsion that now engulfed Christian. Finally, Tomaroa gave the signal to move out.

A young lieutenant spurred his reluctant horse into the water, leading the double files of riders forward. Upstream infantrymen stepped swiftly into the rocking balsas, four in each, clutching paddles; the others forward, peering ahead, weapons ready. Few words were spoken. Soon the flotilla felt the tug of the deceptively strong current and began to lose formation as the more resolute paddlers forged ahead, leading the way. Only the splash of paddles and an occasional grunt broke the silence.

The command passed the midpoint of the river, no longer in any particular order, a dispersion of craft like a scattering of water insects, their only urge to reach the distant shore as quickly as possible. The downstream horses and riders were ahead of the boats, now. They had swum the short first channel, waded belly deep across a submerged bar in midstream, and now were swimming again with only 100 yards to the enemy bank. There was no sign of the Araucanians. The approaching shore loomed dark, ominously silent, still as death. Upstream the balsas moved sluggishly, their green reeds absorbing water swiftly, the craft settling lower in the water. In the foremost there was scarcely a freeboard, the soldiers sitting in sloshing water seeping in. Tomaroa was correct; he would never be able to reuse these craft for retreat. It was conquer—or die!

All the horses were swimming now, their riders being towed along as they clutched the sodden sheepskins, holding aloft with their free hands bundles of arms, keeping precious powder above water. Suddenly from the bank came the insistent chirping of a rainforest bird, loud and foreign to the stillness. From upstream came an answer, then a high-pitched scream of war, repeated four times. Instantly musketry rattled; great flowers of gunpowder smoke fogged the shore, followed by a stinging shower of arrows fired full at the approaching horsemen. A soldier to the right of Christian screamed with pain and surprise, a long shaft penetrating his right eye with its iron head. He drifted away, rolling over and over in the current. Two horses plunged uncontrollably, arrows protruding from their necks. Other animals and men were wounded, though less seriously; the fire had been largely over their heads. The Spaniards closed in on the bank, the horses found footing, and in a splashing stampede they rallied together behind an outcropping of stone, protected for the moment from enemy fire.

Other boats lunged ahead, the soldiers leaping from the foremost into shallow water toward the bank, arms ready. They could see no enemy but were too experienced to waste fire on phantoms. The captain was among the first to gain shelter of the cutbank against which he leaned, urging his men closer. There was no strain, no fear, no emotion on his sardonic face with its spirited mustache. This was soldier's work; for soldiering he was born. The other craft swept in rapidly now, the men leaping from them, huddling under shelter, forming up for the bloody work ahead.

Tomaroa wished the horsemen could have landed farther upstream, closer to his own detachment, but they probably couldn't have done anything in the thick woods anyway. Their mission was to sweep behind the enemy if they could and force him forward, into the field of Spanish musket fire. In the incredible tangle of the forest, that might not be possible. Tomaroa sent auxiliaries into the woods and to either flank, to get some idea of the disposition and numbers of the enemy. Forming his soldiers into a loose skirmish line, he led them up the bank. Araucanian fire had ceased; the enemy also awaited the next move. He lifted a shoulder in a slight gesture of resignation. He signaled his combat line to edge into the thickets, keeping within sight of one another. If they were split, it would be deadly.

Downstream the cavalry unrolled side arms and muskets, thrusting them into belts or saddle scabbards; they loosed their lances and mounted. The woods were too dense for horsemen, but below in a tiny bay, grasslands came down to the water. The officer led his men inland by way of these. It became hard to tell whether his command was paralleling the river, now beyond view, or quartered away from it. One could only hope. No sounds of combat could be heard, only the buzzing of insects. The sun shouldered through the trees, burning away the morning mist.

Tomaroa, meanwhile, commanded his infantry to enter the deep woods. Quickly a clatter of musketry signaled reestablishment of contact with the enemy. He sent a detachment to his left to try to find the end of the hostile line, to see if they could roll it up, giving him room to maneuver. The horsemen, far beyond, heard the fresh firing, realized they were too far from the river, and veered right, rounding a pond along the mudflats, closer to the woods. The lead horse began to flounder, sinking more deeply into the mire. Almost instantly the command broke up into plunging, frightened horses seeking to escape the morass. Some riders leaped to earth, only to become bogged almost waist-deep themselves. Somehow all but one of the horses extricated themselves from the sucking mud. Once more the force assembled, moving on, probing the dense forest, finding the way increasingly difficult.

"Maybe we should retrace our course, try some other way," suggested Christian to the lieutenant. The other shook his head, his face pale; he was frightened.

"There is no other way," he insisted. "The enemy is over there, where Captain Tomaroa is. We have no choice but to go ahead."

All at once Tomaroa's men were having better fortune. His detachment had indeed swung round the enemy's right and by sudden assault surprised the hostiles into withdrawing, slowly at first, then rapidly as the fleeing warriors fell among their companions, adding to confusion. Tomaroa found himself leading his men parallel to the river toward the fortified islands, driving the Indians before him. The Araucanians, many of them, escaped into the shelter of stockades. The captain deployed his men before these redoubts, ordering them to keep up a desultory fire to keep the hostiles behind their walls.

His cavalry now was beyond contact, however, unable to fulfill their mission, while the captain's force confronted the stockaded enemy. Suddenly a fierce beating of drums and wild screeches combined into an unearthly racket. From the dense woods a swarm of countless warriors surged down upon them from behind. Each soldier whirled to face this new enemy. Perhaps they knew it was hopeless, but they were fighters still for that was their trade. Tomaroa, laconic as always, faced the new direction, shouting orders. But mostly he cursed himself for his stupidity in becoming trapped. His right was smashed in upon him, his left rolled up except for a detachment cut off and fighting for its life beyond sight; his center hard pressed, its back to the river and island fortresses from which the Araucanians now sallied. It was enough to make the most resolute man quail, but Tomaroa drew his sword and fought until he was cut down. The firing ceased, and all that was heard were the triumphant cries of the warriors and the frightened screams of the worst wounded being butchered in the utmost agony, for that was the Araucanian way.

The distant horsemen heard the sounds of the battle faintly, muffled by the undergrowth and the dripping trees. They were too removed to comprehend clearly what was happening or to help if they did. Ahead of them a small band of Araucanian horsemen swept into view. The lieutenant ordered a pursuit across a slough and through a neck of woods into a wide theater between the shoulders of twin hills. Too late he saw there were but two exits: the one which they had just entered and a narrow pass far ahead. There was no point in retreat; in that way lay only disaster.

Spurring their tired horses into a run, the lieutenant and his detachment galloped for the pass ahead. The Araucanians had anticipated this and waited. In the middle of it, the blow fell. From both sides and from the front, and soon closing in from the rear, came a hail of missiles such as no man could withstand. Animals screamed and fell, their riders pinned underneath them. Others milled around, their riders seeking sight of the enemy but finding none. Their musket balls expended, swords out, they could find nothing to cut down. Christian, seeing disaster all about, led three or four in a bounding gallop toward the open end of the pass. Soon he was riding alone. And then the enemy bore down upon him too. A giant warrior lunged out from a thicket and expertly swung his mace, crashing it between the horse's ears and felling it like a thunderbolt. Christian rolled clear and leapt upright, his lance clutched firmly in his grip. He wheeled as an enemy mace glanced against his head and stunned him.

How long he was unconscious he could not tell, but he forced his eyes to open against the blinding, searing pain of his head. He focused his gaze by sheer determination upon the figure staring down upon him and saw the bold, ruthless face—of Kolapel.

CHAPTER TWELVE

Christian lay unable to move a muscle, the merciless face above him, a blurred composition of pitilessness. The Araucanian slowly put a leather-shod foot on the Englishman's neck, holding the head for a death-blow. He raised the blood-drenched mace high to finish the task. Then uncertainty raced across his face. He stared down at his victim. Without lowering the club, he demanded, "*Quién es?*"

With an effort Christian collected his thoughts, gestured for the other to remove his foot, rubbed his crushed throat tenderly. He replied slowly: "An officer, Kolapel. I was with Don Ambrosio Higgins at the council. You saw me there."

The Indian lowered the mace a trifle, wrinkled his brow.

"You are Spanish?"

Christian shook his aching head. "I am of the tribe of Don Ambrosio."

He could not have explained why he said this, but in his clouded mind was a dim recollection that Kolapel had differentiated between the Spaniards and Higgins. In this situation the young Englishman clutched at anything. Never had he been so close to death. Kolapel lowered the war club and gestured Christian to his feet. The Indian herded him to a ragged band of prisoners, almost all wounded, collecting in the center of the valley.

"You are my prisoner," he said flatly, little mercy in his voice. "You are not my friend. I give you life, not freedom." With that he turned away. From his retreating footsteps there came a dim echo. Christian heard these mysterious words whirling through his brain: "*Laich! Anochi iemach* . . ." They were not Kolapel's words for he had heard them before, even from the *Bounty* mutiny, it seemed.

Most of the shambling, reeling prisoners seemed stunned, half conscious, and one died apparently from loss of blood before all were gathered. Araucanians, some mounted, more afoot, brought additional captives up, but his friend Guido was not among them. Perhaps, thought Christian, he had been fortunate enough to have been slain outright. Captain Don Guillermo de Tomaroa y Cuernavaca was brought in, however, or part of him—his head on a lance. The sardonic expression still was there, the mustache as jaunty as in life, but his sightless eyes and sockets were smashed. The Indians had multiplied to a horde that herded the prisoners with taunts and jabbing down the valley toward the pass. A few, unable to move, were callously butchered, apparently by those warriors who had captured them. An Araucanian possessed the man he had taken, to do with as he desired, Christian gathered. He felt fortunate again that he had been seized by the one Indian who might have recognized him as an associate of Higgins.

They came at last to an open field, a *canelo* tree in the middle of it, its black shadow grotesque—for until now there had been little sunlight. The prairie teemed with men and women, more arriving by every path and lane.

"Now comes the party," muttered a Spaniard beside him. "Victory dances and rites. None of us will live to see the end of them; we will all be butchered. For some it will be quick and merciful, for others slow and tortuous."

Christian scanned the ragged crowd. His blinding headache was finally lifting. He could see and think more clearly.

"What would the Spanish do if they captured as many Araucanians?" he wondered. His companion chuckled bitterly in response.

The heads of the slain, spiked on lances, were assembled in the center of the field so that the dead with their sightless eyes might "see" the victory celebration. Around the circle of many heads danced the warriors to accompaniment of flutes, drums, rattles, and triumphant chanting. The dancers were garishly dressed in whole animal skins with the creatures' stuffed heads above their own, looking grotesquely alive.

The circling dancers became more frenzied, their leaps higher and more contorted, the drums paced faster until it seemed that human endurance could stand no more. As sharply as a cannon shot it ended. The dust slowly settled, the dancers removed their costumes; a stillness settled across the field. A single flute then sounded, thin and wavering as the recollection from a dim and distant past, rising higher and higher as the dancers and all the people remained motionless, listening. When the tension reached an unbearable peak, the booming of a giant drum took over, setting the blood pounding anew until it likewise crashed into silence.

Warriors now approached the prisoners, each selecting the individuals whom he had captured, directing them out onto the field before the assemblage. These victims were dispatched in many ways, some routinely, others imaginatively. Most of them were lanced, a few mercifully through the heart. Some were clubbed with heavy maces, frequently with direct blows crushing the rib cage; one or two were lingeringly played with, made to toss sticks into holes in the earth, recounting their past deeds, sins, or triumphs as they "buried" each bit of wood before they were slain.

Christian's erstwhile companion was among the final victims. As he was led away, he shouted over his shoulder: "The last shall be best! I'll show these savage cowards how a brave man dies!"

Stripped and forced to his back on the green turf, Indians armed with ritual flint knives clustered about him. Christian could see his body contorting with pain and the pool of scarlet widening around it, but no groan, no cry of agony escaped his lips. He died as he had pledged, a brave man.

Thereafter the victory celebration continued in an uninterrupted frenzy that lasted two whole days until the drink had run out and stupefied bodies littered the field.

Christian knew he could slip away into the forest, but he had no means of providing himself with food, no way of returning to Spanish settlements. So he awaited the pleasure of his captor and new master, whose arms he collected and whose horse he watered and tethered, stacking and caring for the equipment.

Kolapel, among the first to rouse, raised himself upon one elbow as though he were some ancient god in all his barbaric magnificence. His head may have been splitting, but he gave no indication of it, nor did he appear to notice his gathered arms and tethered animal. He roared at Christian to bring him food and drink; then, he drank a little *chicha* left from the debauchery and ate noisily but without speaking. When finished, he motioned for Christian to eat with the women, an indication of his future status in the Kolapel household.

The officer accepted his new role submissively. He helped the women pack family goods and loot on the mules and horses. As Kolapel led the caravan of his family and close followers from the bloody scene, Christian embarked on his life as a drudge slave, learning slowly the Araucanian tongue and much about their customs, almost erasing the memory and the manner of his former lives.

The settlement of Kolapel was in a small valley threaded by a swift-running stream called the Caunahue by the Mapuches. And since the Indian was a war leader of importance, there were eight or more family dwellings with other settlements nearby whose warriors joined Kolapel in the frequent wars and raids on Spanish settlements or in feuds with other bands. War, Christian learned, was the normal state of affairs with these people.

He quickly found he was not to inquire how many wives a man possessed but rather to ask how many fires were in his house, for all of the wives lived in a common house, each possessing an alcove curtained by matting of her own and equipped with a private cooking fire.

Kolapel's house was of moderate size for one of his status, rectangular in form with gabled roof and thatched down to the ground. It was built of sturdy timbers and sheathed with split cane and bark. There were no windows and the holes in the roof were to draw off smoke, so inside at cooking time the air was acrid and heavy. Though Christian's eyes teared and burned, the inhabitants seemed accustomed to it.

Christian was impressed by the fact that the Mapuche were a cleanly people, loving water almost as much as the Polynesians. Whether winter or summer, they took a quick swim and rubdown each dawn in the chill Andean stream boiling past the settlement. But despite daily baths and their passion for clean clothing, they were afflicted with lice. Christian, after a vain attempt to rid himself of these infuriating creatures, finally learned to ignore them as did the Araucanians.

Kolapel's house, atop a bluff, afforded a clear view up and down the valley, an advantage in observing his grazing stock, but even more so in watching for the approach of enemies. A small palisade nearby provided a retreat in the event of attack. As he developed fluency in the language, Christian learned that there was much white and, for that matter, African blood among the Mapuche. Many Spaniards had fled military service to live amongst them; African slaves escaped to join them. The Mapuche welcomed them as recruits, provided they were not taken in battle, and readily absorbed them. In return they bestowed certain skills upon their adopted people, not the least of which involved modern methods of waging war. These the Indians swiftly turned against their enemy.

While they were a carnivorous people, the Araucanian diet was predominately vegetarian except at feast days, for there was not an abundance of meat and game. At celebrations, however, flesh was devoured freely, often raw or only slightly cooked, and near the coast there was an abundance of fish. The Mapuche women were good farmers and assiduously cultivated the fields after the sod had been broken by warriors or strong male slaves, as Christian quickly learned, his back being lame for days after grubbing a few acres with wooden tools. Corn and potatoes were the principal crops with beans, squash, and of course chili peppers, adding spice to everything. Christian could not identify many plants used for food; various grains were grown and from them a kind of bread was fashioned. Sometimes the Mapuche made a ceremony of planting, the warrior calling in his neighbors to help break ground and sow his crops. He would then throw a party and provide great jars of *chicha* to assure that everyone got as drunk as possible.

Christian was not permitted to take part in the rare hunting excursions for more than a year, for this was a pursuit of free men, but there was not much game in the rainforest and because of the undergrowth, what little could be found was hard to pursue. However, Kolapel had a small herd of two species of deer and the guanaco, fed and cared for by Christian.

Livestock also consisted of pigs, chickens, a few horned cattle, sheep, and a few llamas. Sometimes several beasts would be the price of a bride. The Mapuche especially prized their horses. They were superb horsemen who bred and cared for their riding animals intelligently. Their equipment was more simple than that of the Spaniards, a saddletree of light wood, a few brightly woven blankets and an open triangular stirrup to be clutched by the big toe. The bridle and reins were leather or woven hemp and always the lasso was added, the men adept in its use in peace and war. Christian spent weeks, months, practicing with it, clumsily at first but with gradually improving skill until he could not only cast a 25 yard rope expertly, but plait one from long thin strips of hide specially cut for the purpose. In developing his skill with the lasso, he improved his riding. Naturally strong and supple, he had that instinctive feeling for an animal, which makes a fine horseman. He even won approval from the taciturn Kolapel, who allowed only his trusted English slave to care for his war animals. Christian's status thereby rose gradually from that of a drudge captive to one of trust. He did not resent his bondage, given the alternative punishment, and was sure it was temporary, although it continued for the better part of two years.

Riding an old piebald horse Kolapel had bequeathed him for herding purposes, Christian one evening brought stock from the uplands. Nearing Kolapel's dwelling, he detected many packed mules and surmised it was some trading expedition from the Spanish settlements. The Mapuche tolerated these traders at rare intervals, desiring some of the manufactured articles the Spanish offered. The Englishman unsaddled and carried his equipment to his alcove, then joined the women near the door where Kolapel conversed with a Spaniard whose back was to the onlookers. To Christian there was something familiar about the set of his shoulders, the tilt of his hat, the ring of his spurs. When he rose to pluck a gift from a mule's pannier, Christian recognized Bartolome Borja, the frontiersman who, by his vast knowledge and wisdom, had won the admiration of Higgins.

Christian could not bring himself to the other's attention at once, for there was the ritual of presenting trader's presents to Kolapel, so he would permit them to set up shop. Christian completed his evening duties, cut the firewood, brought water, and assisted the women until with the dusk the *chicha* began to flow. At long last he came face to face with the Basque.

Borja would have passed him without more than a cursory glance if Christian had not stirred some faint recollection, some distant wave of memory. He scanned him head to toe, questioningly.

"Welcome, Borja," grinned the Englishman, "to Araucania."

"Mother of God!" Borja breached. "Are you *Fletcher?* I heard you were killed with Tomaroa! How on earth do you come to Kolapel's town?"

Christian threw back his head in laughter.

"I'm the number-one boy around here, Borja. Kolapel spared me because I was of the tribe of Higgins, as I was quick to inform him, and not a Spaniard. But I am his slave, as you can see—and delighted to welcome you here on the part of all drudges!"

Borja's deep brown eyes twinkled. "Wait until these people get drunk, which won't be long, and we shall talk."

Under a full moon Christian and Borja seated themselves on the lip of a bluff, while the settlement lay silent in the sodden grip of *chicha*. The Englishman told the Basque of the ill-fated campaign, the battle, and his years in Kolapel's camp.

"If you want to escape," said Borja, "it could be managed."

Christian shook his head. "For what? I've no particular love for the Spanish, nothing to draw me back there. I'm not unhappy here, except that I'm imperfect in the Araucanian tongue. Neither do I understand all their customs and prejudices."

Borja lost himself in reflection for a long moment.

"What you require is expert instruction," he judged. "Why don't you take a wife—what about Kolapel's sister? I could help you with the price, if you are agreeable. Perhaps I could even persuade Kolapel to give her to you."

Again Christian shook his head. He was not unaware of Pinsha, "the Hummingbird," a beautiful young creature who occupied the honored place in the chieftain's household, but he had never spoken to her nor she to him. Such aspirations could not bode well for him, and Christian said as much. Borja remained unconvinced.

"If Kolapel tells her to marry you, she will marry you," he insisted. "He is master. What he says is *law*."

"I am Kolapel's slave, not his friend. Would he willingly turn his sister over to his slave?"

"Why not become his friend, then?"

"How would I accomplish such a feat?"

Borja tossed a pebble down the hill into the rushing stream, its ripples making silver rings in the moonlight.

"Kolapel honors one thing alone—courage! And he is consumed by one passion—war. If you go with him to war, if you show great courage, murder enough hapless enemy soldiers, you will win his approval. With that, marriage would be possible, even probable. A new life could begin."

Christian reflected, then once more shook his head, slowly.

"Borja, I don't object to war and all that goes with it. War is as natural to men as breathing or sleeping. I know it and have had some experience in the business. I can fight and I can command. But I am not by nature treacherous. I have no more love for the Spanish than have you, or even less. Still I feel some loyalty to Don Ambrosio. So long as he lives, I would never fight against him or his men."

Borja's teeth flashed in the ghostly light. "He would like that," he conceded, "as do I, for treachery is no part of honor, and I believe in honor. But in this case you are free. Don Ambrosio is no longer captain general of Chile. In fact he no longer is even in Chile. Now the army here is Spanish-, not Irish-led."

Christian was startled. "What happened to him?"

"He has become what no Irishman, what no foreigner ever has before. He is the viceroy of Peru, the top dog in the Spanish Empire. Don Ambrosio is in Lima trying to improve the idiots who have made this hemisphere a sinkhole of ignorance, cruelty, and misery. His position in Chile has been given to Gabriel de Aviles y del Fiero, the Marquis de Aviles, who took us right back to the age of stupidity we were in before Don Ambrosio. Your conscience can be clear as gold."

"What sort of man is Aviles?"

"You mean in appearance? His eyes are light brown and shameless. His face is practical, restless, but there is no deep thought there, nor probably even scheming."

"I had meant, rather, his character—is he able, kind, just, dedicated to improvement, to the righting of wrongs, to governing fairly, to the benefit of the people, to settlement of differences between colonial and native?"

"He is Spanish." Borja added, "He spends half of his time in church, I hope at confession—he has plenty to talk to God about. In Peru he took part in the ghastly fighting against Tupac Amaru. When Field Marshal José del Valle died—

of infection from—a rotten soul, many think—Aviles took over. It was by his signature that the captured Quechua chiefs were tortured in one of the most fiendish tragedies under the Spanish Crown. He was named lieutenant general and president of Chile in 1795, and here he is."

Borja cast another pebble into the stream. "You can have a clear conscience to fight Spaniards on still another count." Christian looked at him inquiringly, and Bartolome continued:

"Spain was at war with France, as you may know, and no sooner did the conflict end when she signed an alliance with the French and went to war against England. The French never had the navy to threaten this coast, but England has. That has Aviles quivering with worry. Anyway, your people are at war with Spain. That should cure your scruples."

"Why do you tell me all this?"

"Aviles rebuilt the garrison at Pichura, which Kolapel's Indians flattened three years ago. Higgins made a deal with Kolapel by which he agreed to abandon the Pichura site. Aviles ignores that pledge."

"That makes you angry?"

"It disgusts me. It confirms dishonor as national policy in Chile. Kolapel is furious, not at Higgins whom he still trusts, but at the Spanish. He will fight—and there is your opportunity."

CHAPTER THIRTEEN

Borja evidently spoke well of Christian, for on the morning after he left with his cavalcade of pack mules, Kolapel tossed the Englishman a musket. "Now you are free, a *mosotone*, a warrior—if, as Borja asserts, you can fight." He strode away, but when the horses were driven in that evening, Kolapel picked out three good ones and turned them over to him.

Although Christian continued to dwell in Kolapel's household, now there was a subtle alteration in the attitude of others toward him. No longer did he eat with the women, hew the wood, draw the water, tan hides, herd stock, perform the drudgeries reserved for slaves. Christian also found Kolapel a different person, light-hearted, cheerful, prone to practical jokes on other warriors, generous—all of these things in time of peace; he had yet to observe him in war.

The effect on Kolapel's sister, Pinsha, was even more apparent. For the first time she dared express an interest in the tall, bearded visitor, now treated as a permanent guest.

She was tall for a Mapuche woman, but 6 inches shorter than Christian, and formed as gracefully as a doe, and as light of movement. Her dark flowing hair, which she sometimes wore in twin braids, reminded Christian of Mautea's. In her effervescent enthusiasm, there was a touch of a little girl that delighted him. Still he could not speak to her openly, being poor and an untried warrior. But between them generated a current of knowledge, and each was aware of the other.

The old women who had ordered him about, now became subservient, eager to comply with all his wishes, showing no embarrassment whatever at the abrupt reversal in his fortunes. They accepted it, as did he.

As the full moon waned, Kolapel became more solemn, even morose; and Christian believed he was thinking of Avila's treachery in re-arming Pinchura. Obviously peace palled upon him; war was his business, and the Spanish duplicity made a campaign inevitable, a matter of propriety. Christian, foreseeing war, observed closely the chain of events, the ceremonial preparation leading up to a military expedition.

Kolapel's band, like others of the Mapuche, had many enemies, some of them their own neighbors whom they fought in a light-hearted way, but war with the Spanish was different; it was a consuming passion, the proper outlet for the warriors' implacable hatred and resolution. And Kolapel was determined to move against the Spanish at Pichura. This garrison on the north bank of the Rio Rahue had been overrun and burned to the ground many times in the past; and again many times, the attackers had been repelled. The ferocious war against such outposts had continued now for more than two centuries.

So it was that Kolapel one day silently brought to light from its secret hiding place the battle ax of black obsidian, the ritual arrow, and the quipu. The quipu was a fringe of colored strands whose use Kolapel carefully explained: four knots on the black meant it would be the fourth day after the full moon when the *werquenis*, or messengers, would be sent to friendly bands and possible allies; ten knots on the white thread meant that ten days after the messengers left, the war would begin. Each chief who received the quipu would tie one knot on the red, if he would take part. The position of his knot indicated his identity. If he refused to join this war for any reason, he would tie a knot binding red and blue strands together; and again, the placing of the knot would be his signature. Still other colors indicated the number of warriors each *toqui* would bring and how many were mounted. When the messenger returned, Kolapel would know at a glance how many warriors, how much cavalry and infantry, would be available for the expedition. The quipu also showed who would command the various groupings and the day the campaign could begin—all of this without one word being exchanged. The cords were tied at their upper ends to a stick split in two. Kolapel opened it to show Christian the dried Spanish finger embalmed within, symbol of the quipu's deadly mission.

The messengers were dispatched the next day with their tufted proclamation of war. Christian imitated Kolapel in preparation for the conflict, and under the chief's guidance, experienced older women fitted Christian with a helmet adorned with plumes and a corselet of thick, stiff leather. The Englishman at first found this armor hot and uncomfortable, but in time he became so accustomed to it that without it he felt undressed. A circular shield of several thicknesses of dried bull hide was also made for him, stout enough to deflect arrows and even a musket ball that did not strike it squarely.

On the appointed day, all the bands converged upon the settlement of Kolapel, camping on the flatlands along the river. Christian was amazed at the discipline and order of the soldiers' encampments; these Mapuche had learned well from their enemies what made for military efficiency. The warrior leaders gathered beneath Kolapel's standard to learn why he had decided to fight, against whom, and the provocation that had led to his decision. Kolapel, whose oratory prowess contributed greatly to his leadership, ignited their patriotism, their concern for their homeland, the fear for their liberties threatened now by Spanish betrayal in reestablishing the Pichura garrison. He slyly stressed the unreadiness of the post, the inexperienced militia—or in his words, "dog soldiers"—and hence its weakness, and the loot that awaited a successful assault upon the place.

As his passions soared, Kolapel swung the bloodied war ax twice in enormous circles around his head and drove it into the ground. Two chieftains, armed with long lances raced round the tight throng, piercing the ground with their weapons, crying: "Valiant pumas! Advance to battle! Light-winged falcons! Fall screaming upon our enemies, as the true falcon plunges upon its prey!"

"*Ou! Ou!*" responded the inflamed *caciques*. "*Ea! Ea!*" called the swift war chiefs. "Make the world tremble as you quake your native soil! *Ea! Ea!*" Furious dancing commenced among all the wild chieftains and inflaming ritual.

Oddly, Christian found the barbaric spectacle shoring up his own courage. The rite was reaffirmation of the chiefs' determination, solidifying individual wills, and forging a unified war implement obedient to a single leader—Kolapel.

Christian was a new warrior, his worth still unproven, and so he observed the ritual from afar, but feeling himself strangely stirred, nonetheless. Little wonder that the Spanish had been unable to conquer this savage people.

Kolapel was chosen as their leader, a formality only, and showed proof of his fitness for the honor by causing *chicha* to flow until all lay drunk about the meadow, to awaken with the cold dawn, their aching heads lending a sullenness to their ferocity, making it even more sinister. During the next few days, they disciplined their forces, reducing the food dispensed to each man so that he would be thin and agile during battle, reducing also the fodder for their animals for the same purpose but giving them plenty of a peculiar grass, the chosen food of the *clen-clen*, a dove of swift flight, reasoning that if this grass fueled such velocity on the part of a bird, it might do the same for a horse. Each warrior practiced long hours with the weapon of his choice, drilling himself in leaps, racing, throwing the lasso or the lance, lifting enormous stones to strengthen his muscles.

There were nearly 2,000 warriors, and each was issued his *machica*, the flour of parched grain. A fistful for each day would be mixed with water into a gruel, and upon this meager ration alone, each warrior would subsist until the feast which would greet the conquering horde upon its victorious return, or the lugubrious banquet in the event of its failure.

Aside from the cavalry, the warriors were organized into four squadrons of infantry of approximately equal strength. Each body had its own scouts and its selected route toward the enemy; each had its own standard, banners of bluish-green, the favorite color, emblazoned with a single five-pointed white star. The flag was carried at the head of the marching column. The horsemen followed, coming in to bivouac with the other soldiers each evening. Christian was impressed by the care most riders lavished upon their mounts and the obvious affection between animal and cavalryman.

By the second day the contingents had reached the shores of a mighty lake. In the evening dusk, the stilled surface reflected thousands of tiny fires, doubling those lit by each soldier, giving the sparkling impression of a mighty army camping on this wilderness-girt body of water.

Christian stood on the outer circle of the leaders clustering about Kolapel discussing strategy beside the tiny fire, until at length the *toqui* noticed him. "Ai, foreigner!" he called. "Borja tells me you can fight in many ways—how would you approach this enemy?"

Thus summoned, Christian shouldered in among the leaders and squatted down across the blaze from the chief. He asked Kolapel to sketch a map of Pichura in the dust, inspecting it gravely. The settlement lay on a curve in Rahue, built on a meadow. In rebuilding the post, the Spanish first would construct palisades for protection, then rebuild the settlement behind them. As soon as possible they would mount cannon as their principle defense while the rest of the soldiers worked on restoring the housing. Surprise was the thing.

"Where are the guns?" he asked, studying Kolapel's rude sketch.

"My spies say they are mounted at each end of the palisades and also buried in the earth along it."

Christian understood this meant they were placed in a trench in front of the wall. "It would seem to me, Kolapel, that the attack might be in three stages," he suggested, calculatingly. The chieftains had ceased their chatter and listened gravely to his words. "Do any of your men understand the firing of cannon?"

The chief looked about at the assembled faces as he tried to recollect the talents of his soldiers. He shrugged. "Perhaps," he said.

"I would send swimmers at night and float away the Spanish boats so that none might escape down the river," suggested Christian. "At dawn your swift-mounted riders might run off the herd of horses as they are driven out to graze. Then the garrison and people would be trapped and at your mercy. That would be the first stage, I think. To increase the confusion you might send lasso-armed riders on strong and willing horses to sweep the trench so close beneath the guns on the wall that fire could not be brought to bear on them. Have them rope and drag out the cannon along with what powder and shot is stored there. That would be the second phase. For the third, you could mount the stolen guns here at the edge of the woods—no entrenchments would be necessary since the Spanish could never sally and recover them—quickly blow gaps in the palisades, overrunning the place through them before the enemy could rally. There might be difficulties, but none you cannot overcome. However, you are a veteran of countless engagements against this enemy. What think you? I would like to hear your mature views and will gladly accept what you direct." He realized he might have been trapped by his own enthusiasm, a bit forward for an untried warrior.

Kolapel was an unusual man. He was not offended by another's offering, providing it made sense to him. He had listened gravely, now he considered silently and well. He turned to the assembled *caciques*, discussing with them the scheme in rapid Mapuche, which Christian could follow only broadly, detecting the tenor but not the necessary detail to join in.

There seemed to be a division between those who wished their men to drive against the defenses in open, bloody war and the others inclined to favor the more artful scheme put forward. The final word, however, remained with Kolapel.

"Your plan is good," he said to Christian at last in his fluent Spanish, "if it works. If it does not . . ." He left the remark unfinished, though the Englishman clearly understood the implication.

Like the others, Christian had commenced to feel a ravening hunger, increasing daily, for the tiny allotment of gruel did little beyond sustaining life itself. His spirits sagged from growing hunger while those of the Indians swooped toward their zenith and their pride, their self-assurance swelled. He wished he shared more fully in their tradition, but now the action was approaching.

Under the smoky mist arising from the river and in the ghostly strata over the lowland marshes, the blocky skeleton of Pichura lay half visible. From the rim of the dense forest, thousands of obsidian Mapuche eyes peered relentlessly at the target. Already the swimmers from upstream had glided toward the waterfront in the night, loosening the plank pirogues and other craft, pushing the smaller ones from the beaches into the stream, guiding the larger from their moorings out into the current. At dawn no alarm had been sounded. The Spanish, if they feared attack at all, expected it from the forest, rather than the river. Their sentinels peered languidly into the night to landward and the woods, little suspecting that their river escape route at that moment was being severed. Even the dogs were still.

A cock at long last crowed, and then another and still another across the settlement. The soldiers began to stir in their wooden shacks, secure, they believed, behind their protective wall. Oxen and horses, too, drowsed behind the stone walls of the corrals, which had been constructed even before the palisade could be raised.

This formidable wall was composed of sizable upright *coihué* and *algarrobo* trunks, footed in a trench, the timbers bound one to another by strips of rawhide, which when dried were taut and hard as iron bands. The sullen muzzles of four-pounder cannon, eight of them, protruded through the portholes, the guns squatting like toads upon their platforms, which also supported the gun crews, iron cannon balls, and powder.

Most of the guns, however, were in a trench before the palisade, their barrels raised slightly and aimed at the fringe of woods. There were twenty-seven guns so mounted, also of four-pounder caliber—light perhaps, but powerful enough to decimate any attacking Indian infantry, it was believed. Each was well supplied with munitions protected beneath ground level from musketry.

Christian shook his head in admiration of such defenses in the wilderness. It must have required fearsome labor to get the heavy pieces so far inland, up the twisting streams, along with ammunition and power. But he had learned that problems meant nothing to Spaniards when they were preparing for conquest or war.

The meadow between woods and palisade, 400 yards wide, appeared level in the predawn gloom but a rivulet meandered across it, giving some protection to their placement but offering advantages to an attack force as well. A gulch carved by this watercourse was not deep, but reeds and thickets would cover horsemen for a short distance. Along its bed Kolapel had sent riders to run off the livestock when it was driven out to graze.

Already smoke from morning fires had drifted across the prairie from the awakening village, a pungent summons to action.

CHAPTER FOURTEEN

Christian edged onto the meadow with Kolapel's cavalry from the woods hard on the heels of the small band sent out first to lay an ambush for the stock expected to be driven out of the post to graze at first light. Each of the second detachment of horsemen was armed with a plaited lariat, for they could not use firearms at the outset. Most riders had removed the brilliant plumes from their helmets to aid their concealment, although a few would not give them up, their feathers of bright colors nodding in time with the movement of their horses. However, they were not visible for any distance in the dim predawn.

From the walls a trumpet sounded faintly. The riders, concealed in the creek bed, remained hidden from the palisades. The wide gates creaked open, and livestock straggled out, dragging muzzles through the wet grass as they fed toward the creek where they would water. Christian estimated at least 200 oxen and 175 horses and mules. His pulse throbbed quickly now, the early morning chill forgotten. He rode high in his saddle; eagerness to engage the approaching conflict consumed him.

The last of the livestock ambled from the gates, followed by tousled, yawning soldiers longing for their warm beds. Suddenly, the Mapuche war screeches tore the morning stillness. Swift-mounted Indian raiders thundered in upon the herd, waving ponchos in fluttering confusion to stampede the docile stock and panic their herders. In an instant, the startled animals bolted in a mad race ahead of their new tormentors. Several Spaniards were already lanced and lay dying upon the damp turf; others fled to the gates while the sentinels struggled to close them. Christian and the main body of wildly screeching cavalry swept in new confusion with whirling ropes and raced down the trench close beneath the palisade where fire from upper-level cannon could not reach them. Expert ropers dropped their loops over the squat guns and jerked the heavy weapons from the trench. Each cannon weighed 250 pounds, but this was nothing to riders accustomed to roping 1,000-pound bulls. Within moments two-thirds of the guns were being dragged, twisting, tripping over hummocks, bounding through the air like living hulks, toward the woods.

Seizure of the guns was only half the plan, for without balls and powder they would be useless. Mapuche *arrieros* galloped in on the heels of the first wave to throw what shot and powder could be found onto their pack mules. But now the crews manning the palisades' cannon were at work, the roar of their weapons adding to the shrill cries, the beat of hundreds of hoofs, the squeals and shrieks of animals and men, as the small arms fire through the ports made hazardous work of loading the excited animals, shooting numbers of them down in their tracks. Christian spurred the *arrieros*, who packed their mules within pointblank range of the enemy. They hurried off a few mules but not enough to arm all the cannon even once. The mule carrying gunpowder blew up in a spray of flame and fragments of flesh by a lucky shot. Two or three mules gained the woods unharmed, blowing hard but safe with their cargos.

Christian was startled by a frightened screeching of greaseless wheels upon dry axles. To his amazement the gates swung ajar and a rude cart drawn by two yoked oxen straining under jabbing goads dragged the vehicle toward the field of action. By one of those unpredictable imbecilities of war, some officer had ordered the cart laden with powder and iron shot to the presumed hard-pressed gun crews outside.

Christian leapt upon the vehicle with as many of the laughing Indians as he could muster, and the Mapuche swiftly dispatched the single terrified driver and two assistants. Horsemen roped the axle-hubs on both sides, spurring their mounts so the cart was quickly pulled forward, goading the oxen into a lumbering run, the vehicle banging against their hocks. Another warrior dropped his lasso over the horse of the leader, pulling the animal after him to keep the team headed for the woods; otherwise they might have circled back for the fort. Cannon fire from the palisades dropped shot all around them, but none came close, and the conveyance with its ammunitions gained the forest. The heaving oxen were left yoked while the powder and cannon balls were distributed to the waiting guns.

At Kolapel's direction Christian quickly aligned the heavy weapons, directing the crews of warriors somewhat familiar with their use.

Perceiving the disaster of the munitions cart, the garrison hastily slammed and barred the gates. Aware that those portals represented the weakest portion of the wall, Christian concentrated six guns upon them. The others he split equally, each directing its fire upon a single portion of the palisade. Kolapel now led his foot soldiers across the field at a run, holding their fire, the enemy cannon now so reduced in number as to constitute minimum risks for the darting soldiers. Their front ranks gained the protection of the palisade just as the first volley of Christian's cannon fire lofted splinters and chunks high into the air, making the entire bastion quiver with shock. The shot that struck the gate did greater damage, forcing that portal to sag perilously, held upright by its cross bars alone. Within minutes came a still more disastrous volley, blasting the gates ajar. The Mapuches streamed through the openings crying: "*Lape! Lape!* You die! You die!"

They closed with the defenders in hand-to-hand combat, which the Mapuches dearly loved. Now it was only a question of time, since they heavily outnumbered the defenders; and by noon the battle was over, almost all the Spaniards slain. Women and those children the Mapuche chose to spare were herded upon the meadow. The settlement, looted of every object the Indians might desire, went up in flames, towering black smoke marking the funeral pyre of Pichura. All that Christian retained was a finely wrought gold ring, which had fallen from the hand of some unknown woman into the dust.

Triumphant Indians camped amid the charred wreckage, roasting meat from dead oxen, horses, and mules, commencing the celebration of their victory. Christian clearly recalled what it meant from the loser's viewpoint, and now he one of the triumphant party. Wearily, he reflected that given the choice, he much preferred the latter.

Although Spanish accounts, including the Marquis de Aviles' report to his king, would assert that sheer numbers overwhelmed the defenders of Pichura and at a cost to the attackers of thousands upon thousands of slain, Christian, in his orderly way, could find only 11 Mapuche killed and 18 wounded seriously enough to require attention. He himself also counted 278 Spanish slain and 31 women and children captured. These would be preserved for a life of captivity and eventually, if they survived, incorporated into the Mapuche society. It was a clear victory for Kolapel and not a small one, by any means.

In high good humor, the chief joined him at the edge of the reeking shambles. He accepted Christian now after the great success with an open friendliness, which the Englishman felt marked a new phase of their relationship, one he deeply welcomed since his fate was irrevocably bound to this wild, moody leader.

"Do you move upon Osorno, now?" Christian asked speculatively. A much stronger base, some distance down the river, Osorno would not prove so easy to take as unprepared Pichura.

"No, *mosotone*," Kolapel replied, sobering at the question. "I pledged to Don Ambrosio that he could fortify that place free of Mapuche attack, and I keep my word as he ever kept his with us. The stupid Spaniards tried to reestablish Pichura by treachery; for that we have destroyed it. Osorno was reestablished by agreement. Thus we spare it." He gazed about the leveled ruins of the settlement, smoking still from the last flames. "We have finished here," he murmured. "We must return now, a great feast awaits us . . ." He surveyed Christian thoughtfully but said nothing further.

CHAPTER FIFTEEN

Kolapel, Christian, and the Mapuche warriors rode leisurely back to the settlement north of the Caunahue, reaching it late one afternoon; other bands took their share of booty to their own communities.

Despite the euphoria of his overwhelming success, it took a supreme effort of the will for Christian to wrench his mind from the brutality of the conflict—and the memory of events leading to his own capture. Now he was among the Mapuche for the remainder of his life, he supposed, and therefore an enemy of Spaniards everywhere, save for the nomadic traders like Borja the Basque and the few captives who had joined themselves to Araucanian society. So be it.

In truth, Christian had not only become Araucanian in custom and manners and dress, but almost in thought. He was marked as a foreigner only in the bushy fullness of his beard and the curl of his hair.

Copying Kolapel, he wore the accustomed garb of the Mapuche, woven of the *bayeta,* or llama wool. The *chamall,* a small rectangle of cloth, was thrown over his shoulders and gathered at the waist with a *faxa,* or sash. Below this was a *chiripa,* a cross between a breech-cloth and diaper, which Christian had come to appreciate for its comfort and looseness with some amusement. Of course he carried with him the inevitable poncho against the daily rains. He wore no hat, nor did the other Indians, employing rather a woven fillet round his head to control his hair. As a renowned warrior, this would eventually be replaced by a silver band such as Kolapel wore. Over his feet Christian pulled stockings with rawhide sandals.

He was Mapuche in all but birth and his aversion to sadistic cruelty. And he was content, or as nearly so as a young man ever can be. In this remote land, so far removed from his previous life, he felt he might indeed lead a new existence, as he expressed it, "out from under God, Jesus Christ, or the Holy Ghost." He all but forgot the "stick," the curse put upon him by Bligh. Perhaps he had at long last worn out that imprecation, which may have been nothing but a figment of his imagination. And yet he could not overlook a chain of disasters to those whom he had touched. From the mutineers to Roca Montalván and Tomaroa, he appeared to have been the lodestone that attracted evil.

Christian realized he was hungry and brushed past the curtain-covered doorway into the house of Kolapel to be greeted by a snicker from Pinsha at the glowing fireside, assisting the older women preparing a meal. Always they were charged with feeding the men whenever hunger gripped them, which might be at any time of day or night. Pinsha had been more open in her notice of him since, as a warrior, he had been admitted to the highest rank of Mapuche society. Now she mocked him, tugging at an imaginary beard on her face, flickering down the corners of her mouth, grunting in imitation of his deep voice. She loved teasing him, giggling like a little girl as she saw his discomfiture. According to Mapuche etiquette, since both were single she could not address him formally or openly, but she could slyly torment him and make known her interest. Kolapel, still recovering from the *chicha* consumed during the victory feast, observed the incident but for the moment said nothing. Since both their parents were dead, his sister was in his charge. His slightest wish was a command, which she could never evade.

Christian sat beside Kolapel in companionable silence, devouring the supper Pinsha had brought him. Her *kepam* brushed his shoulder as she laid the bowl in his hands. She was a vixen all right, he mused with a quiet grin.

"Two things you need, *mosotone*-warrior," Kolapel announced with considered finality. "You require a name, a Mapuche name, and you need a woman to cook for you and mother your sons."

Christian considered the suggestions gravely.

"Every man needs these things," he agreed. "How shall I be called?"

"You fight like a puma," Kolapel replied, by way of compliment. "You are nimble, energetic, and wise in battle. It is my thought that you shall be called *Lebitureo*, the 'active lion.' It is a good name, worthy of you."

"Lebitureo," repeated Christian, then again, with mounting pleasure, "*Lebitureo*," becoming accustomed to the sound of it. "I accept. It is good."

"You need a woman, as well," the chief reminded him. Christian nodded, saying nothing, permitting his friend to retain the initiative. "You like Pinsha?" asked the Indian suddenly. "You desire her? She is young and strong."

"I could not pay for so splendid a woman, your sister," protested the Englishman. "I was but yesterday a slave. I own nothing. A girl such as Pinsha would be worth many horses and much silver." He poked the fire, hopefully. "What would you accept for her that I could provide, Kolapel?"

The Indian himself stirred at the fire and considered. He liked this tall, brave foreigner. To have him within his family would be good. Ai! It was worth even making a joke about—he had seen the white man laugh once. He could laugh. Now, Kolapel dolefully shook his head to impress the other.

"I have but one sister," he observed tonelessly. "If a man does not become wealthy by selling the woman he had, how else can it be done? In addition, she is pleasing shaped, and she can skin a guanaco, carry water, cook. She will be warm in winter. There is an old man with cold bones on the edge of the settlement who will give a whole herd of horses for her—all bays and blacks and dark chestnuts. Beautiful horses! Another, not quite so old but much fatter, will give me thirty cows and their calves, and that would be riches indeed! Ai!" he mused upon the incalculable wealth that would be his for the nod.

"Aye," agreed Christian, sadly. "She will go to a very rich man, I suppose, and that means a man very old, for who else is wealthy enough for her?" He stared moodily at the fire.

Kolapel enjoyed his unhappiness.

"It would not be wise, however, to have for a brother-in-law one who was too old for war, one who could do nothing but sit at home all day and pick lice from his head. That would not profit a man, even if riches bought her. I will take six young, good horses of a dark color for her, Lebitureo." As Christian glumly said nothing, Kolapel added, "and six saddles with silver mountings, and Spanish bits, and six sets of spurs of silver also, with rowels as broad as the length of your hand, with a pleasant ring to them, and six firearms, too, either pistol or musket. All this is a fair price, no?"

"Very fair," agreed Christian sadly. "Pinsha is worth it and more still, no doubt. But as you know I have nothing to give for her. I hope she goes to a man who can pay and still keep her happy, but who could that be?"

Kolapel laughed.

"You, of course, Lebitureo, if you wish," he chuckled.

"How?" demanded Christian, his empty hands spread.

"The price I demand must be paid, if you agree," Kolapel explained. "But not now. You may have Pinsha and pay for her when you can. Of course, you will have plenty time with her before I get all of my price—unless we have good luck and good looting." He sobered, calculating. "But you should collect her price in a raid or two. There are rich Spaniards all about the frontier."

As a slave Christian had been amused by Mapuche wedding practices. He realized now what was expected of him, that he and his friends should "attack" the home of Kolapel, seize Pinsha who would struggle, scream, and attempt to escape as though the whole thing were against her will. Kolapel, too, and his immediate followers must be overcome in a rough-and-tumble brawl. Then, and only then, Christian might ride off into the woods with Pinsha for a brief honeymoon. They would return the next night for the recital of ballads newly composed for the occasion, the sacrifice of an animal, singing, dancing, feasting, and for the guests the imbibing of all the *chicha* that could be collected. At long last the couple might retire to their own house, if it was completed, to enjoy their nights of wedded bliss.

And so it was. In the struggle Christian found himself directly opposed to Kolapel. He enjoyed testing his considerable strength against the mighty power of the young *toqui*, who had never known a master. However, Christian might have been overwhelmed had not Kolapel held back his strength and had Christian not been schooled in wrestling as a boy. The holds and maneuvers were unknown to Kolapel, which gave the Englishman an advantage that he pressed by every means.

While they were so engaged, Pinsha escaped and fled, as one of the Indians laughed, "quite like a rabbit," across the fields and pastures, apparently seeking the security of the forest. Christian flung himself upon Kolapel's saddled horse and galloped after her, running the girl down short of the timber, sweeping her up onto the animal in front of him and spurring into the cover of the trees, where they disappeared from view while Kolapel's household began the long preparations for the wedding feast and celebration.

Later, following the ceremony and during a brief interval of calm, Christian bestowed upon his wife the golden ring he had brought from Pinchura. Pinsha had never known the use for a ring as a marriage bond, but somehow she understood.

Some loves reach at the outset as close to true happiness as they can attain, then gradually taper off to nothingness; others grow steadily toward perfection with the years, reaching higher planes than could be imagined at the beginning, and so it was with Christian and Pinsha. Their joy penetrated every aspect of their lives. In every way except appearance, the Englishman became Mapuche.

He and Kolapel were inseparable. Their raidings and warrings with other bands and against the Spanish became legendary. The whites learned painfully to leave Mapuche country alone save for rare punitive sweeps—which as often as not ended with punishment for the legions of the king and triumph for the Indians. Lebitureo became renowned in all that country as the first captain of the dreaded Kolapel and almost as able a warrior if not so implacable an enemy. He returned from martial adventures to delight in Pinsha, and she gloried in him, his fame, his worship of her, and most of all for himself alone.

Two youngsters were born to them in the course of time: a son with the dark curly hair of his father and a girl with the almond loveliness of her mother. For slightly more than five years they were happy.

One day on a routine sweep, an enemy of no particular skill or renown trapped and wiped out Kolapel and a small band of his warriors. By the sheerest coincidence, Christian had not accompanied the party, although he had intended to join it later. By the roll of the dice of fate, his life was spared once more—and with Kolapel's death, forever altered.

With that loss, the life was blown out of Christian like a snuffed candle. It was long before it stirred again, and far away.

CHAPTER SIXTEEN

For more than a century, the diaspora of Mapuche tribes toward the east had been underway. The old ones, reciting legends around smoking fires on rainy evenings, told of the people who had explored the great mountain passes and descended by them onto limitless plains in "the land of the sun coming up." The migration was a gentle dispersion, taking place over many years.

The scouts had learned early that beyond the cordillera was much game and feral livestock, which had escaped from the Spanish settlements, affording plenty of food and high adventure for the Mapuche. True, there were nomadic bands of strangers but so weakly organized, they could never compete with the disciplined Araucanians and dared meet them only by silent ambush or treachery. The land called powerfully.

To a less active people, the stupendous snow-clad range might have seemed an impassable barrier. Peaks to the north rose higher than anyone had ever climbed, lancing upward into lung-burning areas whose lack of air made human penetration impossible. Even the passes between these mountains reached so high that a traveler must wear special moccasins like the feet of a duck to negotiate the snowfields, and sometimes they suffered from the *puna,* the altitude sickness for which there was no cure. In the south the slopes were still more precipitous, volcanoes more active, timber so dense in the foothills that trails could be carved only with difficulty. Yet over the years paths had been worn and explored until the Mapuche settled on the rumpled eastern skirts of the range and their predatory bands ranged beyond to the Spanish settlements squatting almost without defenses on the banks of the great river.

The Mapuche did not remain there; but they raided, adding havoc to the depredations of the Tehuelche and other pampa's peoples, another fount of terror for a terror-prone race who nonetheless rarely permitted hardship or fear, bloodshed, disaster, or abject misery to drive them from their sordid villages. Only death could defeat them.

By Christian's time, the pattern for the diaspora was set, a gradual seeping of family groups, of smallish bands, or even of single couples with their children, searching for a better life, a change, or perhaps to satisfy curiosity about a new and different land. With the death of Kolapel and the dissolution of his following, Christian and Pinsha resolved to attempt the long journey with their children.

"You seem grave, Pinsha," he reproved her upon the eve of their departure. She smiled, though there were tears in her eyes.

"Where you go, I, too, will go."

"Have you been talking to the missionaries?" he chuckled, not explaining the ancient sentiment she had echoed.

"Where . . . will go."– In the Bible, Ruth 1:16, Whither thou goest, I will go; and where thou lodgest, I will lodge: thy people shall be my people, and thy God my God.

"My people, my life is here," she murmured, held close in his arms. "But I know that across the cordillera my people also have settled, so it is well. However, the parting is sad for me."

He held her close, knowing that what she said was truth.

In the morning they saddled their horses and packed belongings and food upon two mules.

Christian had learned that the range, although utterly bleak in its upper reaches and very difficult, was not overly wide. Three days should suffice for a passage through the ice and snow, but there would be no forage, so the mules carried maize for all the animals.

At dawn they set out, consoling those who remained behind with the pledge to return one day or perhaps to send for them if what they found was good.

At first the way was gentle, through thriving lands settled by Mapuche, fields carefully tended and fruitful, livestock fat and plenty. They stopped now and then to help someone clear his land, or plant his crops, or to attend a fiesta, for Indian courtesy demanded as much. At length they reached the Rio Nilahue, which in its bouncing course gave a hint of the wild country from which it poured. The trail grew steeper and more difficult. Dripping timber pressed gloomily in upon them, bringing an almost suffocating sense that they were wandering into the very guts of the earth itself. Pinsha grew more solemn, quite different from her normal self. Christian said nothing about it.

They camped at timberline, which was at no great elevation at this latitude. With the warm, crackling fire, Pinsha recovered something of her spontaneity.

With the dawn they continued their migration across an open meadow whose flowers delighted her. But soon they entered the snow, which appeared at first beneath the ledges, then in the trackless frozen fields, becoming at length a white wilderness broken only by black outcroppings of cruel rocks. Pinsha's muted terror returned. Christian fashioned goggles for them, wooden strips with slits for vision, to protect their eyes from the glare of the sun from the white surface. Thus they were spared snow-blindness. Even so, the trail through this unmarked wasteland was difficult to follow. Frequently they took false courses, and the family huddled half-frozen and miserable while Christian sought the hidden way, beating out a path through the drifted snow and returning, wet and cold, to lead his family on.

All his cruel labor notwithstanding, it was easier for Christian than for the others. For one consumed by a dream, any effort is unimportant so long as the vision is pursued. But for those who only loved him, obstacles seem greater, the goal of dubious worth. Pinsha never voiced her objection, though fear and foreboding consumed her; and in the long cold night, huddled under their llama robes, she wept. Christian gathered her close and murmured words of hope, and they slept. But with the dawn they faced an unending struggle against the frozen world, across an ocean of white wastes with dazzling peaks soaring all about.

This night, too, they chewed the dark thin strips of jerky, their children sucking at the frozen beef because their parents did so, until Pinsha, in compassion, chewed up a bit to soften it for them, placing the half-masticated food in their tiny mouths. Again in the night it snowed heavily, and Pinsha's eyes grew wide with terror.

"I fear, Lebitureo!" she wept. "We shall be frozen, lost beneath these snows; never will our bodies be danced over, as is the custom of our people . . ."

"We shall not perish here, Pinsha," he pledged softly. "The mountains do not go on forever. Beyond them will be warmth, grass, trees, the people with their ceremonies, and happiness." He wished to believe that himself, and she was soothed.

With the dawn he poured generous piles of maize on hides before each of the animals and rubbed the circulation into their loins. His providing the mule loads of corn had been very wise, for the animals were enduring the ordeal well, even if ravenous for pasture. The snowfall continued, but there was no wind and it did not drift. Where its fresh accumulation lay belly-deep, he went on ahead, using the makeshift snowshoes he had fashioned to break a trail. It was brutal work. Their gravest peril was from bridged-over crevices into which the careless might plunge and be lost. He did not know how much farther they still had to go. They had brought food and grain enough for only three full days in the high mountains. Already this was the third day. Perhaps, he grinned, this might be the time to call upon God. He laughed wryly.

Christian moved more slowly, ever mindful that a misstep could prove disastrous, his body tiring under the bitter, incessant labor. He felt stiff and weakened. He rested more frequently. His exhaustion sapped his drive, knowing there could be no turning back. The way lay upward and still higher into the ever-deepening snow, requiring ever greater effort and bringing further weakness. He did not know how much longer he could endure. Forward one step, then another, still another. Rest. Forward one step, then another, still another. A longer rest this time, but he must go on. Behind him the animals with their living burdens followed noiselessly in the thick whiteness. The mules' expressive ears had settled horizontally, denoting patience, resignation. Forward one step, then another, still another. Rest. Mounted upon her horse with their daughter in her arms, Pinsha was terrified but followed wordlessly, faithfully, because she loved him.

A touch of wind brushed Christian's face and quickly passed. A flick of fate, perhaps? Then a stronger blast swept the falling snow aside; and in another step he saw below the sky a deeper blue like the sea. But it was not the sea at all, for they stood at once upon the stupendous rim of the great uplift, the land falling off before them, cascading in white rivers and finally disappearing into the misty green of distant verdure, far, far below. Beyond they could see a hint of the plains and pampa in the remote distance beyond the breaks and foothills and barrancas. They had made the crossing; the land beyond was theirs!

Emerging from the snow, the trail curled, whipping back and forth across the face of the massive mountains, leading downward, ever downward, into a fresh new world. Far to the south a glint reflected as from silvered metal, marking a lake.

They camped that night below the snow in a rocky cove where a wayward creek plunged from the frozen peaks down the mountainside, to join others and merge into a stream flowing eastward.

By evening of the second day, they reached plains and a river flowing to the southeast. Guanacos and *ñandus*, the ostrich of the pampa, whirled away before them. Christian had no idea how to catch the birds, or guanacos either; but there was an abundance of armadillos, which could easily be harvested. He was delighted to learn that roasted in their shells they were the tastiest of food.

The way wound among hills and broken country, and within a day or two they commenced to see more clearly the sheen of the immense lake Christian had sighted from the rim. It gradually assumed the proportions of an inland sea. For three days they continued southeast, along its shores, through open timber. To the northwest and west the metallic surface was bordered by a broken row of gleaming fangs, the snowy peaks of the southern cordillera, walling off the Mapuche homelands beyond.

Christian cut a few poles and erected a hide-roofed shelter, building a leaping yellow fire for Pinsha to cook on after it had died to coals. Taking his son and daughter by the hands, he led them to the shore, and they chased the squawking newborn ducks and tiny fishes, returning wet and exhilarated when Pinsha called them.

While she crooned the children to sleep, Christian sat before the fire and watched the light fading, the snow-covered mountains and the clouds set ablaze by the waning sun. Then the sky was dark. The stars came out and he recalled the distant lochs of his childhood home: Crummock Water, Buttermere, Bassenthaite, Ullswater, and Windermere. This savage land was reminiscent of that well-settled region; but it was magnified as a landscape laid bare and enlarged by a ship's glass. Somehow in this wild glory of lakes and mountains he felt at home. He held Pinsha, and they were again happy.

CHAPTER SEVENTEEN

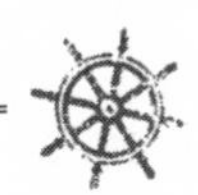

Christian's spirit lifted with a dawn that brought life and color to his soul as it did to the land. A buoyant hope emerged that a new existence might indeed open for them here. With Pinsha he could forge whatever life they willed, and their children would perpetuate it. This was a new land, as different as noon from midnight from the rain and gloom they had left with its cruelty and warfare, enmity, and torture. He stepped down to the graveled lakeshore, bestirring a processional of the young ducks, swimming decorously as though bound for church. A black-headed gull, pirouetting above the water, screamed applause for this fresh new life; and Christian wryly gave thanks for it. To the northwest, well into the lake were islands, bony with exposed rock but forested. He wondered if there were game upon them. A retreat might be found there, if food existed. It would be ironic indeed if amidst all this beauty starvation lurked!

His fear was dissipated with discovery of the water as home for a brown-furred aquatic rodent of beaver size, the coypu, or nutria, whose flesh proved savory. He devised an ingenious trap and with it caught a supply of food for the immediate future. He scrambled among the rocks for ostrich eggs; and Pinsha collected berries and wild fruits endlessly, discovering, too, a wild root like the potato and quite as edible. So they learned to survive in this lush land, a primordial Adam and Eve. There would be time enough to find some wandering band of the people, with whom they could join their lives and fortunes.

Christian returned from a day of exploration along the shore of the great lake and sat alone, as he sometimes did, watching the evening come on while Pinsha fed the children and wrapped them in their robes. He felt strangely uneasy and morose. From the darkling sky descended a mist, not quite rain, which chilled and depressed the soul. Pinsha, her tasks completed, slipped up beside him.

"It looks so sad," she said, responding to his unspoken mood.

He stroked her glistening hair. "Yes, Pinsha, it does. But without the sadness, we would be unable to enjoy the glory, no? One sets off the other. And the sadness even now is lifting—see how the sky is breaking?"

The heavy clouds had weakened; and the moon, now full, shone hesitantly at first, then bringing life and dancing movement once again to the waters and touching the mountains as the chilly air dissipated.

"It makes me happy, Lebitureo, the moonlight," she whispered. He nodded, silently.

With morning his buoyancy returned; and after playing with the children, he kissed his young wife and set out to explore the western lakeshore. He had no tools save knife and fire to build a pirogue, but if he found a log of proper size, one might be worked out that would do to explore the islands and find some nook perhaps for a more lasting home. He had glimpsed a proper fallen tree several miles distant. Now he located it again.

Pacing off its length, he realized it would be an enormous task to shape and hollow it, even with fire, but it might be done. Cutting the great log would be the greatest difficulty; and then the trunk must be divested of its bark, the ends shaped, the top flattened, and the interior burned out before his sharp knife could take over for the finishing work. Christian had closely observed expert Polynesian canoe makers and understood what was needed. Though perhaps he lacked their skill, he was young and strong and felt the lure of the problem, the compulsion to meet the challenge.

It was late afternoon before he turned back toward the camp. One difficulty might be to convince Pinsha that the pirogue was worth the work and time, that it would not delay their finding some band of the Mapuche. A girl did not always see such undertakings with the enthusiasm of a man who is pulled by the urge to prove himself against them. It might take persuasion. Grinning to himself, Christian rounded the point to approach their camp. He stumbled and almost fell across the lifeless body of his son, whose little head had been crushed upon a granite boulder. Fresh blood was everywhere.

The shock of disbelief smothered the horror that lay about the camp he had left only a few hours before. His daughter, her body broken and covered with blood, lay halfway from the point to where the tent had been. Half-in, half-out of the tumbled shelter lay the bleeding, still warm body of Pinsha, whose death had been most agonizing as the gruesome evidence made clear. Viewing the horrible carnage that had once been his beautiful, loving, joyful wife was more than Christian could absorb. He did notice that her index finger was gone, cut off in order, he knew instinctively, to steal the ring he once had placed there.

Disbelief, a numbing sense of unreality overcame him through these moments of incredible savagery. The insatiable fury would set in later. Now he idly looked and wandered about, his mind drained of emotion, his thoughts as always analytical. He roved another world, infinitely removed from this remorseless horror, trying to fathom how and why this had happened. This bloody wreckage could not be all that remained of his warm and vital and loving Pinsha, nor their children who were their future. What kind of demonic evil could have conceived and executed such destruction, and what had become of them? There was no why. Perhaps the Tehuelche, ever the enemies of the Mapuche, were responsible. They roamed as bands of killers and marauders, fleeing ever from the shadows.

A wracking sob tore his body mightily at last, as the catastrophe broke into his mind and awareness. He crumpled across the form of Pinsha, the broken hummingbird, and wept his soul to weakness and from weakness to bitter resignation and finally to immutable hatred. Toward the vanished murders? No. The enemy was unidentified, would probably remain so. No, it was against himself, his captured soul, held prisoner by that all-pervasive evil of whose existence this new horror convinced him, which ever eluded his grasp, even his comprehension. He could see and identify its vile work, but know it, understand it? Never. It pursued him with disaster upon disaster, savagery upon savagery, death upon death. He—*he* was the cause, but never did it strike *him*—no! Always it struck the innocent beings who somehow touched him.

As the night advanced he slipped into oblivion, dreamless. He longed that it might bring Pinsha to him once more, a renewal, however transitory, of a happiness that never was to be again. But there was no dream. With the dawn he set about the last duty he would ever be able to perform for her, the burying of her torn and battered body and those of his children in whom he would never delight again.

He laid them all against a clay bank, well covered with robes and, taking up the lance, pried the sweet-smelling earth down over them, piling rocks upon the sepulcher. Lastly, for some reason he could not explain, he marked the grave with an upright pole, eight feet in length. However, he did not fashion a cross-piece, since it would represent something in which he refused to believe. Then he sought out the animals the raiders had overlooked or ignored. He unhobbled the mules and horses, turning them all loose save his riding animal, which he saddled. Without looking back he rode up the long slope and turned the horse's head southwest, toward land unknown. To the west, beyond his vision, lay the great fallen boat log, to rot into earth-mold with no further service to perform, now that it had lured him away long enough from those he loved above his own life, leaving them defenseless in the face of cruel destruction.

Christian could not have told why he set out in this new direction, except that he felt somehow pulled toward the setting sun. He rode slowly, permitting the animal to select its way and gait. He was an automaton—neither seeing nor caring where he was bound.

The murder of Pinsha and their children wracked his mind, confirming his conviction that the tragedy was not a thing apart, but a continuation of the pattern he had never been able to escape since the day he sent Captain Bligh off to some unknown fate. The late sun slanted through the timber as his mount of its own accord stopped at last, hard by a grove of *arrayánes* trees, their slender yellow-brown trunks vying for the last sunlight. Beyond the grove some distance shone a charcoal lake, its waters dingy but curiously limpid, too, so that from above it one could see clearly into its most profound depths.

Christian dismounted stiffly, unsaddled his horse, and led it into a vale with a cascade of fresh water running through it. Carrying his saddle and blankets, he entered the grove and made his bed upon a spongy mat of ferns and pungent growth. He drifted numbly toward sleep with the coming of darkness. Never could man be more isolated, more cast upon his own resources, more dependent upon fortune, the fickle slave of destiny. Christian slept.

Was it the cold that awakened him? Or the laughter? He recognized the demoniacal laughter by its tone—there could be no other such deep and vicious glee. The mood glittered in upon him in slices through the bars of a cage, and in his clouded state he felt himself entrapped indeed, heavy bars rising all about him. From all directions rocketed the laughter, the high-pitched glee of Captain Bligh whom he had set adrift, whose revenge was even now wreaking itself upon Christian.

Christian crouched in the ghostly gloom and still heard the mad cackling of that bitter throat, louder and louder, flowing over him, an amplification of all the sins of his life. The laughter increased. Christian sought to flee but was half-stunned as he rebounded from the cold waxy bars. He sought another way to freedom and collided with other bars. He clawed frantically for his freedom and at last surrendered, slipped to the damp earth to lie huddled, sobbing, his body bruised, his mind maddened by the imprisonment from which he could never, never, never escape while his mortal life endured.

Weighted down with a massive guilt beyond evasion, Christian drifted once more into sleep. The evil laughter rocketed away over the mountain ridges to its own distant land of madness where he could never follow. But a torrent of evils would be loosed upon him in deadly succession. This he knew.

The dawn, bringing new light and warmth to the grove, revealed that his cage was but the thicket of trees. He felt as though he had not slept at all; and the night's terror remained as powerful. He was unable to dissect the dream from reality, nor could he ever.

CHAPTER EIGHTEEN

Christian devoured a handful of berries, gnawed at a strip of iron jerky as the sun flooded the land, burned off the dew, and warmed him, generating the swarms of flying insects of a new day. Pinsha seemed curiously remote, part of another life. Perhaps it was in dull reaction to the terror of the night; but he wished now to lose himself completely in the wilderness, to destroy the innocent no more. He caught up his horse and set out again on a southwesterly course, chosen, it may be, because he once heard that no man knew what lay between Chile and the Strait of Magellan, save that it was a complex of islands and channels that had never been explored.

He could not in his present state appreciate the late snows that dusted the forbidding upper reaches of the mountains, barren peaks poking through matted forests that clung like fur to their lower slopes. At his level the timber was open enough that through the feathered branches he could see without caring the glisten of countless lakes, one or two always in sight. Their edges often were bordered with beds of reeds or mudflats and meadows no man had ever trod. For half a day or more, he followed what appeared an ancient trail, though whether beaten by animal or human feet he could not tell.

His horror and revulsion from the experience of the night had faded. Too soon, the path disappeared into nothingness; and he must make his own passage forward through an unmarked region. In his path lay not only isolation—and no doubt oblivion—but there, too, lay the sea, the goal of every man with brine in his veins.

For several days he wandered onward, making more south than west; for he sought to pass through the great mountains which now were losing their stupendous height, though snows lay heavy upon their upper reaches. He camped one night near a basalt dike across which twin rivers thundered into the white fury of foam and spray into a common pool, each cascade festooned with a rainbow.

He worked higher into the mountains, threading fields of shrubs with tiny flowers for which Christian had no eye. He followed up a barren floodplain of graveled riverbed, riding slowly across what appeared to be a tossing sea of charcoal pumice and ash. A gleam attracted him and he discovered that he was traversing a true glacier, blanketed by rocks and detritus of seasonal floods, but ice still, a frozen river, a bitter vengeful stream in which there was no life, fearful of exposure to light and air, like the black river of his soul.

To his right as he worked up the black floodplain, there bore in upon his vision a dark ridge of mountain, capped by a lofty cornice of snow like creamed icing. To the south of it there appeared to be a low point, a gap, and he guided his horse toward it, allowing the mount to select its way as deliberately as it chose. He dismounted as it grew steeper, leading the animal across a perilous talus slope. There was no sound save theirs; for they were above the greenery; and all of life was bound nowhere save the eagles, half as great as condors, guarding the pass and inspecting this stranger who came from nowhere.

Breathing hard the cold fresh air, Christian led his horse across the leveling snowfield and found that they had topped out on the range, much sooner and more casually than he had hoped. Tumbled ridges, becoming lower in the western distance, fell away endlessly; but beyond them lay the sea, although before he could reach it he must pass torrents and rivers, mountains and ridges, and at last, inlets and straits.

Still leading his willing mount, he selected a cautious way downward, soon finding the bed of a thundering, mindless creek dashing in a southerly course. Keeping to the easier ridges, he followed it until, in a day or two, it eased its frenzied rush. Here Christian rode, alert to his surroundings but seeking ever the descent. The stream joined a larger, which flowed generally southwest and became a river whose course broadened imperceptibly until within a week or two or a month—he kept no track of time—it entered a long lake in which were giant fish of great number and fatness. Feasting along the way, he traveled the shoreline to the end and, by a steep, though luckily abbreviated gorge, to where the water bore through a range of low and forested hills. He reached still another body of water, and by drinking of it, Christian tasted salt.

It had now been two months or more, he supposed, since the disaster upon the great lake on the other side of the cordillera. He turned his horse loose upon a rich and extensive meadow watered by abundant springs and strode back to the water's edge.

CHAPTER NINETEEN

Christian rolled his belongings into a bundle and set out along the coast toward the west. The waterway would lead to a channel of greater dimension, perhaps eventually the sea. Vaguely he hoped to discover some Eden where he might dwell, remote from his kind, far from their God, where he could escape his apparent destiny and the evil that seemed to hover over him.

On the third day he arrived at a headland, marking the confluence of his inlet with a greater, bearing north and south. He climbed high ground and from its summit could see across the shining surface to swampy lowlands bordering its further shore. The shout of a girl startled him. It rose the several hundred feet from the beach below. To his surprise he caught a Mapuche word or two—her people were Araucanian! She was a member of a fishing party, for drawn up on the shingled beach were half a dozen craft, whose mode of manufacture he could not discern. Their gray pointed shapes reached toward as many driftwood fires, about them a score of people.

He lay concealed until dusk faded into darkness and then a few hours more, measured by the wheeling of the Southern Cross through the black and moonless sky.

At the water's edge he stripped off his clothes, his body alabaster in the gloom. He laid the garments and his bundle carefully atop a bleached log, so arranged that he could find them readily in the darkness. Christian stepped cautiously into the water. It was cold, but he could endure it. With powerful breaststrokes, careful not to splash, he swam soundlessly along the shore, around the point and northward until he came opposite the camp. The glow from the dying fires had all but disappeared, the pungent smoke whipped away by the rising wind. No one was in sight. His feet struck the bottom and he raised slowly, pausing to allow the dripping to still, then waded quietly ashore among the beached craft. Using his sense of touch more than vision, Christian inspected the boats, of the familiar three-plank construction, though they proved too large and heavy for one man to float. He feared they were all built alike.

However, to his joy he discovered a dugout, small enough that he could manage it alone. Christian untied the rawhide mooring line and slowly, cautiously, slid the vessel with its paddles into the bay. He slipped once more into the frigid water and quietly swam out, pushing the boat away from the land. He dared not pull himself aboard until well down toward the point, where he lifted himself in and paddled to his cache. Swiftly he found the bleached log, dressed himself, grateful for his clothing's warmth. He tossed his bundle aboard, paddled away from the land, heading south. As a pirate, he grinned to himself, he was once more a success. At least he was seaborne once more.

A storm broke just at dawn, rain driven in sheets by the wild west wind, making it all but impossible to keep the dugout headed south. Hard against the land the water was calm and the Englishman drove the boat into a secluded cove, behind a gray outcropping of streaming rock, and pulled it far up on the beach, hidden from curious eyes. The rain would wash out the scratchings he had made; and he was secure, though he dared not light a fire; for in the dampness the smell of wood smoke could travel many miles. He ate raw fish and huddled in the shelter of a great tree, wrapped in his sodden poncho. He slept almost the whole day through.

Late in the afternoon he inspected the boat more closely. It had no keel, but a small blocked indentation suggested that a mast sometimes was used. With his knife Christian cut two poles, with strips of leather lashing the shorter across the longer. He stepped the makeshift mast, and having no other material for a sail, bent the poncho to the yard with rawhide thongs. After dark he set off southward up the sound.

For several nights he worked his way, concealing the boat and his camps during daylight. The rain continued but so did the westerly winds; and they drove him faster than he could have paddled. Soon, by the lift and swell of the water, he realized he was nearing a channel leading directly to the Pacific. Christian felt an almost uncontrollable pull, a lure to test it. He had no reason for exploring the strait, except his seaman's inquisitive mind. He bore across the channel three leagues to a shingled beach where he rested, and then continued westward to still another extremity of his land, where it broke into a spray of islets and half-submerged rocks. He landed and climbed a stony peak to survey his wild surroundings.

To landward was a wilderness of broken, forested wastelands. On the south he could detect half-drowned peaks on the far side of the channel, and to the southwest, well out to sea, a dark long shape of an island with its white spray of breakers on its northern point. Christian knew that this land must be the westerly fragment of the continental mass, breasting the Pacific. The sighting sparked his restlessness to explore, though he had no reason to suppose it would differ from what he had left behind.

By now he had widened his crude sail with sealskins sewn as he had observed the natives do, and it was broad enough to draw his craft steadily onward in a moderate breeze. When the general westerly had become a northwesterly, he embarked on a fine reach of sailing that moved the dugout well; and within that daylight, he made his landfall upon an island that seemed barren of human habitation.

Here he might cast aside that caution that had become a part of him during the long days working south when he was wary of encountering native bands of possibly hostile impulse. Over a period of several weeks, Christian explored the island, determining its configuration; and he found that he was not the first to visit it. Hollowed into its westward nose, he discovered a cave. Within it there were human skeletons, seven of them, laid out in a tidy row. On the beach below was the wreckage of what once had been a ship's boat, now smashed by the surf to splinters.

CHAPTER TWENTY

The cave was broad and shallow with a roof sufficiently elevated to permit a man to stand upright. It faced the sea, its floor seventy or eighty feet above the beating surf. The skeletons were garbed in tattered remnants of clothing; and in the rear of the retreat lay heaped materials, such as men might salvage from a foundering vessel. In one corner, a canvas sailcloth seemed sound. Lines were coiled in a careful, seaman's way, boathooks and other metal objects coated thinly with rust from the salt air.

For a long time Christian stared out to sea, the friendly and hostile, boisterous and calm, honest and deceptive, cruel and gentle, the changing sea, throwing its rubbish onto iron coasts like this. Who were these men? What had they experienced? The sea always won. These men had clearly lost. This every sailor knows and shrugs off. He continues to challenge her because he can do nothing else; he becomes addicted. And still there were those who believed in a God, a loving God, who watches over and cares for his creatures! Ha! The sea, the instrument of this God, was merciless, luring, deceiving; then, it smashed its victims. The faithful and faithless perish alike.

Christian rose stiffly to his feet and sorted the equipment he had found, the still-sound canvas, the lines, an oar, a compass, although he rejected the primitive sextant since he had no timepiece to give it usefulness. Atop his pile of salvage he tossed a notebook and pencils he recovered from the dusty floor, not knowing why he saved them.

With a tug at his forelock, the time-honored tiff of the foretop man, Christian quit the cave and its dead. He paddled the dugout round the point and made camp.

Where to go? Christian, perhaps at this time the freest human being upon the globe, yet found himself bound by his prejudices and his sullen awareness of the "stick" hanging over him. He could not return north, for the disasters he had survived and memory of Pinsha would not permit it. Neither could he put to sea without a suitable craft. He must point South, for there was no other direction left.

Utilizing the persistent westerlies and a fresh canvas sail, Christian bore southeast by east at dawn, bound for a headland he could make out on the southern rim of the channel, which forced into the continent eastward. He knew the risk of crossing by daylight but had no recourse since the winds would die with the sun. He could hold the dugout off the land, though close in while inspecting it for human traces, and outrun any pursuing craft. By evening he skirted the northern coast of a sizeable island. He had observed no sign of life, and with driftwood made a tiny smokeless fire, warmed himself, toasted a strip of fish, then huddled into a cleft in the stone forest.

How long he slept he did not know, but he awoke a prisoner. In the murky half-light, silent figures surrounded him. Two prodded him upright with stone-tipped lances and inspected his dugout and its limited cargo. They built up the fire, and he saw it would be hopeless to even attempt to flee. He quietly studied his captors. Since they could not understand him, they ignored him as they squatted, preparing a rude shellfish breakfast, toasting the clams over the coals of his fire. One tossed over a roasted shellfish, and he devoured the hot flat flesh and found it good. 'Twas odd that upon this sparse-inhabited coast he had run afoul of perhaps the only band of nomads in the land.

Of the dozen or so Indians, all but two were armed with lances, crudely made with heavy stone heads. The others carried across their shoulders short bows and a clutch of arrows. Their hair was banged across broad foreheads, they wore it long behind, unkempt and tangled. None was painted or tattooed. Most wore a mantle of curious manufacture across their shoulders; it was not until later that Christian realized these had been woven from the hair of their long-legged shaggy dogs.

Despite their primitive dress, these muscular Indians exhibited the vigor and facial expressions of other men, ranging from the intelligent to the stupid. One of the more alert inspected his dugout so carefully the Englishman felt sure he could have built a duplicate himself.

With breakfast finished, his captors motioned him into his craft in which the interested native rode, facing backward until Christian indicated he should turn about, his open countenance assuring the other that he had nothing to fear at his back. The Indians strained and heaved two of their heavy craft into the water, each fashioned of three rudely-shaped planks, more crudely made than any mainland boats he had seen. They leaked so stupendously that one or two Indians must constantly bail them to keep them afloat. His dugout, far handier and watertight, made the indicated beach some time before the others.

Clouds lay thick and the sea was slowly making up. Christian was glad when the others arrived and led him, no less a prisoner though he was unbound, up a greasy path through the timber to an open *meseta* where the people had established a temporary camp. A dozen or more beehive huts were scattered about. Each had a hole at the top for smoke from the tiny central fire, and they were scarcely the length of a man's body and so low one must kneel when inside to avoid the roof.

Perhaps two dozen people were scattered about the clearing, including a sprinkling of children, the women bulkier generally than the men, though apparently of a more amiable disposition. Now they clustered about to observe him closely. Christian could do little but submit to their curious inspection passively. His eyes scanned the village and quickened as they fell upon one woman who wore a Mapuche headband, her features suggesting she was foreign to these others. When the crowd had thinned, Christian tested her with what he hoped might prove her dialect. Instantly her entire face lightened; and she replied in the rolling cadences of Mapuche. Of middle age, she was more slender and tidier than the others, and her expression seemed more companionable.

Christian asked in her tongue, "How came you here?" He still was neither bound nor otherwise confined, a prisoner more by remoteness of the place than by restriction. She laughed shortly.

"I might ask you that, since you speak Mapuche," she replied. "Some years ago I was half-prisoner, half-traded-for on Chiloé, the big island to the north. Now I am Chono."

"These people?"

"Yes. Chono. So they call themselves. I am one of them now."

"If I could slip away, perhaps I could return you to your people?"

She scanned his face, then looked away.

"I was born Mapuche," she conceded. "I think often of the people and how I lived so many seasons ago. But I am Chono now. I could not be married there, ever, for none would have me. I am content here."

Christian looked about the clearing, then at the woman.

"Tell me, what is to happen to me? Do they torture? Slay?"

Again she laughed. "None of those things. They neither torture nor kill those they seize—they sell them as slaves to the Mapuche. Often they war with the people of the south to capture men and women for the slave trade, but they do not torture nor kill because that would lose them the trade; and they have come to depend upon it."

"And I?"

She surveyed him frankly.

"You will bring a good price. Perhaps a plank boat, much wheat or barley, ax heads—you are young and strong."

She offered him a bowl of seal meat floating in liquid oil. He drank it and found it fishy to the taste but not unpleasant.

"How did you learn our tongue?" she asked.

"I was years among the people." Christian told her briefly how he had come to the Chono islands. She listened, her compassion awakened for this strange man who shared a connection with her past. She wished to help him, for in a way he was her relative.

"Tonight there will be a dance, a barbarous dance. Nothing to drink, for the Chono have no *chicha,* but the dance will continue until all are exhausted and in deep slumber. If you wish, you may go. I will collect and bring your things to your boat. Because it is faster than the Chono boats, none can catch you if you are careful."

"What will happen to you, if you do this for me?"

She smiled at him.

"I shall be beaten."

Christian shook his head. "That I could not permit," he said. "Rather than that, I would stay."

She forced another bowl, a Mapuche bowl, of meat and oil upon him.

"You will go," she directed, with impassive certainty. "My man, Dalco, is not a bad man. He is Chono, a *cacique*. He will start to beat me, but then he will sleep; and when he awakens, I will have hot food ready for him. He will forgive, or forget, which is the same thing; and it will be done with. You will be gone. The punishment means nothing to me. For you it is a free life."

The primitive dance came to pass until at long last the camp was silent. The Mapuche woman swiftly gathered and rewrapped Christian's bundle. Hurriedly she led him down to the sea. The moon cast its light through the fog. She tossed the bundle into Christian's dugout. She untied its line, handing it to him. Christian placed both hands upon her shoulders and stared into her face, her eyes pools of blackness.

"You will come with me?" he invited her, softly.

She shook her head, a tiny spray of droplets from the rain falling about her shoulders.

"No, Lebitureo," she said, remembering his Indian name. "I am Chono."

Christian leaned forward and kissed her on the cheek, the gesture strange to her but whose significance she grasped. With no further word, Christian shoved the dugout into the water and paddled silently away from the shore, the woman's form tall, proud, motionless, until it faded into the gloom.

CHAPTER TWENTY-ONE

From that black night forward and for nearly two years, Christian saw no other human beings except once, at a distance, a ragged settlement soon blocked off by storm and cloud. Soon he came to possess a rudimentary knowledge of the almost endless maze of channels, islands, inlets, bays, and sounds of the most spectacular land-sea environment he could have ever imagined.

He was no geologist, but he soon perceived that the cordillera became less elevated the farther south he journeyed, that the islands he voyaged among were but the near-drowned peaks of the descending mountain range. He reasoned that the central valleys of the range, running north and south, must be reflected by a strait or straits continuing as long as the peaks themselves were visible. He worked out a pattern for the geography, at first bewildering, and discovered that his hypothesis was correct. In the notebook from the cave, he sketched rude maps as he wandered southward, estimating distances and heights and as a seaman of long experience, doing so with a fair degree of accuracy.

This endeavor so consumed his attention that it all but dislodged the bitterness from his heart or, rather, drove it deeper. It remained as leaden baggage, but for long periods he forgot it; and when he did remember, he vaguely hoped only that he had finally managed to outrun his "stick."

There came a day when, rotten and its remaining rigging sagging and worthless, a half-submerged wreck told Christian that he must have entered the western waters of the Magellan Strait near the lower tip of South America, the first bit of geography he could positively identify on his southward odyssey. Here, in the Pacific, the westerlies blew strong and almost without cessation, and he recalled those wracking, bitter weeks when with Captain Bligh on the *Bounty* they had tried so unsuccessfully to round the Cape to the south. They might have had no better fortune in the Strait, yet Christian wondered. Many vessels had traversed it, he was aware, before the passage around Cape Horn was discovered by Drake. Numbers of ships were wrecked. But for a captain who knew the channels, the Strait might yet prove an alternative to the terrible seas below the Horn.

Christian dared not attempt to cross the broad and windswept western entry to this waterway in his unwieldy craft, for it was twenty-five leagues at very least to the southern land. Rather he explored to the southeast until it narrowed, then easily made the forest-grown coast of Tierra del Fuego, where he found some food plentiful but a puzzling paucity of seals. There had been scores of thousands upon rookeries along the coast to the north.

On the third day of his cruising the southern shore, he came upon a village, the first he had seen so close since the Chono camp. It was broad day, and he paddled boldly to the gravel beach below it.

He had been so long without the sight of a human face, the sound of a voice, that it appeared to him simply the time to return to the world of people, however primitive. A man wearies of running when there is no cause; the delusion that he was a man accursed had dissipated, partially. So he nosed the worn dugout in upon the shore. Two or three strange craft lay beside light canoes of beech bark, slabs sewn together with whale baleen and caulked. They appeared seaworthy.

In an indentation of the thick forest lay a haphazard cluster of huts, oval in shape, with doorways covered with ferns to keep out the weather. Fires burned in each of them, and he was to find that keeping the flames going was a constant task because the making of fire was difficult for these people. Like the Chono, they were primitively clothed, wearing very little. A few dogs bounced about, barking. The men were armed with lances, a few with bows, and three or four with rude harpoons. Although all carried weapons, they did not threaten this stranger. One muscular fellow idly scratched his head and leaned upon the haft of a harpoon, its head down, the universal gesture of peace. He stepped forward to help Christian beach his craft. The Englishman grinned his thanks, smoothing with his hand his own thick beard.

"You hunt'm seal?" demanded the Indian.

So unexpected was the query in English that Christian shook his head before realizing that the young man had spoken in that tongue.

"No," he shook his head, wondering. "No hunt seals. No hunt anything."

The Indian gravely inspected his dugout, taking his time, while Christian stared about him. Most of the others squatted nearby, silent. A woman or two lurked in the background, one occasionally carrying an infant upon her hip.

"Me guide. Good guide. You hunt'm seal?" asked the young man once more.

Again Christian shook his head.

"No," he replied, patiently. "No hunt seal."

Christian squatted by the bow of the dugout, waiting. The cluster of Indians remained silent. Even the children grew quiet in the presence of the white stranger. For long the stillness continued, eerily, although no one appeared hostile in any way. No one noticed the rain. Christian felt somehow it would be polite to allow another to break the silence.

The Indian at last shifted his position. The courtesy period was fulfilled. He grinned at Christian. "You like eat?"

While not particularly hungry, the Englishman understood the importance of native customs and nodded. "Come," directed the Indian, leading him to a larger hut than the others. He dropped to his hands and knees and crawled in, thrusting aside the ferns with sprang back into place. Christian followed, finding the interior dark at first, but dry and not as smoky as he had feared. He sat cross-legged on a hide next to his host. A woman, heavy with child, silently turned a chunk of seal meat upon the coals. A small boy sat wide-eyed in the background, silent. The woman retrieved the meat, deftly cut it into two equal pieces with a large mussel shell, tossed half to the skin before her husband, the rest before Christian. The meat was moderately well cooked, and the Englishman carefully followed the procedure of his host. He picked it up with his fingers, ignoring the stinging hot flesh, biting off a chunk, wiping his greasy fingers on the seal skin, and when he had finished, belching as had his host. The men being sated, the woman silently cooked a second chunk for herself.

A stretching frame propped in the rear held an otter skin and another a sealskin, both being dried and receiving some tanning benefit from the smoke in the hut.

"You like sleep now?" asked the Indian, grinning broadly. Two of his front teeth were missing, the others gleamed whitely. Christian shook his head.

After a moment he pointed at his host. "Your name?" he asked. The Indian not comprehending, Christian pointed to himself. "Fletcher," he said. "My name Fletcher."

Understanding at last, the other said, "Lolet." When Christian said it after him, Lolet pointed to the otter skin, then to himself; for he was named after the animal. "Cap'n call me Jack," he added, proudly. "Me Jack, you Fletcher, eh?" He laughed triumphantly. "What Fletcher?" he asked sobering suddenly. Christian drew an arrow from a sealskin quiver suspended near the doorway and gestured to indicate Fletcher was the maker of arrows. "Ah, *annaqua*, eh?" Jack seemed to understand. "*Annaqua*. Fletcher."

So commenced Christian's education among the Alacaluf, one of three tribes of Tierra del Fuego, the most remote peoples on the face of the earth, primitive and yet akin to all others on every continent. Christian found companionship there, for what he was capable of imagining, his hosts, too, could conceive; what they feared, he could learn to dread; their skills became his skills, their tongue his, although only to a rudimentary degree.

The mystery of Jack's English remained. Christian found that the man was the only individual of the band who could speak any English; and while proud of his accomplishment, he would not explain how he had acquired the skill.

Because the weather in the region was so foul, Christian learned with amusement the things the Alacaluf did to improve it, not that they often succeeded according to his observation. They believed that bad weather was caused by throwing sand into the water and shellfish into the fire. When far from home, therefore, the boatmen might eat mussels, but they had to transport the shells to dry land before discarding them. Ashes thrown upon tempestuous seas could bring fair winds, perhaps even clear skies briefly. If a snowstorm blew in from the south, a handful of feathers tossed into the fire would turn the snow to rain, swing the wind around, and probably bring fair weather.

Hunting and fishing were the prime concern of the Alacaluf. Sea lions, if caught ashore, they netted, harpooned, or clubbed. Dogs they trained to corner otters in rock crevices. Sometimes deer were hunted, though they were few. The cormorant chase required special skills. Hunters with blackened faces and hands crept upon a rookery at night and caught one bird after another, thrusting its head beneath its wing, so it would not squawk until enough were taken. Fish the Alacaluf often caught, sometimes with the help of dogs; the women gathered mussels and sea urchins, the food supply augmented by a few wild plants and berries. At these pursuits Christian kept busy with the Alacaluf until one dawn, some months after he had settled in.

He pushed out through the doorway upon Jack's call, confused by sleep, and looked at him questioningly. He said nothing but gestured toward the water. Christian saw standing in toward the beach a brig of about 90 tons, her fore course and mainsail yards braced to a light westerly, drawing full. As he watched, speechless, this apparition out of the night, out of his past, the wind was spilled from her sails and she glided in beyond the breeze. A few yards from the beach her hook dropped, the great anchor swinging her stern around. Christian could read painted there in block letters: *Adder*, STONINGTON—a vessel from Connecticut and not, as was his initial fear, from England. Jack, grinning from ear to ear, gestured toward the vessel: "Cap'n come!" he cried gleefully. "We hunt'm seal! Much whiskey! Much drunk."

CHAPTER TWENTY-TWO

The next day Christian accompanied Jack on board the *Adder*. The Indian skipped to the quarterdeck where a lean and sallow individual in dirty garb lounged beside a three-pounder, his hair, black and stringy, framing his face beneath the officer's hat. "Cap'n," explained Jack to Christian. "Hunt'm seal. 'Allo, Cap'n!" he hailed. "Jack ready to go!"

The captain grunted, said nothing, his shifty gaze flicked over Christian. "Who in blazes are you?" he demanded, with a touch of whine, not of beggary, but of disdain.

"A friend of Jack's," replied Christian. He suppressed an impulse to retort more sharply, knowing that he was as defenseless as Jack. The captain shot a thick stream of tobacco juice over the side where it plunked into the clean sea with a splash. He ignored Christian and spoke to the Indian, his whine even in pitch, neither rising nor falling more than a decibel.

"Got to have lots of seals, Jack," he rasped, his voice penetrating like a saw into hickory. "You fin'um seals, hear?"

Jack chortled gleefully, nodding.

"Me good guide! Know where lots *harkasi*, like before. All you want, Cap'n. We drink'um whiskey, eh?" Again the captain spat over the rail, wiped his whiskered chin.

He grinned sourly at the Indian. "We cotch enough to fill th' *Adder*, an' you'll get enough whiskey to make your whole village drunk fer a week." Christian estimated the crew at about thirty men, including those primarily seal killers and skinners, most of whom apparently doubled as deckhands. In addition to the captain, Obadiah Hanks, and the two mates, there was a foreman of the hunters, a grizzled, leathery individual called Ad by the officers.

At this season there was plenty of daylight so far south, full darkness lasting only about five hours, from 10:00 P.M. until 3:00 A.M.; and the brig's people determined to waste no moment of light. She lifted her hook with the dawn, making use of oarsmen to tow her beyond the point where her sails could fill, and heading then along the labyrinth of rocks, islets, and channels northwest, seeking to round

Desolation Island and hunt along the broken and dangerous southerly coast where, Christian learned, the fur seals had established the greatest number of rookeries in times past. He and two young men of the village shipped with Jack. It was good to feel the deck beneath his feet again, though he gave no hint of his true profession.

For three days the *Adder* lay off Cape Deseado, unable to round the spray-drenched iron headland because of persistent westerlies, then seized advantage of a brief shift in the winds and doubled the point, beginning a search among the incredibly complex fragments of islands, rocks, and storm-lashed coasts for "the rooks," as Hanks called them. Laconic-appearing though he was, he was stoked with nervous frets as several days passed without rookeries being located. Jack only grinned and promised each day, until one dawn he pointed excitedly toward the coast where Christian could see a rock covered with movement, like a carcass alive with maggots.

Instantly the brig was brought about and run in as close as Obadiah Hanks dared. Boats were put over and tumbled full of killers and skinners. They pulled for the islet, against which the breakers boomed, driven by the southern gales, sending white surf half the height of the tallest points. Christian watched from the ship as the boats darted into a cove and were pulled onto a shingle in the lee of the wind.

Hours later, the boats came into view filled to overflowing with bundles of skins of all sizes and shapes. After unloading their cargo, they returned to pick up another load from the massive hunt.

Suddenly the weather changed to bitter cold with a driving rain and slanting needles of sleet. The captain mentally calculated the take.

"Not near enough haul to sail for Canton," he grumbled.

Skins that might bring two dollars each at Mystic or Boston would fetch ten or twenty dollars apiece in China, and a cargo for trade items loaded at South China ports would again bring a handsome profit in New England. There was money to be made all around, but disaster if the holds weren't filled to capacity. Money was Obadiah Hanks' god, if he had one. Before it he groveled, and for profit he bartered his soul—and by so doing, believed himself righteous and worthy of his breed as, in fact, he may have been.

In pursuit of profit, now he drove the *Adder* in a tireless search among the islands and reefs where always before there had been rookeries. He had not the wit to realize that if he, the hunter, did not assure the continuation of fur seals by curtailing his greed, God could not do so, that if there were few seals now, it was because of his own and others' stupidity. Instead he blamed Jack, since one of his kind must always blame someone else. He charged Jack with unwillingness to guide the *Adder* to fresh rookeries, purposely misleading him.

His dour, suspicious, evil mind sent him round the Isla Santa Inés, to beat back up the Magellan Strait toward the Alacaluf settlement, not to return Jack to his people, but to complete his hunt and pick up what otter and other skins the Indians might have gathered. By then the brig stowed only a few more than 10,000 seal skins, one-third her capacity.

Christian hurried ashore in the first boat to reach the settlement, eager to have done with the *Adder* and her merciless crew, to seek some secluded place to sort out his tumbled thoughts, this new evidence of the futility, the lack of value of life, his own in particular. He could hear the whiskey being broken out. Leaping ashore he searched out his dugout, paddled it beyond earshot of the brig, into the solace of the wilderness.

For two long antarctic days he remained apart, roasting a fish but eating nothing else until, in the twilight of the second day, he saw a receding sail against the setting sun. With the ship gone, he determined to return to the village, to Jack and the natives who had become over a period of months his people.

He saw no smoke overlying the sodden community as he rounded the cape. No children played upon the beach. There was no sign of life. Rolling awash at water's edge was a grotesque body, which Christian knew before turning over was Jack, his neck purpled where he had been garroted or hanged. About the settlement were heaped the bodies of the slain—men, elderly, children. All women were gone. Vanished.

Christian cursed that disappearing sail long and bitterly. He swore at the measureless brutality of the drunken sealers, who finding no more rookeries to obliterate had wiped out this peaceful, helpless village, slaying the men in a drunken holocaust, stealing the women whom they would surely use up and discard upon some barren islet.

Rain drenched his head and coursed down his face and beard, but he was oblivious. He had reached once more the base rock of his soul, through this ultimate disaster. At Tierra del Fuego he had reached the known world; still his "stick" hung over him. There was no escape. His curse was to live, while others suffered and must perish. Beyond this land there was nothing save the eternal seas raging against barren and lifeless rocks. "*Laich*," once again the phrase of mystery came faintly to his ears, as with the wisp of breeze. "*Laich* . . . ," but Christian heard no more, for he shook it off.

A rift of cloud to the northward cast the light from the waning sun, beckoning, calling. He shoved the dugout away from the shore, raised the tattered sail and drove with the snow southeastward out of this land of murder and cruelty. Out of these gloomy mountains and forests and ice fields, he rode the craft toward the sunlight, the grassed plains, the sandy beaches of the eastern portion of the archipelago, toward a new way of life. But he was convinced he took the evil with him still.

BOOK III

The LORD sent out a great wind into the sea,
and there was a mighty tempest in the sea,
so that the ship was like to be broken.

JONAH 1:4

CHAPTER ONE

The sullen green cape lay behind the boat, its dingy timber splotched with brilliance, as though to mark the division between gloom and light, evil remembered and something less. Although Christian did not know it, he had rounded Land's End, the southernmost cape of the American continental mass, beyond which lay only the Fuegian islands and the gale-swept seas.

He bore northeasterly now for half a degree of longitude, he supposed. A bulky sea lion, nodding with the wavelets in his bower of the sea, drifted past. Coveys of gold and white penguins exploded in torrents of foam and fright as his craft glided among them. With a swirling boil of sea water, three black-and-white creatures surfaced so close they rocked the dugout: porpoises, most likely, of some new kind. Christian landed on an island, with flints struck a fire, and roasted strips of fish. Before dawn he put into the Strait once more, heading north now for several days. He saw smoke from folds of the land to the south, perhaps communication between bands of nomads. On the fourth or fifth day after leaving the southern cape, he passed a narrows five miles or less in breadth, then put into a bay on the northern coast and beached by a rivulet seeping from the tableland beyond.

Here, for a reason he did not examine, but in obedience to some inner urging, he carefully wrapped his notebook of penciled charts of channels, islands, and sounds of the western coast of the continent and placed it in a cavity, which he lined with flat stones, taking care to protect it against moisture. Atop the cache he built a cairn, visible from the sea. Why he did this he did not know. He never intended to return. But these notes represented part of himself; he could not cast them off.

When he had finished his task, he squatted before his tiny fire in the twilight.

He heard the rattle of stone behind him and spun to see a fur-clad figure arc a bow and aim a stone-tipped arrow at his belly.

Christian returned a gaze as bold as the other's stare. He was not surprised. He had undergone much violence and savagery; and Christian accurately gauged his danger, and was quite alive to it. But he had become in many ways a hard man since his days with Kolapel; and now he waited, his forearms on his knees, his hands hanging loose, seemingly impassive. However, it was not submission which gripped him nor indecision. Some sense told him his opponent was determined only to preserve himself. This savage had seized and meant to hold the initial advantage, for it is only thus that wild men preserve their lives.

Christian smiled, the universally understood gesture of friendliness. The other lowered the arrow a trifle, then raised it again, with fresh purpose as though determined finally upon murder. He was stayed by a shout.

Both men involuntarily swung around. Horses and people exploded over the lip of the bluff, several hundred, including women, children, and the aged, as well as warriors.

A broad-faced rider splashed his piebald pony through the water and pulled up before the agonists, a lance balanced across his wooden saddle. He sat upon the animal easily, carelessly, an expert horseman. He demanded something, and the warrior shook his head, muttering a brief reply. The horseman fingered the greased rawhide of a coiled *boleador* tied back of his saddle. Then he jerked his head, spun the pony, and goaded it forward, the young man motioning Christian to follow. They threaded the chattering throng busily erecting a *toldería* of hide-covered family tents, about twenty in all, of guanaco skins sewn together, smeared with a mixture of grease and red paint, draped over rows of stakes. Fires were already being made under the skin shelters.

To Christian they appeared a robust race, taller than Europeans, some of the men reaching almost seven feet. Their bodies were muscular and hardy, their eyes lively, teeth extremely white and regular, and a few had beards.

Christian arrived within a ring encircling the biggest fire of the camp. The horseman dismounted, turning his animal over to a young woman. He muttered something and one of the men jabbed Christian with a lance. The Englishman realized he was expected to say something. He tried the Araucanian dialect, but the instant anger made him switch to Alacaluf. This stirred no hint of recognition. Finally he lapsed into Spanish, which one or two seemed to grasp. "*Soy cristiano*," he explained, in an unconscious play upon his name.

"*Claro*," muttered one of his captors.

"What are your people called," he asked in the same language.

The other tossed his young head and replied, "Ahonicanka." After a moment he added, "Tschonek," then, "Tehuelche." This last word Christian understood for he had heard of these wild horsemen who ranged from La Plata on the north all the way to the Strait. He only knew that they were bitter enemies of the Araucanians and of the Spanish as well.

Christian answered a question as to how he came there briefly, saying he had escaped from the sealers, arousing approving grunts when translated, for those piratical seamen generated hatred even here. The young warriors were restless for they had come far that day, and the women had not yet prepared food.

"Can you fight?" one demanded suddenly. Christian nodded, unsure of the intent, supposing he referred to war. It was a more immediate challenge, however. The warrior sloughed off his guanaco robe, revealed an athletic build in bronze, clothed only in a *chiripa* breechcloth. In his right hand he loosely clutched a formidable knife. He swept up a hide and began to wrap it carefully around his left forearm, crouched lower, gesturing for Christian to prepare for a duel.

Clumsily Christian wrapped a hide to his left arm, borrowing a *facon*, or gaucho knife fourteen inches in length, from another warrior. Imitating his opponent, he held it underhand, like the abbreviated sword it was. Christian had never received more than cursory instruction in use of an edged weapon. Now he stood flat-footed while his catlike antagonist circled craftily, occasionally twirling his knife, so to loosen muscles or confuse his enemy. Christian ignored the weapon, staring into the other's eyes, for he had long since learned that a man can conceal his intent from neither his eyes nor his hands. Closer and closer the other circled, his black eyes inscrutable, searching for an opportunity to slash and rake. His right hand, clutching the *facon*, thrust a bit forward now, trembled slightly. Christian made ready for the deadly stroke.

A shouted command, "*Ai! Ai! Wati!*" came from behind. His enemy instantly straightened, dropping the weapon arm, and disgustedly turned aside.

Startled, Christian spun to confront an Indian of commanding presence who clutched his robe tightly around his muscular body. He spoke in Spanish, better than the others. "*Christiano?*" he asked.

Christian nodded, tossed his knife to the Indian who had loaned him the weapon.

It was obvious that the old man was a *cacique*, or headman at least. The deference paid him was unmistakable.

"*Pashlik ya*," said the old man, motioning for Christian to accompany him. "*Vamos a comer*—let's eat." Christian followed him silently, toward his *toldo*. Among the dwellings the smell of roasting meat supplied a companionable atmosphere that smothered all notions of enemies, strife, and killing. The declining sun touched the bluffs with red; a twilight chill had already set in.

Before the largest *toldo*, the Indian invited Christian to sit with him. A woman brought them meat and they ate hungrily, in silence mainly, although Christian learned his host's name was Lenketrú, that he had two wives and several children, that all Tehuelches paid him deference. Under his protection Christian would be accepted as a warrior so long as he could fulfill the role.

"*Cristiano?*" demanded Lenketrú again, when they had finished.

"*Cristiano*," agreed Christian, nodding vigorously.

"*Yo, tambien*—I am too," grinned the Indian, making a crude but unmistakable sign of the Cross. Christian was startled to see that ancient gesture of civilization in this wilderness. Perhaps Lenketrú had learned it from itinerant priests sent to work beyond the frontier.

As Christian later discovered, Lenketrú had two sons, Toki and Orleke, both revealing vestiges of their father's strengths, but as unlike as darkness and day. They frequently dropped by, to squat and eat in silence, observing Christian's every action. Orleke was like the full-blown day, merry, full of pranks and laughter; and with him the Englishman felt he would soon be friends. Toki was moody, glowering, and silent most of the time. Both were adept in the arts of the Tehuelche: the skills of war, of fighting, of hunting and roving.

The first night Lenketrú led Christian to sleeping quarters behind the screen of hides, tossing him skins to rest upon. Outside a dog barked. A dolphin, near the shore, leapt from the water and flopped noisily back into it; then, there befell a great quiet as the people and the land and the water slept.

CHAPTER TWO

Fletcher Christian awoke to a new world, that of the nomadic, joyous, murderous, reckless, far-ranging hunters of the Patagonian plateaus, a world freer still than he had known, unconfined by elaborate convention or hoary customs, as free as the ceaseless wind and the driving dust and the heat and the cold.

Lenketrú gave him horses of the knob-kneed, bucket-headed variety native to those wastes along with a horseman's accoutrements, the Englishman was eager to set about learning to hunt the swift rhea and shy guanaco.

One day Lenketrú showed Christian his armor, a coat of stiffened leather, enough layers to stop a lance, a helmet of bull hide, and a circular painted shield of several thicknesses of rawhide. The Indian pointed to where an arrow had struck but failed to penetrate. "*Kelz, kelz,*" grinned the *cacique*; and Christian agreed that it was good.

More than their strength and vigor, it was the self-reliant, noble demeanor of these barbarians that attracted Christian. A weaker, lesser people might have seized upon him to force his submission. They could have made him a slave, but Christian had been generally accepted as an equal by these people who had no need to bolster their self-assurance at the expense of an easy victim.

Their lives centered around the horse, although the people had known this useful creature less than a century. The Tehuelches had many horses and a few mules. The older, more docile animals were used by women and children in moving camp and other domestic chores; but the men each had a string of good horses, some schooled for war, others for hunting, and still others for the simple endurance required by their constant migrations. As a hunting society, they moved frequently to fresh game fields, although their natural restlessness also was a factor.

One dawn the horses were driven in, some saddled for the men, others packed with towering bundles of camp equipage atop which perched a child or oldster amid a tempestuous scene that gradually became orderly as Lenketrú led the way to a beaten trail to the north. They wound up steep bluffs to the gale-swept plateau. A dusting of snow lay on the plain; nothing spread before them but undulating monotony, scrubby *jarillo* brush, and in the frozen distance, black ranges with few distinguishable features. Four days the ragged procession ambled northward before dropping through a cleft in an escarpment to the broad river valley the Tehuelche called Chikrookaik. Christian could smell salt marshes to the east. Even the river tasted brackish and the coast could not be far.

"*Ai*," Lenketrú greeted the white man at dawn. "Today we will hunt guanaco or maybe ostrich." They shared a strip of meat, half-roasted.

"*Aaiyehh!*" screamed Lenketrú, so suddenly his cry startled Christian. "*Aaaiyehh!*" he repeated, passing among the *toldos*, awakening the camp, calling out his decision to hunt. The women roused themselves, cooked breakfast-meat for their men; and the *tolderia* came to life. Christian mounted the hunting animal Lenketrú indicated; and the horsemen quitted the community at a canter to warm themselves, one horse bucking with the cold, to the glee of the men.

The party headed for the high plateaus. Toki and another young man, equally sullen, took dogs and bounded away, followed by other hunters in pairs, scattering to surround the game. On a great semicircle the teams of horsemen fanned out, carrying bundles of firewood to light when they reached the starting point. When the ring appeared complete, Lenketrú ordered fires lit, 200 yards apart. He motioned his riders into a long crescent, advancing over the plain while the distant horsemen drew inward, driving before them bands of startled guanacos and scurries of the small ostriches of Patagonia. Slender-legged creatures, the fleet guanacos resembled the miniature humpless camels they in fact were, about three and one-half feet tall, tan in color, with lighter underparts. Upon them the Tehuelche mainly depended for survival.

Between horsemen and their dogs was abundant space at the outset for the wild creatures to escape; but most ran straight ahead, away from their pursuers, toward the center of the mighty trap. The game bounded in frightened leaps for a few hundred yards, paused, then all took flight for another brief run, while the rheas darted more swiftly and more erratically. Nor were these the only game driven. Christian thought he detected a brown streak to his left. Then he saw another, and this time there was no mistake. He called Lenketrú's attention to it, but the *cacique* had already observed the creature. "*Gol!*" he grinned. "Puma—*leon*," the tawny lion of the Americas. Three of them, fleeing the yapping dogs, bounded into the circle.

The trap closed swiftly now. Christian could plainly see the oncoming horsemen, galloping, driving before them bounding flocks of animals and racing ostriches whose stubby wings were set like studding sails.

Not all of the hunters were engaged against guanacos and ostriches. Orleke and a few others rode boldly down upon the crouching pumas. The Englishman saw the chief's son draw a *bola perida* from his belt, swing it vigorously, and ride down upon a great cat crouching before the assault, a trio of dead or incapacitated dogs attesting to its murderous capabilities. The enormous slate-brown animal raised a forepaw in defense, awaiting its enemy. From its tan muzzle to the dark tip of its lashing tail, the beast measured more than nine feet. It weighed more than 200 pounds. Its beautiful greenish-yellow eyes fixed upon its enemy, yet it made no effort to defend itself, despite its power. Muscles bulged beneath the sleek coat, marking it the most lithe and second largest among American felines, the deadliest predator on the continent save man. Orleke rode directly toward the animal, with difficulty forcing his horse to approach it. He leaned forward whirling the stone weight and smashed it against the creature's skull, crushing the thin bone.

Lenketrú was in enormously good humor at the success of the hunt. His people would eat well for days to come. Division of the meat already had commenced in anticipation of the arrival of the women with pack horses to convey it to the village.

Slaying of the creatures was a time for glorious feasting: hearts, livers, the rest, were devoured. Even Christian consumed some liver and found it palatable, once his scruples were overcome. At the *tolderia* some strips of meat would be sun-dried into jerky, or pounded and mixed with dried berries and ostrich greased into a form of pemmican for use on the endless peregrinations.

A nomadic race from time beyond memory, the Tehuelches quickly became restless in camp. Even a short stay was sufficient to make warriors finger their *facons* in squabbles about very little. At an age when he might have preferred to remain longer in the warmth of this lovely valley, within a few days, Lenketrú called out in a chill dawn the instructions: camp would be moved that day. The animals again were packed, the people filtered out of the campsite, and somehow the mile-long straggle assumed shape. Christian rode wordlessly beside the aged *cacique*, listening to the soft padding of the barefoot horses plodding along the trail, here a braided path worn by the hoofs of generations of Indian animals.

Having been accepted, Christian looked to the headman for leadership as instinctively as did the Tehuelches. Lenketrú was a fatherly figure who never wearied of repeating the name Christian and describing himself as "Christian also," not of course realizing that in Christian's case, the name was not synonymous with the religion.

The northward wandering continued, the daily wind sweeping snow up from the southwest, lancing into the caravan, stinging brown faces, and dusting the windward side of the animals. The movement was a simple struggle of human beings to survive in a harsh and bitter land.

The red sun sank behind them as the multitude tumbled down toward the river, swollen with snow waters from the range, its current sweeping along at perhaps eight miles an hour, very swift for families to negotiate, he thought. The plain on this side, within the bend, was flooded to a depth of a few inches, the water sheeted with an ice film that tinkled like brittle bells as the horde splashed across to the stream proper. Here warriors snatched infants from the busy arms of their women, and pack animals were drawn forward to where Lenketrú had paused while his people assembled. The *cacique* exhibited no concern whatever; this crossing was a routine problem.

A few adventurous young men spurred their mounts in a smother of foam and flying ice past the clustered horde, leaping the excited horses into the river. Lenketrú led the others across more quietly. Once the people had gained the north bank, they struck giant fires. The Indians clustered about, warming themselves, drying out while the camp was erected and they settled in.

CHAPTER THREE

The people migrated leisurely up the Coona Terosh. Hunting was good, guanaco and ostriches abundant. Water birds, bright chips of flamboyant life, thronged the ponds, lakes, and marshes, which occurred more frequently now. Learning new expressions each day, Christian began to communicate with the people in their own tongue.

Reaching the ranges near the Andes, the band left the river and turned northward. Month by month they journeyed on from water to water, one primeval valley to another, savoring the good land and abundant life. Christian learned that the Tehuelche were divided into northern and southern bands sometimes hostile toward each other, with minor differences in dialect, the northerners perhaps influenced by the Araucanians, now pressing over the cordillera by every pass and defile, flowing onto pampa in ever greater numbers. His people, of the southern band, moved on past places they called Toppelaik, Kinck, Gelgelaik, about the latitude of the Chonos on the Chilean coast, then continued north farther still.

They passed places called Yolke, Keinak, Yasaik, Telwecken, and finally reached Geylum, hard by a country abounding in salt lakes and brackish ponds draining eastward across a land shelving downward toward a distant haze suggestive of the flat pampa. Christian sensed that they had now passed the inland sea, Nahuel Huapi, where he and Pinsha had spent the few idyllic weeks before her brutal murder, but the lake did not come into view. He felt again a stab of pain, almost physical, as that bloody incident swept in vivid detail into his recollection. He would never forget Pinsha, nor the way she and their children were killed.

The Englishman found the long journey north, its leisurely pace, its complementariness with the land, the sky, the elements to be therapeutic for his soul; or he wryly acknowledged, it would have been if he had one.

Sunlight, the open land, the healing rhythm of the horse's ambulations, the wild hunts and rousing campfire dances in which he had learned to participate a bit, the occasional skirmishes with outlaw Indians, had bronzed his body while tanning his face and refueling his spirit. The tragedies, the doubts, the disasters that had battered his life since the mutiny now seemed surely dethroned, belonging to some other time, a different life. Had he triumphed at last? With this good people, led by the sagacious Lenketrú whom he had come to revere almost as a father, Christian felt increasingly at peace. Never since his Cumberland boyhood had he been so at peace, so eager for a new day to begin, so content with life, the goodness of being.

"*Ai, Cristiano!*" Lenketrú hailed him one dawn, they the first up. "Come with me today! Let's go pick apple! A Christian apple!"

Christian had neither tasted an apple nor heard of one since 1787 when he had left England, and now it was 1805, as nearly as he could calculate. Apples? In the wilderness far beyond the royal Spanish colony of La Plata? Absurd! Yet he found himself nodding in agreement, and Lenketrú set about assembling an expedition. It would include twenty or thirty warriors, a few women to cook for them, a cavalcade of horses, their hoofs sheathed with rawhide against the stony trail, and several pack animals laden with mantas, blankets, and similar products so that when they encountered the "Manzaneros," or apple people, as the *cacique* called them, they might trade instead of fight.

Within the hour after sunrise, the party clattered out toward the mountains in high spirits at the prospect of adventure. The trail they followed had been beaten by a generation of tribesmen avid for the fruit or a drink of cider. Apparently somewhere to the northwest were apple orchards of some sort; but Christian could not imagine how they came to be there in the first place, how the trees had endured, or in what manner the Indians learned to make cider and ferment it, as Lenketrú indicated they could.

The party crossed a river Lenketrú called the Limay, on the north bank topping a rocky eminence from where Christian could make out a distant haze as of smoke. "*Los* Manzaneros," grinned the *cacique*.

Climbing a further ridge, they gained a startling vista: an orchard of immense proportions, although now with countless gaps where neglected trees had perished from one ailment or another. How came these trees here, in the depths of this savage land, perhaps 400 leagues from sea and settlement? The mystery deepened.

Lenketrú led straight as an arrow toward the smoke, originating in a swale beyond the orchard. Christian eagerly plucked ripe fruit from the trees as they passed, ripping into the crisp sweetness hungrily, finding them juicy and good, if wormy and inferior to English apples. But what a delight to encounter such a vivid reminder of his youth!

The cavalcade careened wildly down the slope toward a community of horse-hide *toldos* and a few reed huts and entered a plaza. Leaping from their horses, the Tehuelches neglected even to unsaddle, so intent were they upon the business of dissipation. The village was Puelche. Men and boys dragged sheepskin containers from every hut, while the Tehuelches spread out on the ground the goods they had brought. Already one or two were joisting the bags of cider to eager lips, gulping down the fermented juice in prodigious quantities. There would be much drunkenness this evening and swollen heads tomorrow. Lenketrú, almost alone, stood aloof, holding his horse. Christian joined him.

"*Ai, ai,*" the chieftain grinned approvingly, scanning the raucous scene. There was no social stigma of any kind among his people for such dissipation. The problem was only to protect the inebriated men, so they did not fall victim while unable to defend themselves. "*Ai,*" mused Lenketrú again, thoughtfully. He would not drink much today. He carefully monitored the trading.

Christian found the Puelches, or Pampas Indians, shorter than the Tehuelches but of similar build, culturally akin, although with their emphasis upon horse products rather than the guanaco or ostrich. A few lived still in reed huts, relics of their pre-Spanish culture. Returning to Lenketrú, seated upon a rock surveying with some delight the scene of debauchery, Christian tasted briefly of the cider the chieftain offered him, finding it more vinegar than sweet. He had never had much affinity for alcohol in any event.

In an amiable mood, Lenketrú pointed beyond the village toward a low plateau and said, "*Cristianos por allá, Cristiano.*"

Curious, Christian mounted his horse and rode slowly through the turmoil to the plain beyond the village. The animal carefully picked its way up the slope to the mesa which extended over several acres. Christian found the rubble of disintegrating buildings, of white men's construction beyond doubt; for mortar had been used between the stones. In addition, tumbled into a ditch before the most expansive ruins was a huge metal bell, its clapper so corroded as to be unusable. The long structure had obviously been a church; and Christian spent most of the midday roaming about the site, wondering.

The sun blazed hotly as he explored. The ruins became a city of shadows that for many years had known no human life. They extended over an acre or more; there was something melancholy about them to the Englishman's mind. Here all was ruin. This was truth. This was what men labored for, to give substance to their own illusions.

One small building alone appeared in good repair. Christian brushed away its doorway skins and peered into the gloom. Here, in its rotten smell, was one answer: the cider plant! The huge vat with its simple press still reeked of use. Here the Puelches pressed the fruit to make the cider, which drew as a magnet all the tribes around! A few skinsful of the fresh liquid, still unfermented, were stacked about, along with baskets full of half-rotted apples.

A shadow crossed the doorway; and Lenketrú grinned his amiable smile, happy to see his friend at this favorite site. "*Cristianos*," he explained, sweeping his muscular arm over the ruin-dotted mesa. "*Aquí yo cristiano, tambien*—here I am a Christian, also"; and the Englishman understood that in their once-thriving mission, Lenketrú and presumably hundreds of others had been Christianized. But who had built it? Why had it fallen into ruin?

The chief shrugged helplessly. "They went away," he muttered, as though recalling some sad event of long ago. "The padres, Padre Juan, Padre Manuel, Padre Frederico—they all went away." He added, with a strange bitterness, "*Prisioneros*," gesturing with his hands behind his back how the priests had been driven away as captives.

"By the Indians?"

Lenketrú shook his head vigorously.

"White devils from La Plata." He insisted, "Devils!" adding, "But I am a Christian still!"

Ransacking his memory, Christian collected wisps of information he had picked up ages ago in Chile. Higgins had told him that the Jesuits had been expelled from all of Latin America—when was it? 1767? Twenty years before the *Bounty* had cleared Spithead. Exiles, he and the Jesuits! Christian grinned sourly. The cause of their banishment had always remained secret. No power on earth—or in Heaven—could force Charles III to explain to the Pope; and the reason died with him. Generations of worthy labors had fallen into decay, as here at the place still called Las Manzanas.

While building their tiny city, it must have been the padres who planted the huge orchard, nursed it to maturity, and established the cider to provide an enjoyable product of their enterprise.

What vision, what generosity, what love for future generations must have prompted the fathers to create in this remote and savage land the plantation that would yield simple pleasures for generations of untamed peoples? How useless it had all been—or was it? The orchards provided seasonal joys in a minor way; but by bringing people together and by imbibing too well the produce of the mill, they became involved in tumults, discord, and, Christian had no doubt, strife, bloodshed, and murder. Was this what the padres intended? Of course not. Yet this is what their labors in a sense had generated. There remained still one thing more: their legacy would inevitably bring the scattered tribes together. To war? Possibly, and perhaps something else: mayhap to learn one day to live together, if the Spanish didn't obliterate them before they wiped each other out.

Christian shook his head in weariness and disgust at such dreaming. Such speculations had no place in the mind of a wanderer. He turned toward the Manzaneros village with Lenketrú following silently.

CHAPTER FOUR

Christian joined Lenketrú at the fire in the gray light before dawn as was his custom. The *cacique* tossed a length of stick on last night's coals, taking up his customary position, hands outstretched toward the warmth, watching the fire's new life. Christian backed to the blaze, peering eastward. His attention was drawn to a movement on the skyline. A horseman bounded into view, then sat immobile as he surveyed the straggling Tehuelche camp along the creek bed. Christian directed Lenketrú's attention to the stranger. The chieftain squinted with experienced old eyes.

"Puelche?" asked Christian.

The *cacique* shook his head.

"Guacho malo," he replied, unconcernedly. *"Renegado."*

Christian watched the renegade, driving a band of a dozen loose horses before him as he guided his mount down the slope toward the camp to Lenketrú's fire where he pulled up, raised a hand in wary greeting, and sat quietly, awaiting a response.

He was young, part-Indian, with a full black beard and black eyes, nervously alert. He carefully appraised Christian, while awaiting the decision: peace or war. He sat his excellent bay with the nonchalant grace of the expert rider, his saddle covered with a wooled sheepskin, the lariat in great coils circling the animal's upper rump, his bolas fastened to his waist. This was the first gaucho Christian had ever seen. With a reckless face and lank and unkempt hair bound in a red cloth knotted behind his head, he wore a shirt which may once have been white, a dark blue *chiripa* covering light-colored pantaloons with finely-turned lace edges reaching halfway down his calves. His feet were shod in the angled skins of a mare's hind legs, toes protruding. The leathern stirrups were caught between his great and second toe, and from his bare heels glittered the silver *nazarenas,* the roweled spurs like the thorn-crown of Christ. The ever-present *facon,* long and razor sharp, was all but hidden at his back, only the end of the shaft protruding at the edge of his belt.

"Cristiano?" demanded the stranger, his bold eyes boring into Christian's.

The Englishman nodded, but Lenketrú replied for him, asserting his right to answer for the people of his camp. "*Cristiano*." It was a synonym for white men, rather than faith, for this individual would have had little to do with religion.

The women were stirring now and poked up the coals, readying breakfast and launching a new day in the endless cycle of their lives.

"*Baje*—get down," invited the chief, after an appropriate interval. The gaucho lightly swung a leg across the animal's withers and vaulted nimbly to the ground without touching a stirrup. He stepped catlike to the fire, opposite the other two, wary in this camp of friends or possibly of enemies.

Lenketrú's woman gave him a foot-long strip of roasted mare's meat. With a little bow and "*Muy gracias*," he acknowledged it politely. He seized one end in his mouth, his eyes never leaving the pair across the fire. He drew his knife and expertly sliced off the tip he held between his teeth, chewing solemnly, holding in his free hand the remaining meat to be consumed as he severed it, bite by bite.

"*De la frontera?*" asked the old Indian, casually.

"*Sí. Hace algun tiempo*." Yes, he had come from the frontier settlements, some time since.

"*Hay indios por allá?*" asked Lenketrú, conversationally.

The other hesitated, then replied he hadn't encountered any wild Indians.

Orleke and Toki silently joined the company at the blaze, their black eyes surveying the gaucho with neither hostility nor welcome. Such castaways were not uncommon, although their quality varied.

The stranger gave his name as Justo—Justo de Galitano, he explained, as though to emphasize his foreign birth. If Justo had been discovered by a party of Tehuelche warriors or even the whole tribe traveling, he would have been slaughtered with no compunction. But because he had willingly entered the camp on his own initiative, he had the courtesy of any honored guest. Despite his reserved exterior, Justo in the days that followed proved to be a merry soul, generous and high spirited, although, as Lenketrú sourly observed to Christian, "Watch out for him; he'll slice your throat between jokes!"

But Christian liked Justo; and the other, in his curious way, returned the friendship, although the gaucho always referred to the Englishman as *el chapetón*, or the tenderfoot, because he was a novice at gaucho skills. The two hunted together, rode and explored in company.

Campfire gatherings were a time of chatting, yarning, or even of songs. But on a particular night, no sooner had Cayuke, the ancient seer, commenced a wailing recital than a nightjar swooped low over the fire, scattering the people like quail. Christian and Justo alone remained seated, startled by the sudden chaos. Lenketrú, obviously shaken, stalked toward his *toldo*. Christian questioned him. The chief muttered that the nightjar was "the bird of ill omen—there will be disease or death," and disappeared into the abode.

At dawn a stone-tipped arrow stabbed through the *toldo* and buried itself quivering less than an inch from Christian's face. The shrieks of attacking warriors followed, and for a moment Christian imagined he was once again in the midst of the indomitable hordes of Kolapel.

He darted for the doorway, colliding with Lenketrú, as a rush of attacking warriors reached the outermost tents. Mindless tumult reigned over the camp as the dawn attack left the Tehuelche no room to organize resistance. The Mapuche surged forward, eager, shouting, a murderous throng among the tents, driving the confused warriors of Lenketrú into the creek bottom, scattering them through the brush and timber when they turned back to the smoking settlement.

Christian huddled on the distant bank, observing the pillage and destruction. Watching helplessly from the perimeter, his qualities as a battle leader surged; and calling to Justo, they found Lenketrú and rallied Toki, Orleke, and most of the warriors. With new leadership, the fighting men eagerly followed. The Araucanians had fallen into the trap of many barbarous fighters—and civilized ones too—for they turned to the women once they had overrun the camp, never suspecting that the scattered enemy might recover.

Justo swept up his murderous *facon* while Christian picked out the two apparent leaders, who watched their fighters milling about, attacking the women and cavorting among the destruction of the camp. Suddenly fire blazed through the tents; apparently they meant to burn the village.

Silently Christian waved his men on and bounded through the screen of huts, the deadly point of his lance centered on the foremost of the leaders. Justo at his side held his knife low, making for the other. Before the chiefs could cry out, Christian's spear was driven through the heart of the one. The gaucho shunted the knife of the other aside; grasping his long hair and twisting back the head, he neatly slit the soft bare throat.

A howl, a moan, arose from the throats of the Araucanians who had witnessed the counterattack. This cry of dismay generated disorderly flight among those who a moment before had been victors. They loosed their captives, dropped the loot, and fled screaming downstream toward the open country.

In moments the village, earlier overrun and helpless, was in the hands of its rightful owners. The attack, counterattack, and rout of the enemy had occupied scarcely an hour.

The keening, the wailing for the dead, had commenced, although few bodies littered the campsite. Among the victims, however, was Orleke, the happy warrior who had fallen without a sound, an Araucanian arrow in his back. Lenketrú, as a war chief must, took this loss of one of his two sons bravely, although the hurt was deep in his eyes. Already many were weeping, scratching their faces, and gashing their cheeks until the blood ran.

Toki, Lenketrú's second son, stood motionless in the doorway of his *toldo* where the body of his young wife lay in a bloody heap. The cry that escaped his lips was animal-like in its anguish, incorporating a ferocity that demanded revenge, as though all the meanness of his short and violent career was loosed upon the sudden debacle. Lenketrú and Christian sped to the scene. Christian peered over the stooped back of Lenketrú at the tragic, twisted form of the dead girl, lying upon her back, her mouth slightly open, eyes staring at the dawning sky, which she would never see again. A gleam of gold glimmered from a leather cord tied about her neck.

Christian's eyes fixed unswervingly upon this gold. He bent forward, tore the thong from the girl's dead body, holding the golden ring aloft, spinning it in the rising sunlight. He glared unbelieving at Toki, whose mourning shriek trailed off and was stilled. Christian's eyes stabbed at the Indian. He hurled the ring at the warrior while the other stared uncomprehending.

"*Where?*" hissed Christian. "Where did you come by this?"

Toki's glittering eyes were fixed on the white man's contorted face. He said nothing.

"The lake? By the great lake?" demanded Christian, the words echoing strangely. Toki nodded once. His eyes narrowed; he knew his peril. Christian bored in, sure now, but desiring admission, confirmation, proof perhaps. "A camp? A woman and two children? Three winters ago?" Toki's eyes were slits. He fingered the *bola* at his waist, the deadly weapon of the Tehuelche, loosed it; but he was too late. Christian tore out his *facon*, gripped it as the gauchos did, low, a short sword, and fell upon the Indian who stumbled backward with the assault. The Englishman was upon him with jungle ferocity, ripping with the long blade, slicing, from the lower stomach upward, the heart of him, slaying as quickly, as though his skull had been crushed with a rock. Toki perished soundlessly; and

Christian, still a captive of his passion, gasped from his emotion. As the rage-filled fog lifted, it seemed to him as though he could not have committed this murder. Heedless of all consequences, in this camp where he had been a guest, he was now at war with these people, his hosts.

He sensed the stooped form of another at his back, but before he could whirl to meet a fresh threat, Justo's reassuring voice came to him: "Circle left, slowly, *tigre*. We protect ourselves, no?" Like wolves at bay, the crouching outsiders, back to back, slowly circled, their knives ready to fight off any threat. There was none.

Lenketrú stumbled forward. Incredible tragedy deepened the worn lines of his old face, tears coursing his cheeks as he raised the limp head of his second son, this last son to die within the hours, lifting the lids, peering expertly into the vacant eyes, turning his own uncomprehending, devastated face up to the man who had been his guest, his companion, his friend. This one had deprived him of his only remaining son, the flesh of his flesh, the bone of his bone, his dreams and hopes for immortality, the future leader he would have left to his people, guide and counselor for them through the seasons and the years to come.

"*Por qué, Cristiano?*" he asked vaguely, incapable of comprehending this greatest of all tragedies. "*Por qué?* Why? Why?" His voice trailed off in a tremulo of tragedy: "*Cristiano? Ah, Cristiano, Cristiano* . . . Why Christian? Why this act of murder? Why, why, why? Ah, Christian, Christian. You are Christian, I am Christian too. Why? Why? Why?" His voice had risen into the wail of mourning, usually sung by women, never by a chief. But he was a chief with no legacy, no hope, an old man, destroyed while still alive, breathing, yet dead, a human tragedy.

Christian and Justo had straightened, sensing that no harm would come to them from the Tehuelche. Without confrontation they caught up their horses, saddled them, mounted, and turned away toward the east. Behind them Christian still could hear the old man's wail as he held his dead son in his arms: "*Por qué, Cristiano?*" Oh, Christian, why, why?

Christian himself felt no emotion, nothing but death in his being, no triumph, no exultation in a vengeance finally exacted for the murder of his beloved and his own children. Nothing. But he felt the grip of the curse more freshly than for many long months. It was once more very real and vivid. Instead of the sweet opportunity for total retribution, Christian saw only the manifestation of the evil, the "stick" laid upon him by that other, years before. Wherever he went, tragedy inevitably must follow; 'twould be so until his day's end. He was death. In his mind, in his soul, he had come to believe this. But he heard another voice too, more faintly, though of substance still: "*Laich!*" It told him, softly, "*Laich, anochi iemach . . . ,*" and once more he thrust it rudely aside, meaningless to him as it had ever been, shivering that the Speaker of these meaningless words seemed aware of his entrapment and offered, if he could only understand, some kind of comfort.

CHAPTER FIVE

They followed down the Limay, riding generally to the east, their troops of loose horses trotting before them. It seemed at first to Christian an empty, even a hostile country; but with experience, his vision widened; and he found it teeming with life. Of guanaco, ostrich, and armadillo, which Justo called the *mulita* because of its ears, there was an abundance.

Lakes and ponds belied the apparent aridity of the land. They teemed with wildfowl: swans, ibises, ducks, great blue herons, bitterns, and tall flamingos, bringing the color and warmth of the panoply of life: a land empty of humans but filled with the goodness of nature. Here Christian found a strange healing or at least forgetfulness under the blaze of the sun, violence of primeval colors, the clean wind and crisp nights, an elemental existence. Humans were made to be healthy rather than ill or morbid; and under the challenge of this land, Christian felt an intelligent interest awaken in his surroundings, a fresh buoyancy.

The region they coursed seemed limitless for horsemen. To the south they sometimes could see the rim of a flattened Patagonia, wooled with shrubs and brush, rising by a series of red or brown escarpments to the high interior plateau Christian had crossed with the Tehuelches, so recently his friends.

For days, weeks, months perhaps—Christian lost count of time—the pair rode on, sometimes through broken country on one side or the other of the river. They worked through a range of charcoal mountains, which supported little vegetation and less wildlife and where Justo was forced to kill a mare for food. As a gaucho he ate meat alone, disdaining the various delicacies that so stirred the native's palate—or a gourmet's. Like others of his kind, he ate red meat, drank red wine, clocked his existence by sun and stars, fashioned his tools of leather, rawhide, and bone, dealt only in *baguales* and fierce wild cattle, savage enemies, and equally barbaric friends; he might be a philosopher as some of his kind were, but he had no patience with soft thoughts or soft people or time for nongauchos except as they presented throats to be cut or authority-by-wealth to command him. Even so, he would obey only while it suited him and fade into his endless land beyond the frontier when it did not. Justo was a gaucho.

"How did you come to the Tehuelche?" asked Christian, by an evening fireside.

"To be a gaucho is to be *matrero*."

"*Matrero?*"

"One good horse and one jump ahead of the authorities," Justo laughed. "Then we go to the *indios*, the Tehuelches or some other. Often I have fled so. Doubtless I will again."

"Won't the Indians remember how you fought them?"

Justo shrugged, sliced off a bite of roasted meat. "If one's luck is bad, and they catch you away from their village . . ." He gestured across his throat. "If one reaches their camp, they ever make a man welcome. They are odd people, I think. *Los cristianos* are more dangerous; they remember better."

"Why do you call the white men '*cristianos*,' Justo? Not all are such."

The gaucho laughed lightly. "What is a *cristiano?*" he demanded. "It is what we call the 'civilized,' rather than the barbarian." I am '*cristiano*,' which is to say, *blanco*, white. It is my race. My faith?" He shrugged again. "I have never seen a priest, only a renegade priest once who was more gaucho than any, and fought better and slit more throats. But a real priest, never. Was I baptized? I don't know. Will I see a priest if I should marry? Hah! Gauchos rarely 'marry'; and if they should, they become no more than *pobladores*." He expelled the word for townsmen so contemptuously that Christian laughed. Justo concluded: "And when gauchos die? No priest then, either. Only the wind, the bones, the dust, and the earth. No more. Am I *cristiano* in faith? *Quien sabe?*"

"A rough sort of life."

"To be born on this land is a kind of curse. I think gauchos have a dark sin deep inside they always must pay for, and so they are born. They pay forever."

The two followed the Limay onward. One evening Christian caught fish with his hands, but Justo refused to touch such flaky white meat. He snorted, "Fish is for nuns!"

At length they arrived at the junction of the river with another from the north, the two flowing eastward as the Rio Negro. In this broad bottom below the confluence, with the tributaries flowing in and the Negro flowing out, it seemed a world of water as much as land. It was summer's end, and the river was brown with silt and uncommonly swift. Christian, like most people, was uneasy where his vision was impaired. The crossing, which Justo called the "ford of the Indians" seemed to the Englishman a dubious gamble; but the gaucho was wholly unconquered. He tossed his riata over the head of a big black, the leader of the troop, and swiftly fashioned a hackamore. "*Vamos*," he called to his companion, spurring his mount into the stream, leading the black after him. The other horses followed willingly; and Christian came after, his qualms settled. The horses came to the swift water. Justo's animal bucked into it, dropping from sight for an instant, the gaucho clinging to the saddle with one hand, swimming alongside in easy strokes with the other, nimbly remounting as it scrambled blowing, into shallower water. In the timber on the far side of the river, Justo quickly struck fire with two flints, and camp was made. Now, he explained languidly, they had entered the country of the Christians. The frontier lay before them.

Ever more wary, Justo was now alert to the reactions of his horses as they rode across endless plains that became increasingly level, the soil thickening from sand to clay and then to loam.

Once he pointed out a nest of a *chuchuento*, an armful of twigs and thorns that Christian thought had been rolled up and bounced into the bristly *jarillo* bush by the wind. Yet it had a fist-sized opening in one end, leading into a three-foot tunnel and the nest somewhere in the interior of the roll. The retreat, Justo assured him, was watertight, designed to keep the eggs safe from fox or other predator.

"The fox is very wise," the gaucho conceded, "but the bird is a devil, wiser than the fox because it not only is a devil, but very old. Because it is so wise it can live forever."

"Do you think it does live forever?"

The other shrugged. "I have never seen a dead one."

"Is the *chuchuento* then as wise as the gaucho?" asked Christian mischievously.

Justo estimated the height of the sun, checked the slant of the ears of his horses, and finally replied: "No, the *chuchuento* is not like the gaucho, because it is elusive, fearful, and takes no chances. No, Englishman. The ostrich is the gaucho bird."

Christian could agree. The rhea was leathery, tough, swift and daring, afraid of nothing; and it had many enemies. Truly it was the gaucho among birds.

The way seemed utterly trackless, but to the gaucho the pampa was as familiar as the sea to a sailor. "Gauchos and Indians carry compasses in their heads," he explained. "Our horses, which can smell their way in the dark, can smell Indians and Christians too. With the horses we are safe."

Christian had noted the pampa's horses' curious customs of traveling through the gloom with the nose held low, brushing the grass tops, as though finding the way through scent. He knew of their astounding vision in open country and suspected that the creatures had developed a sensitivity to vagrant odors. Wildlife now had changed in species, though still was abundant; and vegetation reflected the different soil, more moisture, although this remained a harsh land.

Now they had descended toward the true pampa, the humid plains, a grass ocean, although flatter than any sea. It, too, supported a wealth of life, although dormant itself; and there seemed about it a cruelty, or at any rate heartlessness, that Christian found intriguing in an aloof sort of way. The plains were edged by meadows of rough pampa's grasses, their plumes forming a misty purplish-white sea as far as the horizon, extending upwards eight or nine feet. Justo pulled up his horse and leaped to a standing position upon its back, elevating his eyes, so he could see across the fog of plumes, searching for enemy movement. In this land all strangers were probably inimical. But he saw no one.

More frequently now, Justo drove his long-bladed *facon* into the earth and listened for tell-tale vibrations that might reveal hard-riding men, enemies, who must be avoided. He tasted the grass more often, the better to locate them on the prairies. Christian estimated the pair had traveled about 600 miles since they crossed the Negro. They must be nearing the line of frontier forts, slanting southeasterly from the Buenos Aires-Santiago high trail toward the coast below the capital. Justo took no greater risk than he had to of being picked up by an army patrol or encountering bands of the Pampas Indians. Consequently they moved mainly during the night hours, making for a destination the gaucho called *La riolada de los desterrados*, or "the gathering of the outcasts."

Early one night Justo quietly reined his horse and sat silent. The animal's nose was close to the ground, its ears pointed forward, its nostrils twitching in faintly audible nickering. The gaucho sat still as rock, listening, sniffing the night breezes, peering into the gloom toward an invisible horizon. He slipped to the ground, pulled some grass, tasting it. Christian waited silently. When they moved forward, it was more slowly, even the troop pacing more quietly, as though alert to some danger. For more than a mile they traveled so. Justo again pulled up. He reached over and raised Christian's arm toward the horizon ahead of them, aligning it so that the Englishman might discern the peril. Sighting along his arm,

Christian stared for long moments at what he mistook at first for a star. It was in fact a light of human origin, directly upon the skyline.

"*Chascomué*," muttered Justo softly, identifying the light as that of a Spanish fort. He eased the *tropilla* of horses forward, apparently meaning to bypass the establishment, far enough distant from it to avoid alerting sentry or dogs. Bands of cattle moved off from their course like ghosts; they, silent, too, in the gloom.

The driven horses, trotting easily forward, halted abruptly, milled, confused and unable to go onward. Justo cursed and spurred his mount up to investigate the difficulty. He found they were on the rim of a dark gash that cut across their route as far as they could see in the light of a newly risen moon. It was an abyss perhaps twenty feet across and no one could say how deep, but in either direction it seemed endless. The gaucho grumbled bitterly. "*La zanja es completo!*" The ditch had finally been finished: a barrier in that fenceless, stoneless land against Indian raids upon the settlements beyond, an edging to civilization, or what there was of it. It was a device no barbarian horde could cross, averse as the Indians were to labor and devoid of tools. The great trench, nearly 1,000 miles in length, had been gouged out with thousands of teams of oxen and mules, the labor of countless workmen, slave and free. Now it was obviously done, a barrier to white renegades as to Indians. Justo whistled almost inaudibly. How to cross it? Under his breath he whispered, "A man never plaited a rope that a gaucho couldn't unravel." The question was how to do it.

He eased the *tropilla* north along the *zanja*. Quietly they rode for several miles. Then Justo guided his horses away from the gash, toward the west again. After a mile or so, Christian found they were approaching a herd of range cattle, wild and suspicious. He could make out the dark shapes of the animals. Smelling or hearing the animals approaching them, sensing somehow that they were not harmless wild horses but ridden creatures, the cattle rocked to their feet and faced the danger, faces raised, wet nostrils sniffing. They milled, uncertain, their heads tracing the movement of the riders swinging around behind them.

Reaching position there, Justo took off his poncho, whirled the cloth, snapping it mightily. He screamed out at the cattle, cracking his quirt like a pistol shot, driving home his spurs so savagely that his horse bounded forward, possessed. The charge of this apparition screeching down upon them panicked the cattle. They fled from the thundering riders, breaking into a wild stampede, heedless of their course, terrified in the rush toward safety. The swifter animals gained the fore, followed by the long banner of running cattle trying to escape that mounted storm in their wake. The pursuers pressed upon their heels, goading the stragglers on. The leaders pounded blindly to the lip of the great ditch in a paroxysm of terror. They were smashed into from behind; they tumbled into the ditch stunned as more and more animals crashed down upon them, smothering the bodies of the first, filling the trench with writhing masses of flesh and bone, leveling the *zanja* from side to side, permitting the last few cattle to cross and scramble up the far side of the ditch, where they fled lowing into the night.

The horses and the pursuing riders made their way over the cattle more easily and, reaching the far side, galloped free beyond the barrier. Justo singing a wild gaucho song while Christian, silent, was strangely perturbed by the torn, battered animals they had left heaped in the barrier behind them.

What would happen to all the injured, still-living creatures caught irretrievably in the trench from which they could never escape? The misery they had caused these innocent creatures lay heavy upon his heart. He knew it was useless to carry his concern to Justo, who would have been astounded at such a thought. Were they not safely across? Free as the nightjar? Eastward, then! Eastward.

CHAPTER SIX

The Riolada signaled its presence long before it came into view. The stench that blew from it like smoke from a bonfire warned that strong nostrils would be needed when it was in full flower, so to speak. Christian suspected it lay near to the sea because of a freshness that swept some of the odor away, although he could neither see the waters nor hear the surf. The Riolada, a gaucho hangout, was an *estancia*, centered around a low blocky building with only a single window covered with hide. The roof had been thatched by some more provident owner in the long ago, and traces of his workmanship remained; he had even white-washed the coating of clay-and-dung, which covered much of the adobes, although patches of the rough blocks were everywhere exposed. Obviously no one had cared for the structure for a long time. Back of the main building were others in a similar state of disrepair. A few corrals of upright stakes, bound with strips of rawhide, held many horses, dowsing slope-hipped, along with a steer or two. Chickens scratched in the dust for grubs; and a welter of mangy, flea-ridden dogs sprawled about sleeping, occasionally rousing to scratch or fight.

The layout seemed to float in a thick sea of offal in all stages of decay, the debris of thousands of butcherings, giving rise to the overpowering stench. Hordes of rats worked everywhere, gorging themselves with no fear and no ambition save gluttony. Flies, in swarms and clouds, caused Justo to slip his neckerchief over his mouth and nose. *Surely if there is a hell, this must be it,* Christian thought dourly. *But a person can always adjust.*

No human was visible, however, as Justo herded the leg-weary troop into a corral where they unsaddled, the animals rolling luxuriously in the warm dust to soothe their lathered backs. The two carried their saddles to the main building, entering by the single door, grateful for the shade and coolness and relief from the flies. They dropped their trappings and seated themselves in front of the fire around which a dozen or more figures hulked. Two or three women, of indistinguishable features, bulky in the cumbersome clothing of the pampa's tradition, were shadows in the background, like their men saying nothing.

Justo grunted a greeting. No one replied. Piratical band as they seemed, all were dressed like Christian's companion. For long moments they remained silent, each lost in his own thoughts if he had any, in a state of torpidity, like a chilled reptile.

"*Indios?*" demanded the one with the bushiest mustache, the visage most fierce. Obviously he was leader of this outlaw crew.

"We saw no one," replied Justo, lapsing into silence again.

"*Ejercito?* Army?"

"*Tampoco*. Neither."

Once more the stillness of death, or decay, reigned, except for eating noises and the squeaking of a maté gourd suddenly gone dry.

"Did you find him among the Indians?" demanded the *patron*, nodding at Christian.

"*Si*, Ruffino," replied Justo. "With the Indians on the Limay. He fights bravely, if not very well. The *facon* is foreign to him. He is *Inglés*."

"Ah." He stroked his mustache. "He rides an Indian saddle; that is why I asked. Like a barbarian. Miranda was killed, it makes a few days ago."

"That is a pity," sighed Justo.

"So many beautiful horses die," replied the leader, philosophically. "The stranger can have Miranda's saddle so that he may appear as one of us, properly mounted in a proper outfit." Only the gaucho did things correctly; others must conform, obviously.

Often Christian had observed Justo preparing a riding animal, but the elements of the *recado*, or saddle, seven or eight pieces if he counted them correctly, confused him still, although if he were to learn gaucho skills and become one of them, it was now time to learn. With much practice, Christian was soon able to saddle a horse within two or three minutes, comparing favorably with the gauchos themselves.

Eager to breathe clean air once more, the Englishman accompanied a gang of riders one day to bring in salt, necessary, Justo said, to cure hides. He explained no further.

They herded before them eight or ten mules, fitted with packsaddles, proceeding inland several miles to an expansive basin into which two creeks had brought brackish water for ages past, which the withering sun had evaporated, leaving the earth white with a thick incrustation glittering under the clear sky. Tasting proved the white substance to be salt, and at the near side, the surface was broken where holes had been drilled with sharpened stakes to be used then as levers. A *riata* was attached to the upper portion of the pole, tied to a cinch ring, and a horseman goaded the animal away until a lump of salt was broken free. When the mules all were packed, the party returned to the Riolada where a few gauchos reduced the lumps to powder with stone mallets.

On the fourth day, the gang set out before dawn under the leadership of Ruffino. He once more took them inland. After three hours, Ruffino gradually fanned them out until they commanded an enormous sweep of country, virtually from horizon to horizon. At long last one of the teams of gauchos encountered tracks of cattle, summoned the others, and pressed along the trail as swiftly as they could, mindful that they had no spare horses on an expedition such as this. After an hour Christian detected a scattering of dots, black with distance; and toward them they rode, the ever-advancing mirage before them and between them and the quarry.

As they neared the cattle, Ruffino separated the horsemen into two bands, one for each side of the grazing animals. The gauchos rapidly circled the herd, fanning out to come down upon them from the west. Now aware of the threat, the prey came instantly to the alert, those lying down bounding to their feet, tails roiling, ears sharply forward, nostrils distended, twitching. Fluttering their ponchos, the riders bore in upon them until the herd exploded, running wild, almost as swiftly as the horses. Nor did the riders try in any way to control them, except to drive them forward.

For mile upon mile they raced across the level plains. By the time the hacienda buildings came into view, the cattle were blowing, badly winded, exhausted, becoming manageable. The riders swept up along their flanks and began to turn the leaders until the herd was brought into a full circle at the outskirts of the ranch bone yard; and the dust grew thick and dense as the restless animals milled more and more slowly, at a trot and finally a walk. The butchery could begin.

The process was long, and the Englishman never knew how he completed that grisly day. Somehow he performed creditably enough that Ruffino, wiping his knife at long last against a drying carcass by the light of the moon, said "*Bueno*, gaucho," and Christian knew himself accepted.

He awakened again before dawn, stiff, nearly dead from exhaustion, only to discover that the work was not yet ended. It was necessary now to drag the hides, two or three roped together and pulled with a cinch-ring lariat, to the *estancia* where the white salt lay. Here the skin was spread flat, flesh side upwards and dashed with salt to preserve it. The crystals were shoveled up with a stiff rawhide and sprayed across the skin; another was laid on top and the process repeated. When a dozen hides were so salted and stacked, the whole was roped together, fastened once more to the cinch ring by a riata, and skidded off toward the east by a gaucho, riding unconcerned and never glancing back at his trailing cargo. Christian moved his horse into position, and when a load was secure, slowly moved off on the trail, not knowing where he was bound but following along, doing as others had done.

For several miles the odd procession continued easterly. Christian became aware of the sea before it came into his view, though how he sensed it he could not have told. Perhaps it was an imperceptible change in temperature, a taste of salt air, or maybe the foamy seething of distant surf, inaudible to the ear yet boring in upon the consciousness of a sailor. When his horse topped the hill, before him lay the gray-green reaches of the South Atlantic. With a seaman's natural affinity for the ocean, the sight brought him peace he had not known for months. It was a broad sea and wholly empty; not a sail broke the endless vacancy of it. Christian's horse carefully chose its way down the quickening slope.

They rounded a gray bluff, and the puzzle of the destination was resolved. Here in a wide-mouthed cavern overlooking a shingled beach the loads were loosened, the skins stacked in the recesses of the cave out of the weather. There were also many casks of suet or tallow, and Christian noted that the barrels were European-made. The cavern opened on a gorge leading to the water, its mouth an inlet free of surf and the beach suitable for boat landings. Christian dismounted and joined the men stacking skins as long as he could stand the odor in the cave, where earlier bundles of skins bordered on decay despite their protection of salt. He then went down to the beach.

A fork-tailed royal tern, its gracefully angled wings too fragile seemingly to support it, drove in tight maneuvers across the inlet. It had been nearly twenty years since he had seen the South Atlantic, as second in command of the *Bounty*. In that day his future lay before him—and what a future! Had he known what it was to be, he might have leapt overboard into this cold southern ocean and have done with it. But he shook the notion off; he knew he could never end this mysterious life by his own hand. He would, rather, live out this existence he had not sought, did not savor, and would not end. There were many who held that this life was but a foretaste, a preparation perhaps for some dreamlike existence later on, but he knew this was not so. Let them revel in their hallucinations; as for him, this one was enough, more than sufficient.

The sea lapped gently at the polished black stones at his feet. He listed to the whisper of the waters, the clopping sounds, softly hollow. In his mind they assumed form; shaped in his brain those mysterious words he had heard so often on so many winds: "*Laich*," they seemed again to say. "*Anochi iemach.*"

He listened, perturbed. That was all. The substance of the sounds drifted off, and his mind returned to the soft, hollow clopping of the wavelets. The tern swung in close again, uttering its shrill "Keer! Keer!" as it drove past. Christian broke from his bond with the water.

For three full days the toil went on, mounted gauchos dragging bundles from the butchery to the sea, filling the cavern. Christian had taken to sleeping beyond the stench and near to the coast where he could smell the salt and feel the freshness and wash his soul in the chill brisk air, purified by a thousand leagues of open water. He laid out his saddle parts and rolled up in his poncho upon the soft wool and slept beneath the galaxies and the Southern Cross. Justo joined him the third night; the gaucho, restless as always, arising before dawn.

"*Ai!*" he called, as light flowed across the sea. "The ship is here, Englishman! The ship!"

Christian bounded to his feet, sped to the top of the sea-cliff where he could see the water.

She was a little brig, a cargo vessel, though armed with a few cannon in prudent fashion as were most ships of the time. She flew no flag; bore no identification visible from this distance.

CHAPTER SEVEN

The brig dropped anchor as close inshore as she dared, no doubt the only foreign vessel on that forbidden coast. Ruffino led several gauchos to the beach to meet the boat. Graceful enough on a horse, the outlaw chieftain walked, or rather waddled like a goose when afoot, but he was the leader beyond question. When the ship's small craft nosed to the land, he stepped aboard first, followed by another of his men and Christian, included because Ruffino suspected he was knowledgeable about ships, or at least foreigners.

Despite reluctance to fly her flag, Christian saw the smuggler was Portuguese by the weathered name, *São Tomé*, on her stern. Ruffino, puffing mightily, waddled aft to the captain, an asp-eyed man with whom the gaucho had obviously done business before.

In the administrative morass of Spanish America, Spain sought to wall off her possessions from outside commerce and, in the process, almost choked them to extinction. To smuggle was to live; to be caught was to die. But the risk was less than might be supposed. Both the captain and Ruffino were well past their prime, they had engaged in illegal trade all their lives and were in excellent health still.

Aft of the mainmast were displayed samples of the goods the *São Tomé* had brought to barter for hides, horns, and tallow: clothes to delight a woman or a dandy; iron mallet heads and plows; combs, needles, thread, and pins; horse gear—harness and iron rings for shoes for mules, horses, and oxen. Ruffino knew what such things were, though he had never used them. He touched one disdainfully with his toe: "Why should *plateños* pay four *reales* to shoe a horse they can buy for two?" He demanded testily. The captain shrugged.

Other things, too, were laid out, some useful, others less to a gaucho's taste: pitchforks and money boxes; twine and rope of fiber instead of rawhide; cinch rings and firearms; and powder, balls, and flints; chains, nails, buckets and hinges; goods to satisfy every colonial want. Ruffino selected what he thought marketable. The captain wanted to know about the hides, tallow, and horns for glue. They haggled like fishwives at a Friday market but reached agreement at long last because each knew that he must.

Christian had spent the hour unnoticed, pacing the littered ship, lost in a sailor's reveries. She was an untidy gypsy, but she awakened nostalgia in the seaman, even though he had no impulse whatever to serve on her. A man who felt he had lost his soul was convinced he never would recover it aboard a Portuguese smuggler. So he inspected the *São Tomé*, but he had no designs upon her.

The captain ordered his two other boats into the water to ferry hides to the ship and, in return, take merchandise ashore. He and Ruffino, despite the fact that they had dealt for years past, or because of it, trusted each other like two tomcats. They bickered over whether the initial load of merchandise should be sent to the land or the first boatload of hides come to the ship. The impasse was settled when Christian suggested that the boat taking Ruffino and his men ashore start back with hides while the other boats left the ship with his goods, the two parties passing each other in midchannel, as it were, with neither having any advantage. So it was agreed.

For a couple of weeks the trade continued, the enormous piles of hides from the cave disappearing into the holds of the brig and her stores of trading goods piling up inside the grotto. Christian worked as often in the holds as at the cave. The hides were laid carefully on dunnage of brush and packed systematically because they represented money, and it was only by careful planning that the greatest number of skins could be stowed. The captain did not wish to leave ashore a single one, which might be converted into cash at Oporto.

Thus when the hides had been stored to within a few feet of her beams, steeving began. By this process, a number of skins, up to a hundred or so, were stacked, the lot folded in half, and the bundle inserted by greased ways between two skins as far forward as the bulkhead. Wedgelike spars, were pressed against the inner spine of the folded hides. Pushed with the aid of tackles, the hides were levered forward so tightly that even if the *São Tomé* had burst her seams in some gale, she could not sink. In return for the hides, the captain sent ashore sufficient merchandise to load hundreds of mules at 200 pounds of cargo for each animal.

One morning when Christian awakened, the ship was hull down on the horizon. Given good weather and no chance encounter with a Spanish frigate, she could raise the Portuguese coast in six weeks, poor sailor though she was. He watched until her tops and topgallants slipped into the sea, then joined the gauchos at the cove.

Ruffino had sent several gauchos north toward a La Plata River settlement near Buenos Aires, a hangout for smugglers and fences. During the four weeks of their absence, pack mules moved the goods to the hacienda where they were stored in the outer sheds. Christian thought it risky to bring it within easy reach of authorities on a raid, but Justo disagreed.

"Ruffino wants to move it north as soon as can be done," he said. "Besides, a *rastreador*—a scout—would locate it easily in either place. If we get caught, we will die just as quickly, no matter where they are concealed."

"Die?" Echoed Christian sharply. The possibility for some reason nettled him.

Justo laughed. "The pampa along this coast is littered with gaucho bones and those of soldiers. Ruffino makes much money, but he should spend it quickly, I think. He will not live to count it often."

"And you?"

Justo lifted his shoulders. "The law is like a *facon*, useful for the one who handles it," he sighed. "It's made for everyone, but it rules only half—the bottom half. We have enough: we fight, we steal, we die—it makes no difference. All die, gauchos and soldiers alike. There's no man's time that does not end, no rope that doesn't break."

Until now the smuggling had been an adventure, a novel exploit and little more; but with Justo's fatalism, Christian sensed its more sinister aspect or at least its deeper meaning. To colonists faced with unendurable deprivation and, to their minds unnecessary restrictions, there was no other recourse. However perilously they did it, Ruffino and the others like him thus served a useful purpose; many became wealthy at this underground trade, but many more died because of it. The business was for neither weaklings nor the timorous, and this gaucho crowd included neither.

Sorting and packing the goods went on, pending return of the emissaries to the north. Ruffino directed the operations, and nearly three weeks had elapsed when the gaucho emissaries galloped in from the north with a note for Ruffino that none could read, save Christian. "Bring your cattle to Magdalena when you are ready. I will read brands there and compensate you, although hide and jerky demand is slow. There is little money, times are hard. Go with God. Marcos."

Marcos, whoever he was, had prepared himself should the courier be caught by the army. Ruffino snorted and tore the message from Christian's grasp, scanning it quickly, although he could not decipher a word of it. He cast it aside. "We risk our throats and he cuts the prices," he growled. He mumbled on and on in the weary fatalism of the eternal middleman whose profession is the pivot upon which others prosper. Ruffino at last gave directions for a northward start in the morning and went to sleep against a wall, snoring peacefully.

No hint of approaching daylight had penetrated the thick walls when the door exploded with grotesque forms crowding inside, firing aimlessly into the blackness. Bursts of flame and crashes of gunfire echoed from wall to wall, filling the room with pungent smoke. The gauchos came awake with a leap, drawing their deadly knives, slashing. Screams of the wounded filled the tumultuous darkness, Ruffino shouted commands. The men cursed and flailed. More assailants tumbled into the crowded room, swinging their firearms like bludgeons, stabbing with short lances. The trapped outlaws fought savagely; but it was hopeless. In moments it was over, save for the groans of the wounded.

A Spanish officer with a high-pitched boyish voice directed lights to be struck, prisoners secured, the damage assessed.

A shambles was revealed in the flickering glare of grass torches where a few minutes before all had been serene. The lieutenant was garbed as if for parade, a shiny black *casco* with white and black plumes, a scarlet tunic with gold bands crossing his chest, his uniform touched with the yellow stripes of the dragoons. His bearded soldiers, all former gauchos and of gaucho mentality still, were dressed alike in blue blouses and the lace-edged pantaloon Christian had found so incongruous above their toeless boots of horse hide.

"Tie them up," repeated the officer, the squeak of his voice weighted with the air of absolute command. A black-bearded corporal saluted this stripling who might have been his grandson. "There are two dead and three badly wounded, *señor* Lieutenant," he reported.

"They'll fight no more," promised the officer, grimly. "Who is the leader? Is he alive?"

"I think that one, *señor* Lieutenant. The fat one. He is the bull, I think."

The officer stroked his mustache. It wasn't much, for he was very young, but it was the best he could raise. "You," he called. "Where is the contraband? That which you sought to trade at Quilmes?"

Ruffino grunted, said nothing. He knew that with daylight the smuggled goods would be instantly located, but he would never tell anything. He had been a *gaucho malo* most of his life. Now that he was to be executed, he would die one.

The officer selected a knife from the heap at his feet, placed the point against Ruffino's throat. His hands bound, the gaucho stared at the officer with glittering black eyes. This young fool thought his weak threats could make a man speak when he chose to be silent! The knife pressed in through the wiry black beard upon his throat. "Tell me!" commanded the lieutenant, "or I'll make you cry tears of blood!" Ruffino laughed. His teeth gleamed in the dancing light.

"Where is your guitar, child?" He fueled the immature rage of the young officer. "With your soprano and an instrument, you might sing for us. But I'll never make music for you, *niño*. Slice yourself and leave the real men to—" His voice drowned in a gurgle. A gush of red flooded his front; and he died staring implacably at his murderer, the grin still twisting his bearded face.

The officer tossed the glistening weapon upon the pile and directed the prisoners outside in the growing light and aligned them against the wall of the house. A search group instantly located the plunder. The officer hastened to estimate its worth—not that he would receive any financial reward for his diligence, but he must stress in his report the great value of his efforts to the Crown. Promotions came slowly in such a remote province as this; and one must overlook nothing that might influence his superiors or, hopefully, even the king. The lieutenant was in an improved humor when he rejoined his men for a breakfast of roasted meat. This had been a very good haul indeed, the best of his experience, limited as it was.

The corporal wiped his greasy knife upon a tuft of grass and looked inquiringly at his officer. The latter shrugged. It was time. There was nothing more to be done.

Christian sat next to Justo at the end of the line of gauchos, bound like the others, facing into the rising sun on this, his final day, reflecting upon his eventful life. Lazily he traced it from first to last: from his boyhood home in Cumberland to the sea; from the sea to the *Bounty;* from Bligh to Mautea to Pitcairn; to Ishmael, Higgins, and Bernardo; to Borja and Valdivia and Roca Montalván, to Kolapel and Pinsha. Then came the cold and rainy strait and Obadiah Hanks, to Lenketrú and Ruffino. What a mixed bag! His personal disasters commenced with the "stick," the curse laid upon him by Bligh. From that evil moment to this, his life had been a downward spiral, bringing destruction upon all he touched, or at least to many. And if not death, then disaster, and always he was the cause. What else was there to think? And now he wished only that his baleful influence might extend after his death to wipe out this detestable excuse of an officer.

The corporal roused two soldiers from a nearby fire. One was small and active as a fox, the other huge, slow-moving, as inexorable as a glacier. Starting at the opposite end of the line of prisoners, the larger soldier twisted the first prisoner's head back, holding the beard out of the way while the smaller wordlessly and neatly sliced the throat. The executioners moved on to the second man and the third. No word was spoken. The courier, named Gregorio, was fourth; and as the soldier grabbed for his beard, Gregorio's eye caught the giant's and he cried, "Esteban!"

The executioners paused. The huge man replied questioningly: "Eh, *amigo?* Esteban? I am he—who are you?"

"Gregorio, uncle! The son of your sister, my mother. Do you not remember?"

A wide smile spread slowly over the broad face of the soldier. He opened his arms. "Gregorio! Ah, yes, Gregorio, my relative! How are you my son?"

"Until now, well, uncle. Until this moment!"

"Yes, it is sad," agreed the other. "A pity. But it is nice to have seen you, and I shall make it very swift for the sake of my sister."

"Will you tell her that I die with her name on my lips, uncle?"

"That indeed I will, my son. Easy now. This will be too fast for the pain. I am skilled, an expert, as you can see." Swiftly he cut his nephew's bared throat, sighed and turned to the next in line.

The corporal walked over to the officer, who was sipping maté by himself, for one of His Majesty's lieutenants must never eat, drink, or associate with common soldiers. The corporal saluted stiffly.

"Sir, two of our men are dead, three wounded, and already we were under-strength, as the lieutenant informed me last night."

"Yes?"

"Perhaps we could enlist replacements from this band, if the lieutenant thinks it wise and so wishes."

The officer considered the suggestion carefully. He must not appear guided by an enlisted man, and yet the proposal was worthy. Truly the company was so shorthanded it fulfilled its duty with great difficulty. Yes, this would be a solution.

"Very well, corporal," he replied, returning to his maté. "Select two or three to enroll. Young, strong ones with good faces, if possible, but not so lively they will instantly desert."

And so it happened that Christian and Justo, the last two on the line, were spared at this final moment. The soldiers, gauchos all, lost no time rounding up the mules, driving them out, as though they themselves were *contrabandistas*, as they might well have been had fate cast differently. The captive pair, duly enrolled as soldiers of the Crown, followed.

The lieutenant, in advance of the column, rode silently on his bay as Christian and Justo rode well behind, side by side.

"I do not like the army," muttered Justo, almost to himself.

"It may be better than death, Justo."

"In what way?"

It was Christian's turn to shrug. "Death I have not tried and do not understand," he returned. "This life I have tried and do not understand, either. But at least it is known."

The pair rode wordlessly for some moments.

"I do not think we will be soldiers long," Justo mumbled, more brightly. "We are gauchos. We will find a way out. While the army has horses, we shall obtain liberty." After a moment he added, "The army is Spanish. We are not. We are gauchos!"

CHAPTER EIGHT

Justo was right. Desertion from the poorly led, low-morale frontier army of the viceroyalty of La Plata was frequent and usually successful. Fleeing soldiers were rarely apprehended. Recruiting procedures were so brutal and oppressive that there was a constant need to replenish the garrisons. Soldiers fled, therefore more must be brought in; the means to do this were ruthless, for soldiers could be secured in no other way. It was a bitter cycle.

When deserting soldiers fled across the frontier, they generally found a hearty welcome among the Indians, particularly if they brought along their weapons, which most deserters were careful to do. Many became so entranced with the wild, free life that they settled in among the tribesmen, fought and raided the Spanish settlements with them, and never had any desire to return to their former lives.

The new recruits did not suffer from a lack of rations, being issued their six pounds of beef a day or, when vegetables or grain were available—an anathema to gaucho soldiers—three pounds of meat. The horses were not fed at all, however, beyond what they could gather when grazing under herd guard.

"Why don't they feed the stock grain or corn?" wondered Christian while he and Justo were on herd guard.

The other shrugged. "Corn only pampers a horse," he said and so believed.

It also strengthens the animal, Christian thought, *and gives it endurance*.

Christian quickly became accustomed to army life on the pampa as he once had under Viceregent Higgins across the Andes. The bugle at dawn signaled the unvarying commands: "*Cinchar!*" "*Enriendar!*" "*Montar!* "*En marcha!*" And the column would set off on its mission of the day. Christian, by diligently performing his duty and keeping his mouth shut and his eyes open, came to be accepted as part of the organization. He never received the *cepo*, or stocks, as most soldiers did, but by meticulously caring for his animals, he prepared for the day when he could flee.

An occasion arrived more quickly than he had hoped, and quite unceremoniously. Christian and Justo, along with a noncommissioned officer they detested, were on herd guard near a post called Cabeza de Buey, or "ox head." It was early morning. The herd had grazed two or three miles from the fort. They were idly chatting when the corporal assailed them savagely, ordering them to separate, to better herd the horses. His directive was sensible, but his manner irritated Justo. Awaiting his opportunity, the gaucho stabbed him fatally, grinning at Christian, "So, no more army! We have already been here too long, no?" Together they drove the loose horses northward at a run, selecting a dozen of the better ones and abandoning the others. They had no wish to put the company afoot but to make immediate pursuit less likely. Now they could truly become *gauchos malos*.

As free and rich as birds that never want for anything, they were also as poor as birds which never have anything. Month after month, for the better part of a year, the pair wandered. They rarely worked except at some accommodating hacienda for a few days and avoided the towns with their constables, dodging the army recruiters. They floated like thistledown, drifting with the breezes of their whims.

One day they sighted in the distance a black spot, a rarity on the featureless grass plains. As they advanced it grew slowly in size until it could be distinguished as a tree. "*El ombú*," Justo explained, idly.

"The only one in the world?"

The gaucho shook his head. "There are others, here and there. They grow always singly save at some haciendas where five or six are planted. It is the only tree of the pampa, except what the Spanish brought to remind them of Spain, though if they wanted to remember Spain they should have remained in Spain. A snake does not crawl into a Vizcacha burrow to remember that he has just left."

"Perhaps the Spaniard is not a snake."

"What's the difference, *Inglés?* He travels on his belly, or at least for the sake of it. He ingratiates himself until he can strike and strikes without mercy. He seizes from his victims whatever he wishes, and soon he owns the colony and thrusts the others out. I see no difference between them."

"You are a philosopher, Justo."

"I think *Inglés*. We *criollos* always think, but someday we will act too."

The *ombú* indeed was an inviting tree. It was thirty feet or more in height, its crown circular and gracious in form and its shade dense. Immediately above the ground, the root system sprawled in all directions, smooth flowing masses, as though eager to hold as much of the rich dark earth as could be managed. At this season the *ombú* was in flower, trusses of tiny buff-colored blossoms, each collection four or five inches long and an inch in diameter. The bare space beneath the tree was littered with them in scented profusion.

"A good time to boil maté," Christian suggested.

"No dung for a fire," replied Justo lazily. Christian laughed. "With all this wood, you are concerned about dung?"

"*Ombú* doesn't burn *compadre*," Justo replied. "Look—I will show you."

He snapped a green branch from the tree. "Test the weight of it," he urged, tossing it to Christian. It was heavy. Justo found a limb of similar size broken off in a storm. He slung that to his companion. It was so light that it floated through the air like down. The Englishman squeezed it, and the material turned to dust between his fingers.

"Like a man," he mused, casting it aside. "When full of life, he is substance; when he dies, he is no more than dust."

"Dust thou art, and unto dust shalt thou return," murmured Justo, sententiously. Christian was startled.

"Where in God's name did you learn that? He demanded, irritated as he ever was at the mention of Scripture.

"I am *Cristiano*," he shrugged. "All Christians know that verse, if none other. Are you not Christian?"

"Only in a sense, Justo," he parried. "I am Christian, but not as you are."

Traveling north Justo detected a haze to the east, identifying it as the dust of the *salineros*, or salt-gatherers. They followed a course that would intersect the caravan, of greater size than anything of the kind Christian had ever seen, or that had been observed by anyone else for that matter.

The governing *cabildo* of Buenos Aires assembled this mighty train of carts to be sent to the Salinas Grandes for salt this year, the mineral destined for use not merely as seasoning, but to cure hides and meat for shipment abroad. Christian found the caravan to include 600 carts; 12,000 oxen; 2,600 horses; 600 bull drivers and half that many wagoners to keep the vehicles in condition; 400 infantry and 65 cavalrymen; 4 pieces of artillery and scores of individuals of other specialties. The journey of about 350 miles southwest of Buenos Aires required 3 months in going and coming and loading the carts with a ton and one-half of salt each—about 2 bushels of which the *cabildo* demanded as taxes, taxes being a mark of civilization more unfailing than the arts or the law.

Justo had learned that mule drovers were sought to the north; and the pair eased up that way, quitting the open pampa for a better-watered, more-wooded country with tall *ceibo* trees. In the midst of these prairies and woods and sluggish streams, a hacienda had been built, and Justo led the way unerringly to it.

It lay east of the Rio Areco. The hacienda proper formed a rectangle, walled and moated with a crude drawbridge perhaps patterned after some ancient and primitive European castle. Rawhide ropes attached to a crude windlass raised it.

The manor house—long, low, and of several rooms—sprawled at right angles to the bridge entrance, behind it the usual assortment of buildings and sheds surrounding a grassy patio, in the center of which was a well. Defenses of the place included four small cannon, a scaffold of poles and cross-pieces rising 25 feet above the ground, and nearby a pit large enough for the watchman if Indians swept in to attack the place.

Christian and Justo rode across flowered meadows with tall, rich grasses and through shaded groves where numerous herds of mules grazed, each held in by a hobbled bell-mare, the small bronze instrument ringing with each movement of the animal's head. The mules seemed to pay no attention to the mare but in fact were tied to her by the invisible bond of the bell and the curious affection each mule had for the horse. As long as the bell-mare was restrained, there was no concern that the mules would wander off. When it was desired to bring them in, all that was necessary was to free the mare and lead her in, bell tinkling, when her gaggle of mules would trot obediently in her wake. Mules, Christian learned, were the easiest of all creatures to herd.

Justo led the way to a central fire where he nimbly leaped to the ground and greeted a bushy-bearded drover of the fiercest visage.

"*Ai*, Sebastian!" Justo proclaimed.

"Aha, gaucho!" Acknowledged Sebastian, flashing a grin of delight. "You have survived against all my predictions. What a pity!"

Justo grunted at the jibe. "More mules for Peru, eh?" he said.

"Always the mules," Sebastian sighed. "Last year there were 50,000. This year there will be more—probably 80,000. There is no end." He shook his head, almost sadly.

"Ha, it is a good thing, Sebastian! If there were an end, you would be unemployed and a gaucho again. What a tragedy for the rest of us, having again a man among us whom we could neither whip nor disobey. It is better that you are with the mules. We would go with you, to Salta at least."

"*Con el mayor gusto,*" Sebastian accepted the suggestion with alacrity. "We need riders who understand mules. Mule drovers I have few. Of mules I have many."

Three days later the great drive toward the northwest commenced, not one massive movement, but as a number of smaller bands with up to 1,000 head of mules in each. The animals made a colorful migration: blacks, browns, whites, yellows, blues, sorrels and chestnuts; pintos, flea-bitten grays, brown-nosed black mules , yellowed-nosed brown mules, roans, creams, and bays: more variety of color than Christian had dreamed existed for such a common animal. So young, the mules were almost at the end of their lives, for they were bound for the mines of Peru where cruelty and neglect would wipe them out swiftly. Had they foreseen their fate, they might have burst the bonds of the bells and sought safety and happiness and long life on the pampa. But then again, they might not. For they were mules.

The herds followed each other up the post road toward Cordoba. There the way would divide, one road curving southwest along the eastern slope of the Andes, up through ancient Tucumán Salta, Jujuy, and on into Upper Peru, the wrinkled brown tableland of stupendous altitude guarding the mines of the land of the Incas more effectively than the highest wall might have done.

Cordoba was the second down in size to Buenos Aires, 468 miles from the capital of the viceroyalty. The mules were herded on an immense grassed flat, south of the old city. At the point where the great road divided, Christian and Justo quickly found a sizable *pulpería* flying the red flag, which meant it sold even meat, although wine and brandy were its main attractions

A wickedly mustached *pulpero*, a former gaucho himself, was protected from others of his lawless kind by a grill of upright bars. Having received a few coins of their eventual pay, the pair threaded through a swarm of trail-dusty drovers to the grill. Justo purchased wine, Christian brandy. They lounged against the far wall, gouging out the wooden stoppers with their *facons*, slushing their throats with deep draughts of the sour-smelling liquors.

Amid the clatter and the racket of the *pulpería*, Christian imagined once more he heard that voice, that mysterious, familiar summons of his soul: "*Laich . . .* ," it began. "*Laich . . .*"

Savagely he lifted the dusty bottle to his lips to drown that persistent, unintelligible command. The fiery liquor scorched his throat when he heard another voice behind him. "Eh, eh, eh!" A voice he would recognize among a thousand, though he had not heard it for a decade now. "Eh, we must be off. There is no time to tarry here, amid these raucous drovers. *Bueno, amigo*. Come!"

Christian spun and stared full into the face of Ishmael!

CHAPTER NINE

"Raucous drovers, is it?" demanded Christian in English. "And where must ye be off to so quickly, old man?"

Ishmael stared at him like a bird, unblinkingly, not recognizing this leathery, bearded gaucho, yet conscious of a faint whispering in the wrinkles of his memory. "Eh, eh, lad—ye speak like a native-born Englishman. Who be ye?"

"Why, Ishmael," laughed Christian, "don't you recognize me, the castaway you plucked from the sea and left in Santiago with Higgins so many years ago?"

Ishmael peered more closely at Christian then drew back with a grin of unabashed delight.

"Can it be?" The old man cried. "The arrow-maker, Fletcher! How is this, lad? I heard you were sent south to your doom with Spanish soldiers against the Mapuche. And here ye be, alive—or are we both dead?"

"Alive we are, Ishmael—never more so," Christian assured him, alight with a strange happiness. "The other soldiers died by Kolapel's hand; but being of the Higgins' 'tribe,' I was spared and now am here, gaucho as an ostrich, to greet you in this raucous pub. Let's go outside and talk."

They found their way outdoors and sat apart in the shade, filling in the years since they last were together, omitting nothing likely of interest to the other.

"And how are ye with the struggle against evil, the fight all of us must wage, Fletcher? Have you won out? Found peace of mind at last?"

Christian shook his head, recalling the "stick" that beat the buoyancy of life from him.

"I have not lost my curse, Ishmael," he replied, thinking now of the strange series of catastrophes affecting those whom he had loved or known. "It strikes those I have made mine, punishing me through others, a cowardly way, surely. You must know that you, too, are in great danger because of it, do ye not?"

Ishmael laughed his high-pitched cackle.

"'Tis other subjects I have to concern me, lad," he reassured Christian, who accepted the other's desire to speak of different things.

"And where to now?" he asked Ishmael. "And who was it that you spoke English to in the pub?"

The old man's face grew solemn. "A friend, nothing more . . . an acquaintance named Burke." His voice trailed off, then resumed again on a fresh tack. "The English have taken Buenos Aires, Fletcher," he announced. "They took it with a regiment or less, a miracle! But I doubt they can hold it unless massive reinforcements have reached the city in the four months since. Buenos Aires is a city of 40,000 now, including one-third or more slaves."

"Won't they fight on the side of the English, to be freed?"

"Beresford, who took the place, blundered I do believe. The slaves offered their numbers in return for liberty. But he hesitated to accept for fear of offending the citizens and their owners, and so he stands to lose the city. Without their thousands, I doubt he can hold out."

Christian gulped more brandy. "What concern of yours is all of this, Ishmael? Why do you leave Chile for Buenos Aires?"

"Because I am an Englishman."

"There is no other reason?"

Ishmael hesitated. "It is my duty," he said, simply. "Would you go with us, Fletcher? You know the post road, the pampa, the people, while I am a stranger to them all. So is my companion, young Burke."

"What is your mission?" insisted Christian.

The old man drew a circle with his toe in the dust. He dropped a pebble in the center. "I belong there, Fletcher," he said. "I cannot tell you why. Our mission may be nothing. It may prove perilous; it may require skill, imagination, courage—but it is my duty. I need you. Will you come?"

Christian laughed. "You know I will, Ishmael! I wouldn't miss it!"

The Englishman parted abruptly from Justo and Sebastian, telling neither Ishmael's news nor his intention; and with Burke, they were soon galloping swiftly 80 or 100 miles a day with many changes of horses down the post road toward the great port city. Approaching Esquina de la Guardia, 244 miles from Buenos Aires they saw shimmering in the sunlight before them an immense encampment, where on the mule journey to the northwest they had found only distance and a handful of frontier dragoons.

Christian signaled a halt. "This must be a La Plata force mustering for a counterblow," he muttered. "They are athwart our course. We've got to pass directly through their camp, I think."

Ishmael held his tongue. Burke seldom said anything, nor did he now. The old man seemed wearied by the furious riding of the past few days; it had even taxed Christian's strong body. Now it was midday and very hot. Christian dismounted, gathered up some dried cattle dung, and struck a fire.

"Can we not go on, Fletcher?" demanded Ishmael with some irritation.

Christian placed the *maté* pot on the fire.

"Dismount, Ishmael," he urged, kindly. "Let us take maté, a gaucho custom I have grown fond of at times like this." He waited patiently for the water to boil. "We will pause here until darkness, then attempt to pass through the camp. It will not be without risk."

"Could we not go around?"

"'Twould take several days, Ishmael, and it would be dangerous. Should we be detected trying to circumvent this camp, we would be done for. Our only chance is to go straight ahead. I shall talk—you two hold silence. There will be sentries."

With dusk the three herded their loose horses down the road toward the encampment. At their approach, a sentinel armed with a musket as tall as himself hailed them. He was a Spaniard, aloof from the barbarian ways of *el campo* rascals. "*Quienes son?* Who are you?" he demanded, as Christian neared.

The Englishman, muffling his voice in his poncho, replied, "Scouts from Cordoba, soldier. Our troops follow to join you. Who is in command? Where shall we report?"

The other hesitated but slightly. The enemy was English, not Spanish colonials from the interior. Reinforcements would be welcome, more rabble to fight rabble. It was not in his hands, anyway. He shrugged and stepped aside. "The viceroy, the marquis of Sobremonte, is encamped along the road. Headquarters is at this tent. Pass, *baqueanos*. How soon will the Cordoban arrive?"

"When we return, we shall guide them in," answered Christian vaguely.

The trio rode silently onward, passed the great tent that must be the viceroy's, lit within; at this hour his eminence would be dining. Without pause the three moved toward the eastern bounds of the bivouac. Nearly at that point, they put spurs to their horses, swept past a startled sentry who flung a shout after them as they darted by; then they were in the open, feeling the cool of the night on their faces, racing down the dark road.

Buenos Aires was a compact city on the pattern of all Spanish towns, with its streets neatly right-angled. Spreading on a slight summit overlooking the brown and shallow La Plata stood an arched and white-towered *cabildo*, or government house. Christian and his companions searched out a corral for their spare horses. Passersby paid them not the slightest attention, being principally concerned with avoiding puddles and mud sinks in the streets. The city did not appear to be under British control. Nor was it, any longer.

An aged, white-bearded gaucho with the inevitable *facon* protruding from his belt came up as they led their stock into the walled corral. He called to someone to help unsaddle and feed their animals; when that worthy appeared, he was wearing what must have once been a British army tunic with chevron-shadows still visible. There was an expression in his face and blue eyes that marked him as neither *plateño* nor Spanish.

"Who are you?" Christian blurted in English.

The hostler blinked his surprise. His smile however hesitant, revealed delight at hearing an English voice in this remote land of unhappy memory.

"Late of His Majesty's seventy-first Highlanders. Sergeant Campbell, sir."

"What is a British noncom doing tending livestock in this mud corral?"

"I was one of the fortunate ones, sir," the sergeant replied. "The others are scattered all along the rivers north. Them that survived."

"Survived?"

"We come in with our pipes skirling and took the bloody place, held it for two months and then got ourselves whipped. Ain't you heard?"

Christian shook his head. Ishmael, as nervous as a bird, danced around eager for news. "Tell us, tell us about it, sergeant," he urged.

"It's a bit of a story, sir," said the soldier. "And calls for a bit of vinegar-wine to aid in the telling."

He led the way to a corner café where he found them a remote table. A grinning slave brought them mugs of wine. None of the natives paid the slightest attention to them—such was the self-confidence, the pride, of the newly liberated colonials.

Campbell was equally oblivious to what he referred to as the "little people" who had spared his life and come to own it. He grew loquacious after a drink and proved both intelligent and knowledgeable; obviously he had earned his stripes.

"Late in 1805 we shipped for the Cape under Popham—Sir Home Riggs Popham of the Diadem, 64 guns," Campbell began. "Sir David Baird commanded the troops. We easily whipped the Dutchmen—They call 'em Boers—but Popham had come south for a fight, and he commenced looking somewheres else for glory; an' he thought of this place, God forgive him." The soldier said it without rancor.

"About 1,900 men was put under General Beresford—One-eyed Billy, we calls him—and Colonel Denis Pack and shipped for here with three frigates, three corvettes, and five transports—178 guns in all. Off Montevideo across the river, we captured a Spanish schooner with a royal pilot named Russell from Glencoe, where I come from too; but that's neither here nor there. He'd lived down here so long all he could speak was Spanish, anyways."

"Whose notion was it, lad, to attack this place—Popham's alone?" asked Ishmael. Campbell shook his head.

"I'm a line soldier, old man, an' not such as officers take into their councils," he replied. "Some says Popham met a Yank merchant captain what told him these Spaniards was ripe for the pluckin', but I doubt he would gamble the king's men an' ships unless old Pitt shoved the thought into him. I'll wager he gets court-martialed, now it's failed."

"Go on," prodded Christian. "Let's hear the rest of it."

"We crossed the river to a place south of Buenos Aires the Spaniards call Quilmes," continued Campbell. "It was raining so hard when we landed you couldn't tell the river from the land. We had to harness men to the guns to pull 'em ashore." He sighed as he recalled the miserable labor.

"It's so shoal," he recalled brightening, "that one day th' wind blew off shore and blew the water out to sea, leaving nothin' but a wide mud-flat. One of our ships, the *Justinia,* was beached, an' a cloud of them Spaniards on horseback galloped out to her. She listed so her larboard guns was full of mud an' her starboard guns aimed skyward, and them horsemen took her, crew an' all! Did you ever hear the like? Horsemen capturing one of His Majesty's ships, even if she was a sixth-rate!"

Campbell downed another deep draught, had his mug refilled, and continued. "Billy Beresford and Pack had less than 2,000 men when we mucked ashore, an' 'twas raining hard. But fat old Sobremonte wouldn't believe we was comin' in, even when he was told we were landin' men and guns.

"We heard he was at the theatre; and by the time Sobrie came out of the show, we was already skirmishin' with 'em. There was a couple thousand of them, mostly cavalry, along with brow of a hill. They had eight guns, we was told; but they was poorly manned. When we come up the hill, the Spaniards split, leaving us four of their field guns.

"We pushed on after a rest. The enemy opposed our crossing over a little river next day, but their hearts wasn't in it. Billy sent our grenadiers and a light company across by raft to rout 'em, and we come in on the city with no further opposition at all. We found that the militia had been given arms but no cartridges, an' their guns had no flints. That's the way these people does things. They rung all their bells like madmen when we come in; but it wasn't to welcome us, but to alarm th' populace; an' they took off.

"Old Sobrie'd heard the shootin' and he careened out of the city beyond our reach. He ordered the treasury to follow him, but Billy with some engineers captured that. In all 'twas a million dollars. 'Twas sent to England, every dollar of it."

"How then did the city become lost?" asked Ishmael.

Campbell sighed noisily. "'Twasn't but a couple of months at most, we held it. Long enough for the ships to withdraw to a better anchorage across the river, off Colonia and Montevideo. This was a city of many thousands, and we was few. Beresford and Pack tried to fool 'em into thinkin' we was more than we was, by orderin' more rations than we could eat and like that. But we couldn't keep them in the dark forever.

"Th' Spaniards, who had lost old Sobremonte—an' little loss it was—found a man name of Jacques de Liniers, a froggie; and he armed 'em somehow—drilled 'em, and put some fight into 'em. Then they had us boxed up to rights, because we couldn't get out, and no relief could get in. On August 12, they swarmed over the walls and it was all over. Billy, bless him for the soldier he is, got us terms, but the Spaniards never kept them. Now he an' Sir Denis is prisoners like us." The sergeant glumly finished his drink. "They's better off, I must admit, since they've got a house and the run of the city, but no better future they can look forward to, I believe."

There was silence following Campbell's recital. Then Ishmael asked, "Is it possible for us to see Beresford?"

"See Billy Beresford? Why, I suppose ye can. I see him all the time. He ever has a bit of a smile for me, too, I must say, for all of his worries. Why did ye want to see him?"

Ishmael gave no answer for the moment. Then he called for a pen and bit of paper. When the paper at last was brought, the old man penned a note, folded and handed it to the sergeant along with a silver *reale*. "Will you get this to him, Campbell?"

The sergeant tossed the *reale*, caught if deftly, pocketed it, and tucked the note into his army blouse pocket.

"I will that, sir," he pledged.

CHAPTER TEN

General William Beresford was short, dark, of incisive movement and speech. Colonel Pack was his complete opposite. Where Beresford was short, Pack was tall; where Billy was filled with bustle, Pack appeared more languid, reasoned, relaxed. Each complemented the other, comprising a completed professional whole, an effective team. Now as captives of war, they shared a comfortable, if unpretentious villa with an enclosed patio bordered by flowers and with servants suitable to their rank and their status as the most exalted prisoners ever to fall into the hands of the viceroyalty of La Plata. The Spaniards had not yet decided what was to be done with them, and so the two waited, bored almost beyond endurance. There was little to do except carry on with their studies of the Spanish language, which one day might prove of value to an officer of the king.

Now they sat in the center of the patio, speaking little because everything had been said long ago.

They looked up with interest as the strangers were ushered in. In the dusk Beresford's black eye patch seemed like a cavern into his skull. "Yes?" he demanded, in his commanding officer's bark. "Yes? I received your note, sir—you are English, I take it?"

"English we are indeed, or at least to that tongue were born, so I suppose 'tis English we are," answered Ishmael.

"Are you citizens of Buenos Aires, then?" wondered Beresford. "How do you survive—how does anyone survive this stagnation?"

"We are citizens of nowhere, sir," replied Ishmael, in his enigmatic way. "We are here to serve the wishes of the officers of His Majesty in any way we can."

"Our wishes are to be out of this God-forsaken city of mud," drawled Pack. "If you can do that, we shall be in your debt. If you cannot, there is little else that will serve us." He yawned. "Ah boredom, thy name is Spain!"

"Can you tell us what is the situation in the estuary?" asked Christian, who thus far had not spoken. Beresford looked at him with quickening interest.

"In what way?" he asked.

"Well, sir, who holds what land? Is the English force with their ships withdrawn entirely? Will there be no counter-attempt of any sort against the Plata cities?"

Beresford examined the face of Christian with his sparrow's eye and precision judgment, seeking to assess his character, liking what he saw. So, too, did Pack from beneath hooded lids.

"A fresh assault?" demanded Beresford. "Who can tell? Who but Wellesley, or Buckingham, rather? We intended at the outset to seize Montevideo and Colonia when we came in. Montevideo alone is visited by 600 or more coasters a year and 130 ships, according to our intelligence. The lifeblood of war is commerce, or at least greed." He paused, reflected. "I would imagine they have been captured; and we may hold them still, if Popham has not pulled out. I sent a million dollars to London; and if it was landed properly, it would certainly stir the avaricious; and there are none more so than my dearly beloved countrymen. With the great profit from these miserable plains, they would push His Majesty's government for relief for our forces—in no uncertain terms."

"When would it arrive?"

"Not before spring, I would suppose. They must realize our force was very small, too small."

"Eh, precisely what is your status, sir?" asked Ishmael. "Are you under pledge of some sort? Word of honor?"

Beresford glanced at him sharply.

"We have given our word, yes," he replied. "We pledge not to take flight, to not attempt escape." Beresford pursed his lips thoughtfully. "However, I might point out that Liniers gave us his pledge that our men would be held together here, pending some sort of exchange."

"And instead they've been dispersed to the four winds," rasped Pack with bitterness. "So much for the word of the Spanish."

"Liniers is French, Denis," corrected Beresford. "He's a man of honor, I think."

"Perhaps so; but he spoke for the Spaniards who are without honor, apparently."

"In any event," Beresford continued, "I consider my pledge lifted, since theirs was not sustained." He sighed, picked up his maté gourd, quickly setting aside with a grimace. "This is a pathetic excuse for tea."

Christian drew at a *bombilla* with more contentment. "Then why," he asked, "do you not leave? There must be a craft on the river to get you to Montevideo. It would be no great matter to sail across the estuary, to see if His Majesty's ships are still there. That is what I would attempt in your place, since you say you are released from your pledge and owe these people nothing."

Beresford inspected Christian again, finding his suggestion as satisfying to his daring nature as it was to fulfill the duty of a captured soldier to rejoin his comrades if at all possible.

"I come from Yorkshire, a long way from the sea; Pack is from Ireland, also a landsman. We know little of boats, nothing of sailing, navigation. If we sent out at night, we would be just as likely to sail out into the open ocean as to make the opposite shore. The estuary is more than 100 miles in width with a wild shore to land upon, even if it were possible for us to cross." But his imagination had been stirred; and Beresford quickly added: "Are you a seaman, sir? Could you obtain a craft of some sort, setting out with us, if we should elect to leave?"

Fletcher Christian found himself torn by opposing impulses. These men were Englishmen and he felt a bond with them. On the other hand, 'twould be highly dangerous to consort in any manner with Royal Navy seamen, even though it was now twenty years since he had seized the *Bounty*. English memories were long.

"I—I could not bind myself to deliver you to His Majesty's ships; but possibly I could see you across to the northern coast, where, if it is in British hands, you could perhaps return to your regiments."

"I see," murmured Beresford. He was not a fool, and this was no time to insist upon conditions. A bearded Englishman wandering in the remotest corner of the Spanish empire reluctant to approach British warships no doubt had sufficient cause.

"Your services would be of the greatest importance to us, Fletcher—is that your name? We are men of honor and would pledge you our support. In any event, we would respect your wish for anonymity. We acknowledge our obligations, sir, and would repay them in any manner of your choosing."

"Repayment I do not anticipate, sir," countered Christian. "Money would have little value to me at this moment, and in favors I have no—" He caught himself. "We shall see. Who knows the future?"

CHAPTER ELEVEN

Through the darkness Christian found the water's edge where a silent creek entered La Plata, its confluence flushing out a channel of some slight depth. This channel would continue into the riverbed, permitting the small boats to approach the shore, although larger vessels were anchored to buoys well offshore; by means of such channels crews rowed out to the anchored craft. Through the silty soup of the river, one could see nothing, even by daylight. The existence of the channels could be discerned only by skilled observation of the choppy wavelets that the wind stirred up.

Locating a suitable boat and gathering the party had been no simple matter, but it was done. The British officers, thanks to judicious bribes of their guards by Ishmael together with Burke and Campbell, were now collected in the darkness, relying upon Fletcher Christian to guide them to freedom. For several days he had carefully reconnoitered the long stretch of coast, discovering finally a craft anchored far enough offshore so that it might be loosed and slip away unseen, one seaworthy enough to get them across the river.

The boat was invisible from shore this night, but Christian sloshed out into the shallow waters with assurance. The others followed before he was lost from sight. For a quarter mile the tall figure of Christian led the way, striding through the turbulent stream as though it were a field of wheat. Steadily the party splashed on across the barely submerged mudflat, the silt hard and packed and giving them secure footing. The water gradually deepened, reaching almost to their waists when the vague form of an anchored sloop loomed ahead. No guards were stationed on La Plata boats, since none had ever been stolen—until now.

The light wind was from the northwest, which suited Christian perfectly. With a low voice he directed his companions, and a gaff-rigged, fore-and-aft sail was hoisted, the rattling and creaking gear sounding overloud in the night. The boom was swung into the wind; and the boat and her tiny crew gradually gathered headway, the vessel cutting her bone in style. They had seen no one since they had left the land. They were free!

So they imagined; but they were not to be loosed so smoothly; for the vast and bitter land they quitted would give them one final salute, an unforgettable reminder of its ferocity.

The day dawned hot with the shoreline low and indistinct to the west and nothing but open water before. It was as if they were navigating a flat, waveless sea, but this was the yawning mouth of one of the world's great river systems. The frightful intensity of the sun seemed to boil off the breeze, leaving them baked, listless.

Then, in midmorning, with his seaman's eye Christian detected a haze to the south, a murk filling the sky as the north wind stilled. A dark mountain of cloud built rapidly to the southwest so swiftly it appeared driven by an elemental force more furious than the wind itself. Soon an entire half of the heavens was overcast by a boiling darkness, a shadow of evil, hurtling swiftly over the land toward them. Flashes of lighting laced its forward edge; the rumbling sounds of battle quickened to sharp crashes, with the uproar accompanying the demoniacal fury of the wind.

"'Tis the pampero," announced Christian matter-of-factly to his companions. "The pampero everyone dreads for it sweeps all before it. We shall be fortunate if this craft survives." Billy Beresford and Pack assessed his serious face with little emotion. Death in any form was their constant companion; and they had no awe of it, even here.

Christian quickly got in the mainsail and had a jib raised to give the boat steerage before the gathering storm, now close upon them. Swept wildly overhead, the terrified harbingers of the blow came, the fluttering gulls and other birds, seeking to escape its fury, winging broken paths barely in advance of the boiling turbulence of yellow dust, the torrents of rain and pounding hail.

With the storm came an abrupt chill. The temperature in an instant plummeted thirty degrees. The little sloop quivered, as if from the ague, then rose to meet the onslaught.

As the wind beat down, the water swept up in tumult. Only the consummate skill of Christian preserved the craft that otherwise would have been smashed into pieces, hurtling the victims into the water. He kept the tiller steady despite the lashing rain, the hail, and the great plumes of white, the charging savagery of the waves. How he did it, none could say; but Christian managed to hold the boat against the wind for upwards of an hour until the gale swept past, leaving only the cold driving rain.

"We should have perished in that storm," murmured Beresford, quietly.

"Perhaps," replied Christian at long last. "But 'tis quickly over. At this season these southwest storms are not uncommon, but the danger they present always seems new."

"Aye," agreed Pack. "It would take some getting used to, I'll concede."

Colonia, an ancient Portuguese settlement, was now held by the Spanish. There were no signs of the British fleet in the evening sunlight. Christian held the sloop well out into the river, taking advantage of a rising wind in the wake of the pampero, though with none of its violence or hatred.

Twilight melded into the darkness of early night. The shore they coasted was of a still deeper shade, a deserted, desolate land. "Do you wish to put in along there somewhere, sir? Christian asked the general. "We might possibly strike a fire, but I doubt we'd find anything to eat, unless we killed a wild cow."

Beresford settled deeper against the bulkhead. "No, I don't think so, Fletcher," he replied. "We'd be better off cruising the coast than visiting it. How far do you estimate Montevideo to be?"

"I am not familiar with this shore, sir; but I've heard it is forty leagues below Colonia; we ought to be in its vicinity shortly after sunup. I hope we don't overrun it in the night."

It was midmorning before the fugitives discerned the *cerro*, the 500-foot, conical peak that bestowed upon on Montevideo its name. After another hour of slow progress, the Englishmen perceived British men-of-war standing off the landing. There were two third-rates blocking the harbor and one flying the admiral's pendant farther out.

The Portuguese-built fort revealed a broken outline, as though smashed under bombardment. From the city itself rose the twin domes of a new cathedral, nearly 150 feet high, and opposite the white tower of the *cabildo*. But it was toward the flagship that Christian directed the sloop, now heeling a bit under a freshening breeze, the ocean character being felt this far inland.

Swollen oaken sides of the great ship marked her style of architecture as British. She had swung around revealing a name, *HMS Audacious*. Above the green copper sheathing, a wide black stripe was painted right round the ship, as high as the lower gun deck. Above this she was brownish-yellow, the paint discolored by her long passage down the reaches of the Atlantic from Portsmouth. She was a taut ship, the mark of a proud, efficient commander.

A scarlet-jacketed marine with crossed belts hailed the sloop from the main deck entry, attempting to call to them in halting Spanish. Finally he gave it up and demanded in English: "What boat is that? Stand off! Don't approach until cleared, you!" A midshipman appeared at his side.

"Whose ship?" demanded the general, his one eye scanning her to find a clue somewhere to her commander. "Beresford, Colonel Pack here, late of the Seventy-First Highlanders, and late of Buenos Aires, too, if it comes to that." His voice trailed away.

The midshipman hastily disappeared. In a moment a roar of command surged out from the quarterdeck: "*Beresford! Pack!* Get them on board, you nincompoop! Don't just stand there, for the love of God! Bring them up!"

Then a somewhat quieter voice, but equally of command: "Pipe them on board, Mr. Stevens. At once, sir! At once!"

The thin, wobbling note of the high-pitched boatswain's whistle sounded as two ranking officers—one of the ship's captains, the other an army officer—joined the marine at the rail. Laboriously Pack started up the ladder, and Beresford prepared to follow him.

"Will the General have any further need of the boat—or of us?" asked Christian hesitantly.

The officer turned, surveyed him with his good eye. "Why, I don't know, Mr. Fletcher," he replied slowly. "Won't you come aboard with us? You have earned a bit of rest. At least have some food with us, perhaps a reward of some kind. After all, you did rescue us from Buenos Aires and save our lives on the river."

"I'd rather not, sir, though I'm grateful for your kindness," replied Christian. "But 'tis possible these others might like to remain with you."

Again Beresford hesitated.

"At any rate, Fletcher, I wish you would hold your craft here for the present. I pledge you, sir, that you shall be entirely safe. No one will in any way interfere with your liberty to leave when you desire to do so. But do stand by for a brief time."

He turned then, as though certain his suggestion would be accepted, and climbed the ladder. The boatswain's piping continued without interruption until the figures disappeared onto the deck.

For more than an hour the sloop, her canvas neatly furled, was held in close to the warship. Christian listened with nostalgia to the sounds of the great ship-city, with its working crew, its drilling marines, a ruffle of drums, an occasional cry of command. He had forgotten almost that such a ship lived, that it reflected so self-contained a community, having its own rulers, its own hierarchy, labors, leisures, friendships, and hatreds—His Majesty's vessel, a world apart, autonomous, fulfilling the will of the king, but independently of his voice, almost of his scepter.

She carried 74 guns, capable of slamming a broadside of 1,764 pounds of shot into an enemy, with short-range carronades in addition. Her complement numbered about 650 men and a few women; and her main gun deck was nearly 200 feet in length, her displacement 1,700 tons. She was indeed a city, a fortress.

A call from the deck interrupted Christian's reverie.

"Mr. Fletcher!" cried a midshipman. "The admiral wishes you aboard, sir. Will you come up?"

Again Christian hesitated. Memory of the *Bounty* warned from an impulse to accept. A single glint of recognition from some sailor or officer, one whisper of suspicion might prove his undoing, leading to his hanging from those very yardarms etched against the afternoon sky. While he paused Beresford appeared and cupped his mouth in his hands, "Operations are planned still against Buenos Aires, Mr. Fletcher," he called. "Your counsel is needed—do come up, please! Bring the others along, if you care to, sir!"

Gaining the spar deck, Christian instinctively saluted the quarterdeck, a gesture Beresford did not miss. He followed the general into the captain's cabin under the poop deck, feeling vastly out of place in his gaucho's *chirips* and *potro*-boots. He remembered protocol, however, and removed his head covering before ducking through the low entryway. On the long curved bench opposite, under the glazed ports, sat several officers, Pack among them, apparently as many from the army and marines as from the navy. The ship's captain, in sharply turned blue coat, lace, white cuffs, and gold buttons, his cockaded hat laid aside, sat at a polished table at the head of which was Admiral Stirling.

The admiral, who had a rather chilled cast to his stern features had been newly appointed to command the fleet in these waters. He succeeded Popham who had been ordered home in some disgrace for having quitted the Cape for La Plata in the first place, although he would receive huge honors from admiring Londoners for his successes in doing so. Next to Stirling was a neatly-bearded soldier of the rank of brigadier general, introduced as Sir Samuel Auchmuty, whose clear, loud voice Christian recognized as the source of the bellow when Beresford and Pack had announced themselves. Born in America and raised in that land, Sir Samuel had brought his Loyalist sentiments to New England, which had forced him to flee the continent's eastern seaboard. Profane and quite outspoken, he was nevertheless a competent officer, one whom men would follow anywhere with devotion and faith.

His gray eyes studied Christian's face with intelligence and perception.

"Mr. Fletcher has extensive and, if I may so, intensive knowledge of the Spanish viceroyalty," Beresford said by way of a beginning. "He is an honest man as I believe." The other officers observed him with varying degrees of interest. Beresford turned to Christian. "We would be interested in your evaluation of the strength of the colony, sir," he said. "What force you believe could take it—and hold it this time: anything of that nature. Anything at all."

Christian's eyes swept the faces before him and settled upon that of Auchmuty as the key to the adventure. He spoke as though to him alone.

"Of organized defenses, the *plateños* have very little, and that not much of consequence. But of spirit—well, General Beresford can attest to that better than I. In Liniers they appear to have a competent organizer and commander. He is to be feared, I think."

"Has he authority?" the bearded general asked.

"Sufficient for his purpose. Sobremonte, I believe, is through; and the man in charge now would be Liniers, unless orders from the king should say differently. In any event, orders would be long in arriving."

A marine colonel interposed. "The king of Spain is unlikely to say anything whatever about the affairs in this remote area. He is occupied sufficiently for the present with Napoleon, I should think."

It was a new name for Christian; having no knowledge of that person, he said nothing.

"As to their spirit, I've been well introduced," growled Auchmuty, painfully. "We lost 600 men storming Montevideo, but take it we did after it proved unfeasible to capture Buenos Aires with the force I brought. We can hold Montevideo, I believe. If we could now gather sufficient force to smash into Buenos Aires and seize it, could we hold it?" He cleared his throat. "And what about the hinterland? Is there strength there? Are they organized? What about food and supplies—would they support an army? Would the people prove amenable to our occupation? Are they discontented, would fair rule by foreigners seem to them acceptable? These are the questions which concern us."

Christian shifted his position, considering the questions carefully.

"The Spaniards are brave people, as you know, sir, even if they are sometimes weak, cruel, and treacherous. They also are very proud. To be forced to submit to foreign rule would only generate hatred. And as their fury increased, so would their blind determination to oppose, at any cost. I do not believe they would ever submit for long to foreign control, however just. That is my belief. A strong force, well managed, could of course seize the city, but the city could never control the countryside. The *campo* is so vast, so trackless, that it would be impossible to control it without hundreds of thousands of troops, mostly of well-mounted cavalry, able to move swiftly, strike hard, and pursue the enemy relentlessly. I do not believe, sir, that Englishmen could do it."

"Could any people?"

Christian hesitated. "Yes, by overwhelming them it might eventually be accomplished by some persistent, stubborn nation. But it could not be done quickly by military means alone, but only by settlers, farmers, and villagers fanning out over many years from Buenos Aires. No nation, I believe, could accomplish this, no European nation, unless it intended to make this conquest its primary effort. As a bit of dilettantism, a mere exercise in empire, I do not believe it can be done, no matter what initial force might be mustered."

Auchmuty inspected Christian's face closely for a long moment. A slow grin gradually lightened his expression.

"You are aware, of course, Fletcher, that those remarks are scarcely calculated to enhance your popularity among this motley company of adventurers?"

CHAPTER TWELVE

As a civilian of possible value to the expedition, Christian was quartered and rationed aboard the *Audacious*, his fears gradually fading from his mind. Having neither duties nor responsibilities, he lived a shadow existence, quick to serve while not subject to demand. He fit smoothly into the ship's life, almost as though the intervening twenty years had never existed, even though he felt a man apart, as indeed he was.

The British expeditionary force gathering to retake Buenos Aires in the River Plate, as the English called La Plata, seemed stronger, almost each hour. From the river-sea in the eastern first light, tall pyramids of sail moved in to join the fleet, among them the flagship of Sir George Murray who assumed command of naval operations. Soon a fleet of eighteen war vessels and more than eighty transports had assembled, all awaiting the arrival of the frigate *Thisbe* with Lieutenant General John Whitelocke who had been named to command the landing forces. This had grown to impressive proportions: 1,400 men from Cape Colony, plus General Auchmuty's contingent of 4,400, and another 4,000 under quick-tempered Robert Crauford of India fame, to bring the total to nearly 12,000 men, 5 or 6 times the ragtag force Buenos Aires was believed to be capable of arraying against them. All that was required, it seemed, was a resolute, imaginative commander, and it was hoped Whitelocke would prove such a man.

Christian never forgot his first meeting with the pasty-faced general aboard the *Audacious* in the middle of May, 1807. Whitelocke reminded him in some ways of Bligh, though not with his precision, crudity, nor peremptoriness. Quite the reverse. Where Bligh had been decisive, Whitelocke was infirm of purpose; Bligh was resourceful, while Whitelocke seemed utterly to lack that quality. The general appeared to lean upon any shoulder within reach. From the outset Christian was wary of this man, as he had learned to be of Bligh.

Whitelocke was bald as an ostrich egg, except for a white fringe that touched his ears. About his mouth there was the slight sneer of a man contemptuous of those with whom he is forced into contact, or perhaps because of a secret conviction that, while superior in rank, he was basically inferior in quality to virtually all of them. His well-tailored blouse with its stiff collar, the epaulets and the gold braid, concealed a somewhat portly figure, but it served to identify his rank; and in this army, rank was everything, even authority to lead men into disaster. Christian, summoned to council the first day after the general's arrival, was the subject of disdain amounting to aversion. As for Ishmael, the commander gave neither a word nor a glance. Major-General John Leveson-Gower, Whitelocke's second in command, also owed his appointment to politics and was living evidence that in the British army of the day, rank—not ability—was supreme. Good and brave men fell like rain at the inept orders of creatures whose rank supported their wicked commands.

Addressing Christian, Whitelocke's voice was imperious, strident, impatient. "You!" he turned at last to Christian. "What is your name? What experience have you had with these people, this place? List for me their defenses."

Christian endeavored to conceal his distaste.

"I know nothing of the numbers, arms, training, or the officer quality of the defenders of Buenos Aires, sir," he replied, softly. "I know only of the general ability of the people, their spirit, their method of fighting, their temper, their resourcefulness—"

Whitelocke impatiently gestured him silent.

"I have not time for such general philosophy," he said curtly. "I deal in guns, not emotions—soldiers, not rabble. Answer my questions, please."

Christian shook his head. "Of the sort of information you demand, sir, I fear I have little."

Whitelocke spread his hands helplessly and swiveled to stare with exasperation at his assembled retinue. "Why are we wasting time with this fool?" he demanded. Have we not an expedition to prepare? Have we not?"

Most of his officers remained silent. Auchmuty, however, was not easily impressed by mere rank.

"Mr. Fletcher," he said quietly, "our proposal is for infantry, marines, and generally dismounted cavalry to—"

Whitelocke interrupted him.

"I do not favor discussing our plans before idiots who can easily pass word of them to the enemy."

General Auchmuty heard him tolerantly. His Yankee independence may have bordered upon insolence, but too much was at stake to ignore the basic elements of success. His own command was semi-autonomous, in any event.

"I do not see any possibility of our decisions being carried to the Spaniards because of questions we ask this man," he insisted. "He has given much proof of his general loyalty to our flag. I do believe that an army without all the information it can get is at least partially blinded. Blindness leads frequently to disaster, it seems to me. I cannot so cavalierly jeopardize my troops." Without awaiting permission, he turned back to Christian.

"We intend to land south of the city and drive in toward it with our foot supported by considerable artillery. Our force will be impressive in numbers, if somewhat lacking in mobility."

Christian considered the prospect thoughtfully.

"I am confident, sir, that the *plateños* can muster no organized force capable of opposing you effectively," he said, "but their strength is not in ranks of trained soldiers; rather 'tis in the spirit of their people, if suitably aroused. The hinterland is vast and can conceal hordes of mounted irregulars who would cut you to pieces, given time to gather them together and to become motivated. It would appear to me that your cavalry should be mounted against them, that your attack be swift and concentrated, and your position ashore made secure before opposition can coalesce."

Auchmuty considered Christian's views with care, his fingers tapping upon the table.

"We cannot mount our cavalry without horses," he grumbled, "and horses cannot be ferried by transports any distance such as this and arrive in fit condition to work, so we brought none."

"La Plata is full of horses, sir."

"How does that avail us?"

"Give me a few able men, and I can bring in all the horses you need, sir, in two or three weeks or a month."

Whitelocke burst into the conversation with irritation.

"We have no time for such ridiculous enterprises, Auchmuty," he railed, "Even if this man can do as he says, more probably he would employ the occasion to muster opposition to us and inform this rabble of our intentions. Let us be on with our work. Fletcher, you may go."

Thus dismissed, Christian returned to the spar deck, where he had left Ishmael drowsing in the sun. The old man peered quizzically at him. "Ye look displeased, Fletcher," he observed, not without a certain humor. "Ye must have been talking with the supreme ruler of the fleet, the army, the expedition, the empire?"

Christian managed a grin.

"You describe him well, Ishmael." He stared aloft at the network of lines, spars, upper masts, furled sails, the most intricate composition that had ever been invented by man and the most useful and durable employer and exploiter of the elements. That so efficient and lasting a machine as the ship might be used with incompetence bothered him.

"Have plans been completed as yet for furtherance of the kingdom?" asked Ishmael.

Christian did not reply for a long moment.

"'Twill be no conquest, Ishmael, and well ye know it," he murmured. "Even if their plans are drawn to perfection and command falls into hands competent and dedicated, it will fail. And do you know why? Not for any fault of its own. It will fail because I am associated with it. *I* will doom it. My 'stick' is heavy upon it, heavier because of the incompetence of the commander. This mighty force is doomed, and I am the cause of it more than any man, more even than Whitelocke himself, because he will not be able to help himself. I have touched him."

Ishmael had raised himself and now stared unblinkingly at Christian.

"Will ye never lose this obsession, Fletcher? I would think it had long since worn out and been forgot, that foolishness of yours, that—that superstition, for I can call it nothing else."

Christian shook his head. "The truth never wears out, Ishmael. What a novelty, I instructing you! But 'tis I who have had the experience of this thing; and you cannot detect it. You have never seen the disaster it has wrought."

Ishmael sank to the deck again.

"How can I convince ye, Fletcher, that your 'fatal touch,' as you conceive it lies within your mind? It will grow not stronger with the years, but weaker. It is the one obstacle that ye must climb over to preserve your sanity, let alone your happiness."

"Of happiness I have no hope, Ishmael. I have tasted it; and I have destroyed it, not once, but frequently. I am afflicted with the incurable disease; and there is no gainsaying it, for the proof is ever at my hand."

"Fletcher," Ishmael replied at last, "ye are an obstinate man, though not without reason, I suppose. Do you not realize that a delusion such as yours cannot be run away from or escaped save by a greater idea, a belief that can rout it out by its own purity, its own strength? If you believe you are possessed by this evil, then only good will supplant it. For your devil there is but one answer: God. Why are you so blind to this truth? It was evident in the time of Moses and has been for all the ages; it should also be for you. Truth, as you yourself have said, never alters, never fades—"

A savage irritation all but blinded Christian. He leaped to his feet and strode away. A tide of anger overwhelmed him that he could neither grasp nor control.

CHAPTER THIRTEEN

Late in June, Whitelocke left a garrison of 1,350 men at Montevideo and moved an attack force of 7,822 rank and file across the wide river toward a landing at Ensenada de Barragon, a tiny port eighteen leagues southeast of La Ciudad de la Santíssima Trinidad, Puerto de Santa María de Buenos Aires. His men composed 9 battalions of infantry, 2 ½ regiments of cavalry, although only 150 men were mounted, and 16 field guns, a powerful force—if ably led.

The English troops were colorful enough, the infantry in blue knee-breeches and scarlet jackets with gold epaulets, a black three-cornered hat with a white, scarlet-tipped feather to top it; dragoons in scarlet and white with bearskin helmets, and grenadiers in blue and gold. All this composition of color and discipline and efficiency would face a populace drab enough—but commanded by Liniers.

Jacques de Liniers, or Santiago de Liniers as he was known to the Spanish, now viceroy and commander in chief for the defenders, was no fool. Energetic, bold, wise, and swift in decision, he may have been guided by volatile emotions; but none could question his loyalty, his perception, nor his effectiveness. The English troops, impressive in numbers, tautly disciplined, fearsome in guns, frightened Liniers not a whit. Chess was a game he understood; a checkmate was gained not by bluff, but by movement, by power, by blows, by truth.

Whitelocke, for his part, leaned heavily upon Gower, his staff chief, for planning the drive into the city; and Gower was no armchair soldier. He urged upon his general a Napoleonic scheme by which the army would swing around west of the city, hook its left arm upon the wide La Plata, and, choking in upon the settlement, bring cannon to bear upon its principal buildings and centers until surrender was forced, hopefully with only minor British losses. Crauford and Auchmuty argued bitterly against this proposal, which was suited to the capture of fortified European strong points but scarcely to a scattered community of 50,000, with only 6,000 indifferently armed and trained militia and soldiers to defend them. These defenders, it was learned with Christian's help, were organized into several regiments, such as the *Catalanes*, who thought of themselves as Spanish;

the *Patricios*, of peasants and journeymen; and the *Castas*, a slave regiment assigned to the artillery.

"Gower's plan would be the best means to assassinate civilians and alienate us all irretrievably," Auchmuty growled to Whitelocke. "I doubt an empire could be built in Spanish America or anywhere else by such measures. All it will do is encourage irregular resistance until the citizens learn military skills. And that is could bring disaster down upon us, turning our 'empire' to ashes."

"What do you propose, then?

"Drive in with every man we've got in two or three columns, seize the *cabildo* and *plaza de toros*, and control the heart of the city. Then hold it with a tight, well-organized force until the inhabitants, with no relief in sight, are forced to surrender. Make generous terms, share the rule, give the citizens the impression that we favor their peace and prosperity and are here only to assure and protect them and raise a generation of subjects devoted to His Majesty. That is the way to do it, for Gower's plan can't work. I never heard of a man with a bloodied nose who didn't swing back."

Whitelocke adopted something of his subordinate's views, and more of Gower's, and came up with a combination strategy worse than either's. While he hesitated, his troops gradually advanced from Ensenada toward Buenos Aires.

Arriving at the outskirts, they found the waters of a stream separating them from the city subsided and fordable. On July 2, Gower took an advance guard across it and in a sharp action drove the defenders back into their city, while the British took up positions awaiting the main body. These troops arrived the next day.

Buenos Aires was not fortified, since it never had considered itself a pawn in colonial struggles, so remote was it and so well protected by the wide mud flats of La Plata and the limitless plains of the interior. Now it found itself quite unexpectedly the target for a European invasion. The citizens were not only startled but conscious of a surge of pride that they were not so neglected as they had supposed, that somebody did indeed desire the place. They felt more important than they were, perhaps; but danger invigorated them and brought them a fresh life and élan of a sort.

The prospects facing the British the next morning were quite different from that of the previous night. They found an enemy even more resolute and determined to resist them than during the previous evening's skirmish. "Don't fight unless you are ready to capitalize on the decision, and when you rout an enemy, crowd him hard!" recited Auchmuty to his respectful breakfast audience. He had invited Christian to eat with them. "Now the general is drafting an ultimatum to people in a city we've not entered, and before he has even decided how he is going to take it. What a war!"

"What will the ultimatum say, sir?" asked Colonel Pack.

"I've only seen a draft," replied Auchmuty. "It demands delivery of British subjects, the imprisonment of Spanish soldiers, the surrender of all arms, and all the loot Whitelocke could think of. They'd be insane to accede to it without a battle, and they won't. We sound like a crew of bloody pirates."

As Auchmuty predicted, Liniers wrote that it was absurd to demand that the Spanish lay down arms they had not yet used. Whitelocke, still convinced that the bluff would work, wrote him the next day of his additional forces within call, other troops waiting to disembark, his warships eager to join in a bombardment of Buenos Aires, and the impossibility of the Spanish getting support from anywhere.

Liniers laughed. At least his reply sounded as though he were laughing. While he had ammunition, he wrote, and his people were filled with the spirit of resistance and anticipation for battle, the English could do whatever they wished; he would meet it.

With positions now drawn, Whitelocke's army prepared to begin hostilities. His own commanders were disgruntled. The scheme of attack was enough to confuse any soldier. The assault plan was as indecisive as the mind of Whitelocke itself and his officers, professionals all, fretted under it.

"Look at this fool's dream!" exploded Auchmuty as the troops got underway. "Look! Here, Fletcher, look at this ridiculous thing! All the officers are busy, and I've got to share it with someone. Just look!"

Christian scanned the neatly penned page, written by Whitelocke's clerk.

"We're to be organized, our eight battalions in thirteen columns, to clear out as many streets, to enter the town with arms unloaded, and to meet along the river front!" exclaimed the general. "Sixteen hundred left here and the rest of us marching into a town like a bloody parade! What are the Spaniards going to do while we're prancing through their streets without cartridges in our guns? They'll cut us to ruddy ribbons. We'll be lucky if anyone gets out of Buenos Aires alive!"

Auchmuty's own regiment was the Ninth Light Dragoons, also known as the Queen's Royal Regiment of Lancers. It was formed in brigade with four troops, dismounted as well, of the Sixth Dragoon Guards, the Carabineers, and Colonel Thomas Mahon's Fortieth and Forty-fifth Regiments of foot. After a light skirmish in which Gower had dispersed the enemy, Auchmuty's column had driven into the southern suburb of the city and bivouacked upon the central avenue, driving straight as a lance at the center and the viceroy's quarters. Other troops edged into the town by other thoroughfares. And so it was when the fateful July 5 dawned, rainy and cold and with a chill wind sweeping in upon their backs, they commenced their march dully as ghosts, eager for the clash and warmth of battle.

Attached informally to Auchmuty's headquarters, Christian listened to his directives: four troops of the Sixth Dragoon Guards and three of the Ninth Light to force the street, supported by two six-pounders, with the remaining five troops of the Ninth forming the reserve. Auchmuty and most of his staff would come in hard upon the heels of the assault force.

The city itself lay silent now just before dawn, its roofs wet and glistening. No person could be seen. In the distance a burro sawed mournfully. Once its wracking sobs abated, complete silence fell again like a fog over the city.

A cannon boomed. With a loud forceful ruffle, drums beat out from Whitelocke's post. The rattle was taken up by various drummers, followed instantly by the shrill high bellows of noncommissioned officers as they ordered their units into motion. Then the whisper of many feet, the music of marching men, the clatter of accoutrements, the banging of provision carts and gun carriages, the sharp cries of teamsters, all the sounds of a moving army proclaimed the ominous motions of war.

"Like men sucked into a whirlpool," muttered Auchmuty. "We'll see some of them alive no more after this fateful day!"

Rank upon rank they advanced, the foot armed with carbines, four and one-half feet long or the five-foot rifles, curved wooden cartridge boxes, well japanned, with twenty-one sockets each for cartridges, now covered against the rain. The officers stuffed their belts with *bachorrillos*, the small brass-mounted pistols easily concealed for personal protection at close quarters.

The men marched steadily in their closed columns, inward upon Buenos Aires, striding through the mud and muck of the street. The unpaved road became an ankle-deep morass of soup that sloshed and splattered their feet and legs, staining them to their knees with brown La Plata mud. Bayonets fixed, the men marched with their unloaded weapons on their shoulders, properly angled, seeming oblivious of impending doom, as though on parade before the monarch of the House of Hanover.

The columns had progressed two-thirds of the way into the city by eight o'clock in the morning. A break in the clouds permitted the sun to blaze through for one brief instant, glittering upon the smartly uniformed ranks, reflecting the glory of marching men, a well-ordered contingent of the armies of George III invading the realm of his distant cousin, Charles IV for honor, for profit, . . . and because they could.

From the twin white towers of the Church of Santo Domingo, bells tolled, their rhythmic boom clear as brass in the morning stillness, their summons unmistakable. From one tower came a shot, then from the other. From the rooftops of the street's canyon walls erupted a maelstrom of musketry, cries, a hail of crude hand grenades, even stones, bricks, and hurled clubs. Such a storm these British troops had never before experienced. It forced even the most experienced veterans among them to turn and dodge—losing their precious formation. As though sliced with a knife, the columns split, men scuttling to either side to the bare cover of the walls, leaving the street vacant except for the cannoneers and Auchmuty and his staff storming angrily down upon the gun crews.

"Take fire at that church!" cried the general. The dull boom of artillery punctuated the action, clouds of blue smoke engulfing them in choking swirls, confusing the cries, shots, screams of wounded and dying men and animals, as strife boiled along the way. Nor was Auchmuty's unit alone. On every avenue the assault had commenced; and soldiers were fighting for their lives, struggling to advance as ordered, beating in doors with musket butts and racing upstairs to clear the roofs. But the enemy fled from one rooftop to another, protected by the thick adobe walls. The defenders returned time and again like relentless waves to renew the assault upon the trapped invaders below.

The maelstrom flowed over the city. The cannon proved virtually useless, for there were no ranks of troops to destroy, no firm body of the enemy to shell. The British were fighting against mists of men who appeared to assault, then disappeared to recoup, and slashed back into action from another base. They were here, there, before, behind, always in superior position, fearless, exhilarated, that day all but unbeatable, though armed with the crudest of weapons. They fired their clumsy 6-foot muskets that were so long they required a stake to aim, but just as deadly as any other weapon. The sheer discipline of the well-oiled British tradition enabled most of the invaders to survive and drive forward.

"We are exposed to murderous attacks from myriads of enemy behind parapets and everything else they have at hand," scribbled Auchmuty in a hurried note to Whitelocke. "Even their slaves are fighting us! We are continuing to advance but with difficulty. A barricade in our front must be carried. We are doing our best."

Crauford, whose column was trying to make way down the street to Auchmuty's left, was under even heavier fire. Ditches and barricades prevented his contacting Whitelocke. Other columns were assailed savagely. Reserves were pushed up, and artillery sought to blast away the defenses; but as often as holes were blown, they were dammed by fearless citizens, plugging boards, doors, furniture, or anything else at hand into the breech. Directly to Auchmuty's front, a platoon had stalled on the lip of a carefully dug ditch, too wide to jump, too deep to penetrate, too well defended to bridge, even if the engineers had brought materials for such an eventuality, which they had not.

"Get more men up there!" screamed the general. "Storm those works in some way!"

Christian thought of Justo's expedient in crossing the great *foso,* but there were no vast numbers of livestock to sacrifice; and the only bodies apt to fill this trench were British. Now and again the dragoons fought to its very lip, but they could not cross in the face of heavy small-arms fire. Cannon were trundled forward; and after blasting down the barricade and smashing houses on both sides, the rubble partially filled the excavation, forming a feasible, if perilous route, though at what cost! British dead littered the street.

Other columns, evidenced by heavy firing and outcries, were having difficulties quite as momentous. Only Auchmuty's and Colonel Thomas Backhouse's commands reached their goals that day, the viceroy's residence for the former and the Plaza de Toros for Backhouse. They fanned their forces defensively while awaiting orders from Whitelocke. From the roar at different points about them, they judged the battle heavy still. Whitelocke rushed up, his face pasty, his eyes wide and staring, his voice high and thick. He was terrified, Christian observed impassively but said nothing to anyone. He had seen disintegration before. When it reached this state, everything would be lost.

And so it was. Buenos Aires was lost through a failure of nerve on the part of a single man in authority. His weakness destroyed the expedition.

Ensigns burst in upon them now and again with reports, news, and dispatches. It was all bad. Crauford had surrendered, finding himself hopelessly trapped, trying thus to save his men from massacre. Pack had been wounded thrice, once severely, and was incapacitated. Other columns had failed or were bucked up tight, short of their objectives. Casualties were heavy. British loss in prisoners alone that day was 1,676 men, including 120 officers, and in dead wounded there were 1,130, including 70 officers. One-third of the assault force was destroyed.

"So much for the noble plan of attack," growled Auchmuty, disgustedly. "We'll be lucky if we can fight our way out. All there is to do now is wait."

"Wait, sir? For what?" asked Christian. He had taken no active part in the engagement but had been at Auchmuty's side throughout. An affinity, almost a friendship, had formed between the two; but Auchmuty now stared at him as belligerently as if they had been rival bulls.

"For what?" he echoed. "Why for that lucky Liniers, of course! For the ultimatum, his terms! What else? If I were in his place, I'd bloody well ram them down our throats. What can we do but accept? Commit suicide? Look at that gibbering old fool over there. He's too scared to shoot himself and would miss even if he tried, worse luck!" He jerked a thumb at Whitelocke contemptuously. "He'll give away the empire if Liniers wants it!"

The ultimatum was not long delayed, brought by a captured English officer escorted by two Spaniards, stovepipe-topped officers under white plumes, with their red-collared blue jackets, gold buttons, and crossed-pipe clayed belts. One was Juan Manuel de Rosas, the other an individual named Abánipal.

Whitelocke had the communication read aloud at an officers' call. It had been written in fair English, to insure the conquered foe would understand it:

> The same sentiments of humanity which induced your Excellency to propose to me to capitulate, lead me, now that I am fully acquainted with your force, that I have taken 8 officers and upwards of 1,000 men and killed more than double that number, without your having reached the center of my position; the same sentiments, I say, lead me in order to avoid a greater effusion of blood and to give your Excellency a fresh proof of Spanish generosity, to offer to your Excellency, that if you choose to reembark with the remainder of your army, to evacuate Montevideo and the whole of the River Plata, leaving me hostages for the execution of the treaty, I will return all the prisoners which I have now made. At the same time I think it necessary to state that if your Excellency does not admit to this offer, I cannot answer for the safety of the prisoners, as my troops are so infinitely exasperated against them, and the more so as three of my aides-de-camp have been wounded bearing flags of truce; and for this reason I send your Excellency this letter by an English officer and shall await your answer one hour.

Whitelocke, his bald pate glistening with sweat despite the chill in the evening air, his hand quivering as he snatched the document from the adjutant and scanned it himself, raised dully eyes to the assembled officers, weary with battle and short of temper. "Gentlemen," he croaked, "gentlemen, I see no alternative."

A rumble of dissent arose from a score of throats.

"No!" roared Auchmuty, heedless of impropriety in contradicting his superior. "Not by this officer, sir! This is not an agreement, 'tis a call for capitulation! To a band of semibarbarians who have not yet trounced us!"

Whitelocke hesitated, more anxious for guidance than to reprove one of his officers for insolence.

"What do you suggest, Auchmuty?" he asked, weakly.

Auchmuty tugged at his beard, spat contemptuously to one side, glared at his commanding officer, and in his gravelly voice rasped: "Fight!" He spat again, then added, still spirited:

"We hold both flanks with my column and Backhouse's. We hold the arsenal, what there is of it. We still have more than 5,000 effectives ready for action. We hold the riverfront, have contact with our ships, even if they can't lay in close. But they can supply us all we need. I doubt Liniers has at his command a force as large as ours, nowhere near as well supplied. We have not only men, but we have British discipline, too, sir. That rabble can never crack it, once we are dug in along these positions. We can hold our own, wear them out, and take over the bastard—all it will take is time, sir. Time and *courage!*"

His voice broke into as near to pleading as Auchmuty would ever come.

"Don't surrender, sir. Don't give up your men! Things look gloomy now, in all this devilish rain; but we can win. Let us fight!"

"Aye, sir," seconded Backhouse, heartily. "I would approve our continuing as best we can."

Still undecided, Whitelocke glanced up at Auchmuty.

"What about our prisoners? Do you condemn them to execution perhaps, or worse? After our reverses we have no way to assure their safety other than to accept Liniers' terms."

"Being captured is a chance a soldier takes, sir," Auchmuty argued, his emotions in conflict. "Sometimes 'tis an evil choice, but it's a hazard of war. We do those prisoners no favor by cravenly abandoning what they fought for, saving our own skins by surrendering to the enemy they fought so bravely. That would make their sacrifice meaningless. What we need in this situation is iron, not mud in our craw. How can you win a battle if you don't fight it out to the last gasp? Liniers is as beaten as we are, but his ultimatum was written first, is all."

The officer walked away in disgust, aware that Whitelocke was in no condition to listen, that they were whipped not by the enemy but by their own indecision and lack of will.

Yet if his arguments did not stiffen Whitelocke's spine, they did at least temper his determination to capitulate, postponing until the following day his reply. Then his communication, if placating, did not entirely give in to Liniers' imperious terms. Almost, but not entirely.

The following morning, July 7, an agreement was reached at the white-plastered *cabildo*. The corps was transformed by the surrender from an elite band of veteran officers into a pool seething with repressed fury, a sense of outrage, their valor destroyed by an impotent fool, any one of them convinced he could have better commanded the expedition than Whitelocke.

"What does the agreement provide, sir?" asked Christian, presuming upon him the informal friendship with Auchmuty. The other snarled the provisions at him, ticking them off on his fingers, twisting them as though to wrench them from their sockets and hurl them into the mud at his feet:

"Cessation of hostilities, not only here, but in the *Banda Oriental* of Uruguay. Our withdrawal to Montevideo for a couple of months. Mutual restitution of prisoners. We must be gone in ten days with our tails between our legs. We are to give up Montevideo in September, every single soldier paroled not to fight against South American colonies again, at least until we reach Europe. We should be dictating to them, and with a bit more fighting we might have done it; but this fool surrenders all."

"Is the agreement signed?"

"It will be, tomorrow, when Admiral Murray comes ashore for it. It's too late now. On the other side, those cigar-smoking Indians are ready. Liniers is happy and his second in command, Cesar Balbiani, and somebody named Velasco or something will sign for them. I will never sign the thing. Never. It'd be like treason to me. Treason!"

"It may not seem treason to Whitelocke, sir."

"Treason, sir, is treason, whether for Auchmuty or Whitelocke. Mark my words, Whitelocke will be court-martialed for this and, in my judgment, cashiered—I hope. His action is inexcusable, utterly inexcusable. The army, the government will not tolerate it. No, sir, never. *Never!*"

Treason it might be, Christian mused. But Whitelocke had been unable to help himself or save the situation. He had been doomed from the outset not by the military situation, not by his own incompetence nor lack of decision. No. He had been destined to failure because his expedition had been touched by another, at whose hands all things ended in disaster. The fault was not entirely Whitelocke's. The fault lay with Fletcher Christian. Of this he was convinced.

CHAPTER FOURTEEN

Self-recrimination beat upon Christian as though he alone had doomed the military gamble. The long and melancholy string of disasters could not, he felt, be chance alone. He had roved one-third of the world, from the Edens of the southern ocean to the ice-covered rocks of the Antarctic coasts, but he could neither escape his "stick" nor exhaust its malignancy. His obsession now occupied most of his waking thoughts.

Physically he was stronger than ever, thanks to his vigorous life. He was as strong as a pampas ox, as agile as one of its great wild lions; but his fixation was wringing the juices from his mind and bid to press him into madness.

"Aye, ye look as pale and wan as if ye had lost the battle by yourself," clucked Ishmael, peering anxiously into his face.

"Perhaps I did lose the battle," Christian replied slowly. "How else account for it? This finely-tuned superior force thrashed by a rabble with no training."

"Spirit sometimes can accomplish what training cannot . . . I thought ye did not believe in miracles?"

"Enough, Ishmael! I do not hold with religious miracles. This I witnessed, and so did you."

"Blessed are they that have not seen and yet have believed!"

"I do not wish to be blessed, only to be relieved of this great millstone round my neck that brings tragedy upon every man and woman who touches me."

Ishmael laid a hand on his arm. "Ye have not brought disaster upon me, Fletcher. Does that destroy your gloomy theory?"

"But I *will*, Ishmael!" Christian whispered hoarsely. "If ye do not abandon me, if ye do not shun me, I shall destroy you!"

Ishmael linked his arm through Christian's, giving what consolation lay within his power, as they paced the shoreline of the river.

"If ye feel it so deeply, this thing that has captured your mind, it may be as real for you as were the visions for Saint John. If ye cannot beat it down, then ye must root it out, Fletcher. There is no other way."

"I do not grasp your meaning."

There was about the old man's face a melancholy gentleness, a love that encompassed Christian and somehow bestowed courage upon him and if not the faith, then at least a bit of the inner goodness that was Ishmael.

"Go to England," said the old man, softly. "That is where all began. If ye are to pry this obsession loose, ye must return to your beginning. That is the way I believe ye can rout it. If ye do not, I am truly convinced ye might lose your mind, as ye fear."

Christian mulled over the suggestion. "I cannot do this," he answered quietly. "I—there is a price upon my head. 'Twould mean my death."

Ishmael spun him around brusquely.

"Death? Nothing is certain but death, lad. Ye cannot evade it; only time it, if you must. But death or madness—which do you prefer? I should choose the former, Fletcher, and so upon reflection will you—because you must!"

Evacuation of the British expeditionary force began at once. By July 12, one week to the day after crossing the tributary and entering Buenos Aires, the last wounded soldier and every gun and bale of supplies were ferried out to the transports, taken aboard, and stowed away. The mighty fleet of conquest drifted with the current out into the channel, raised what sail was required, and glided from the city and viceroyalty forever, beaten and shamed.

The convoy dropped anchor amid the warships clustered off Montevideo, 140 miles east of Buenos Aires. The harbor itself was paced with merchant vessels laden with the goods of commerce, brought in to profit mightily in a conquered, hungry, greedy land where luxuries of any sort, and even necessities, were always in short supply.

Soldiers and seamen wandered and caroused about in the city they had won so bloodily.

Montevideo appeared almost English, with placards in that language everywhere. English shops were stuffed with English goods at prices much lower than the smuggled wares of the Spanish colonials. Even a newspaper was printed half in English, called the *Star of the South*, and the remainder in Spanish, *La Estrella del Sur*.

Throughout the captured town, where the colonials fraternized cheerfully with their conquerors, there existed a common unhappiness with the debacle at Buenos Aires. Disgust focused upon one individual, Lieutenant General John Whitelocke. A favorite toast heard everywhere, at cafés and dusky taverns, was "Success to gray hairs, but bad luck to white locks"; and every man approved.

Christian came across Auchmuty sipping coffee at a sidewalk table and was invited to sit with him.

"You'll do yourself no service, sir, to be seen at table with a pampa wanderer," sighed Christian. Auchmuty gestured impatiently.

"I speak with whom I like, associate with those I enjoy, protocol be hanged," he growled. "That's one American trait I brought into this British caste system. Back home my joy as a lad was listening to yarns of the woods runners who brought their furs for sale once or twice a year. They sat around gossiping, half-drunk, with others of their calling. I wanted to make for the frontier, like most boys, and might have if the rebellion had not broken when it did." He slipped into a pleasant haze of memory of those vanished days, swirling his drink idly. "At any rate its better here than in Sydney with old Bligh." Christian thought he had not heard correctly.

"With whom, sir?"

"Bligh. Billy Bligh—do you know him?"

Christian flushed.

"Possibly. I knew one of that name long ago. Doubtless, however, 'tis the same man."

Auchmuty spoke as though to himself. "There can't possibly be another man like this one. From the time he lost his ship to those South Seas pirates until the report now that he is about to lose New South Wales to a mutinous army, he has ever been the same cursed soul." He shook his head in dismay. "He must be a hard man to serve. I was happy we were ordered here instead of Sydney, where rumor had it we were to be sent."

So Bligh lived! Christian had *not* been the cause of his murder, though Bligh's curse had all but murdered the soul of Christian. There was vast relief in this fresh awareness and a profound disturbance as well, although he could not quite define it.

"We'll lift anchor shortly," Auchmuty was saying. "What will you do then, Mr. Fletcher? Go back into the interior?"

Christian shook his head.

No sir, not unless 'tis forced upon me." His words came with a rush, without conscious thinking. "I wish to—I hope to return to England myself, if I can sign on one of these ships. I trust 'twill not be impossible."

"Sign on? Of course not. Go as my guest, sir! It can be arranged. I'll speak to captain Lanceton of it at once."

"Why would you do that for me, sir?"

Auchmuty scratched his shoulders comfortably against the back of his chair. "Beresford, that one-eyed Yorkshireman, has told me much about you, Mr. Fletcher, before he left. We owe you a great deal. A passage to England would be very slight payment, indeed. Do let me arrange it."

It was Christian's turn to decline.

"I appreciate your kindness more than I can say, but I should prefer to make my own way, before the mast." He grinned sheepishly at Auchmuty, who studied his face.

"And what will you do when you get there? It is not easy for a seaman or even an officer to quit one of His Majesty's ships, you know. These, after all, are war conditions, most of the time anyway."

Christian glanced across the bustle of the city, and for the first time in many years the land seemed foreign.

"I don't know, sir," he confessed. "I simply have the feeling that I must return. I cannot predict how nor what will happen there. 'Tis a compulsion, almost—an obsession. But I must go."

Auchmuty smiled.

"As you wish," he agreed. "I will speak to the captain, and I am confident you can sign on the transport of your choosing. May you discover in England whatever you seek. If I can be of further service at any time, never hesitate to call upon me."

Christian signed aboard the *James and Rebecca*, a fair ship in a good wind, though her bottom had become so fouled having been so long at sea that it took a gale to move her. Besides her complement of more than 100 officers and seamen, she carried nearly 400 troops. She was so crowded there was no space for drill, little hope of discipline, and no room for more than the universal longing to be home.

Christian reported to the mate, signed the ledger, and was assigned with the elder, better seamen to the forecastle crew, a step above able seamen, though not quite so exalted as the topmast hands. He set to work with a will to perform his duty smartly and well. He had all but forgotten the pride in the ordered life of a vessel at sea, though now he melded back into it with a smoothness and alacrity that amazed him. As with all hands, he had shaved and scrubbed and had his hair queued by a shipmate. He drew clothing and what scant supplies he required and within a few hours of coming aboard was indistinguishable from the crew.

Two months to the day after leaving Montevideo, the *James and Rebecca* raised the white fringe of the blue-black knobs of the Scillys, five inhabited islands where the hardy colonists made most of their income salvaging wrecks of ships that dashed to pieces upon their coasts. The *James and Rebecca* passed them early in the morning, however, well out to sea and within half a day had raised the iron-bound coast of Cornwall. A cheer arose from dragoons and crew alike when the foretop lookout sang down the news, for the men had endured many battles and long months away from home. None was more stirred than Christian.

He felt an odd thickening of his throat as the country of his birth rose into view. From it he had been sent to sea, toward it he now was returning, as though directed by some unseen hand. He was British, England was home, and yonder Cornwall was part of his land. Its wooded, cove-indented shoreline appeared more English than any other. The north coast of the Cornish peninsula, by contrast, was swept bare of trees and shrubs by the great north winds that hurtled across the confluence of Saint George's Channel and the open Atlantic and slammed into the land.

At eight bells and off duty, he resumed his position at the bulwark, reveries flooding him anew. On this late November day, the winter scud swept low and darkness already was assembling over Gwennap Head. Finally, he abandoned the rail and went below to draw his grog, to sup, and returned to duty on the second dog watch. This coast had seen the wreck of uncounted ships, and her officers guided the *James and Rebecca* cautiously by the channel lights off Mount's Bay. To Christian, who had had no knowledge of this course, the lanterns seemed unusually bright and close in, but he shrugged and went below, unrolling his hammock by the light of the flickering torches. It was nine o'clock when he turned in, and almost instantly he was asleep.

Two hours later he was thrown from his hammock by a grinding collision that wracked the ship to her keelson, with thunderous crashes of collapsing masts and spars and the tumult of stove timbers. He felt the inrush of icy water, surging and washing through demolished bulkheads over the orlop deck, lower deck, and beating at the scuppers of the main deck. Bounding past his struggling shipmates, heedless of the cries of the injured and the havoc, Christian gained topside, glimpsing the foamy line of spray marking the meeting of sea and rock perilously at hand. The *James and Rebecca* was hard aground. The dancing lights of Mount's Bay mocked and jeered at her dismay beyond the boom of winter breakers.

orlop deck-
the lowest deck in a wooden ship. The lower deck was above the orlop deck.

The captain and his mates surged to and fro and up and down the decks, ordering the clearing of rigging and poles, trying to cut a boat free and get it over into the seething water. The ship was in peril of being dashed to pieces by each pound of surf against her wounded hull. Guns of distress were fired to bring the Cornish to the coast, to assist as they might in salvaging her people.

Somehow a boat was cleared and a crew got into it, Christian among them. Coils of line were passed into her while she rose and fell, 15 or 20 feet with each mighty wave, a fragile toy she seemed in such monstrous weather, but a stout and nimble craft at that. They cleared the ship and pulled for shore like a water spider with eight legs to a side. The boat seemed to progress little at first; then, as they neared the brutally-pounded beach, too fast. Seamen jumped overboard and pulled her in and held her with all their strength against the ebb of the sea until they were joined by others who dragged the boat beyond reach of the waves. With the assistance of the gathered Cornish, accustomed to such disaster, they set about rigging a traveler to bring survivors ashore.

"Ye must be daft to run aground on a fair night like this!" cried a Cornishman. "I hav'n seen th' like, hav I!" Although the stormy vapors hung low and heavy over the land, 'twas fair Cornwall.

The boatswain answered: "I hear th' lieutenant say to th' captain the lights was mistook for guidin' us fair into th' channel, instead of onto th' rocks."

Christian labored with the rest to rig the traveler and help the first dragoons ashore, their bodies streaming from sea and spray. The Cornishmen lit great bonfires and about them the survivors huddled, grateful for the warmth, dazed and clustered mutely under the sweep of winter gale.

Systematically more and more men were lofted ashore through the darkness. It would soon be dawn; work would hasten then. With luck the ship would not finally break up before noon. By then the last of the shipwrecked probably would be ashore, those who had survived the collision and the sea.

Christian, his services no longer needed, and indeed no one seemed to be even aware of his presence, faded into the darkness. He stumbled across a trail bound upward over the cliff to the moor; and in lonely solitude he moved toward Saint Ives Bay, while in the drumming of his ears he heard once more that mysterious, distant murmur: "*Laich!*" it seemed to say, "*Anochi iemach . . .*" It was still night, and he was on English soil. For the moment he was free—and almost home.

BOOK IV

The men knew that he fled from the presence
of the LORD, because he had told them.

JONAH 1:10

CHAPTER ONE

How well Christian remembered each wrinkle of this North Country road, the lanes wandering quietly as tributaries through picket gates, neglected now much as they had been twenty years earlier. He had met no one he knew, none who recognized him. Approaching Cumberland he had traveled most commonly in the dusk of evening or dawn, and now it was broad day. It was a kind of madness to risk returning to his boyhood home with a king's price on his head and near certain death should he be discovered. Yet Christian could do nothing else.

This was Lamplugh Road. Behind lay the villages of Lamplugh and of Loweswater, Mockerkin, and Parshaw and most recently Eaglesfield, all to be avoided or traversed at night. Ahead of him a couple of miles was the familiar Cockermouth, at the confluence of the Derwent and the Cocker, streams he had fished and near the place where he had gone to grammar school at All Saints'. Now his heart lifted as he espied the familiar whitened gate between the gray stone guards his father, Charles Christian, had built as an ornate touch to the driveway. Opening the gate and latching it carefully behind him, he strode up the gentle rise toward the still-invisible house.

Still he was not sure. What misery might he bring to those he cared for? Might his return loose disaster upon them as he had brought destruction to so many others? If he truly believed this, he would turn back. But he still held that wisp of hope that dies last in every man: a wish that perhaps he erred in what he thought was truth. And so he walked up that empty lane.

He came to a thick-boled oak, which he well remembered since it still bore the battens he and Edward had nailed to its rough bark as a ladder to their tree house, long since vanished. Christian leaned his back against the warm rough surface, trying to iron out his motives and his thoughts.

It had been months since the Cornish shipwreck. He had drifted from one job to another until his courage and determination were strong enough to bring him north to Cumberland. He had been a roadster for a period and plugged muck for a North Country husbandman who asked no questions, appeared bereft of curiosity.

This was true of much of the society. So savage was the law, so cruel and merciless and even unjust, that it had alienated a vast body of Englishmen. They lived among their kind by their own "law" which, though unwritten, suited them and supported them in their struggle for survival against the oppressive upper classes. Within this strata, Christian found that he was accepted for what he was and was asked few questions. No demands were made upon him except that he accommodate himself to the curious culture.

Now he scanned the horizon, familiar as the knuckles on his hand, although he had not seen it for near a quarter century: to his right the blue, sullen mountains, Skiddaw, Scafell Pike, Grasmore, Whiteside, and the others, whose folds and nooks had seemed mysterious to a youngster who believed their peaks to be lofty. Before him, across the swoop and swale of fell and pasture was the valley of the rivers and Cockermouth where he could make out the tortured outline of its castle, ruined by Cromwell a century ago and more.

Just beyond the shrubs and trees ahead lay Mairlanclere, or Moorland Close, his home, with its guardhouse, erected to shield cattle and sheep from the raiding Scotsmen who in olden times had swept down upon the Cumberland farmers to fight and kill if necessary, though mainly to steal what loose livestock was about. Christian had never experienced such a raid. But the old men told stories of them on winter evenings, and boyish imaginations were stirred by the tales.

How this lush greenery, the chestnuts and brambles, the sycamores and oaks and ash and larch, holly, thorn, juniper and yew, the buttercup-spangled grass and the tidy fields of oats and Swedes, checker boarded by neat hedgerows, how it contrasted with the ice fields and cold salt channels and inlets of Magellan-land! Now he was part of it again.

Christian gathered himself and trudged on, straining for the first glimpse of Moorland Close beyond the gentle rise.

Now he could make out the gray slates of its gabled roof. The house, a stocky pile of stone structures in the fashion of a medieval manor, half-castle and half-farmstead, was shaded by immense sycamores, tossing their upper branches in the slight breeze, as though in welcome. No one appeared about, the men doubtless working in the fields or, it may be, at market. Christian slipped in through the gate, past the stone globe-topped guardian posts, which in his boyhood had suggested the great round earth whose distant seas and coasts he would some day visit. He strode down the cobbled roadway, the stones pressed into parallel depressions by iron wheels of generations of carriages and carts. He passed beneath the windowed arcade where the coaches sometimes waited and stepped toward the doorway.

Christian raised the metal knocker on the paneled door and let it fall once. Its brassy summons rang through the stillness, and almost instantly there came a voice from within. Familiar? He could not determine, but it lifted his heart a beat or two.

Then she stood before him, small and gray, her face a bit lined with age; but the black eyes were alert, knowing.

"Aye?" she said with a touch of impatience. "Yes, what is it, sir?"

Christian grinned in nervous embarrassment.

"Don't ye know me, then, mother? Your son, home from the sea?"

Her hand fluttered to her throat, her eyes widening, her mouth slowly opening. Recognition flooded in and she clutched him, tugging his body to her, sobbing wildly. Christian, too, allowed the tears to fall unchecked.

"My boy!" she sobbed. "My boy, my Fletcher! How I have prayed that this moment would come! Here again, after all of these years. Home!" No word about his crimes, nothing of troubles, only love and gladness that he was returned safely to her once again. Christian felt a happiness sweep over him he had not experienced for ages.

Anne Christian led him through the rooms he remembered as though it were but yesterday, rooms that seemed smaller but old and familiar and comfortable still. There was the aroma of sage in the hall, drying before being hung in tiny bundles from the kitchen rafters for use with country pork and roasted geese at Michaelmas and Yuletide, and from the upper floor came the faint scent of lavender. The bustle of the house emanated from the kitchen, where his mother joyously led him.

Christian hesitated at the door but was quickly enfolded by friends and relations, the passionate interest of all. There was James, his older brother, still the hunter and mountain rover, bulging with questions about the exotic past of this adventurer come home. "Worsta gawn?" he demanded in his thick Cumbrian accent, so natural for him that Christian instantly replied in kind: "I'm gawn yam, Jimmy. Here I be."

"Did ye shut the yat?" he demanded seriously.

"Aye," replied Christian. "Ye knew I'd not forget t'keep the stock in an' the toon-folk oot!" They both laughed heartily.

There was Peggy, his sister, unmarried, but in her late thirties, bound to wed soon, if ever she would; Agnes, the aged charwoman whom Christian recalled as always at the beck and call of everyone; and Jane, the other maid, whom he remembered from his adolescence when she was young and pretty.

"Why ha' ya never married again, mother?" Christian asked, suddenly. His mother sobered, looked down at her folded hands.

"Because I still love Charles," she replied, simply. "It's not that I hadn't the opportunity. A widow with an estate has no lack of suitors. But I never felt I should, nor desired to, nor do I now. One marriage is all I felt would be mine, although I miss the companionship . . ."

Christian, too, fell silent, remembering his distant past.

"And Isabella?" he asked. "How is she? Do you suppose she remembers?"

"Aye, son. She would never forget yan," his mother reassured him. "She is now an invalid, though beautiful as ever. She and John live on Belle Isle, and I see them rarely. When we do meet, she ever has a word about ye, an' 'tis invariably a warm one."

A smile touched Christian's lips.

"Is John still enamored of the Quakers, the Society of Friends?"

"Aye. 'Tis a life's persuasion with him, Fletcher. He is a Whig, also, a power in North Country politics."

"Oh?"

"He has refused a peerage, I'm told. He changed his name to Christian Curwen, partly for his wife's family name of Curwen and in part because of—well, I suppose, because he wished to do so."

"To avoid a stigma?"

"I did not say that."

Here in this mix of relatives and friends, Christian felt the weight of his ancient restlessness drop from him. Twice had Christian created a family; twice had it been stripped from him in the cruelest fashion. Now he had returned to the family that no fate could take from him while he retained his mind and memory.

Christian spent idle afternoons in the "summer house," as the guardhouse had come to be called. It had been erected at the corner of a walled acre that once had protected their cattle and sheep from raiders of across the Solway Firth; now the area was given over to an orchard of ancient apple trees.

It was hot, this particular summer afternoon. Christian's gaze swept the pastures grazed by fat red and white cattle of the Ayrshire breed originating perhaps with raids by Cumbrians upon the Lowlands. A few long-horn black Welsh animals were sprinkled among them for beef, while the black-faced heath sheep, or the Herwicks, all bore the painted "CC" to mark them as belonging to the estate of Christian's father.

He climbed to the roof of the guardhouse to extend his vision, to Cockermouth in the north, or Brigham to the northwest. He lay against the warm plates, his feet pressed to the rim of the leaden gutter, flat and just wide enough for his shoe. Half in jest, he opened his sailor's knife and with a tile fragment for a hammer, pounded a row of tiny pits around the outline of his foot in the soft lead. As youngsters carve names on trees, so Christian traced his shoe for possibly the same reason: to leave the record of his passing, a wry attempt at immortality.

He smiled down at Peg who called him to "tea," a custom he much enjoyed since his return from the sea, and especially when accompanied by cold-boiled ham or pork pie, hot bread, thick country butter, and bramble jam. Tea was an occasion for gossip. Then he refreshed his memory of Cumberland mores and learned of the contentions and loyalties of the clannish North Country relatives of the Christians: the Christians, the Vanes, the Curwens, the Flemings, and their more distant kin: the Wilsons, the Washingtons, and the Wordsworths.

His mother refilled Christian's cup and turned to her favored son, "Will ye be stayin' long, my dear?"

A faint troubled frown drifted across his face. His eyes became old, touched with apprehension.

"I don't know, Mother," he replied, slowly. "I would never want to put you and the family in any danger. I don't know."

His mother reassured him. "Edward can manage the risk, Fletcher. Ye are safe here as anywhere. There's not a one in Cumberland 'twould turn ye in, unless he be a stranger or an outlander, an' there's not many of them hereabout."

"There's few in England remembers the *Bounty,* except the vengeful," interposed James. "Bligh's gone to Australia where 'tis said he's havin' trouble that might dwarf that one on your ship, e'en if he returns. If you keep low an' no tread overmuch in broad day, I think ye'll be as safe here as on some far continent."

After a pause Anne Christian, her twisting hands betraying her nervousness, turned to this stranger son. "I've a favor to ask of thee," she whispered.

"Anything, Mother," he pledged.

Her worn finger traced a pattern in the lace of the table cover.

"Would ye accompany me to services Sunday?" she asked, her voice all but inaudible.

A shadow of dismay flashed across his face, gone in an instant. The request was not one he could ever deny her.

"Aye, Mother," he agreed, "if ye wish it."

CHAPTER TWO

Preparations for Sunday were as ritualistic as the custom-bound North Country itself. Christian smiled as he watched the women under direction of his mother go about their duties. They started Friday and continued most of Saturday: sweeping the hearth, polishing the ornaments; and the tidy Betty, scrubbing stoops and flagstones which must be whitened at the edges, the window leads touched up, small panes wiped. Clothes had been washed on Tuesday, dried by Thursday, then folded and tucked away. The Friday-churned butter was packed for Saturday market, to which James and Agnes fetched in the trap.

"Aye, Sunday is a day o' rest because it requires so much," Christian chuckled to Agnes.

Pleasant as it was on Sunday morning, riding with his mother and sister in the cart along satin-smooth dirt lanes the mile and one-half to Brigham, Christian felt a twinge of apprehension. The square-gabled tower of Saint Bridget's Church came gradually into view. The lush greenery and bright flowers of this summer day were reassuring, however, bringing the soft glory of England home. Christian was glad he was home, even though his soul was disturbed at the prospect of attending his first prayer service in thirty years. His mother wished it. He glanced at her aged face with lines that time and he himself had etched there. Her black eyes danced with happiness this Sunday morning, pleasure that he had brought her. And for that he would be content for this day.

The weathered freestone church had come into full view now, gray and solid on the further side of Brigham. On each of the four sides of the stumpy tower was a tall arched window, shuttered against the flitter mice, the dozens of bats that drowsed beneath the torn oak beams from which they clung. When its three great bronze bells were sounded, shaken loose, they swirled about until the shattering reverberations ceased.

To Christian, the squarish church seemed like a miniature fortress. Built in approximately 900 B.C., it was the mother church of the diocese, older even than All Saints' at Cockermouth or the Carlisle cathedral. While portions of the church had been added on, the tower was ancient. Yews of dark green foliage and red berries graced the yard, planted centuries before; and they had remained, forever guarding the bodies and souls beneath tilted tombstone slabs raised everywhere. The seaman scanned some unfamiliar inscriptions: John Danton, who had entered his reward, whatever that might be, March 15, 1799; Joe Sproat, buried two years earlier; and the others, some known to Christian from his boyhood, now all equal in death and dust. Such was the destiny of man; any who claimed more was a fool. This Christian felt sure.

They entered the sanctuary beneath the arch, through inner doors, their weight suspended by ornate iron hinges, the flanges splayed against the dark wood like tails of devils. The primordial architect who had conceived this church had been devoted not only to his God, but to the arch as the ultimate expression of human creativity and worship. Wherever one looked were arches and more arches—over windows, the apse and transepts, and between the sanctuary and the chapel. Christian and his mother seated themselves toward the tower in the rear, inconspicuous in the shadows. The wooden pews were hard and uncomfortable, darkened by time and candle smoke.

His mother knelt in prayer. She then selected a prayer book and, opening it, began to read silently, her lips moving with the familiar words. To please her Christian also took up a volume, but instead of reading, he scanned the congregation in the dim light, all of them good friends of long standing, their lips sealed against the king's men or any outlander who did not belong in the North Country.

The priest entered now, a dignified figure with a voice like a rogue quarterdeck master but a light in his eye of loftier origin than *Naval Rules and Regulations*. He read the Scripture, his voice reverberating, blasting away the mists of idle daydreaming of his flock, forcing them to concentrate upon the passages. Christian read the words in his worn prayer book:

"When the wicked man turneth away from his wickedness that he hath committed, and doeth that which is lawful and right, he shall have his soul alive," the priest read from the Book of Ezekiel. And from Daniel: "To the Lord our God belong mercies and forgivenesses, though we have rebelled against Him; neither have we obeyed the voice of the LORD our God, to walk in His laws, which He set before us." And from Saint John's first epistle: "If we say that we have no sin, we deceive ourselves, and the truth is not in us. If we confess our sins, he is faithful and just to forgive us our sins, and to cleanse us from all unrighteousness."

With irritation Christian shut the volume and shoved it into place before him, but the rector's words summoned his attention, stabbing at the recesses of his mind:

"Dearly beloved brethren, the Scripture moveth us in sundry places to acknowledge and confess our manifold sins and wickedness; and that we should not dissemble nor cloak them before the face of Almighty God our heavenly Father, but confess them with an humble, lowly, penitent, and obedient heart, to the end that we may obtain forgiveness of the same by his infinite goodness and mercy—"

Despite his lack of belief, Christian found his lips moving into the General Confession, although the words remained unspoken save to his deepest mind.

He felt a pressure on his hand. His mother sought to take his strong fingers in her worn, dry ones. He returned the grasp in an outpouring of love and gratitude, a token of regret for the years of concern he had caused her. Together, more closely linked than anytime since Christian's childhood, they listened as the priest ruffled heavy pages of the great Bible, "Here beginneth the First Lesson, with verse 7, from Psalm 139 of David." He cleared his throat noisily:

"Whither shall I go from thy spirit? or whither shall I flee from thy presence? If I ascend up into heaven, thou art there: if I make my bed in hell, behold, thou art there. If I take the wings of the morning, and dwell in the uttermost parts of the sea; even there shall thy hand lead me, and thy right hand shall hold me. . . . Yea, the darkness hideth not from thee; but the night shineth as the day: the darkness and the light are both alike to thee. For thou hast possessed my reins. . . . Search me, O God, and know my heart: try me, and know my thoughts: and see if there be any wicked way in me, and lead me in the way everlasting."

Christian went through the motions—kneeling, bowing his head dutifully, standing for the hymns, sitting when the others did so, but it was as though another person did these things.

From the pulpit, Father Plumberry, himself of the North Country, peered across his congregation with keen blue eyes beneath shaggy brows, his massive head a repository for his people's strengths and loyalties, their sins and weaknesses, seeking to translate with his understanding the concern for them of the Almighty, to make the One intelligible to the many.

"Brethren, I would talk today about sin, for that is ever with us, an' as much wi' me as wi' yan." He plucked at the notion of evil, turning it over and over, examining its every side, endeavoring to open the minds before him, striking at the evil of self-righteousness, which dwelt upon another's errors rather than one's own.

"There be two species of sin," he confided. "There is first the kind familiar to every one o' us, sin against neighbor, like robbery an' murder, but also like jealously an' greed an' the sins o' the night, which had best not be listed in the house of the Lord. But there are sins against God as well, such as blasphemy, an' havin' other gods before him such as money or success or fame.

"But brethren, these two kinds o' sin come together here, for a sin against neighbor is a sin against God, an' those who would deny it are deceivin' themselves or have not read the New Testament. One is as great an evil as 't other . . ."

Fletcher Christian's mind wandered to the sunlit southern ocean and that fresh April morning when the boat was got ready and the captain, about to step down into it, had laid the "stick" upon him, and so diseased his life . . .

"And to correct yan's sin against God, ye must acknowledge his grace an' ask for it, an' to correct yan's sin against neighbor, ye must beg forgiveness at once or thereabouts, not alone from God but from the other as well, since sin against a neighbor is sin against the Father." Christian's irritation had vanished, but his mind still avoided acceptance with protestations and rationalizations. However, without his awareness, the priest's views became part of his memory.

"How did yan enjoy the service?" queried his mother hesitantly, as the cart jounced along toward Moorland Close.

"'Twas—it was—very fine, Mother," he replied, awkwardly, slapping with the reins at the rump of the old gray horse. "I trust 'twas not risky, our being there."

She shook her head positively.

"They all be Cumbrians, lad," she assured him. "There is no gossip in them that's apt to hurt one of our own." In a moment, she added, "Anyway, the service did ye no harm, an' I thought the message contained wisdom."

Again her son held his silence for a long moment.

"It did that, Mother," he agreed, then humoring her, said, "I thought so at the time, an' I think so still. Aye, he's a wise man, if one could . . ." His voice trailed off. He clucked at the horse again.

"Ye do not believe, do ye, Fletcher?"

Christian slapped the reins. The stubbornness of his mind would not let him grant her ease; he shook his head.

"'Tis given to some to believe, and from some the gift is withheld," he murmured. His voice scarcely rose above the whishing of the cart's wheels on the soft earth, against the grass sprays. "Sometimes I want to believe, but permission is denied me. 'Tis a thing I cannot control. I feel some days able to cope with all the world, an' again unable to manage even the smallest obstacle. 'Tis a mental thing. I cannot help it." Again he paused. "No, Mother," he summed it up, frankly. "I do not believe—not as you do. Would that I might."

Silence came upon them for a space, the man's mind in turmoil, the woman's with love and hope surviving as it does in every mother, confident that the future would solve all problems, even those compounded with evil, the nature of which she had not explored. She had never questioned him about the mutiny, nor had he volunteered information. Her faith in him rose above all such matters, and the issue was too painful for him to explain even to her.

At last she spoke again. "I have invited him to call one day soon," she said in the low, firm voice he remembered well. When she spoke thus, the matter was decided. "Father Plumberry," she explained, needlessly. "I sent him a note."

Once more Christian slapped the horse, but this time there was purpose and command in the gesture. The creature lumbered into a heavy trot, which soon subsided however into the same old leisurely walk.

"As you wish, Mother," her son replied. Then, quickly, he relented. "He's a fine man, I think."

CHAPTER THREE

Father Plumberry rode his venerable flea-bitten gray up the long lane from Lamplugh Road like a missionary approaching a strange camp of heathen. His flowing white hair was capped against the mist, and he wore a thick woolen jacket for equal protection for his active body. Red stockings added the touch of color he loved. The clergyman had come to Brigham as a young man fifty years before; never had he had another parish, nor did he wish any other, though now he was older than all but a few of the people to whom he ministered. He was opinionated, as befits one looked up to for so long, but with a kindness and curious gentleness. His compassion extended to all, *even pirates*, as Father Plumberry mused to himself. *No doubt Fletcher deserved the price on his head.* He sighed. He had no sympathy with outlawry, yet pirates were people and had need of clergy quite as much as anyone—more, if truth be told.

"Do come in, Father," Anne Christian said, holding the door wide for him. He slapped the moisture from his cap and jacket and strode into the house, dominating it, following his hostess to the kitchen. He greeted Christian gruffly, seriously. "Aye, I have heard much of thee, an' recall a bit as well. I have seen thee at worship, the first occasion in many a year. Ye look the same, though older than long ago, an' wi' creases about yan eyes that tell of far places and many lives."

Christian nodded, making no reply. He was uneasy in the presence of this churchman for he was but a faint memory from his childhood.

Father Plumberry accepted a tart and cup of tea with grace, eating noisily and with pleasure.

"What be yan's plans?" he demanded abruptly, staring with his blue eyes directly into Christian's own. The younger man flushed, hesitated.

"What can they be, Father?" Christian's mother interrupted. "Fletcher's come home as I've prayed for years that he might, an' now he is among us again, but how can his safety be assured, with the threat of—of death, over him, over us all? For if he dies, I die too, an' so do others since he is a part of all of us."

"Aye," the priest said, as if to himself. "Aye, a problem 'tis, right enough. Aye." He sipped again at his tea, then looked squarely into Christian's face once more.

"What I would recommend, ye will not do," he said flatly. "By the trial of *Bounty* people they caught, 'tis hangin' the law allows ye, an' little else. No matter whose be the fault of yan incident, yours or Bligh's. From what your brother Edward has collected an' written, 'twas as much the captain was to blame as you. But that would not hold up in a court of naval law unless pressure be brought. The Christians an' the Curwens an' all they're blooded to, which is aplenty, men of mighty influence amongst 'em, could bring pressure that perhaps might save your life, by pardon if not by judgment. But nothing is certain, except death for each of us eventually."

Agnes, completing her task of blackening the stove for the weekend, sniffed loudly. The priest cast his bright eyes upon her, for she, too, was of his flock.

"Eh, Agnes?" he demanded. "Is that sniff a token of disagreement? Or do I mistake it for a coming chill?"

"'Tis no chill, Father," retorted Agnes. "But you're little help to them as needs it, I'm thinkin'. Ye speak as if Judgment Day was here in Coomberland, an' ye be the Great Judge hisself!"

Father Plumberry laughed, his eyes twinkling. He and the maid were nearly of an age. For half a century they had carried on a ceaseless banter, which both enjoyed, unseemly as it might appear.

"'Tis not a matter of 'judgment,'" he said, soberly. "'Tis rather one o' law, an' the safety of yan's kin. Here on Moorland Close ye'll be safe enough from it. Law 'twill not likely reach ye here. But how long can a man bury himself from humankind an' life? How long can one nurse a sore tooth without havin' it oot? I am a direct man. I believe the way to solve a problem is to go to its heart an' root it oot. If a man has sinned, or even if he has been sinned against, th' long nursing festers it. Instead of wearin' oot, it blows up like a cancer until it smothers the life o' him. Which is the better way: a quick death by cryin' cockles or a long drawn out affair by gradual strangulation?"

Christian smiled, without much amusement, however.

"I asked for bread, and ye gave me a stone, Father."

The old priest snorted.

"Gwan, lad!" he growled. "Ye came here with a stone. I offer ye bread, rather, but ye prefer the stone! A man must make his own choice, ye know." He relented, slightly. "I cannot choose for ye, Fletcher, but I know how I would choose."

"There are others to consider."

"Aye, that there be," agreed Plumberry, wagging his head vigorously. "An' the same situation lies before 'em: wi' quickness or wi' deliberation, wi' the end result the same. There is no other choice."

"While he lives there is ever hope," replied his mother, gently.

Father Plumberry fixed her with an unblinking ice-blue eye, a smile lurking beneath his stern exterior.

"I am supposed to mention that to solace *thee*, not yan to bring remembrance to this old priest," he protested.

"Then do so, Father."

"Aye." He held his cup for a freshening. "Now, Fletcher, ye are a man wi' a price on yan's head, but also ye are a relative of several who have great political power or potential. They are good men wi' powerful enemies. An' these enemies will use any means, *any* means whatever, to secure advantage for themselves and to harm those in their way. I needn't belabor the point, my lad. You are not only vulnerable yourself, which assuredly you are, but you might bring down the whole house wi' yan, should your presence here become widely known. That is the potential evil of it. I know the powers that wish ye to have your freedom also are vast. In truth, I cannot say they're wrong. An old man just does not know. He can see, an' he can point to what he sees, but judgment is beyond him—no matter what Agnes thinks."

After pausing, he concluded: "I know—I knew it from the first—that the course I would choose ye will not accept. So be it. 'Tis in the hands of the Lord, not ours. I cannot change my view, but I can offer ever my priestly office an' sympathy—an' what spiritual assistance ye have need of, an' will accept. That I can ever do."

Anne Christian bit her lip: "Ye will keep this—our secret, Father?"

Plumberry looked down upon her haughtily, as befits a minister of the Word and a gentleman, and her senior, too, by many years.

"Madame," he intoned with an inflection almost pompous, "I am a priest. I keep many confidences, not one of which I have ever divulged to another. In addition," he said, turning toward the door, "I am Coombrian."

Christian settled smoothly into the life of Moorland Close as he had among the Tahitians, or the Mapuche, the Tehuelche, or the gauchos, but there was a difference: here there was a relapse into a former existence. The painting of him on his piebald pony above the fireplace was not the only reminder of his boyhood on the estate. No turning failed to reveal something to stir his memory. He did not flaunt this presence in any way, but assumed a role in the management of the comfortable acres, while remaining aloof in the daylight from the town and from strangers.

Only with the dusk of twilight or at dawn, or when sleep eluded him, did he dare to penetrate the village of his boyhood. He walked by the hour about the darkened, still streets, a stalking ghost of the past, avoiding the fitful lamps from open doorways, becoming so accustomed to Cockermouth once more that he dangerously believed it also had accepted him.

Frequently he swung down Lamplugh way, reaching Crown Street opposite the Wordsworth House where William, six years his junior and a distant relative, now lived and wrote his amiable poetry. Since the year 1221, Cockermouth had been a market town, and had grown in three separate bursts of prosperity. Christian often crossed the old arched bridge over the Cocker, passing Moot Hall, the meeting place where the law was administered, and the corn market. Sometimes he climbed the hill past the ancient blue-slate shops with the twin bowed windows to Castlegate, pausing in the lane of the deep shadows under the great old trees to view again the focal point of all the North Country thereabouts, the ruined castle itself.

Sometimes he passed the decaying mansion of Henry Fletcher for whom he supposed he had been named, a wealthy merchant and a stubborn one who, on May 17, 1568, had been host, and a gallant one, to the fugitive Mary, Queen of Scots. Christian sometimes climbed the hill to All Saints', where he had tied his pony while attending grammar school with many another lad.

But these places lived in his memory only, and only stressed the gulf between his former way of life and this, for now and forevermore he was a man apart. This he knew. So passed the summer and autumn and winter and spring. And so passed the second winter and spring.

With James, the man of fells and mountains, of the rivers and woods and still waters, Christian roamed on frequent hunting or exploring trips. He was safe from the fear of recognition in the wild reaches of the Cumbrians, and even further from denunciation, since the reserved and suspicious hill folk had little truck with outsiders, and none with the "law" under any circumstance. They would never "denounce even a Scot for slaying their kin," James observed sourly, preferring to handle retribution in their own way; lawlessness which did them no harm was not considered a social evil. Over this lovely countryside, the two roamed freely, hunting as an excuse but in truth eager for the other's companionship, the roaming a pretext to forget the ache of uncertainty that clung like a cloud over Christian and hence troubled his brother even more.

On brisk days they hunted the red grouse or the golden plover on the uplands, or mallard, teal, pintail, or grebes among the marshes. From this wild country Christian won a healing and new confidence. He felt as one with the foxes, the pine marten, stoats, and the hares, the red and fallow deer that dwelt in the craggy recesses of the mountains.

As Christian lost his dread of capture, his wariness also gradually left him. He did not now recall when he first had entered the Crown and Mitre for a mug of ale, but by the second spring he had come to do so once a week. None paid him heed; he was a neighbor, a countryman, a Cumbrian; he was accepted. He stood against the outside wall in the evening, watching the life of the town and market place and green. Almost he forgot that he never again could be truly a part of this community, for over his head lay the black flag. One day it must be faced, barring a miracle. He did not believe in miracles.

In the warm dusk of one summer evening, Christian stood against the white-plastered facade of the pub. A stillness in the dark air seemed almost oppressive, and he stirred uneasily; possibly the unfelt ripples of some approaching storm had laid themselves upon him. He felt a lift in his awareness, an alteration, a shift in the smell of the air, although he did not attempt to define it.

A great clatter signaled the approach of a carriage and pair up Crown Street. Perhaps the coach came from one of the Tory manor houses north of the village; some of those who lived there were said to be followers of the late bad Earl and had profited from his political machinations and conspiracies. The carriage drew up, its liveried coachman ramrod stiff in the box and beside him his shadow, the footman.

The polished coach halted directly opposite the entrance to the Crown and Mitre. Through the carriage door, a short individual of middle-aged portliness emerged and moved toward the inn. Casually Christian observed his face in the dusk just as the visitor glanced up at the tall stranger by the side of the entrance. At that instant a reveler flung wide its door, flooding them both with light, and Christian stared full into the face of John Hallet, late midshipman of HMS *Bounty*. One April dawn long ago, Christian personally had knocked him from the deck of the ship into the castaways' boat.

CHAPTER FOUR

Frozen, Christian could only stare, powerless to move. Hallet returned the inspection, unbelievingly. Then the door swung to, blotting out the light. In the sheltering darkness Christian ran, looking over his shoulder only after he had crossed the green. No one pursued him. The carriage-and-pair remained silhouetted, still as a painting, against the white of the Crown and Mitre. Raucous sounds drifted from the tavern.

He stumbled down Lamplugh Road, once hiding among the brambles as a half-drunken carter trotted an old gray horse homeward, singing of his happy state for all of the fells and woods to hear. A mist began to fall, and then, with a thunderclap, the rainstorm was upon him, boiling upon road and field, turning thick dust into deep mud. Christian swung across the fields approaching Moorland Close over the meadow. He stepped through the door into the serenity of the warm interior, standing for a moment, back against the wood, his clothes dripping, his eyes staring into nothingness. His mother, bearing a sputtering lamp, found him so.

"Fletcher!" she cried, startled to see him there. "Fletcher, my son! What is it? Have ye seen a ghost?"

Christian shook his head violently. "Aye, Mother. A ghost indeed! An evil recollection from my past, but 'twas no spirit but the end, Mother. The end of all!" He clutched her blindly to him, heedless of his sodden clothes. She led him gently into the lighted kitchen where the others were. Haltingly he related the unbelievable encounter.

"Aye, 'tis odd indeed," murmured James, then lightened. "Perhaps we look enough alike so I could swear 'twas I he met? He saw you for a moment only."

"'Twould never do, Jemmie," Christian moaned. "We were not three feet from each other. He *knew,* I'm positive. And he's a small man, in form and character. A man of hate. Revenge would be his obsession."

James, wise in the way of Cumbrians, leaned back.

"From yan's description of the' carriage an' coachmen, 'twas from the manors north," he said. "They are neither Whig nor Tory but grasping at both. 'Twould be to their advantage, as they conceive it, to use yan for political purposes, a tool to pry oot whatever they want, rather than to turn ye in for cold justice. If that be so, ye become not a fugitive from justice, but just a lever to be used to shape others to their thinkin', to discomfit 'em."

Christian shook his head slowly.

"I cannot chance it, Jemmie. It would more likely bring nothing save catastrophe upon this house an' all I love here. I must flee."

Anne Christian, the etched lines upon her strong face grown deeper as the moments passed, seemed lost in thoughtfulness. Then she brightened.

"One moment, Fletcher," she interrupted. "A message came this very day for thee—from Isabella. A friend met the post at Carlisle an' fetched it. I had forgotten till this moment, such a start ye have given me." She handed him a folded paper sealed with the Curwen crest, tannish, thick and yet elegant. Even as he tore it open, Christian felt a warm anticipation rise from the paper, a faint joy that stirred memories:

July 7, 1810

F.

At last we've heard of your safe arrival many months ago. Word travels so slowly here! We trust very shortly to have the honor—the dearly anticipated pleasure—of a visit, whenever you feel free to come to Belle Isle. John joins me in this wish, and together we send you and your mother our love,

As ever,
fondly,
I.

Christian scanned the letter a second time. "'Tis over late, too late," he murmured softly. His mother caught his hand.

"Why, son? Why over late?" she demanded. "A retreat for thee until our fears can subside! 'Tis my prayers answered, Fletcher! The answer to my prayers."

Once more he shook the notion off, feeling the weight of his "stick" this night as he had not detected it for so very long.

"Already I have brought disaster upon all I have known. I cannot bring it down upon Isabella too. I cannot."

Anne Christian pressed his calloused hand.

"Yes, Fletcher, yes!" she whispered hoarsely. "John is a man of power in his district. He knows what he is about. He sanctioned this invitation, for Isabella would not have sent it otherwise or phrased it so. John can protect you—no agent can search his island without his let. Ye'd be as safe from the king's law as across the channel in Napoleon's army. Go, Fletcher! Go. Perhaps John might even obtain a pardon for you, and you can come back. Go quickly, while ye may."

CHAPTER FIVE

Christian set out in the rain that very night, the storm soon blowing itself away over the mountains. He followed the cart road from Eaglesfield eastward toward the Cocker and up the river toward the high country. He did not hide by day but avoided drawing attention to himself, trusting that farmers passed would think him an ordinary roadster, unworthy of note or recollection.

The hill and lake people were kind and open, ready to share a hot loaf of fresh bread and mug of warm milk, or sometimes tea, sending him refreshed upon his way with no questions. Sometimes he performed a few chores in payment for food and lodging; more frequently the country folk waved him off, glad for a brief conversation with someone from "outside." He threaded Honister Pass to the upper Derwent, pursued a forest trail to Great End and Stake Pass and by way of Langdale Pikes to the River Brathay and down that to Lake Windermere at its northern tip. He worked along the western coast to the shore opposite Belle Isle, unobserved for the latter part of his journey.

Windermere was considered by many the largest and among the most beautiful lakes in all of England. It lay in a trough with wooded mountains pressing upon it. The water was long and as narrow as an eel, scarce a mile across at its broadest point. A cluster of islands divided Windermere into northern and southern seas, and its fjordlike setting made of it a safe haven, his senses told him. Belle Isle, guarded by a screen of wooded reefs at the throat of Bowness Bay, was nearly thirty acres in extent, the largest, assuredly the loveliest, of its islands. The only inhabited isle, it had been brought as dowry by Isabella to her marriage and was wholly owned by the Christian Curwens, assuring its privacy.

Hailing a fisherman, Christian was quickly rowed to the landing on Belle Isle with its trim, newly painted boathouse facing the eastern shore. Already it was midafternoon; the sunlight gleaming on the waters made him pause a moment to savor the tranquility of this island jewel in its golden setting. He turned toward the house, a spacious structure of stone with a patina of ivy brightening its outer walls. To keep up the place, there must be a large staff, but there were neither stables nor livestock, a retreat indeed for one wishing to live apart.

A butler showed Christian into a drawing room and after a few moments returned and guided the visitor to a sunlit study fitted with chintz curtains and polished dark furniture tastefully arranged before an inviting grate. Christian moved swiftly toward the woman awaiting him with outstretched arms from the chaise to which she was confined.

"Fletcher!" she cried. "Dear, dear Fletcher! How good, how blessed to have you here at last after all those distant oceans! How I have waited, how I've prayed for this moment."

Isabella Curwen, though for many years confined to her chair or bed by crippling disease, had lost none of her beauty. It flamed outward to brighten those about her. Her glossy black hair fell in rippling waves, her dark eyes were animated, her face, pale for want of sunshine and exercise, had lost none of the loveliness Christian remembered. He dropped to his knees at her side and kissed her check gently, holding her close with a great affection. He had always held her in high regard—more as a close sister than a distant cousin.

She sensed something of his agony for her invalid condition. "'Tis nothing," she breathed. "I have grown accustomed to it so that I no longer pay the slightest attention. John, too, has resigned himself so that we scarcely think of it anymore. You must tell me of your travels, dear Fletcher, but first of your family. How is your mother? Your brothers and sister? How was Moorland Close? The same? Such lovely old manors change little with the generations."

He told her, in as lively a manner as he could manage, all that she wished to know, keeping the conversation light. She sensed a depth, a hidden reserve in him, however, which she had never detected before. It was more than maturity.

"Your face has altered, Fletcher," she said. "It is more—more experienced, of course, but 'tis changed more deeply than that, I think." She studied him thoughtfully. "'Tis as though you have waged a long difficult battle with some inner torment, and the lines are drawn but the decision not yet reached. Is it anything like that? Is it the—the mutiny, perhaps?"

Her husband strode into the room, and a maid began preparations for tea. The time for serious talk had passed—for the moment.

Christian sensed the solidity, the friendliness of this man he had known from childhood, though never well. There was an indefinable power, an outflow that reached toward Christian and from which he cautiously withdrew, if ever so slightly.

John Christian Curwen appeared to Christian to be the antithesis of his wife. Where she was grace and loveliness, he was as squarely built as a merchant brig, as deliberate in ordinary dealings, unimaginative, although he could let his lightning strike when he was aroused. Her emotions were changeable as Glasgow weather, though she kept them light and joyous. Her husband seemed anchored to an acceptance of all things, a refusal to become disturbed by changing events or mercurial shifts in the social and political life about him. His dress reflected his character, dark and gray or black, with a white shirt, and white cuffs to brighten it, and a black brimmed hat which he rarely removed, even indoors, putting it aside only when busied at his desk. His blue eyes were the one engaging feature of his otherwise immobile face. They gleamed with a lively interest and shone with a kindliness that quickly won him friends. There was nothing of the introvert about John Christian Curwen.

"'Tis good to have thee here, Fletcher," he greeted his guest. "Isabella and I have discussed thee often and even fretted about thy distant life."

Christian stirred his tea absently.

"Aye, John. Aye. I suppose I've been a concern to many I love." He set the cup aside. "It was not something I wished. I had no desire to bring a stigma upon my people, to induce them to change their names because of my past. Do believe me!" His deep concern led him to plunge directly into this grave issue.

"I did not expand my name because of any fancied 'stigma' thou brought the house of Christian," John protested. "Rather 'twas to wed great families, the Christians and the Curwens. I did not abandon the name of Christian, but multiplied it with Isabella's family. 'Twas not stigma but to honor her and them, Fletcher. It was just a coincidence that the change occurred when word of thy adventure reached us."

Christian placed his cup and saucer upon the polished table and arose, standing with legs slightly spread and hands folded behind him like a sea captain pondering an action.

"I fear you've underestimated the blackness which has descended about me, John. 'Tis not stain alone, but disaster I bring upon those whose lives I touch. Disaster, blood, shame! I should never have come here. I tell you this to forewarn you and to explain why I must leave at once, before the infection roots in my dearest friends, you and Isabella."

Curwen faced Christian with fresh interest, deepened concern, understanding for the first time that he was a man not merely of violence, but of thought, with great torment of soul. "We will not permit you to depart for now, Fletcher," he said quietly. "Isabella and I have long awaited this visit. We fear no disaster, nor have we ever. Ye must abide with us for the present, for thou art of us, and we of thee; and 'twould be unseemly to abandon us so hastily. It might even be rude!" The phrase was a passing joust by which this odd man tried to lighten Christian's burden. Christian could not help but stir to his warmth and that of Isabella, who spoke not, yet seemed as much part of the conversation as either of these men she loved so deeply.

"I bring disaster, John—disaster," repeated Christian hoarsely, his eyes feverish. "Suppose king's men come for me and ye were found to house me? What would happen then to Isabella, let alone to you? Don't you see, John? At Cockermouth I was discovered by one who hates me and who will not rest until I am captured even here! I must leave at once."

Curwen shook his head stubbornly. "You cannot leave, Fletcher, torn and troubled as thou art. We forbid it. Think naught of any danger to us, your being here. We own this island, and we say who shall set foot upon it, even upon one square inch of it. I am not without influence, here and in London too. The king's men are well aware of my power, although I do not wield it carelessly. But no man ever seizes what is ours without my let, nor enters my house without permission, nor threatens my wife or guests while I live. No, Fletcher, thou are safe in this house. Ye must abide with us for the present. We will have it no other way."

CHAPTER SIX

The Christian Curwens sought delicately in succeeding weeks to draw from their guest the account of his years of outlawry. They felt that the mutiny could not be the sole cause of such deep turmoil. Christian was frank enough about the events on the *Bounty* and sketched his subsequent adventures, but an inner reserve seemed to keep hidden the things that most wracked his soul. John and Isabella were very wise people. They were deeply involved in seeking to bare the root causes of human conflicts and human troubles and were interested in Christian for himself and also because of his apparent problem in itself.

Christian cooperated as fully as his personality permitted, though his temper flared briefly at their questions on occasion, perhaps when they struck too closely to the truth. Understanding, the Curwens never resented his outbursts, feeling they signified an ever closer approach to the bedrock.

"Why?" demanded Christian. "Why do you bother me? I tell you I am not worthy of your concern!"

Isabella reproved him gently: "Thou are a man, Fletcher. Therefore thou are worthy, as are all men. Made in the image of God there is within thee spark of God. Besides we love thee."

Christian flushed at this fresh evidence of their affection and at something else, as well.

"I do not believe in God. I know you do, Isabella, so I would not deny Him here, for that would pain you; and pain I would not bring. But as for me, since I cannot accept the notion of God, I find I get along well without."

She arched her brow. Again he flushed. "My problems are of my own making, I would think," he continued, "or because of bad luck or something." He could not bring himself to define his "stick," for the idea of it seemed preposterous in this light-flushed island, and he felt they would be unable to accept his explanation of it.

John had just entered the room from the library with a small leather-covered book, a finger marking his place.

"As thou knowest," he said, "we are Friends, called by our enemies, although we recognize none, 'Quakers.' Our beliefs were formalized by George Fox, who died little more than a century ago."

"I thought Quakerism—pardon me, Isabella—the Friends—"

"Think nothing of it, Fletcher," she laughed. "We are accustomed to being 'Quakers' in the general mind. Call us so, if it comes easier to thy tongue."

"Well, I thought the movement to be one of country people, shepherds, farmers, shopkeepers. How could it appeal to those of your position and culture?"

John smiled, explaining, "So 'twas in its origins but its social character has altered and its acceptance broadened. We anticipate 'twill one day sweep the world."

"Like the faith of Christ, eh?"

"It *is* the faith of Christ! Yes, Fletcher, the faith of Christ will one day cover the earth. Here, let me read a bit of what George Fox wrote. I think you will find it not without meaning. Fox observes that the Quaker belief embraces the idea of God in every man, to which the Christian in the presence of evil is called on to make an appeal, following out a line of thought and conduct which, involving suffering as it may do, is in the long run most likely to reach the inward witness and to change the evil mind into the right mind."

Christian grinned mirthlessly. "'Tis that I have an evil mind, eh? I do not doubt it," he added, thickly. "But of whose creation? Placed within me from without by some supreme being or by my own hand and action? I do not believe in your God, yet sometimes I sense an evil that has clutched me and uses me for sinister purposes I cannot fathom. Nor explain."

"Is not such present in every man?"

Christian glanced at his host. "I cannot judge—can you? If you believe in God, how do you explain this evil? For that matter, if *I* do not believe in God, how do I?"

"Robert Barclay, another Friend," John continued, without answering directly, "has written that 'When I came into the silent assemblies of God's people—meaning the Friends—I felt a secret power among them, and I found the evil weakening in me and the good raised up.' My object in citing this is to stress our feeling that evil cannot be driven out by itself but must be replaced by something; and that thing can only be good, which we call God, or the 'light within.' 'Tis that which we urge thee to accept, Fletcher."

"Why cannot man, recognizing evil, simply have done with it?"

"We do not believe this is possible. Another of our writers believed that 'Nothing divine, nothing that has religious value can originate in man, as man.'"

"I do not recognize the value of the religious."

John Christian Curwen shook his head stubbornly.

"Not to be religious is not to be human," he insisted. "To be human is to be religious, however dormant that impulse. It is what raises us above the beasts; and, I might add, 'tis the only thing that does so."

"What about love?"

"Love is a reflection of the religious. If 'tis only lust, it is nothing."

"Religion, or the religion in which I was raised, is based upon the Bible. Many believe it written at a time of revelation whether by dictation of God, as some suppose, or by mental visions or aberrations. At any rate, that time is past. Those who accept it seek to resurrect a relic, no more."

"'Tis no relic," insisted his host. "The one great message is that revelation is continuous, available to the soul of every man. It fuels the inward light."

"And if I cannot accept the revelation within the individual, or your Bible, or your God—what then?"

"Then thee must fight evil by thyself alone, and that is futile. No man can be as strong as evil, nor as cunning."

"How did it enter your life—this evil that so greatly troubles you?" asked Isabella.

Christian looked away. It seemed incongruous to speak of dark and sinister mysteries in the presence of this woman, so gentle, so good—and so helpless. Of what benefit was faith in God to her, crippled, maimed by disease as she was? Did it heal her, make her whole, keep her so? Yet her infirmity had deepened his affection for her, and for John, so faithful to their love. Christian could no longer be secretive in replying to their questioning. Recalling now that decisive incident in his life, that continental divide from which the years of wandering had flowed, frankness opened his mind to them.

"It was at the moment of the mutiny, I believe, Isabella. Captain Bligh then leveled upon me what I can only consider an imprecation. I shrugged it off, at the time. But still I hear his voice, sense his unswerving hatred. I can feel his words lance into me. I can feel the dark and burning malevolence in his eyes. If I absorbed evil, 'twas from the captain's will that black morning. Into my soul it came, from the soul of him. I feel it now. This hated curse has been confirmed by a thousand incidents, over 10,000 leagues. It endureth forever."

John turned Christian's words over in his analytical mind. "If Bligh bestowed it upon thee, Fletcher, Bligh must lift it."

"I do not understand."

"When one disagrees with another, however slightly, he must take the first opportunity to talk it out with him," John replied. "Otherwise the difference will rankle, convert itself into poison, and generate an insoluble hatred. Speaking of it frankly provides the only way out from such a personal catastrophe."

"One of my former rank does not talk out a situation with a tempestuous superior like Captain Bligh, John. One might as well attempt to settle differences with a lion—or a viper. Were I inclined toward suicide, I should choose another way than throwing myself upon his mercy, a quality that for him does not exist in any event."

"Are you not committing suicide in another, more painful way? There is no other course, Fletcher. If he should bring the weight of naval law against you, remember that I am not without influence, nor are others. We should not permit injustice to be done."

"He feels I was unjust to him, and the law would provide mere retribution."

"Perhaps you were. In that case, why avoid punishment? But if instead he were to prove unjust also, or if the fault were equally placed, bringing it to light could not but benefit you both."

Christian sighed.

"Would that this were so," he murmured. "But I fear the scales of justice never truly balance."

Fletcher Christian was a man who felt the need for solitude at intervals. Whenever his thoughts became unclear, his frustrations flared, he sought out loneliness. Belle Isle heavily wooded and abounding with rocks and rills was perfect for securing isolation. He formed the habit of slipping away in the long twilight, to sit upon a rock at the north end of the island or in some sheltered cove to rest for hours, allowing fantasies and half-formed thoughts to assume what shape they would.

One afternoon in early autumn so occupied, he saw the dispatch boat leave Bowness-on-Windermere and pull strongly toward the island. The passage seemed hurried. His curiosity aroused, he watched the boat bang into the side of the little pier. A passenger leaped ashore and sped toward the house. Seized by a foreboding, he was not surprised when Tim, one of the gardeners, was sent to fetch him. Christian made his way toward the house with deliberate apprehension, while overhead the gulls screamed a sailor's warning that all was not well.

Isabella and John greeted him gravely. Christian shook off the suggestion he take tea. "What is it?" he demanded, his voice strained, harsh. "I realize the news must be bad; I am prepared whatever it may be."

"Fletcher!" cried Isabella. "Dear Fletcher, we love thee so—"

"We have received disquieting information from Cockermouth, Fletcher," John interrupted.

"Moorland Close!" gasped Christian, remembering Hallet. "My people!"

"Aye, Fletcher. It has to do with Moorland Close—and thy people."

"My mother! She's, is she—"

"Thy mother is safe, Fletcher. Do allow me to read the dispatch." He read the folder paper slowly, unemotionally:

> Aware of your relationship with the family at Moorland Close, Mr. Curwen, I send you the lamentable news that it was savagely attacked two nights hence by a band of ruffians thinly disguised as Scots, and left something of a ruins, although it is reparable. The purpose of the attack is not known here. The attempt to disguise the assailants suggested to some that it was political in motive and was set in motion by dissident elements along the Solway who are neither Whig nor Tory, fish nor fowl, but reckless pursuers of the phantasms of the late Earl.
>
> Although it is not known exactly what their mission may have been, James Christian resisted the ruffians, was struck on the side of the head by one of them, and expired yesterday morning. Mrs. Anne Christian, fearing another attack, removed as swiftly as her things could be got ready and arrangements made, to her people on the Isle of Man. Indications are that she will not return. The sympathy of the community goes out to her, while authorities are seeking the perpetrators and reasons for this rude incident. We send assurances of our highest esteem, and please believe me to be,
>
> Y'r ob't s'v't

John handed to Christian a second folded paper, which he had neither opened nor read, though it was unsealed. "'Tis from thy mother, Fletcher, and I know it is for thee."

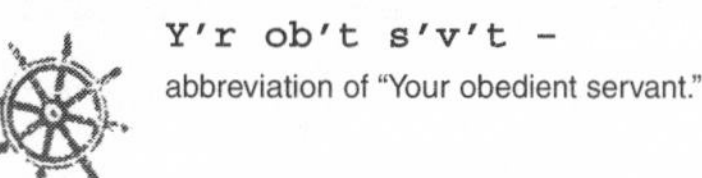

Y'r ob't s'v't – abbreviation of "Your obedient servant."

The letter bore no name at its beginning, nor at its ending:

> My son, my son! With this comes all of the love a mother can express to an honored child whom she bore and whom she reared, and whose progress through the world she has watched as she could, and in whom she had great pride, and has so still. It has given us to be touched by tragedy, tragedy manifold; but I know you never willed it, and in this mother's eyes you ever will be innocent of any wrongdoing. The assailants, who numbered above a score, were disguised and told us not what they were in pursuit of, save that they secured no information from any of us, nor would they ever.
>
> I believe that whatever you do is right, as you see the right and good; and I live in pride of you and will die in pride of you when my time comes. Nothing can ever alter that, my son. As you will have heard, Moorland Close can no longer be sanctuary for you and, therefore, no longer for us; and poor James lies savagely beaten because he tried to defend it, and none knows at this writing whether he will live or die. But if he dies, know that he did so bravely, defending your home to the last and with no regrets, and that you are not the cause of his tragedy.
>
> Although I shall leave this place forever in a few hours, I pray you to be ever aware that my love will always accompany you for the remainder of our lives here and for eternity afterward. You are my dearly beloved son, in whom reposes my boundless joy and my affection now and forevermore. Go with God, my son. May we each be sustained.

The letter required no other signature than the hand that wrote it. Christian crumpled it in his great fist, then smoothed it out, read it over again and folded it carefully, slipping it into his pocket.

He raised a lined, anguished face. "She has gone," he muttered. 'Tis a book closed, a tragedy completed. Did I not warn you? To touch me brings disaster!"

"Not disaster for her, Fletcher," John protested. "You brought her great happiness, the assurance that you lived and loved her. What more could any mother ask? 'Twas not disaster. It was life!"

"And James?"

"James was a brother faithful, loyal unto death. It is given to each man to die, and only the circumstances remain to be decided. A death is a tragedy, but more for the living than for the dead. That is our faith. We regret his passing as we treasured his life. But I cannot believe that he now regrets his death. The tragedy is ours, not his."

"Ye talk like a priest, John," said Christian, near the breaking point.

"Priests speak truth."

A moan escaped Christian's lips. He covered his face with his hands and sank into a chair. "Mother, mother!" he sobbed. "Mother and James. What blackness have I brought you? Why am I afflicted so?"

He felt upon his shoulder the hand of John Curwen. He looked up. "Can you help me, John? Can Isabella? Can anyone? The more I love people, the harsher the anguish I seem to bestow upon them. It is ghastly, John, to be the tool of evil when I wish only to be the instrument of good. How can I escape?"

"Would that you had faith, Fletcher," cried Isabella. "Faith can conquer all things!"

"Faith is not for me; it is not within my power."

"Faith is not a matter of power, Fletcher. It is a question of acceptance, of openness, not of thy will."

John broke in harshly. "Go to Bligh!" he commanded. "Seek out this captain, talk with him, allay his hatred as you can, or at least allay yours. Win his release from that accursed imprecation, or become convinced that it was meaningless. You can never do it any other way, Fletcher. That is the first step *within* your power. Do it! For 'tis the only way through the morass of misunderstanding. For our sakes—if not for your own—do this thing, whatever the peril for you!"

Christian's face twisted with a grimace.

"Shall I go to Australia for this, John?"

"'Tis not necessary. I have received information that Bligh will reach England shortly, perhaps already has done so. He has added one more mutiny—his third—to his wake! The Australians whom he was to govern revolted against him, arrested him, packed him home. He returns to England even more controversial than when he left."

"Shall I leap then from the snake pit into the lion's den?"

"My God, man, you already believe yourself wrapped in disaster! What is one more peril if you might win release? Peace of mind? Rest of soul? Compared with that, what is death?"

CHAPTER SEVEN

Upon the plains of middle England, summer lingered still, the fields of barley white where the harvest had passed, smoke from thatched cottages drifting over them. Herons in the shallow water looked for a last fish before the ice sent them in search of warmer lands. The valley of Trent was dotted with gray haycocks signaling the end of the season and preparations for the time of snow; thick wool on the black-faced Hampshire confirmed it. All roads led to London—one of these Christian followed, indistinguishable from any tramp, stepping aside for the mail coaches or the skimming carriages, walking the dirt roads with the carters and freighters or occasionally hitching a ride on a canal barge, slowly approaching the great city of the south. As he entered London, he was like an automaton in progress toward disaster, but of iron, inflexible will in seeking it out.

He had been driven to the utter limits of despair. He thought no thoughts, dreaded no fate, possessed a sole ambition: to have done with it. The Curwens' argument that this could be accomplished only by confrontation of Captain Bligh had taken root, flourished, become an obsession. Yet his fixation was well concealed.

Christian well remembered the address of the three-story home where William and Elizabeth Bligh had lived for so many years, maintaining the residence even when the captain had been posted to Australia. He would never forget that summer evening of so long ago when he had been brought to Bligh to be introduced by his cousin, now long dead. And then he had signed on the voyages, to the West Indies and to the South Seas . . .

Bligh lived in a quiet nook in Lambeth, not far from the right bank of the Thames, where the ferryman deposited him for a copper. Christian first sauntered through Astley's Circus and fashionable Vauxhall Garden, before embarking upon what was likely to prove his fatal, last adventure. His plan was to come upon the captain so abruptly that he would have time to speak and allay Bligh's understandable apprehensions. This would require resourcefulness, and luck.

Durham Place appeared deserted, save for a waiting carriage, its coachman and footman idly chatting beside it. Christian approached the house, then stepped aside as a tall man swooped down the steps and darted past him, swiveled forward at the hips so that he seemed in imminent jeopardy of falling, his dark eyes intent on the way ahead, his expression mobile. Passing Christian, he whirled and stabbed at him with a long finger.

"Who are you?" he demanded testily, as though he owned creation and everyone in it. He wore a huge gold ring with the three crowns and the *tria juncta in uno* legend of the Order of the Bath.

"Why—why, sir—what do you mean?" stammered Christian.

"You are quite obviously a ship's officer! What ship, sir? Who are you? I haven't got forever, you know!"

"I'm—I'm Lieutenant Fletcher, sir. From—from the Admiralty. Here to see Captain Bligh."

"Oh, from the Admiralty!" growled the other. "I thought you were serving usefully, somewhere." He whirled to resume his lurch toward the carriage. "I believed for a moment I had known you."

He pulled himself aboard before the footman could say, "If you please, m'lord," slamming the door on which Christian had only time to see *Cochrane* and the crest on its lacquered surface before the vehicle whipped off.

Fletcher Christian mounted the three stone steps of the home of Captain William Bligh. He raised the glittering brass knocker and let it fall, its boom reverberating through the house. In a moment the captain's aged houseman stood there, weak eyes blinking. "Yes, sir? What is it, sir?"

"Captain Bligh?"

"Whom shall I say is calling?"

Christian hesitated. "I have a communication for the captain from the Admiralty," he announced. "I am to place it in the captain's hand personally. Please inform him of that."

"This way, sir," said the butler, showing Christian into a drawing room of delicate French furniture, lit by three lamps, a fire smoldering in the grate. Elizabeth Bligh had lived long alone in this house, and its decor was hers, not that of a gruff sea captain.

Christian, his hands clasped behind him, faced toward the grate, his back to the door. There was a heavy step, a rasping voice he knew so well growling, "Yes, sir? What is it?" A vague impression of a bulky figure approached him. Christian whirled about, closed the door and stood with his back to it, staring into the startled sea-colored eyes of William Bligh.

"What is the meaning of this, sir? What message from the Admiralty requires such an interruption . . ." His voice trailed off as he struggled to place this disturbingly familiar figure from out of the past. From where, how far back? A figure seen through the wrong end of a glass. From Botany Bay? Hardly. Too recent. Some ship, perhaps? The *Porpoise? Lady Sinclair? Warrior—Irresistible—Monarch?* Could he be from the old *Glatton?* The seventy-four-gun *Director,* his first line of battleship? Or perhaps from the little old *Providence?* The *Bounty?* The *Boun*—ah, could it *be?*

"My God!" Bligh stepped backward, his face ashen, his brilliant eyes glazed with emotion. "Mr.—Mr. *Christian!*"

"Aye, Captain Bligh," returned Christian warily. "Christian, late of the *Bounty*, sir."

"My God!" repeated Bligh, strangely at a loss, his hands gesturing at nothing. "How came you here, Christian? What insanity is this?" A bit of arrogance reappeared in his voice as he roused from shock. Christian remained unsure what he was about, where the dialogue would lead.

"It does seem mad," he agreed, "but madness is not so foreign to our lives, I think."

A shrewdness grew in the captain's eyes. "How did you survive, reach England?" he wondered, sincerely curious. "The Admiralty heard last May from Sir Sidney Smith at Rio de Janeiro, relaying a yarn from a Captain Folger of the American sealer, *Topaz*. His log reported a landing at Pitcairn Island. Little attention would have been paid his story save he brought the Kendall Chronometer from the *Bounty* herself."

Christian hesitated, bit his lip. "Who was—did Folger say who remained on Pitcairn?"

Bligh laughed a laugh of self-considered righteousness. "Everyone—every man had perished save Alexander Smith, or John Adams, as he now chooses to call himself. Most of the native women still live and numerous children. The men killed each other off as might be expected from such unprincipled wretches."

"All dead, sir?"

"So says Folger. Being an American his account is somewhat suspect. Folger reported that you, too, had perished," he stared at Christian defiantly, "a statement that gave me considerable satisfaction at the time." Bligh shifted uncertainly. The business of Christian's return might throw his whole case into hopeless confusion, even doubt! First the mutiny on the *Bounty*, then the great mutiny at the Nore, and now the court-martials and the troubles relating to the Australian mutiny—'twas enough to give a man a fit. How many rebellions could an officer's record endure, even if the fault was in no way his?

He well understood why the Admiralty had not followed up on the Folger report and sent a warship to ascertain the Pitcairn facts: let sleeping dogs lie. Navy men had long memories—but they were realists. They would allow the hangings of Ellison, Burkitt, and Millward atone for the *Bounty* affair and get on to other things. Now this rascal would likely reopen the whole affair of twenty years ago, in the midst of the far more important—and urgent—matter of the mutiny in New South Wales. And through his powerful relatives, Christian might even drag politics into this mess. What a mess!

"William?" a woman's voice came through the door. Christian stared at Bligh, uncertain, both of them.

"Yes, my dear?" replied the captain, after a pause.

"Are you all right? Is anything wrong?" Her voice was insistent.

"Yes, yes, my dear," he reassured her. "Quite all right. Go upstairs, Betty, and retire. I'll be along directly. I am engaged in an important matter for the moment, with a—a gentleman from the Admiralty."

Christian relaxed. "Captain Folger reported I, too, had perished?"

"Yes, sir, that he did. I had hoped 'twas true."

Christian nodded, wonderingly. "Adams was loyal as he had promised."

"Loyal! Loyal to whom? Why he was a ringleader, after you! He was a *mutineer!* Guarded me with a musket himself, he did! You have a pathetic notion of loyalty, Christian. But then you ever had. You always were a fool."

"Perhaps, sir." Christian's face clouded. "Did Folger's story include any details on how the Pitcairn debacle occurred?"

"Not specifically. He said you had died and the others fell to wrangling. They killed each other off. He gave few details."

"Disaster!" groaned Christian, more to himself than to the other. "One more disaster I've caused. What misery . . . what evil . . ."

Bligh peered curiously at Christian's contorted face, uncomprehending, wholly unfeeling of the other's agony, as he ever was oblivious to the sensibilities of others. Still his curiosity grew. "Christian, why in the name of God did you come here? You were as safe as any bloody renegade ever could be with a crime such as yours on his conscience. You must have known that I would set the dogs on your trail instantly when you approached. You would never get out of London alive. Your execution would be certain. Were you unaware of all this?"

"No, sir."

"Then why the devil did you do it? Is this suicide?"

"Because I had to. I was forced."

"By whom?"

"By events, Captain Bligh."

"What events?"

Christian's face twisted with the recollection of many disasters, a series that seemed endless. "That morning off Tofua," he said hoarsely, "in April of 1789, I was scarcely sane, a state to which you had driven me."

"I drove no man daft, Christian, no man intent upon his duty. If you were crazed, it was your own foolishness that led you to it, not I. All I demanded was duty and reasonable efficiency in its performance."

"The men of Nore? Of New South Wales? They, too, revolted because of their own foolishness? Is that the formula for all your insurrections?"

Bligh flushed. "They had other causes," he admitted. "But ever the same damned irresponsibility, a cavalier attitude toward duty."

"As we put you into the boat, Captain, you leveled against me an imprecation—some would call it a curse—that I overlooked and then forgot for a time. But it has pursued me from place to place, disaster following upon disaster, half way round the world, leaving my wake strewn with broken bodies, broken lives, and all because of me. Or rather, because of you."

"All this because of a curse?" Bligh's forehead wrinkled as he searched his memory, sought for understanding. "You speak like a child, a common illiterate! By God, sir, you make no sense!"

Christian waved his protest. "At the outset I paid little attention to it," he repeated. "I no more believed in curses than I believed in anything. Then events commenced to overwhelm me, and I was left no room for doubt. I can no longer disbelieve it."

"'Tis a childish thing, you know."

"Aye. That it is."

"Even supposing there's something to it, what has this to do with me? 'Tis past, these twenty years. I presume you would like to undo the past. I am told criminals sometimes are driven to remorse if they are capable of it. Perhaps you are to some slight degree."

"Remorse? For what? For seeking justice from a tyrant? No, Captain, I have no remorse save as others have suffered because of those events. I was driven here not in remorse but to seek such rectification as we find possible."

"We?"

"Aye. I have come to believe this imprecation is real. I never suffer from it. The innocent with whom I come into contact do bear its burden. That is where lies its injustice. I came not seeking from you mercy, for that is foreign to your nature, nor compassion for that, too, is unknown to you, but justice for the innocent who yet will suffer because of deeds of which they are wholly ignorant, that brings upon them disasters they do not merit. I ask for your assurance that this curse has been lifted."

"And in return?"

Christian spread his hands helplessly.

"I am at your service, sir. Even unto the yardarm."

Bligh, his mouth slightly open, stared at him. For long moments they gazed at one another, Christian's eyes pleading with this harsh man who had more than control of life and earth over him, the power of the living death. Bligh was lost in a whirl of speculations. This was far better than he had hoped. Retribution to the man who had injured him most deeply and with little risk of enhancing his Australian difficulties. What had appeared at the outset as catastrophe now seemed the reverse: revenge and satisfaction beyond his dreams! A fitting end to what had been an ugly chapter in a worthy life as His Majesty's loyal and dutiful officer.

His stomach commenced to quake and from deep within came a distant rumbling, mounting as a rolling, heavy laugh of sheerest triumph tumbled from his lips. He threw back his head and roared with wild, relieved gusts of joy, pouring his laughter over Christian like deluges of iced salt water, leaving him helpless, confused, wordless.

"Cursed!" cried Bligh with tears of violent mirth. "Cursed ye were and cursed ye still be! Now you want me to *lift* your affliction? The punishment? For that is what it is. Divine retribution. Divine! By God, know ye the taste of revenge? Ah, 'tis perfection. You desire me to raise the curse? Hah! That I shall *never* do. Never! Nor will I turn you in for a court and legal punishment to atone for your crimes. No, you will pay a price far greater than any court could levy. The weight of its punishment you bear, and will forever, as long as you live and for generations to come!"

A mad gleam burned in the eye of the captain. "You are free, Christian, *free!* Free to become the living dead! May ye live long and regret every moment of it! I will never release you. Never! Not in this life or any other!"

CHAPTER EIGHT

His spirit as lowering as the wooled November day, Christian moved southwesterly, as a sailor in trouble, depressed beyond measure, migrating as his kind ever does toward the sea. His was not a conscious choice. He knew not where he was bound, nor why, nor did he truly care. He sought oblivion in mind, although he would not seek it in body.

Finally, rounding the head of Mill Bay, Christian passed through Stonehouse, crossed a mossy stone bridge, climbed a ridge, and swung down into Davenport, the old sea village on the slopes above the king's dockyard. Already more than a century old, the yard's hundreds of acres were littered with lumber sheds, mould-lofts, drydocks where one or two first-raters were in the stocks, and slips for lesser vessels, the skeletons of which, in every stage of construction, rose along the waterside. Some already were being dressed alongside sheer-hulks offshore.

Davenport dockyard was a hub of the empire, or at least of its naval might. Thousands of craftsmen and artisans swarmed over hulls in various degrees of completion. The racket of hammering and sawing, the screeching of booms and tackles lay over the port like a noisy cloud. Davenport was a haven for the seamen, for the haunted—or wanted—soul; but he must be wary and alert if he wished to elude the press gangs that roved the streets and penetrated the taverns, running down and seizing men like wild game for gun-deck service or duty aloft aboard His Majesty's men-of-war.

Christian secured a room above the tavern on Fore Street where most of the time he hid. He was no less a fugitive because Bligh had refused to turn him over to a naval court in favor of sending him packing under his cloud of guilt. The sentence of death hung over him still and always would; his record could never be truly cleared while he lived, and this he knew. It guided his every moment. Christian was unsure why he had come to Davenport at all. In this naval center, every man who had ever served with him and still followed the sea would turn up sooner or later. He had no ambition and no notion of what his future should be. He supposed he might one day be impressed and serve out a short remaining life on a gun deck or in the tops. He considered enlisting in the marines but decided against it. He was almost wholly without hope, yet his wariness never quite abandoned him.

One morning he chanced to walk down Fore Street toward the docks. After a night's rain, the air smelled clean and salty, lifting Christian's spirit for the first time in months. He shied from happiness for it seemed to him that simple lightheartedness led inevitably to the blows of fate. He heard a quick step behind and instinctively, even amid the bustle and racket from the king's dock, felt the step was in pursuit of him. He hastened, then slowed his pace, but he could not throw off his mysterious pursuer. He paused at the window of a chandler's, to cautiously peer at the individual who drew up beside him. Christian turned—and found himself face to face with Peter Heywood!

"Christian!" cried Heywood, in the uniform of a navy captain. Christian whirled away, bounding the down the crowded street, threading its traffic with astounding agility. He dodged up a side street, doubled through another. He heard the pursuing steps fade and slipped through a tavern door into an ale room, seating himself in the corner murk among seamen indistinguishable in the gloom. There he rested and waited, his heart beating with the fury of the race and narrowness of his escape. Heywood! *Bounty* midshipman and closest friend whom he had sent to Cumberland with the dreary account of the mutiny—a naval officer still, and risen now to the rank of captain.

Even if Heywood had been delighted to see him, because of duty he could not have failed to report his presence in Davenport. The result could only have been to undo the cruel structure Bligh had erected, to erase the hope for life which was beginning once again to stir if still without conscious reason. Now his only escape lay in the chance nature of the encounter. May Peter not have been positive of his identity? If so, would he not report his presence to anyone? He could not depend on it. His safety lay once more in flight. But where? Where, indeed? With the other's discovery, a place aboard a man-of-war would be akin to suicide. Christian sat long over his ale. The fates had boxed him in. Still uncertain, he paid his copper and warily made his way to his quarters, but the streets seemed clear. He climbed the outside stairway, opened his door, and entered the darkened room, drawing aside the curtain from the sole window.

"Mr. Fletcher Christian, I believe!" grated a harsh voice behind him. He spun, then dropped back from the muzzle of a pistol at his head. There was a weathered, fearless face behind it, and in the gloom of the corner three other figures. He could no longer flee. He was trapped!

"Who are you?" sighed Christian wearily. His mind would scarce accept this abrupt ending of twenty-two years of fugitive liberty.

"That is not the proper question," parried the other in a dry policeman's voice. "It is, rather, you are Mr. Christian, are you not?"

Christian shrugged helplessly.

"Yes."

"As we had thought," replied the other with satisfaction. "Would you be so good as to sit over there, sir? We will not bind you, for the moment; but we are quite alert and will not tolerate foolishness."

He scribbled something on a paper and handed it to one of his colleagues. "Take this at once to Sir Harry," he directed. "Tell him we await his pleasure."

Silence descended upon the room and its occupants. Christian sat erect while his captors lounged between him and the door. These were veteran man hunters who could neither be outwitted nor easily defeated. Suddenly Christian felt very tired, very old, resigned to the end of his long flight and even, yes, to his all-but-inevitable execution. He would not have tried to escape now, if he could.

In half an hour the messenger bounded up the stairs. "Sir Harry says bring him along," he reported to his chief, who nodded coldly to Christian.

"We must go now, sir," he said in his flat monotone. "It will necessitate passing through the streets. We would prefer not to draw unnecessary attention by binding you, but we assure you that a false move means your death. Is this understood, sir; or must I restrain you?"

"I understand," replied Christian, his voice already dead. "I'll make no effort to flee."

"Let us be off, then."

Once again, this time with his captors, he set out along Fore Street toward the mast pond, threading the midday crowds. Short of an Admiralty administrative structure, he was led to an old converted cottage, set well back from the street, with guards lounging before it, the building having about it the unmistakable aura of a law-enforcement headquarters. Christian paused at the lower steps to gaze once more at the sky and hills, sea and forest, the busy clattering community of relatively free men, his last view of these, as he supposed. Then he was hurried into the dusky interior, down a long corridor to a tastefully furnished, if somewhat Spartan, office.

Behind a desk sat a white-haired man of striking, if not precisely handsome, appearance. His white mustache drooped definitively, giving his mouth a bulldog appearance; and his lively eyes were pale in color, a sort that conveyed a remote inner fire; none could avoid those eyes entirely. Sir Harry Gladden-White, known to every policemen in Britain as Whitey, although never called that to his face, was not a man to trifle with. He wasted no time on preliminaries.

"Mr. Christian?" he asked. "Do sit down, sir, and tell me of yourself."

"I do not understand," mumbled Christian.

Sir Harry waved the other men from the office, then faced Christian alone. His demeanor was neither lordly nor hostile, but Whitey was not one with whom one could be evasive. "Tell me of your movements after the mutiny," he directed.

Christian looked down at the desk, his thoughts glum, wholly resigned to his denouncement. "Well, sir, after some years in the islands, I went to South America and eventually returned to England. There is not much more—"

"Let me refresh your memory with what we already know, Mr. Christian," Whitey interrupted, impatiently. "You set Captain Bligh adrift in late April, 1789, then made your way to the island known as Pitcairn's where you established a colony."

His recitation was in clipped accents, his fingers from either hand touching their tips, his eyes scanning Christian's face and shifting now and then to the thicket of masts beyond the window.

"In approximately the year 1793, you quit Pitcairn by boat and landed upon the western coast of South America, where, after a series of adventures, you became associated with the natives," he pursed his lips, "about 1797. You attained a position of some importance among them, though why you left we have not yet ascertained—perhaps you will supply that information. Eventually you wandered into the viceroyalty of La Plata as a—a gaucho, I believe they call them—a semi-barbaric horseman at any rate, but a breed demanding skill and doubtless much experience to be accepted among them. You came to the assistance of Beresford at Buenos Aires and later of Auchmuty. You returned to England with the convoy, were shipwrecked upon the Cornish coast, made your way to Cumberland, thence to London and now here, which brings us up to date. There are some gaps, which I should like to you fill."

Christian was speechless.

"Who could have told you all of this? Bligh? Some at Cumberland, perhaps? Who knew—"

"No one in England has told us a thing," interrupted Whitey testily. "We have our own sources of intelligence in many places. What I have told you is merely a survey of your dossier, information gathered over many years and from—ah—varied sources. We have quite a bit, sir. I am counting on you to complete what we lack."

"Perhaps you could remind me of things I had forgotten," Christian grinned wryly. "The only major events, other than purely personal matters which I am sure would not interest you, were those after I left the Mapuche, the Chilean Indians, until I became associated with the gauchos. I spent much time of that period wandering southward, as far as the Strait and even to Tierra del Fuego. Then after some—uh, dismal experiences down there, I returned northward along the eastern slope of the Andes with the Tehuelche. They are an Indian people like the Mapuche but much more primitive. Fine horsemen. I found them possessed of certain lofty qualities, as I believe."

"Excellent," mused Sir Harry. "Splendid. We could not have asked for better."

"There really is not much more to relate, sir."

Gladden-White turned his pale eyes full upon Christian, a strange fire kindled in them.

"The government as well as certain private sectors of our economy have great interests involved in the expansion of our flag and influence at the—well, the expense of certain others," he said. "This is why I am speaking to you now. As you doubtless are aware, our empire is developed in many ways, as the vitality and creativity of the nation and its agents make possible—in part by military means; at other times—by commercial or subtler means in many parts of the world."

"I grant what you say, sir, although I never glimpsed the overall view you present. I still do not quite see how this applies to me—to my predicament."

"Oh, forget your predicament, Christian. We are not speaking of that at all."

"Then what, sir?"

"If you possess eyes and wits, as I have reason to suppose you do, you know that Spanish America is in utter turmoil. England is watching like a goshawk, hoping to plunge in where, until now, it has not been feasible. The revolutionist, Francisco de Miranda, works for independence of the northern part of the continent, helped by an arrogant young whipjack named Bolivar. If the situation develops favorably, as we expect it will, we shall send—or permit to go—5,000 'volunteers' to aid the colonial cause, and incidentally further your own."

"You desire that I become one of them?"

"Heavens, no! That is not your field, the area or the people you know." He put his irritation aside. "In the southern reaches of the continent, the situation also develops. You may not have heard, but on May 25, the colonials, under someone named Manuel Belgrano, set up a form of self-government at Buenos Aires. So much for Napoleon's effort on the Peninsula and Whitelocke's blundering. We can most assuredly profit from this event.

Christian's interest quickened. "Can their independence be assured so easily?"

"I doubt it," Whitey replied tersely. "Spain remains a power still, and unquestionably much fighting remains before independence is secure on La Plata, to say nothing of Chile, Peru, and Upper Peru. Spain's armies in the hemisphere are intact and will naturally oppose the colonial bid for freedom, so they must fight it out. It could well be a long time and difficult struggle."

"I agree," reflected Christian.

"We would be unlikely to sanction any considerable number of 'volunteers' for the southern effort, but that doesn't mean we shan't attempt to influence the course of events for the common good and our advantage."

"Of course."

"Thank you for understanding," responded Whitey wryly. "No leader has yet emerged to whose standard we might rally with confidence, although we are searching for such a man. The colonials no doubt are also seeking a professional military man who might lead them to success. Is Belgrano such a one? I doubt it. He is not positive enough. We do have our eye upon a possibility for La Plata, another for Chile, in both cases men with some experience in England."

"And I?"

Gladden-White shifted position and stared directly into Christian's face.

"You have many qualities that fit you for this situation," he said. "You are young enough to be active, old enough for mature judgment. You are a man of proven courage on many battlefields, intelligent, not rash, able to assess situations and make sound judgments. You are habituated to the command. You are more familiar with the geography of southern South America than perhaps any man alive; and you have lived with a wide variety of its peoples, learned several of their languages, understand their diverse cultures. You are a man of discretion, and you are an Englishman. However—well—reprehensible some of your previous actions may have been, you have never betrayed your English tradition. Also, you are very lucky. What more than all this could be desire in an unofficial agent?"

"Agent?"

"Precisely. To serve with and support colonial forces in ways that you see fit and wherever possible to influence them to think not unkindly of Britain, so that when independence comes, as it surely must, our government will have at least an equal opportunity with all other nations to supply and invest in their future. That is all we ask. We do not fear competition for goods and services and financial advantage. All we ask is an equal go at it.

"Your conscience should be clear on all counts: you are furthering the cause of human freedom and justice, while seeking to better the lot of the natives and colonials by offering them our help and services."

Christian hesitated.

"You speak for His Majesty's government, sir?"

Whitey grinned.

"I do," he replied. "None more clearly. Do not ask me to specify my official position, but believe me, I speak for Whitehall."

"Would there be compensation for my services?" asked Christian, more to gain time to consider this astonishing offer than to bargain.

"No. Other than transportation down there and a letter or two. Of course you are at liberty to prosper as you may. I should think your opportunities might prove rather stupendous."

Christian leaned back. "Why would you trust me in an endeavor such as this, a man with my background and record?"

"We are building an empire. Sometimes we are forced to gamble. In your case, however, we entertain few reservations."

"I realize that my anonymity must be preserved in England, but would I be permitted to inform my mother, now on the Isle of Man, that I have gained a reprieve of sorts and would serve abroad? It would greatly ease her anguish, I am sure."

Whitey nodded. "If you are discreet."

Still Christian hesitated.

"Sir, considering that I am yet under a cloud, that execution would in all likelihood be my lot should I be tried, it seems inconceivable that His Majesty's government would assign me to extend the empire, even informally. What about English justice? What about the majesty of the law and all those things drilled into the marrow of every Englishman about the inevitability of punishment for wrongdoing?"

Gladden-White stared silently at Christian's earnest, troubled countenance. Gradually there spread across the older man's face the ghost of a grin, which broadened until it gave it an impish cast.

"Mr. Christian," he replied, slowly, arching a brow, "have you heard of Morgan?"

"Morgan, sir? You mean Henry Morgan? What has he to do with me?"

"Morgan, Mr. Christian, was one of the most conscienceless rascals in the history of the world. He was up to his neck in human destruction, and much of it was English. Yet when Britain cast about for a man to control piracy—most of it generated by Morgan himself—and to contain the Spaniards in the West Indies, Morgan was chosen for the job—he was the only man who could do it. Not only was he named lieutenant governor of Jamaica, but he was knighted in the bargain. So much for English justice and law when empire considerations are involved."

"Are you offering me a knighthood, sir?" asked Christian, slyly.

"Most certainly not!" he exploded. "I am offering you life and freedom—outside of England, of course—in exchange for your services. Naturally 'twould be unwise for you to return to this country."

"And if I reject your offer?"

Gladden-White touched his fingertips again, leaned back in his chair, and glanced through the window at the tangle of ship's masts and spars.

"There is ever the yardarm."

BOOK V

When my soul fainted within me I remembered the LORD: and my prayer came in unto thee, into thine holy temple.

JONAH 2:7

CHAPTER ONE

William Parish Robertson tilted the letter to the light, while the dark stranger who had brought it lounged against a counter, studying the stock of dried foods, *monturas*, bottled wines, *boleadoras* and other goods displayed by a Buenos Aires general merchant:

London, November 27, 1811

Dear Billy:

This letter will introduce a gentleman who is in our confidence. He will inform you of his name and enterprise. He is trustworthy, I believe, and will prove a loyal friend. Any assistance you may be willing and able to afford him upon his arrival or thereafter, so long as he requires it, will be appreciated by me personally and professionally. You may rely upon his courage, intelligence, discretion—and his good fortune. With kindest personal regards, I remain,

Y'r ob't s'v't, etc.,
Harry, C.B.E.

Robertson carried the letter to a charcoal brazier and laid it upon the coals, watching until it was wholly consumed. "Welcome to Buenos Aires, sir," he said then, with a trace of a smile. "I would be pleased to know your name?"

"Fletcher, Mr. Robertson, if that will do."

"Perfectly. I gather you have come to observe the independence movement and mayhap nudge it along a bit?"

"If I can. But I don't even know who the leaders are at this moment."

Robertson grimaced. "'Tis a bloody mess," he sighed. "Half a dozen misfits are vying for leadership here, the men who should have it fighting Spaniards on the frontier, and no one equal to the task of guiding and organizing anything. And if Napoleon is beaten, freeing Spain to move strongly again into Montevideo, we shall all hang."

"Who're the leaders, such as they are?"

"Buenos Aires is run by a triumvirate, like ancient Rome. Nobody ever heard of any of this trio before, nor will they be heard of again if a strong man appears to depose them. At any rate they are an improvement over the Junta, a body of Creoles, each wishing to run the country himself.

"Well, there must be someone capable of organizing an independence movement."

Billy Robertson smiled wryly. "There was Jacques Liniers, the Frenchman, for one. He and his colonials beat the British twice, I am embarrassed to say. He then became viceroy; and when he tried to force reason on the Junta, they executed him, an example of gratitude, that. Then there was Manuel Belgrano, a school teacher who had at least some control over his ambition and emotions—they call passions 'human fire' down here, where it substitutes for brains. The Junta sent him to Paraguay to try to inject some independence spirit into the Guarnís Indians, but they beat him twice instead. Of course he had only 700 men and needed 10 times that. Belgrano is the best now available, I would judge. I understand he's on the way to Upper Peru to try to find some Spaniards and whip them. They are not so easy to defeat, those Spaniards, as he will discover. The problem, you see, is to find a strongman."

Christian sympathetically shook his head. It was a problem.

He arranged to live with Robertson, assisting as he might in the Englishman's business enterprises, which included not only the Buenos Aires store but trading caravans reaching well into Paraguay and across the pampa to Córdoba. Although caustic and cynical, Robertson was a sharp observer, well informed, and rather honest. And so the months passed. The summers of 1811-1812 dwindled away, a hot season, the air humid and sticky. The people were happy to remain within the coolness of their thick adobe houses, barely existing, waiting for the blessed freshness of autumn, which seemed overlong in coming.

On March 9, Christian, seeking some relief from the oppressive air, strolled along the Alameda, as the bank of the La Plata was called. A carriage road followed the breakwater, which served as an all-season landing for freight arriving by sea. Scores of vessels were anchored seven to nine miles offshore, where the Plata ran deep enough for ocean-going bottoms. From the anchorage, goods and passengers were transported by shallow draft luggers against the current and breezes to within 80 yards of shore. Here they were transshipped to high-wheeled carts, drawn by mules wading to knee-depth to meet the boats.

So on this afternoon Christian stood observing the unloading of the *George Channing,* fifty days out of London. Several passengers were aboard a cart, splashing through the river toward the landing, one of them at least a head taller than his companions. He was dressed in an odd combination of uniform and civilian clothing, the soldierly elements indistinguishable by rank or nation, the whole revealing a disregard for any ostentation of dress. But his garb was unimportant in any event, once the face with its dark eyes—black pools of fathomless magnetism—had captured one.

The cart bounced ashore, the mules straining under the whip of the *arriero*. A few paces beyond, an effusive companion of the tall man was hailed with obvious delight by a local dandy, who opened wide his arms: "Carlos!" he cried, they joining in the *embrazo* of the race, hugging each other with every manifestation of joy, both talking at once and understanding one another by sheer osmosis. Swiftly Carlos María de Alvear introduced his companions, including the dominating figure proclaimed as José de San Martín who, Carlos proclaimed proudly, was a "veteran of the Peninsula wars who had outfought the finest Napoleon could hurl at him!" His voice reflected the awe that San Martín frequently generated in those about him.

Christian later made a point of questioning Robertson about the mysterious stranger. "San Martín?" Robertson asked distractedly as he attempted to complete a page of his ledger, scratching the crown of his shaggy head with the tip of his quill. "There was one of that name at Yapeyú, in Misiones, many years ago, a soldier from León. The reason I recall his name is that he married his wife by proxy, being called to the frontier before the ceremony could be performed. This San Martín could be their son. 'Tis an uncommon name, prosaic as it sounds."

The *Gaceta Ministerial*, official publication of the government, announced the arrivals, asserting they had come to offer their swords to the cause of freedom. Alvear, a native of Buenos Aires, had friends everywhere, but San Martín, after twenty years of loyal service to the king of Spain might have come under suspicion had not his imposing and his distinguished courtliness disarmed the most critical detractors. He quietly laid before the triumvirate a plan for a unit of the Mounted Grenadiers. He personally would raise, train, and command them, he said, they to be employed for "the defense of this noble city"—which appealed to the trio mightily—and wherever else they might prove useful. Impressed beyond measure, the triumvirate promptly commissioned San Martín a lieutenant colonel "in view of his merits, services, and military knowledge," the last being the most necessary quality since no one else possessed much of it.

Initially the triumvirate authorized a mounted force of 300 men. San Martín personally chose from the better families of Buenos Aires the blades who would be cadets for his officer corps. On the other hand, he selected his soldier material from the illiterate, bearded, ugly gauchos who flocked into the encampment. San Martín selected his gauchos as one would choose prize bulls or dogs, by conformation rather than anything else, picking the tallest among them so that when garbed in their striking uniforms they would be as imposing as possible. The Mounted Grenadiers were to be his instrument, the core of the independence movement;

and he fashioned it with precision and the utmost care. San Martín's objective was to build pride with loyalty—pride in country, pride in regiment, pride in self.

Carefully Christian read the regulations posted publicly by San Martín. Christian had come to headquarters to offer his talents to the colonial army, convinced that even if San Martín should prove not to be the man to free southern America, the true leader must surface through the vehicle the officer would forge. Christian was ushered in and stood at attention until San Martín deigned to notice him.

"*Sí, señor?*" He turned his black eyes upon the visitor, surveying him with a glance, unsmilingly courteous yet conceding nothing. It was his army, his country; and he was in command.

"Sir, my name is Fletcher," said Christian. "I have had some military training, as well as naval experience in various parts of the world. I believe in the freedom of Spanish America. I've come to offer my services for any use you may care to make of them."

An indefinable warmth, perhaps appreciation, passed briefly across San Martín's face. Then he shook his head.

"I appreciate the offer of your person for our sacred cause, but I regret that I cannot accept it. My regiment is being formed of my countrymen only, for if they are to deserve freedom, they must win it themselves, without assistance, however well intentioned. Your offer, however, is much valued as an endorsement of our dream, which is honorable and just and which will be realized!"

Christian shifted his weight from one foot to the other. San Martín still had said nothing to indicate he should be at ease.

"Sir," he argued, stubbornly, "it has been my experience, as it no doubt is that of other soldiers, that war is as indifferent to race as to motives; that a bullet has no conscience and will destroy the just as quickly as the scoundrel; that battles are won by force and tactics, rather than by principles; and that power, assembled from any source, may win out over the rightness of one's cause. In spite of all this, it is for the triumph of freedom that I made my offer."

"You speak as one of us," he conceded, smiling. "It is a pity we cannot accept your sword—now. Later, perhaps. We are in process of creating the genesis of our movement, and it must be drafted of men who think alike because they were born and bred and matured alike. They will form a cord no blade on earth can sever! With them I will organize and develop an army that can fight and win battles. However, the day may come when you may indeed have a role suited to your talents and experience, if you wish."

"The answer is, not now, sir?"

"Not now!"

CHAPTER TWO

In a gleaming carriage Billy Robertson led his caravan of carts northward, carrying his trading goods and wines. It would have been cheaper to send the merchandise by boat, but the Spaniards controlled the river wherever their gunboats could float. Fortunately Robertson had company, for Christian had accepted his invitation to come along in order to sound the sentiment of the upcountry people toward the political freedom movement.

Three weeks after leaving Buenos Aires, they had traveled only 200 miles to Rosario, where the garrison was commanded by Major Celedonio Escalada. For some months Robertson had been a primary supplier for the Mounted Grenadiers, endeavoring always to be meticulously honest with them; and thus, he had formed a working friendship with the new commander. He well knew that come independence or tyranny, law or outlawry, order or chaos; people must eat, clothe themselves, and have wine to drink. A merchant could prosper, if he were not slain nor his goods confiscated as had sometimes been the case under Spanish rule. As they continued northward, Robertson raised his eyes to Heaven, "May that evil day never return!"

Seated beside him, Christian squinted through the January mirage. "There appears to be a tower alongside the river."

Robertson flicked his long buggy whip across the team to stir them up.

"That must be the chapel at the Franciscan monastery. We can camp in the orchard and perhaps a breeze will blow in from the river. The bank is high enough."

From the lip of the bluffs, a panorama of river and lowland unfolded, a symphony of wilderness. Here bronzed, quiet-flowing, less wind-tossed than the Plata into which it flowed, the river fashioned an immense arc bending westward to carve these bluffs and enfolded an endless thicket of swamps and forests to the east. In midstream lay the long, scrubby island of San Lorenzo.

Padre Flores greeted them at the monastery that evening, delighted to have visitors. During the evening meal, he proved to be a wealth of information as he meandered through rumors, truths, myths, and reports of Spanish activity along the Paraná.

"Last October the monasteries of San Nicolas and San Pedro were cannonaded and sacked," he confided. "Ruiz, a smuggler and a very bad man (God forbid that I should condemn him so, but it is the truth) commanded the flotilla, about eleven vessels in all. Another flotilla operating in this direction has some hundreds of infantry aboard, so I have been informed. Zabala commands. I hear of all things along the Paraná, in time."

"Do the Spanish have control of the river?" asked Christian.

"Who is to prevent it?" exclaimed Padre Flores indignantly. "I am informed that Colonel San Martín has been ordered to Santa Fe with two squadrons of his Grenadiers, but he has not yet passed this way as yet. Now I understand that Zabala's flotilla with the infantry is working its way upstream. They were delayed by a north wind which was God-sent obviously. No man can predict what the Spaniards will do when they run ashore at a place like this, especially if they suspect gold or silver is stored here. We have little of that, I assure you; but it is useless to attempt to persuade a Spaniard that there is no gold when he smells gold, or thinks he does."

"Does the north wind still hold?"

"I think not. Probably the Spanish even now are ascending the river. I wouldn't wonder but San Martín is keeping pace with the fleet along the shore, watching their movements. That is what I should do if I were a soldier."

Bivouac was made near the monastery whose evening bells tolled their message of faith eternal or, as Christian mused, myth eternal, matching their tones to the copper gleam of the dying sun. At that thought, he felt the attention of the quiet Listener deep in the depths of himself, but he shrugged the feeling off. He would not back down before mere feeling. Robertson had a pipe; and he and Christian retired shortly; three o'clock would come all too soon.

It was near midnight, judging from the stars, when the muffled figure of Padre Flores announced the news that the Spanish fleet had arrived, dropping anchor in the lee of San Lorenzo. There were many craft, surely the entire royalist flotilla. Something must be done, but what? Padre Flores would help, but what could he do? A poor Franciscan, and an aging one, at that. One thing he would never do was submit to the Spanish. Never! He was *criollo*, as well as a Franciscan.

"Perhaps they will not land," suggested Christian. "There is little here for them, I should think."

Padre Flores wagged his massive head. "They are Spaniards. They see that this is a chapel, a church; and they smell gold here, so they will land. We have no gold, but they will seize our chickens and demolish much in their search."

Robertson yawned. After a moment he spoke quietly, sensibly, as an Englishman should.

"Fletcher, you've been something of a gaucho. Take one of the carriage mules and ride south toward Rosario. Urge Escalada to come here with what men he can muster. He might be able to discourage any Spanish foraging parties if they are not too large. Padre, have some of your *mozos* drive your cattle westward a few miles and hold them until Zabala leaves. We will take our carts with the cattle beyond the road. Zabala will seize any stock he finds; but being sailors they won't forage the interior, I shouldn't think."

Major Escalada swept into instant action, mounting thirty horses, rousing twenty-two musketeers, and ordering ox teams to bring along the gun and ammunition. The cannon's effectiveness was minimal, but it was a symbol of pride for Escalada. At Christian's suggestion Escalada sent a dragoon to accompany him southward in search of San Martín to urge him along with his squadrons.

By the following morning with his tiny force no more than a company in size, Escalada hastened up the post road toward the white steeple of the monastery, its red tiles reflecting the morning sunlight. Towering dust accompanied their movement, which would surely warn any Spanish foragers, but this could not be helped. At the monastery a hundred of the enemy's soldiers had labored up the bluffs and were rummaging the grounds, chasing squawking fowl, scouring the premises for anything of value, while the junior officer endured the frantic expostulation of Father Flores. One of the faithful himself, he dared not run the priest through as he might some lesser mortal; but he didn't want to listen to him, either. The sub-lieutenant leaped to his feet and scanned the haze of dust growing larger to the south. Now he could make out dark figures of a formation of mounted men. No estimate of their numbers, but it was time to leave. Quickly he summoned his drummers.

Escalada's approaching force scattered to the edge of the bluffs and fired at the withdrawing Spanish, who got away to their boats so swiftly there was no time for even a token cannon blast. His men lit cooking fires close enough to the rim of the bluff, so the smoke would warn the enemy that the region was held. The fires also served as a beacon that night for a Guaraní taken prisoner by the Spaniards to serve as a guide. He escaped, floated ashore on a bundle of faggots, and crept into Escalada's camp, seeking sanctuary. He brought information that the enemy had about 350 foot soldiers and were readying two guns. They were planning to land with the dawn, sack the monastery, which they still believed must have riches buried somewhere; then, they would proceed upriver, hoping to cut the route to Paraguay.

However, Zabala had not counted upon Padre Flores.

Flores knelt before the altar in the silence of the sanctuary. He prayed, volubly of course, for that was his way, but nonetheless clearly, pleading with God to save this lonely church from destruction. Perhaps God humored this earnest, if garrulous priest. Who knows? It can only be affirmed that as his prayer finished, a soft breeze arose from the north and blew more strongly, becoming a gale with a force that the Spanish ships could not withstand, not even when they were anchored in the lee of the low island. The violent wind tore and whipped through the stubby trees and undergrowth and heaved the vessels, straining them against their groaning moorings. Lines were cast off, and the vessels ran for it, under bare sticks mostly and the push of the current. They were swept south for many miles until a curve of the river with its high steep banks afforded shelter. Not for two or three days would they be able to beat up the Paraná again to San Carlos, though they would do so. Zabala still smelled treasure there.

During these events, Christian and his gaucho companion came upon the tents of San Martín just two days hard ride south of the monastery. A rigid, correct sentry, helmeted and sabered, escorted them to the colonel's tent. San Martín, poring over his maps of the river between sips of deep red wine looked with irritation at the intrusion.

"Yes?" he questioned. "Yes, what is it?"

"Sir," explained the grenadier at stiff salute, "these men say they are from San Carlos, near San Lorenzo. They say the Spanish fleet is there, that an attack is expected. They have come to seek your assistance."

San Martín inspected the visitors, lingering upon Christian.

"Have I not seen you before? Oh, indeed. You are the foreigner who desired to serve with us! What brings you to this frontier, Englishman?"

Christian unaccountably found himself standing at attention before the patriot officer. "I am merely accompanying a merchant, William Robertson, with his goods toward Paraguay, sir. We reached the chapel at San Carlos the evening the Spanish fleet came up the river. There were eleven in the convoy, from brigs to luggers, escorted by three small warships, lightly gunned. The cliffs there are 100 feet in height. The place need fear nothing from the Spanish vessels, but if they can land infantry, they could cause damage."

"Will you guide us to San Lorenzo?"

"Willingly, sir."

Moving swiftly northward, San Martín's force of 120 grenadiers flowed almost silently, smoothly, its discipline never faltering. It was for this purpose these chosen men had been enlisted and trained. Onward to battle! If they could catch the Spaniards ashore, there would be combat; but San Martín was too much the fox to challenge the vessels. The Spanish must come ashore, or there would be no contest.

The command approached San Carlos in deep darkness, fanning out to see whether any enemy had yet landed. The patriots filtered into the compound at the monastery, dismounting to hold their horses close up during the predawn hours. San Martín climbed to the belfry where even in the darkness he could inspect the dim outlines of the enemy flotilla—now returned upstream to anchor north of the island. Even as he watched they commenced to disgorge cargoes of men and munitions, flags, drums, and fifes, and four small cannon, four-pounders perhaps. Christian was silent as was his custom, yet there, for any directive.

"The enemy has double our number, true enough," the colonel muttered. "But I doubt he gets the better of us this day!"

He led down the spiral stairs and called his second in command, Captain José Bermudez, directing him to ready the second squadron, reserving command of the first for himself. He warned Christian to remain out of the way. "This is not your duty, sir," he told him, courteously. "We are trained for this. I will give you a fresh horse. If the Spaniards get the better of us, ride for the interior. Being boatmen, they will not follow."

Christian stubbornly shook his head.

"I will not fight if you order me not to do so," he replied, "unless it is necessary, sir. But I will not run. If you fall, I fall. However, I am sure I will celebrate your undoubted victory!"

San Martín appeared taken aback by this unaccustomed defiance from a stranger. Then he turned away. "As you will." He had given no further order to remain aloof, Christian noted.

A level prairie, a mile wide, extended to the edge of the cliff, providing room for cavalry to maneuver and fight; it was like an immense sporting field. Two paths, only one suitable for infantry in formation, were the most prominent routes up from the river bottom. San Martín separated the squadrons now, ordered girths tightened and grenadiers to stand to horse on both sides of the monastery. Major Escalada and his fifty men were ordered within, as a reserve. Daylight swept in with full strength, and the colonel made a final hurried ascent of the tower. Boats laden with armed men were already approaching the shore, soon disappearing from sight beneath the bluff overlooking the beach. At half-past five o'clock, two small columns of infantry appeared above the edge of the plains. In the early heat they were already sweating, drops glistening at their temples, running down stubbly cheeks.

Running past Christian at the foot of the stairs, San Martín mumbled, "Two minutes more and we shall be upon them, splitting their heads!" He vaulted into the saddle of the bay held by his orderly and spurred to the forefront of his command. Drawing his Moorish sword, its jet-black hilt gleaming with gold lacery, he cut the air above his head with great sweeps:

"Grenadiers!" he shouted. "We have come to battle! Fight bravely! Use lances and sabers, no pistols, no muskets! No retreat!"

He ordered Bermudez to swing wide and come in behind to cut off the enemy's retreat. He led the charge of his squadron full into the Spaniards' formation, moving in parallel columns of half-companies, with two four-pounders between each set of files. The grenadiers, settled firmly in the saddle, their horses chafing, heard the trumpet blasts calling and swept to the attack, San Martín on the left, Bermudez on the right. The colonel struck the center of the Spanish advance, finding as his immediate opponent the red-haired Zabala himself. They drove the royalists back initially in the confusion. But now the enemy cannon, roaring twice, caused disorder in some of the patriot ranks. Spanish musketry poured a rattling volley into the grenadiers, suddenly slaying San Martín's horse. It crashed heavily on its left side, pinning the colonel's leg under its body, holding the officer helpless. His glittering sword became useless in his hand. The battle raged about the fallen commander amid clouds of dust, milling hoofs, trampling feet, pungent fogs of gunpowder, the clashing of blade on metal and bone, screams of the wounded and of hysterical combatants, the mad whirling maelstrom of hand-to-hand combat. The weight of the greater Spanish numbers at last threatened to swing the tide.

Christian, his hands crossed before him on the saddle, observed the strife while remaining aloof in accordance with San Martín's wish. Seeing the colonel fall, he came to a quick decision. He loosened his bolas, swinging one of the stone balls in murderous crescendo about his head. He spurred his horse into the midst of the battle, reaching San Martín's helpless form precisely as a royalist infantryman, musket raised, prepared to drive his bayonet through the heart of the fallen commander. With a brutal force, Christian crushed the Spaniard's head like a melon. He then leaped to the ground and clutched the short tail of the dead horse, heaving it sufficiently for San Martín to pull out his trapped leg.

"Is it broken, sir?" the Englishman shouted.

San Martín, his face streaming crimson from a saber cut, rubbed life back into the stiffened limb and shook his head.

"I think not. But I need your horse!"

Mounted once again, San Martín rallied his cheering men. Christian now armed with sword and musket from the fallen enemy, helped the grenadiers drive the Spaniards back toward the bluff. Bermudez, desperately engaged on the other side, renewed the efforts of his men; and they, too, began to press more heavily upon the enemy. At the edge of the cliff, the Spaniards attempted frantically to form a defense square under cover of guns from their fleet. Bermudez, leading a second charge upon them, fell dead. Lieutenant Velez misgauged the terrain. With his horse he rocketed over the edge of the precipice. He had already received twin bayonet wounds in his chest and a ball in the forehead and was dead before his body crashed onto the beach below. The Spaniards turned and fled down the paths, leaving behind forty dead, fourteen prisoners, their flag, their guns, and fifty muskets. However, they managed to take with them most of their wounded, including the savagely cut Zabala, who would not fight again for many a long and painful day.

"We have fifteen killed, sir, and twenty-seven wounded," an orderly reported. San Martín nodded as he surveyed the tormented field. The blood on his face had dried to form black ribbons bordered by rivulets of sweat. He rode slowly over to where Christian stood alone. Neither spoke for a long moment. The sun scorched the prairie, tingeing the clouds of dust with gold. Flies buzzed hungrily over the dead while Padres Flores labored with oil and busy fingers, giving the rites of extreme unction.

"Now, sir?" asked Christian.

San Martín smiled ever so slightly. Gently he shook his head.

"Mr. Fletcher, you are a brave man, a gaucho, a warrior. You do not run. But I am a man of my word. My Grenadiers are the fledglings of an empire. I cannot give command to one not of us by blood. You, sir, because of foreign birth, and only because of that sad fact, cannot be a part of it, although you deserve it fully."

Christian's gaze dropped to the torn ground before him. He turned dejectedly toward the chapel, where Robertson and the other civilians waited.

San Martín called him back. "I cannot commission you in my Grenadiers, Mr. Fletcher," the officer repeated gravely. "But neither can I ignore your bravery, your talents, your eagerness to serve our cause—nor my debt to you. Therefore I name you my aide, without commission but with all privileges due the rank immediately beneath my own—if that meets with your approval."

CHAPTER THREE

Christian stirred from the stupor induced by the blazing endless heat and glanced back at the way they had come. The road, as well defined as the hoofs of thousands of mules could etch it, had been the principal artery between La Plata and Peru for centuries. Today it appeared void of all life save for the military expedition of which he was a part. The Englishman spurred his horse up once more to his proper position behind the carriage of the commander.

He and San Martín had become old friends in the months since San Lorenzo. San Martín found himself able to confide in Christian more easily than in his countrymen for several reasons. San Martín had become convinced of Christian's sympathy for and support of the independence movement. Professionally he appreciated Christian's martial qualities, soldierly skills, and courage as he had demonstrated in that skirmish along the Paraná. He also was aware that Christian, an Englishman, a foreigner, was wholly uninvolved in the many plots and intrigues squirming below the surface in the colonies. A leader must confide in someone. Thus, the supreme commander and his aide had established a bond more durable than that made possible by military structure alone.

Once more Christian peered back down the long trail winding between the foothill range to the east and the massive Andes cordillera to the west. They had followed the Rio Sali for a long time. A sergeant muttered that before them lay the village of Yatasto, where they were to find General Manuel Belgrano and perhaps the mysterious Martín Guemes too. There must be a meeting of minds to decide what must be done next. The carriage lurched, then righted itself. They had come 100 miles above Tucumán now and were only 60 miles from Salta, key to all this region and currently held by the Spaniards.

Topping a ridge, the column came in view of an encampment of three large white tents housing the general and his staff and an irregular scattering of the more humble abodes of his soldiers. A broad white canvas sunshade marked the hospital, such as it was. Well upstream and more scattered in the near distance was another grouping of rude shelters of heaped brush. These no doubt sheltered Guemes' gauchos, a particularly independent lot. Little held them together but their deep, unshakeable loyalty to Guemes himself. No man on the frontier was capable of such deviltry, no man could so harass the Spaniards. None other proved so agile in striking, vanishing, and reappearing to attack again. Guemes! Uncontrollable, yet indispensable.

San Martín's escort led the way down the road toward the tents of Yatasto, followed by the jouncing carriage and green-uniformed guards and finally the squadron of scarlet and blue uniformed Grenadiers. Long before the company reached the tents, a trumpet flared; and a contingent of battle-scarred and ragged soldiers lined up in an uneven presentation of arms. The formation opened toward the center to frame the thin, nervous general and members of his staff. With respectful salutes the visitors drew up, and San Martín descended stiffly from his carriage and stepped forward to embrace Belgrano.

"I have come to place myself and my command at your service, sir," announced San Martín earnestly. Belgrano shook the suggestion off. "Ah, no, indeed!" he exclaimed. "You cannot know how I have longed for this day." His voice mirrored his physique, reedy, high pitched as the restless dry wind in these elevated deserts. He sounded like the onetime schoolmaster he was, yet he was the foremost patriot officer because of his devotion, his intelligence, his eagerness to learn the trade of a soldier and his astounding good fortune, which made up for any lack of professional training in the art of war. "Because God so willed, I am a general, though without knowledge of what I am about. This is not my career. I must study constantly to avoid being overrun, to learn what must be done next. I've made war like an explorer, ever plunging into what I do not know. I am glad you are here, sir. You are to be not only my friend but my teacher and my chief, if you wish. I plead with you to accept that charge!"

San Martín's face flushed in momentary embarrassment. He peered intently into Belgrano's face as though to read what lay behind the words. Reassured, he nodded once, as though the issue was resolved; he might move ahead.

"We shall see, sir," he replied. "May I inspect your camp, hear your view of the situation?"

It was indeed a dismal encampment, the men dispirited, unpaid, mired in despondency, a ragtag collection of rabble. Could these "sad fragments of a beaten army," as Belgrano frankly called them, whip the fierce disciplined armies of Burgos and Castile? It seemed incredible, unbelievable. Only the genius of San Martín could see in them the elements, the nucleus of conquerors.

"Would you review for me the events since you took command, sir?" the colonel asked of Belgrano in his clipped, businesslike tones. They were seated in the shade of a tattered tent, its sides rolled up to admit the slightest stir of air. "I have heard of your marvelous successes—"

"And doleful defeats," muttered Belgrano.

"Principally your triumphs, General. But I know few details, nor do I have any clear understanding of the situation on this frontier."

Manuel Belgrano arranged his facts in the precise fashion befitting a schoolmaster preparing a lecture. His mind was attuned to the classroom rather than rugged field duty, yet paradoxically he was one capable of extreme daring when high risks were called for and even of impulse on occasion.

"I was directed after independence seemed assured in 1810 to occupy Upper Peru, if we could take it with what force we could collect," he commenced, slowly. "Initially we saw little action. We drilled our men and learned what we could of the military profession.

"Meanwhile the royalists were advancing south through Upper Peru past Salta and toward Córdoba. Our mission was to destroy them; but they reached and occupied Tucumán, pushing us before them, although contact was slight. We had never yet fought a battle in this theatre, but the royalists, acclimated to the 15,000-foot plateaus of Upper Peru, came down into our lowlands to which they were unaccustomed. Sickness and weakness and a consequent enervation of spirit began to afflict them.

"I received positive orders from Buenos Aires to fall back on Córdoba rather than risk untrained men against skilled professionals. But," he permitted himself a wisp of a smile, "an opportunity afforded itself, and we attacked near Tucumán. Fortune attended our endeavors, and we won."

"I received word of that," approved San Martín, warmly. "You attacked the Spaniards with half their strength, routed them, captured flags and cannon, and saved the revolution. A feat indeed for a 'nonprofessional,' as you put it. No wonder the twenty-fourth of September is honored everywhere in La Plata! Do go on."

A trace of color appeared in Belgrano's cheeks, then ebbed. "We had no choice but to follow the Spanish in their retreat to Salta," he said. "Once again we were gifted with fortune, and they were driven out."

"I've heard that at Salta the Spaniards were entrenched. Despite that you beat them badly," murmured San Martín, with appreciation. Belgrano once more hesitated, then continued:

"They withdrew rather hastily; and we pursued as best we could, although not very effectively, I fear. At any rate, they turned upon us, caught us unawares, defeated us badly at Vilcapugio on October 1, and almost destroyed us at Ayohuma on November 14. We were lucky to escape, those who did, and all we brought back was 36,000 dollars from the treasury at Potosí. Vilcapugio is seventeen miles southeast from Challapata, east of Lake Poopó; and Ayohama is west of Sucre. Neither is important, save that we were shipped there.

"Joaquín de la Pezuela pursued us as far as Salta. I think his energy was fueled as much by desire for the loot we had seized as anything. Now he is entrenched about Salta once more with his 5,000. This time he will not be surprised, nor will his defenses be turned. At least not by me."

Reflecting upon what Belgrano had told him, San Martín opened his map case, never far from him, and drew out a folded chart. Silently he traced names and places, his lips pursed, his brow furrowed.

"I thank you for what you have told me, General," he said at last. "As can be plainly seen, the task before us is stupendous, but it can be accomplished with your army, plus my command, and with the others we shall attract and forge into the tempered steel of liberty." He turned back to the map. "As we know, the Spaniards hold Montevideo and their ships control La Plata estuary and its rivers, save where they have been—well, discouraged."

"As at San Lorenzo?"

"A skirmish. Little more. But it gave them a clue to our determination. Our siege at Montevideo goes on with no decision, though the final outcome cannot be in doubt. Paraguay is independent now but of little consequence because of its remoteness from everything. Spain has crushed the revolt beyond the Andes, and Chile once again is firmly under their control. Peru! Ah, that is indeed the stronghold, the bastion, of royalist strength in America. That is the heart of it. Until Peru falls and becomes liberated, there will be no freedom anywhere else that can be considered secure. There in Peru, before the throne of the Incas, must freedom be won."

"What about Upper Peru?" Belgrano was earnest in his questioning. San Martín shrugged.

"Your noble effort there demonstrates the futility of seeking a decision in Upper Peru, which some call Bolivia," he said, stabbing at the map with his finger. "That province may be an avenue for the Spaniards, but it is a bottomless morass for the patriots. It is an elevated wasteland, a lure, a trap, sucking up armies from the south, wearing them out with impossible geography, beating them more by distances and unlimited space than by military prowess. And even if it could be seized and made secure? Is it possible to use Upper Peru as a base from which to conquer Lima? Ridiculous! From Upper Peru, one is as distant from Lima as at Tucumán from Upper Peru."

"Then what, sir?"

San Martín gave his curious nod again, as though the decision were reached. "If Lima cannot be seized from the land side—and it cannot, I think—then it must be taken from the sea. The patriots must gain access to the sea. How?" He traced the long western coastline. "Chile! We must capture Chile and make it our base. *Then* we can work northward to Lima."

"You are no doubt correct," Belgrano murmured. "But I see problems, many problems."

San Martín's eyes fired, but the flares quickly subsided. He glanced at the map, then at Belgrano, his expression fathomless, his eyes those of a visionary, almost a madman. "Yes, yes. There are problems. Also there are solutions."

"Sir, I know neither tactics nor strategy," said Belgrano, "but would it not be dangerous to concentrate upon Chile while the Spaniards are free to drive a sword through our armies at any time from Upper Peru? We have limited men and supplies. How can we contain them to the north and simultaneously beat them to the west?"

San Martín laughed.

"And you say you are no soldier! That is the point only an astute commander would note. It is well taken—one of the problems. I think that here we shall have a gaucho war, with mounted guerillas harassing and keeping the Spaniards occupied while we busy ourselves elsewhere. By driving down here with 5,000 men, the enemy was not perceptive. He has fallen into our trap, rather than we into his. We shall keep him engaged—eternally! What is this fellow's name? Guemes? The gaucho from Salta? He must carry the battle for us, if he will. If he will."

CHAPTER FOUR

On the bony black horse, General Belgrano led the way as San Martín, Christian, and an aide rode up the stony valley toward the gaucho camp. Guemes would not be surprised. Shortly the party was stopped by a lean horseman whose dark face and lank hair gave evidence of his Indian blood. He wore a tattered poncho, once red, great *nazarenas* on his heels, and athwart his forearms bore an iron-tipped lance decorated with a scarlet rag, a war banner. His only other weapon was a *boleadora*. Now he raised the lance and sat silently, his glittering eyes inspecting them, until their horses almost touched.

"Eh?" he said, warily. He had seen much, much killing. Those not gaucho did not impress him.

"We wish to see Major Guemes," said Belgrano, shortly. "Take us to him."

The gaucho scanned the general from plumed helmet to booted foot.

"Guemes is busy," he said. "He sees no one when he is busy."

"You do not understand, gaucho!" protested Belgrano, his reedy voice rising. "We have matters of importance to discuss with him. This is Colonel San Martín. I am General Belgrano. We must have audience with Guemes."

The outpost spit carefully to one side, his eyes never losing their hostility nor leaving the face of Belgrano.

"Maybe that's why he is busy," he retorted. "Guemes said no one was to interrupt him today. No man will."

Belgrano flushed. San Martín took the impasse more casually. "If you won't take us to Guemes," he said, curtly, "bring Guemes to us."

The rider shook his head.

"Then take a message to him."

Once more the rider shrugged the suggestion aside.

"Guemes isn't partial to pretty officers," he growled. "He fights—they talk and pose. He doesn't like that. He would kill me if I interrupted him on your behalf. He gave me orders. Come back another time."

Two or three mounted gauchos had appeared upon the knolls to the rear of the outpost. They were armed; it would be futile to attempt to override them. The party sat in helpless anger before the statuelike horseman. Christian concealed his momentary amusement, then broke in: "Would the colonel permit me to talk with this man?" he asked courteously. "He is a gaucho. I have been a gaucho. Perhaps we speak the same tongue."

"Do what you can, Mr. Fletcher," snapped San Martín, his irritation rising.

Christian coolly addressed the outpost. "You fight Spaniards. We fight Spaniards," he said. "We can cut more Spanish throats together than alone. But if we fight each other, the Spaniard says of us, 'The gaucho kills five patriots. The patriots kill five gauchos. That's ten dead for us.' To squabble among ourselves is to be as stupid as the *viscacha*. Guemes knows that. So do you."

The gaucho rubbed his tousled head. He was interested. "You talk like a gaucho," he admitted, "but you dress like a *pueblero*."

"I am gaucho."

The outpost shrugged slightly and nodded toward the hill behind him.

"You want to see Guemes?" he demanded. "If he finds you are not a gaucho, he will kill you, maybe me too. But you sound gaucho. Go ahead, if you want, but the others stay here. All I know is they don't pass unless Guemes says they pass."

Christian glanced questioningly at San Martín, who gave a single nod, more impatiently than ever. "We shall wait here," he announced crisply. "Do what is possible."

The Englishman guided his horse up the rubbled path, under close scrutiny from hilltop sentries. He reached a second outpost, three riders manning it, peering suspiciously at him. They said nothing. He guided his horse atop the ridge and across a barren flat to a makeshift shelter where a cluster of men watched a game of *treinta y uno*. Christian sat quietly scanning the crowd, unwilling to disturb them until he could identify the leader. The head man appeared to be the bearded fellow winning at cards. He slapped down the cards at last and stared directly at Christian, his gaze piercing as an eagle's, cold as a wolf's. "You interrupt?" The question was flat as the mesa. Christian lifted his shoulders.

"A cactus pricks because it has thorns," he said. "Ants never visit an empty skull. I would have words with Guemes. Therefore I go where Guemes is. You are he?"

The leader turned away for an instant, presenting his profile, his drooping nose giving the impression of a hawk's beak, to match the fierceness of his eyes. There was calculation in them when they returned to Christian.

"An eagle does not write his name in the sky for his prey to read," he growled. "His name is known from the savagery of assault, the swiftness and sureness of his kill. You talk gaucho. What are you?"

Christian returned the stare. "Test me!" he invited.

Guemes gained his feet from his cross-legged position, rising smoothly, flowing upward. He borrowed a *facon* and tossed it to Christian, who slowly dismounted, untying his poncho, carefully draping its folds over his left arm, neither dreading nor welcoming what was coming. This was a gaucho test. It must be met. Christian stepped into the clearing, waiting. Guemes had made no move to draw his own knife; it would be beneath him to fight a stranger, a mounted wanderer. He called to someone behind Christian, motioning him forward to test the visitor, blade for blade. Christian crouched, shook the folds out from his poncho, his knife held low, forward, in dueling position, whirled, and faced—Justo!

"*Madre de dios!*" cried the gaucho, "*Madre de dios! El cristiano!*" His long knife dropped. He plunged it into the earth and spread his arms. They embraced in the manner of all gauchos, danced about one another, grinning, slapping backs, both talking at once.

"*Ai*, Guemes!" shouted Justo in boyish glee. "Look! This is my friend! With him I escaped from *los indios* the last time, and from the police several times, and from the army! He helps me escape from everybody!" He thumped Christian again between the shoulders.

The men who had gathered swiftly to see a fight were transformed from enemies to brothers. Christian was wholly accepted, as gauchos always take in one of their kind, for it is ever the gaucho against a hostile world.

So it was that for a second time Christian approached Guemes, who was sitting cross-legged, sipping maté through a silver *bombilla*.

"A fox does not announce himself," Christian said quietly, "but he comes for a purpose."

"*Ai*," responded Guemes soberly, "to devour the mouse. But I am not a mouse. I, too, am a fox—ask the Spaniard!"

Christian grinned.

"That is well known from Montevideo to the Andes, from Potosí to Tucumán," he agreed. "But while one fox may nip the enemy's heel, it will take many to eat him up—foxes of all sorts—for the enemy is numerous and he multiplies like mice. So long as such enemies exist, no one fox, however brave, is safe."

"*Ai*," assented the other glumly. "You speak the wisdom of the pampa, if with a barbarous accent."

Christian accepted a gourd, sucked the tea, and peered earnestly into the face of the chieftain.

"I come not on my own behalf, Guemes, but on that of men greater than I, General Belgrano and Colonel San Martín, commanders of the force below. They would speak with you."

"They are not gauchos."

Christian smiled slyly.

"What is a gaucho? I have heard that Guemes was born under a roof, upon a proper bed, in Salta—not to a lass beneath the open sky upon the endless pampa. Does that make him less a gaucho?"

"The difference between a townsman and a gaucho is his inclination, not his restlessness nor lack of shelter. So long as he shares the skills and character of gaucho, he is gaucho."

"Exactly. A fox is told not by his coat but by his spirit, the sharpness of his teeth, his tenacity of life, how hard he is to kill."

"These foxes of yours, they are hard to kill? They fight like gauchos and do not run? That is hard for me to believe."

"I have seen San Martín in battle," said Christian. "In a sharp action against the Spaniards, his horse fell upon him—"

"No gaucho would be trapped so."

"There were circumstances . . . his horse died upon his leg, only one hand free against a powerful assault. Many men would have been finished there, would have surrendered. But San Martín had not yet begun his fight. He never gives up. He never runs. He stands and fights."

"And the other?"

"Belgrano. Surely you know of him? He was beaten in Upper Peru, but he brought his men back—what was left of them—despite the best the Spaniards could do. Belgrano never surrenders, either."

Guemes considered Christian's arguments long and carefully. Then he balanced his gourd in the vacant eye-socket of a sun-bleached cow's skull. He rose fluidly to his feet.

"I will go with you, gaucho," he announced.

Justo and two others followed them down the twisting trail, more from curiosity than as escort. Christian introduced the bearded Guemes to the senior officers. The preliminary courtesies were minimal; these were soldiers, men of action, not of words.

"We would compliment you upon your many victories over the Spaniards, Guemes," said Belgrano, with a thin-lipped smile. The gaucho nodded. "We control the countryside where we rove," he agreed.

"But it is far from Lima," San Martín pointed out. Guemes inspected him sharply—not disapproving of what he saw.

"*Ai*," he assented. "The country is endless and the Spaniards are many. My men are brave, though few, their horses swift, but acclimated to the lowlands. It is indeed far from Lima. How to drive there? That is a problem."

"With a proper plan and working together, we can accomplish it, Guemes," began San Martín. He outlined his concept, speaking plainly as an engineer describing the construction of a wall, yet injecting the project with his enthusiasm and vision. As he explained what must be done and how the parts fit together. Guemes was struck by his fire, for the first time seeing the goal as grander than even a gaucho war.

"*Ai*," he agreed. "*Ai*, we can do this. The gauchos of Salta will take part. We will hold the Spaniards here and beat them when they stir!"

With San Martín exuding his trademark enthusiasm, confidence, and vision, the Army of the North almost instantly began to stir from its melancholy slumber. Under his direction the money seized at Potosí was doled out in payment to the men and officers who had fought for it in Upper Peru. Spirits lifted instantly, even though most of the soldiers squandered their allowances in the *pulperías*. San Martín ordered the camp and hospital tidied up, the paths wetted and brushed down daily. The men were rigorously drilled, not for extended periods but enough to help instill discipline. He insisted upon an officers' call each morning, the commanders to be properly dressed and precise in fulfillment of their soldierly duties. During this interval, the harassing of the Spaniards was left to Guemes and his mamalukes—as his gauchos were sometimes called. With joyous ferocity they pursued their mission.

After a short period of time, San Martín and Belgrano moved the Army of the North away to Tucumán, a harshly rectangular city softened by tree-lined streets and softly hissing irrigation canals. North of the town, San Martín selected an isolated hill to fortify as his citadel. He entrenched it, protecting its crest by low walls, not as formidable as some redoubts, but if resolutely garrisoned, capable of resisting much greater forces than the Spaniards possessed in this region. Beyond Tucumán the patriots would never retreat; it was to be the Gibraltar of the North, the fortress city holding the frontier, providing a base beyond which Guemes and his irregulars could harass the Spaniards, keep them on edge, wear them down, force them into submission so that this region might remain secure. Then Belgrano's army could get on with the principal task.

Much of the populace turned out day after day to watch construction of the fortress, help out where they could, or offer unsolicited advice. Among those frequently inspecting the works was a red-bearded blue-eyed monster of a man of foreign visage whom Christian discovered to be an American, William Colisberry, a physician. "I am in the process of establishing a practice here and learning the language. One is as difficult as the other," he confided.

"Why don't you acquire a dictionary?"

The doctor laughed. "If only it were that simple," he replied.

On April 25 of the year 1814, San Martín awoke from a brief siesta, suddenly violently ill. Christian, from an adjacent room, rushed to his side but was waved away as the officer retched vomit that was bright scarlet; his face, flushed and then quickly ashen, his eyes dark and glazed, a curious rasp emanating from his throat. Christian guided him to a couch and dispatched a messenger after Colisberry, the only physician he knew. The gruff American scurried into the room with his kit and made a hasty examination, slowly folding the foot-long wooden tubes he used for a stethoscope. He selected a vial from his satchel, prepared a mixture and directed the half-conscious San Martín to drink it. Almost instantly the officer's moaning ceased, his legs straightened, his expression relaxed, a glaze of peace settling over his burning eyes. "I do not know what that was," he sighed, "but it relieved me of a fearful pain, for which I am grateful." His voice tapered off as he drifted into a relaxed sleep from the opiate.

Colisberry bustled about with his paraphernalia, oblivious to his illustrious, though dormant, patient. "I've seen other such cases," he muttered to Christian. "They are difficult to treat. I recommend most importantly that he be taken to a more beneficial climate, perhaps to Córdoba—'tis his lungs that are infected. If he is not removed to a drier climate, I firmly believe he will not live six months!"

He added, "I think I will try to obtain some alder bark, which is very useful as a cure for bleeding of the lungs and numerous other ailments, including scrofula and blood disease. I will make a steep of it; and you must see that he ingests some of the fluid, perhaps five times a day."

"Suppose that does not work?"

"Then we will try other effective remedies for his symptoms. However, the most important thing is to get him away from here into bracing air, sir; and I highly recommend it."

The physician packed his kit, engaged Belgrano for a moment's conversation, and bustled off. The general slowly entered, his face sober. He hesitated beside the couch until San Martín opened his eyes.

"Do you wish for a priest, my friend?" asked Belgrano, gently.

"A priest! What for?" Incredulity raised San Martín's voice an octave. "Am I so ill I must arrange my passage elsewhere?" His breath rattled through a strictured throat. "Even if that were so, it would not be a priest I'd seek but a soldier to impart my vision, my life, my mission!"

"A priestly need is a personal thing, my friend. Not a mission, I think."

"My 'person' *is* my mission. No more than that. I have little use for priests."

Christian smiled inwardly. The words might have been his own.

CHAPTER FIVE

At Dr. Colisberry's insistence that San Martín must seek a better climate, they set forth with a small escort for the region of Córdoba. In the cool of one early evening, they reached at last the rancho-estate once presented by a distant king, who did not own it, to the Miraval and Tejeda families who themselves had seized it only by force of arms from natives who valued it less. Here San Martín rested his aching, ravaged form; and here in the high thin air, under a sun toasting the earth through cloudless skies, within short weeks he found a healing peace for body and soul.

In midwinter he received the news of the first great patriot triumph. Don Gervasio Antonio Posadas, the supreme director at Buenos Aires, proudly reported that on July 4, his nephew, Carlos Alvear, had seized Montevideo, the city across from Buenos Aires and the key to La Plata estuary and its waterways. "Let your heart breathe," the old man wrote San Martín. "Carlos, your good friend has taken Montevideo, and our navy has seized its harbor!" San Martín was aware young Alvear not only had been his good friend but now would become his rival; undoubtedly he would be made supreme director when opportunity arose; and what then would that mean for the grand vision of freeing the southern continent?

Well, no matter, for vain and ambitious as Alvear was, he would be most interested in keeping San Martín far from Buenos Aires, in distant Córdoba or even more remote Cuyo. Cuyo! There San Martín could resume forging his weapon; there he would create the army to truly win the long struggle.

On July 11, Carlos Alvear himself wrote San Martín, the letter thinly disguising his determination to keep the two ambitious men ever separated: "Fortune has favored me admirably in all my undertakings," he gloated. "May she be favorable to you in the same manner."

Christian occasionally joined the guards in drill or firing practice to vary his days. He rarely entered the town of Córdoba itself; there was no need. His life was here at the estate, where San Martín sought health and dreamed glorious dreams. Christian had been gravely presented by his commander with a brace of pistols in recognition of his service and friendship. These cavalry weapons of

Spanish manufacture were like all complicated mechanisms—subject to failure—but nonetheless seemed an improvement over the bolas and *facon*, which had become Christian's favorite close-range weapons. He eagerly accepted instruction in mounted drill and firing practice. A snapped frizzen spring ended his use of one pistol until it could be repaired, no simple thing on this frontier, but he continued practicing with the other until he became fairly proficient in its use, though scarcely an expert.

On August 10, 1814, Posadas of Buenos Aires formally named San Martín governor of the remote province of Cuyo. A governor of a region so distant from the capital city was commander, jurist, legalist, autonomous—in effect a little king. He was an ally of the home government to be sure, but an emperor, nonetheless. "Your health, my dear José, will prove more robust in distant Mendoza than it could ever be at Buenos Aires," the uncle of the ambitious Alvear seemed to be saying to him. "Go with God—but go!"

"It is of little consequence," the officer muttered to Christian upon receipt of the order. "My ultimate desire coincides with the wishes of Posadas and Alvear, if for opposite reasons."

"Yes, sir," agreed Christian, understanding. "Cuyo it is."

Three Andean realms, those of Mendoza, San Juan, and San Luis, were grouped to form the Province of Cuyo when San Martín become its governor, a kingdom with some 40,000 subjects. They were hardy, brave people, disciplined by the harshness of their environment, thrifty as they must be to wrest their living from the elevated valleys and stony mountainsides, astute enough to trade across the Andes into Chile and across the pampa to Buenos Aires. Bold they must also become to fight the Indians who looked with covetous eyes upon the riches passing in trade caravans beneath the points of their lances. From Cuyans, San Martín might indeed forge a formidable army.

Mendoza, the capital, lay upon a plain coursed by the knee-deep Rio Mendoza which supplied irrigation waters for its oasis. Normally it accommodated fewer than 10,000 souls, the city all but hidden under tossing plumes of poplars. Convents, churches, and monasteries were scattered throughout the community, and the cathedral fronted the two-block long Plaza Pedro del Castillo. San Martín and his party bivouacked about the city as soldiers must, the leader establishing himself upon an estate, donated for his use, a short distance south. He installed his secretaries and his staff, set about creating a recruiting center, and directed his aides to organize the cadres that would become his battalions, his regiments, his divisions, his army.

The government of Buenos Aires, perhaps thinking to soothe the vanity San Martín did not possess, had finally named him a brigadier general—a title he reluctantly accepted "temporarily." In anticipation of a lengthy stay on these acrid plains, he sent to Buenos Aires for his wife, Remeditos. Doña Remeditos at eighteen, barely out of girlhood, crossed the pampa in a state carriage with her slave, Jesusa. She was eager, though a little fearful, to rejoin her husband, a thirty-three-year-old stranger consumed with ambitions she could not share.

A few weeks after San Martín's arrival and while the community bustled with unaccustomed activity, there trickled into Mendoza the first refugees from Chile—harbingers of a mighty flood to come. Countless men, women, and children arrived, fleeing Spanish arms with the remnants of the patriot forces shattered at the flaming city of Rancagua. From the ashes of their revolt, they washed through the defiles and down the mountainsides and into the arms of San Martín and his fledgling army of revenge.

Day by day the tide waxed stronger until the refugees, half-starved and dispirited, crowded the streets of Mendoza. Dependent on the meager rations provided by the general, they milled about the dusty roads, idling in groups and for the most part remaining silent; for there was little to discuss save grim defeat. It was among them one day that Christian saw a bandy-legged individual he could never under any circumstances forget.

Ishmael walked with a gray-robed friar with more hair upon his chin than upon his head, a priest whose friendly, darting eyes enlivened a face marked by intelligence and good humor. This, said Ishmael, was Friar Luis Beltran. "A genius," he explained, simply.

"Genius?" echoed Christian in mock wonder. "Genius? Idling away all his time with the likes of you, old man? What kind of wisdom is that?"

Friar Beltran laughed, and they sat in the warm sunlight at an outdoor table over tiny cups of sugared coffee.

"If you are a genius, sir, may I ask what direction your talents take?" asked Christian.

Ishmael replied for the friar. "My friend is a genius with guns and mules, bridges and corduroy, forges and anvils, and hammers and files. He can make anything, do anything, create anything, repair anything. Also he is a man of faith. And a patriot."

"If what you say is true, Ishmael, let him repair my pistol," Christian said, with a grin. He drew the weapon with the broken frizzen spring and laid it upon the table. Eagerly Luis Beltran snatched it up, his agile fingers testing lock, trigger, turning it from side to side, his mind expertly weighing the firearm, mumbling to himself under his breath, the words keeping pace with his busy fingers.

"Yes, yes. A cavalry weapon of the newer type, manufactured at Burgos for army and colonial use. Yes, durable and useful, except for the spring, which is overly weak, a pity." He looked up suddenly at Christian, his eyes intense. "I can fix it sir, if you wish?'"

"Please do."

Beltran dove into the bulging pouch slung from his shoulder. He rattled around inside it, his hands emerging with handmade tools and, astonishingly, a whole spring of somewhat similar manufacture but stronger, as though from a musket.

"Useful item to keep, sir. One never knows when it will be needed," he explained. With his implements he swiftly removed the damaged spring from the pistol and efficiently filed, perfected, and fitted the substitute. Within moments it was in place. He emptied the pistol of its powder and ball, tested the lock and firing action, reloaded the weapon and handed it to Christian. "Quite as good as new, sir," he said gravely. "Better in fact, for this spring is stronger. It will not break."

"I am indebted to you, Father," acknowledged Christian. "Ishmael was correct, as usual. You would be an asset to any army, I am sure." He smiled. "You might even *be* an army!"

"Not enough of one, I am afraid," said the friar, not joining in their laughter. "I was of little help at Rancagua, except to the dying and a few to whom I offered solace."

Christian brusquely shifted the subject, requesting the story of the battle, knowing the general would be interested.

"It was a disaster, Fletcher," replied Ishmael, "compounded by treachery and defined by heroism of the most astounding quality. You could say it was the struggle of good and evil in miniature."

"Whose was the treachery and whose the gallantry?"

"The Carreras are filled with evil designs, yet Bernardo O'Higgins is a valiant man of honor."

"O'Higgins?" repeated Christian, startled. "Bernardo? An odd name, that. Who is he?"

"Ah, surely you remember his father, Fletcher? The viceroy, Ambrosio Higgins? The boy is his natural son, born with the name Riquelme, now Bernardo O'Higgins and famed from one end of Chile to the other. A man honest, enduring, and a very bold fighter—though more crafty than skilled. But he is impetuous enough to carry it off. If the Revolution has developed one hero beyond the Andes, Bernardo O'Higgins is he!"

So Bernardo Riquelme, who was sixteen when Christian had known him twenty years before, had returned from England to become a warrior-hero of his people! Would Bernardo recognize him? This young Irish-Chilean might prove the key to independence in his important sector, a fitting counterpart to San Martín, if he could be contacted. But who were the Carreras?

"The Carreras are—well, the Carreras. And quite unbelievable," said Ishmael. "Ye know I speak no ill of no man, but some I can speak well of only in part, and of the Carreras—I can speak of very little at all."

"A large family?"

"Rather. But the four who count are José Miguel Carrera—erratic, unreliable, vain, ambitious, thoroughly untrustworthy. Then there is Luis Carrera, who is the best of the family and with whom honest patriots might deal, if it were not for the influence of his brothers and Juan José Carrera, of whom I will not speak."

"Then there is Javiera, the goddess of the clan, as a mythologist might describe her, and she rules over all. If she were a man, she would be emperor, brigand chief, or governor. The only safety for Chile is that she is a woman; her tools are her brothers, and in the end she will be the death of all of them. You will see."

"They will come here?"

"Where else? There is nowhere else for them to go. You will see them and judge for yourself!"

CHAPTER SIX

"If the choice were yours," said San Martín over a glass of red wine as they finished their roast beef lunch, "which way would you go? O'Higgins or the Carreras? Neither choice jeopardizes my position, I think, but who would prove most useful for the reconquest of Chile and a continent?" He sometimes discussed questions in this manner with the Englishman, more to clarify his own thinking than to secure advice. "The Carreras are more able, more brilliant. But in war that is not everything."

"O'Higgins I know," said Christian, sipping his dry wine, slightly bitter with the purple grapes of Mendoza. "The Carreras I do not. The general must judge for himself. But if the choice were mine, I would elect bravery, honor, and intelligence over brilliance, questionable trustworthiness, and possibly even treachery—although that has not been proven."

"Both factions appear to have important followings."

"That is true, sir. But from what I hear of the Carreras, their support can only dwindle."

"Perhaps." It was time for San Martín brief siesta. "I wish you would contact them in some discreet manner, assess them so far as possible, and make arrangements for them to come to dinner."

"The Carreras and O'Higgins together?"

"I think not. There might be sparks and smoke, through which one could observe only with difficulty."

As fortune would have it, Christian was at his favorite café with Ishmael when the Carreras arrived like conquering heroes, rather than as the fleeing fugitives they were. Outriders preceded them. The quartet was followed by a uniformed retinue in excessive finery; there was no evidence that they had narrowly escaped destruction at the Spanish sword. The three brothers—and the sister—dismounted and made their way through the loiterers who parted ranks for them as for royalty. They approached the café where Christian sat, looking neither to right nor left, haughty monarchs, rulers over all within their sight.

José Miguel, the nominal leader, was twenty-nine, tall and dark, his animated face aflame with delight at having reached this sanctuary. Luis, twenty-three, had the best countenance of the three, although it lacked José's charm. As for Juan José, thirty-two, one look at him and Christian understood why Ishmael would not speak of this man. However, his glance was completely arrested by the woman. At thirty-three and the oldest of the Carreras, Javiera Carrera was the most strikingly beautiful woman Christian had ever seen. In all the years of his roaming, he had never beheld a face and figure so remarkable in every detail. She was dark like her brothers, with waves of lush black hair and full red lips. And if her figure approached perfection, the animation of her face made the Carrera men appear dull and plain; for Javiera was the mistress of all, her brothers included, woman who knew how to employ her beauty as well as her wits to attain whatever goal she sought.

Upon reaching the table next to his, Javiera met Christian's eyes for the fraction of a second. In her glance Christian saw evidence that she, too, bore a "stick," although she may have been unaware of it. He recognized that hers was a curse by which her touch, reaching for greatness, brought death instead. There was a subterranean kinship between the two of them, a compulsion toward doom. He sensed this, and Javiera, too, may have caught something of it; for she started as her glance met his. She recovered almost instantly and busied herself in quiet discussion with her brothers.

Christian finished his drink and stepped to the Carrera table, oblivious to the curious glances of all but the woman, who silently appraised him with more calculation than curiosity. She lifted a brow as though to inquire his reason for the interruption.

"You are the Carreras?" asked the Englishman. The woman nodded, a silent, tiny gesture.

"I am aide to General San Martín," explained Christian. "He has directed me to invite you to dine with him—this evening, if you like."

Javiera glanced at her brothers. Luis grinned, Juan José remained inert, and José Miguel shrugged. She spoke for all: "Tell your general that we accept—with the greatest of pleasure." Her voice had a compelling quality and, though her appraisal of Christian had previously been businesslike and cold, her expression softened as she realized that this quite presentable man was in the confidence of the governor and general of Cuyo; he might prove useful. "We shall be there."

The Sierra de Uspallata hovered dark and massive to the west as the group sat over wine at the long table in the twilight, a glow from the declining sun touching its ridgeline with gold. The conversation had been animated, stirred up now and then by the general and taken up with spirit by Javiera and her brothers. Christian was silent. He was a necessary element, having brought the group together, but he remained apart from it, though nothing escaped his careful observation.

"Why did the patriots lose at Rancagua?" wondered San Martín aloud, fingering his long-stemmed glass. José Miguel flushed.

"It became a trap of O'Higgins' own making," he muttered. "He remained there when he might have withdrawn. He must have been aware that the enemy was superior in force and artillery. His final salvo, I have been told, was of *pesos*, not cannon balls, so low was he in ammunition!"

"Then the Spaniards were superior to all of you together?"

José Miguel reddened.

"It is useless to throw good men and units into a hopeless situation," he argued. "Better to wait until a more advantageous occasion presents itself, do you not agree, General?"

San Martín again twirled his glass, stared full into the face of the Chilean unblinkingly.

"A man who values honor above life, who realizes the military value of impulse and vigor over cold wisdom, could never betray allies or friends, even if the result is annihilation," he replied coldly.

"Is the general suggesting that my honor was at fault?"

"I suggest nothing. I was not there. But I will never abandon my allies, my friends, nor could I accept the support of anyone who would."

Javiera leaned forward, using her allure to full advantage.

"We have much support in Chile still, my general," she assured him softly. "We can always rally it. With San Martín in command here at Mendoza and with the Carreras commanding the patriots of Chile, we can clear all the lands south of Peru of the Spanish. We can control the continent! We invite you, we plead with you, to join in this noble endeavor!"

"With no more Rancaguans?" demanded the general bluntly. "With no more occasions when it may prove useless to rescue a situation? I could not risk that, madame. Rancaguans are always possible. I am the governor of Cuyo. I am commander of the Army of the Andes! I must select the officers who will not fail me in this massive undertaking. I do not know who those officers will be—perhaps a

Carrera will be among them—but that will be for me to decide, not for a Chilean, no matter how competent, how skilled, or how noble. My colleagues must be patriots first, officers second. They must be able and willing to submerge their persons, their vanities beneath the supreme cause of liberty. And they must above all be officers whom I can trust when the situation proves hopeless. Those qualities must be theirs, the selection mine."

A few days later, Christian learned from Ishmael that O'Higgins had slipped into Mendoza from the high Andes among the last of the refugees. The problem was to find him, but this was accomplished in time. The Englishman spotted him resting in front of a modest *pensión*, scanning the latest *Gaceta* established by the general for his proclamations and to disseminate news from any source that might filter in. It was only a single small sheet, printed on both sides, but it served its purpose. Christian pulled up a chair next to O'Higgins without disturbing him. The young leader, his dusty boots with the giant spurs resting upon a ledge, finished reading and offered the paper to Christian with no comment, scarcely a glance at him.

"Thank you, Mr. Riquelme," said Christian gravely, in English.

O'Higgins started, for the first time looking at Christian squarely in the face, puzzled. "Do I know you, sir?" he asked politely.

"I do hope so, Bernardo," Christian laughed. "Or did London schooling blot out all recollection of those who persuaded you to attend?"

A slow grin dawned across his handsome face, and O'Higgins bounced up and impulsively embraced Christian. "Mr. Christian!" he cried. "How often I have thought of you! How I wished to tell you that the schooling wasn't so bad after all. You were right to force me to go! Not only were you my rescuer, my adviser, but you grew to be ever my friend in my thoughts. I am grateful to you. To see you now, here, after all these years is—why, 'tis the work of the saints!"

"Saints be hanged, Bernardo," retorted Christian. "'Tis the luck of the Irish, no more. But it *is* luck."

Arm in arm the two crossed the street to Christian's favorite café, sitting at an outside table but somewhat apart from the milling crowd. They spoke of long-gone days in Chile, of Bernardo's mother, still living in seclusion, dreaming no doubt of old Ambrosio and their son. They discussed the battle for independence and even the Carreras. Bernardo, whatever he may have thought, would scarcely speak ill of them. "They are patriots, too, I think," he mused. "But mercurial."

"Untrustworthy," corrected Christian, "or so I've heard. A more accurate description, I believe."

That night, they rode south from the city together toward San Martín's hacienda. As on the earlier evening, there was something of a state banquet, this time more congenial, much more frank. Even the general's bride, Remeditos seemed animated; and while she spoke little, she at least listened with pleasure.

"The Carreras told me of Rancagua, that the situation was so hopeless that you fired coins instead of cannon balls at the Spaniards," said San Martín gravely. "Others have affirmed that you performed an impossible exploit, cutting your way free from Spanish encirclement while the city burned all about and guns were bearing on you from every side! A most heroic feat."

"'Twas that or perish, sir. We had lost most of our effectives and could not even take our wounded with us." He shook his head in dismay. "A man can lose his following if he doesn't care for those who rally to him."

"You will never lose your following, I am confident. Your men know loyalty. Tell me, sir, what was the Carrera role at Rancagua?"

O'Higgins hesitated. This was a topic he would have preferred to avoid, but the question had been direct.

"Their role was exactly what they made it. They were to support us with artillery and men. They did not arrive, at least until the Spanish had already trapped us. Even then I think a resolute force could have—might have . . ." His voice trailed away.

"Was their failure to support you deliberate?"

O'Higgins' blue eyes rested solemnly upon San Martín's face.

"I mean to say," pursued the general, "you were rivals. If the Spanish disposed of you, the patriot cause would have remained wholly in Carrera hands—surely that thought must have occurred to them?"

O'Higgins waited a long moment, before replying.

"I believe, sir, you had better inquire of the Carreras upon that subject."

San Martín flushed. "I am convinced it was as I have suspected, then." He toyed with his glass. "What are your plans now, may I ask?"

O'Higgins deliberately took a bite of red meat, sloshed it down with wine, and leaned back in his chair.

"I have not yet entirely decided, sir. I am *Chileño* and the liberation of that land is my life, but I wish to go to Buenos Aires for some months, to ascertain what support I may expect and from whom. Of course, I shall return. The way to Chilean freedom is over the mountains, not around by sea; and Mendoza is the gateway."

San Martín chuckled.

"So it is, O'Higgins. So it is." He lifted his glass. "That is why I am here, as well. When the hour comes, may we strike together!"

Leaving O'Higgins at his lodging, Christian, not yet ready for bed, strolled along the Alameda, the mile-long walk between two of Mendoza's irrigation ditches with their rows of poplars. Midway along the path, Christian came upon the Carreras, or two of them, Javiera and her brother, Juan José. They were seated at a table enjoying the cool night air and tunes of the strolling musicians. They were all but indistinguishable among the shadows, and Christian might have passed them by had not a throaty whisper summoned him to their table. He lifted his hat and stood beside them silently until Javiera invited him to be seated. As Christian took a seat, Javiera dismissed her brother with a pointed look.

"I have been thinking of you," she said softly to the Englishman. The dark wells of her eyes matched the raven flow of her hair.

"To what purpose?" asked Christian lightly. He was amused, for she was not a woman who spoke without purpose.

"I am a woman. You are a man," she shrugged, a hint of question in her voice. "Need there be any deeper reason?"

"With you, *señorita* Carrera, I think there must."

She straightened as though with irritation, then relaxed again.

"Had we a few moments together, I might perhaps convince you otherwise," she laughed. Then she added, "I have rooms not far distant, if you would escort me there?"

Amused, intrigued as well, and if truth be known—flattered by the attention of this remarkable woman—Christian nonetheless realized her intent.

"Javiera, Javiera," he sighed. "I would not unduly use my influence upon the general, even if I possessed any. And," he stood up, "since you will not ask me directly, I must tell you that I prefer O'Higgins myself to your brothers."

He stood abruptly and turned to leave.

"Fletcher!" her voice now lower and more insistent, halted him like an iron tether. "I shall not forget!"

CHAPTER SEVEN

It was miraculous that an army could be created in a place like Mendoza, midway between the remote principalities of La Plata to the east and Santiago to the west, themselves distant from Peru, the stronghold of Spanish power, and Peru being very far indeed from Madrid.

Yet here in a center named Plumerillo, so undistinguished that Ferdinand VII had difficulty locating it even upon his most skillfully inked maps, San Martín labored in ceaseless activity, generating the soldiers, the battalions, the regiments, an army out of the wind and the leaves. He had a tiny cadre to commence with: an auxiliary force of 300 Cordobans and Mendozans under Juan Gregorio de las Heras, raised to match a Chilean force early in the patriot war. Two companies of the Eighth Regiment marched out from Buenos Aires to join with him, and Colonel Matías Zapiola, former naval officer turned cavalryman, brought two squadrons of Grenadiers. Later the Seventh Infantry under Ambrosio Cramer, a French soldier of fortune who had served under Napoleon, moved out from La Plata, and the various regiments were redesignated under different names.

Thus by September of 1815, the army numbered 2,300 effectives, still far short of the force required but a healthy nucleus. At Tucumán, the new revolutionary capital, it was rumored that freedom would be given to all slaves who would enlist. Christian commented on this to San Martín.

"With a judicious hint that freedom would be inevitable in any case, perhaps slave-owners would free those who enlist in order to retain the others for a while."

"There would be much resistance, Mr. Fletcher," objected the general. "You are speaking of slaves as men, but their owners think of them as gold; and landowners would rather volunteer the services of their brothers than lose the labor of their slaves and the wealth they produce. Besides, they will say, the effect of these freed men, even if serving in the army, will be harmful to discipline over those still enslaved. And that will interfere even more with profits."

Christian stubbornly shook his head.

"Perhaps the general could persuade them to enlist a small proportion of their slaves but grant their freedom only after they have crossed the Andes into Chile, beyond any influence upon their bonded fellows."

San Martín agreed. By this means two battalions, comprised of 710 men, were raised among the slaves. They were destined for heroic service.

Chilean refugees, among them followers of O'Higgins and others of the Carreras, enlisted in their own units which they hoped would form the kernel of a Chilean army. All of these units, in O'Higgins' absence, José Miguel Carrera sought to control. With his brothers and sister, he established a headquarters in a barracks apart, commenced playing at independence through proclamations, even created a toy government, taking upon himself powers for which he had neither the taste nor stability to do justice. His followers seemed as arrogant as the Carreras. They were unwilling to submit to general discipline because, they said, they were subjects of an "independent state."

When not squabbling with authorities, they fought with Chileans devoted to O'Higgins, a small-scale replica of the internal strife that had so recently cost them Chile. At length the Carreras had gone too far. San Martín deemed them a nuisance that must be removed so that honest men might get on with their vital work.

Consequently, one day before dawn, their barracks were surrounded by troops. Carrera was called out and presented with a one-word ultimatum: *Leave!* A pragmatist, even if a proud and willful one, he instantly saw that he could do nothing else. Under guard he moved his family and a tiny escort out of Mendoza, down the long road toward Buenos Aires.

Christian silently observed the departure, although he had taken no part in this decision. He was given a lasting impression of Javiera, coldly surveying him from the carriage with her eyes of death.

With the Carreras out of the way, the general dispatched a messenger to Buenos Aires, urging O'Higgins to return and assume command of the Chileans, which he promptly did.

The general and his staff dealt endlessly with a myriad of problems and needs, and in these situations Friar Luis Beltran often proved a key man. He had been introduced to San Martín by Christian, and the value of his unique talents was instantly perceived.

The good friar had many skills besides his ability with mechanics. Although an artilleryman by preference, he was also a self-taught mathematician and chemist, a maker of fireworks, a carpenter, architect, blacksmith, cobbler, and physician. He was, said the general one evening, "a division in himself, sparing neither virtue nor fault."

He charged the friar with establishing a chemist's shop to produce medicines and chemicals for the army, and before that was fairly underway, ordered him to create an arsenal. Beltran gathered and trained more than 300 specialized workmen. He cast cannons and shells, using melted down church bells when iron ran out. He made limbers for the guns, saddles for the cavalry; and when Christian urged that the horses and pack mules be shod to protect their hoofs from Andean stone, Beltran and his aides hammered out 50,000 shoes, training farriers in the unaccustomed fitting and use.

limbers-
two-wheeled vehicle to which a gun may be attached for transport.

Under his genius, canteens were contrived of stoppered cows' horns, shoes made for the infantry, muskets repaired and sometimes manufactured, and on the sooty walls of his shop, plans sketched for mountain conveyances to negotiate the high passes. From *caliche* beds in the range, he drew sodium nitrate; from a volcano to the south, sulphur; and with charcoal added, he turned out immense quantities of high-quality gunpowder. Beltran established a factory to make army cloth, dyed the product blue, green, and red; and from it the women of Mendoza made the thousands of uniforms for the infantry, the artillery, the *cazadores*, and the sappers. Having the time of his life, Beltran was the Leonardo da Vinci of the Southern Andes.

"One thing more, Merlin," San Martín jested one day. "We need wings for the cannon, to hoist them over the mountains!"

The friar chuckled.

"Very well, sir," he replied in kind. "If Archimedes could move the earth with a fulcrum and a lever long enough, we can make wings sufficiently great for cannon. But they might come with long ears and a bray."

Alvear was finally named supreme director at Buenos Aires as San Martín had sourly predicted. However, he did not last long for he possessed too many similar characteristics to the Carreras. Deposed within months, he was succeeded by General José Rondeau, just returned from a defeat by the Spaniards in Upper Peru.

La Plata's formal independence from Spain was proclaimed in 1816, at Tucumán. Juan Martín de Pueyrredon was elected first president of the new republic, a man at last with whom the general could work. Pueyrredon supported San Martín hugely with supplies, with men, with hope, and with humor. As the long training of the army drew to a close, Pueyrredon wrote from Buenos Aires:

> Besides the 4,000 blankets sent from Córdoba, there go now 500 ponchos, the only ones I could find. You requested 1,000 arrobas of jerked beef. It shall be

> sent. Here go the clothes ordered and many shirts. Here go saddle blankets. Here go the only 2 bugles I could find. Here go the 2,000 sabers you requested. Here go 200 tents and there are no more. Here goes the world. Here goes the devil. Here goes the flesh. How shall I ever extricate myself from the debts I have incurred for this? One of these days I shall go bankrupt and go over to you, so you can feed me the jerked beef I am sending you. Don't ask for anything else, if you don't want to hear I have been found hanging from a rafter!

San Martín chuckled upon reading the report, handing it to Christian. "You can always depend on Juan," he said, still laughing. "They ought to call him Saint John. Perhaps one day they will!"

"If the campaign succeeds," agreed Christian.

"When," corrected the general.

Some days later Christian was summoned to headquarters. He stood patiently at attention while San Martín hustled his secretary out and closed the door, leaving the two of them alone. Upon the wall behind his desk was a huge map of the middle Andes, showing few details but sketching the upthrust in general terms, more decorative than useful.

"Mr. Fletcher," the general said, "having been a ship's officer, you understand navigation thoroughly?"

The Englishman nodded.

"You must have had at least rudimentary training in map making?"

Christian recalled his two years exploration of the southernmost Chilean islands and channels and his years with Bligh, a master chart-maker. "A bit, sir. I do not know how my work would compare with that of professional cartographers."

"No matter," replied the officer impatiently. "You know more about map-making than my officers." He moved behind the desk and with a quill pointed to the map. "This range is our barrier, our protection. It is also our ally, permitting us to descend upon the Spaniards unexpectedly and from unanticipated directions. Unfortunately, we have no satisfactory charts of the major passes, a fact which hinders planning. Therefore I intend to entrust you with a very delicate—perhaps perilous—mission, if you will consider it."

Christian was somewhat amused. "Delighted, sir," he replied.

"With no questions? Ah, that I like. On the surface, Mr. Fletcher, your mission will be diplomatic. I will send to President Francisco Marcó del Pont of Chile, the formal proclamation of independence, drafted at Tucumán. He may have already heard of it anyway. But for our purpose it is only a pretext." He waved toward the map with the feather end of the quill. I wish you to journey to Chile by way of the pass of Los Patos, about thirty leagues north of Mendoza. It also is well above Uspallata Pass, which is the principal route across the mountains. This map-making expedition will take you two or three weeks, even with good fortune." He mused for a moment, then continued. "When you deliver the sealed proclamation to the Spaniard, he will without question be very angry; and no doubt you will be hustled back to this side of the Andes by the shortest route, which is Uspallata Pass. I want you to take no notes, either going or coming. If such should be discovered on your person, you would be hanged, which is a distinct possibility anyway. But I wish you to memorize every stone, every detail of both routes so that when you return you may draw us maps to chart the way through the defiles for our army.

"Naturally I cannot force you to undertake such a dangerous mission. But I request it."

"I accept, sir," replied Christian without hesitation. "May I choose a companion?"

"If you wish, and if he is discreet, and if he will not talk even under torture, as I know you will not."

"He is all of those things my general—and more."

"Who is this paragon?"

"Ishmael, sir. A very old acquaintance of mine. He is familiar with Chile, though an outlander. He is discreet, and slips about like a ferret. He was with O'Higgins during the Patriot War and knows the situation there perfectly. My thought would be to leave him in Chile to assemble a report on such patriot elements that may still exist for the information of our army when it arrives."

"Obviously that would be of immense value, if we can depend on the judgment and loyalty of this Ishmael. What nationality did you say he was? His name sounds Jewish."

Christian searched his memory. "I don't really know, sir. I know only that Ishmael is what he calls himself. I suppose he is British, from his accent. He has good judgment. I would trust him as my brother."

"Very well, then. Good luck to the both of you."

Mounted upon mules, one gray and the other brown, and leading a single pack animal, Christian and Ishmael camped the first night at a mountain watering site against the sunrise flank of the Sierra de Uspallata, well north of Mendoza. On the third day at dusk, there loomed on their left hand the enormous barrier of the Andes. They continued north along its shoulder until they rounded the foothill range called the Cordillera de Tigre, rising to 16,000 feet or more. After gaining the Rio de Los Patos, the men made their way toward the head of the stream in the royal range. Beaten by *contrabandistas* and others with no legitimate business but plenty of illegal reasons for taking this circuitous route, a trail led them by the correct tributaries, one after another, upwards toward the pass. Christian mentally recorded the twists and turns, the width of trail, depth of stream, possible obstacles for guns and packs, presence or absence of forage, and even the existence of the *vicuñas*, which might serve as emergency food for patrols or a few lost men. The little golden camels with the silky coat and the grace of antelopes, bounded easily up and down the mountainsides, curious about these clumsy intruders infringing on their wild and lofty principality.

On the sixth day, the pair bivouacked at a spring of cold water in the lee of a black stone ledge well within the pass, the elevation, Christian calculated, being about 12,400 feet. He suffered slightly from the *puna*, a high altitude disorder which enhanced one's irritability. It depressed him; but Ishmael, wholly unaffected, rocked back and forth on the hard ground within inches of the tiny fire, his hair frosty, his eyes as bright as ever. Nothing ever seemed to change Ishmael.

The night was like ice, the sky black and bitter. There was utter loneliness in this windswept defile; even the mules were listless, standing without forage, nothing in their bellies, heads low, long ears drooping, waiting for an end to the cold dark night and a descent to good grazing with tomorrow's sun. Christian broke out two pieces of jerky, tossed one to Ishmael and gnawed at the other. It was brittle, hard to chew. He huddled closer to the fire. "What a miserable wind," he muttered.

"Aye, lad, 'tis harsh, no doubt of it," agreed Ishmael. "Soon perhaps our army will lead the wind down into the vale of Chile where it is ever warm."

"If 'tisn't warm enough, the Spaniards will heat it up for us, I have no doubt," grumbled Christian.

"Eh, eh," Ishmael chortled. "There is a rhythm to this land, no doubt of that; cold and warmth, peace and war, tranquility and violence. One balances t'other. No man can doze for long."

With daylight Christian stiffly arose and stamped circulation into his feet. He was getting old, he reflected bleakly—nearly half a century of age to his bones this morning, and they felt it. He rubbed the backs of the mules to comfort them a bit, stroked their soft muzzles to extend companionship, saddled the two and packed the third, and carefully affixed a white rag of peace to the tip of a lance, which he bound upright to girth and saddle. Then the whole party, empty-bellied, picked their way downward into Chile. It was the first time he had been in that country in fourteen years; it seemed like a homecoming, however dangerous it might prove.

As he had expected, they stumbled across a royalist picket halfway down the mountain trail, its sentries awaiting them, having heard the click of disturbed rocks and seeing them high on the uplift, long before their arrival. A fiercely mustached *huaso,* who obviously could not read a word, gravely accepted the letter they bore, turned it over and over while he considered what to do with these strange wanderers and how to deal with their determination to see the governor. Ah, well, it was not for him to decide. And so he passed them on. As they moved southward, day by day and further up the chain of command, an officer at each level judiciously avoided responsibility for shooting them, preferring that a more exalted official—or someone else, at any rate—make that grave decision. And so they came at last to Santiago.

It was heavy dusk when they reached the outskirts, and in the growing blackness they were guided as captives toward the center. Now and then a chaise passed them on its way from the theatre or dinner. They crossed the Mapocho by the stone bridge and came at length to the great plaza and to the single-storied palace, sprawling ominously out into the darkness. Shown to the anteroom, their letter from San Martín taken from them, they waited under heavy guard for the better part of an hour. Distant whispers of marching men reached them, becoming louder and louder. Suddenly Governor Don Francisco Marcó del Pont stood in the room, his hand bearing the Tucumán declaration.

A man of middle age, wigless at this hour and with full red lips twisted into a disparaging sneer, Marcó confronted the foreigners, "This—this note, this communication from your master, I will deal with suitably," he squeaked contemptuously, his voice a tone or two higher than it should have been. "It would give me great pleasure to deliver the two of you to the hangman for a public burning on the plaza. But," he added, contempt still coating his tongue, "I will need you to carry my reply back to San Martín, and so I will reluctantly forego that pleasure." He turned to a small, highly polished desk, and in bold flourishes composed an elegant reply, glancing up before signing it.

"I inscribe this with the white hand of loyalty, not with San Martín's black hand of treachery," he proclaimed haughtily. "You will so inform your master!"

In the darkness, without ceremony, they were hustled from the city. In the murky outskirts, Ishmael, as they had planned, escaped back into the town. By morning Christian was alone at the foot of the Andes. In due course his mission was completed in his thorough manner, even reporting Marcó's jibe to San Martín. The general smiled grimly. He would remember it.

CHAPTER EIGHT

Christian nodded to Zento, San Martín's secretary, who lifted reddened eyes from a ledger and grinned. "At his map again," he whispered. "I can tell that the army will march soon. The map, always the map! Go on in. He expects you."

The general stood with his back to the entrance, gazing at the chart, his hands folded behind him. He did not turn around.

"Mr. Fletcher," he said. "Come here, sir." With a baton he swept the Andes from the top to bottom of the map. "Our problem," he began as though addressing a class in strategy, "is to convey our forces from this side to this other side of the barrier range in condition for battle. Our choice of route through the mountains is limited to the several known passes. The Spaniards cannot predict which will contain our main thrust, and we must endeavor to enhance their confusion. I have already decided where this principal effort will be made, but I must keep the knowledge to myself, for his spies are busy and alert. We must persuade Marcó that we will attack in force through other passes than those we shall actually employ."

"May I make a suggestion, sir?"

"Of course."

"This," said Christian, raising a ruler and brushing the range south from Uspallata Pass, "as you are aware is the country of the Puelche and the Mapuche, those who left Chile and crossed the Andes to make their homes on our slopes. They were my people. I lived among them for several years, married into the tribe, speak the language, and have friends among the Mapuche to the west who have relatives and friends among these people. Perhaps with the Puelche, they are the jealous guardians of the southern passes. If you were to summon a congress of these people and let it be known that your army intends to cross into Chile by way of the southern passes and you desire their permission and assistance, word of this design would certainly be passed on to traders. Marcó quickly would hear of it and deploy troops to counter an invasion from that direction. This would weaken him in the region of Santiago. The disadvantage to such a procedure, of course, would arise if you really intend to launch your invasion through the southern passes."

San Martín smiled, tapped Christian companionably with this baton. "Your plan, sir, is excellent," he declared. "Perhaps that is why I had already thought of it myself!"

Fort San Carlos lay forty leagues south of Mendoza, an adobe-walled defense works erected against roving bands of Indians where the Yaucha and Papagallos meet before joining the Rio Tunuyán. Southwest of it lay the best-known southern passes through the Andes: Portillo, above the headwaters of the Rio Diamante, and Planchón Pass, south of Portillo. San Martín's couriers summoned the Puelche and Mapuche *caciques* and war leaders to San Carlos. Even before he arrived, the pampa about the post was emblazoned with lance-born banners, dotted with Indian *toldos* as brightly colored as the horses that had given their hides to cover them.

Horseman cavorted everywhere, scampering from tent to tent across the plains, some racing, others showing off. When the general's column approached, Indians bore down upon him in tumbling haste, anxious to see this white commander, his armed escort, and the gifts he brought, especially to taste his brandy.

San Martín rode out in front of his escort accompanied by Christian as interpreter and counselor. Christian dismounted to warmly embrace a half-clothed Indian, the head chief of all those present. Huanguenecul was tall, perfectly formed, of an indeterminate age and intelligent lively countenance, lightened now by broad smiles. Although he and Christian had never met, the Englishman's Mapuche war name of Lebitureo opened all doors; for Araucanian memories are long and admiration for courage limitless.

Christian translated carefully. It would not do for either party to gain a misapprehension of the other's views, even on trivial matters.

San Martín's grenadier officers stood at attention to one side, their bicorned hats, with tall soft plumes of dyed ostrich feathers; their blue coats and white trousers, high polished boots and gleaming swords added color and dignity to the scene. Before the Indians, gifts were splayed out in profusion and, to their eyes, of incredible richness. Open panniers revealed cloth, richly colored with Friar Beltran's liveliest dyes, beads and tinted feathers, knives, pistols, ammunition, horse gear, cooking pots, needles—items that to a native mind were more precious than gold. And in addition there were great jugs of wine and brandy. The treasure represented not a promise of a better life to come but of riches now, at hand today. The Indians were hugely interested.

At the great council San Martín cited the evil natures and manifold sins of the Spaniards and explained his desire for assistance and the need for permission to use the passes. *Ai*, here was a warrior to humble the proud Spaniards! Here was a captain worth joining! Yes, indeed, they would fight as they had ever fought, valiantly and to the death. This was a day of joy!

While cannon boomed in salute from the fort, the parade grounds became a festive maelstrom, filled with colorful dances until the brandy began to take hold, further sealing the new fellowship. For six days the bacchanal continued until, drunken to weariness but still joyfully determined to move from festival to war, Huanguenecul and the other chieftains made their sign to the paper, each embracing the general. San Martín, with his treaty, now returned to Mendoza, leaving Christian with their new allies for the remaining festivities.

CHAPTER NINE

By January 1, in the midsummer of 1817, the Army of the Andes had been honed to an edge for war, prepared to scale the great Andean barrier, cross its elevated passes, and strike a mortal blow at the southernmost reaches of the Empire of Spain.

Forges had glowed day and night; munitions were manufactured and packed. Beltran had devised special slings for the guns to suspend the heavy barrels between two or sometimes four mules trained to work as unyoked teams. "The general wanted wings for the cannon," the friar recalled happily. He gestured toward the stacked rawhide slings. "Well, there they are—wings! With those the guns will soar over the Andes and reach the valleys beyond without a scratch, ready for action. Wing! Hah!"

The friar had created rope and tackle mechanisms to hoist the cannon over ledges or other obstacles. Four cables, each 170 feet long, and two grapnels formed a portable bridge for each column. Nor were the needs of the individual soldier neglected.

From jerky a form of pemmican was made, the dry strips of meat as hard as metal, pounded to dust, mixed with melted fat, and, instead of the fruit of the North Country, laced with chopped chili peppers. These were packed into daily rations in many thousands of tiny leather bags. Mixed with water and heated, the pemmican made a nourishing meal, and the peppers kept the men from realizing how bad it tasted.

The Army of the Andes at this point counted 3,988 regulars, of whom 204 were officers. San Martín was in command and O'Higgins commanded a division, while brilliant, but vain and erratic, Miguel Estanislao Soler served as chief of staff. Other officers included Cramer, De las Heras, Zapiola, Rudecindo Alvarado, and Pedro Conde. The artillery, with Luis Beltran as "enabler," was commanded by Pedro Regalado de la Plaza. Seven hundred slaves, augmented by gauchos and others, were among the 1,200 militia; and unassigned officers included San Martín's brother-in-law, Manuel Escalada, Fernando Ramallo, and Mariano

Necochea. The whole force totaled about 5,000 men, plus the Chilean patriots and thousands of packers, artisans, and others accompanying the army.

There were more than 7,000 saddle mules, nearly 2,000 pack mules and 1,600 horses, with 600 cattle to be driven along and slaughtered as required. Supplies included 2,000 cannonballs, 2,000 rounds of shrapnel—an English invention of a dozen years earlier—and 600 specialized charges of some variety in addition to more than 900,000 musket loads for the foot soldiers.

Of course a formal farewell to Mendoza was necessary, to take place some time before the actual departure since it was in the nature of a fiesta. Dressing his units as nearly in parade uniforms as circumstances permitted, San Martín led them to the square before the cathedral where the priests blessed them. Doña Maria Remeditos, San Martín's bride, and her ladies had completed work upon the silken flag of the Army of the Andes; and this, too, must be blessed since otherwise it would have no protective value. It was in the purity of white and the pale blue of the pampa sky, with a coat of arms between a laurel branch and one of olive, symbolizing on the one hand victory and merit, on the other, peace. Above the Andean crest, with the sun of the Lautaro Lodge rising over it, two hands lifted the Phrygian cap of liberty.

"Soldiers!" announced the general, standing bare-headed with the banner, newly sanctified, floating above his tousled hair, "This is the first flag of independence to be blessed in America!"

It wasn't, of course, but the multitude roared its approval, cannon thundered, and church bells pealed.

Lamps burned brightly in San Martín's study that evening, the light reflecting from the great wall map. The general had invited Christian to join him for coffee in the late stillness. Now, bemused and mellowed slightly by brandy, he felt the need to talk with this Englishman, who had never betrayed a confidence or failed to deserve a trust.

"There are six viable passes across the barrier, over a spread of 140 leagues," he remarked. "I have decided to employ them all, in order to confuse Marcó until the last moment and hopefully cause him to split up his forces until each fragment is too weak to contain any thrust of ours. If he does that, he is a fool, but wars are won against fools, or rather because of foolish mistakes."

"Quite so, General."

"The first of these will be organized in La Rioja in Córdoba Province, which has ancient commercial ties with such trans-Andean mining towns as Copiapó and Huasco. With our skilled officers, about 200 volunteers, some of them Chileans and the other *riojanos*, will make up the endeavor. They are imperfectly armed but have plenty of enthusiasm, will cross the Andes and fall upon the Copiapó district, which our spies assure us is very lightly held."

"And the next expedition?"

"That will come from the district of San Juan. Sixty soldiers and about 400 militia will cross the mountains by either Calingasta or Azufre Pass. They will strike at La Serena on the coast."

"Those columns are so small their operations amount to guerilla actions."

"Almost, but not quite, Mr. Fletcher. Guerillas operate without plans to advance or withdraw, seizing what opportunities present themselves. These forces will operate under tight control as part of a master plan. They are regulars, not bandits."

"And to the south, sir?"

"One column is of much more respectable size, the other smaller. The weaker will thread Portillo Pass, that closest to Santiago. The other, by Planchón Pass, will be commanded by Ramon Freyre and hopefully will accomplish a great deal in the central valley of Chile south of Santiago. It is small, but the area to be penetrated is a hotbed of patriot activity and it will draw much strength from Chilean irregulars."

"What about the central passes, sir?"

"On the basis of your maps, our principal command, under myself and with O'Higgins, will go by way of Los Patos. The artillery, however is a problem. The only pass through which it can move is Uspallata where Marcó already is entrenched and will defend himself resolutely."

"Unless we cross in force through Los Patos first, luring his men away."

"Exactly. Las Heras is directed to leave here on the eighteenth, cross to Chacabuco if he can, and entrench himself. Beltran, with the artillery, will leave two days later, to follow him up. But I do not wish to risk loss of the guns. Their protection is Las Heras's principal mission."

On January 9, the officers left to take over the northern columns, whose operations had to be timed meticulously to bring the offensive units into Chile at the precise instant. January 14, Freyre left for the south. Four days later Las Heras pulled out with his command for Uspallata. The general and O'Higgins quitted headquarters January 24, with the Los Patos command.

Las Heras, as it turned out, struck the most opposition initially when Marcó's field commander, Marqueli, fearing that the principal threat would come through

Uspallata Pass, sent a reconnaissance force under Colonel Miguel de Atero to scout the defile. It surprised a patriot post half a day's journey from the pass, taking seven prisoners, none of them fortunately cognizant of San Martín's plans or the movements of the other units of the army and, thus, able to give no information of consequence to the Spaniards. After a second light skirmish, Atero became convinced the patriots were quitting the mountains entirely and pulled back. Thus he inadvertently opened the way for Las Heras and Beltran.

San Martín and O'Higgins meanwhile had swung north until they reached the Los Patos River, following it as had Christian earlier toward the snow-capped upper Andes. The worst of the climb was above 9,000 feet where altitude sickness was as much a threat as the cold, although most of the soldiers rode mules; so only a few were afflicted by the *puna*, becoming so ill they had to be sent back.

The upward march continued in good order. By meticulous attention to the instructions of the general, who had anticipated everything, the army persevered. Each day's march was short, in order to give men and beasts maximum rest. Hannibal and Napoleon, crossing the Alps, had encountered rather fewer difficulties because their transits were made at two-thirds the altitude of the Andean passes and while the way was longer, their road was easier and better defined.

On February 2, the army began its long descent toward the valley. San Martín dispatched 200 men, under Major Antonio Arcos of the engineers, by forced marches down the hideous slopes, to wrest control from the first royalist outpost in the lowlands.

Las Heras moved ahead cautiously, meanwhile, through more-traveled Uspallata Pass, his command a day or two ahead of Beltran's artillery and baggage, confident of the ability of that amiable friar to follow swiftly. Beltran was in his glory with a challenge to his ingenuity at every moment. If the trail was too narrow for gun carriages, sappers widened it; if the way was too steep, ropes were manned to hold back or pull onward the carts and guns; if torrents must be crossed, his prefabricated bridges were thrust across; if wheels could not negotiate a steep pitch, rawhide slings were passed under canon and guns enabling them to skid across.

The army inched forward with not an ounce nor a mechanism lost, everything dragged, pulled, rolled, skidded onward, ever onward, over the rocky summit of the highest mountains of the New World. Scouts well in advance occasionally sighted royalist patrols, but none of the enemy apparently were aware of the doom lowering upon them. Las Heras and Beltran gained the valley without further clashes.

"May I congratulate you, General," smiled Christian, below Los Patos Pass to the north, "on a difficult undertaking accomplished successfully?" The last of the army filed down from the high reaches toward the Putaendo River. San Martín had drawn his saddle mule up on a stony promontory to observe the parade of men and animals and supplies passing before him. Restlessly eager, the Englishman had joined him, sensing no fear of the approaching actions, only the joyous anticipation that he was coming home again—to Chile, the land he had made his own.

"Congratulations are not yet in order, Mr. Fletcher," said the general, with a worried frown. "If Las Heras has not arrived on this side and Beltran, with the guns, we ride into a trap. We are doomed."

Swiftly San Martín dispatched the arrogant Soler, impossible to manage, whose only priceless qualities were his brilliance, his superb competence as a soldier, his tenacity in battle—his, well, his exasperating indispensability. With two squadrons of grenadiers, he was directed toward the enemy by three captured royalists who under persuasion had given up important details of the Spaniard presence in the valley. Joined then by his cavalry, Soler led into the valley of the Putaendo at last. Eager to plunge into the sweet, cruel, flowered land of his adoption, Christian secured the general's permission to join the advanced elements under Captain Necochea, scouting toward San Felipe, an important crossing of the Rio Aconcagua.

The royalists awaited them at San Felipe, but suddenly they were worried. Fugitives from the north staggered into the Spanish camp after midnight, almost at the same hour as the arrival of other refugees who had fled before the advance of Las Heras, now nearing the community of Santa Rosa. Each party reported the patriots' advance in widely-separated forces, apparently of some strength. The engineer officer, Atero, now commanding at San Felipe, was deeply concerned. He was not a line officer; this situation clearly was beyond his training, although he was a brave man. He sped couriers to Marcó, in Santiago, with his disquieting intelligence, and prepared to face the enemy. But which enemy? In which direction?

Atero had about 400 men, among them excellent veterans of the Talaveras Regiment of Toledo in Spain, but others were green recruits, or worse. It would be better, he decided, to withdraw toward Santiago and fortify the crest of the Chacabuco Mountains, probably defendable, while strong royalist forces rallied behind him. They could come to his support in time, if they hurried. He ought first to send a reconnaissance to the north, to test that wing of the invaders, see what it was made of, he thought; but the operation would be risky because it would bare his back to any advance from Santa Rosa. Nervously Atero considered his dilemma from all sides. Then he pulled out his main body for the south and the Chacabuco range.

Scarcely had he gained the Chacabucos when he ran into a travel-stained command of 200 carabineers under Colonel Quintanilla, up from Santiago and full of fight. Reinforced, Atero moved back into San Felipe, which the invaders had not yet reached. Now Atero could scout to the north, and at two o'clock in the morning of February 7, a strong royalist contingent moved out. It struck a small unit of mounted chasseurs under wise old Necochea. He lured 300 royalist cavalry in pursuit of him, pulling them away from their infantry and guns. When well clear he turned like a puma, cutting up the enemy so badly that Spaniards pulled back to San Felipe once more, destroyed the bridge across the river, and withdrew finally toward the south. Could such tigers be anything but the vanguard of a mighty force?

On February 8, the patriots camped in the valley of the Putaendo so recently evacuated by the enemy. A scouting force was sent to the south toward the Chacabuco range. These mountains, nearly 4,000 feet in elevation, oddly slashed east and west across the valley, forming a perfect screen for the Santiago region beyond. Christian, with eight men, had been sent to probe the steep skirts of the range. He observed some movement to his left and laid a careful ambush, a Mapuche ambush, easily capturing a patrol as small as his own. But it was not royalist. It was a reconnaissance from Las Heras! Eagerly Christian dispatched a note to San Martín with the longed-for news of the reunion of the two forces.

"And Beltran?" demanded the general tensely.

The courier grinned. "Yes, sir," he replied. "He lost many mules in the crossing, but he is down safely."

"The guns?"

"Every gun has arrived. All are already on limbers, ready to fire. The gun crews are intact. Chaplain Beltran directed me to request your orders."

CHAPTER TEN

Withdrawal of the royalists cleared the valley of the Rio Aconcagua of Spanish troops. Now, with the joining of the two divisions, the patriot army would be ready to move south, given a few days' rest for the men to recuperate from the arduous passage over the high mountains. The two armies thus could muster their strengths; the issue would become a decisive test of their power.

Although San Martín would not hear of it immediately, success had attended the two light columns operating in the north. They had reached the coast and had easily seized their objectives. The two commands to the south of Santiago could not make their fortunes known to the general until later.

Scouts now reported to San Martín that the royalists were bivouacked near the Casas de Chacabuco, a nest of adobe buildings a mile or two south of the Chacabuco Range, with a screen of riflemen to defend the crest against a patriot advance. At a staff meeting, the commander appeared thoughtful, consumed by the myriad details of the impending battle.

"Marcó is uncertain," he said, considering each word carefully. "He has issued an astounding proclamation telling the Santiguenos of an enormous 'defeat' we have suffered, though conceding that we hold this entire valley. He affirms faith in victory, yet holds all ships at Valparaíso in case he has to abandon Chile. If his deductions convince him that our main threat is from this valley, Marcó would have but one recourse: attack. This he will do, coward though he is. It is here, gentlemen, that the fate of Chile—for the moment, at least—will be decided.

"Our mission is to sweep their riflemen from the ridge and get our chasseurs, infantry, and guns up there ready for deployment," San Martín continued. "We must hold our attack until the Spaniards are fully assembled to make the test as decisive as possible. I have no wish to break up their units merely to occupy territory. Only so will our road to Santiago and central Chile be open with no fear of a mightier engagement sometime later."

"Do you know their strength now?" asked Christian.

San Martín indicated a small bright-eyed man, disguised as a peasant. "Juan Estay tallied them as they left Santiago," he assured his officers, "and estimates the enemy as fewer than 1,800, including two companies of the Talaveras Regiment from Toledo—they will not run—and what is left of the Abascales carabineers, also good soldiers."

"The general is well informed."

"Juan Estay also tells me that Colonel Ildefonso Elorreaga has arrived at Chacabuco, or should have, with the Brigadier Rafael Maroto who is in overall command. We can handle the Spanish force readily, I think, if we fight to the limit of our capability and above all, tenaciously. Stubbornness wins battles more than strength. Stubbornness and will."

San Martín then turned to his battered field desk and picked up a paper. "This is the order of the day for the Army of the Andes, February 11, 1817," he read, slowly. "The army will be split into two principal divisions and a small reserve corps. The first division, of about 2,000 men, commanded by Soler, will include the chasseurs battalion . . ." He detailed numerous instructions, then concluded:

"Soler will take the right, scaling the Chacabuco Range and moving to the right of the Casas de Chacabuco from where he will launch the principal assault on the enemy's left flank. O'Higgins will work up the ridge directly to our front, clear it of enemy riflemen, and descend against the Casas. He should wait until Soler is in position, however, before attacking seriously."

San Martín finished reading, laid the paper down, and faced his officers for the last time.

"Mr. Fletcher, you will accompany O'Higgins. The positions and assignments for the rest of you have been cited. The army will rest until midnight. We will move out with moonrise at 2:00 A.M., to reach the crest of the mountains by daylight or shortly before. *Vaya con Díos*, gentlemen."

The divisions marched south by the same road for a time, Soler in advance, O'Higgins following a league in the rear. After some distance, Soler sheered off to the right. O'Higgins continued by the "Royal Road," as it was called, winding and zigzagging laboriously up the steep sides of the mountains toward the crest. They gained the ridgeline, meeting no obstacle; then, the Spaniards finally detected the unavoidable sounds of moving men and animals. Though they could not clearly identify the threat in the darkness, with the first light they sounded an alarm, which brought assistance under command of Marqueli.

Marqueli dispatched a courier to Brigadier Maroto at the Casas for reinforcements. He then ordered a volley loosed at the oncoming patriots, but since his men were firing downhill, their shots did little damage. O'Higgins' soldiers contemptuously continued upward, holding their fire. As they approached to almost within bayonet range, Marqueli saw that he was about to be overwhelmed. Rapidly he withdrew, sending his soldiers tumbling and racing down the southern slope of the ridge toward the Casas to rejoin the main Spanish force. By eight o'clock, O'Higgins was master of the crest.

Through a telescope, Christian observed the royalists breaking up their bivouac below them and, with the swiftness and sureness of the veterans they were, assembling in good defense order.

Meanwhile, on the right side the column led by Soler labored around the rugged western side of the bowl of Chacabuco, seeking to gain the flank of the Spaniards. To the left rose the high Andes they had crossed, still streaked with snow, glittering in the early light. Much lower and closer in, dyed black and sullen red, a range of volcanic hills thrust southeasterly, enclosing the cup on the side opposite Soler. Only to the south, toward Santiago twenty leagues beyond and not quite in view, was the way open, a fact that Maroto no doubt had considered.

It was calm and still on the height. Only the gasping of the men and the stamp of a mule broke the quiet. The guns were far below, their location revealed by the curses of struggling artillerymen, desperately trying to wrestle the heavy guns upward. At O'Higgins' feet a canyon plunged down the slope, directly toward the Casas de Chacabuco. Bernardo was eager and determined to throw his force down this canyon, assembling and reforming at its mouth in preparation for the battle he anticipated before the Casas.

Finally, O'Higgins' advance units leaped down the slope in pursuit of the fleeing Spaniards. The fiery leader, his blue eyes dancing, drew his sword and slashed forward, calling over his shoulder: "Onward men! Already they are in flight! Onward!"

"But, sir," protested Christian, "we must await Soler! The general said that Soler must be in position so that the attack can be coordinated!"

"Nonsense, Fletcher," retorted O'Higgins, his face flushed. "They are fleeing. We cannot waste this opportunity!"

Heedless, he plunged down the slope after the skirmishers. Fletcher shrugged helplessly and bounded after him, and the army, in a straggling column rather than battle formation, swept downward in magnificent pursuit hard upon the enemy's heels.

Maroto was scribbling a dispatch to Marcó, at Santiago, for reinforcements when a courier burst upon him, telling of the commencement of the battle. He ordered his junior officers to hold their positions at any cost, sent some support to Marqueli hoping to blunt the assault, and hastily formed the main body of royalists and moved them up the valley. He had covered half a league, or midway to the foot of the mountains when the first fleeing segments of the defenders fell amongst them, sporadic firing revealing how closely they were pursued. Maroto formed a battle line, its flanks anchored upon breaks and hills on either side. Although the site was impromptu, the terrain favored the royalists, for the patriots would have little room to maneuver. Maroto ran up two cannon while O'Higgins had far outdistanced his own guns, and the royalists commander placed two rifle companies on a small hill to his right to harass oncoming enemy. This veteran officer knew what he was about.

O'Higgins' advance slowed, his view of the enemy screened by hills. His vanguard of Mounted Grenadiers came under royalist fire and pulled back in order to avoid useless sacrifice, as their leader prepared to form up his major battle lines.

"To attack, eh, General?" demanded Christian mischievously.

"You are ready now, eh Fletcher?" retorted Bernardo, the glory of impending battle shining on his face. "I thought you advised us to wait!"

Christian laughed. The exultation had infected him too.

"It's too late now, Bernardo!" he cried. "We have chased them this far. Now they are ready. Soler or no Soler, San Martín or no San Martín, we have got to fight. Aye, we've got to win!"

"For Chile and for glory!" cried the officer.

It was now ten o'clock. The midsummer sun blazed with suffocating power. No one knew where Soler was. He had vanished among the high folds of the foothills. No matter. O'Higgins ordered the grenadiers to sweep the right flank, break through the enemy, and roll him up. He would command the shock troops, aligned and eager for battle.

"Soldiers!" O'Higgins cried in a penetrating tenor. "Chileans! *Plateños!* I pledge you death or freedom! *Vivir con honor o morir con Gloria!* Live with honor or die with glory! The brave follow! Columns to the charge!"

Drums sounded, trumpets blared. The men surged forward through the heat and the dust with O'Higgins at their head, shouts upon their lips. Christian had no choice but to follow the Irish-Chilean, and no wish to do otherwise.

But almost at once the fight turned against the patriots. Because of the terrain, O'Higgins' remounted cavalry could not turn the royalist left or even bring battle to it. The infantry of some 800 effectives possessed spirit in great measure but not the muscle to split a such a large and disciplined enemy line.

O'Higgins' assault was hampered by a shallow ravine and, although the royalists suffered some losses, they did not give one inch.

San Martín, meanwhile, descending from the ridge with Soler, was warned by the banging of royalist artillery and the battle smoke that action had commenced. He directed Soler to hasten so as to bring the great weight of his command into action, for without this support he feared that O'Higgins might come to disaster.

Although repulsed, O'Higgins had suffered only slight losses. He busied himself straightening out the confusion in his ranks, swiftly reorganized the division, and, better informed of the natural obstacles confronting him, prepared to move forward again.

Christian quickly swept up firearms from three wounded soldiers; and running ahead of the advancing patriots, he gained a small cover two-thirds of the way to the royalist positions. Throwing himself prone in the deep shade of a *quillay* shrub, he carefully placed the three weapons before him and awaited some movement by the armies. He had a clear view of the royalist forces, now readied and standing at ease, a cluster of 5 or 6 officers behind them, perhaps 200 yards distant. Christian thrust a rifle before him, carefully hollowed depressions for his elbows. Timing, he knew, was of the greatest importance. The effect of his shots would be doubled if they came at the height of action, when the issue was in doubt.

Patiently he waited. A *tábano* buzzed noisily past his head, settled voraciously on his bared wrist. He blew it away and wiped the moisture from his brow lest it dribble into his eyes at a critical juncture. Behind him came the urgent cry of bugles, the ruffle of drums, the shuffle of marching feet through the thick sand. In a moment the patriot formations swept past him. Their fire rattled and plunked into the royalist formations, dropping a few men, spinning others wounded against the earth where they writhed in agony. Two slave battalions were in the foreground, led by O'Higgins, Cramer, and Conde, advancing at a dead run toward the Spaniards, bayonets fixed, screaming war cries as they came.

The shock of battle reached Christian. In a moment of intense confusion, he clutched the first of his weapons. He held his breath and aimed carefully at the glittering uniform of the field director, standing in full view studying the battle. He squeezed the trigger. The target humped in startled anguish as the heavy leaden bullet appeared to break him in two, his hands flying out from his sides as though grasping for eternity. He bounced upon his back, leaving a gap in command that would not be filled in this battle. Swiftly Christian reached for the second of his weapons and fired at another officer. He sent the second reeling to earth as well. Never had Christian been so calm, his aim so sure, his confidence so great. With his third weapon he put still another officer out of combat.

With the destruction of their chief and his two principal assistants, the royalists began to fold in upon themselves. Then the fury of a charge with leveled bayonets shattered their spirit. The lead battalions were irresistible in their assault, engulfing the enemy like a torrent, crying "Victory!" as they plunged through the Spanish lines. Directed by their officers, they turned back and chopped the royalists' shattered elements to pieces. The cavalry under Captain Necochea and Zapiola had finally pierced the enemy positions. They swung around at a gallop where terrain permitted, hacking with bloody sabers at reeling fragments of the Spaniards. The battle in these moments was decided with startling swiftness, though far from finished.

The patriots had smashed the provincials, but the Talaveras veterans moved forward against the liberator flank, disorganized in its pursuit of the enemy. Upon a relatively open field, the Spaniards abruptly sensed a fresh danger. They sought to form a defensive square against the still greater division of Soler, now crowning a nearby hill, at last having negotiated the tortured terrain in its long march down the divide.

The Andes chasseurs poured rapidly down upon the battle scene, falling like a thunderbolt upon the Spaniards, breaking up their defensive formation. Then they advanced irresistibly upon those royalists still in position about Maroto, who had watched the two-hour engagement from a safe distance. Observing that all was lost, he turned and, with what effectives he could salvage, fled. The straggling remnants of his command dribbled after him, futilely trying to avoid slaughter, the tempest on all sides howling and cackling at their heels.

Disintegration of the Spanish forces had begun with Christian's destruction of the point of the enemy pyramid, its command; it was sealed by Soler's crushing assault. San Martín, hastening onto the field on a lathered horse, took over command; but the battle itself was finished. The grenadiers chased the fleeing fragments three leagues on the road to Santiago, slaughtering the fugitives at will, before pulling back to the field of victory.

By two o'clock the patriot units had reassembled near the Casas de Chacabuco. The Army of the Andes had suffered negligible losses, not more than 150 dead and wounded, although the former included two gallant captains.

By contrast the royalists losses were enormous: more than 500—some said 600—slain, including three of their most prestigious officers. Six hundred men were captured, 32 of them officers including Major Vicente San Bruno and Sergeant Villalobos, both believed to be guilty of atrocities against patriot irregulars; their fate was predetermined by their own cruel natures. The San Martín forces also captured immense battlefield loot including two cannon, more than 1,000 muskets and rifles, proud battle flags, and vast stores of powder, balls, and food. "Almost enough for a second battle," calculated Christian as he watched the arms and stores being collected.

O'Higgins grinned. "With you on our side, we scarcely need it. Again I owe you my gratitude. Had it not been for you and your marksmanship, the result may have been disastrous."

Christian, as a man ever aware of his own weakness, was embarrassed; he had not realized that the other was aware of his feat nor that it was anything but a soldierly effort to affect the outcome. He said as much, mumbling to himself; but O'Higgins shook off his protestations.

"No, Fletcher," he declared. "In the heat of battle, winning is the only thing. But reflection afterwards enables one to see more clearly wherein the victory and credit lies. Had you not wiped out their command, they might have triumphed. At least success would have been Soler's and not of this division. I shall never forget it!"

CHAPTER ELEVEN

O'Higgins, still flying high from the glory of victory, presented a strange contrast to the reserved and almost melancholy San Martín at officers' call that evening. The reeking funeral pyres had consumed the enemy dead; and San Martín, weary with war, seemed almost to regret the action; but perhaps he was simply preoccupied with plans yet to unfold.

Christian brooded quietly at the outer fringe of the group, saying nothing, thinking upon the mysterious destiny, which had brought him to this region and this company, yet whichever held him apart. A man of the sea, he now appeared wedded to this land. By inclination he was a man of peace, yet he found himself inextricably embroiled now in war. Life indeed was unfathomable, an endless, cruel mystery.

"Gentlemen," began the commander when all had assembled, "the first battle is ours. It did not develop quite according to plan; but battles rarely do, and success is the important thing. That we have achieved. The glory is yours, and I congratulate you." Even in the hour of triumph, San Martín could not quite overlook that the engagement had not been carried out in accord with his plan, with its meticulous attention to detail and the strategy over which he had labored so long. Rather, it had been won by impetuosity, doggedness, and the luck of war.

"Sir!" O'Higgins exclaimed, "now that the Spaniards are on the run, if the general will assign me 1,000 mounted men, I believe I can cut off the fugitives between Santiago and the sea, thus separating them from Valparaíso. That would prevent them from reaching Peru and fighting us one day again."

San Martín turned his brooding gaze upon the young man for a long moment, then thoughtfully shook off the suggestion.

"It will not do, my friend," he replied, "although your bravery and efficiency are well proven this day, to the gratitude of all who would liberate the land. We have fought here fewer than 2,000 of the enemy, and he had 6,000. Thus he still has four. Should you be trapped and destroyed, we would lose not only a friend and comrade but our only opportunity to free this realm. I cannot permit it. We shall remain here for the present until the situation better defines itself."

"Are we not even to harry them? Drive them like lemmings into the sea?" questioned Soler boldly. "Not even occupy an abandoned Santiago?"

"We do not know that it is abandoned," the general sighed, wearily. "However I have decided to send Necochea with 200 grenadiers toward the city to determine its status. If it is clear, the army will follow."

Christian readily secured permission to accompany the cavalry. It met no royalists, no one in fact but Indians and sturdy laborers on the forty-mile march to the Mapocho.

The command clattered openly across the bridge and into the city as swarms of Chileans howled their greetings. Not even a vestige of royalist forces remained in Santiago. Drawing his horsemen up before the government palace, Necochea conferred briefly with Don Francisco Ruiz Tagle who had hastily been elected provisional president by citizens anxious to preserve order; and a courier was dispatched to San Martín to inform him that the capital city was open to the Army of the Andes.

Christian listened idly to the chatter about him as he wandered along the facade of the cathedral, his mind turning from this day to that lonely night of long ago when he had been a silent witness at its great Mass. Many a league had been covered since then, but some things had progressed little, including the prejudices of his mind, and somehow that disturbed him. With that thought he grew once more aware of a Presence quietly waiting for him to make a move, to say a word. He cast such thoughts from him with irritation. Turning away he all but collided with a figure darting out from the great doors. He sensed before actually recognizing him that 'twas Ishmael.

"Eh, eh, Fletcher!" greeted the old man, a grin splitting his ancient face. "I thought I would find you at Santiago. I hurried here, in fact, to welcome you."

"I thought you were with Francisco Villota or some of the mountain boys harassing the Spaniards in the south. How do you come to be here?"

"Pancho is dead. He died a hero, trapped in a defile holding off the royalists, so his patriots could escape. He is gone."

"And Freyre?"

Ishmael chortled. "Eh, eh! As successful as a bishop. He negotiated the pass and collected the patriots to him like a cow gathers ticks. After a skirmish or two, he inveigled Moraga out of Talca, then occupied Curicó and San Fernando. A great soldier is Freyre. He has so tightly held the southern valleys that Marcó feared to flee south and now can easily be penned up at Valparaíso, when the beach is occupied by San Martín."

"He won't do it."

Ishmael stared open-mouthed, speechless briefly, for once. "How—how is that, Fletcher?" he asked then. "Why, he can destroy the royalists with little risk and only a passing effort. Ye say he will not?"

"He will not. He is a wary man, Ishmael. His strategy binds him. Brave, but cautious."

"To the point of timidity?"

"No. But he must be certain before he will act. Certain and ready. That takes time."

"Chacabuco will have to be fought again, in that case," Ishmael muttered. "Perhaps more savagely than before. Without control of the sea, he must either vanquish the royalists on land or wait for them to muster enough to destroy him, which they surely will attempt to do. Victory lies within his grasp. This reluctance to engage could lead to a debacle."

"Aye, my own."

Ishmael turned quizzically.

"My 'stick,'" explained Christian, wearily. "My ancient, enduring 'stick' that I keep hoping has dropped from my back but never quite does. In one form or another it brings disaster. It was always so. In my bones I feel it again."

"Bosh. 'Tis ever in your mind alone."

"Where else? Where else could it be? Is not the mind sufficient?"

Ishamel turned away to scan once more the unfinished cathedral, listening to the hum of the crowd. At length he and Christian found a bale of dried hides at one end of the plaza and rested upon it. The afternoon faded into dusk. Cathedral bells called the hour to the citizens. Soon almost no one was about.

"Abascal will no doubt send reformed regiments back," mused Christian.

"José Fernando de Abascal is viceroy of Peru no more," corrected Ishmael. "Joaquín de la Pezuela has taken over—an even better soldier, a graver threat."

"I remember him from Salta," said Christian. He fell silent, then demanded sharply: "How do you know everything, Ishmael? You are a library of facts, possessing more than any mortal man ought."

Ishmael responded after a breath or two. "I have good ears. A good memory. I am interested."

"Why?"

Ishmael stirred uneasily. "If San Martín gains command of the sea," he blurted, shifting the subject adroitly, "he might prevent the royalists from returning."

"And transport his own Army of the Andes to Peru when ready," agreed Christian. "I have no doubt Chileans would make good sailors, given time—and ships. They might have the time, but they cannot manufacture the vessels."

"They could seize them, when they put in."

Christian laughed. "*If* they held the ports, and if the ships put in, and if they are of Spanish flag, and if they are poorly manned. Those conditions cannot all be met, not even with the help of your all-powerful God."

"Perhaps, Fletcher. There are other means, however. Ships may be obtained elsewhere, in America, or in England, and a sea captain of competence and courage could be employed. I see no other way to bring this war to a happy conclusion now but by attacking the royalists from the sea. Can you?"

"I suppose not."

"Could you bring up the subject with the general?"

"Perhaps within a week or two, if I have the opportunity. The idea would be meaningless, however, without some assistance from abroad."

"What kind of help?"

"Oh, someone who would know ships and seamen, who might suggest men and cull out the worthless scoundrels who would flock about such a mission. A guide, a mentor, a friend."

Ishmael scribbled on a paper he had drawn from his pocket.

"Give General San Martín this, Fletcher. Tell him to instruct his emissary who would go to England, I presume, to find this man, who can be very easily located, since many know of him. He will provide all the things you mentioned. He is privy to funds that will be of great assistance and to powerful forces too."

Christian turned the paper against the flickering light of plaza torches. He made out the dim writing with some difficulty, but with greater wonder: "Sir Harry Gladden-White," it read. "Of Plymouth Docks."

Christian raised his eyes and stared at Ishmael. Their glances locked. Ishmael did not speak, nor did Christian. Christian refolded the paper and pocketed it. He lifted his shoulders ever so slightly, but the unanswered questions remained.

And so it was that a noble-minded patriot, Don José Condarco, was dispatched to England. He was commissioned to seek out and enlist a suitable naval officer, if possible, or a sea captain with sufficient battle experience and the luck of victory upon his shoulders. Don José was granted authority to borrow money, to purchase warships or have them built, and in every way to develop and expedite the patriot cause. He was to reach England, according to his initial report, in the last days of April or early in May.

CHAPTER TWELVE

Christian had no concern for politics, so he scarcely noticed when San Martín was offered the political leadership of Chile, nor his rejection of it. Bernardo O'Higgins accepted the post of supreme leader, bearing the role as easily as the embroidery on his cuffs, with grace and integrity. The independence of Spanish America would come, Christian believed, by arms, by fighters, and by guns and ships—never by politics. Of course, once the soldiers win the war, the politicians would inevitably corrupt the freedom and engage in small-minded rivalries over power, graft, and greed to their hearts' content.

In the weeks following Chacabuco, the military situation clarified gradually, like standing water losing its silt. The Rio Maule, which severed Chile from the Andes to the sea immediately to the south of Talca, formed the new frontier between patriot-held territory to the north and the royalist empire to the south. Within the patriot region, in addition to Santiago and Talca, lay San Fernando and Curicó. Beyond, in territory held by the Spanish, were Concepción, Talcahuano Bay, Chillán, and Valdivia. Unless the patriots could somehow seize Concepción and Talcahuano Bay, reducing the enemy to dependence upon distant Valdivia, the final decision for independence must come north of the Maule.

Once the provisional government was firmly established, San Martín made a hurried trip to Buenos Aires to confer with his old friend, Pueyrredon, incidentally meeting José Miguel Carrera, who refused to even shake his hand. Carrera's head buzzed with conspiracies for his own return to Chilean power, now that the Spaniards had been bested. His brothers were actively engaged in the plotting, but the real instigator no doubt was Javiera, whose home had become a nest of sedition. Ah, well, all that could be dealt with later. Yet an eye must be kept on the sinister family. San Martín secretly persuaded Pueyrredon to recall the valiant Soler, if not partisan, at least a friend of José Miguel Carrera, and thus no longer to be fully trusted—whatever his magnificent military contributions.

Upon his return to Chile, San Martín plunged into study and planning of patriot operations south of the Maule directed against Concepción, and he dispatched Christian to assist as he might. Royalist forces in that region were commanded by Colonel José Ordoñez, a veteran of the Napoleonic wars and the most able of

Spanish officers. Ordoñez had strongly fortified the Tumbez Peninsula, above Concepción and confined the important Talcahuano Bay on its western side.

Freyre had kept the enemy to the south well occupied. He was joined in early March by Las Heras, down from Santiago, who assumed overall command. Las Heras and Freyre plunged into royalist territory through Chillán and on Easter Sunday occupied Concepción itself, abandoned by Ordoñez and his Spanish forces, which retreated to their protected Tumbez Peninsula. The opponents glared menacingly at each other across the great military works, the one too strong to be easily crushed, the other too weak to successfully attack. Upon Las Heras' request, O'Higgins was sent south to assume command of the patriot forces; but before he arrived, the royalists were reinforced; and on May 5, Ordoñez attacked, only to be driven back with sizable losses.

O'Higgins bustled in, fairly bursting with ideas. He conceived the idea of attacking the Tumbez royalists by land and sea, in a manner of speaking. Five large and unwieldy rafts were to be constructed and 300 men embarked upon them by night, hopefully to land on the lightly-guarded west coast of Tumbez.

"'Tis a venturesome business," muttered Christian dubiously. "Risky. Ordoñez has as many defenders as you have for the assault, plus guns of his ships and their crews. Can your luck carry such obstacles?"

"I've sent to the general for reinforcements," defended O'Higgins stubbornly.

Winter rains set in before the attack could be launched. The countryside became a swamp. Fever decimated the ranks. The clumsy rafts could not be satisfactorily moved. Finally even O'Higgins gave up his dream. It was just as well. He could never have breached the royalist defenses and at length came to recognize that fact. The stalemate continued almost without incident.

San Martín, meanwhile, busied himself recruiting at Santiago and elsewhere in free Chile, the new volunteers more than balancing the desertions of those who were tired of war and slipped away. By December 1, the patriots numbered 4,400 men, well-drilled and many of them proven soldiers. But Chile sorely needed naval strength as well, a fact of which the general became increasingly aware. North American whalers, engaged in illicit trade along the coast, could sometimes be persuaded to serve as privateers, for the loot might be significant, but the patriot naval element remained negligible and of little combat value.

San Martín sent three ranking officers to O'Higgins in the hope they might prove of assistance and lend sorely-needed military expertise: Miguel Brayer, who had been a lieutenant general under Napoleon; Alberto Bacler d'Albe, a military engineer of great skill; and Captain Jorge Beauchef, also an engineer. Brayer was quickly named chief of the general staff for the Army of the South, although Christian dourly considered him too old for useful service and overranked. Yet O'Higgins welcomed the trio with confidence and anticipation.

Brayer immediately organized an elaborate attack on the Tumbez Peninsula royalists, which proved a disaster. "His plan was too complicated for our forces and the leadership we have," Christian growled to O'Higgins.

"With a renewed effort, we still might launch a successful attack."

"You cannot be serious!" Christian exploded, "You could bang away with every man you've got and never overrun them now. Ordoñez is no fool. He learns from every failure of ours. You'll never take him—not here. The best we can do is withdraw north of the Maule and unite with the general. We can only hope the Spaniards will follow us out to some place where we can fight them on even terms. We aren't equipped, manned, or gunned for sieges or to attack fortresses."

"I thought Brayer was supposed to give military advice, not you."

"You can see what kind of advice he gave you. I could do as well. I am no trained officer, but I have eyes."

O'Higgins set down his coffee mug. "Well," he sighed wistfully, "we failed to take them that is certain. The general has informed me that his prisoners report a major Spanish contingent of veterans are about to embark for Talcahuano Bay, bringing a new commanding officer."

"Who?"

"He is one who served in Chile before. Also, he is a relative of Pezuela and that does his military future no damage. His name as prisoners reported it, is Mariano Gregorio."

"Mariano *who?*"

"Gregorio. Have you heard of him?"

Had he heard of him? Memories drenched him like a tidal wave. Valdivia. Roca Montalván, reduced to a quivering mutilated wretch, destroyed by this arrogant reptile who felt no emotions but his own. Yes indeed, he had heard of Gregorio. He had known him, would never forget him. He still had a score to settle with him. Or did he? Somehow the hatred, his desire for vengeance, seemed a bit forced now. It had happened so very long ago. Gregorio had drifted into a dungeon of his mind and would ever remain there. If opportunity afforded, Christian would gladly kill him; but wearily he found he had lost the compulsion to do so; Gregorio did not seem now to be worth the effort. He hated him, but no longer with the old passion to make his death a matter of utmost requirement. Let Gregorio determine his own fate; 'twould be savage enough, if there were any justice. But justice there was not. Only power, and luck.

CHAPTER THIRTEEN

The dispatch to Chile of heavy royalist forces did not generate the panic one might have supposed but rather a general belief that this was a move of desperation on the part of the viceroy. Thus there grew a confidence that Chile could well defend herself. Every movement of the enemy, rather than concealed from public view, was given the widest publicity to arouse the general ardor. San Martín stated frankly that the royalist maneuvers would bring about the long-anticipated decision so much the quicker, that thereby Chile would confirm her freedom forever. It would require only sacrifice and devotion on the part of everyone. More sacrifice. More dedication.

San Martín wrote to O'Higgins confirming Christian's advice that he fall back, hoping to draw the enemy after him to where he could meet the Spaniards in open battle. The royalists lacked cavalry, O'Higgins possessed it in abundance; the enemy, therefore, might be sabered to bits.

Reinforcements assembled by Pezuela for use in Chile included nearly 1,000 men of the veteran Regiment of Infante Don Carlos and 1,000 provincials of the Regiment of Arequipa. These, together with artillerymen, sappers, dragoons, and lancers to an overall number of about 3,300 men, were destined for Talcahuano Bay. The plan was that the united force would destroy O'Higgins, move quickly by sea to Valparaíso, and smash the patriot forces gathered at Santiago. It was a masterful plan, but it had to contend with the luck of war.

Before even the advanced elements reached Talcahuano Bay, O'Higgins had withdrawn northward toward the Maule River, leaving a wasteland behind him. Fifty thousand refugees accompanied the patriots in a massive exodus of misery and fear. By late January they were north of the river, and O'Higgins was settled at Talca, on the Lircay River.

Gregorio meanwhile had disembarked his troops and learning that the Chileans had evacuated Concepción, resolved to pursue the withdrawing enemy as swiftly as possible, which was exactly what O'Higgins had hoped he would do. The royalists outnumbered the patriot Army of the South, although they in turn would be outmanned if O'Higgins and San Martín could combine forces.

Toward the end of the month, tentative contact was made between Gregorio and O'Higgins, and a decisive action seemed in the making. On March 4, the royalists occupied Talca, from which the Chileans had withdrawn. The armies, almost equal in discipline and spirit, jockeyed cautiously, each attempting to learn more of its enemy. San Martín hastened south to assume overall command of the patriot forces, bringing some strength with him.

Gregorio and his able second in command, Ordoñez, were as eager at first for a general engagement as were the Chileans, although as the action neared, Gregorio found his resolution ebbing. He had been assured by Pezuela that he was to fight a rabble, an enthusiastic but untrained peasantry. Instead, he learned he was faced with a military force almost equal to his own, uniformed, ordered, well led, proud of past victories. It was unnerving. He owed this command to Pezuela, his relative, not to his experience nor his record as a soldier, which included no field experience whatsoever.

While the royalists formed their major defenses at Talca, the patriots drew up theirs a league or two northward at a place called Cancharrayada on a tributary of the Lircay on whose banks, contemplating the distant view of Talca, Christian once more reunited with Ishmael who had come south with San Martín.

Below them the patriot soldiers and camp followers—the men who yesterday had been *huasos* and clerks, laborers and farmers—and their women busied themselves establishing their camp. Cannon were being dragged into position and ponderously hoisted around into firing readiness. The camp was a busy, noisy place but strangely set apart.

"If I were the general, and especially since 'tis Holy Thursday, I would call the soldiers to prayer," said Ishmael, solemnly.

Christian exploded into laughter. "Why, Ishmael, don't you suppose the clerics with the Spaniards are praying also? What is God going to do—count the prayers on either side and deliver the victory to the most numerous? I think the number of cannon is likely to prove more decisive!"

"One doesn't pray for victory unless one is a child," Ishmael replied. "He prays only that what he does is right, is somehow in tune with God's will, and that God's will be done."

"Even unto defeat?"

"If one's cause is not just, yes."

"'Tis my observation that the cause your God is apt to favor is that with the most muscle," jeered Christian. "I think he likes to be on the winning side, rather than to see that the right side wins."

"Ye should not speak so, 'tis blasphemy, or near it."

"How can one blaspheme something in which one does not believe, Ishmael? You know I do not believe in your God."

"Believing or not believing on your part has nothing to do with his existence. You could 'not believe' for eternity; and that would have no effect whatsoever upon his control over the destinies of men and nations, or upon your fate, for that matter. It might show your obtuseness but would say nothing for his omnipotence."

Christian flung a pebble far down the slope, watching it bound and rattle among the talus at the foot. He felt the Presence again, listening intently, waiting for him. And somewhere inside, a part of his heart frightened him by yearning to respond.

"Life is like that fringe of rubble down there," he said bitterly, flinging the words like stones into the deep silence inside where the One waited, unperturbed. "Scattered shapes heaped in no order, no purpose. How do you *know* that God exists? How do you know that he controls men or nations? To me it all seems chaos. The only rightness is that which is nurtured within men's souls; some having it, others not. I suppose you would say that it is all revealed in Scripture? I have tried to read Scripture. I found it a meaningless collection of words. Scripture, I've found, is unreadable."

"No, Fletcher, that is not so. The pattern is there. It can be discovered. You have difficulty reading the scripture? Would you not have equal difficulty reading an arithmetic book? A medical tome? A dictionary? Those must be studied, not read, yet few would belittle their importance. So it is with scripture. If you approach it honestly, study diligently, you will find the pattern. And you are unlikely to find it anywhere else. Nor is that all. It behooves you to intelligently seek that pattern, for otherwise your existence becomes a shambles, meaningless, purposeless. Your life becomes death. With the Bible, death becomes life."

"You speak in riddles."

"Which, too, are a pattern. So is prayer. Prayer cannot alter battles, but it can influence purposes and improve the men who fight, exalt their motives."

"Possibly," said Christian without conviction. "If you'll excuse me, however, I will go and see to my guns while you pray for us both."

The patriot army was camped in two principal divisions, the right commanded by an officer named Quintana, the left by O'Higgins; and by seven in the evening, the soldiers, some wearied by several days of forced marches, had settled down peacefully. The full moon was obscured occasionally by rolling masses of clouds that threatened but appeared to have no rain in them.

This scene of peace contrasted vividly with that at Talca, where the royalist encampment was in ferment and so was Mariano Gregorio's stomach. He did not know what he should do but shrink from committing his army irrevocably to battle. Perhaps he might withdraw to the south and hope for an improved opportunity in an unpredictable future. Ah, perhaps that would be best. He brightened.

"It is my wish," the royalist commander said to his officers, "that we pull out under cover of darkness and strike for Talcahuano Bay where we can defend ourselves as before until we get further reinforcement or in some other way find it possible to fulfill our mission."

A murmur of dissent rippled through his assembled officers, but it was the resolute Ordoñez who replied. He had no confidence whatever in this perfumed and supercilious gadfly and had followed his aimless directives only because of the iron discipline of his two decades of service in one of the finest military organizations of the world.

"That cannot be done, sir!" he countered now, with spirit, his tone one of near-defiance. He had served under such superiors before, many of them. Too many. One might humor them for a time, but when a campaign might be won or lost, one could no longer defer. Risking insubordination, he said: "We can strike them tonight, hit them hard and generate enough confusion to render them incapable of defense, put them to flight or at least secure an advantage we can employ with benefit tomorrow. There is no safety in retreat, no desirable end in submitting to besiegement in this miserable hamlet or even at Talcahuano. It must be attack and attack now, within minutes. Attack, sir! There is no other way."

A chorus of officers roared approval. Gregorio paled in the heat of it because of Ordoñez's soldierly defiance and doubtless through nervous fear, as well. This sort of battle, this fighting in the blackness of night where success depended upon the superb handling of a mighty force in the face of one nearly equal to his own, was not to his taste. Abruptly he turned command over to his subordinate and retired to a village convent.

At eight o'clock with the clouds covering the moon, three columns of royalist infantry and four squadrons of cavalry moved as silently as possible upon the distant campfires of the patriots. Ordoñez commanded the center column, Colonel Primo de Rivera and Colonel La Torre the other two. A battery of a dozen cannon was left on the outskirts of Talca to cover a retreat, should that become necessary.

From spies San Martín had heard of unusual enemy movements and rightly calculated that these foreshadowed a nighttime attack. He began to reshuffle his forces so that they might counter any enemy assault, but the attack came before his dispositions were complete and in the precise turmoil of this movement. It struck vigorously at the patriot left wing, the engagement soon breaking into a confusing maelstrom of small actions in which soldiers fired as often upon friends as foes. O'Higgins had a horse shot under him, a musket ball smashed through his right elbow, and in the confusion patriot cannon were abandoned. A detachment of grenadiers fled in panic and an aide-de-camp of San Martín was slain within a few feet of the general. By eleven o'clock, the disorganized and battered patriot elements had swirled backward across the river, small groups streaming northward after what had been a disaster.

To Christian the outlook could not have been more bleak, eased only by his survival and the grim option open to him still of fleeing over the mountains to safety. Yet he knew he would not go. It would be better to face execution, death, in this land than life elsewhere. He had become too old to run. The years were piling up swiftly; there were not many left. Why should he seek to extend them unduly? To what end?

With daylight and reassessment it became clear that disaster was but a partial debacle, perhaps not irretrievable after all. The right wing under Las Heras, who had assumed command when Quintana wandered off into the obscurity, had withdrawn in fairly good order, though he had lost about 500 men through desertion. By forced marches he moved his command toward San Fernando to the north, where within two days it rejoined the gathering remnants of the left, along with most senior officers. The nucleus of the army had been saved, and with it rose anew a confidence in the "independence of America," as San Martín gravely observed. He ordered the reunited command to fall back on Santiago, to reorganize rapidly, to meet the inevitable royalist pursuit.

The defeat and the recovery from it proved not to be the sum of his concern at this critical juncture. Christian and Ishmael had been with the right wing with Las Heras and so had missed the principal action. Twenty-two hours after Cancharrayada, Christian reached San Martín's headquarters upon an exhausted horse, bringing a Sergeant Rodolfo Flores with him. He found San Martín white-faced, the strain of battle, sleepless nights, and ancient ailments had etched deep lines into his face, though the old cordiality remained.

"I would not have troubled the general at this time except that Sergeant Flores has a report on a matter of pressing concern," blurted Christian.

Flores said that he had been urged to desert "for the good of the fatherland" during the dark hours following the attack, that half a thousand of his comrades also had been contacted and had melted away from the army into the night.

"So?" demanded San Martín, with a touch of impatience. "Who urged you to do this? Spanish agents? Dissident officers, perhaps?"

"None of these, my general," replied the sergeant. "The voices were those of the Carreras—their agents."

San Martín started. The weariness vanished. "How so, sergeant?" he asked. "The Carreras are jailed at Mendoza or in exile at Montevideo. How could they be in Chile?"

"No, sir, not the Carreras in person. But Carrera men, nonetheless, sir. They started rumors which circulated like grass fires among the ranks that night when all was confusion. The word came: 'The Carreras will save the army, will save Chile! Desert, make for the mountains, wait. The Carreras are coming!'"

"It is a fact, sir, that our column lost upwards of 500 men that night," said Christian. "And since then others have not returned. I thought the general ought to be aware of how this may have come about."

"You did well, Mr. Fletcher. You invariably do well." He hurriedly dispatched an aid to awaken O'Higgins. That officer, his bandaged arm bulky and still causing intense pain, hastened to the headquarters tent.

"Always the Carreras," he sighed, after hearing Flores' report. "They are my enemies. They invariably appear at times of crisis, only to make the crisis worse. The only freedom they seek is chaos, to make a profit for themselves from other men's struggle for liberty."

"The solution?" demanded San Martín, knowing well the solution. "They are your problem. What do you wish done with them?"

Bernardo shrugged. He glanced in hesitation at Christian, questioning.

"I am a seaman, sir," Christian said slowly. "The punishment for mutiny—mutiny at sea, is hanging—if the mutineer is caught. You have already caught yours." He added, with a faint grin, "But mutiny is scarcely proven. We have only the word of—"

"The word of an honest soldier," interrupted O'Higgins. "We know the double-dealing we have always had from the Carreras." He had made his decision; General San Martín instantly grasped it. This was war, a time for harshness. The entire Revolution might well depend upon elimination of this cancerous group.

"I will send Dr. Monteagudo, our quartermaster general, to Mendoza," said San Martín, his voice flat as a calm sea. "He has been with me a long time. He will be discreet. None will ever know or be able to prove anything until long after this war is over—win or lose. Then it will not matter."

"Except that Chile will have a larger measure of peace," added O'Higgins.

"Precisely."

CHAPTER FOURTEEN

Rumors of the catastrophe of Cancharrayada preceded the first couriers to Santiago, and no man could explain by what means the news had arrived. It generated panic in the capital, largely because those in power, wishing to "spare the populace terror," tried to withhold the facts and consequently magnified the turmoil they sought to avoid.

And turmoil it was. The populace flowed to the plaza before the government palace that Bernardo's father, Ambrosio Higgins, had helped create, frantically seeking details. Since accurate information was not forthcoming, they came to believe the disaster had been of more than human proportions. There was an "eye-witness" report of the death of San Martín; another "saw" O'Higgins fall, mortally wounded; another reported that the royalists were sweeping unopposed up the high road to Santiago, and nothing could stop them. The only recourse was to flee—up over the Andes to Mendoza once again. Women wailed and wept at leaving their homes; men flung saddles on mules and loaded them with what valuables might be at hand. Provisions were rounded up; caravans clattered toward the mountains. Church bells tolled, more from fear than because this was the end of Holy Week. Santiago was on the brink of becoming a ghost city. The furor was contagious and deadly.

A few quavering shouts of "Long live the King!" were raised here and there, and one optimistic royalist shod his best horse with silver to present to Mariano Gregorio for his triumphal march into the city. If half a hundred organized royalists had appeared, they could easily have swept into Santiago and presented the city to Ferdinand VII. But none appeared. For Gregorio again was in command far to the south, and he was no Tamerlane; he dallied fearfully, and that was fatal for him and for his king.

Amidst the tumult one figure galloped about on horseback, calling for a semblance of order. This was Don Manuel Rodriguez, veteran and honored guerilla—although rumored to be a friend of the Carreras. He called a mass meeting on the plaza to elect him emergency dictator, raised a squadron of horses which he called the Hussars of Death to defend Santiago, or as some suspected, to turn it peacefully over when the enemy appeared. His efforts, however, did promote a measure of tranquility; and after three days and two nights, the panic had subsided. Now the people were wary, resigned, fatalistic.

Fugitives from Cancharrayada swooped in upon the city like driven birds. The patriots had indeed suffered a reverse, they said, even a measure of disaster, but perhaps all was not lost. Much of the army seemed intact, though scattered. No one knew where the ranking officers were. San Martín was out of contact. So was O'Higgins. Brayer arrived on jaded horse, fleeing with professional skill. The defeat appeared irreparable; and he said he would leave for Buenos Aires within a few days, although he did not leave.

At this point Bernardo O'Higgins and a few others, among them Christian and Ishmael, clattered up to the palace on horses trembling with exhaustion. Despite his wariness, the agony of his wound, and the underlying anxiety, O'Higgins immediately signed a decree "thanking" Rodriguez for helping to reestablish order while moving at once to thwart Rodriguez's more elaborate aspirations.

Christian awoke at an early hour, stiff and sore from the bone-pounding ride to the capital, reflecting on what age did to a man. He glanced across the room at Ishmael, flat on his back, the white fringe of his halo rising and falling gently in rhythm to his light snoring. Ishmael almost never seemed visibly tired, never seemed to ache, appeared as enduring as the mountains or the sea. Who was he? What was he? Christian knew almost as little about Ishmael now as he had when the old man had fished him out of the sea nearly a quarter of a century ago. How could a man be so mysterious and yet so open? And that one so inherently sensible could have such unbelievable theories was beyond belief, at least to a man of any sense. He stared as a harsh rap at the door interrupted his meditation.

"General O'Higgins requests your presence, sir, when convenient."

"Very well, corporal," replied Christian, grimacing as he swung his aching legs free and groped for his boots. He knocked once at the general's door and found the other all but surrounded by aides, orderlies, and papers, the place a turmoil.

"Ah, good morning," grinned O'Higgins. "Slept well, I hope?" He seemed to pay no attention to his own painful wound. His injured arm was in a fresh sling, held close to his chest.

"For all of three hours," growled Christian. "But enough. Is the war still on?"

O'Higgins laughed. "So far as I know it is." He closed the door after clearing the room; and when he turned to the Englishman, his face was grave, solemn.

"You have been my mentor, whether you were aware of it or not. Perhaps because I need to share responsibility for distasteful tasks. Not really, though. The question of war will resolve itself within a week or so, when San Martín arrives and we have our big battle somewhere. But the question of treachery remains." Christian lifted an eyebrow, and the Chilean continued. "Rodriguez. Ah, he is the problem. You will shortly observe how the people follow him. Well they might. His record is a heroic one. For a year he alone rallied the patriot bands in the mountains and fought the Spanish occupation bravely and well. That is what makes him so difficult to handle. If he had only proven a traitor. Just once!"

"Why not use him then, as he is?"

"Aye, we could do that, Christian. But the war, the land war, is nearly over for Chile. The peace still must be won, and that will prove more difficult. Rodriguez will figure largely in that and, I'm afraid, to the disadvantage of the nation."

"How so?"

"He has a single weakness, but 'tis major—he is a Carrera man."

"Are you sure?"

"Yes. He was their secretary for a time, when they were active in Chile. He has since become a lawyer."

"Naturally."

"How so? Oh, never mind. In any case, he is still prominent in the Carrera faction. He is popular, and he is brave and impetuous and presents us with a hopeless impasse."

"So he must be eliminated."

O'Higgins flushed. "I would not put it so, so bluntly, but—well, yes. I dread it but see no other recourse. Do you? It seems too much like murder for my taste."

"War is murder. Thousands have died already. More will die. Some of them will be as good men, and as worthy, and possess qualities as fine as this Rodriguez. Deaths in wartime are fate, the fate of the losers, perhaps the sacrifices to victory, the payment for—for something. I know not what." Christian hesitated, then continued. "But if I may make a suggestion? Do not be hasty in disposing of this man. If it is done before the Carreras are dispatched, trouble surely will erupt. There is time enough. By himself he is harmless, however much of a nuisance he may be. Wait. Set the hour but by the proper clock."

"I had thought that you—"

"That I would kill him?" Christian shook his head. "You knew that I would not do that, Bernardo, although I have no scruples against it that I can summon to mind. But to me it smacks overmuch of assassination. I can understand the need, but something within me prevents my executing such an order. Is that as weakness? If it is, so be it."

The other was silent, brooding.

"'Tis not that I lack the courage, Bernardo."

"Oh, I know that, Fletcher," agreed O'Higgins testily. "I also knew somehow you would not do it. I understand. And I am grateful for your views, reinforcing my own." He smiled, ruefully. "I'll find another, whom I can trust as I trust you. But later, as you suggest. Not now."

San Martín reached Santiago at twilight on March 25, accompanied by his aide and a small picket of cavalry, trottering smartly despite their weariness to the government house where he conferred briefly with O'Higgins. News of his arrival spread swiftly; and the general, resignedly, addressed a worried crowd that clustered beneath a balcony on which he stood:

"Chileños!" He cried, in the only speech of his life. "By reason of one of the misfortunes men cannot evade, our army has suffered a reverse. But you will observe that the army is resurrected, that it faces the enemy as before, secure in the inexhaustible resources of our country, in your valiant support, in the glory of their courage and discipline. While the tyrants have advanced fearfully, I have assembled a force of more than 4,000 men to face them, without counting the militia.

"Shortly I shall return to my field headquarters. I assure you we will very soon give you a day of glory such as southern America has never known before! Courage, faithfulness, honor! That we possess. That we demand of you. Victory! Victory over the Spaniards will be ours!"

San Martín was as good as his word. At the head of the veterans who had dribbled into Santiago to be reassembled, he shortly left for the Plains of Maipó, two leagues toward the southwest, where he had determined the royalists would be met as they crept up from the south, resolutely, if slowly.

The other division of the patriot army, salvaged from Cancharrayada, worked north under the acid-tongued Las Heras who shortly deferred, by reason of rank, to Colonel Ramon Balcarce. Balcarce arrived with his new command at Maipó on March 28, where the work of forming a new army out of pieces of the old continued at a feverish pace. And within the incredibly short span of ten days after the patriot's debacle, the banners floated proudly again over the "miracle of San Martín," as Christian put it, a united force, ready for battle, risen phoenix-like from ashes.

The army was composed now of 5 battalions of Chilean and 4 of *Plateños* infantry, in all nearly 4,000 rifles, 2 regiments of Plateño and 1 of Chilean cavalry, for an additional 1,000, and 22 guns with their crews, a combined force of more than 5,000 men. The royalists, too, had been reorganized after their victory, numbering about 5,500 men. The enemy command reached the Maipó River on April 2.

The Maipó Plains are bounded on the east by the Mapocho, flowing southwest from the city of Santiago; on the north by the range of hills separating the prairie from the Valley of the Aconcagua River; on the south by the Maipó River. To the west the plains rise gradually. From Santiago pointing toward the heart of the plains is a stretch of rather elevated land, the *loma blanca*, so named by reason of the whitish chalk of its formation. On this broad ridge the patriot army was encamped. Beyond the western extremity of the ridge and across a shallow valley rose an isolated hillock of triangular shape, low in profile, soon to be occupied by the royalists. Beyond the far angle of this hill was the Espejo Hacienda, from which a gently rising roadway mounted the slope, being bordered by vineyards and the mud walls of corrals. Between the royalist and patriot forces lay a swath of open ground, varying in width from 300 to more than 1,000 yards.

San Martín, leaving semitrained militia to protect the capital, now divided his regulars into three divisions, commanded respectively by Las Heras, Rudecindo Alvarado, and Quintana, while Balcarce was in overall command of the infantry and the general retained that of the cavalry. He issued minute instructions to the troops to guide their conduct in the impending action and to promote their aggressiveness.

A day of indecisive skirmishing occupied the advanced units of the opposing sides as the royalists completed their crossing of the Maipó. By the evening of April 4, the antagonists were in position, as ready as they ever would be.

Shortly after dawn, San Martín, attended by Christian, Ishmael, and a small escort, rode to the lip of the *loma* to observe the final preparations of the foe. "I feared that they would extend far west and secure the road to Valparaíso for the retreat," he mused, studying with field glasses the sprawling enemy emplacements. "But the fools did not. We have them! What primitives these Spaniards are!

Gregorio is a greater dunce than even I thought. I take the sun for witness that this day is ours!" Christian grimly smiled. He hoped the general was right.

What San Martín did not know was that Gregorio, fearful as ever, had indeed ordered that the Valparaíso high road be occupied to assure his escape should a reverse occur; but doughty old Ordoñez, grim veteran that he was, had foiled the directive. He had ordered a favorably-inclined officer to move up within sight of the road but not to seize it. Like Cortez burning his boats at Vera Cruz, like Darius destroying the bridge of escape over the Danube, Ordoñez sought to make impossible Gregorio's escape from this battle before its decision. "I will make the coward fight," he assured his aides. "There will be no convent for him this time—he will bear arms or be butchered with the rest of us!"

Sunday, April 5, was one of those rare perfect fall days in the southern hemisphere, fitting indeed for the fate of a continent to be decided. The royalists swung into a crescent-shaped line along their triangular hill, a line that was bowed slightly inward at the center. The Spaniards were under the command of Ordoñez, who controlled the right wing battalions with supporting elements, Colonel Lorenzo Morla leading the center, and the right wing commanded by Colonel Primo de Rivera. With armies so evenly matched, the victory would go to the best led and the troops imbued with the greatest spirit and determination. It has always been so in war but never more so than on this bright day in central Chile, where 300 years of Spanish domination were to be tested against the worldwide surge of revolt, the struggle for independence on the part of diverse peoples everywhere who wished to be finished forever with foreign rule.

Desultory fire had been maintained all morning by both sides, merely to remind each other that a general engagement was imminent; but at half past eleven, San Martín ordered his artillery to open in full force upon the royalists. Half an hour of cannonading did not suffice to move the enemy from a single position, and the general directed his right and left divisions to move forward on the attack. The enemy responded as heavy fire was instantly poured upon the advancing patriots. From his vantage point with the staff, Christian could watch the action as though on a chessboard before him, the racing figures of men and horses. He could hear only the distant thunder of battle, nothing of the cries of battle fury, the screams and moans of the wounded, the dust, the sweat, the agony, the glory of action. Yet Christian could feel it all, sensing it more strongly than if he had been directly engaged in the battle.

The attack progressed in the face of stubborn resistance as Las Heras advanced swiftly toward the two squadrons of dragoons pouring down out of the hills to receive him. But furiously attacked by this saber-wielding horsemen, the royalists quickly fled back into the high ground. Infantry fire repulsed Las Heras at last. Regrouping, he attacked again and again, causing growing tumult in royalist positions.

On the opposite flank, three patriot infantry battalions under Alvarado hammered home a vigorous assault with artillery and cavalry support. Their advance was halted and disorganized by the resistance; the patriots, with heavy losses, pulled back to their original positions. Defeat seemed not only possible then but actually imminent.

Observing the Chilean difficulties, Ordoñez ordered his troops to pursue. But once they had dropped to the lowlands separating the two sides, patriot artillery, loaded with grape, caused such fearful casualties that they, too, were forced to withdraw. The royalist center now came under the concerted attack of two patriot battalions, one hastily formed at Santiago from such artisans and locals as could be assembled, hastily drilled and disciplined, who now fought with fearsome valor. This gave the Chileans time for reserves to be pushed forward.

San Martín, surrounded by his aides, watched the engagement unfold with his customary detachment; but the mounting strain was evident in the deepening lines about his hard mouth. He directed the reserves to race to Alvarado's support and carry the drive once more to the enemy. In the furious fighting that followed, the day was decided. The royalists abandoned the high ground on their left in order to reinforce their center. In doing so they abandoned four cannon, reducing the fire they could deliver. The chasseurs of Freyre and Santiago Bueras now seized this unexpected advantage and fell as a lightening bolt upon the Spaniards. Although Bueras died, Freyre pushed on, dispersing the royalist horsemen in all directions. He swung about then to reattack the enemy center. The royalists, deprived of their cavalry and artillery on this wing, still resisted fiercely. The Spaniards were compressed now into a more compact line, royalist foot soldiers contending valiantly with an enemy that had somehow become more numerous, more vicious.

A determined bayonet charge was decisive, attended by strong and persistent blows against the wings. The royalists began to fall back, although still in good order, tightly reined in by their officers. However, their losses had been relatively enormous. The butchery mounted as the patriots pressed their advantage.

San Martín hastily scribbled a note to O'Higgins who had been forced to remain in Santiago because of his wound and fever: "We have completely dominated the battle. A small remnant fled. Our cavalry pursues them to finish it. The fatherland is free. God guard your Excellency many years—*San Martín*." A courier dashed for the capital, bearing this first announcement of victory, but he was too late.

For already O'Higgins was galloping across the tortured field toward the general's position where the tricolor floated lazily and the knot of aides and officers pressed about him in this moment of supreme triumph. Bursting through these people, brushing past Christian, O'Higgins spurred his horse alongside that of the general, leaned forward and threw his one good arm around his neck, shouting: "Honor to the savior of Chile!"

"Excellency," cried San Martín, at once in high humor, "Chile will never forget the name of the illustrious invalid who this day of days presented himself on the battlefield in such a state!" Side by side the two raced their horses forward toward the houses of Espejo, to direct the final stages of engagement. Behind them, struggling to keep pace, rode the others, Christian bringing up the rear. Their services had not been required this day, but their places of honor had been assured by their service on the long, rocky road to liberty.

Mariano Gregorio, escorted by his dragoons, was already prepared to flee of course; but nearly 2,000 royalist soldiers, though bereft of cavalry and cannon, still defended themselves vigorously, determined to fend off the patriot attacks and die, if they must, valiantly. In their hopeless struggle, Ordoñez seized overall command, with no thought of victory, only of fighting like the professional he was until destroyed. Perhaps when night came, some Spaniards might cut their way through the south, possibly even gain the old sanctuary of Talcahuano. Meanwhile, one must fight, for that was to be a soldier.

But the patriot force was too overpowering now. Though suffering grievous losses, they stormed across the open field toward the hacienda irresistibly. The assault was renewed; patriot cannon battered down the walls. Troops overran the outer defenses.

They pinned their victims within the shattered structures while the guns chewed them up. The patriots burst into the central plaza, under intense fire from all around. Infuriated rather than cowed by this, they smashed through hasty barricades, knifing, bayoneting, shooting every living thing save those who surrendered, sweeping the houses with fire room by room until the hacienda was blanketed with dead and washed with blood. Christian, Las Heras, Freyre, and other officers with great difficulty managed at last to still the tempest, cool the flaming embers of hatred, saving the lives of some few hundred remnants of the enemy. Finally, between five and six o'clock, the struggle was over.

A few Spaniards escaped to the south, across the Maipó, racing against destruction toward distant Concepción. An additional handful fled with the terrified Gregorio. But these were the only significant members avoiding the holocaust. The victory was complete and decisive.

The enemy had suffered losses of 1,500; 2,289 were taken prisoner, many others declared missing. Among those seized were 174 officers, including Ordoñez himself; Primo de Rivera; and many others. The patriots, too, had suffered: 800 or more slain, 1,000 wounded. But they won the field—and the nation—and the continent. No wonder the whole valley of Santiago was filled this night with delirious joy!

"The men deserve to howl," grumbled Las Heras, wearily. "The wolves have fought their war. The monster is slain."

Christian nodded, reflecting upon the thousands of brave men who had begun that day with health and spirit, hopes and ambitions, and who now lay contorted, shattered, and stiff with death in order that their cause might triumph.

CHAPTER FIFTEEN

San Martín lounged at a table with a few faithful officers and friends, among them O'Higgins, Las Heras, Freyre, Christian, and Ishmael. It had been a long day, hard and brutal, with a riotous city eager to do the general every honor for his glorious victory at Maipó. Now it was late. The others had departed, full of wine and exhausted with patriotism. Only the tight inner circle of battle-forged companions remained, to finish off the bottles and relax in their knowing that the war had been won, even though mountainous problems remained.

"We still face the most difficult part, do we not, General? Winning control of our coasts and the sea, defeating the Spaniards in Peru? And then what?" The questions were common to all minds present, voiced by no one in particular.

San Martín stared owlishly at the group, his face flushed with wine. Rarely, perhaps never before, had he allowed himself to drink too much, but this was a great occasion. For this one brief moment, it was appropriate.

"Then what? When it is over? Oh, we shall all go into exile," he sighed. "Those of us who survive." He twirled the glass once more.

"That is the fate of the Latin liberators, you know. We win our people freedom, and then they exile us. Now the English, Mr. Fletcher's compatriots, do it differently. They revere their heroes, place them in high office, and keep them there until they are old, and tenderly care for them into senility and until they die. But we Latins exile ours. This is the story of Latin Americans, over and over, and I am one of them."

Christian listened to the general and thought of his own "stick"—how San Martín reflected it! And how could Christian's curse possibly influence the lives of San Martín, O'Higgins, and these others? Yet he was convinced that it somehow did. The debacle the general predicted would come about not through blemishes in the Latin American character, but through the moral blemish within Christian, their friend and colleague.

"So," San Martín swayed slightly, turning to leave, "so we shall give them liberty, and when they choose to make swine of themselves, they will have the freedom to do so, and we shall be exiled. But first we must assure their freedom to treat us so."

San Martín dispatched word of the victory of Maipó to Buenos Aires, along with a note to Dr. Monteagudo at Mendoza; and the same day that the news of the victory passed through that city, Luis and Juan José Carrera were led from the city jail and shot in the plaza. No one, of course, knew who had directed that it be done, although the authorities went through the motions of a brief inquiry. News of the double execution was overshadowed by the report of the great victory, and Javiera wept bitter tears more from frustration than sorrow. Quickly she sent the unhappy report across the wide river by dispatch boat to José Miguel, self-exiled at Montevideo, warning him to remain away and brood about vengeance at some later time. Carrera, with the printing press he had brought with him, ground out sheet after sheet of diatribe against the victorious leaders; but his influence was dwindling as his remoteness from events grew and he could no longer be considered the leader of a potentially powerful cabal.

Not only had he lost the help of his brothers, but Dr. Rodriguez, who alone remained a potent threat to the inner stability of the newly freed land, was taken from Santiago toward Valparaíso, though destined never to reach that city. The official story held that he was shot while attempting to escape. From this incident, José Miguel Carrera found still more ammunition for his shrill printing press; but by this time, almost no one was listening.

"Too bad," murmured O'Higgins when he heard of the assassination. "Pity," echoed San Martín. Christian said nothing. Had it not been inevitable?

Several days later he met with O'Higgins in a quiet office of the government house at Santiago. San Martín had already departed for Buenos Aires to seek financing for the naval and expeditionary phase of the war.

"Our principal objective now is to create a fleet," the supreme director announced. "That's why I called you here, other than to enjoy your company, of which I have not seen much during recent hectic days."

O'Higgins quickly turned to the matter on his mind. "We've had some good fortune at sea, largely because the Spanish are overcommitted and undergunned along our coast. We've captured some vessels, seized a couple by subterfuge. But it's one thing to gather in a chance ship and another to organize a fleet."

"Aye. Who captains the vessels you have?"

"English and American adventurers. They are brave enough, but it's the lure of prize money that holds them. Few have any affection for our cause."

"To be expected."

"Captain George O'Brien, late of the Royal Navy, took out the *Wyndham*, which he renamed the *Lautaro*, a forty-four-gun onetime East Indiaman, and engaged the Spanish *Esmeralda* of equal battery off Valparaíso. He almost took it. Had he not lost his life, he would have attained everlasting fame. We have heard from Condarco at London, however. He reports he has found us the perfect commander for our fleet, when we get one."

East Indiaman-
a merchant ship used to trade with East India.

"Oh? Who is he?"

"Lord Cochrane! England's boldest and most successful sea dog, victor in a score of engagements. Do you know him?"

Christian's mind whirled backward to that fearsome evening in London so long ago on his way to meet Bligh. He remembered as vividly as though the encounter had only the moment before taken place, that tall, intent figure bounding down the walk upon him, then hastening away in the carriage marked *Cochrane*.

"Aye. I have met him briefly. When will he arrive?"

"His heart was set upon bringing us a new war-steamer, which is being constructed to his specifications in British yards; but there are many delays, and perhaps he will come without her. Just as well. I have never seen a vessel driven by steam rather than the faithful wind, have you? I could have little trust in it, but to Lord Cochrane 'tis a novel toy; and considering his unbelievable record, we have to take his notions seriously; he has earned a right to them."

"Any idea when he will show up?"

"In midspring, I think. November, if he can round the Horn in good time. That is always uncertain."

"I remember."

O'Higgins looked sharply at him, then continued: "We must present him with the components of a fleet, if we can. That is why I am asking you to go to Valparaíso and assemble it. You are the only ranking man among us with extensive sea experience."

"How do you know about my extensive sea background, Bernardo?"

"Didn't Ishmael pluck you from the waves?" teased the other. "Do you think a man can hide his profession? I imagine you fight as well on the sea as on land. We trust you. That is more than can be said for the lot of adventurers we have skippering our vessels."

"What would be my rank, or am I merely to be an agent of the government?"

O'Higgins spread his hands. "I would suppose your rank should await Cochrane, to see what he selects; but for the present it could be almost whatever you wish—enough to impress that assortment of captains, surely."

The first warship to fly the Chilean flag had been the 16-gun Spanish brig, *Aguila*, lured into Valparaíso harbor where she was seized and renamed the *Pueyrredon*. She was immediately employed to rescue a number of patriots exiled to the Juan Fernandez Islands, 400 miles off the coast. Among those brought back was a young artilleryman, Manuel Blanco Encalada, once a naval ensign. Since he was the only native-born officer with any naval experience at all, he was named admiral of the fleet—a fleet which did not yet exist.

The *Lautaro* shipped a crew of 100 foreigners and 250 Chileans, including marines. All of her officers were English or North Americans, not one capable of giving orders in Spanish. A 20-gun American privateer was bought and renamed the *Chacabuco*; a 16-gun American brig was renamed the *Araucano*. Later the 64-gun *Cumberland* was sent out by Condarco and renamed the *San Martín*. These were all reliable ships; but they ill-compared with the Spanish naval power in the Pacific, which counted fourteen vessels mounting 331 guns and an additional 27 gunboats with more coming out from Spain, according to report.

On May 21, 1818, the fifteenth Spanish expedition to reinforce garrisons in America since the Revolution broke out sailed from Cadíz for the Pacific under escort of the 50-gun *María Isabel*. It included 2 armed vessels among its 11 transports with more than 2,000 men. One transport was forced to drop out at Tenerife. On August 26, a second transport, the *Trinidad*, with 180 soldiers aboard, cast anchor at Ensenada, near Buenos Aires, the crew having mutinied and shot their officers. Thus the plans and destination of the Spanish convoy became known to the patriots on the east coast and, as rapidly as horses could race, to those in Chile. O'Higgins sent a copy of the intelligence by swiftest post to Valparaíso for the information of Admiral Blanco Encalada and Christian.

Christian had already reported to the admiral aboard the *San Martín*. "The supreme director suggests that you serve as sailing master and executive officer," grinned young Blanco. "I think that is a splendid notion, especially since I scarcely know a foresail from an anchor and have never fought a ship! I suppose if you do not assist me, I would have to turn to those ruffian countrymen of yours, whose barbarous language I do not even speak."

Christian threw back his head in laughter. "As the admiral wishes," he agreed. "But I want only to serve under your command. I am too old and have no desire to seek fame or fortune or anything else, save to be useful."

Raising anchor in obedience to orders, the *San Martín* put to sea in late September, accompanied by the *Lautaro*, *Chacabuco*, and *Araucano*. The directive from O'Higgins ordered the patriot ships southward toward Santa María Island, which Christian remembered off Talcahuano Bay, to look for targets of opportunity, being aware of the possible approach of the Spanish convoy.

The sea was calm but not dead calm, long swells rolling the ship pleasantly, reminding Christian that he was now in his primordial element, on a quarterdeck, a situation he had not enjoyed for almost thirty years. He returned to this pattern as though in naval command all of his life, so lasting is the training of youth! Ishmael, his cheeks pale beneath the white fringes of his beard, had not yet found his sea legs, Christian noted with amusement; but as for himself, the roll of the ship and the creak of her timbers, the full-bellied straining of her sail, the orderly discipline of top and gun decks were a balm to his soul. This was where he belonged.

Christian employed the voyage south to put the ship in order, drill the gun crews, create some sort of system for the disparate elements who manned this vessel. He found the complement willing and diligent, primarily due to the prize money in the offing, naturally.

Three ships of the Chilean squadron slipped in behind the northerly marker-rocks of Santa María and anchored in the cove on its southwestern coast. The *Chacabuco*, separated by a strong wind and imperfect handling, remained somewhere out to sea; and the *Araucano* was sent about fifteen leagues north to reconnoiter Talcahuano Bay. The Chilean ships flew the Spanish flag for the benefit of any spies ashore, the maneuver proving profitable when a small cutter appeared shortly, bearing a letter to any friendly ships along the coast. Seizing the cutter and its letter was quickly done.

Blanco scanned the missive quickly. "He says that he has dispatched two transports on to Callao. His ship, the *María Isabel,* remains at Talcahuano to gather in any other transports which make a landfall. I suppose that he is in the bay alone."

"The convoy must have been scattered rounding the Cape," said Christian, thoughtfully. "Little wonder." He leaned against the bulwark. "Let's seize her, sir!" he blurted suddenly. The fire of adventure brightened his eyes.

"Do you think it practical, *señor* Fletcher?" asked Blanco dubiously. "She must be anchored directly under the guns of the fortress guarding the beach. I admit that the *María Isabel* would be a most worthy prize if she could be taken. But could we cut her out? The firepower would be overwhelming, I would expect."

"No, Admiral Blanco! Half her crew will be ashore. We can run down on her and drive her men below decks before they can collect their wits. The shore cannon are of no importance. Our ship is a gun platform, more than equal to any minor fortress. She can maneuver at will, swing her broadsides at the whim of her master. A fortress's guns are fixed. They must be moved and aimed individually, and that allows for a great deal of human error. If we are damaged heavily, we can always stand off to sea."

"If you think it prudent, *señor* Fletcher," the young admiral reluctantly consented. "But you assume command. I do not feel adequate to undertake so risky an adventure, and I should not wish to jeopardize it."

"It shall not fail, sir!" Christian promised in high good humor. "Or, if it does, perhaps we shall sink together."

Christian ordered the *Lautaro* alerted and both ships made ready for sea. They arrived off Talcahuano in good order, the harbor being protected by two fixed batteries, placed separately to deliver crossfire upon the roadstead. By adroit maneuver, much of their firepower could be nullified, Christian believed. The emplacements were several hundred yards inland from the beach, and their gunners must take care not to inadvertently hammer their own *María Isabel*.

On October 28, driven by a fresh northerly, the patriot craft glided into the harbor and bore down upon the Spaniard anchored under the shore batteries. As Christian predicted, at least half of her crew was ashore. She greeted the vessels, flying British flags, with a gun salute that was promptly replied to. Then within musket range, the Chileans ran up their own flags with loud cheers. Outmanned and outgunned, the Spaniard delivered something of a ragged broadside which, aimed and fired in haste, ripped holes in the sails but did little other damage. The *San Martín* replied with a broadside of her own, scarcely more effective, but the commander of the *María Isabel,* faced with overwhelming odds, cut the cables and ran the ship aground, part of the crew pulling for shore in long boats, the remainder maintaining a light and ineffective fire with the poop guns. The Chilean banged away until the *María Isabel*'s flag was run down, two boatloads of marines were aboard her, and seventy-five infantry and the remnants of her crew were taken prisoner.

But now the captors themselves were trapped. They couldn't work the ship clear because of a sea wind that held her fast to the land.

Blanco, at Christian's suggestion, put some marines ashore. But before they could attack the land batteries, Spanish reinforcements were doubled out from Concepción and the patriots were forced to race back to the protection of their ships. During the night, the Spaniards placed a battery of four guns on the beach. Christian directed the marines to tow the *San Martín* around at anchor, bringing her broadsides to bear upon the new emplacements. At dawn in the dead calm, the opponents suddenly opened fire within pistol shot of each other. Despite the roar and scream of shells and mist of powder smoke, the land fire proved ineffective and very little damage was done.

Christian directed a boatswain's mate to bend a cable from the *San Martín* to the *María Isabel,* leaving them separated by scarcely 100 yards. Until about eleven o'clock there was not sufficient breeze for the *San Martín* to even lift the cable from the water, and Christian did his best to disguise his apprehension.

Finally, a quickly vanishing ripple across the glassy surface of the bay foreshadowed the longed-for breeze. The wind strengthened. The foresail and main course suddenly filled on the patriot ship, and canvas raised on the prize—or prize-to-be if she could be dragged off the beach. Slowly the cable tightened and lifted, dripping from the sea. And slowly, almost imperceptibly at first, the great Spanish third-rater was towed into deep water, free at last of the clinging land. Even the shore gunners ceased their futile firing to watch the endeavor until, with both ships well out into the bay, they remembered their duty and loosed a few aimless shots as the craft moved beyond range.

With a prize crew placed aboard the *María Isabel,* the ships bore northward, the *Araucano* watchfully bringing up the rear and the tiny squadron picking up the wayward *Chacabuco* at sea.

"What would the admiral think to rename the *María Isabel?*" asked Christian.

"Any suggestions?" smiled Blanco. "The prize is yours!"

"The prize is Chile's, sir, for I am in her service. We have a vessel named *San Martín*. Of comparable rate, this ship ought to be called the *O'Higgins,* it seems to me."

The *O'Higgins* she became.

Several of the Spanish transports, dispersed in rounding Cape Horn, slipped by with about 1,000 reinforcements in all, but the patriot squadron picked up 5 others with 700 men. Leading their captives like hens lead their chicks, they reached Valparaíso in mid-November. All of the thirteen vessels under the Chilean flag lined up at anchor to make as impressive a show of naval strength as possible for O'Higgins to review. The only significant lack was an experienced admiral to command these vessels, to use them as the tool for opening the western ocean to the forces of freedom.

"And he will not be long delayed, I am confident," the supreme director pledged to Christian. Blanco had generously informed him of Christian's role in the seizure of the *María Isabel,* further reinforcing O'Higgins' respect for the fighting qualities of the Englishman. "Upon Admiral Cochrane's arrival, I wish you to greet him, introduce him to the port, and escort him to Santiago. Instruct him of our movement, its recent history, our aspirations. I will await you at the capital."

CHAPTER SIXTEEN

The merchantman *Rose,* 105 days out of Boulogne, dropped anchor in Valparaíso Bay one month to the day after the action at Talcahuano. Christian, coming up the ladder from his bobbing ship's boat, sensed what a disreputable appearance he must cut in his worn and patched uniform and wide-brimmed hat, when compared with this spotless British vessel. He brushed aside the restraining arm of the wary British guard and stalked along the deck to the quarter where he had spotted Captain Barnstaple, Lord Cochrane, and his handsome wife with two wide-eyed children clutching her hands. The admiral wore the epaulets of his exalted rank and had dressed himself in naval finery for his arrival: sea-blue jacket, high collar with a red bow tie, and beneath it a cluster of lace, white linen trousers, and his officer's gold-hilted sword. His thick dark hair was neatly combed and short enough save for the carefully-brushed sideburns common to men of his station. He was a commanding figure with an expression just short of arrogance, saved by his intense curiosity, openness, and vigor.

"Captain Barnstaple?" Christian addressed the ship's commander, who nodded coolly. "I represent Supreme Director Bernardo O'Higgins, sir, come to welcome Lord Cochrane and your ship to Chile and to escort his lordship to Santiago, at his pleasure."

"Ah, ah, you speak English like an Englishman, sir!" blurted Cochrane, without waiting for Barnstaple to reply. "Who the devil are you?"

"You asked me that once before, sir," grinned Christian courteously, sweeping off his *huaso*'s hat. His ingrained British sense of order caused him to defer to the other's title and rank, and Cochrane's singular naval career was sufficient to demand respect from any seaman in the world. As the admiral peered closely at him, his eyes widened.

"Now what is the admiralty up to in Chile?" he demanded. "No good, I'll warrant!"

"Your lordship's memory is excellent," said Christian, laughing. "No, I am not on the admiralty's business here, nor was I in London. I only stated such in order to avoid unnecessary questions, I suppose. I now represent Mr. O'Higgins and am to conduct you to the capital when you are ready to undertake the journey."

"How far is it?"

"Nearly 100 miles."

"I suppose we shall have to travel by horseback, a difficult means of transport at best and very cruel for women and children," sighed Cochrane.

"Oh, no, sir. There is a graded carriage road, thanks to the supreme director's father, the late viceroy Higgins who was a military engineer. Three days 'twill be, with stopovers at post houses where arrangements already have been made for the comfort of you and your family."

"Good. Excellent. Better than I had expected. Perhaps the land is not so barbarous as I had supposed. Whose ships are those, sir?" Cochrane's hand swept the bay, where the thirteen patriot vessels where anchored.

"Ours, sir. That is the patriot navy, although officered for the most part by Englishmen, Irishmen, and North Americans; the crews, however, are largely Chilean."

"What kind of fighting men are they?"

"Surprisingly good, your lordship. Brave, enduring, and quick to learn—although little trained. Still, they will do, in my judgment."

"I accept your judgment," Cochrane snapped. "I trust you, sir." His keen eyes swept the bay again. "That frigate there, she has French grace about her, but she is not quite French—what was she?"

"Spanish, sir. Lately the *María Isabel*. Now the *O'Higgins*."

"Oh?"

Christian made no reply. In a moment Cochrane asked, "What of Spanish strength?"

"It includes at least three frigates, and there are four brigs. They are reported to have a schooner carrying one large gun and twenty culverins. Spain also has at her disposal in these waters several armed merchantmen. Many, however, are not fit for sea. Naval stores said to be in short supply."

"Where are they?"

"Most of them are at Callao, the port for Lima, Peru, sir. One or two may be at Guayaquil, up the coast, and one or two others probably at Valdivia. Valdivia is protected by an interlocking system of forts and is well manned."

"Hmm," murmured Cochrane. He folded his hands behind him and galloped about the deck in his curious stride, as though fending off frustrations forced upon him by his driving restless ambition. "Hmm," he repeated, stopping alongside Christian once more. "Protected by a single ship or two, you say?"

"And the forts—seventeen of them. All heavily gunned. They are considered by the Spanish to be impregnable. Quite impregnable, sir."

"Hmm," murmured Cochrane, once again.

The admiral was wildly honored at Santiago with such succession of banquets, fiestas, and parties that at length he was forced to remind his hosts that he had come to fight. He said he must be about it or lose his commission as vice admiral of Chile and admiral and commander-in-chief of the naval forces of the Republic. Therefore, just before Christmas he returned to Valparaíso. His flag was hoisted aboard the *O'Higgins* as the flagship of the fleet.

By mid-January it had become apparent that more time would be required to ready half of the ships for sea. Cochrane, increasingly restless, formed a squadron of four of them, the *O'Higgins, San Martín, Lautaro,* and *Chacabuco,* to cruise northward against Spanish power and to reconnoiter the coast. Admiral Blanco would follow if he could fit out the remainder of the patriot vessels.

"Let us hope we don't run into the Spanish fleet," muttered Christian to Ishmael as the *O'Higgins* rolled and wallowed. "Individually these ships are not a match for a well-gunned enemy. Together they are practically a disaster."

"Perhaps a confrontation may be avoided for now," replied the old man. "I heard the admiral remark that he 'had sufficient experience to know that moral effect even if the result of a degree of temerity may not infrequently supply the place of superior force.'"

Christian snorted. "To put that clumsy phrase into seaman's English, he means that a bluff sometimes works; and I suppose he's right. But I prefer more muscle, and I imagine so does he. He is a great seaman, a notable fighting captain. This cruise should provide an education in many things. Not excluding bluff."

Five days out, off La Serena, Christian stared moodily across the waters, attempting to pick out the *encomienda* where thirty years ago Manuel had suffered so terribly in reprisal for attempting to protect his tortured wife. Silently he wondered whether such evils had now been done away with by the patriots since conquest of this land from the Spaniards.

"I would think so, lad," said Ishmael at his side.

"I asked no questions, old man."

"Ye need not. 'Twas on your face. Seems a long, long time ago, eh?"

"Aye," he paused. "Do you think the people are happier, more content, with freedom? What do you make of it, Ishmael?"

"They cannot be less happy than they were, the Indians. Whether they are more content, who knows? 'Tis the nature of man to be discontented with his lot."

"So it is, I know. But is there hope? A man with hope can be a man. Without hope, he is nothing."

"Eh, eh, now ye talk as a philosopher. But 'tis truth. There is movement, now. Even if there is no great improvement, the door is open for it. Once a revelation succeeds, no repression can persist for long. Men tasting freedom will not easily give it up."

In early February, the squadron arrived off San Lorenzo Island, a rocky bit of land rising 1,400 feet out of the sea off Callao, whose port it shielded from the rare Pacific gales. Spies informed the admiral that the land batteries on San Lorenzo and Callao totaled 160 guns, in addition to those of the vessels within the harbor. Mentally, Cochrane cursed the late Sir Francis Drake who had sacked the port and caused the wary, long-memoried Spaniards to fortify it so heavily.

After several days voyage northward, he neared Callao again on the evening of February 20, 1819. The port lay on the north coast of a thin land mass protruding westward into the Pacific like an aged finger pointing at San Lorenzo. Nine miles inland from Callao rose the skyline of Lima, pierced here and there by the towers of a cathedral or church. Behind Lima lifted the tawny mountains, savage and steep, the precursors of the mighty Andes. To the seaward of Callao on a point of land rose three defense turrets capped by gun platforms. These were the principal works for the safety of the port aside from the ever-threatening broadsides of the several warships anchored there. It was a difficult place to attack or for that matter, to defend.

Cochrane, with his long nose sniffing the air for news of any sort, learned that two North American warships were expected sometime during the coming months. "Perhaps we could use that information, sir," he remarked to Christian as they dined in the admiral's cabin.

"This might be a good season for some adventure," agreed Christian. "It is carnival time, and the Spanish will be involved with their masked balls. But one disadvantage is that 'tis a time of heavy fog, and we might succeed in attack only to fail in finding our way to sea again."

"I'm lucky," replied Cochrane, exuding confidence.

He was not so fortunate on this occasion as he would have liked to have been, however. He thought to enter the port under the guise of the North Americans and once well into the bay to send a boat ashore with "dispatches" requesting permission to anchor and land. While the boat was pulling for shore, Cochrane planned "suddenly to dash at the two Spanish frigates and cut them out" before their guns could be manned. If successful the exploit would reduce Spanish power at Callao to near-impotence.

Nonetheless, as Christian had feared, a heavy fog floated in at the last moment and persisted day after day, preventing any warlike movement on the part of the patriots. When it finally lifted, one or two indecisive skirmishes produced little profit, although Cochrane's marines captured the island of San Lorenzo and liberated thirty-seven hapless Chilean prisoners who for eight years had been shackled and worked as slaves. They reported that other captives, under even more brutal conditions, were held in Lima dungeons. With humanitarian intentions, the admiral sent a courteous note to the viceroy, Pezuela, suggesting an exchange of prisoners. His proposal was haughtily refused.

"Read it to me!" the admiral demanded of Ishmael when the boat brought him the Spaniard's reply. Ishmael translated the first part of it, then paused uncertain whether to continue.

"Read me the rest of it, immediately," demanded Cochrane with irritation. "I'm not a patient man!"

"'I am astonished,'" Ishmael translated the final sentence, "'that a British nobleman should come to these distant shores to fight for a rebel community unacknowledged by all the power of the globe.' That's quite all of it, sir." Cochrane snorted with disgust. He paced back and forth for a heated moment. Then he swung savagely about and directed Ishmael to translate his reply:

"A British nobleman," he dictated slowly, "is a free man. Therefore he has a right to assist any country that is endeavoring to reestablish the rights of aggrieved humanity!" He paused to let Ishmael devise a version in Spanish, adding under his breath, "That ought to explain things a bit for the insolent fool." He continued his message: "I have adopted the cause of Chile with the same freedom of judgment that I previously exercised when refusing the offer of an admiral's rank in Spain, made to me not long ago by the Spanish ambassador in London . . . Add this, Ishmael," he amended his directive: "I declare the coast of Peru under blockade as far north as Guayaquil, from this moment onward. All shipping, Spanish or foreign, enters these waters at its own risk, and are subject to having cargoes removed and to being captured, sunk, or both." He cleared his throat, "Let it go that way."

"When we return with more ships," Cochrane said to Christian, "we shall be better equipped and, I have no doubt, will blast them out from behind their defense boom. If we can destroy one or two of their great ships, I believe we can take the port; and by holding that narrow spit of land, we can choke Lima to death and old Pezuela as well." Cochrane delighted in the thought of his enemy's destruction. "However, we need more ships. More ships. But where on earth to get them? Where upon this coast?"

Where indeed? From Mexico to Tierra del Fuego there were no vessels known to be in port save Spanish warships, and seizing them one by one, in action after minor action, would be of little benefit, since such engagements often would result in crippling one's own vessels and thus maintaining the forces at about the same level unless by lucky chance.

Cochrane roved the coast north and south of Callao, now and then putting a landing party ashore to loot towns, collect booty and food supplies, or simply to exercise his men. More often than not he came to assign Christian to lead such tasks. His confidence in his countryman waxed swiftly, and Christian was equally impressed by the strategic and fighting qualities of the admiral. Their talents complemented each other and when meshed, were more likely to produce good results than when used separately. Thus they learned to operate as a well-knit team, at sea and ashore, each magnifying the other's capability. A certain friendship developed, or as much of a kinship as could be forged between such different men.

CHAPTER SEVENTEEN

Admiral Cochrane chafed under action considerably less than his grand dreams had anticipated and eagerly accepted an invitation to confer with the supreme director at Santiago. Christian, as friend and confidante of both, was invited along; and Ishmael came uninvited, as was his way. They reached the capital and following a state dinner gathered at the working office of O'Higgins. San Martín was still on the other side of the Andes with his wife, Remeditos, who was in no condition to undertake the arduous passage over the mountains.

"We would be farther along, sir, had we the necessary ships," grumbled Cochrane, rancor in his voice. "The vessels we possess are serviceable, but they are too few to risk in a decisive action and far too few to transport a large enough land army to take Peru, as the general intends."

"What you say is true enough," conceded O'Higgins, his blue eyes restless. "More ships undoubtedly will be necessary to end the war."

"We can prick the enemy, strike where his power is weak, seize a strong point here and there, but decisive action cannot come until we can launch a concerted attack on Callao."

O'Higgins stared at the ceiling, studying the upside-down flies. "The need for bottoms is obvious," he agreed. "We cannot purchase more, since a frigate costs nearly $200,000 and we do not have that kind of money in our impoverished treasury. That leaves La Plata as the only source. I believe we could borrow three or four vessels if General Pueyrredon no longer fears a Spanish expedition to recapture the city. The real problem is delivery. If we leave it to individual captains to bring their ships around the Horn, they will probably make a pretense of doing so but at the first gale turn back and report that they could not proceed."

"You appear to have little faith in the willingness of the *Plateños* to come fight our mutual enemy, Bernardo," said Christian.

"I am not speaking of the *Plateños* captains, Fletcher, as well you know because there aren't any, but of your own countrymen who fight well if there's a prize in the offing, but otherwise suit their ideals to the risks."

"I do not believe all my countrymen are so base."

O'Higgins dropped his gaze. "Of course not," he agreed. "I was being ungenerous in the presence of those who illustrate the reverse. I beg forgiveness—truly I do. In this very room we have sterling examples of unshakable ideals, in Lord Cochrane and yourself—" O'Higgins paused, staring at Christian. "*You*, Fletcher! You can bring the ships!" The words came in a rush, now. "You can confer with General San Martín, secure his assistance, and then proceed to Buenos Aires and meet with Pueyrredon, assemble the bottoms and crews there, and convoy them around Cape Horn to Valparaíso! Why didn't I think of this before? We shall have a fleet—if the *Plateños* will loan us the vessels. But of course they will! The cause is theirs, as much as ours. You must make them see that!" He touched fingertips with the complacency of a man who has checkmated his opponent.

"You don't know if I am capable of fulfilling this task."

"Don't I though!" retorted the director. "I know you've been a seaman and a ship's officer all your life, in preference at least; I know you for a loyal friend, one wedded to our cause. If I searched the world over, I could find no man whom I would trust more wholly, and I'm sure Lord Cochrane shares my confidence."

Cochrane nodded. "I do. Of course I believe that I might be a preferred choice, but I shall be otherwise occupied; and you would be my selection for such a sensitive job in my place."

"You will leave in the morning with his lordship's permission."

"Capital!" cried Cochrane, bouncing to his feet and pacing back and forth. "Ideals and ships! Fighting ships . . . or any ships, we can fashion warships from them, and clear the entire Pacific of Spanish sail. We can transport the army anywhere!"

"Ships is it?" grimaced Juan Martín de Pueyrredón, the droll and youthful head of the Buenos Aires government. "Ships this time!" He spread his hands in mock despair. "First San Martín takes away my army. Then Alvear robs me of my militia. The Spanish cut off my merchant fleet. The gauchos are off fighting the Indians. The Indians are off fighting the gauchos. All I have left is the pampa. What a place this is!"

Christian laughed. "I guess it is just the Revolution, your Excellency," he soothed him. "Sacrifices. That's all. Sacrifices."

"Sacrifices, hah! Soon I shall have nothing left to sacrifice. In fact, that is the case already as any sensible man can see."

Pueyrredón wore the gold-spangled uniform beloved by the Latin revolutionaries: blue and snow white, with touches of scarlet and gold and a swathing of lace. A lean vigorous man, there was a regal expression about his face which lent substance to his outspoken leanings toward divine right. He firmly believed that a king would lend his stability and viability to the La Plata settlements. The major problem, as he saw it, was what strain of royalty to invite here—and who with any pretense to royal blood might actually be persuaded to reside and rule in these mud cities with their largely barbarous peasantry. Independence, however, must come before a monarch; and for independence it now seemed necessary to loan this Spanish-fluent Englishman three or four ships of war. "Demands!" He sighed audibly. Always there were demands.

"If O'Higgins needs ships, if San Martín needs ships, if Cochrane needs ships, they must have ships. We have them. We have also rumors that the Spanish have dispatched one more great convoy, better escorted than before, from Cadíz for the Pacific coast. As least we have heard the fleet is destined for the west coast—wouldn't it prove embarrassing if it sailed up La Plata instead? Hah! Well, if it does I will be executed like a barbecued pig anyway, so the ships I loan you won't make much difference. But we hear the convoy is bound for Callao. That is more logical, since if the Spanish hold Peru, they will hold America; if they lose Peru, they lose the continent. That is our task: to see that they lose Peru. We cannot take it without warships and transports, and that brings us again to the ships you must have."

Captain Thanatopsis Carver—called Tad by his peers—welcomed Christian aboard with an off-hand salute, which meant that, although in the employ of the Plata Republic, he was the equal of any man and would remain in its hire only so long as it suited him. "Admiral Fletcher, eh?" he mused, scanning the imposing parchment of commission shown him by Christian. He ever so slightly stressed the title, as though to emphasize his disbelief, but it also suggested that he would go along with it because it somehow might pay off. He handed the sheet back.

"'Tis fortunate we're all sick to our guts with laying flat on this sea o' mud," he said with a nasal twang, which in no way belied his obvious competence; the cleanliness of his vessel attested to his quality. "There ain't no profit here, I can tell you. Mayhap there'll be some in the Pacific. I'll go along, Adm'ral, an' I s'pose these other captains will too for they're sick to death o 'idlin' an' there ain't no other war now."

The small squadron, counting only four sail, was impressive as a fleet, though it could make a difference between victory and defeat, Christian believed. He examined each of the vessels in turn through his glass: the *corbeta* or sloop of war, *Invincible*, a gaff-rigged topsail schooner mounting 18 guns; the sloop of war, *Juliet*, 20 guns; the frigate, *Pampero*, 46 guns; and, putting the glass aside, his own frigate, *Hercules*, 48 guns. All were in full sail, drawing well, favored by a light northerly in the course toward the southeast, plowing the hissing brown waters of the muddy Plata estuary. Christian pushed the glass closed, listening to its familiar clicks. The day was fine, only few mare's tails promising continued fair wind. The four vessels were remarkably even sailors, and that was unexpected. No captain was forced to furl sail to remain in convoy.

The waters turned from clay-brown to greenish as they felt the initial motion of the swells and the sea began taking over from the estuary. Screaming about the vessels came the South Atlantic gulls, black on top with white piping edging their upper wings. The morning sun gleamed across the restless gold of the flowing sea. Far to the south lay a rising bank of dark clouds, forewarning of the gales and howling winds and the brutal suffering that lay ahead.

All four vessels raised good canvas, for the wind was strong, though not a gale. No other vessel had been seen, though lookouts were kept in the foretop from dawn to twilight. Christian frequently swept the horizon eastward for some indication of—what? The Spanish convoy mentioned by Pueyrredon? Possibly. Yet this was a lonely ocean.

During the two weeks the ships bore south, they were made ready for the storms to come, their ports battened down, the heavy square wooden lids banged shut and bound tight to keep out the sea water. The cannon, in all likelihood to be unneeded until the Cape was rounded, were strongly secured, for a loose roving gun of many tons could cause fearful damage and maim and cripple men who sought to fetter it under the heaving and rolling of stormy seas. Wise captains employed the fine weather to ready their vessels for the trials to come, and Christian hoped that the skippers on the other ships were attending to this.

By the time the squadron reached 53° South, the sky had turned the color of worn canvas and was darkening; the sea was moderate, but any sailor could tell that foul weather lay ahead. They had found 65° of longitude west of Greenwich as nearly as they could judge with uncertain chronometers.

"Sail, ho!"

The call from the foretop came thin and clear. The sailing master peered aloft, cupped his mouth, "Where away?"

"Abeam to larboard! A sail hull-down and p'raps a second. Can't be sure."

"What is she . . . Spanish?"

"I cannot tell! But it appears she's bearing south."

Seizing his glass Christian sprang to the ratlines, clambering upward to get a clearer view across the heaving water. He could not sight the sail and soon joined Carver.

"If it's a single sail it, might be anyone." Christian said. "If there are two or more, they must be Spanish—what else?"

"Do you think we should run for Thetis Bay?" Carver wondered. "We could lay over a week or two, allow them to reach the Cape afore us." Thetis Bay was at the head of Le Maire Strait, between Staten Island and Tierra del Fuego. Christian shook his head.

"'Twould do no good," he judged. "If the passage is rough as the season promises, their ships will scatter. One refuge is no better than the next. Cochrane sorely needs us. We had best keep our course at least until we make her out, or lose her."

CHAPTER EIGHTEEN

The squadron neared Le Maire Strait, leading toward the southernmost headland of Tierra del Fuego, about midday, the water turning green-gray to reveal to mariners that the bottom shelved here. The ships dropped anchor ten fathoms in the lee of the Fuegian coast while the highlands were scaled and with a glass the seas combed to the south for strange sail. Christian little expected to sight any, since navigators unfamiliar with the region would round the land well out to sea and start their wresting in the open ocean too far to be observed.

Before daylight sail was loosed and the ships glided southward, rising to the ocean swells by daylight. All day the squadron plowed forward, wallowing more now with the weather making up and the wind rising and the ships close-hauled to within six points of a rising gale. A flurry of snow gave a foretaste of weather soon to come.

All day and through the long winter night, the ships drove on, lanterns on their poops giving fitful lights that held them together. At daylight all remained in view, though scattered a bit because of a building storm. As they made their southerly reach, the great winds blew harder, the seas developed strength, the trial commenced. By nightfall they were in the approximate latitude of Cape Horn. The ocean upon which they had entered swept all longitudes right round the globe, building strength and fury beneath sullen gales the like of which are found nowhere else on earth. They howl and bowl along without hindrance round and round the world until their mighty force seems too great for puny wood and sail devices.

poops–
poop decks.

Great rollers a mile in length and half of that from crest to crest, their height thirty, forty, even seventy feet from trough to fringe, now smashed successive blows against the vessels which bounced and rolled and yawed from side to side. Their sodden canvas was swollen with wind and spray, masts cracking as though to snap, the vessels groaning mightily, sighing and creaking as only a live ship can, lending weight to sailors' claims that a vessel is a thing alive and struggling and sometimes deadly. The *corbeta* seemed to weather the gale most readily under tops and fore-and-aft courses; but the frigates rolled and pitched unmercifully, although the greater weight of their gun decks lent them stability of a sort. The passage would prove of no delight to either class of vessel, however, nor to the crews who manned them.

tops and fore-and-aft courses-
minimum sails, the topgallants, in addition to the small sails at the front and back of the ship.

The second day the skies cleared for a moment in the early afternoon; and the *Hercules* found herself southeast of Cape Horn, its bold southern face, wetly green and jagged, rising to nearly 1,350 feet. Then the scud and the mark closed in again and the rock was blotted from their view forever.

The great storm winds screeched to a greater intensity, howling and beating down upon them. The courses were taken in with enormous difficulty, since the gaskets were frozen stiff, the yards glazed with ice, the footropes white with frosted spume, and the ship bucking and rolling so that 'twas difficult to stand aloft and work. The ships wore southerly, seeking to gain a southing, then tacked northward, trying to gain an inch or two on the Cape, but it was no use. For every half-mile gained, a mile most often was lost; and the squadron threatened to be driven apart in the determination to make headway under the battering of the seas and the wind.

southing-
a distance traveled or measured southward.

Day after day the vessels sailed full and by, northward or southward, futilely sawing away against the monstrous elements which forced them to a standstill or even backward as if by a giant hand. Some days the gale would lessen, or steady, and a bit of progress might result. Then, as though eager to disillusion men who thought the elements were surrendered, the storm and seas crashed down once more, driving into the brave little crafts, sending them reeling to where they had been before or even farther eastward.

"I've been around the Cape three times an' I never seen wind an' seas like these!" shouted Captain Carver to Christian. The Englishman nodded, huddling in his sodden jacket under the drive of snow, sleet, and spume. "We'll wear our ships out afore we can make a northing!" Carver glumly added.

Christian recalled the little *Bounty*, thirty years ago, which had attempted for six weeks to round the Cape without success. Finally it was given up as impossible and the ship put about to make for the South Pacific, proving that a straight line is not always the shortest distance. He thought, too, of the hundreds of ships whose bones moldered beneath these seas because of careless handling or elements too savage to contest.

Now it was the thirteenth day of their own epic battle, and they still had not reached the longitude when they could expect to "turn the corner," as old seamen put it. The wind roared across the seething waters with increased fury; the rollers grew in size; the cold, if not more intense, yet by its prolongment seemed even less endurable. The interior of the ship reeked of wet wool and sodden bedding and ever-sloshing gun decks, whose crews, unable to endure the cold and wetness, sometimes even volunteered for deck duty in order to get topside and stretch aching muscles.

It was late on the afternoon of the fourteenth day that disaster struck the squadron. The tiny fleet was widely scattered now, with the *corbeta* and sloop hull-down on either horizon, struggling still. The frigates, almost twin ships in form and outline, alternately rose high on a crest and settled for a deck-flushing in a trough with only tops visible to the other craft. The wind stilled for the space of a heartbeat. Captain Carver was below; and Christian, instantly alerted by the gap in the storm, glanced forward and saw by an onrushing fury of spindrift and boiling spume that the gale had shifted in a twinkling by forty-five degrees. Where it had blown from the northwest, it abruptly swung about and now was bearing down upon them from dead ahead, a disaster most feared by all seamen.

"*Hard a-starboard!*" bellowed Christian to the men at the wheel. "Spoke by spoke, lads! Lose your grip and we lose our rudder! We lose our ship!" Jordan, the sailing master, raced aft along the greasy deck, fighting for his footing as it bucked and tossed. "Wind's shifting!" howled Christian. "We'll be taken aback if she doesn't come about!" Jordan shouted at the deck crew to haul the yards across, sent a boy racing below to bring up the off-duty watch. The storm-swept deck erupted with frantic activity and well-directed movements to bring the vessel onto her new tack before the wind slammed into her. The helmsmen strained, eyes bulging as they beheld the disaster thundering down upon them. Slowly, imperceptibly at first, the bow swung over, almost completing its movement by the time the new wind struck them, but they were far enough around so that the sails boomed full and the vessel straightened out. She was saved.

Not so fortunate was the *Pampero*. Whether the deck officer failed to recognize the new direction of the onrushing hurricane or the ship could not be swung over in time, the result in any case was the same. She was suffered to meet the shifted wind head-on, a collision that no ship ever built could have withstood.

"The *Pampero*'s caught it, sir!" cried Jordan to Carver. The two with Christian clutched the stays, rocking with the heave of the ship as they stared disbelievingly as their companion vessels, only a quarter of a mile off, caught in disaster. In a twinkling, as though she were a match-built toy, the masts snapped before their eyes. As she rode a crest her tracery of spars and sticks crumbled from foremast to mizzen, as though brushed by some mighty hand, the seas surrounding her were instantly afloat with a tangle of lines and splintered wood and sodden canvas which no crew could disengage under the fearful conditions.

At the same instant, the *Pampero* slid into an even greater calamity, her bowsprit aimed pointlessly at the storm-rent sky, her battered, glistening hull fighting against the litter of her rig, sliding backward down the long and fearsome crest. "She's going to poop!" screamed Jordan, his anguished howl chilling the officers next to him even more than the ghastly sight across the heaving deep. The *Pampero,* clearly visible in the fading light, was driven aft by the wind down the long slope until her stern was caught by the opposing roller which crested high above, smashing down upon the hapless wreck. Thousands upon thousands of tons of green water flooded her deck, cascading down her companionways, staving her hatches, swamping her holds, her lower decks with sea and no doubt tearing loose even the tethered guns and sending them bounding about, smashing bulkheads and men with utter abandon. The useless hull, top-heavy with water, rolled over and over to plunge below, joining countless wrecks from similar disasters, the sea floor littered with the bones of seamen. Only the wreckage of what had been a ship scarred the water with its ever-widening design of fragments.

"Gone!" cried Carver, his ghostly face staring where only a moment before there had been a proud ship, a community of men and tools. Now she was gone and her crew with her. Those few men swimming, if any indeed had survived this long, were doomed since no ship could put about to search for them and in this frigid sea no human being could survive more than a few frozen minutes.

"She's gone, indeed," sighed Christian. His "stick" again, that evil old wolf that had pursued him all his roving life, had snapped existence from these hundreds of men, had crushed their ship; and through the howl of the wind, he heard Bligh's maniacal laugh from which he knew he could not escape, ever.

The signal lights drew in the remaining vessels of the squadron during the night, but that was not all: their lure attracted other ships as well. For with the first glimmer of dawn the foretopman called, "Sail, ho!" And then again, "Sail, ho!" And above the screaming of the wind: "Sails to larboard an' starboard. I see four or five strange sails!"

"How far off?" called the deck.

"One to starboard is closing in. She looks Spanish, sir, but I cannot make her out."

"Run up some colors, Captain," Christian directed. "British, American, anything you have so long as it's not of a new republic. They cannot identify us by line."

"Thank God the sea is over-rough for guns," muttered Carver. The union jack was shaken out and run aloft where the stiff gale spread it out for strangers to identify. The two other vessels of the reduced squadron, standing in closer in obedience to the lights, did likewise, but the problem eased not a whit. Amid a Spanish convoy Christian felt himself trapped as he had never been in his life before. Surrounded by enemy ships, outgunned by veteran seamen as good as any he commanded; what would happen if they could not lose them and turn the corner and come upon calmer seas above the Horn? What indeed, save loss of ships, loss of life, loss of everything?

Even were he able to lose the enemy convoy under cover of darkness or a sharply different tack, this would not elude but only postpone the decision; for there yet remained thousands of miles of sea to Valparaíso. In those far reaches, he would be found again, in circumstances under which he would have to fight. From disaster to debacle in less than a night and day! Did any hope remain? The ship was wrenched and tossed all the dark-and-gloomy morning as he struggled with the problem in his tortured mind. The Spanish ships expertly maneuvered closer, appearing and disappearing through mist and spume, riding the contorted sea as did the *Hercules* but daring not to close within a mile because of the difficulty of maneuvering in the great swells. The Spaniards could not make them out but were too suspicious to let them go. Christian had no doubt that her glasses were turned to inspect every line and marking, assessing the probability of ownership and true flag.

Christian's mind raced from one problem to the next. Where might safety lie? How to lose the Spaniard, gain their goal, fulfill their mission—for that matter save the Revolution? How?

A startling idea surfaced in his brain, and with it a strange rift appeared in the western clouds and a shaft of sunlight stabbed strangely down to highlight the *Hercules*. So it was, so other-worldly that Christian stared up into the mysterious light, unreal but intensely tangible at the same moment. Then it was gone and once again the vessel rose and plunged in the misty gloom. He directed a shrill command to Carver and Jordan: "About ship! Bring her about! Signal the others! Let us run before this storm to safety!"

A question flashed across the face of the captain as he stared at Christian to determine whether he had gone daft, but he saw only deadly earnestness. Driven by the discipline of the sea, he loosed orders that sent men scurrying up the ratlines. There was no possibility of swinging her about head-on into the face of the terrible storm, for she surely would have been destroyed like the *Pampero*. She fell off, rolled almost on her beam ends—her rail awash, the water quartering up the deck—but recovered like the sea lady she was, and shook her skirts, came around, and raced away downwind. The bucking and the plunging eased, and her two surviving sloops-of-war followed in her wake. Being largely fore-and-aft in rig, they had completed the maneuver more handily than the frigate. In an instant it appeared the enemy convoy was forgotten, attempting still to make headway westward. The tiny Republican squadron raced freely toward the east.

CHAPTER NINETEEN

The reduced flotilla lay safely in Possession Bay at the eastern mouth of the Strait of Magellan. Christian in a long boat was pulled toward the dun clay bluffs rising for a hundred feet or more. To the west a sand spill swept in by Patagonian winds plunged like a breaker to the water, frozen in yellow time. How well he remembered! So long ago he had paddled to this very shore alone in a crude dugout. Fifteen years ago? Eighteen? No matter. It was all done with; and today he was admiral over a squadron of four—no, three vessels to be conducted to Chile to reinforce the war for independence. What changes the years had wrought! His only task now was to guide these ships safely to Chile. Unable to round the Horn, all but ensnared by the Spanish convoy, he had had little choice but to break and run for the Strait. This had been accomplished. Could the vessels be gotten through it? Who could tell? It had been negotiated: Magellan, Drake, half a hundred others had proven the passage, tortuous by reason of its narrows and head winds, at least possible under some conditions.

Why then was he being rowed ashore while the ships rested in the bay?

The boat touched the beach; and Christian leaped to the land, startled—as always after long at sea—by its solidity, its lack of motion. He stood with arms akimbo, staring upward at the rim of the bluff, half expecting a ragged line of Lenketrú's horsemen to file over the crest. But there was no sound save the lap of the water, the sigh of the constant Patagonian winds above him. Christian found the ancient trail and began his climb upward. Although it was midwinter and streaks of snow lay in the crevices, the warm sunlight and exertion brought a tingling to his body and damp sweat. He topped out to gaze across the endless, brush-grown plains he had once known so intimately. A guanaco pirouetted and raced into the distance.

There, scarce 100 paces off, was what he sought! A heap of stones with which he had formed his cairn so long ago. Christian picked away at the rocks slowly at first, then more rapidly, feverishly. He bared its base and the flat stones, providing a dry space beneath them. He cast the fragments aside and beheld the ancient bundle he had wrapped so carefully. He had no idea at the time why he had done so, a parcel he surely never expected to see again—and now had desperate need of! He carefully drew it out, hastily unwrapped the thick leather-clad book he had left behind so long ago. In it he had jotted his meticulous navigator's notes of straits and sounds, channels and lagoons, passages and inlets and bays of the convoluted western Strait and coast. This was a region that he alone of all the seamen in the world had studied and now understood. Within this bundle, with its finely penciled calculations and notations, he might guide his tiny fleet not only to the western ocean but northward through that intricate maze of islands, rocks, headlands, and channels, safe from detection until they passed the danger and could make a run for Valparaíso. This book might prove the key to survival, to success for the independence effort.

Impatiently Christian riffled the pages, the writing on them as clear and legible as if it had been penciled yesterday, the notations as comprehensible as a master seaman could make them. Thrusting the book inside his shirt, the Englishman swung down the trail, running the last few paces. He reached the boat, ignoring curious glances from the oarsmen, and was pulled back to the *Hercules*.

"You have the look of a man who has found success!" Nobbs greeted him as he stepped to the deck. Christian smiled. He said nothing but went instantly to his cabin, opened the volume, and pored over his earlier calculations. What foresight he had used—through luck, of course. Only a fool could discern anything other than that. Using his notations carefully, he plotted the course of the squadron down the eastern leg of the Strait toward its northwesterly reach. There was where the difficulty would begin! There the williwaws were an ever-present threat, the channels too narrow for maneuvering. Frequently the great west gales thrummed down the canyons to meet probing vessels head-on, driving the water with it at a velocity sometimes of eight knots or even more. No headway could be made until those conditions ceased. Still, many vessels *had* negotiated the Strait. With luck, these could too.

williwaws-
a sudden, violent gust of cold land air common along the mountainous coasts of high latitudes.

The squadron proceeded up Possession Bay through a narrow, into another great basin, and across that to the southwest. Distant views of snowy mountains loomed before them, the low and sullen southerly extensions of the Andes, as Christian remembered. Toward evening the lone Tehuelche-hut peak of Christian's recollection, streaked top to bottom with winter snow, rose as a landmark. It must be rounded to gain the southernmost cape before the trial would finally commence. The ships dropped anchor a short distance from the mountain. A slight storm with a bit of driving snow howled about them during the late night, dusting the worn decks with white. But 'twas gone by day and they continued on, rounding that great green headland marking the southernmost extremity of the continent and altering their course a full thirty degrees to starboard.

The cape was brilliant green, the first hint of dense Andean timber on the moisture-laden western slopes. Driftwood became more common. Sand gave way to shingle beaches. The bony exposures of the mountains, now glistening with snow and ice, gave evidence of harsher conditions to come. When the ships were tied up, it was with a staysail set and sea anchor out to keep their prows directed up the channel. Soon the shoulder of the passageway would crowd in.

Now began the trial. The difficulty was not for want of wind. Frequently it roared down driving snow so thick that even vision proved difficult, the sky merging with hanging glaciers, descending from ice fields dimly seen through beech forests and low clouds. But there was no room to tack. No means by which the wind could be used upon the sails until it shifted. On one occasion it required three days and three nights to move the vessels one-quarter mile. However, inch by inch on some days, mile by mile on others, they labored up the passage. At last they broke free above the Strait, into the bay that led to the western ocean. Christian did not even glance at the island to the south where he had camped with the hapless Fuegians destroyed by the sealers. The memory rankled still; he would not bruise it farther.

During all the passage, he had had no time for anything but his calculations and the work of moving the flotilla. He conversed companionably with Nobbs frequently, however. The mate had a flair for navigation and closely observed the plotting of their course, commenting intelligently on the process. Nobbs had a curious, probing mind. They became friends of a sort, as much as the difference in their ages made possible.

"'Twas a memorable passage, sir," remarked the mate one day.

"Aye, so it was," agreed Christian. "But a much more difficult passage lies before us now."

"Why can we not move out into the Pacific and run north along the coast, with no more trouble than from rough water and high wind?"

Christian shook his head.

"'Twould never do. The Spaniards await us there, I feel; and we could not outrun them nor much less outgun them. But this interior passage is like a secret channel unknown to them. Once above it, we will come out into sunny skies and calmer water and be aided by a strong current flowing northward along the coast. The run to Valparaíso will be hastened and much safer."

"'Tis a varied land down here at this southern end of the world," Nobbs mused. "And 'tis a varied sea out there in the western Pacific—still imperfectly known, as I suppose."

"Aye," agreed Christian. "And 'twill be mostly unknown for your lifetime, lad. There are islands out there with life as easy as in most men's Heaven. There is no cold, few storms, no struggle for food or shelter, no cruelty or misery save what man himself concocts, which is aplenty, if it comes to that! And there are other islands, too, remote, where a man can live his life as he devises, up to his honor and ingenuity." For a moment nostalgia overcame Christian, remembering Pitcairn and its colony, and George Nobbs listened well, fascinated by what he heard. Possibly one day he would touch upon that secret island. Perhaps.

After a lengthy parley to assure the other captains of his plans and the reasons for them, the three-vessel fleet moved northward, the *Hercules* in the vanguard, guided carefully by Christian's notes. Without them the squadron would have become speedily trapped or lost in myriad fjords and waterways that were inlets only, while what appeared to be a dead-end sound would open up at the last moment into a further channel. It would have been a miracle, this passage north, save that it was no miracle at all but the product of a careful study, made with no apparent purpose by a lost and lonely seaman before many of the crew now traversing it even had been born.

Captain Carver marveled at the passage and the fact of its discovery.

"One time out of Boston I took the ship *Behemoth* to th' northwest coast tradin' for sea otters," he recalled. "North of Nootka Sound there is an inland passage northward, about like this but broader, easier to follow, not so broke up by false channels as this one is. I never seen one like this, but that other resembles it somewhat."

On one or two occasions, the vessels emerged into the swells that told them they had reached the rim of the sea, but shortly they darted once more behind the sheltering screen of land and continued their cautious passage. Two weeks and four days after leaving the western outlet of the Strait of Magellan, they hove to at the southern edge of a wide bay clearly of the Pacific Ocean.

Captains and navigators gathered in the high cabin of the *Hercules*, while Christian explained their position and the options. The room rocked ever so slightly with a hint of rollers coming from the ocean, but they paid no heed, concentrating instead upon the crude chart Christian had sketched for them.

"We have reached approximately this point, gentlemen," he said, a wisp of gray hair falling over his brow. "This gulf before us is landlocked on its northern coast, so here we must put to sea. We must round that peninsula to the northwest, tipped by the three peaks you can make out from the deck, and then if the weather is foul or if we sight enemy sail, we could drop inland by another bay and resume our passage until we round Chiloé Island to the north. But that is hazardous, because Chiloé is a Spanish stronghold and 'twould only be by sheer luck if we missed encountering hostile ships.

"What's your recommendation then, sir?" asked Carter, the respect in his voice genuine.

"I have none," replied Christian, slowly. "If 'twere left to me, I should make a run for it from here. That is to say, put out early enough in the day to safely round the Three Mountains Peninsula by light and late enough to break for the open sea by darkness, hoping to get far enough offshore during the night to get outside the course of the Spaniards, if they are coasting north, and be seaward of them by daylight next day. They should be hugging the coast, since they would intend to put in to refit at either Chiloé or Valdivia."

There was little doubt they would have it. Being sea captains, they had felt uneasy during their closely landlocked passage. Upon a landless ocean they felt at home. Water, gales, and storms they understood and could manage. In a single voice they seconded the opinion of their admiral and opted for the sea.

None of the three vessels was a swift sailor and their bottoms now required, in a sailor's term, half a gale to move them. But move they did. With all the sail they could carry, they gathered way and plowed across the gulf, feeling the reassuring heave of good sound swells, wallowing in the security of the wide ocean, and bearing more northerly until by daylight only the merest tracing of the land outlined the horizon. They were free—as free as possible in waters contested by a powerful, vigilant, relentless enemy. But they had negotiated the passage, the first vessels of record to complete it as they had done. They drove northward with a fine wind under clearing skies, spirits soaring to match the happier clime.

CHAPTER TWENTY

Valparaíso Bay was all but emptied of warships as the squadron anchored in the spring of 1819, three months out of Buenos Aires. Cochrane was on a cruise along the coast. He would attempt to seize Callao but failing that, attack targets of opportunity as distant perhaps as Guayaquil. He was expected to return shortly, but with Cochrane one ever knew. Like an angler, he would remain at his favorite sport so long as nibbles were to be had.

Christian reported to the supreme director. Then he ordered his vessels careened, scraped, cleaned, and tarred, putting everything in order for sea duty when the admiral should arrive. While so engaged, sails were observed standing in for the coast, being identified shortly as the *O'Higgins*, Cochrane's flagship the *Lautaro*, and a couple of strangers, which turned out to be prizes. All anchored in the bay December 16.

Christian was piped aboard the flagship and joined Cochrane below for a glass of brandy, the admiral impatiently pacing back and forth, the only man of Christian's experience who could lope in the confines of the ship's small cabin.

"Good, fine!" exclaimed Cochrane, rubbing his hands as Christian reported on his mission. "Sorry about the *Pampero*, but it couldn't be helped, I suppose; although I've always thought that a ship taken aback was the deck officer's fault, though perhaps not. Perhaps not. At any rate, I must congratulate you, sir, on bringing in the others."

"Thank you, sir."

"You have secured the Revolution, you know—its ultimate success. No matter what those land-minded army officers say. With control of the sea assured, they *can't* lose, although the way they fight it might take a thousand years."

"I've found them brave enough, sir," Christian said, stubbornly.

"Oh, of course, yes, Fletcher. I'm not imputing cowardice to them. Just confounded indecision and dilatoriness. Quibbling fools, they are. You say you saw nothing of the Spaniards after your adventure off the Cape? Odd. Odd, indeed."

He rubbed a forefinger along the side of his great nose. "Which port do you think they would make for initially: Chiloé or Valdivia—or neither, perhaps?"

Christian glanced at the map. "After rounding the Horn in winter, sir, the fleet I am sure would require much refitting. Valdivia is primarily a fortress while Chiloé has facilities for working ships. I would suppose those vessels that survived the Cape passage would put into Chiloé before resuming their progress for Callao."

"Avoiding Valdivia entirely, is that it?"

"They would have no reason to put in there, in my judgment."

Cochrane rocked back on his heels. "What would the people think, sir, if I took the *O'Higgins* and captured Valdivia, their 'Gibraltar of the Pacific'?"

Christian's mouth dropped open. "They would—they'd—why, sir, the *O'Higgins* would have to go it alone! My ships—those I brought in—will not be ready for use for weeks. Your own vessels have been long at sea and no doubt are in very poor trim. They would think you—the plan—quite mad, sir!"

Cochrane chuckled. "Well, well, well. Perhaps so."

"I have seen the fortresses of Valdivia, m'lord. There is not such another system of defenses in all of America, perhaps in the world! If not impregnable, they are very nearly so, sir!"

"Eh? What's that you say? *You* have seen the forts? You know them? Capital! Together we shall seize them, Fletcher! You and I—eh? The Chilean people expect the impossible. We cannot take Callao until the ships are ready for it, but by God we can take Valdivia! Their impossibility they shall have!"

"It would be a most desperate enterprise, sir."

"Desperate? I hardly think so. A gamble? What is not?"

"Don't you feel, sir, that it might prove . . . rash?"

Once more Cochrane chuckled, less than the gesture of a madman, possibly, but at least that of a genius.

"Rashness is often imputed to me," he acknowledged, with quiet pride. "But falsely so. When consequences are considered carefully, where lies the rashness? It no longer exists." His mind galloped along. "The first thing we must do is get there and reconnoiter the place. I must bring Major Miller in and inform him of what we have decided, then secure his assent—he is sure to agree if fighting is the prospect!"

Christian smiled. First Lord Cochrane would inform Billy Miller of his plans, then solicit his assent. What marine officer could withhold it under such circumstances? Support for Cochrane's project was assured.

Cochrane, Christian, Miller, and his marines all crowded into the *O'Higgins* and put to sea, reaching Valdivia's Coral Bay on January the 18, 1820. Viewed from the sea, the familiar geography and installations appeared unchanged to Christian, as he remembered from long ago this most distant fortress in the Spanish Empire, at the extreme southern tip of Chile. Below it, he knew, was the great island of Chiloé, where the Spanish convoy may well have put in for its own refitting, but it was too distant from Valdivia, communications were far too poor for Chiloé to be a defense factor for the complicated fortress. Christian had busied himself sketching charts to instruct the admiral in the defense of Corral Bay and environs making up the Valdivia complex. Now he pointed out their features as the ship glided inward toward the land, faintly obscured by light rain. It always rained here. "'Tis a strong place, m'lord, providing the Spaniards are alert."

"We shall see. We shall see," murmured Cochrane, orienting the sketches with the features he could observe.

He ordered the vertically-striped yellow and blue flag raised, demanding a pilot. It was run up beneath the Spanish colors flying at the masthead as the ship stood into the bay, almost within range of the brooding guns of the major forts. A pilot, accompanied by a junior officer and four-man escort for distinguished visitors, pulled out from Corral fortress and came unsuspectingly aboard. As they stepped onto the deck, they were quickly seized and ordered to guide the ship into the bay. The pilot shrugged and complied readily enough; after all piloting was his profession. The officer, *Subteniente* Sanchez, knowing that there was little likelihood of his rejoining his fellows until this issue was decided, responded readily to requests for information about emplacements and garrisons which, Christian found to his relief, were virtually unaltered from his own time. Most Spanish strength long since had been withdrawn to Chiloé and Callao, the port for Lima. Yet the place remained formidable.

"If you will pardon my lack of faith, sir, I do not see how a single ship is going to silence all those guns of far greater caliber than any of ours," muttered Christian.

"It does sound a bit reckless, I must admit, Fletcher," agreed the admiral, as he scanned the shoreline through the glass. "So I suppose we had better not attempt it."

"You mean quit the enterprise?"

"Abandon it? Oh, good heavens, no," rejoined Cochrane, testily. "I never drop anything I embark upon. Never!" He clicked the telescope shut with finality. "This place can be taken, if not by sea, then by land. I really am not such a fool as to attempt to out-duel those 25-pounders with the *O'Higgins'* guns. No indeed.

But the Spaniards can't swing them around; and if we can get into their works, we'll quickly make an end to them."

Christian remained dubious. We might take one position and then another, perhaps. But to reduce all the forts on both sides of the bay will require more men than we now have, no matter how resolute they might be."

Cochrane clapped him on the back.

"Then let us get some more men, Fletcher. "We'll run up to Talco—Talcahuno—how do you pronounce the name of that abominable place? Talcahuano Bay and borrow some from your General Freyre. Surely he would loan us two or three hundred for a project worthy as this! But let us proceed now with our reconnaissance, which will require our moving into the inner harbor. I am certain we will come under fire of those shore batteries, and we can assess them better."

Cochrane proved correct. Detention of the pilot quickly generated suspicion ashore. A heavy fire abruptly opened upon the *O'Higgins* as she cruised into the bay. It was erratic and distracted, the naval officer not a whit from the mission he had set for himself. As the vessel cruised about, sounding waters and improving the charts Christian had sketched, the officers estimated the calibers of the shore guns, which had no more chance to score a hit on the Chilean vessel than they would have upon a moving fly.

"Seventeen forts they are indeed, Fletcher," Cochrane agreed on the second day. "But many can be discounted. Only four or five are of concern to us. I do not consider them impregnable at all, except perhaps from the sea. Given a few more men, good fortune will attend our effort—let us hope."

The shore guns quieted as the *O'Higgins* sailed beyond their reach; but she still flew her Spanish colors, which Cochrane had allowed to remain aloft as an insult rather than any further disguise. It was fortunate he did so, for as they rounded the headlands, they found themselves hard upon the 20-gun Spanish brig *Portillo*. The Chileans quickly boarded her, taking the vessel without firing a shot. This small ship was a welcome addition to their strength, but to add to the delight of the men, she was found to be bringing 30,000 *pesos* in back pay for the Valdivia garrison. This sum the admiral promptly impounded as prize money, he informed his men, for distribution upon their capture of the fortress.

At their resounding three cheers, he remarked to Major Miller, "I imagined that would stoke their enthusiasm!"

"Yes, sir," agreed the marine officer, cheerfully. "Not that they needed it, but a bit of gold will ever lift their spirits."

Cochrane sent aboard the *Portillo* a prize crew, and the two vessels proceeded northward to Talcahuano Bay and Concepción where Freyre readily loaned him the service of Major George Beauchef, a French volunteer, and 250 foot soldiers. Freyre urged Cochrane to take along a Chilean schooner, the *Montezuma*, and a Brazilian brig, the *Intrepido*, which volunteered her services for a share in any booty. With these additions to his strength, the admiral sailed southward once again toward Valdivia.

En route Cochrane explained the mission for the benefit of newly recruited army and sea-going officers. "I must admit that one or two questioned the prudence of attacking so great an installation with a force so modest," he conceded happily. "But I explained that if novel projects are undertaken with sufficient energy, they almost invariably succeed in spite of odds. This convinced them."

At any rate, mused Christian, *those that do succeed are reported by history.* The others are forgotten. No one is interested in perpetuating the memory of debacles.

On the night of January 29 the *O'Higgins* lay in a dead calm off a coastal island. Cochrane had left the deck watch in charge of the lieutenant who also turned in, surrendering the watch to a midshipman, who promptly lay down upon a pile of sacking and fell asleep. A sudden breeze swung the ship in toward the land and the midshipman, springing to his feet, attempted to bring her around but instead ran her with a grinding crash upon a submerged rock where she hung on her elm keel, the powerful rollers beating her savagely, rocking her back and forth under their sledgelike blows. The other vessels had not hove into view. Christian rushed on deck at a cry to lower the boats and abandon ship, a howl stilled at his authoritative bellow:

"Hold up, men! There is no immediate danger; I've survived many such incidents. If you go over the side, all 600 of you, three-fourths of you will drown. The boats can take only 150. Any who reaches the coast of Arauco will meet nothing but torture and death from the Indians—I know them too! Help us salvage the ship. She is hung up but not damaged seriously, yet. We can float her off! I'd wager on't!"

Cochrane at this moment rushed on deck in his night clothes and seconded Christian's plea. Chains of bailing crews were organized as the pumps were out of order. There was now five feet of sea in the bilges, and it was deepening. Christian and Cochrane labored in the darkness to repair the pumps since they had no carpenter aboard familiar with such devices. By midnight they had them working once more. The hold water began decreasing.

"By God, I believe she'll swim!" cried Cochrane.

"Aye, sir. With a kedge I think we can pull her off. We'll soon see!"

With difficulty the frigate was heaved off the rock. Her hull appeared fairly sound—at least would keep her afloat—and there were plenty of hands to man her. Unfortunately her magazine had been under water and the gunpowder rendered useless save for a little that was on deck and what the troops retained in their cartouche-boxes.

"Oh, confound it!" grumbled Cochrane. "We'd not try to outgun the Spaniards anyway. It will force us to the bayonet, and that is the best weapon against them!" His case of battle fever by now was too far advanced for any rational cure.

Christian silently shook his head. However harebrained he thought the expedition, he would make no protest. All men must die sometime. One might as well perish trying to take Valdivia as keel over some morning reaching for his boots.

Once floated free, the *O'Higgins* stood off the island until daylight, when she was joined by the *Montezuma* and *Intrepido*. Cochrane selected the *Montezuma* as his new flagship; and the *O'Higgins* was ordered to stand off to sea, limping along in the wake of the expedition, to be used for reinforcement in case of need.

So it happened, with men so crowding the decks that the two small craft seemed near to foundering, that Lord Cochrane and his wild undertaking ventured into Valdivia harbor to tackle Spanish might—and the most elaborate fortification system in the Western Hemisphere. It was February 2, 1820.

CHAPTER TWENTY-ONE

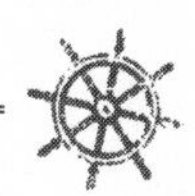

The sides of the estuary at the neck of the inner harbor were only three-quarters of a mile apart, and their artfully-constructed forts lined them so that cross fire could be directed at any approaching enemy. But outside the inner harbor, in the bay opening to the Pacific, were the preliminary works. El Ingles was that farthest toward to the ocean, facing a narrow beach. Progressing inward, on the southern shore, were the principal fortresses of San Carlos, Amargos, Corocomayo, Alto, and finally, the stoutest of all, Corral Castle. On the opposite coast was Niebla, carved from living rock eighty feet above the sea. In addition there were the brooding guns of the fortress on the island of Mancera, which lay athwart the entryway to the river system leading to the city of Valdivia, as Christian well remembered.

Above the forests on either coast rose low mountains, their woods dense and all but impenetrable, and over all lay invariably the thick clouds and fog.

"The most practical plan would be to take the outer fort first, then roll them up, one by one, toward the strongest," mused Cochrane. "If we can get the movement started with enough spirit, the panic will increase as we move from one to another. By the time we get to the great fort, fright alone may topple it into our arms." No thought of failure ever passed his mind; his brain was geared to triumph.

"Yes, sir. The Spanish flags, again?"

Cochrane flashed his rare smile. "Of course, Fletcher. Of course. First, however, lower the boats on the lee side, so they will be hidden from the shore—we don't wish to reveal our plan of attack. All our foot soldiers are to remain below until the last moment."

"Aye, sir."

Flying the red and gold, the *Montezuma* and *Intrepido* approached within hailing distance of the shore. A Spanish prisoner was made to call for a pilot, while the raiders washed inland slowly toward the greatly restricted landing space below the works.

"What does he say, eh?" demanded Cochrane as a wavering call floated from the shore. The translator turned to him.

"He says to send one of our boats in for the pilot—a ruse, I think."

"Yes, yes. No doubt. Tell him—tell him we lost our boats rounding the Cape. He must send us the pilot in his own bottom."

At the moment Christian appeared, grinning. "And tell him to forget that boat of ours, which has drifted free and is in his plain sight! Tell him we don't know whose boat that is."

Cochrane roared with laughter as he peered over the side to see the errant craft. "Well, 'the best-laid plans—' It would be difficult to force a landing in that surf if they oppose us strongly. We had best wait."

The swell had grown high, solid breakers crashing onto the beach with the roar of artillery, sending white spray in clouds against the green hills beyond. While they temporized, the Spanish mustered defenses, firing alarm guns, swiftly trotting up reinforcements from neighboring garrisons to bolster El Ingles, which appeared to be armed with twelve or fifteen guns.

Cannon of the fort suddenly opened fire upon the brig and schooner, a lucky shot crashed into the *Intrepido*, killing two men and instantly arousing to still a higher pitch Cochrane's fiery combativeness. He ordered the two vessels to swing in close to shore and prepare landing parties, surf or no. Hard under the enemy guns actually proved safer since the muzzles of the fortress cannon could not be depressed sufficiently. The landings at once commenced with great difficulty through the heavy seas.

Cochrane descended into a gig; and Major Miller with forty-four marines shoved off, instantly coming under small-arms fire from positions above the landing place. The marines leaped ashore, driving the Spaniards before them at bayonet point and clearing the beach. A second launch, bringing more marines, now approached while the first was sent to the ships for infantry. With each boat-load, the landing zone was extended. In less than an hour, 300 men were ashore; and as darkness fell, offensive operations were quickly planned.

"The only approach to Ingles is by a precipitous path, sir, where the men would have to pass single file," said Christian. "I don't believe we can get our people into the fort without a ladder."

"Take a prisoner for a guide, Fletcher, and let us see what can be done. Try to get above and behind the place. Perhaps you can find a back entrance."

Christian carefully chose the reconnaissance unit. With these few men, he slipped into the hills behind the fort under guidance of a captured Chilean who leaned toward the patriot cause anyway. In silence they secured and held their new positions, which the main attack force moved up by another way, making all the noise they could to distract attention from Christian's important work. Fire was poured through the darkness toward the noisy patriot column; but little damage was done; and there was no cannon support since the great guns were wrongly aimed for this kind of attack, as Cochrane had known they would be. With the 800 defenders so busily engaged and amid the great uproar, Christian and his second in command, Ensign Francisco Vidal, improvised a bridge to cross the fort's deep moat. On the other side, they found a magazine door left ajar by scurrying powder boys in their haste—or perhaps it was rarely shut. Christian instantly deployed his sharp-shooters along the bluff to the rear of the immediate works. At his signal they loosed volleys into the backs of the defenders, at the same time uttering such ferocious cries that panic gripped the Spanish who imagined themselves assailed from the rear by a vastly superior force.

They plunged from their secure positions down the road toward their great neighbor Fortress San Carlos, overrunning and spreading their terror amongst 300 reinforcements sweeping to their support. The Chileans, their bayonets well bloodied, swiftly followed them up, swarming into fort after fort, almost as fast as the fugitives. Cochrane screamed at them: "Speed! Hurry! Don't let the panic subside! Multiply it! Right on their heels, lads! After them! Hound them!" His words may not have been comprehensible to all, but his tone and wild enthusiasm were; and the effect was instantaneous. The Chileans and marines put each position to the blade as they ran on, none of the forts having defenses organized for such sweeping, all-powerful land attack; and each had been looted of all effectives who could be spared to bolster El Ingles during the previous afternoon.

Mighty Corral was stormed with the others, in the full flush of the patriot success. Some of the enemy escaped in light boats, fleeing all the way to Valdivia up river, while others plunged into the forest to become lost. Before midnight the entire coast was in patriot hands with even Cochrane astounded at the stunning success, which exceeded his wildest aspirations; and with Cochrane these visions were extravagant indeed!

The total patriot loss was but seven killed and nineteen wounded. Upwards of 100 prisoners were seized; more than that total had fallen to patriot bayonets, as dawn revealed. But his miraculous success must be repeated upon the opposite shore where the forts were even more formidable, if held with resolution and spirit. They were not.

Cochrane, realizing that the impetus of an assault depended upon the freshest of troops, gave his fighters a one-day layover. Then he embarked with 200 men on the *Montezuma* and *Intrepido* for the short run across the estuary to assail the remaining forts. At this very moment, the damaged *O'Higgins* hove in sight. Thinking only of the demonstrated invincibility of the invaders and presuming mighty reinforcements coming up on the frigate, the Spaniards panicked without firing a shot, tumbling out of their strong redoubts into their boats and pulling hard up the river.

"We should pursue them vigorously, sir," urged Christian. "We should not wish to lose our momentum."

"Right you are, Fletcher," agreed Cochrane. "And since you know the river well and have turned the tide with our attack upon these forts, you may lead the pursuit! And good hunting!"

Embarking with a strong force of marines and infantry in the many boats the Spanish had abandoned, Christian moved his improvised flotilla swiftly upstream, expertly selecting the correct channels amid the maze of islands. It seemed as yesterday when he had come this way before. Upon reaching the mud bank landing at Valdivia, he half expected to be opposed by Gregorio himself. Instead he was greeted by a delegation of frightened citizens bearing a flag of truce. The enemy had abandoned the town after plundering it of everything portable and with the civil officials had fled overland toward Chiloé. They left only military booty but an enormous collection of that. Cochrane instantly set his secretaries to inventory the loot, though it would take many days to complete it.

The admiral resolved meanwhile upon a preliminary distribution of spoils among his officers and men. They never had been paid in full since the squadron was organized, had suffered much, endured much; and compensation was past due them. Besides, he was convinced, it would fire their enthusiasm and fortify their faith in him. Until captured ships and military stores could be converted into money, he had no funds save the 30,000 *pesos* seized from the *Portillo*. This he now determined to share among the men.

Christian, with no formal commission, could lay no claim to any of the spoils, but Cochrane was well aware of his countryman's services and value and allotted him a share only slightly less than his own: 1,000 *pesos* "as a commencement upon what Chile owes you." While embarrassed a bit by the praise, Christian accepted the award. With the novel weight of this large amount of money in his belt, he set out through the rain to discover Valdivia anew, already alive with memories that warmed, even as the day chilled into night.

He visited an old *pulpería*, where he once drank with his fellow officers, though now deserted since the Spaniards had taken flight. Christian sat alone over a bottle of wine, calling to memory those earlier days when all the world seemed, if about as evil, better organized, more stable. He put aside the emptied bottle at last and stepped out into the night.

Christian climbed the hill on slippery planks and gained the plaza here on one side of the square where the brothels lay silent, all but abandoned now with the royalist soldiery gone. Cochrane's men had not arrived save for a vanguard; the main body of troops would be along, perhaps tomorrow. Christian started to move on when a low call halted him, as if by a rawhide leash.

"*Señor!*" came the cry again, from a bundle of rags half-hidden in a doorway, only faintly revealed by some interior light. "A little coin, *señor?* A little money to help an old woman?" He made to move on, but she called to him again, "Please, *señor*—anything. A small something you might spare? I will help you, *señor*. Only a *peso*. One *peso—anything, señor!*" Christian shook his head and turned away, into the rain. Once more the call reached him, pleading, touching him in some way he could not explain.

"Then give me just a peseta, *señor*—only one little peseta for a splash of wine to warm my gut. 'Tis a cold night, *señor*. I have a chill. One tiny peseta?"

With irritation Christian finally reached into his pocket, drew a coin to toss to the woman, then unaccountably stepped into the doorway and handed it to her. She reached out with long spidery fingers to clutch it, turning it toward the light as she did so. Christian drew back in horror. Her face! It was white, bloated a bit, but disfigured by a hideous slash that had left it noseless, a caricature of a woman's features. Even as he recoiled memory stabbed him.

"Who are you, woman? How are you called?"

She smiled at him, or grimaced, rather—an attempt at a smile; and despite the horrible appearance, there was a flash of something from long ago that jarred his recollection.

"Roca," she replied. "Roca is what they call me, those who call me anything."

"Roca what?"

"Just Roca, *señor*. Everyone knows Roca. Oh, once, long ago, I had another name, but no one uses it now. I do not even remember it, except sometimes. I am Roca, just Roca. It is enough."

"Roca—Roca Montalván? Could that be it?"

Her face stilled. Her body, loose beneath the rags, tensed. Her voice firmed. "How did you know?" she asked, wearily.

"Roca Montalván! You remember Gregorio? I am the other—do you remember, Roca? Do you recall the foreigner long, long ago? The man for whom you gave your beauty, your face at the hands of that Spanish dog, Gregorio? Do you remember, Roca?"

She covered her mutilated features with her long fingers and bent forward as though trying to recall, or in an effort to forget. Her shoulders quivered, then pulsed with sobs, the first tears in her memory, for tears were as foreign to her as hope. Christian waited for the weeping to subside.

"I remember," came the dead voice. "Yes, I remember."

Christian leaned forward.

"Invite me in, Roca," he urged in a strange tone, pleading. "Now—invite me in!"

She peered at him slyly through the bony fingers. "A *peso, señor?* A whole peso, perhaps?"

He brusquely but not unkindly bundled her through the door, into the crib illuminated by a single flickering oil lamp. Here in the dim light, Christian was able to see her better, her tortured face turned toward him openly now, with no apology, the woman awaiting she knew not what. To her, Christian, standing just inside the door, appeared to fill the room. His handsome face creased with concern, or perhaps with recollection as he stared down at this shell of a woman he once had briefly loved. Once loved? He did not know, it was so long past. But as he looked at her, within him glowed a strange warming that he could not identify, but it moved through pity, nearing the province of love itself—not a harsh, carnal love, but an emotion deeper, more inclusive, an emotion he had never detected before. It was intense, personal, and yet impersonal. It flowed through his being and clouded his mind and lost itself there. And the woman waited. Watched.

Christian took his heavy belt, containing the 1,000 silver *pesos*, an incredible fortune for one not accustomed to wealth, and placed it gently in her hands.

"Your *peso*, Roca." He smiled as she gazed disbelieving at the belt, weighing it in her hands, searching his face with unbelieving eyes.

"If you guard it wisely, it will assure your future," he promised softly. "With wisdom it may even grow."

She reached for his hand, but he forestalled her, raising her grimy fingers to his lips, brushing them lightly.

"I shall not see you again, Roca," he said. "But somehow I love you, in a way I cannot understand. In spirit I shall be with you always."

He turned and passed through the doorway, stepping down into the mud, striding across the plaza, his mind full of what once had been and what might have been. He scarcely noted when Ishmael joined him, trotting beside like a shadow until Christian came to himself, turned and saw him as they faced again toward the brown river, the reed beds, the boats, and down the stream beyond to the fortresses and the harbors, and the sea.

And Christian's strange restlessness shouldered strongly into him, his dissatisfaction, his irritation with himself and with others. There was the old, old question when he looked once again at Ishmael, as he might have gazed at a reflection in a mirror. "Why?" he asked, needing to say no more.

"Ye have done many things right of late, Fletcher," said the old man, halting. "As far as you've gone, that is to say."

"Then why do I feel empty suddenly, when for a moment, back there, I felt so complete?"

"Because you have not done it all, Fletcher. You overcame repugnance with the greater power of love, extending compassion, instead of insisting upon pride. This is good; the faithfulness to yourself, to your duty, and the love for another. They show that you pursue a course that is right and true."

"I repeat the question then, old man, my mentor, my conscience I suppose: Why then am I so empty, dissatisfied? Why does the rain rinse out my guts, the wind blow through my soul?"

Ishmael's face lightened. "Because you have yet to admit that you are not complete unto yourself. You have not accepted the fact that you are not independent, but dependent. You can not be truly independent until you recognize that you are not alone, not self-sufficient, but a member of the Company."

"And how do I acquire this singular knowledge, for Christ's sake? To whom do I turn?"

Ishmael's smile broadened now, giving his face an impish caste. He spread his hands as though to suggest how obvious it all was.

"You just said it yourself! To Christ, to God—who else?"

The momentum of Ishmael's thought clashing with his rising frustration caused Christian's face to flush, his eyes to reveal his rising tenseness. He did not know why he feared the waiting Presence whom Ishmael called to his remembrance. "Sometimes, Ishmael, if you goad me beyond my reason, I will destroy you. Not because I wish to, but because you will drive me to it!"

Christian saw in Ishmael's face the recognition that the fury in his own voice reflected only the torment in his soul, that he was struggling with the pressure of his stream-of-life backing up against the dam of Ishmael's faith. The conflict was building, swelling, pressing, warning of cataclysm. Not now. But soon.

CHAPTER TWENTY-TWO

Cochrane summoned Christian to his cabin as the flagship wallowed listlessly in the slight sea within Valparaíso Bay. The fleet had returned from Valdivia and now lay at anchor.

"Your wishes, sir?"

"I must discover what lies in the minds of San Martín, and O'Higgins. Is there any future on this coast for a sea dog, at least in the hire of others? Perhaps you can discover these things? You know these people."

"Possibly. I had thought we were engaged in a Revolution?"

"The 'Grand Revolution' seems to be falling apart," Cochrane growled. "I have received word of a growing debacle on all sides, mutiny everywhere."

"Where is San Martín? O'Higgins?"

"I don't know. The *generalissimo* went toward Buenos Aires, the last I knew. I understand he is headed back, due to cross the Andes in a litter! He thinks he suffers from rheumatism, or something like it.

"And O'Higgins?"

"At Santiago, up to his neck in difficulties with his civil government. Quite unable to give the necessary attention to winding up this Revolution. What a contemptible mess!"

Cochrane stroked the side of his nose with a finger, then continued:

"Discover their plans—if they have any! If they would name me commander-in-chief of all their forces, land and sea, I would end this bloody war within weeks."

Christian found O'Higgins at the Chilean capital, his cordial self. "Magnificent, Cochrane's action at Valdivia!" he cried. "Incredible! Only a fool would think otherwise; try to make political capital out of it."

Christian raised a brow.

"Some fools condemn Cochrane for acting without orders! Jealousy! What more do I have to put up with?" His eyes rolled upward in mock despair. "I trust San Martín will not listen to such idiocy. Be careful when you talk with the general—no one knows what suspicions may have been implanted in his mind. He is not well."

Christian discovered San Martín at the Andean mineral baths, treating his ailment while wallowing in dismay at the threatened political ruin.

"The La Plata government is threatened by a pampa uprising," he said, despair in his black eyes. "Intrigues are reported from Paris for royalty to rule in the United Provinces. Buenos Aires is almost in anarchy. I am ordered there to restore, but our own army is near mutiny in Cuyo. If I return to La Plata, the dream of continental freedom is destroyed, for we shall never muster another force capable of seizing Peru; while the Spanish hold Peru, they hold America, or the heart of it. I am a man among ruins!"

"How can there be nothing but ruins while you live? While O'Higgins remains the supreme director of Chile? While Cochrane commands the sea?" argued Christian heatedly. "Sir you underrate the invincibility of such talents!"

"Spain continues to be formidable at Lima."

"In numbers, perhaps. But in genius, in dedication, Peru can never match the forces of liberation, General."

The commander's gloom refused to lift.

"This 'genius' as you call it, can be brought to bear only through rebellion against our own," he sighed. "I must disobey Buenos Aires. O'Higgins must defy his Senate. Cochrane must defy everyone to fulfill the goals he could never even explain to landsmen."

"True, of course."

"Liberation designed to be of benefit to everyone can come about only by destruction of those of us who have achieved it, destruction that defies the will of the majority, which is often contrary to their own best interests."

"I perceive you have listened to the critics of Cochrane?"

"I listen to them, all. I believe no one."

"None but your inner voice?"

San Martín looked at him sharply.

"None other."

"And the voice insists that you go not to Buenos Aires but to Lima?"

"Yes."

"Cochrane, O'Higgins—they, too, share your vision, your—integrity of purpose. You insist you believe no one other than yourself? But they are moved by the same voices! Believe theirs; believe in *them*. Together you can conquer Peru—while separately you can do nothing. Come, talk with them! They await your leadership, even if they do not always recognize their need for it!"

CHAPTER TWENTY-THREE

Peru and its sister territory, Upper Peru, possessed about 2 million souls, Indians making up the majority. Indigenous races numbered more than half the total and mixed races one-fifth, while Spaniards consisted of a bare one-seventh of the population. Its strength was found in Spanish arms and a potent military clique, which ruled the country. The army which held Lima included about 8,000 men, that of Upper Peru about 7,000, and detached garrisons and other forces brought the total to some 23,000, against whom San Martín had sought valiantly to organize a liberation expedition of 4,000. But there was much dissension among the Peruvian forces—insurrections and revolts had eroded their loyalties; and the cruelties with which they were suppressed only succeeded in stoking the fires of freedom. It was a singular thing that the flames of liberalism burned most hotly within the corps of Spanish officers, while they were almost non-existent among colonial officers.

In July of 1820, San Martín gathered an expeditionary force at Valparaíso. Renamed the Liberating Army of Peru, it consisted of 4,450 officers and men, making up 6 battalions of infantry, two regiments of cavalry and support units, with additional equipment for 15,000 freedom fighters in Peru who might defect to the patriot cause. The escort squadron included 8 ships of war, led by the refitted *O'Higgins*, the *San Martín*, and the frigate *Hercules*, the warships mounting a total of 247 guns; in addition there were 16 transports and 11 gunboats. By mid-August all was in readiness.

With this great expedition, the Revolutionary movement in the south edged toward its climax as did the career and the life of Christian Fletcher. He was now 57. He had reached an age when the issue of soundness comes into view as more momentous than any other, the stage for the intelligent man when stability becomes the thing, with himself and for himself. Then one's life must become ordered, logical—or nothing.

Possibly the long idle hours floating northward gave him pause to examine his store of unanswered questions. He sought answers to riddles he could scarcely identify. He was a man, but to what purpose? There was none to ask save Ishmael, and

Ishmael replied in riddles that only added to his frustration. Christian knew that he was driven now toward some unknown destination with relentless urgency.

"The battle that is every man's," murmured a voice at his elbow.

It was Ishmael, of course, and Christian, staring across the purple sea, scanning the waters for a rock, asked, "What battle?" It was early. They were alone. Time stretched before them.

"The struggle that's within thee," said Ishmael, softly. "The battle of thyself against thy destiny, of arrogance against acceptance, of heedlessness against reason, the realization of your mortality and your blind progression into nothingness. A contest that must be resolved by each person alone, by application of no formula save one."

"That one?"

"Faith, man. Faith in God. In submission. The only purpose humanity has ever found. As God's creation, one must fit into the pattern. There is no other."

"It sounds over simple for a solution to the ache of desolation I feel."

"'Tis simple. Yet 'tis the most profound step one can take, for it turns the world around. It is a decision based upon who is in command, who is the master, who is the pilot. The right decision revises one's view on every bearing."

"If 'tis as important as all that, why not just voice submission, no matter what you truly believe?"

"Because you deal with God. God you cannot toy with, for he knows the truth. With others you may dissemble, you may lie, you may procrastinate. But with God that is not possible. On that frontier you come up against a wall of stone. You conceal truth at your peril."

Christian felt the old surge of impatience, now become near-defiance. Ishmael clouded his vision like a Channel mist. He hammered at the rail and groaned: "I cannot believe, Ishmael! I will not!"

"Aye," the other responded, quietly. "That is the thing: ye will not. 'Tis not that ye cannot accept, but that ye contort your mind so that it becomes a contest of will, and that's the heart of the matter. Will—or pride."

"I shall not become another's slave, not even the slave of your God, Ishmael."

"'Tis not a slave you become, but free! The greatest, most absolute freedom known to man, the only freedom. For 'tis freedom from the tyranny of your own will and your desire and frustration. All of those burdens are lifted and placed in another's hands, when ye accept your proper role and at last become yourself. There is no other solution to avoid descent into hopelessness or destruction. No other solution."

Christian broke into a humorless grin, though his voice revealed his inner turmoil.

"How could this God, whom you call good, sign me on, a man whose life is drenched with evil?"

"You exaggerate. You equivocate. You rationalize. You do not understand. To God there is no such as good or evil before the contract is drawn, the ship's papers signed. There is only hope, and waiting, and joy when a man comes to his senses and acknowledges the bond, the reality of the strakes and timbers of his life. Have you never read the parable of the wayward son? A son with no evil design within his soul, but evil done because he failed to recognize the goodness of his father and his true place within that household? With recognition came peace, no further desperation, a purpose to his life."

"I once had faith as a child, I suppose. It wandered off, somehow."

"Faith never leaves a man. He becomes lost from it, is all. He must return in this life, for he has no other destiny. The more firmly he holds to his illusion of independence, the more distance he must recover; but he cannot escape the journey. He may delay it only, thus making it more difficult for himself."

"To the point of impossibility?"

"Perhaps. Who can say? At any rate he is a fool who creates such monstrous problems for himself."

"So say you."

"No. *I* say nothing. I merely repeat what I have learned."

"I think faith in God belonged to an earlier, simpler time; it was easier in the years of my father and my mother. We have advanced so far, explored the whole world and found God nowhere, nor His Heaven. Our science has improved beyond measure, no doubt will progress farther still. We have guns of greater caliber, ships of more range, spy-glasses that can pick out distant galaxies, and we can see neither Heaven nor your God. I think we have outlived any need for Him. He cannot be proven to exist, therefore does not exist—for me, at any rate." Christian felt the burning in his soul at that lie thrown in the face of the One who waited so patiently.

"Nor can He be proven not to exist, Fletcher. Ye speak of not finding Him 'out there,' as though God were a person, an old man like me or you, and Heaven a place, like England. Both concepts are those of infants, as well ye know. Ye speak of modern contrivances and discoveries, yet by conceding they but foreshadow far greater ones to come ye admit that they are but as toys, and we, their users, are but children. Your denial is like a lad in his sandbox having learned to create and manipulate his simple inventions, believing thereby that he has no parents and has outlived the need for them! What nonsense! His parents exist whether he wishes to believe in them or not. They control his destiny, even though he controls some part of it himself, in a limited sense. His denial of them means nothing save future hardship if he persists."

"I believe I am a unit apart, with no hold on the past nor legacy to leave, here for a moment only, then returned to dust forever."

"Like all men you are the product of your father's seed and hence his endless chain of forefathers; of your mother's womb and thus of her people for all ages past. You have in turn influenced in some way many thousands of other people, in your passage, by your thought, your reactions to them, your participation in events which will mold all generations to come. How can you say you are 'apart'? That, too, is childish, unworthy of your intelligence. No man is a separate creation, nor is any man without responsibility for past and future. It is only when he recognizes his true role, however, and to whom he owes obedience, that his influence befits his destiny."

"Adam and Eve and all that?" Christian grinned.

"There is Adam in every man," countered Ishmael, grimly. I am Adam and so are you."

"In what manner?"

"Because we know what we should do, yet we do what we should not do; and because of this we are estranged from God. It is our willfulness, our desire to do what we know is wrong that is the Adam in us; 'tis a universal failing."

"Then why try to improve?"

Ishmael reflected upon the blunt question, then shook his head.

"Aye. Aye, there is reason there. Why indeed? I suppose because there is not only some Adam in everyone, there is also some Christ. Because they cannot help it. Because in their souls they know that they should point toward Christ and not toward Adam." He held his silence for a moment. "Thus is humanity," he sighed. "We can wonder, we being the plague, the riddle; once in awhile, the glory of creation."

Christian frowned. "Humans are only wretches with the potential of nobility but cursed with such untidy instincts as avarice, selfishness, arrogance, jealousy—all the malevolent impulses. They are creatures who are base, who barter souls for gold, who slay their mothers for a profit, abandon their wives, sell their children, grovel in slime, do all or any of these for wealth—for money alone. They are a most unpleasant, unlovable, disreputable, despicable lot."

"You are not so."

"Don't be oversure. I am human, therefore I am potentially worthless. This God you speak of could not be God and still love humans; for they are soul-less monsters nothing truly good could ever treasure. They exhibit all the characteristics foreign to the God you describe. How could one love what is foreign to Him?"

"You concede that we have the 'potential of nobility.' Perhaps God loves the noble in us."

Christian snorted. "I doubt it." He looked gloomily at the far horizon. "We are an experiment that failed." Having so declaimed, he sought again to bring reason to the matter. "You have often said that acceptance brings peace and goodness to men's minds and actions. Yet you have seen with me the savagery of Spaniards who profess the faith of Christ and practice the devil's own! Would you have me become as they? 'Tis lost I'd rather be."

Ishmael raised a warning finger. "Ye cannot judge the faith you should possess by the appearance of another's," he cautioned. "Nor should you judge some other's, nor thank God you are not as they may be, for if you do so you are worse. Your faith is an inward thing, of yourself alone; ye are bound not to imitate any other but to obey the voice ye hear. That path is the course to growth. In that way it becomes worthy of you and you of it."

"And the Spanish?"

"Forget the Spanish, or condemn not them but the evil that they do, and do no evil yourself, not because you are good or can make yourself good, but because you follow One who is good, and in imitation have ye hope and trust."

"There is no goodness aside from him?"

"Not truly 'goodness.' Only an absence of evil."

"Then why not rely upon that?"

"It cannot be depended upon since 'tis an accidental thing, and we cannot abide existence by happenstance, but must have a chart for what we do. That is what troubles you, Fletcher. That and your eternal, blinding pride."

"I do not feel this pride."

"Pride in self. Arrogance. The fiction that you are master of your soul, definer of your destiny, fashioner of your fate. The unwillingness to accept the truth that you are not the captain but foremast hand, that without a captain you are lost, that there can be no triumph—only death—in mutiny!"

The thrust drove him home, but only briefly.

"'Tis not pride I feel—only my accursed 'stick,' that mace swings about my head and smashes not my skull but those of others who have no fault, no guilt, or at least do not share mine. That is the thing, Ishmael."

"Your 'stick' you say? You have no 'stick'! Your curse? You have no curse, save within your stubborn mind. Your curse is not something laid on you by another. Your curse is your disbelief."

"Disbelief?"

"Aye. Disbelief in your servanthood. In your duty to Another, greater than any captain of this life. Duty owed by Fletcher, by all people, by all nations. 'Tis all the same."

"What about the disasters I have wrought to countless others?"

"Aye, the disasters were real enough, but your being instrument for them is another thing, and 'tis not real, in any sense. All men feel a curse—feel cursed by what they do. All must atone, in mind, in commitment to another, and there is no other way. You are human. You have no other recourse, yet acceptance is available for you, as for all men. The life of Christ provides you an escape. One person is never master of another, at least of his spirit, his true life. Each one, each individual, must tread alone. The incidents upon which ye brood are incidents not for you but for others, fitting into their web of existence, not cast there by you or any other mortal being. Far from being cursed, as ye so fondly hold, you are greatly loved, for you have been spared from a succession of events such as have befallen few others within my knowledge or, for all of that, my imagination.

"And for what have you been spared? Because you have not yet run out your ribbon, nor reached that maturity, that state, when you have done what you can do and are ready to accept new work. 'Tis your own development, your own adulthood, your own character that should concern you, not the mythic influence of some 'stick' belaboring others. When your time comes, Fletcher, you will move on, and 'tis for the greatness of it I would make you ready."

"Move on to what?"

Ishmael smiled. "If I knew that, I would not be mortal," he replied. "Being mortal I know it not, but I know it."

"Riddles, again."

"Aye. Riddles. But one thing is not a riddle—that you are important because you are unique. There was none like you before, nor will there ever be again, through all of time to come."

"That's fortunate."

"Aye, for everyone. There are no duplicates."

Dimly, from the far recesses of his mind, there swept upon Christian words, out of a formless void to assume shape and beat against his consciousness: "*Laich!*"

they called, "*Laich, anochi iemach . . .*" thundering upon his mind until, his face ashen, his lips trembling, he all but collapsed against the rail. Ishmael caught at his arm and steadied him. "What is it, lad?"

"Those words, those words have hounded me all of my life since, since . . ."

"What words?"

"Would I knew, Ishmael. I know not whose they are or what they say, but only their sound: '*Laich,*' they seem to say, '*laich, anochi iemach,*' and that is all, but clearly they come to me! There is no more. Never is there more!"

"'*Laich? Anochi iemach?*' They are Hebrew, lad. 'Go!' is what I make of them: 'Go—I am with you!' And curse is it ye fear? Tosh, man! With words like those, ye are above the curse of anyone!"

Perhaps he felt crushed by the weight of Ishmael's words and struggled so against them; or it may be that the arguments fell upon more receptive ground; but whatever the cause, the battle was joined as never before within his churning soul. The words of Ishmael released a flood of passion within Fletcher Christian, made more overwhelming because of the long delay in its release. They thundered in upon his mind, foaming and beating at his resistance as with the force of the sea itself. He even raised his fists above his head in frustration and smashed them at the rail before him, then turned aside and stumbled off below, his mind rent, but not yet broken.

When he emerged again long after upon the sunlit deck, he spoke no word to Ishmael, though his whitened face revealed his inward battle, the struggle between his willful faith in nothing and the old man's unshakeable confidence in his tomorrow. He wished to believe in nothing. He insisted he did. And yet he could not—quite. Into the edges of his consciousness the words of Ishmael over the long decades had commenced at last their work, their emergence into awareness before acceptance. So the struggle at last was joined. The prize was not ethereal, nor even earthly. The prize was Christian.

CHAPTER TWENTY-FOUR

The convoy transporting the Liberating Army of Peru wallowed north, reaching the hook of Pisco, fifty leagues southeast of Lima, on September 7. Cochrane wished to cut off and seize the town and garrison. San Martín, more prudently or as the admiral believed, more timidly, forbade the troops to advance upon the settlement until fully 3,000 were put ashore. The landing force under Las Heras moved out gingerly for Pisco itself, while the general aboard the *Montezuma* ran down the bay to spy out the movements of the enemy. His glass and informants told him that the royalist force was negligible, and so it proved: 40 regulars and 200 undependable militia directing the panicked evacuation of the residents of the place, with all their goods.

"Why must they flee?" wondered San Martín with irritation. "We come not as conquerors but as liberators!"

"Perhaps, General, but they do not wish liberation; they fear it," murmured his aide. The officer sadly shook his head; he had not prepared for this.

But the operation had effects that reached much farther than the thoroughly undistinguished hamlet of Pisco. A few days later, a Spanish vessel hove into view, flying a white flag. An officer representing viceroy Pezuela boarded the *O'Higgins* to confer with San Martín and Cochrane, initiating talks that continued the better part of a week, but an accommodation could not be reached and hostilities resumed in October.

A patriot column on October 5 occupied Ica, on the plateau twenty-five leagues southeast of Pisco, capturing two companies of royalist infantry, the first crack in the enemy facade, though not a very meaningful one. A few more small actions, inconsequential in every way, were pursued in this direction, but it became obvious even to San Martín that little of a decisive nature could be accomplished so far to the south of Lima, their principle objective. Cochrane already had reached that decision; he had arrived at it in fact before such brushfire operations were even commenced, and his irritation with them mounted steadily. San Martín had sought to ignite a conflagration. He had assumed that the liberators would be met with joy and open arms, but apathy greeted them everywhere. "The most revealing thing is the reluctance of the slaves to come forward," the general glumly conceded. "It was a mistake to launch our initial effort so far south."

"Then what do you intend to do?" demanded Cochrane bluntly. "If the choice were mine, I should land every man I have on the coast south of Callao, and I'd have a decisive victory within forty-eight hours!"

San Martín turned his opaque gaze upon the restless Englishman silently. None could discern what went on in his mind. There was little love between the two, but each was intelligent enough to realize he had need of the other. The general slowly shook off the suggestion.

"It would not do, sir," denied the other. "If we won the battle, it would never prove decisive while Peru seethes with twice the number of troops available in that area. The capital is too large for us to garrison against a still-strong enemy. No, we must stir up a patriot conflagration, or we must chew up the royalists piecemeal. There is no other way." San Martín nervously drummed the tabletop with his long fingers. "I think we must reembark our people and move north, perhaps to Trujillo, and try again."

"What foolishness is this?" seethed Cochrane. "Trujillo is 100 leagues north of Lima. How do you expect to take Peru from there?" He shook his head in disgust. "I refuse to transport you and your shirttail army completely out of the region of operations, sir! I will not do it! You must stay and fight it out or accept my resignation. Give me a ship and crew, and I will return to nations where fighting men do not fear battle." He relented then, if slightly. "Or avoid it, at any rate."

San Martín flushed hotly. "Sir, my courage has never before been questioned. If you choose now to make an issue of it, I shall be happy to oblige you!"

Stirred from the lethargy into which he had fallen, Christian leaned forward, his voice quiet, but insistent.

"Gentlemen, may I have a word?" His interruption seemed to well from his subconscious. "There is truth in both of your positions, and they are not wholly irreconcilable. Let the army be reembarked and landed to the north of Callao within easy striking distance of the port, yet above the city so that the temper of those people may be tested. On the beach the army would rest under protection of the guns of the fleet. The troops would also be within attacking distance of Callao, should that port become the target for operations as your lordship urges."

Cochrane spumed and grumbled, San Martín glowered and said nothing; but so at length it was decided, for no alternatives remained except defeat; and defeat was unthinkable equally to both. The troops were picked up and the convoy arrived on October 29 at San Lorenzo Island, with Callao in clear view across the strait.

Christian lounged at the rail, staring at the distant city without truly seeing it, his mind again in turmoil, his face heated by more than the Peruvian sun. About the *O'Higgins* glided transports crowded with soldiers, marines, or sailors eager for a glimpse of this heart of the empire. Only Ishmael was absent. Indeed, Christian had not seen him since the day of their long discussion. Perhaps Ishmael did not exist at all, save in the mind! Christian all but laughed aloud at the notion. Ishmael was real, right enough!

He started as a heavy hand clapped him on the shoulder and turned to see the admiral beside him, glass searching the vessels anchored before Callao, protected by their booms of floating spars and timbers and the guns of the land emplacements. Cochrane put aside the telescope.

"You look not well, Mr. Fletcher," he said. "Is it the fever, the ague? What is it? Tired of the expedition? Here we have scarcely arrived!" His attempt at humor was heavy but his solicitude warming.

"No, sir, nothing like that," replied Christian. "'Tis rather nothing at all. A slight indisposition, sir." He gestured toward the land. "The Spaniards appear to be awaiting us."

"They fear us," replied the Admiral, confidently. "Dread us, rather." He laughed shortly. "They are so terrorized they will not emerge from behind their accursed boom!"

He placed the glass to his eye again, scanning the enemy ships.

"I can make out the *Esmeralda*, clear enough, and she's the most important," he muttered. "But where are the others, the *Prueba* and *Venganza*? Nowhere to be seen! Do you suppose they have put to sea or run up the coast? No matter, they have gone; that's plain enough."

"Perhaps we could put San Martín ashore at the base of the spit," suggested Christian. "He might cut off all their ships and leave Lima unprotected from the sea, sir?"

Cochrane clicked the telescope shut with finality. "Oh, San Martín, the fool," he growled. "He has his heart set now on landing to the north as far removed from Lima—every inch—as I will take him. If Callao and Lima are to be reduced at all, 'twill have to be by attribution, inner collapse, sheer luck, or my marines and myself!" He sighed, the exhalation of a grievously wronged man.

Christian held his silence for a moment. When he spoke it was as though he had swept aside all uncertainties and was once again the resolute, daring adventurer he had been for so long.

"Sir, if I may make a suggestion? The frigate *Esmeralda* remains the only potent sea force the royalists have, at least here. If you were to seize her, 'twould seal the fate of Peru. You would then control the coast beyond question, and without command of the sea or access to it, the king's land forces must wither and die—in time. The war could be won by this single action, sir. The Spanish Empire in this hemisphere would be wrecked, and independence for the continent would follow inevitably."

Cochrane's dark face flushed as he considered the daring proposal. He scanned the shore again with his powerful glass.

"I don't know, sir," he replied slowly, although with his combative spirit simmering. "I don't know. She is well protected, I think. I can make out a dozen gunboats, two schooners and brigs, and at least three armed merchantmen in addition to the boom and the guns of the forts and shore batteries. I do not know. Still, it *would* be a feat, would it not? Yes, indeed! They would speak of such an exploit at Whitehall and Greenwich, you may be sure! But 'twould be risky, very much so. The first thing to do," he spoke softly now, as though to himself, "is to get rid of San Martín and his army. He would only hinder the enterprise, I fear."

Cochrane decided to hold most of his warships to maintain a blockade of Callao, while the transports proceeded to the Bay of Ancon, nine or ten leagues north of the port and there effect the landing, placing San Martín well out of the way during the heavy sea action to come.

Meanwhile Cochrane could not resist a show of bravado to demonstrate his professional contempt for the enemy but, like all his spectacular displays of cold courage, with a purpose more sound than mere boastfulness.

"If we pretend to strike," he confided to Christian, "it may draw the *Esmeralda* out to challenge us. If she emerges, we can destroy or capture her without the painful necessity of going in after her. At any rate 'tis worth the gamble, I think. Don't you?"

No seaman in his right mind would dare disagree with Lord Cochrane and his battle plans, and Christian readily assented.

Cochrane already had sounded the Boqueron Passage between San Lorenzo Island and the mainland and assured himself that its depth was satisfactory. He determined to run the *O'Higgins* through it, within distant cannon range of the royalists' shore batteries. Never had the Spaniards attempted to sail through the strait with a vessel of more than fifty tons. They manned their gunboats now, expecting to see the mighty frigate founder at any moment and formed into line to attack the instant the *O'Higgins* should strike. The shore emplacements were crowded with spectators to cheer on the attack against Cochrane's helpless giant. But the Chilean warship did not ground, the passage was smoothly completed to the cheers of her crew, and not a gun was fired. The *O'Higgins* joined the ships gathered beneath the cliffs of San Lorenzo to implement plans for a final action.

While boats were bringing the captains in for a council, the admiral summoned Christian to his cabin.

"I called you first, Fletcher, to give you instructions which I did not wish the others to be aware of, for the moment," Cochrane said. "I have revised my plan somewhat. I wish you to take the *Hercules*, ostensibly to assist in escorting San Martín's army into Ancon Bay, making sure that he is landed safely and out of the way for the time being, for I have determined to seize the *Esmeralda* as—uh—as has been recommended."

Aware of the admiral's conviction that all sound plans originated in his own mind, Christian smiled inwardly but did not protest.

"Your mission, however, is more extended than overseeing the landing," Cochrane was continuing. "On your return here, I wish you to sweep to sea and ascertain definitely that it is clear, that the *Prueba* and *Venganza* are not lurking in the vicinity nor capable of coming to the relief of the *Esmeralda* while we are hotly engaged with her. And I want you to do that quickly. If you see sail, run it down to ascertain what flag 'tis flying; but more importantly, determine that the waters are bereft of Spanish vessels, so we may proceed to neutralize the *Esmeralda* unhindered. Is that understood?"

"Indeed it is, sir. When am I to return?"

"Well, Mr. Fletcher, you are to have a part in this great adventure, you know. If you wish it, of course." It was Cochrane's concession to the originator of the plan. He could scarcely conceive of a seaman not eager to participate in an action so spectacular. Nor did Christian disillusion him.

CHAPTER TWENTY-FIVE

Under Christian's command, the *Hercules* stood well out to sea during the disembarkation of San Martín's troops at Ancon Bay. He tacked back and forth less to protect the landing than to assure San Martín that the naval force was sufficient to hold off any seaborne action against him. Once the operation was complete, Christian crowded on sail. The old warship heeled over at the wind's thrust and stood off northerly before being brought about for the long sweep of the coast. Two sails were raised. One proved to be English by flag with merchandise presumably destined for clandestine barter with the Spaniards ashore. The other was the royalist schooner, *Alcance*, eight days out of Guayaquil, bringing news of a patriot coup in that city and having testimony of it aboard in the persons of the former Spanish governor and other authorities, seeking to escape to Lima.

"The Revolution has swept the whole coast, save for Peru," Christian mused, not realizing he had spoken aloud. He watched the schooner beat southward toward Callao, having made no attempt to capture her.

"Aye," agreed a voice at his elbow. "Now to see what they make of their new freedom."

Christian spun in astonishment. Ishmael grinned happily. "Where you go, I go also . . . to paraphrase," he chuckled. Christian turned from him in some irritation.

"Then go silently!" he growled.

As the *Hercules* completed her northern reach and bore out to sea, the wind died off. Beyond sight of land she wallowed lastly, her canvas slack, the ship rolling to the great Pacific swells that never ceased. She made no headway; and her crew seemed infected with that mass depression sailing masters ever dread, superstitiously convinced that it foretold dire events. Christian sensed this foreboding even more than his deck officers, for it fitted the mood of black pessimism which had overtaken him ever more strongly in recent weeks. The depression touched all things but focused upon lack of confidence in the value of his life. And a man cannot live without cause or hope if he is such as man as Christian.

The sky commenced to pearl, the sun gleaming from a yellowing sea of its own, an unreal, luminescent canopy of sheerest gauze that was not quite mist, nor yet of cloud, but appeared to have a magnifying effect upon the ocean so that what one saw seemed bolder, clearer, greater than normal; and one's own moods and thoughts were enlarged accordingly. No sound accompanied this weird phenomenon, no hint of wind. It had no cause, no meaning readily apparent, no beginning and no end, yet was more real than any atmospheric effect of Christian's experience; and while he did not fear it—he feared nothing at this late stage of his life—yet it disconcerted him, stirring his soul as never before. When Ishmael stood again beside him, he did not protest, rather found himself engaging the ancient one in discourse, as though he had never denied him before.

"Is this the end, Ishmael?" he wondered. His voice was detached, almost disinterested.

"I think not. 'Tis not as I would have conceived it, at any rate."

"What then does it mean?" Christian peered skyward into the golden haze beyond the rigging, the lines, the stays and shrouds.

"You are the seaman. Not I," shrugged the old man.

"Is this for a seaman to explain? It looks like something out of your Fletcher mythology."

"Mythology, is it? I can near taste it! A man may regard fact as fiction until he discovers too late that it is not myth but truth. And the truth will wreck him before he can convert to it."

"Now 'tis conversion?"

"*Yes!*" Ishmael's sharp assent came explosively. "Yes, Fletcher! I do not know what the strange sky portends, but I know what is our destiny, *yours*. Accept, Fletcher, acknowledge what you *know* is true. Allow yourself to follow this new course! Instead of life closing in upon you, it will unroll before you; rather than barred doors you will find yourself in a passage with no end and new light, which grows stronger and more intense as you advance. Try it, Fletcher. Test it!"

Christian's face flushed with emotion. Perhaps the amber sky, the aura of fallen sunlight all around intensified his passion. As he spoke his voice rose, the surge of chaos revealed at last. "You ask that I renounce my pattern of life and thought, for near three-score years? You are a fool, Ishmael! I am a man grown dependent on no other, nothing save myself and my strength and mind and will. Through all of my life I have not depended upon your God but upon myself, and so it shall ever be. *I do not believe, I cannot* believe, *I will not* believe in your fiction because to do so would mean that I am less than a man, that my life has been in error, a mistake from first to last. You demand that I deny *myself,* and I will not do it—I cannot do it!"

"No! I ask that you *find* yourself. Your suspicions are correct that your life has been lived wrongly, but now you can mend it, make the past of value, a prelude to fulfillment, become complete! The choice is yours, Fletcher! The time is now. You may have no other, for each one's days are numbered and no one knows when they will run out. *Now!*"

"I cannot!" Christian's face was dark with passion.

"*Yes!* You must! Your reason, your conscience, your soul bids you to! Only your will holds you back. Your will must be overcome, Fletcher, now!"

Driven to near madness by his inner confusion, the unreal atmosphere, and the demands of Ishmael, Christian raised his fists overhead, towering above the diminutive tormentor whose back was to the rail. At this very moment the ship jolted, shuddered, as though driven hard aground, but this was no rock she had come upon. A sea-shock far beneath the surface, originating in the liquid darkness robbing the quake-ridden and trembling continental edges caused almost instantly the dreaded tsunami to sweep forward like a cavalcade of death, raising the sea in an onrush of a great tidal wave that caught and heaved the vessel like a toy, slammed Christian against the bulwark and cast Ishmael into the boiling water. His white-fringed face, wreathed in foam, appeared for one last moment far below, his screaming words reverberating through Christian's mind: "*Accept your God!*" and the echo appeared to the man on deck to parade down that long corridor into infinity: "*Accept your God . . . God . . . God . . . God . . . God . . .*"

Christian lowered his white-knuckled hands slowly to the rail, speechless horror suffusing his countenance. He had not struck Ishmael—or had he? Were not his fists raised for that purpose? Was he not responsible for the old man's death? This was his "stick" come to its final dimension. It had first appeared when he had driven his enemy Bligh to his apparent death; now it had brought upon his friend, his alter-ego, doom as well. This ghastly "stick" had run the full course, from enemy to friend, causing the destruction of both. He was evil. He was helpless. He too was doomed—unless Ishmael, by his death, could somehow accomplish what he could not do in life.

Far to the southeast, the tsunami boiled onward at its racing velocity of several hundred miles an hour, losing strength as it progressed, its height and violence diminishing, until at Callao it rocked the vessels of the squadron no more than slightly, causing a seaman or two to look up, wondering why the ships so oddly shifted. Cochrane tilted his head as though listening, seeking the cause of the curious motion. There was no apparent answer. It was a mystery of the sea, a manifestation of the ineffable hand of God. No more.

Lord Cochrane polished his plans for the seizure of the *Esmeralda* which, if successful, would probably seal the fate of Peru and accomplish freedom for America. He awaited only the return of Christian and the *Hercules*. Early in November this ship, concluding its protective sweep, raised San Lorenzo and, as quickly as anchors were dropped, Christian reported to the admiral who scanned the other's whitened face.

"What ails you, Fletcher? You look ghastly! And where is your ancient companion, who boarded the *Hercules* just before it set sail?"

Christian nervously looked away. "Ishmael—Ishmael—he is dead, sir. He was buried at sea. I—I miss him."

"So you must, my boy. So you must! It has come to every man, however; and far better to be buried in the clean ocean than in a stinking cemetery plot by filthy-handed ghouls, I would say. Glad you returned safely, Mr. Fletcher. Now my plans are ready, providing that you found the sea to be clear."

Cochrane had requested volunteers for the perilous mission. So many had leaped forward that he had no difficulty selecting 160 sailors and 80 marines for the 14 ships' boats comprising his attack force. His proclamation read to them promised that "One hour of courage and resolution is all that is necessary to triumph!" It also promised that the value of the loot and vessels taken would be fairly divided, and this was the ultimate incentive.

On November 4, the boats were collected and fully manned, leaving their various ships at half past ten at night for a drill, after which they were concealed behind the *O'Higgins* and the men taken aboard the frigate.

"It will be necessary to delude the enemy somehow," Cochrane said to Christian, "for if he expects us, it would be most difficult to take that ship."

"Could we not raise a signal at San Lorenzo," suggested Christian, "as though a sail or two had been sighted, and have the fleet put to sea as if in pursuit? The *O'Higgins* could be left here with her brood of boats. Under cover of darkness we could then surprise an unsuspecting enemy."

"Capital!" cried the admiral, his spirits soaring. "I should have thought of it myself!"

When the signal flags were raised, in full view of the Spaniards at Callao, the patriot fleet stood out from the coast, except for the flagship. Interpreting the departure as indication that the blockade had been raised, at least for the moment, the royalists celebrated with a wine-drenched banquet aboard the *Esmeralda*. This was what Cochrane had hoped for. He dressed his men and officers in white, that they might be identifiable in the gloom, and he and Christian wrapped blue bands around their arms that, should fire commence aboard the prize, they might be readily be distinguished.

At ten that night, the admiral ordered men into the boats; and thirty minutes later he and Christian led the two columns of craft, the sailors stroking with muffled oars toward the narrow opening in the boom, three miles across the star-reflecting water. One boat, its crew having lost its nerve, defected to the protection of an alien frigate anchored in the bay, but the remaining thirteen pulled faithfully in Cochrane's wake until they reached the narrow passage through the float. It was midnight.

The entrance through the boom was guarded by a small gunboat. Cochrane himself, pistol in hand, sprang aboard, threatening instant death to any who cried out. The terrified Spaniards held their silence, surrendering to this single intrepid commander and his followers. Thus the passage into the harbor was secured; and the attack boats stroked through, only an occasional squeak of an oarlock marking their passage. Fortunately there was no moon, and from the muted noises on the *Esmeralda* it appeared that the royalist officers were playing cards in the great cabin. The deck was sparsely guarded, since no danger was anticipated. The boats slipped into either quarter undetected. Christian and Cochrane leaped simultaneously for the chains, vaulting the bulwark as one.

The admiral instantly was bludgeoned by the one sentry on duty who recovered from his astonishment at the white-garbed ghosts, and belayed about viciously with the but of his musket. He fired at Christian, the flash scorching his white uniform. Christian drilled the sentry through the forehead with his pistol from point-blank range.

"Up, lads! She's ours!" cried the indomitable Cochrane, rising from the deck to lead the onrush. He sent the most agile of his men scrambling up the rigging to the tops. The deck almost instantly was covered with racing Spanish marines, sweeping into view with cries and a rattling volley of shots. Cochrane and Christian had boarded from the starboard quarter, the other boats from port, the two parties sweeping across the beam and meeting amidships, clasping hands in the insane glee of battle. A pocket of resistance held out on the poop, the boarders largely ignoring it as they swept up against the weight of the defense. The Spanish, barricaded on the forecastle, loosed volleys of deadly fire. Cochrane with his aching head bound by a rag was shot through the upper leg. He collapsed upon a gun where he coolly bound the wound tightly with a large handkerchief. Leaping again to his feet he raised his sword and led his men in a new attack upon the resolute enemy but was driven back.

Christian, lagging a bit as he surveyed and assessed the situation, searched for the officer directing the defense, spotting him among the fire flashes high on the forecastle. With sword in hand, the Spaniard stood aloof from the action but seeing everything, directing it in the most minute detail, calm, resolute, a professional.

Racing nimbly along the deck, Christian leaped up the companionway and brushed past two marines so startled they had no time to deflect him. Gaining the upper forecastle deck, he ran forward, sword in hand, toward the ice-cold Spanish officer who calmly waited, his blade raised, anticipating the decisive duel.

The Englishman slowed, calculating, as he approached his antagonist, then lifted the sword, its point circling tentatively. He thrust it forward in an exploratory fashion, rather than deadly intent. Then Christian moved in to the assault. The ringing metals, the cacophony of battle around them suddenly stilled, as though in witness to this decisive contest which seemed to determine not only the fate of the ship, but of the war, of the crusading human struggle for liberty, for freedom, for destiny.

The conflict was brief. Christian, aided by the impetuosity of his rush, found his opening and drove his blade home. The Spaniard fell to his knees, staining the deck with his life's blood. In that moment the Englishman heard another voice as clearly as though it were shouted into his ear, the voice of an old man filled with ancient wisdom and with truth: "You must, Fletcher! Now! You *must!*" and raising his face Christian gasped, "My God!" Whether in submission to Ishmael's final plea, or in resigned recognition of his own servanthood, or perhaps in reaction to the dagger thrust into his body by his mortally-wounded enemy, nonetheless he finally cried out—broken before God.

EPILOGUE

The capture of the *Esmeralda,* as Christian had predicted and Cochrane believed, made certain the ultimate surrender of Peru as well as the dissolution of the Spanish Empire in America, for without access to the sea, attrition alone would doom a landlocked power. Then Cochrane passionately urged a crushing blow against the royalists, but San Martín, a strategist, rejected the suggestion to allow time for the rotting fruit to fall of its own weight. San Martín was right. After the new viceroy and his loyalists were evacuated from Lima on July 28 1821, the country proclaimed independence.

A secret and mysterious conference between San Martín and Simon Bolivar followed; and the former, as he had known was inevitable, went into a self-imposed exile; he died in Boulogne in 1850. Cochrane was cheated out of just payment for his services and left the west coast of South America under something of a cloud, at least of disillusionment. O'Higgins was deposed and exiled in 1823; he died at Lima twenty years later. Attempting to slip into Chile, José Miguel Carrera was captured at Mendoza in 1821, and beheaded; Javiera, her former power in ashes, married and lived out her days obscurely. Las Heras served briefly as governor of the Province of Buenos Aires and was deposed. He exiled himself to Chile. Guemes was killed in a civil disturbance at Salta in 1821. Ramon Freyre, who succeeded O'Higgins at Santiago, lasted just three years. And George Nobbs *did* reach Pitcairn Island, arriving November 5, 1828, becoming a confidante of John Adams (Alexander Smith), by then the patriarch of the colony, and was appointed by Adams as his successor. In due course Nobbs was ordained an Anglican clergyman, being removed by death from the spiritual and temporal leadership of the *Bounty* colony fifty-six years to the exact day after he had joined it.

Liberty for the southern part of the South American continent brought only disorder. Chile endured a decade of nearly-complete anarchy; in the La Plata provinces the situation was worse. Governments fell; leaders fled or were slain; all order dissolved until the region at last came under the strong gaucho hand of Juan Manuel de Rosas, who had fought with the ill-fated Liniers and negotiated with Whitelocke. He brought a bloody peace to the country for nearly a quarter of a century, became mad, controlled at last by terror. He was deposed, bound into exile abroad, although he left as his legacy a unified Argentina.

And so the conquerors themselves were conquered by events, though not until they had completed their courses. If disorder followed their footsteps, it also planted the seeds of liberty they had sown, seeds that would sprout and grow into a mighty forest of freedom, strong and enduring—and equally forgetful of its past.

> Should not I spare . . . persons that cannot discern
> between their right hand and their left hand?
>
> JONAH 4:11

DAN L. THRAPP

Born on June 26, 1913, Dan Thrapp lived a life that aptly suited him to be the creator of an adventurer like Fletcher Christian. After graduation from high school at age 16, wearing his Eagle Scout uniform, he hitchhiked from his suburban Chicago home to the Pacific Ocean and gleaned a taste for travel that he never lost. After a year of college, he went back west to travel through every state west of the Mississippi. After working for the American Museum of Natural History in New York and in Wyoming digging for dinosaur fossils, Dan Thrapp took a leave of absence to make a solo exploration of cliff-dweller ruins in an unmapped canyon area of southern Utah. He had taken in two weeks of food and two pack horses and was presumed lost or dead until he reappeared four months later.

He received a Bachelor of Journalism degree in 1938 from the University of Missouri and went on to become a United Press news correspondent in Chicago, New York, and from 1940-1942 in Buenos Aires, South America. When World War II broke out, Thrapp made a two-month journey through South America, traveling by mule over the Andes on his way back to the US to join the WWII military. He served as a Mule Pack Specialist in China and Burma, earning four battle stars from the US Army and a medal from the Chinese government.

He rejoined United Press in 1946 and worked until 1948 as a news correspondent in London, Greece, and Rome, and then freelanced through Africa. Continuing his career as a journalist, Thrapp worked for the *Los Angeles Times* as the religion editor from 1951 to 1975. Thrapp was the author of fourteen books, including six books on the Apache Indians and the highly praised *Encyclopedia of Frontier Biography,* a four-volume series, greatly valued by writers and scholars of the American West. In preparation of this novel, Thrapp did research in England and took a voyage through the Magellan Straits to the Pacific, visiting both Easter Island and Tahiti. Thrapp died in 1994. *Mutiny's Curse* is his final work.

Additional copies of this book and other titles by RiverOak Publishing are available from your local bookstore.

Other fiction from RiverOak Publishing:

A Place Called Wiregrass
Avenged
Flowers for Victoria
Malchus
Murder in the Mummy's Tomb
Q

If you have enjoyed this book, or if it has impacted your life, we would like to hear from you.

Please contact us at

RiverOak Publishing
Department E
P.O. Box 55388
Tulsa, Oklahoma 74155
Or by e-mail at *info@riveroakpublishing.com*